Praise for the Mon

'The novels of Andrea Camilleri breathe out the sense of place, the sense of humour, and the sense of despair that fill the air of Sicily. To read him is to be taken to that glorious, tortured island'

Donna Leon

'The seal of the best foreign crime writing is as much the stylish prose as the unfamiliar settings. When both ingredients are presented with the expertise shown by Andrea Camilleri, the result is immensely satisfying'

Independent

'For sunny views, explosive characters and a snappy plot constructed with great farcical ingenuity, the writer you want is Andrea Camilleri'

New York Times

'It doesn't get much better than this! Inimitable'

Choice

'The mixture of wit, irony, cynicism and a sexy but troubled hero with a combative girlfriend far away, and constant niggles with his police underlings as well as superiors, remains irresistible'

Marcel Berlins, *The Times*

'Among the most exquisitely crafted pieces of crime writing available today . . . simply superb'

Sunday Times

'One of fiction's greatest detectives and Camilleri is one of Europe's greatest crime writers . . . As ever, at the heart of this artfully constructed yet utterly gripping story is the play between perception and reality, the mafia and the truth, all dusted with carnal desire'

Mirror

'Beautifully written and brilliantly observed'

Books of the Year, *Independent*

'The popularity of Camilleri's clever, bitter-sweet novels comes from their human comedy, their commitment-phobic central figure, and from the quality of the writing'

Times Literary Supplement

'Montalbano's colleagues, chance encounters, Sicilian mores, even the contents of his fridge are described with the wit and gusto that make this narrator the best company in crime fiction today'

Guardian

'Over a dozen evocative mysteries, Camilleri has turned Inspector Montalbano, his gourmet Sicilian detective, into a national treasure in Italy'

Independent

INSPECTOR MONTALBANO: THE FIRST THREE NOVELS

Andrea Camilleri is one of Italy's most famous contemporary writers. His Montalbano series has been adapted for Italian television, broadcast on BBC4 in the UK, and translated into several languages. He lives in Rome.

Stephen Sartarelli is an award-winning translator. He is also the author of three books of poetry, most recently *The Open Vault*. He lives in France.

Discover more at
facebook.com/AndreaCamilleriAuthor

The Inspector Montalbano series

THE SHAPE OF WATER

THE TERRACOTTA DOG

THE SNACK THIEF

THE VOICE OF THE VIOLIN

EXCURSION TO TINDARI

THE SCENT OF THE NIGHT

ROUNDING THE MARK

THE PATIENCE OF THE SPIDER

THE PAPER MOON

AUGUST HEAT

THE WINGS OF THE SPHINX

THE TRACK OF SAND

THE POTTER'S FIELD

THE AGE OF DOUBT

THE DANCE OF THE SEAGULL

THE TREASURE HUNT

ANGELICA'S SMILE

ANDREA CAMILLERI

INSPECTOR MONTALBANO

THE FIRST THREE NOVELS

Translated by Stephen Sartarelli

PICADOR

The Shape of Water first published 2002 by Penguin Books,
a member of Penguin Group (USA) Inc., New York
First published in Great Britain 2003 by Picador
Originally published in Italian 1994 as *La forma dell'acqua* by Sellerio Editore, Palermo

The Terracotta Dog first published 2002 by Penguin Books,
a member of Penguin Group (USA) Inc., New York
First published in Great Britain 2004 by Picador
Originally published in Italian 1996 as *Il cane di terracotta* by Sellerio Editore, Palermo

The Snack Thief first published 2003 by Penguin Books,
a member of Penguin Group (USA) Inc., New York
First published in Great Britain 2004 by Picador
Originally published in Italian 1996 as *Il ladro di merendine* by Sellerio Editore, Palermo

This collected volume published 2013 by Picador
an imprint of Pan Macmillan
20 New Wharf Road, London N1 9RR
Associated companies throughout the world
www.panmacmillan.com

ISBN 978-1-4472-4519-3

9 8

A CIP catalogue record for this book is available from the British Library.

Typeset by Intype Libra, London
Printed and bound by CPI Group (UK) Ltd, Croydon, CR0 4YY

Contents

Introduction

The present 'omnibus' volume includes my first three novels featuring Inspector Salvo Montalbano as protagonist, originally published from 1994–96 in Italy.

It all started with a 'historical' novel I had set out to write in 1993 but which wasn't published until years later in Italy, *Il birraio di Preston* ('The Brewer of Preston'). At that time, when working on that novel, I came to realize that my personal way of putting a story down on paper was, well, a bit disorganized.

To explain: everything I had written up to that moment had sprung from a few powerful ideas (the memory of a story told to me, or a page of history), and I had always started composing my fictions on the basis of these ideas. Once the novel or novels were finished, these original starting points never constituted the first chapter, but found their place instead somewhere within a broader sequence of events already unfolding. In other words, the first chapter I set down on paper would end up, once the novel was completed, as the fifth chapter, or the tenth, or what have you.

And so I asked myself: Was I capable of writing a novel by starting with the first chapter and proceeding straight through to the end, with no leaps of logic or temporal sequence? My answer was that yes, perhaps I would be able to do this if I got caught up inside a sufficiently sturdy narrative structure.

At this point I remembered something Leonardo Sciascia had once said in an essay on the detective novel about the rules that an author of mysteries is expected to follow. At the same time I remembered a statement that Italo Calvino once made: that it was impossible to set a detective novel in Sicily. And so I decided to take up a twofold challenge, with myself and with the unsuspecting Calvino.

But before setting pen to paper, I thought for a long time about my choice of protagonist, of detective.

I'd had a lot of past experience with the detective genre, since, as production coordinator at the RAI, the Italian state television network, I oversaw the entire Maigret television series and another series featuring Inspector Sheridan. And I also directed some mysteries for television. But what had the most influence on me of all was the way the playwright Diego Fabbri adapted Simenon's novels for the television screen. He would deconstruct them as novels and then restructure them as TV scripts. Working alongside him was like attending the workshop of a watchmaker who would dismantle a watch and then reassemble it to fit a new watchcase of a different shape.

I'm convinced that I learned the art on those occasions and then, without realizing, tucked it away for later use. As a result, my detective took shape at once not as a private eye or 'dick,' as the Americans call them, but as a policeman, a law-enforcement officer, either a detective or *commissario,* a chief of an investigative branch. Why not a marshal or officer of the carabinieri? I was tempted for a long time by the idea of creating a *maresciallo* of the carabinieri, especially since the investigator in my very first novel *Il corso delle cose* ('The Way things Go') was precisely that. But in the end I opted for a *commissario,* because I realized that, as such, he would be less obliged to uphold certain rules of conduct that the carabinieri, who are a part of the military, cannot escape.

What would be my character's main personality traits? I must admit that they were clear to me from the start. He had to be an intelligent man, true to his word, uncomfortable with useless heroism, cultured, well-read, quietly rational, and free of prejudice.

The sort of man you could feel comfortable inviting home to dinner with the family. The kind of man who, 'when he wanted to get to the bottom of something, he did,' as I wrote in the first book in the series.

I was tossing around two different names for him: Cecè Collura and Salvo Montalbano, both very common in Sicily.

I decided to call him Montalbano in homage to Manuel Vásquez-Montalbán, because one of his novels, *The Pianist,* had suggested to me what became the definitive structure of *The Brewer of Preston.* Once I had clarified these things for myself, I wrote my first 'detective' novel, keeping to the rules I had imposed on myself (the first chapter actually begins at dawn, like every subsequent novel in the series). Sellerio publishers, of Palermo, brought it out in 1994 with a delightful cover. Having won my first challenge with myself – and quite possibly my challenge with Calvino as well – my immediate inclination was to end things there.

I didn't obey this impluse because I felt less than fully satisfied with how the figure of Montalbano had come out; I felt as if I had painted an incomplete portrait of him, favouring his role as a detective while neglecting certain aspects of his character. In short, he seemed only half resolved. And it bothered me a lot to leave him unfinished. I always try to bring everything I start to completion.

And so, out of some sort of concern for craft, I decided to write a second novel featuring this police inspector and thereby conclude my brief career as a mystery writer.

I think it is obvious to most readers, already by the first few lines, that there is a substantial difference between the first and second novels. In the first book, it's the two garbagemen who witness the dawn, while in the second it is Montalbano, as it will be in all the novels that follow.

This means that, from the second novel on, everything that happens will be viewed through Montalbano's eyes. The stories will all be a series of point-of-view shots. Nothing happens, so to speak, outside of him; he sees everything, or almost everything, and the things he doesn't see are recounted to him by others. In this way the reader has the same cards in hand as the inspector.

I'd decided that the second novel would also have a *sui generis* subject. While the first one, so to speak, essentially revolved around a crime of image, the second would be an investigation into memory, based on a crime committed many years before that had long since fallen under the statute of limitations. This second novel, *The Terracotta Dog,* was first published in 1996, at which time I considered my incursion into the field of detective fiction definitively over.

The only problem was that, for reasons that remain inexplicable to me, the character became a tremendous success. Not only that, but his success dragged the previous books I'd published along in its wake, so that Sellerio had to republish them

I started to receive dozens, then hundreds, of letters urging me, in more or less peremptory fashion, to keep writing about Salvo Montalbano. On the other hand, the character actually didn't need the readers' support to keep nagging at me. He began to reappear to me in the most unlikely situations and torment me. I had read about authors supposedly obsessed with their characters and had considered it to be nothing more than a literary affectation.

I was forced to acknowledge that it was indeed a reality. In fact, I eventually found myself in the absurd situation where I couldn't even think about a 'historical' novel unless I was thinking at the same time about a new investigation of Montalbano's. Otherwise I was unable to proceed.

And so I found myself 'forced', and with a certain urgency, to write the third novel, *The Snack Thief*, highlighting an entirely personal aspect of the inspector's character in it.

I was under the illusion, yet again, that I had at last closed the file. I simply didn't feel like becoming a mystery writer focused on a single character, who was, moreover, serial.

Instead it was like throwing gasoline on the fire.

Andrea Camilleri

THE SHAPE OF WATER

ONE

No light of daybreak filtered yet into the courtyard of Splendour, the company under government contract to collect trash in the town of Vigàta. A low, dense mass of clouds completely covered the sky as though a great grey tarpaulin had been drawn from one corner to another. Not a single leaf fluttered. The sirocco was late to rise from its leaden sleep, yet people already struggled to exchange a few words. The foreman, before assigning the areas to be cleaned, announced that this day, and for some days to come, Peppe Schèmmari and Caluzzo Brucculeri would be absent, excused from work. More than excused, they'd been arrested: the previous evening they'd attempted to rob a supermarket, weapons in hand. To Pino Catalane and Saro Montaperto – young land surveyors naturally without employment as land surveyors, but hired by

Splendour as temporary 'ecological agents' thanks to the generous string-pulling of Chamber Deputy Cusumano, in whose electoral campaign the two had fought body and soul (and in that order, with the body doing far more than the soul felt like doing) – the foreman assigned the jobs vacated by Peppe and Caluzzo, that is, the sector that went by the name of the 'Pasture,' because in a time now beyond memory a goatherd had apparently let his goats roam there. It was a broad tract of Mediterranean brush on the outskirts of town that stretched almost as far as the shore. Behind it lay the ruins of a large chemical works inaugurated by the ubiquitous Deputy Cusumano when it seemed the magnificent winds of progress were blowing strong. Soon, however, that breeze changed into the flimsiest of puffs before dropping altogether, but in that brief time it had managed to do more damage than a tornado, leaving a shambles of compensation benefits and unemployment in its wake. To prevent the crowds of black and not-so-black Senegalese, Algerians, Tunisians and Libyans wandering about the city from nesting in that factory, a high wall had been built all around it, above which the old structures still soared, corroded by weather, neglect and sea salt, looking more and more like architectures designed by Gaudi under the influence of hallucinogens.

Until recently the Pasture had represented, for those who at the time still went under the undignified name of garbage collectors, a cakewalk of a job: amid the scraps of paper, plastic bags, cans of beer and Coca-Cola, and shit piles barely covered up or left out in the open air, now and then a used condom would appear, and it would set one thinking, provided one had the desire and imagination to do so, about the details of that encounter. For a good year now, however, the occasional condom had turned into an ocean, a carpet of condoms, ever since a certain minister with a dark, taciturn face worthy of a Lombroso diagram had fished deep into his mind, which was even darker and more mysterious than his face, and come up with an idea he thought would solve all the south's law and order problems. He had managed to sell this idea to a colleague of his who dealt with the army and who, for his part, looked as if he had walked right out of a Pinocchio illustration, and together the two had decided to send a number of detachments to Sicily for the purpose of 'controlling the territory', to lighten the load of the carabinieri, local police, intelligence services, special operations teams, coastguard, the highway police, railway police and port police, the anti-Mafia, anti-terrorism, anti-drug, anti-theft and anti-kidnapping commissions, and others – here omitted for the sake of brevity – quite busy with other business. Thanks to the brilliant idea of these two eminent statesmen, all the Piedmontese mama's boys and beardless Friulian conscripts who just the night before had enjoyed the crisp, fresh air of their mountains suddenly found themselves painfully short of breath, huffing in their temporary lodgings, in towns that stood barely a yard above sea level, among people who spoke an incomprehensible dialect consisting not so much of words as of silences, indecipherable movements of the eyebrows, imperceptible puckerings of the facial wrinkles. They adapted as best they could, thanks to their young age, and were given a helping hand by the residents of Vigàta themselves, who were moved to pity by the foreign boys' lost, bewildered looks. The one who saw to lessening the hardship of their exile was a certain Gegè Gullotta, a fast thinker who until that moment had been forced to suppress his natural gifts as a pimp by dealing in light drugs. Having learned through channels both underhanded and ministerial of the soldiers' imminent arrival, Gegè had had a flash of genius, and to put said flash to work for him he had promptly appealed to the beneficence of those in charge of such matters in order to obtain all the countless convoluted authorizations indispensable to his plan – those in charge being, that is, those who truly controlled the area and would never have dreamt of issuing officially stamped permits. Gegè, in short, succeeded in opening a specialized market of fresh meat and many and sundry drugs, all light, at the Pasture. Most of the meat came from the former Eastern Bloc countries, now free at last of the communist yoke which, as everyone knows, had denied all personal, human dignity; now, between the Pasture's bushes and sandy shore, come nightfall, that reconquered dignity shone again in all its magnificence. But there was also no lack of Third World women, transvestites, transsexuals, Neapolitan faggots, Brazilian *viados* – something for every taste, a feast, an embarrassment of riches. And business flourished, to the great satisfaction of the soldiers, Gegè and those who, for a proper cut of the proceeds, had granted Gegè permission to operate.

Pino and Saro headed toward their assigned work

sector, each pushing his own cart. To get to the Pasture took half an hour, if one was slow of foot as they were. The first fifteen minutes they spent without speaking, already sweaty and sticky. It was Saro who broke the silence.

'That Pecorilla is a bastard,' he announced.

'A fucking bastard,' clarified Pino.

Pecorilla was the foreman in charge of assigning the areas to be cleaned, and he nurtured an undisguised hatred for anyone with an education, having himself managed to finish middle school, at age forty, only thanks to Cusumano, who had a man to man talk with the teacher. Thus he manipulated things so that the hardest, most demeaning work always fell to the three university graduates in his charge. That same morning, in fact, he had assigned to Ciccu Loreto the stretch of wharf from which the mail boat sailed for the island of Lampedusa. Which meant that Ciccu, with his accounting degree, would be forced to account for the piles of trash that noisy mobs of tourists, many-tongued yet all sharing the same utter disregard for personal and public cleanliness, had left behind on Saturday and Sunday while waiting to embark. And no doubt Pino and Saro, after the soldiers' two days off duty, would find the Pasture one big glory hole.

When they reached the corner of Via Lincoln and Viale Kennedy (in Vigàta there was even a Cortile Eisenhower and a Vicolo Roosevelt), Saro stopped.

'I'm going to run upstairs and see how the little guy's doing,' he said to his friend. 'Wait here. I'll only be a minute.'

Without waiting for Pino's answer, he slipped into one of those midget high-rises that were not more than twelve storeys high, having been built around the same time as the chemical works and having just as quickly fallen into ruin, when not abandoned altogether. For someone approaching from the sea, Vigàta rose up like a parody of Manhattan, on a reduced scale. And this explained, perhaps, the names of some of its streets.

Nenè, the little guy, was awake; he slept on and off for some two hours a night, spending the rest of the time with eyes wide open, without ever crying. Who had ever seen a baby that didn't cry? Day after day he was consumed by an illness of unknown cause and cure. The doctors of Vigàta couldn't figure it out; his parents would have to take him somewhere else, to some big-shot specialist, but they didn't have the money. Nenè grew sullen as soon as his eyes met his father's, a wrinkle forming across his forehead. He couldn't talk, but had expressed himself quite clearly with that silent reproach of the person who had put him in these straits. 'He's doing a little better, the fever's going down,' said Tana, Saro's wife, just to make him happy.

*

The clouds had scattered, and now the sun was blazing hot enough to shatter rocks. Saro had already emptied his cart a dozen times in the garbage bin that had appeared, thanks to private initiative, where the rear exit of the factory used to be, and his back felt broken. When he was a few steps from the path that ran along the enclosure wall and led to the provincial road, he saw something sparkle violently on the ground. He bent down to have a better look. It was a heart-shaped pendant, enormous, studded with little diamonds all around and with one great big diamond in the middle. The solid-gold chain was still attached, though broken in one spot. Saro's right hand shot out, grabbed the necklace, and stuffed it in his pocket. The hand seemed to have acted on its own, before his brain, still flabbergasted by the discovery, could tell it anything. Standing up again, drenched in sweat, he looked around but didn't see a living soul.

*

Pino, who had chosen to work the stretch of the Pasture nearest the beach, at one point spotted the nose of a car about twenty yards away, sticking out of some bushes a bit denser than the rest. Unsure, he stopped; it wasn't possible someone could still be around here at this hour, seven in the morning, screwing a whore. He began to approach cautiously, one step at a time, almost bent over, and when he'd reached the taillights he quickly stood straight up. Nothing happened, nobody shouted to fuck off, the car seemed vacant. Coming nearer, he finally made out the indistinct shape of a man, motionless, in the passenger seat, head thrown back. He seemed to be in a deep sleep. But by the look and the smell of it, Pino realized something was fishy. He turned around and called to Saro, who came running, out of breath, eyes bulging. 'What is it? What the hell do you want?' Pino thought his friend's questions a bit aggressive but blamed it on the fact that he had run all that way. 'Get a load of this,' he said.

Plucking up his courage, Pino went up to the driver's side and tried to open the door but couldn't: it was locked. With the help of Saro, who seemed to have calmed down, he tried to reach the other door, against which the man's body was partially leaning, but the car, a large green BMW , was too close to the shrub to allow anyone to approach from that side. Leaning forward, however, and getting scratched by the brambles, they managed to get a better look at the man's face. He was not sleeping; his eyes were wide open and motionless. The moment they realized that the man was dead, Pino and Saro froze in terror – not at the sight of death but because they recognized him.

*

'I feel like I'm taking a sauna,' said Saro as he ran along the provincial road toward a telephone booth. 'A blast of cold one minute, a blast of heat the next.'

They had agreed on one thing since overcoming their paralysis upon recognizing the deceased: before alerting the police, they had to make another phone call. They knew Deputy Cusumano's number by heart, and Saro dialled it. But Pino didn't let the phone ring even once.

'Hang up, quick!' he said.

Saro obeyed automatically.

'You don't want to tell him?'

'Let's just think for a minute, let's think hard. This is very important. You know as well as I do that Cusumano is a puppet.'

'What's that supposed to mean?'

'He's a puppet of Luparello, who is everything – or was everything. With Luparello dead, Cusumano's a nobody, a doormat.'

'So?'

'So nothing.'

They turned back toward Vigàta, but after a few steps Pino stopped Saro.

'Rizzo, the lawyer,' he said.

'I'm not going to call that guy. He gives me the creeps. I don't even know him.'

'I don't either, but I'm going to call him anyway.'

Pino got the number from the operator. Though it was still only seven forty-five, Rizzo answered after the first ring.

'Mr Rizzo?'

'Yes?'

'Excuse me for bothering you at this hour, Mr Rizzo, but . . . we found Mr Luparello, you see, and . . . well, he looks dead.'

There was a pause. Then Rizzo spoke.

'So why are you telling me this?'

Pino was stunned. He was ready for anything, except that bizarre response.

'But . . . aren't you his best friend? We thought it was only right—'

'I appreciate it. But you must do your duty first. Good day.'

Saro had been listening to the conversation, his cheek pressed against Pino's. They looked at each other, nonplussed. Rizzo acted as if they'd told him they'd just found some nameless cadaver.

'Shit! He was his friend, wasn't he?' Saro burst out.

'What do we know? Maybe they had a fight,' said Pino to reassure him.

'So what do we do now?'

'We go and do our duty, like the lawyer said,' concluded Pino.

They headed toward town, to police headquarters. The thought of going to the carabinieri didn't even cross their minds, since they were under the command of a Milanese lieutenant. The Vigàta police inspector, on the other hand, was from Catania, a certain Salvo Montalbano, who, when he wanted to get to the bottom of something, he did.

TWO

'Again.'

'No,' said Livia, still staring at him, her eyes more luminous from the amorous tension.

'Please.'

'No, I said no.'

I always like being forced a little, he remembered her whispering once in his ear; and so, aroused, he tried slipping his knee between her closed thighs as he gripped her wrists roughly and spread her arms until she looked as though crucified.

They eyed each other a moment, panting, when suddenly she surrendered.

'Yes,' she said. 'Now.'

At that exact moment the phone rang. Without even opening his eyes, Montalbano reached out with his arm to grab not the telephone so much as the fluttering shreds of the dream now inexorably vanishing.

'Hello!' he shouted angrily at the intruder.

'Inspector, we've got a client.' He recognized Sergeant Fazio's voice; the other sergeant, Tortorella, was still in the hospital with the nasty bullet he'd taken in the belly from some would-be Mafioso who was actually just a pathetic two-bit jerk-off. In their jargon a 'client' meant a death they should look into.

'Who is it?'

'We don't know yet.'

'How was he killed?'

'We don't know. Actually, we don't even know if he was killed.'

'I don't get it, Sergeant. You woke me up to tell me you don't know a goddamn thing?'

Montalbano breathed deeply to dispel his pointless anger, which Fazio tolerated with the patience of a saint.

'Who found him?' he continued.

'A couple of garbage collectors in the Pasture. They found him in a car.'

'I'll be right there. Meanwhile phone the Montelusa department, have them send someone from the lab, and inform Judge Lo Bianco.'

*

As he stood under the shower, he reached the conclusion that the dead man must have been a member of the Cuffaro gang. Eight months earlier, probably due to some territorial dispute, a ferocious war had broken out between the Vigàta Cuffaros and the Sinagra gang, who were from Fela. One victim per month, by turns, and in orderly fashion: one in Vigàta, one in Fela. The latest, a certain Mario Salino, had been shot in Fela by the Vigatese, so now it was apparently the turn of one of the Cuffaro thugs.

Before going out – he lived alone in a small house right on the beach on the opposite side of town from the Pasture – he felt like calling Livia in Genoa. She answered immediately, drowsy with sleep.

'Sorry, but I wanted to hear your voice.'

'I was dreaming of you,' she said. 'You were here with me.'

Montalbano was about to say that he, too, had

been dreaming of her, but an absurd prudishness held him back. Instead he asked: 'And what were we doing?'

'Something we haven't done for too long,' she said.

*

At headquarters, aside from the sergeant, there were only three policemen. The rest had gone to the home of a clothing-shop owner who had shot his sister over a question of inheritance and then escaped. Montalbano opened the door to the interrogation room. The two garbage collectors were sitting on the bench, huddling one against the other, pale despite the heat.

'Wait here till I get back,' Montalbano said to them, and the two, resigned, didn't even reply. They both knew well that any time one fell in with the law, whatever the reason, it was going to be a long affair.

'Have any of you called the papers?' the inspector asked his men. They shook their heads no.

'Well, I don't want them sticking their noses in this. Make a note of that.'

Timidly, Galluzzo came forward, raising two fingers as if to ask if he could go to the bathroom.

'Not even my brother-in-law?'

Galluzzo's brother-in-law was a newsman with Televigàta who covered local crime, and Montalbano imagined the family squabbles that might break out if Galluzzo weren't to tell him anything. And Galluzzo was looking at him with pitiful, canine eyes.

'All right. But he should come only after the body's been removed. And no photographers.'

They set out in a squad car, leaving Giallombardo behind on duty. Gallo was at the wheel. Together with Galluzzo, he was often the butt of facile jokes, such as 'Hey, Inspector, what's new in the chicken coop?'

Knowing Gallo's driving habits, Montalbano admonished him, 'Don't speed. We're in no hurry.'

At the curve by the Carmelite church, Peppe Gallo could no longer restrain himself and accelerated, screeching the tyres as he rounded the bend. They heard a loud crack, like a pistol shot, and the car skidded to a halt. They got out. The right rear tyre hung flabbily, blown out. It had been well worked over by a sharp blade; the cuts were quite visible.

'Goddamn sons of bitches!' bellowed the sergeant.

Montalbano got angry in earnest.

'But you all know they cut our tyres twice a month! Jesus! And every morning I remind you: don't forget to check them before going out! But you arseholes don't give a shit! And you won't until the day somebody breaks his neck!'

For one reason or another, it took a good ten minutes to change the tyre, and when they got to the Pasture, the Montelusa crime lab team was already there. They were in what Montalbano called the meditative stage, that is, five or six agents circling round and round the spot where the car stood, hands usually in their pockets or behind their backs. They looked like philosophers absorbed in deep thought, but in fact their eyes were combing the ground for clues, traces, footprints. As soon as Jacomuzzi, head of the crime lab, saw Montalbano, he came running up.

'How come there aren't any newsmen?'

'I didn't want any.'

'Well, this time they're going to accuse you of trying to cover up a big story.' He was clearly upset. 'Do you know who the dead man is?'

'No. Who?'

'None other than the engineer, Silvio Luparello.'

'Shit!' was Montalbano's only comment.

'And do you know how he died?'

'No. And I don't want to know. I'll have a look at him myself.'

Offended, Jacomuzzi went back to his men. The lab photographer had finished, and now it was Dr Pasquano's turn. Montalbano noticed that the coroner was forced to work in an uncomfortable position, his body half inside the car, wiggling his way toward the passenger seat, where a dark silhouette could be seen. Fazio and the Vigàta officers were giving a hand to their Montelusa colleagues. The inspector lit a cigarette and turned to look at the chemical factory. That ruin fascinated him. He decided he would come back one day to take a few snapshots, which he'd send to Livia to explain some things about himself and his island that she was still unable to understand.

Lo Bianco's car pulled up and the judge stepped out, looking agitated.

'Is it really Luparello?' he asked.

Apparently Jacomuzzi had wasted no time.

'So it seems.'

The judge joined the lab group and began speaking excitedly with Jacomuzzi and Dr Pasquano, who in the meantime had extracted a bottle of rubbing alcohol from his briefcase and was disinfecting his hands. After a good while, long enough for Montalbano to broil in the sun, the men from the lab got back in their cars and left. As he passed Montalbano, Jacomuzzi said nothing. Behind him, the inspector heard an ambulance siren wind down. It was his turn now. He'd have to do the talking and acting; there was no escape. He shook himself from the torpor in which he was stewing and walked toward the car with the dead man inside. Halfway there, the judge blocked his path.

'The body can be removed now. And considering poor Luparello's notoriety, the quicker we do it the better. In any case, keep me posted daily as to how the investigation develops.'

He paused a moment, and then, to make the words he'd just said a little less peremptory: 'Give me a ring when you think it's appropriate,' he added. Another pause. Then, 'During office hours, of course.'

He walked away. During office hours, not at home. At home, it was well known, Judge Lo Bianco was busy penning a stuffy, puffy book, *The Life and Exploits of Rinaldo and Antonio Lo Bianco, Masters of Jurisprudence at the University of Girgenti at the Time of King Martin the Younger (1402–1409)*. These Lo Biancos, he claimed, however nebulously, were his ancestors.

'How did he die?' Montalbano asked the doctor.

'See for yourself,' said the doctor, standing aside.

Montalbano stuck his head inside the car, which felt like an oven (more specifically, a crematorium), took his first look at the corpse, and immediately thought of the police commissioner.

He thought of the commissioner not because he was in the habit of turning his thoughts up the hierarchical ladder at the start of every investigation, but merely because some ten days earlier he had spoken with old Commissioner Burlando, who was a friend of his, about a book by Ariès, *Western Attitudes Toward Death,* which they had both read. The commissioner had argued that every death, even the most abject, was sacred. Montalbano had retorted, in all sincerity, that in no death, not even a pope's, could he see anything sacred whatsoever.

He wished the commissioner were there beside him now, to see what he saw. This Luparello had always been an elegant sort, extremely well groomed in every physical detail. Now, however, his tie was gone, his shirt rumpled, his glasses askew, his jacket collar incongruously half turned up, his socks sagging so flaccidly that they covered his loafers. But what most struck the inspector was the sight of the trousers pulled down around the man's knees, the white of the underwear showing inside the trousers, the shirt rolled up together with the undershirt halfway up his chest.

And the sex organ obscenely, horridly exposed, thick and hairy, in stark contrast with the meticulous care shown over the rest of his person.

'But how did he die?' he asked the doctor again, coming out of the car.

'Seems obvious, don't you think?' Pasquano replied rudely. 'You did know he'd had heart surgery,' he continued, 'performed by a famous London surgeon?'

'No, I did not. I saw him on TV last Wednesday, and he looked in perfect health to me.'

'He may have looked healthy, but he wasn't. You know, in politics they're all like dogs: the minute they realize you can't defend yourself, they attack. Apparently he had a double bypass in London. They say it was a difficult operation.'

'Who was his doctor in Montelusa?'

'My colleague Capuano. He was getting weekly check-ups. His health was very important to him – you know, always wanted to look fit.'

'You think I should talk to Capuano?'

'Absolutely unnecessary. It's plain as day what happened here. Poor Mr Luparello felt like having a good lay in the Pasture, maybe with some exotic foreign slut, and he had it, all right, and left his carcass behind.'

He noticed that Montalbano had a faraway look in his eyes.

'Not convinced?'

'No.'

'Why not?'

'I don't really know, to tell you the truth. Can you send me the results of the autopsy tomorrow?'

'Tomorrow?! Are you crazy? Before Luparello I've got that twenty-year-old girl who was raped in a shepherd's hut and found eaten by dogs ten days later, and then there's Fofò Greco, who had his tongue cut out and his balls cut off before they hung him from a tree to die, and then—'

Montalbano cut this macabre list short.

'Pasquano, let's get to the point. When can you get me the results?'

'Day after tomorrow, if, in the meantime, I don't have to run all over town looking at other corpses.'

They said goodbye. Montalbano called over the sergeant and his men and told them what they had to do and when to load the body into the ambulance. He had Gallo drive him back to headquarters.

'You can go back afterwards and pick up the others. And if you speed, I'll break your neck.'

*

Pino and Saro signed the sworn statement. In it their every movement before and after they discovered the body was described. But it neglected to mention two important things which the garbage collectors had been careful not to reveal to the law. The first was that they had almost immediately recognized the dead man, the second that they had hastened to inform the lawyer Rizzo of their discovery. They headed back home, Pino apparently with his thoughts elsewhere, Saro now and again touching the pocket that still held the necklace.

Nothing would happen for at least another twenty-four hours. In the afternoon Montalbano went back to his house, threw himself down on the bed, and fell into a three-hour sleep. When he woke, as the mid-September sea was flat as a mirror, he went for a long swim. Back inside, he made himself a dish of spaghetti with a sauce of sea urchin pulp and turned on the television. Naturally, all the local news programmes were talking about Luparello's death. They sang his praises, and from time to time a politician would appear, with a face to fit the occasion, and enumerate the merits of the deceased and the problems created by his passing. But not a single one of them, not even the news programme of the opposition's channel, dared to mention where and in what circumstances the late lamented Luparello had met his end.

THREE

Saro and Tana had a bad night. There was no doubt Saro had discovered a secret treasure, the kind told about in tales where vagabond shepherds stumble upon ancient jars full of gold coins or find little lambs covered in diamonds. But here the matter was not at all as in olden times: the necklace, of modern construction, had been lost the day before, this much was certain, and by anyone's guess it was worth a fortune. Was it possible nobody had come forward to declare it missing? As they sat at their small kitchen table, with the television on and the window wide open, like every night, to keep the neighbours from getting nosy and gossiping at the sight of the slightest change, Tana wasted no time opposing her husband's intention to go and sell it that very day, as soon as the Siracusa brothers' jewellery shop reopened.

'First of all,' she said, 'we're honest people. We can't just go and sell something that's not ours.'

'But what are we supposed to do? You want me to go to the foreman and tell him I found a necklace, turn it over to him, and have him give it back to its owner when they come to reclaim it? That bastard Pecorilla'll sell it himself in ten seconds flat.'

'We could do something else. We could keep the necklace at home and in the meantime tell Pecorilla about it. Then if somebody comes for it, we'll give it to them.'

'What good will that do us?'

'There's supposed to be a percentage for people who find things like this. How much do you think it's worth?'

'Twenty million lire, easy,' Saro replied, immediately thinking he'd blurted out too high a figure. 'So let's say we get two million. Can you tell me how we're going to pay for all of Nenè's treatments with two million lire?'

They talked it over until dawn and only stopped because Saro had to go to work. But they'd reached a temporary agreement that allowed their honesty to remain intact: they would hang on to the necklace without whispering a word to anyone, let a week go by, and then, if nobody came forward, they'd pawn it.

When Saro, washed up and ready to leave, went to kiss his son, he had a surprise: Nenè was sleeping deeply, peacefully, as if he somehow knew that his father had found a way to make him well.

*

Pino couldn't sleep that night either. Speculative by nature, he liked the theatre and had acted in several well-meaning but increasingly rare amateur productions in and around Vigàta. So he read theatrical literature. As soon as his meagre earnings would allow him, he would rush off to Montelusa's only bookshop and buy his fill of comedies and dramas. He lived with his mother, who had a small pension, and getting food on the table was not really a problem. Over dinner his mother had made him tell her three times how he discovered the corpse, asking him each time to better explain a certain detail or circumstance. She'd done this so that she could retell the whole story the next day to her friends at church or at the market, proud to be privy to such knowledge and to have a son so clever as to get himself involved in such an important affair. Finally, around midnight, she'd gone to bed, and shortly thereafter Pino turned in as well. As for sleeping, however, there was no chance of that; something made him toss and turn under the sheets. He was speculative by nature, as we said, and thus, after wasting two hours trying to shut his eyes, he'd convinced himself it was no use, it might as well be Christmas Eve. He got up, washed his face, and went to sit at the little desk he had in his bedroom. He repeated to himself the story he had told his mother, and although every detail fitted and it all made sense, the buzz in his head was still there, in the background. It was like the 'hot-cold' guessing game: as long as he was reviewing everything he'd said, the buzz seemed to be saying, 'You're cold.' Thus the static must be coming from something he'd neglected to tell his mother. And in fact what he hadn't told her were the same things he, by agreement with Saro, had kept from Inspector Montalbano: their immediate recognition of the corpse and the phone call to Rizzo. And here the buzz became very loud and screamed, 'You're hot hot hot!' So he took a pen and paper and wrote down word for word the conversation he'd had with the lawyer. He reread it and made some corrections, forcing himself to remember even the pauses, which he wrote in, as in a theatrical script. When he had got it all down, he reread the final draft. Something in that dialogue still didn't work. But it was too late now; he had to go to Splendour.

*

Around ten o'clock in the morning, Montalbano's reading of the two Sicilian dailies, one from Palermo and the other from Catania, was interrupted by a phone call from the commissioner.

'I was told to send you thanks,' the commissioner began.

'Oh, really? On whose behalf?'

'On behalf of the bishop and our minister. Monsignor Teruzzi was pleased with the Christian charity – those were his exact words – which you, how shall I say, put into action by not allowing any unscrupulous, indecent journalists and photographers to paint and propagate lewd portraits of the deceased.'

'But I gave that order before I even knew who it was! I would have done the same for anybody.'

'I'm aware of that; Jacomuzzi told me everything. But why should I have revealed such an irrelevant detail to our holy prelate? Why should I disabuse him, or you, of your Christian charity? Such charity, my dear man, becomes all the more precious the loftier the position of the object of charity, you know what I mean? Just imagine, the bishop even quoted Pirandello.'

'No!'

'Oh, yes. He quoted *Six Characters in Search of an Author,* the line where the father says that one cannot be held forever to a less than honourable act, after a life of great integrity, just because of one moment of weakness. In other words, we cannot pass on to posterity the image of Luparello with his pants momentarily down.'

'What did the minister say?'

'He certainly didn't quote Pirandello, since he wouldn't even know who that is, but the idea, however tortuous and mumbled, was the same. And since he belongs to the same party as Luparello, he took the trouble to add another word.'

'What was that?'

'Prudence.'

'What's prudence got to do with this business?'

'I don't know, but that's the word he used.'

'Any news of the autopsy?'

'Not yet. Pasquano wanted to keep him in the fridge until tomorrow, but I talked him into examining him late this morning or early in the afternoon. I don't think we're going to learn anything new from that end, though.'

'No, probably not,' Montalbano concurred.

*

Returning to his newspapers, Montalbano learned much less from them than he already knew of the life, miracles, and recent death of Silvio Luparello, engineer. They merely served to refresh his memory. Heir to a dynasty of Montelusa builders (his grandfather had designed the old train station, his father the courthouse), young Silvio, after graduating with highest Honours from Milan Polytechnic, had returned to his hometown to carry on and expand the family business. A practising Catholic, he had embraced the political ideals of his grandfather, a passionate follower of Don Luigi Sturzo (the ideals of his father, who had been a Fascist militiaman and participated in the March on Rome, were kept under a respectful veil of silence), and had cut his teeth at the FUCI, the national organization of Catholic university students, creating a solid network of friendships for himself. Thereafter, on every public occasion – demonstration, assembly, or gala – Silvio Luparello had always shown up alongside the party bigwigs, but always one step behind them, half smiling as if to say that he stood there by choice, not out of hierarchical protocol. Officially drafted numerous times as a candidate in both the local and parliamentary elections, he had withdrawn every time for the noblest of reasons (always duly brought to the public's attention), invoking that humility, that desire to serve in silence and shadow, proper to every true Catholic. And in silence and shadow he had served for nearly twenty years, until the day when, fortified by all that his eagle eyes had seen in the shadow, he took a few servants of his own, first and foremost Deputy Cusumano. Later he would likewise get Senator Portolano and Chamber Deputy Tricomi to wear his livery (though the papers called them 'fraternal friends' and 'devoted followers'). In short, the whole party, in Montelusa and its province, had passed into his hands, as had some 80 per cent of all public and private contracts. Not even the earthquake unleashed by a handful of Milanese judges, unseating a political class that had been in power for fifty years, had touched him. On the contrary: having always remained in the background, he could now come out into the open, step into the light, and thunder against the corruption of his party cronies. In barely a year's time, as the standard-bearer for renewal, he had become provincial secretary, to the acclaim of the rank and file. Unfortunately, however, this glorious appointment had come a mere three days before his death. One newspaper lamented the fact that cruel fate had not granted a man of such lofty and exemplary stature the time needed to restore his party to its former splendour. In commemorating him, both newspapers together recalled his great generosity and kind-heartedness, his readiness to lend a hand, in any circumstance, to friend and foe alike, without partisan distinction.

With a shudder, Montalbano remembered a news story he'd seen the previous year on some local TV station. In the town of Belfi, his grandfather's birthplace, Luparello was dedicating a small orphanage, named after this same grandfather. Some twenty small children, all dressed alike, were singing a song of thanks to the engineer, who listened with visible emotion. The words of that little song had etched themselves indelibly in the inspector's memory:

What a good man,
What a fine fellow
Is our dear
Signor Luparello.

In addition to glossing over the circumstances of the engineer's death, the newspapers also carefully ignored the rumours that had been swirling for untold years around far less public affairs in which he'd been involved. There was talk of rigged contract competitions, kickbacks in the billions of lire, pressures applied to the point of extortion. And in all these instances the name that constantly popped up was that of Counsellor Rizzo, first the caddy, then the right-hand man, and finally the alter ego of Luparello. But these always remained rumours, voices in the air and on the wind. Some even said that Rizzo was a liaison between Luparello and the Mafia, and on this very subject the inspector had once managed to read a confidential report that spoke of currency smuggling and money laundering. Suspicions, of course, and nothing more, since they were never given a chance to be substantiated; every authorization request for an investigation had been lost in the labyrinths of that same courthouse the engineer's father had designed and built.

*

At lunchtime Montalbano phoned the Montelusa flying squad and asked to speak to Corporal Ferrara. She was the daughter of an old schoolmate of his who had married young, an attractive, sharp-witted girl who every now and then, for whatever reason, would try to seduce him.

'Anna? I need you.'

'What? I don't believe it.'

'Do you have a couple of free hours this afternoon?'

'I'll get them, Inspector. Always at your service, night and day. At your beck and call, even, or if you like, at your whim.'

'Good. I'll come and pick you up in Montelusa, at your house, around three.'

'This must be happiness.'

'Oh, and, Anna, wear feminine clothes.'

'Spike heels and slit dress, that sort of thing?'

'I just meant not in uniform.'

*

Punctually, at the second honk, Anna came out the front door in skirt and blouse. She didn't ask any questions and limited herself to kissing Montalbano on the cheek. Only when the car turned onto one of the three small byways that led from the provincial road to the Pasture did she speak.

'Um, if you want to fuck, let's go to your house. I don't like it here.'

At the Pasture there were only two or three cars, but the people inside them clearly did not belong to Gegè Gullotta's evening shift. They were students, boys and girls, married lovers who had nowhere else to go. Montalbano took the little road to the end, not stopping until the front tyres were already sinking into the sand. The large shrub next to which Luparello's BMW had been found was on their left but could not be reached by that route.

'Is that where they found him?' asked Anna.

'Yes.'

'What are you looking for?'

'I'm not sure. Let's get out.'

As they headed toward the water's edge, Montalbano put his arm around her waist and pressed her toward him; she rested her head on his shoulder, smiling. She now understood why the inspector had invited her along: it was all an act. Together they would look like a pair of lovers who had found a place to be alone at the Pasture. In their anonymity they would arouse no curiosity.

What a son of a bitch! she thought. *He doesn't give a shit about my feelings for him.*

At a certain point Montalbano stopped, his back to the sea. The shrub was in front of them, about a hundred yards away as the crow flies. There could be no doubt: the BMW had come not by way of the small roads but from the beach side and had stopped after circling toward the bush, its nose facing the old factory; that is, in the exact opposite position to that which all the other cars coming off the provincial road had to take, there being absolutely no room in which to manoeuvre. Anyone who wanted to return to the provincial road had no choice but to go back up the byway in reverse. Montalbano walked another short distance, his arm still around Anna, his head down: he could find no tyre tracks; the sea had erased everything.

'So what now?'

'First I have to call Fazio. Then I'll take you back home.'

'Inspector, may I tell you something in all honesty?'

'Of course.'

'You're an arsehole.'

FOUR

'Inspector? Pasquano here. Where the hell have you been hiding? I've been looking for you for three hours, and at headquarters they couldn't tell me anything.'

'Are you angry at me, Doctor?'

'At you? At the whole stinking universe!'

'What have they done to you?'

'They forced me to give priority to Luparello, the same way, exactly, as when he was alive. So even in death the guy has to come before everyone else? I suppose he's first in line at the cemetery, too?'

'Was there something you wanted to tell me?'

'Just an advance notice of what I'm going to send you in writing. Absolutely nothing: the dear departed died of natural causes.'

'Such as?'

'To put it in unscientific terms, his heart burst,

literally. In every other respect he was healthy, you know. It was only his pump that didn't work, and that's what screwed him, even though they made a valiant attempt to repair it.'

'Any other marks on the body?'

'What sort of marks?'

'I don't know, bruises, injections . . .'

'As I said, nothing. I wasn't born yesterday, you know. And anyway, I asked and obtained permission for my colleague Capuano, his regular doctor, to take part in the autopsy.'

'Covering your arse, eh Doc?'

'What did you say?'

'Something stupid, I'm sorry. Did he have any other ailments?'

'Why are you starting over from the top? There was nothing wrong with him, just a little high blood pressure. He treated it with a diuretic, took a pill every Thursday and Sunday, first thing in the morning.'

'So on Sunday, when he died, he had taken it?'

'So what? What the hell's that supposed to mean? That his diuretic pill had been poisoned? You think we're still living in the days of the Borgias? Or have you started reading remaindered mystery novels? If he'd been poisoned, don't you think I would have noticed?'

'Had he dined that evening?'

'No, he hadn't.'

'Can you tell me at what time he died?'

'You're going to drive me crazy with questions like that. You must be watching too many American movies, you know, where as soon as the cop asks what time the crime took place, the coroner tells him the murderer finished his work at six-thirty-two p.m., give or take a few seconds, thirty-six days ago. You saw with your own eyes that rigor mortis hadn't set in yet, didn't you? You felt how hot it was in that car, didn't you?'

'So?'

'So it's safe to say the deceased left this world between seven and nine o'clock the evening before he was found.'

'Nothing else?'

'Nothing else. Oh yes, I almost forgot: Mr Luparello died, of course, but he did manage to do it first – to have sex, that is. Traces of semen were found around his lower body.'

*

'Mr Commissioner? This is Montalbano. I wanted to let you know I just spoke with Dr Pasquano on the phone. The autopsy's been done.'

'Save your breath, Montalbano. I know everything already: around two o'clock I got a call from Jacomuzzi, who was there and filled me in. Wonderful, eh?'

'I'm sorry, I don't understand.'

'It's wonderful, that is, that someone in this fine province of ours should decide to die a natural death and thereby set a good example. Don't you think? Another two or three deaths like Luparello's and we'll start catching up with the rest of Italy. Have you spoken to Lo Bianco?'

'Not yet.'

'Please do so at once. Tell him there are no more problems as far as we're concerned. They can get on with the funeral whenever they like, if the judge gives the go-ahead. Listen, Montalbano – I forgot to mention it this morning – my wife has invented a fantastic new recipe for baby octopus. Can you make it Friday evening?'

*

'Montalbano? This is Lo Bianco. I wanted to bring you up to date on things. Early this afternoon I got a phone call from Dr Jacomuzzi.'

What a wasted career! Montalbano thought furiously to himself. *In another age he would have made an excellent town crier.*

'He told me the autopsy revealed nothing abnormal,' the judge continued. 'So I authorized burial. Do you have any objection?'

'None.'

'Can I therefore consider the case closed?'

'Think I could have two more days?'

He could hear the alarms ringing in the judge's head.

'Why, Montalbano? Is there something wrong?'

'No, Your Honour, nothing at all.'

'Well, why then, for the love of God? I'll confess to you, Inspector – I've no problem doing so – that I, as well as the chief prosecutor, the prefect, and the commissioner, have been strongly pressured to bring this affair to an end as quickly as possible. Nothing illegal, mind you. Urgent entreaties, all very proper, on the part of those – family, political friends – who want to forget the whole sad story as soon as possible. And they're right, in my opinion.'

'I understand, Your Honour. But I still need two days, no more.'

'But why? Give me a reason!'

He found an answer, a pretext. He couldn't very well tell the judge his request was founded on nothing, or rather on the feeling that he'd been hoodwinked – he didn't know how or why – by someone who at that moment was proving himself to be shrewder than he.

'If you really must know, it's out of concern for public opinion. I wouldn't want anyone to start whispering that we closed the case in haste because we had no intention of getting to the bottom of things. As you know, it doesn't take much to start people thinking that way.'

'If that's how you feel, then all right. You can have your forty-eight hours. But not a minute more. Try to understand the situation.'

*

'Gegè? How's it going, handsome? Sorry to wake you at six-thirty in the evening.'

'Fucking shit!'

'Gegè, is that any way to speak to a representative of the law? Especially someone like you, who before the law can only shit your pants? And speaking of fucking, is it true you're doing it with a ten-and-change black man?'

'Ten-and-change what?'

'Inches of cock.'

'Cut the shit. What do you want?'

'To talk to you.'

'When?'

'Tonight, late. You tell me what time.'

'Let's make it midnight.'

'Where?'

'The usual place, at Puntasecca.'

'A big kiss for your pretty lips, Gegè.'

*

'Inspector Montalbano? This is Prefect Squatrito. Judge Lo Bianco communicated to me just now that you asked for another twenty-four hours – or forty-eight, I can't remember – to close the case of the late Mr Luparello. Dr Jacomuzzi, who has politely kept me informed of all developments, told me that the autopsy established unequivocally that Luparello died of natural causes. Far be it from me to think – what am I saying, to even dream – of interfering in any way, since in any case there'd be no reason to do so, but do let me ask you: why this request?'

'My request, sir, as I have already explained to Justice Lo Bianco and will now reiterate, was dictated by a desire for transparency, to nip in the bud any malicious supposition that the police department might prefer not to clarify every aspect of the case and wish to close it without due verification of all leads. That's all.'

The prefect declared himself satisfied with the reply, and indeed Montalbano had carefully chosen two verbs ('clarify' and 'reiterate') and one noun ('transparency') which had forever been key words in the prefect's vocabulary.

*

'Hello? This is Anna, sorry to disturb you.'

'Why are you talking like that? Do you have a cold?'

'No, I'm at the squad office, but I don't want anyone to hear.'

'What is it?'

'Jacomuzzi called my boss and told him you don't want to close the Luparello case yet. The boss said you're just being an arsehole as usual, which I agree with and actually had a chance to tell you just a few hours ago.'

'Is that why you called? Thanks for the confirmation.'

'There's something else I have to tell you, Inspector, something I found out right after I left you, when I got back here.'

'Look, Anna, I'm up to my neck in shit. Tell me about it tomorrow.'

'There's no time to lose. It may be of interest to you.'

'I'm going to be busy here till one or one-thirty this morning. If you want to drop by now, then all right.'

'I can't make it right now. I'll see you at your place at two.'

'Tonight?!'

'Yes, and if you're not there, I'll wait.'

*

'Hello, darling? It's Livia. Sorry to call you at work, but—'

'You can call me whenever and wherever you want. What is it?'

'Nothing important. I was reading in a newspaper just now about the death of a politician in your parts. It's just a brief notice. It says that Inspector Salvo Montalbano is conducting a thorough investigation of the possible causes of death.'

'So?'

'Is this death causing you any problems?'

'Not too many.'

'So nothing's changed? You're still coming to see me on Saturday? You don't have some unpleasant surprise in store for me?'

'Like what?'

'Like an awkward phone call telling me the investigation has taken a new turn and so I'll have to wait but you don't know how long and so it's probably better to postpone everything for a week? It certainly wouldn't be the first time.'

'Don't worry, this time I'll manage.'

*

'Inspector Montalbano? This is Father Arcangelo Baldovino, secretary to His Excellency the bishop.'

'It's a pleasure. What can I do for you, Father?'

'The bishop has learned, with some astonishment, I must say, that you think it advisable to prolong your investigation into the sad and unfortunate passing of Silvio Luparello. Is this true?'

It was indeed, Montalbano confirmed, and for the third time he explained his reasons for acting in this manner. Father Baldovino seemed persuaded, yet begged the inspector to hurry up, 'to avoid untoward speculation and spare the already afflicted family yet another torment'.

*

'Inspector Montalbano? This is Mr Luparello.'

'What the hell! Didn't you die?' Montalbano was about to say, but he stopped himself in the nick of time.

'I'm his son,' the other continued, in a very educated, polite tone that had no trace of dialect whatsoever. 'My name is Stefano. I'm afraid I must appeal to your kindness and make what may seem to you an unusual request. I'm calling you on my mother's behalf.'

'By all means, if I can be of any help.'

'Mama would like to meet you.'

'What's unusual about that? I myself was intending to ask your mother if I could drop by sometime.'

'The thing is, Inspector, Mama would like to meet you by tomorrow at the latest.'

'My God, Mr Luparello, I really haven't got a single free moment these days, as you can imagine. And neither do you, I should think.'

'Don't worry, we can find ten minutes. How about tomorrow afternoon at five o'clock sharp?'

*

'Montalbano, sorry to make you wait, but I was—'

'On the toilet, in your element.'

'Come on, what do you want?'

'I wanted to let you in on something very serious. The pope just phoned me from the Vatican, really pissed off at you.'

'What are you talking about?!'

'He's furious because he's the only person in the world who hasn't received your report on the Luparello autopsy. He felt neglected and told me he intends to excommunicate you. You're screwed.'

'Montalbano, you've completely lost your mind.'

'Can you tell me something, just out of curiosity?'

'Sure.'

'Do you kiss arse out of ambition or natural inclination?'

'Natural inclination, I think.'

The sincerity of the response caught the inspector by surprise.

'Listen, have you finished examining the clothes Luparello was wearing? Did you find anything?'

'We found what you'd expect. Traces of semen on the underwear and trousers.'

'And inside the car?'

'We're still examining it.'

'Thanks. Now go back to the toilet.'

*

'Inspector? I'm calling from a phone booth on the provincial road, near the old factory. I did what you asked me to do.'

'Tell me about it, Fazio.'

'You were absolutely right. Luparello's BMW came from Montelusa, not Vigàta.'

'Are you certain?'

'On the Vigàta side, the beach is cordoned off by cement blocks. You can't get through. He would have had to fly.'

'Did you find out which way he might have come?'

'Yes, but it's totally crazy.'

'Why? Explain.'

'Because, even though from Montelusa to Vigàta there are dozens of roads and byways that one can take to avoid being seen, at a certain point, to get to the Pasture, Luparello's car would have had to pass through the dry bed of the Canneto.'

'The Canneto? But it's impassable!'

'Well, I did it, and therefore somebody else could have done it. It's completely dry. The only problem is, my car's suspension is ruined. And since you didn't want me to take a squad car, I'm going to have to—'

'I'll pay for the repairs myself. Anything else?'

'Yes. As it was pulling out of the riverbed and turning onto the sand, the BMW's tyres left some tracks. If we tell Jacomuzzi right away, we can get a cast of them.'

'Fuck Jacomuzzi. '

'Yes, sir. Need anything else?'

'No, Fazio, just come back to headquarters. And thanks.'

FIVE

The little beach of Puntasecca, a compact strip of sand sheltered by a hill of white marl, was deserted at that hour. When the inspector arrived, Gegè was already there waiting for him, leaning against his car and smoking a cigarette.

'Come on out, Salvù,' he said to Montalbano. 'Let's enjoy the fine night air a minute.'

They stood there a bit in silence, smoking. Then Gegè, having put out his cigarette, began to speak.

'I know what you want to ask me, Salvù. I'm well prepared. You can ask me anything you like, even jumping around.'

They smiled at this shared memory. They'd known each other since La Primina, the little private kindergarten where the teacher was Signorina Marianna, Gegè's sister, some fifteen years his senior. Salvo and

Gegè were listless schoolboys, learning their lessons like parrots, and like parrots repeating them in class. Some days, however, Signorina Marianna wasn't satisfied with those litanies, so she'd start jumping around in her questions; that is, she wouldn't follow the order in which the information had been presented. And this meant trouble, because then you had to have understood the material and grasped the logical connections.

'How's your sister doing?' asked Montalbano.

'I took her to Barcelona. There's a specialized eye clinic there. They say they can work miracles. They told me they can get the right eye, at least, to recover in part.'

'When you see her, give her my best.'

'I will. But as I was saying, I'm well prepared, so you can start firing away with the questions.'

'How many people do you have working for you at the Pasture?'

'Between whores and fags of various sorts, twenty-eight. Then there's Filippo di Cosmo and Manuele Lo Pìparo, who are there just to make sure there's no trouble. The smallest thing, you know, and I'm screwed.'

'You've got to keep your eyes open.'

'Right. Do you realize the kind of problems I'd have if there was a brawl or somebody got knifed or OD'd?'

'Still sticking to light drugs?'

'Yeah. Grass, coke at the most. Ask the street cleaners if they ever find a single syringe, go ahead and ask 'em.'

'I believe you.'

'Then there's Giambalvo, chief of vice, who's always breathing down my neck. He says he'll put up with me as long as I don't create any complications and bust his balls with something big.'

'I know Giambalvo. He doesn't want to have to shut down the Pasture or he'd lose his cut. What do you give him, a monthly wage? A fixed percentage? How much does he get?'

Gegè smiled.

'Get yourself transferred to vice and you'll find out. I'd like that. It'd give me a chance to help out a poor wretch like you, who lives only on his salary and goes around dressed in rags.'

'Thanks for the compliment. Now tell me about that night.'

'Well, it must have been around ten, ten-thirty, when Milly, who was working that night, saw some headlights coming from the Montelusa side near the sea, heading up toward the Pasture at a good clip. Freaked her out.'

'Who's this Milly?'

'Her real name's Giuseppina La Volpe, thirty years old, born at Mistretta. She's a smart girl.'

He took a folded-up sheet of paper out of his pocket and handed it to Montalbano.

'Here, I've written out everyone's real name. And address, too, in case you wanted to talk to somebody in person.'

'Why did you say Milly got scared?'

'Because there's no way a car could come from that direction, unless it passed through the Canneto, which would be a sure way to bust up your car and your arse into the bargain. At first she thought it was some brilliant idea of Giambalvo's, a surprise round-up or something. Then she realized it couldn't be vice: you don't do a round-up with only one squad car. So she got even more scared, because it occurred to her it might be the Monterosso boys, who've been waging war on me, trying to take the Pasture away, and maybe there would even be a shoot-out. So, to be ready to hightail it out of there at any moment, she kept her eyes on that car, and her client started complaining. But she had enough time to see that the car was turning and heading straight for the bushes nearby, driving almost into them. And then it stopped.'

'You're not telling me anything new, Gegè.'

'The guy who'd been fucking Milly then dropped her off and went back up the path, in reverse, to the provincial road. Milly waited around for another trick, walking back and forth. Then Carmen arrived at the spot where she'd been a minute before, with a devoted client who comes to see her at the same time every Saturday and Sunday and spends hours with her. Carmen's real name is on that piece of paper I gave you.'

'Her address, too?'

'Yes. Before the client turned off his headlights, Carmen noticed that the two inside the BMW were already fucking.'

'Did she tell you exactly what she saw?'

'Yes. It was only a few seconds, but she got a good look. Maybe because it had made an impression on her, since you don't usually see cars like that at the

Pasture. Anyway, the girl, who was in the driver's seat – oh, I forgot to mention, Milly said it was the girl who was driving – she turned, climbed onto the lap of the man beside her, fiddling around with her hands underneath, but you couldn't see them, and then she started going up and down. You haven't forgotten how people fuck, have you?'

'I don't think so, but we can check. When you've finished telling me what you've got to tell me, drop your pants, put your pretty little hands on the trunk, and stick your arse up in the air. If I've forgotten anything, you can remind me. Now go on, and stop wasting my time.'

'When they were done, the girl opened the car door and got out, straightened her skirt, and shut the door. The man, instead of starting up the car and leaving, stayed where he was, with his head leaning back. The girl passed very close by Carmen's car, and at that exact moment a car's headlights shone right on her. She was a good-looking lady, blonde, well dressed, and she had a shoulder bag in her left hand. Then she headed toward the old factory.'

'Anything else?'

'Yes. Manuele, who was making the rounds in his

car, saw her leave the Pasture and walk toward the provincial road. Since she didn't look to him like Pasture material, by the way she was dressed, he turned around to follow her, but then a car came by and picked her up.'

'Wait a second, Gegè. Did Manuele see her standing there, with her thumb out, waiting for someone to give her a ride?'

'Salvù, how do you do it? You really are a born cop.'

'Why do you say that?'

'Because that's exactly the point Manuele's not convinced about. In other words, he didn't see the chick make any signal, but the car did stop. And that's not all: although the car was moving along at a pretty good clip, Manuele had the impression the door was already open when it put on the brakes to pick her up. But Manuele didn't think to take down the licence number – there wasn't any reason.'

'Right. And what can you tell me about the man in the BMW, Luparello?'

'Not much. He wore glasses, and he never took his jacket off to fuck, even though it was hot as hell. But there's one point where Milly's story and Carmen's don't jibe. Milly says that when the car arrived, it looked like the man had a tie or a black cravat around his neck; Carmen maintains that when she saw him, he had his shirt unbuttoned and that was all. But that seems like an unimportant detail to me, since Luparello could have taken off the tie while he was fucking. Maybe it bothered him.'

'His tie but not his jacket? But that's not unimportant, Gegè, because no tie or cravat was found inside the car.'

'That doesn't mean anything. Maybe it fell out onto the sand when the girl got out.'

'Jacomuzzi's men combed the area and didn't find anything.'

They stood there in silence, thoughtful.

'Maybe there's another explanation for what Milly saw,' Gegè suddenly said. 'Maybe it was never a question of ties or cravats. Maybe the man still had his seat belt on – after all, they'd just driven along the bed of the Canneto, with all its rocks and sticks – and he took it off when the girl climbed onto his lap, since the seat belt would surely have been a bother.'

'It's possible.'

'I've told you everything I was able to find out

about this, Salvù. And I tell you in my own interest. Because for a big cheese like Luparello to come and croak at the Pasture isn't good for business. Now everybody's eyes are gonna be on it, so the sooner you finish your investigation, the better. After a couple of days people forget, and we can all go back to work in peace. Can I go now? These are peak hours at the Pasture.'

'Wait. What's your opinion of the whole thing?'

'Me? You're the cop. But just to make you happy, I will say that the whole thing stinks to me. Let's imagine the girl is a high-class whore, a foreigner. Are you gonna tell me Luparello doesn't have a place to take her?'

'Gegè, do you know what a perversion is?'

'You're asking me? I could tell you a few things that would make you puke on my shoes. I know what you're going to say, that they came to the Pasture because they thought it would make it more erotic. And that does happen sometimes. Did you know that one night a judge showed up with his bodyguards?'

'Really? Who was it?'

'Judge Cosentino. See, I can even tell you the name. The evening before he was kicked out of office, he came to the Pasture with an escort car, picked up a transvestite, and had sex with him.'

'What did the bodyguards do?'

'They went for a long walk on the beach. But to get back to the subject: Cosentino knew he was a marked man and decided to have a little fun. But what interest could Luparello have had? He wasn't that kind of guy. Everybody knows he liked the ladies, but he was always careful never to let anyone see him. And where is the woman who could make him risk everything he had and everything he stood for just to get laid? I don't buy it, Salvù.'

'Go on.'

'If we suppose, on the other hand, that the chick was not a whore, then I really don't know. It's even less likely – downright impossible – they'd let themselves be seen at the Pasture. Also, the car was driven by the girl, that much is certain. Aside from the fact that no one would ever trust a whore with a car like that, that lady must have been something to strike fear in a man's heart. First of all, she has no problem driving down into the Canneto, and then, when Luparello dies between her thighs, she gets up like nothing, closes the door, and walks away. Does that seem normal to you?'

'I don't think so.'

At this point Gegè started laughing and flicked on his cigarette lighter.

'What are you doing?' asked Montalbano.

'Come over here, faggot. Bring your face to the light.'

The inspector obeyed, and Gegè illuminated his eyes. Then he extinguished the lighter.

'I get it. All along, you, a man of the law, were thinking the exact same thoughts as me, a man of crime. And you just wanted to see if they matched up. Eh, Salvù?'

'You guessed right.'

'I'm hardly ever wrong when it comes to you. Gotta go now. Ciao.'

'Thanks,' said Montalbano.

The inspector left first, but a moment later his friend pulled up beside him, gesturing for him to slow down.

'What do you want?'

'I don't know where my head was. I wanted to tell you this before. Do you have any idea what a pretty sight you made this afternoon, hand in hand with Corporal Ferrara?'

Then he accelerated, putting a safe distance between himself and the inspector, his arm waving goodbye.

*

Back at home, Montalbano jotted down a few of the details that Gegè had provided, but tiredness soon came over him. He glanced at his watch, noticed it was a little past one, and went to bed. The insistent ringing of the doorbell woke him up. His eyes looked over at the alarm clock: two-fifteen. He got up with some effort; the early stages of sleep always slowed down his reflexes.

'Who the fuck is that, at this hour?'

He went to the door just as he was, in his underpants, and opened up.

'Hi,' said Anna.

He'd completely forgotten; the girl had indeed said that she would come see him around this hour. Anna was looking him over.

'I see you're wearing the right clothes,' she said, then stepped inside.

'Say what it is you have to tell me, then go back home. I'm dead tired.'

Montalbano was truly annoyed by the intrusion. He went into his bedroom, put on a pair of trousers and a shirt, and returned to the dining room. Anna wasn't there. She had gone into the kitchen, opened the refrigerator, and was already sinking her teeth into a bread roll filled with prosciutto.

'I'm so hungry I can hardly see.'

'You can talk while you're eating.'

Montalbano put the espresso pot on the stove.

'You're going to make coffee? At this hour? Will you be able to fall back asleep afterwards?'

'Anna, please.' He was unable to be polite.

'All right. This afternoon, after we split up, I found out from a colleague, who for his part had been told by an informer, that starting yesterday, Tuesday morning, some guy's been going around to all the jewellers, receivers of stolen goods, and pawnbrokers both legitimate and illegitimate to alert them that if someone came in to buy or pawn a certain piece of jewellery, they should let him know. The piece in question is a necklace, with a solid-gold chain and a heart-shaped pendant covered with diamonds. The kind of thing you'd find at some cheap department store, except that this one's real.'

'So how are they supposed to let him know? By phone?'

'It's no joke. He told each one of them to give a different signal – I don't know, like putting a green cloth in the window or hanging a piece of newspaper from the front door, things like that. He's shrewd: that way he can see without being seen.'

'Fine, but I think—'

'Let me finish. From the way he spoke and acted, the people he approached concluded it was best to do as he said. Then we found out that some other people, at the same time, were making the same rounds in all the towns of the province, Vigàta included. Therefore, whoever lost that necklace wants it back.'

'Nothing wrong with that. So why, in your opinion, should this interest me?'

'Because the man told a certain receiver in Montelusa that the necklace might have been lost in the Pasture on Sunday night or Monday morning. Does it interest you now?'

'Up to a point.'

'I know, it may be only a coincidence and have nothing whatsoever to do with Luparello's death.'

'Thanks anyway. Now go back home. It's late.'

The coffee was ready. Montalbano poured himself a cup, and Anna naturally took advantage of the opportunity.

'None for me?'

With the patience of a saint, the inspector filled another cup and handed it to her. He liked Anna, but couldn't she understand he was with another woman?

'No,' Anna said suddenly, putting down her coffee.

'No what?'

'I don't want to go home. Would you really mind so much if I stayed here with you?'

'Yes, I would.'

'But why?'

'Because I'm too good a friend of your father. I'd feel like I was doing him wrong.'

'What bullshit!'

'It may be bullshit, but that's the way it is. And anyway, you seem to be forgetting that I'm in love, really in love, with another woman.'

'Who's not here.'

'She's not here, but it's as if she were. Now don't

be silly and don't say silly things. You're unlucky, Anna; you're up against an honest man. I'm sorry. Forgive me.'

*

He couldn't fall asleep. Anna had been right to warn him that the coffee would keep him awake. But something else was getting on his nerves: if that necklace had indeed been lost at the Pasture, then surely Gegè must also have been told about it. But Gegè had been careful not to mention it, and surely not because it was a meaningless detail.

SIX

At five-thirty in the morning, after having spent the night repeatedly getting up and going back to bed, Montalbano decided on a plan for Gegè, one that would indirectly pay him back for his silence about the lost necklace and his joke about the visit he'd made that afternoon to the Pasture. He took a long shower, drank three coffees in succession, then got in his car. When he arrived in Rabàto, the oldest quarter of Montelusa, destroyed thirty years earlier by a landslide and now consisting mostly of ruins refurbished and damaged higgledy-piggledy ramshackle hovels inhabited by illegal aliens from Tunisia and Morocco, he headed through narrow, tortuous alleyways toward Piazza Santa Croce. The church stood whole amid the ruins. He took from his pocket the sheet of paper Gegè had given him: Carmen, known in the real world as Fatma Ben Gallud, Tunisian, lived at number 48. It was a miserable *catojo,* a small ground-floor room with a little window in the wooden door to allow the air to circulate. He knocked: no answer. He knocked harder, and this time a sleepy voice asked, 'Who that?'

'Police,' Montalbano fired back. He had decided to play rough, catching her still drowsy from the sudden awakening. Certainly Fatma, because of her work at the Pasture, must have slept even less than he. The door opened, the woman covering herself in a large beach towel that she held up at breast level with one hand.

'What you want?'

'To talk to you.'

She stood aside. In the *catojo* there was a double bed half unmade, a little table with two chairs and a small gas stove. A plastic curtain separated the toilet and sink from the rest of the room. Everything was so clean and orderly it sparkled. But the smell of the woman and her cheap perfume so filled the room that one could hardly breathe.

'Let me see your residence permit.'

As if in fear, the woman let the towel fall as she brought her hands to her face to cover her eyes. Long legs, slim waist, flat belly, high, firm breasts – a real woman, in short, the type you see in television commercials. After a moment or two, Montalbano realized, from Fatma's expectant immobility, that what he was witnessing was not fear, but an attempt to reach the most obvious and common of arrangements between man and woman.

'Get dressed.'

There was a metal wire hung from one corner of the room to another. Fatma walked over to it: broad shoulders, perfect back, small, round buttocks.

With a body like that, thought Montalbano, *I bet she's been through it all.*

He imagined the men lining up discreetly in certain offices, with Fatma earning 'the indulgence of the authorities' behind closed doors, as he had happened several times to read about, an indulgence of the most self-indulgent kind. Fatma put on a light cotton dress over her naked body and remained standing in front of Montalbano.

'So . . . your papers?'

The woman shook her head no, and began to weep in silence.

'Don't be afraid,' the inspector said.

'I not afraid. I very unlucky.'

'Why?'

'Because you wait few days, I no here no more.'

'And where did you want to go?'

'Man from Fela he like me, I like him, he say Sunday he marry me. I believe him.'

'The man who comes to see you every Saturday and Sunday?'

Fatma's eyes widened.

'How you know?'

She started crying again.

'But now everything finish.'

'Tell me something. Is Gegè going to let you go with this man from Fela?'

'Man talk to Signor Gegè, man pay.'

'Listen, Fatma, pretend I never came to see you here. I only want to ask you one thing, and if you answer me truthfully, I will turn around and walk out of here, and you can go back to sleep.'

'What you want to know?'

'Did they ask you, at the Pasture, if you'd found anything?'

The woman's eyes lit up.

'Oh, yes! Signor Filippo come – he Signor Gegè's

man – tell us if we find gold necklace with heart of diamond, we give it straight to him. If not find, then look.'

'And do you know if it was found?'

'No. Also tonight, all girls look.'

'Thank you,' said Montalbano, heading for the door. In the doorway he stopped and turned round to look at Fatma.

'Good luck.'

So Gegè had been foiled. What he had so carefully neglected to mention to Montalbano, the inspector had managed to find out anyway. And from what Fatma had just told him, he drew a logical conclusion.

*

When he arrived at headquarters at the crack of dawn, the officer on guard gave him a look of concern.

'Anything wrong, Chief?'

'Nothing at all,' he reassured him. 'I just woke up early.'

He had bought the two Sicilian newspapers and sat down to read them. With a great wealth of detail, the first announced that the funeral service for Luparello would be held the following day. The solemn ceremony would take place at the cathedral, officiated by the bishop himself. Special security measures would be taken, due to the anticipated arrival of numerous important personages come to express their condolences and pay their last respects. At the latest count they would include two government ministers, four under-secretaries, eighteen members of parliament between senators and deputies, and a throng of regional deputies. And so city police, carabinieri, coastguard agents and traffic cops would all be called into action, to say nothing of personal bodyguards and other even more personal escorts, of which the newspaper mentioned nothing, made up of people who certainly had some connection with law and order, but from the other side of the barricade on top of which stood the law. The second newspaper more or less repeated the same things, while adding that the casket had been set up in the atrium of the Luparello mansion and that an endless line of people were waiting to express their thanks for everything the deceased had dutifully and impartially done – when still alive, of course.

Meanwhile Sergeant Fazio had arrived, and Montalbano spoke to him at great length about a number of investigations currently under way. No phone calls came in from Montelusa. Soon it was noon, and the inspector opened a file containing the deposition of the two garbage collectors concerning their discovery of the corpse. He copied down their addresses, said goodbye to the sergeant and the other policemen, and told them they'd hear from him in the afternoon.

If Gegè's men had talked to the whores about the necklace, they must certainly have said something to the garbage collectors as well.

*

Number 28 Gravet Terrace was a three-storey building, with an intercom at the front door. A mature woman's voice answered.

'I'm a friend of Pino's.'

'My son's not here.'

'Didn't he get off work?'

'He got off, but he went somewhere else.'

'Could you let me in, signora? I only want to leave him an envelope. What floor is it?'

'Top floor.'

A dignified poverty: two rooms, eat-in kitchen, bathroom. One could calculate the square footage the minute one entered. Pino's mother, fiftyish and modestly attired, showed him in.

'Pino's room's this way.'

A small room full of books and magazines, a little table covered with paper by the window.

'Where did Pino go?'

'To Raccadali. He's auditioning for a part in a play by Martoglio, the one about St John getting his head cut off. Pino really likes the theatre, you know.'

Montalbano approached the little table. Apparently Pino was writing a play; on a sheet of paper he had lined up a column of dialogue. But when he read one of the names, the inspector felt a kind of shock run through him.

'Signora, could I please have a glass of water?'

As soon as the woman left, he folded up the page and put it in his pocket.

'The envelope?' Pino's mother reminded him when she returned, handing him his water.

Montalbano then executed a perfect pantomime, one that Pino, had he been present, would have admired: he searched first in the pockets of his trousers, then more hastily in his jacket, whereupon he gave a look of surprise and finally slapped his forehead noisily.

'What an idiot! I left the envelope at the office! Just give me five minutes, signora, I'll be right back.'

Slipping into his car, he took out the page he'd just stolen, and what he read there darkened his mood. He restarted the engine and left. 102 Via Lincoln. In his deposition Saro had even specified the apartment number. With a bit of simple maths, the inspector figured that the surveyor/garbage collector must live on the sixth floor. The front door to the block was open, but the elevator was broken. He had to climb up six flights of stairs but had the satisfaction of having guessed right: a polished little plaque there read BALDASSARE MONTAPERTO. A tiny young woman answered the door with a baby in her arms and a worried look in her eye.

'Is Saro home?'

'He went to the drugstore to buy some medicine for the baby, but he'll be right back.'

'Is he sick?'

Without answering, she held her arm out slightly to let him see. The little thing was sick, and how: sallow, hollow-cheeked, with big, already grown-up eyes staring angrily at him. Montalbano felt terrible. He couldn't stand to see children suffer.

'What's wrong with him?'

'The doctors can't explain it. Who are you, sir?'

'The name's Virduzzo. I'm the accountant at Splendour.'

'Come on in.'

The woman felt reassured. The apartment was a mess, it being all too clear that Saro's wife was too busy always attending to the little boy to look after the house.

'What do you want with Saro?'

'I believe I made a mistake, on the minus side, on the amount of his last payslip. I'd like to see the stub.'

'If that's all you need,' said the woman, 'there's no need to wait for Saro. I can get you the stub myself. Come.'

Montalbano followed her, ready with another excuse to stay until the husband returned. There was a nasty smell in the bedroom, as of rotten milk. The woman tried to open the top drawer of a commode but was unable to, having only one free hand to use, as she was holding the baby in her other arm.

'I can do it, if you like,' said Montalbano.

The woman stepped aside, and the inspector opened the drawer and saw that it was full of papers, bills, prescriptions, receipts.

'Where are the payment envelopes?'

At that moment Saro entered the bedroom. They hadn't heard him come in; the front door to the apartment had been left open. The instant he saw Montalbano rummaging in the drawer, he was convinced the inspector was searching their house for the necklace. He turned pale, started trembling, and leaned against the door frame.

'What do you want?' he barely managed to articulate.

Frightened by her husband's obvious terror, the woman spoke before Montalbano had a chance to answer.

'But it's Virduzzo, the accountant!' she almost yelled.

'Virduzzo? That's Inspector Montalbano!'

The woman tottered, and Montalbano rushed forward to support her, fearing the baby might end up on the floor together with his mother. He helped sit her down on the bed. Then he spoke, the words coming out of his mouth without the intervention of his brain, a phenomenon that had come over him before and which one imaginative journalist had once called 'that flash of intuition which now and then strikes our policeman'.

'Where'd you put the necklace?' he said.

Saro stepped forward, stiff from struggling to remain standing on his pudding-legs, went over to his bedside table, opened the drawer, and pulled out a packet wrapped in newspaper, which he threw on the bed. Montalbano picked it up, went into the kitchen, sat down, and unwrapped the packet. The jewel was at once vulgar and very fine: vulgar in its design and conception, fine in its workmanship and in the cut of the diamonds with which it was studded. Saro, meanwhile, had followed him into the kitchen.

'When did you find it?'

'Early Monday morning, at the Pasture.'

'Did you tell anyone?'

'No, sir, just my wife.'

'And has anyone come to ask if you found a necklace like this?'

'Yes, sir. Filippo di Cosmo came. He's one of Gegè Gullotta's men.'

'And what did you tell him?'

'I said I hadn't found anything.'

'Did he believe you?'

'Yes, sir, I think so. Then he said that if I happened to find it, I should give it to him right away and not mess around, because it was a very sensitive matter.'

'Did he promise you anything?'

'Yes, sir. A deadly beating if I found it and kept it, fifty thousand lire if I found it and turned it over to him.'

'What did you plan to do with the necklace?'

'I wanted to pawn it. That's what Tana and I decided.'

'You weren't planning to sell it?'

'No, sir, it didn't belong to us. We saw it like something somebody had lent to us; we didn't want to profit from it.'

'We're honest people,' said the wife, who'd just come in, wiping her eyes.

'What were you going to do with the money?'

'We wanted to use it to treat our son. We could have taken him far away from here, to Rome, Milan – anywhere there might be doctors who know something.'

They were all silent a few moments. Then Montalbano asked the woman for two sheets of paper, which she tore out of a notebook they used for shopping expenses. Holding out one of the sheets to Saro, the inspector said, 'Make me a drawing that shows the exact spot where you found the necklace. You're a land surveyor, aren't you?'

As Saro was sketching, on the other sheet Montalbano wrote:

> I the undersigned, Salvo Montalbano, Chief Inspector of the Police Department of Vigàta (province of Montelusa), hereby declare having received on this day, from Mr Baldassare 'Saro' Montaperto, a solid-gold necklace with a heart-shaped pendant, also solid gold but studded with diamonds, found by Mr Montaperto around the area known as 'the Pasture' during the course of his work as ecological agent. In witness whereof,

And he signed, but paused a moment to reflect before adding the date at the bottom. Then he made up his mind and wrote, 'Vigàta, September 9, 1993.' Meanwhile Saro had finished. They exchanged sheets.

'Perfect,' said the inspector, looking over the detailed drawing.

'Here, however, the date is wrong,' Saro said. 'The ninth was last Monday. Today is the eleventh.'

'No, nothing wrong there. You brought that necklace into my office the same day you found it. You had it in your pocket when you came to police headquarters to tell me you'd found Luparello dead, but you didn't give it to me till later because you didn't want your fellow worker to see. Is that clear?'

'If you say so, sir.'

'Take good care of this statement.'

'What are you going to do now? Arrest him?' asked the woman.

'Why? What's he done?' asked Montalbano, standing up.

SEVEN

Montalbano was well respected at the San Calogero trattoria, not so much because he was a police inspector as because he was a good customer with discerning tastes. Today they fed him some very fresh striped mullet, fried to a delicate crisp and drained on absorbent paper. After coffee and a long stroll on the eastern jetty, he went back to the office. Fazio got up from his desk as soon as he saw him.

'There's someone waiting for you, Chief.'

'Who is it?'

'Pino Catalane, remember him? One of the two garbage collectors who found Luparello's body.'

'Send him right in.'

He immediately noticed that the youth was tense, nervous.

'Have a seat.'

Pino sat with his buttocks on the edge of the chair.

'Could you tell me why you came to my house and put on the act that you did? I've got nothing to hide.'

'I did it simply to avoid frightening your mother. If I told her I was a police inspector, she might've had a heart attack.'

'Well, in that case, thanks.'

'How did you figure out it was me who was looking for you?'

'I phoned my mother to see how she was feeling – when I left her she had a headache – and she told me a man had come to give me an envelope but forgot to bring it with him. She said he'd gone out to get it but had never come back. I became curious and asked her to describe the guy. When you're trying to pretend you're somebody else, you should cover up that mole you've got under your left eye. What do you want from me?'

'I have a question. Did anyone come to the Pasture to ask if you'd found a necklace?'

'Yes, someone you know, in fact: Filippo di Cosmo.'

'What did you say?'

'I told him I hadn't found it, which was the truth.'

'And what did he say?'

'He said if I found it, so much the better for me, he'd give me fifty thousand lire, but if I found it and I didn't turn it over to him, so much the worse. He said the same thing to Saro. But Saro didn't find it either.'

'Did you go home before coming here?'

'No, sir, I came here directly.'

'Do you write for the theatre?'

'No, but I like to act now and then.'

'Then what's this?'

Montalbano handed him the page he'd taken from the little table. Pino looked at it, unimpressed, and smiled.

'No, that's not a theatre scene, that's . . . '

He fell silent, at a loss. It occurred to him that if those weren't lines of dramatic dialogue, he would have to explain what they were, and it wouldn't be easy.

'I'll help you out,' said Montalbano. 'This is a transcript of a phone call one of you made to Rizzo, the lawyer, right after you found Luparello's body, before you came here to headquarters to report your discovery. Am I right?'

'Yes, sir.'

'Who made the phone call?'

'I did. But Saro was right beside me, listening.'

'Why'd you do it?'

'Because Luparello was an important person, a big cheese. So we immediately thought we should inform Rizzo. Actually, no, the first person we thought of calling was Deputy Cusumano.'

'Why didn't you?'

'Because Cusumano, with Luparello dead, was like somebody who, when an earthquake hits, loses not only his house but also the money he was keeping under the floorboards.'

'Give me a better explanation of why you called Rizzo.'

'Because we thought maybe something could still be done.'

'Like what?'

Pino didn't answer, but only passed his tongue over his lips.

'I'll help you out again. You said maybe something could still be done. Something like moving the car out of the Pasture and letting the body be found somewhere else? Were you thinking that's what Rizzo might ask you to do?'

'Yes.'

'And you would have been willing to do it?'

'Of course! That's why we called!'

'What did you expect to get out of it?'

'We were hoping maybe he could find us other jobs, or help us win some competition for surveyors, or find us the right job, so we wouldn't have to work as stinking garbage collectors any more. You know as well as I do, Inspector, you can't sail without a favourable wind.'

'Now explain the most important thing: why did you write down that conversation? Were you hoping to blackmail him with it?'

'How? With words? Words are just air.'

'So what was your reason?'

'Well, believe it or not, I wrote down that conversation because I wanted to study it. Something didn't sound right to me – speaking as a man of the theatre, that is.'

'I don't follow.'

'Let's pretend that what's written down is supposed

to be staged. I'm the Pino character, and I phone the Rizzo character early in the morning to tell him I've just found his boss dead. He's the guy's secretary, his devoted friend, his political crony. He's more than a brother. But the Rizzo character, he keeps cool as a cucumber, doesn't get upset, doesn't ask where we found him, how he died, if he was shot, if he died in a car crash, nothing. He only asks why we've come to him, of all people, with the news. Does that sound right to you?'

'No. Go on.'

'He shows no surprise, in other words. In fact, he tries to put a distance between himself and the dead man, as if this was just some passing acquaintance of his. And he immediately tells us to do our duty, which is to call the police. Then he hangs up. No, Inspector, as drama it's all wrong. The audience would just laugh. It doesn't work.'

Montalbano dismissed Pino and kept the sheet of paper. When the garbage collector left, he reread it.

It did work, and how. It worked marvellously, if in this hypothetical drama – which in the end was not really so hypothetical – Rizzo, before receiving the phone call, already knew where and how Luparello had died and anxiously wanted the body to be discovered as quickly as possible.

*

Jacomuzzi gaped at Montalbano, astonished. The inspector stood before him, dressed to the nines: dark-blue suit, white shirt, burgundy tie, sparkling black shoes.

'Jesus! Going to your wedding?'

'Have you done with Luparello's car? What did you find?'

'Nothing of importance inside. But—'

'The suspension was broken.'

'How did you know?'

'A little bird told me. Listen, Jacomuzzi.'

He pulled the necklace out of his pocket and tossed it onto the table. Jacomuzzi picked it up, looked at it carefully, and made a gesture of surprise.

'But this is real! It's worth tens of millions of lire! Was it stolen?'

'No, somebody found it on the ground at the Pasture and brought it in to me.'

'At the Pasture? What kind of whore can afford a piece of jewellery like that? You must be kidding!'

'I want you to examine it, photograph it, do all the little things you usually do. Then bring me the results as soon as you can.'

The telephone rang. Jacomuzzi answered and passed the receiver to his colleague.

'Who is it?'

'It's Fazio, Chief. Come back to town immediately. All hell's breaking loose.'

'What is it?'

'Contino the schoolteacher's shooting at people.'

'What do you mean, shooting?'

'Shooting shooting! He fired two shots from the balcony of his apartment at the people sitting at the café below,. screaming something nobody could understand. Then he fired another shot at me as I was coming through his front door to see what was going on.'

'Has he killed anyone?'

'No. He just grazed the arm of a certain De Francesco.'

'OK, I'll be right there.'

*

As he travelled the six miles back to Vigàta at breakneck speed, Montalbano thought of Contino the schoolteacher. Not only did he know him, there was a secret between them. Six months earlier the inspector had been taking the stroll he customarily allowed himself two or three times a week along the eastern jetty, out to the lighthouse. Before he set out, however, he always stopped at Anselmo Greco's shop, a hovel that clashed with the clothing boutiques and shiny, mirrored cafés along the *corso.* Among such antiquated items as terracotta dolls and rusty weights for nineteenth-century scales, Greco also sold *càlia e simenza,* a mixture of roasted chickpeas and salted pumpkin seeds. Montalbano would buy a paper cone full of these and then head out. That day, after he had reached the point, he was turning around, right under the lighthouse, when he saw an elderly man beneath him, sitting on a block of the low concrete breakwater, head down, immobile. Montalbano got a better look, to see if perhaps the man was holding a fishing line in his hands. But he wasn't fishing; he wasn't doing anything. Suddenly he stood up, quickly made the sign of the cross, and balanced himself on his tiptoes.

'Stop!' Montalbano shouted.

The man froze; he had thought he was alone. In

a couple of bounds Montalbano reached him, grabbed him by the lapels of his jacket, lifted him up bodily, and carried him to safety.

'What were you trying to do, kill yourself?'

'Yes.'

'Why?'

'Because my wife is cheating on me.'

This was the last thing Montalbano expected to hear. The man had surely passed his eightieth year.

'How old is your wife?'

'Let's say eighty. I'm eighty-two.'

An absurd conversation in an absurd situation, and the inspector didn't feel like continuing it. Taking the man by the arm, he forced him to walk toward town. At this point, just to make everything even crazier, the man introduced himself.

'I am Giosuè Contino, if I may. I used to teach elementary school. Who are you? If, of course, you wish to tell me.'

'My name is Salvo Montalbano. I'm police inspector for the town of Vigàta.'

'Oh, really? Then you came at just the right time. You yourself can tell my slut of a wife she'd better stop cuckolding me with Agatino De Francesco or one of these days I'm going to do something crazy.'

'And who's this De Francesco?'

'He used to be the postman. He's younger than I am, seventy-six years old, and he has a pension that's one and a half times the size of mine.'

'Do you know this to be a fact, or are you just suspicious?'

'I'm absolutely certain it's the gospel truth. Every afternoon God sends our way, rain or shine, this De Francesco comes and has a coffee at the café right under my house.'

'So what?'

'How long do *you* take to drink a cup of coffee?'

For a minute Montalbano went along with the old schoolmaster's quiet madness.

'That depends. If I'm standing—'

'What's that got to do with it? When you're sitting!'

'Well, it depends on whether I have an appointment and have to wait, or if I only want to pass the time.'

'No, my friend, that man sits there only to eye

my wife, who eyes him back, and they never waste an opportunity to do so.'

They had arrived back in town.

'Where do you live, Mr Contino?'

'At the end of the *corso,* on Piazza Dante.'

'Let's take a back street, I think that's better.' Montalbano didn't want the sodden, shivering old man to arouse the townspeople's curiosity and questions.

'Coming upstairs with me? Would you like a coffee?' he asked the inspector while extracting the front-door keys from his pocket.

'No, thanks. Just dry yourself off and change your clothes.'

That same evening he had gone to speak with De Francesco, the ex-postman, a tiny, unpleasant old man who reacted quite harshly to the inspector's advice, screaming in his face.

'I'll take my coffee wherever and whenever I like! What, is it illegal to go sit at the café under that arteriosclerotic Contino's balcony? You surprise me, sir. You're supposed to represent the law, and instead you come and tell me these things!'

*

'It's all over,' said the municipal policeman keeping curious bystanders away from the front door on Piazza Dante. At the entrance to the apartment stood Sergeant Fazio, who threw his arms up in distress. The rooms were in perfect order, sparkling clean. Master Contino was lying in an armchair, a small bloodstain over his heart. The revolver was on the floor, next to the armchair, an ancient Smith & Wesson five-shooter that must have dated back at least to the time of Buffalo Bill but which unfortunately still worked. His wife was lying on the bed, she, too, with a bloodstain over her heart, her hands clasped around a rosary. She must have been praying before agreeing to let her husband kill her. Montalbano thought again of the commissioner, who this time was right: here death had indeed found its dignity.

*

Nervous and surly, Montalbano gave the sergeant his instructions and left him there to wait for the judge. He felt, aside from a sudden melancholy, a subtle remorse: if only he had intervened more wisely with the schoolmaster, if only he had alerted Contino's friends and doctor in time . . .

*

He took a long walk along the wharf and the eastern jetty, his favourite. His spirits slightly revived, he returned to the office. There he found Fazio beside himself.

'What is it? What's happened? Hasn't the judge come yet?'

'No, he came, and they've already taken the bodies away.'

'So what's wrong?'

'What's wrong is that while half the town was watching Contino shoot his gun, some bastards went into action and cleaned out two apartments top to bottom. I've already sent four of our men. I was waiting for you to show up so I could go and join them.'

'All right, go. I'll be here.'

He decided it was time to play his ace: the trap he had in mind couldn't fail. He reached for the phone.

'Jacomuzzi?'

'What, for God's sake! What's the rush? I still don't have any report on your necklace. It's too early.'

'I'm well aware you couldn't possibly tell me anything yet, I realize that.'

'So what do you want?'

'To advise you to maintain total secrecy. The story behind that necklace is not as simple as it may appear. It could lead to unexpected developments.'

'You insult me! If you tell me not to talk about something, I won't talk about it, even if the heavens fall!'

✡

'Mr Luparello? I'm so sorry I couldn't come today. It simply wasn't possible, you must believe me. Please extend my apologies to your mother.'

'Just a minute, Inspector.'

Montalbano waited patiently.

'Inspector? Mama says tomorrow at the same hour, if that's all right with you.'

It was all right with him, and he confirmed the appointment.

EIGHT

He returned home tired, intending to go straight to bed, but almost mechanically – it was sort of a tic – he turned on the television. The Televigàta anchorman, after talking about the event of the day, a shoot-out between petty Mafiosi on the outskirts of Miletta a few hours earlier, announced that the provincial secretariat of the party to which Luparello belonged (actually, used to belong) had convened in Montelusa. It was a highly unusual meeting, one that in less turbulent times than these would have been held, out of due respect for the deceased, at least thirty days after his passing; but things being what they were, the troubling situation called for quick, lucid decisions. And so a new provincial secretary had been elected, unanimously: Dr Angelo Cardamone, chief osteologist at Montelusa Hospital, a man who had always fought with Luparello from within the party, but fairly and courageously and always out in the open. This clash of ideas – the newsman continued – could be simplified in the following terms: Engineer Luparello was in favour of maintaining the four-party governing coalition while allowing the introduction of pristine new forces untrammelled by politics (read: not yet subpoenaed for questioning), whereas the osteologist tended to favour a dialogue, however cautious and clear-eyed, with the left. The newly elected secretary had been receiving telegrams and telephone calls of congratulation, even from the opposition. Cardamone, who in an interview appeared moved but determined, declared that he would commit himself to the best of his abilities not to betray his predecessor's hallowed memory, and concluded by asserting that he would devote 'his diligent labour and knowledge' to the now-renovated party.

'Thank God he'll devote it to the party,' Inspector Montalbano couldn't help but exclaim, since Dr Cardamone's knowledge, surgically speaking, had left more people hobbled than a violent earthquake usually does.

The newsman's next words made the inspector prick up his ears. To enable Cardamone to follow his own path without losing sight of the principles and people that represented the very best of Luparello's political endeavours, the members of the secretariat had besought Counsellor Pietro Rizzo, the engineer's spiritual heir, to work alongside the new secretary. After some understandable resistance, given the onerous tasks that came with the unexpected appointment, Rizzo had let himself be persuaded to accept. In his interview with Televigàta, Rizzo, also deeply moved, declared that he had no choice but to assume this weighty burden if he was to remain faithful to the memory of his mentor and friend, whose watchword was always and only: 'to serve'.

Montalbano reacted with surprise. How could this new secretary so blithely swallow having to work, with official sanction, alongside the man who had been his principal adversary's most loyal right-hand man? His surprise was short-lived, however, and proved naive once the inspector had given the matter a moment's rational thought. Indeed, that party had always distinguished itself by its innate inclination for compromise, for finding the middle path. It was possible that Cardamone didn't yet have enough clout to go it alone and felt the need for extra support.

He changed the channel. On the Free Channel, the voice of the leftist opposition, there was Nicolò Zito, the most influential of their editorialists, explaining how in Sicily, and in the province of Montelusa in particular, *mutatis mutandis* – or *zara zabara,* to say it in Sicilian – things never budged, even when there was a storm on the horizon. He quoted, with obvious facility, the prince of Salina's famous statement about changing everything in order to change nothing and concluded that Luparello and Cardamone were two sides of the same coin, the alloy that coin was made of being none other than Counsellor Rizzo.

Montalbano rushed to the phone, dialled the Free Channel's number, and asked for Zito. There was a bond of common sympathy, almost friendship, between him and the newsman.

'What can I do for you, Inspector?'

'I want to see you.'

'My dear friend, I'm leaving for Palermo tomorrow morning and will be away for at least a week. How about if I come by to see you in half an hour? And fix me something to eat. I'm starving.'

A dish of pasta with garlic and oil could be served up without any problem. He opened the refrigerator:

Adelina had prepared a hefty dish of boiled shrimp, enough for four. Adelina was the mother of a pair of repeat offenders, the younger of whom was still in prison, having been arrested by Montalbano himself three years earlier.

*

The previous July, when she had come to Vigàta to spend two weeks with him, Livia, upon hearing this story, became terrified.

'Are you insane? One of these days that woman will take revenge and poison your soup!'

'Take revenge for what?'

'For having arrested her son!'

'Is that my fault? Adelina's well aware it's not my fault if her son was stupid enough to get caught. I played fair, didn't use any tricks or traps to arrest him. It was all on the level.'

'I don't give a damn about your contorted way of thinking. You have to get rid of her.'

'But if I fire her, who's going to keep house for me, do my laundry, iron my clothes and make me dinner?'

'You'll find somebody else!'

'There you're wrong. I'll never find a woman as good as Adelina.'

*

He was about to put the pasta water on the stove when the telephone rang.

'I feel like crawling underground for waking you at this hour,' was the introduction.

'I wasn't sleeping. Who is this?'

'It's Counsellor Pietro Rizzo.'

'Ah, Counsellor Rizzo. My congratulations.'

'For what? If it's for the honour my party has just done me, you should probably offer me your condolences. Believe me, I accepted only out of a sense of undying loyalty to the ideals of the late Mr Luparello. But to get back to my reason for calling: I need to see you, Inspector.'

'Now?!'

'Not now, of course, but bear in mind, in any case, that it is an improcrastinable matter.'

'We could do it tomorrow morning, but isn't the funeral tomorrow? You'll be very busy, I imagine.'

'Indeed. All afternoon as well. There will be some

very important guests, you know, and of course they will linger awhile.'

'So when?'

'Actually, on second thoughts, I think we could do it tomorrow morning, but first thing. What time do you usually get to the office?'

'Around eight.'

'Eight o'clock would be fine with me. It will take but a few minutes.'

'Listen, Counsellor, precisely because you will have so little time tomorrow morning, could you perhaps tell me in advance what it's about?'

'Over the phone?'

'Just a hint.'

'All right. I have heard – though I don't know how much truth there is in the rumour – that an object found by chance on the ground was turned over to you. I've been instructed to reclaim it.'

Montalbano covered the receiver with one hand and literally exploded in a horselike whinny, a mighty guffaw. He had baited the Jacomuzzi hook with the necklace, and the trap had worked like a charm, catching the biggest fish he could ever have hoped for. But how did Jacomuzzi manage to let everyone know things he wasn't supposed to let anyone know? Did he resort to lasers, to telepathy, to magical shamanistic practices? Montalbano heard Rizzo yelling on the line.

'Hello? Hello? I can't hear you! What happened, did we get cut off?'

'No, excuse me, I dropped my pencil and was looking for it. I'll see you tomorrow at eight.'

*

As soon as he heard the doorbell ring, he put the pasta in the water and went to the door.

'So what's for supper?' asked Zito as he entered.

'Pasta with garlic and oil, and shrimp with oil and lemon.'

'Excellent.'

'Come into the kitchen and give me a hand. Meanwhile, my first question is: can you say "improcrastinable"?'

'Have you gone soft in the head? You make me race all the way from Montelusa to ask me if I can say some word? Anyway, of course I can say it. No problem.'

He tried to say it three or four times, with

increasing obstinacy, but he couldn't do it, getting more and more marble-mouthed with each try.

'You have to be very adroit, very adroit,' said the inspector, thinking of Rizzo, and he wasn't referring only to the lawyer's adroitness in casually uttering tongue-twisters.

As they ate, they spoke of eating, as always happens in Italy. Zito, after reminiscing about the heavenly shrimp he had enjoyed ten years earlier at Fiacca, criticized these for being a little overdone and regretted that they lacked a hint of parsley.

'So how is it that you've all turned British at the Free Channel?' Montalbano broke in without warning, as they were drinking an exquisite white wine his father had found near Randazzo. He had come by with six bottles the previous week, although they had been merely an excuse for them to spend a little time together.

'In what sense, British?'

'In the sense that you've refrained from dragging Luparello through the mud, as you would certainly have done in the past. Jesus Christ, the man dies of a heart attack in a kind of open-air brothel among whores, pimps and buggers, his trousers down around his ankles – it's downright obscene – and you guys, instead of seizing the moment for all it's worth, you all toe the line and cast a veil of mercy over how he died.'

'We're not really in the habit of taking advantage of such things.'

Montalbano started laughing.

'Would you do me a favour, Nicolò? Would you and everyone else at the Free Channel please go fuck yourselves?'

Zito started laughing in turn.

'All right, here's what happened. A few hours after the body was found, Counsellor Rizzo dashed over to see Baron Filò di Baucina, the "red baron", a millionaire but a communist, and begged him, with hands folded, not to let the Free Channel mention the circumstances of Luparello's death. He appealed to the sense of chivalry that the baron's ancestors seem, long ago, to have possessed. As you know, the baron owns eighty per cent of the network. Simple as that.'

'Simple as that, my arse. And so you, Nicolò Zito, who have won the admiration of your adversaries for always saying what needed to be said, you just say, "*Yes,* sir" to the baron and lie down?'

'What colour is my hair?' asked Zito by way of reply.

'It's red.'

'I'm red inside and out, Montalbano. I belong to the bad, rancorous communists, an endangered species. I accepted the whole bit because I was convinced that those who were saying we shouldn't sully the poor bastard's memory by dwelling on the circumstances of his death actually wished him ill, not well, as they were trying to make us think.'

'I don't understand.'

'Well, let me explain, my innocent friend. The quickest way to make people forget a scandal is to talk about it as much as possible, on television, in the papers, and so on. Over and over you flog the same dead horse, and pretty soon people start getting fed up. "They're really dragging this out!" they say. "Haven't we had enough?" After a couple of weeks the saturation effect is such that nobody wants to hear another word about that scandal. Now do you understand?'

'I think so.'

'If, on the other hand, you hush everything up, the silence itself starts to talk, rumours begin to multiply out of control until you can't stop them any more. You want an example? Do you know how many phone calls we've received at the studio precisely because of our silence? Hundreds. So is it true that Mr Luparello used to do two women at a time in his car? Is it true that Mr Luparello liked to do the sandwich, fucking a whore while a black man worked on him from behind? Then the latest, which came in tonight: is it true that Luparello used to give all his prostitutes fabulous jewels? Apparently somebody found one at the Pasture. Speaking of which, do you know anything about this story?'

'Me? No, that's just bullshit,' the inspector calmly lied.

'See? I'm sure that in a few months some arsehole will come to me and ask if it's true that Luparello used to bugger little four-year-olds and then stuff them with chestnuts and eat them. The slandering of his name will become eternal, the stuff of legend. That, I hope, will help you understand why I agreed to sweep it all under the carpet.'

'And what's Cardamone's position?'

'I don't know. That was very strange, his election. In the provincial secretariat they were all Luparello's men, you see, except for two, who were Cardamone's, but they were there just for the sake of appearances, to show that they were democratic and all. Clearly the new secretary could have been and should have been a follower of Luparello. Instead, surprise: Rizzo stands up and proposes Cardamone. The other members of the clique were speechless but didn't dare object. If Rizzo's talking this way, it must mean there's something lurking beneath all this which could turn dangerous; better follow the counsellor down that path. And so they vote in favour. Cardamone gets the call, accepts the post, and himself proposes that Rizzo work alongside him, to the great dismay of his two representatives in the secretariat. But here I understand Cardamone: better to have Rizzo aboard – he must have thought – than at large like a loose cannon.'

Zito then proceeded to tell him about a novel he was planning to write, and they went on till four.

*

As he was checking the health of a succulent plant, a gift from Livia that he kept on the windowsill in his office, Montalbano saw a blue government car pull up, the kind equipped with telephone, chauffeur and bodyguard, the latter of which got out first and opened the rear door for a short, bald man wearing a suit the same colour as the car.

'There's someone outside who needs to talk to me,' he said to the guard. 'Send him right in.'

When Rizzo entered, the inspector noted that the upper part of his left sleeve was covered by a broad black band the width of a palm: the counsellor was already in mourning for the funeral.

'What can I do to win your forgiveness?'

'For what?'

'For having disturbed you at home, at so late an hour.'

'But you said the matter was improcr—'

'Improcrastinable, yes.'

Such a clever man, Counsellor Pietro Rizzo!

'I'll come to the point. Late last Sunday night a young couple, highly respectable people, having had a bit to drink, decided to indulge an imprudent whim. The wife persuaded the husband to take her to the Pasture. She was curious about the place and what goes on there. A reprehensible curiosity, to be sure, but nothing more. When the pair arrived at the edge of the Pasture, the woman got out of the car.

But almost immediately people began to harass her with obscene propositions, so she got back in the car and they left. Back at home she realized she'd lost a precious object she was wearing around her neck.'

'What a strange coincidence,' muttered Montalbano, as if to himself.

'Excuse me?'

'I was just noting that at around the same time, and in the same place, Silvio Luparello was dying.'

Rizzo didn't lose his composure, but assumed a grave expression.

'I noticed the same thing, you know. Tricks of fate.'

'The object you mention, is it a solid-gold necklace with a heart studded with precious stones?'

'That's the one. I'm here to ask you to return it to its rightful owners, with the same discretion, of course, as you showed when my poor Mr Luparello was found dead.'

'You'll have to forgive me,' said the inspector, 'but I haven't the slightest idea of how to proceed in a case like this. In any event, I think it would have been a different story if the owner herself had come forward.'

'But I have a proper letter of attorney!'

'Really? Let me see it.'

'No problem, Inspector. You must understand that before bandying my clients' names about, I wanted to be quite sure you had the object they were looking for.'

He reached into his jacket pocket, extracted a sheet of paper, and handed it to Montalbano. The inspector read it carefully.

'Who's this Giacomo Cardamone that signed the letter?'

'He's the son of Dr Cardamone, our new provincial secretary.'

Montalbano decided it was time to repeat the performance.

'But it's so strange!' he mumbled again almost inaudibly, assuming an air of deep contemplation.

'I'm sorry, what did you say?'

Montalbano did not answer at once, letting the other stew a moment in his own juices.

'I was just thinking that in this whole affair, fate, as you say, is playing too many tricks on us.'

'In what sense, if you don't mind my asking?'

'In the sense that the son of the new party secretary happens to be in the same place at the same time as the old secretary at the moment of his death. Curious, don't you think?'

'Now that you bring it to my attention, yes. But I am certain there is not the slightest connection between the two matters, absolutely certain.'

'So am I,' said Montalbano, adding, 'I don't understand this signature next to Giacomo Cardamone's.'

'That's his wife's signature. She's Swedish. A rather reckless woman, frankly, who seems unable to adapt to our ways.'

'How much is the piece worth, in your opinion?'

'I'm no expert, but the owners said about eighty million lire.'

'Then here's what we'll do: later this morning I'm going to call my colleague Jacomuzzi – he's got the necklace at the moment – and have it sent back to me. Tomorrow morning I'll send it over to your office with one of my men.'

'I don't know how to thank you—'

Montalbano cut him off.

'And you will give my man a proper receipt.'

'But of course!'

'As well as a cheque for ten million lire – I've taken the liberty of rounding up the value of the necklace

– which would be the usual percentage due anyone who finds valuables or large sums of money.'

Rizzo absorbed the blow almost gracefully.

'That seems quite fair. To whom should I make it out?'

'To Baldassare Montaperto, one of the two street cleaners who found Luparello's body.'

The lawyer carefully wrote down the name.

NINE

Rizzo had no sooner finished closing the door than Montalbano already began dialling Nicolò Zito's home phone number. What the lawyer had just told him had set in motion a mechanism inside his brain that outwardly manifested itself in a frantic need to act. Zito's wife answered.

'My husband just walked out. He's on his way to Palermo.' Then she said, suddenly suspicious, 'But didn't he stay with you last night?'

'He certainly did, signora, but something of importance occurred to me just this morning.'

'Wait, maybe I can still get him. I'll try calling him on the intercom.'

A few minutes later he heard his friend's panting, then his voice, 'What do you want? Wasn't last night enough for you?'

'I need some information.'

'If you can make it brief.'

'I want to know everything – but really everything, even the most bizarre rumours – about Giacomo Cardamone and his wife, who seems to be Swedish.'

'No "seems" about it. She's a statuesque six-footer with tits and legs like you wouldn't believe. But if you really want to know everything, that would take time, which I haven't got right now. Listen, let's do this: I'm going to leave now. On the way I'll give it some thought, and as soon as I arrive I'll send you a fax.'

'Send a fax to police headquarters? Here we still use tom-toms and smoke signals!'

'I meant I'll send a fax for you to my Montelusa office. You can pass by later this morning, or around midday.'

*

Montalbano had to do something, so he went out of his office and into the sergeants' room.

'How's Tortorella doing?'

Fazio looked over at the desk of his absent colleague.

'I went to see him yesterday. They've apparently decided to release him from the hospital on Monday.'

'Do you know how to get inside the old factory?'

'When they built the enclosure wall after shutting it down, they put in a tiny little door, so small you have to bend down to pass through it, an iron door.'

'Who's got the key?'

'I don't know. I can find out.'

'Don't just find out. I want it before noon.'

He went back into his office and phoned Jacomuzzi, who let him wait a bit before deciding to answer.

'What's wrong, you got dysentery?'

'Cut it, Montalbano. What do you want?'

'What have you found on the necklace?'

'What do you think? Nothing. Actually, fingerprints, but there are so many of them and they're such a mess they're indecipherable. What should I do?'

'Send it back to me before the end of the day. Understood? Before the end of the day.'

He heard Fazio's irritated voice shout from the next room. 'Jesus Christ! Is it possible nobody knows who this Sicilchim belonged to? It must have some sort of bankruptcy trustee, some official custodian!'

And, as soon as he saw Montalbano enter, 'It'd probably be easier to get the keys to St Peter's.'

The inspector told him he was going out and wouldn't be gone more than two hours. When he returned, he wanted to find that key on his desk.

*

As soon as she saw him in the doorway, Montaperto's wife turned pale and put her hand over her heart.

'Oh my God! What is it? What happened?'

'Nothing that you should worry about. Actually, I have good news for you, believe it or not. Is your husband home?'

'Yes, he got off early today.'

The young woman sat him in the kitchen and went to call Saro, who had lain down in the bedroom at the baby's side, hoping to get him to close his eyes for just a little while.

'Sit down,' the inspector said to Saro when he appeared, 'and listen to me carefully. Where were you thinking of taking your son with the money you would have got from pawning the necklace?'

'To Belgium,' Saro promptly replied. 'My brother

lives there, and he said we could stay at his house for a while.'

'Have you got the money for the journey?'

'Scrimping and saving here and there, we've managed to put a little aside,' said the woman, without repressing a hint of pride in her voice. 'But it's only enough for the trip.'

'Excellent. Now I want you to go to the station, today, and buy the tickets. Actually, no, take the bus and go to Raccadali – is there a travel agency there?'

'Yes. But why go all the way to Raccadali?'

'I don't want anyone here in Vigàta to know what you're planning to do. While you're doing that, your wife should be packing for the journey. You mustn't tell anyone where you're going, not even family. Is that clear?'

'Perfectly clear, as far as that goes. But excuse me, Inspector, is there anything wrong in going to Belgium to have your son treated? You're telling me to do all these things on the sly, as if we were doing something illegal.'

'You're not doing anything illegal, Saro, no need to worry about that. But there are a lot of things I want to be absolutely sure about, so you'll have to trust me and do exactly as I say.'

'All right, but maybe you forgot. What are we going to Belgium for if the money we've got is barely enough to get us there and back? To go sightseeing?'

'You'll get the money you need. Tomorrow morning one of my men will bring you a cheque for ten million lire.'

'Ten million? What for?' asked Saro, breathless.

'You've earned it. It's the percentage you're entitled to for turning in the necklace you found. You can spend the money openly, without worry. As soon as you get the cheque, cash it immediately and then leave.'

'Who's the cheque from?'

'From Counsellor Rizzo.'

'Ah,' said Saro, turning pale.

'You mustn't be afraid. It's all legitimate, and in my hands. Still, it's best to be as careful as possible. I wouldn't want Rizzo to change his mind, out of the blue, like some bastards. Ten million lire, after all, is still ten million lire.'

*

Giallombardo told Montalbano that the sergeant had gone to get the key to the old factory but wouldn't be back for at least two hours; the custodian, who was not in good health, was staying with a son in Montedoro. The policeman also informed him that Judge Lo Bianco had phoned, looking for him, and wanted to be called back by ten o'clock.

*

'Ah, Inspector, excellent, I was just on my way out, I have to go to the cathedral for the funeral. And I know I will be assaulted, literally assaulted, by influential people all asking me the same question. Do you know what question that is?'

'Why hasn't the Luparello case been closed yet?'

'You guessed it, Inspector, and it's no joke. I don't want to use harsh words, and I don't want to be misunderstood in any way . . . but, in short, if you've got something concrete in hand, then out with it. Otherwise close the case. And let me say I simply don't understand: what do you think you're going to discover? Mr Luparello died of natural causes. And you, I have the impression, are digging your heels in only because he happened to die in the Pasture. I'm curious. If Luparello had been discovered at the side of the road, would you have found anything wrong with that? Answer me.'

'No.'

'So where do you want to go with this? The case must be closed by tomorrow. Understood?'

'Don't get angry, Judge.'

'Well, I am indeed angry, but only at myself. You're making me use a word, the word "case", that really should not properly be used in this case. By tomorrow, understood?'

'Could we make it Saturday?'

'What are we doing? Bartering at the market? All right. But if you are so much as an hour late, your superiors will hear about this.'

*

Zito kept his word, and the Free Channel office secretary handed him the fax from Palermo. Montalbano read it as he headed off to the Pasture.

> Young Mr Giacomo is a classic example of the spoiled rich kid, very true to the model, from which he hasn't the imagination to deviate. His father is

notoriously honourable, except for one peccadillo (more of which below), the opposite of the late lamented Luparello. Giacomino lives with his second wife, Ingrid Sjostrom, whose qualities I have already personally described to you, on the second floor of his father's villa. I shall now enumerate his exploits, at least those I can remember. An ignorant dolt, he never wanted to study or apply himself to anything other than the precocious analysis of pussy, but nevertheless he always passed with flying colours, thanks to the intervention of the Eternal Father (or more simply, his father). He never attended any university courses, though enrolled in the medical school (just as well for the public health). At age sixteen, driving his father's powerful car without a licence, he ran over and killed an eight-year-old boy. Giacomino, for all practical purposes, never paid for this, but the father did, and handsomely at that, compensating the child's family. As an adult he set up a business in services. Two years later the business failed, Cardamone lost not a penny, but his business partner nearly shot himself. A revenue officer trying to get to the bottom of things found himself suddenly transferred to Bolzano. Giacomino is currently in pharmaceuticals (imagine that! Daddy's the brains behind it, of course) and throws around a lot more money than he probably takes in.

An enthusiast for racing cars and horses, he has founded a polo club (in Montelusa!) where not a single game of that noble sport has ever been played, but there is plenty of snorting to make up for this lack.

If I had to express my sincere opinion of the man, I would say that he represents a splendid specimen of the nincompoop, of the sort that flourish wherever there is a rich and powerful father. At age twenty-two he contracted matrimony (isn't that how you say it?) with one Albamarina (Baba, to friends) Collatino, from a wealthy Palermo business family. Two years later Baba went to the Rota with a request for annulment, on the grounds of manifest *impotentia generandi* on the part of her spouse. I forgot to mention that at age eighteen, that is, four years before the marriage, Giacomino got one of the maids' daughters pregnant, and the regrettable incident was, as usual, hushed up by the Almighty. Thus there are two possibilities: either Baba was lying or the maid's daughter was lying. In the uncensurable opinion of the holy Roman prelates, it was the maid who had lied (how could it be otherwise?), and Giacomino was incapable of procreating (and for this we should thank the Lord in heaven). Granted her annulment, Baba got engaged to a cousin with whom she'd already had relations, while Giacomino headed toward the foggy lands of the north to forget.

In Sweden, he happened to attend a treacherous sort of rally race, the course of which ran around lakes, crags, and mountains. The winner was a tall, beautiful blonde, a mechanic by profession, whose name is, of course, Ingrid Sjostrom. How shall I put it, my friend, to avoid having it all sound like a soap opera? *Coup de foudre,* followed by marriage. They have now been living together for five years, and from time to time Ingrid goes back home and enters her little auto races. She cuckolds her husband with Swedish ease and simplicity. The other day at the polo club, five gentlemen (so to speak) played a party game. One of the questions asked was 'Will anyone who has not made it with Ingrid please stand?' All five remained seated. They all had a good laugh, especially Giacomino, who was present, though he didn't take part in the game. There is a rumour, totally unverifiable, that even the austere Dr Cardamone père has wet his whistle with his daughter-in-law. And this is the peccadillo I alluded to at the start, Nothing else comes to mind. I hope I've been enough of a gossip for your purposes. Vale –

NICOLÒ

Montalbano arrived at the Pasture about two. There wasn't a living soul around. The lock on the little iron door was encrusted with salt and rust. He had expected this and had expressly brought along the oil spray used to lubricate firearms. He went back to the car and turned on the radio, waiting for the oil to do its work.

The funeral – as a local radio announcer recounted – had reached some very high peaks of emotion, so that at one point the widow had felt faint and had to be carried outside. The eulogies were given, in order, by the bishop, the national vice-secretary of the party, the regional secretary, and, in a personal vein, by Minister Pellicano, who had long been a friend of the deceased. A crowd of at least two thousand people waited in front of the church for the casket to emerge, at which point they burst into warm, deeply touched applause.

'Warm' is fine, but how can applause be 'deeply touched'? Montalbano asked himself. He turned off the radio

and went to try the key. It turned in the lock, but the door seemed anchored to the ground. Pushing it with his shoulder, he finally managed to open it a crack, just wide enough to squeeze through. The door was obstructed by plaster chips, metal scraps, and sand; obviously the custodian hadn't been around for years. He noticed that there were actually two outer walls: the protective wall with the little entrance door and a crumbling old enclosure wall that had once surrounded the factory when it was running. Through the breaches in this second wall he could see rusted machinery, large tubes – some twisted, some straight – gigantic alembics, iron scaffolds with big holes, trestles hanging in absurd equilibrium, steel turrets soaring at illogical angles. And everywhere gashes in the flooring, great voids once covered with iron truss beams now broken and ready to fall below, where there was nothing any more except a layer of dilapidated cement with yellowing spikes of grass shooting up from the cracks. Montalbano stood motionless in the gap between the two walls, taking it all in, spellbound. While he liked the view of the factory from the outside, he was thrilled by the inside and regretted not having brought a camera. Then a low, continuous sound distracted his attention, a kind of sonic vibration that seemed to be coming, in fact, from inside the factory.

What machinery could be running in here? he asked himself, suspicious.

He thought it best to exit, return to his car, and get his pistol from the glove compartment. He hardly ever carried a weapon; the weight bothered him, and the gun rumpled his trousers and jackets. Going back inside the factory, where the noise continued, he began to walk carefully toward the side furthest from where he had entered. The drawing Saro had made was extremely precise and served as his guide. The noise was like the humming that certain high-tension wires sometimes make in very humid conditions, except that here the sound was more varied and musical and broke off from time to time, only to resume almost at once with a different modulation. He advanced, tense, taking care not to trip over the rocks and debris that constituted the floor in the narrow corridor between the two walls, when out of the corner of his eye, through an opening, he saw a man moving parallel to him inside the factory. He drew back, sure the other had already seen him. There was no time to lose; the man must have accomplices.

Montalbano leapt forward, weapon in hand, and shouted, 'Stop! Police!'

He realized in a fraction of a second that the other had anticipated this move and was already half bent forward, pistol in hand. Diving down, Montalbano pulled the trigger, and before he hit the ground, he managed to fire another two shots. But instead of hearing what he expected – a return shot, a cry, a shuffling of fleeing steps – he heard a deafening explosion and then a tinkling of glass breaking to pieces. When in an instant he realized what had happened, he was overcome by laughter so violent that he couldn't stand up. He had shot at himself, at the image that a large surviving pane of glass, tarnished and dirty, had cast back at him.

I can't tell anyone about this, he said to himself. *I would be asked to resign and ridden out of the force on a rail.*

The gun he was holding in his hand suddenly looked ridiculous to him, and he stuck it inside his belt. The shots, their long echo, the crash and the shattering of the glass had completely covered up the sound, which presently resumed, more varied than before. Now he understood: it was the wind, which every day, even in summer, lashed that stretch of beach, then abated in the evening, as if not wanting to disturb Gegè's business. Threading through the trestles' metal cables – some of them broken, some of them taut – and through smokestacks pocked with holes like giant flutes, the wind played its plaintive melody inside the dead factory, and the inspector paused, entranced, to listen.

It took him almost half an hour to reach the spot that Saro had indicated, having had, at various points, to climb over piles of debris. At last he figured he was exactly parallel to the spot where Saro had found the necklace on the other side of the wall, and he started looking calmly around. Magazines and scraps of paper yellowed by sun, weeds, Coca-Cola bottles (the cans being too light to be thrown over the high wall), wine bottles, a bottomless metal wheelbarrow, a few tyres, some iron scraps, an unidentifiable object, a rotten wooden beam. And beside the beam a leather handbag with strap, stylish, brand-new, stamped with a designer name. It clashed visibly with the surrounding ruin. Montalbano opened it. Inside were two rather large stones, apparently inserted as ballast to allow the bag to achieve the proper trajectory from outside the wall to inside, and nothing else. He took a closer look at the bag. The owner's metal initials had been torn off, but the leather still bore their impressions, an *I* and an *S*: Ingrid Sjostrom.

They're serving it up to me on a silver platter, thought Montalbano.

TEN

The thought of accepting the platter so kindly being offered him, along with everything that might be on it, came to mind as he was refortifying himself with a generous helping of the roast peppers that Adelina had left in the refrigerator. He looked for Giacomo Cardamone's telephone number in the directory; his Swedish wife would probably be home at this hour.

'Who dat speakin'?'

'It's Giovanni. Is Ingrid there?'

'I go see, you wait.'

He tried to guess from what part of the world this housekeeper had landed in the Cardamone home, but he couldn't figure it out.

'Ciao, monster cock, how are you?'

It was a deep, husky voice, which fit the description Zito had given him. Her words, however, had no erotic effect whatsoever on the inspector. Actually, they made him feel upset: of all the names in the world, he had to go and pick one belonging to a man Ingrid knew down to his anatomical proportions.

'Are you still there? Did you fall asleep on your feet? Did you fuck a lot last night, you pig?'

'Excuse me, signora . . .'

Ingrid's reaction was immediate, an acceptance without surprise or indignation.

'You're not Giovanni.'

'No.'

'Then who are you?'

'I'm an inspector with the police force. My name is Montalbano.'

He expected an expression of alarm but was promptly disappointed.

'Ooh, how exciting! A cop! What do you want from me?'

Her tone remained familiar, even after she knew she was speaking with someone she didn't know. Montalbano maintained his formality.

'I would like to have a few words with you.'

'I can't this afternoon, but I'm free this evening.'

'All right then, this evening.'

'Where? Shall I come to your office? Tell me where it is.'

'Better not. I'd prefer somewhere more discreet.'

Ingrid paused.

'How about your bedroom?' The woman's voice had grown irritated. Apparently she was beginning to think that the person on the line was some imbecile trying to make advances.

'Listen, signora, I realize you're suspicious, with good reason. Let's do this: I'll be back at headquarters in Vigàta in an hour. You can phone there and ask for me. All right?'

The woman didn't answer immediately. She was thinking it over before making up her mind.

'No, I believe you, cop. Tell me when and where.'

They agreed on the place, the Marinella Bar, which at the appointed hour, ten o'clock, would surely be deserted. Montalbano advised her not to tell anyone, not even her husband.

*

The Luparello villa stood at the entry to Montelusa as one approached from the sea. A massive nineteenth-century building, it was surrounded by a high defensive wall with a wrought-iron gate at the centre, now thrown open. Montalbano walked down the tree-lined lane cutting through one part of the park and came to the huge, double front door, one half of which was open, the other half draped with a large black bow. He leaned forward to look inside: in the vestibule, which was rather vast, there were some twenty people, men and women, looking appropriately grief-stricken, murmuring in soft voices. He thought it unwise to walk through the crowd; someone might recognize him and start wondering why he was there. Instead, he walked all around the villa and at last found a rear entrance, which was closed. He rang the bell several times before someone came and opened the door.

'You've made a mistake. For condolence visits use the front door,' said a small, alert housekeeper in black pinafore and starched cap, who had classified him at a glance as not belonging to the category of caterers.

'I'm Inspector Montalbano. Could you tell one of the family I'm here?'

'They've been expecting you, Inspector.'

She led him down a long corridor, opened a door, and gestured for him to enter. Montalbano found himself in a large library with thousands of well-kept books neatly arrayed on enormous shelves. There was an immense desk in one corner, and in the corner opposite, a tastefully elegant sitting area with a small table and two armchairs. Only five paintings adorned the walls, and with a shudder of excitement Montalbano immediately recognized the artists: there was a Guttuso portrait of a peasant from the forties, a landscape in Lazio by Melli, a demolition by Mafai, two rowers on the Tiber by Donghi, and a woman bathing by Fausto Pirandello. The selection showed exquisite taste and rare discernment. The door opened, and a man of about thirty appeared: black tie, open face, stylish.

'It was I who phoned you. Thank you for coming. Mama was very keen on seeing you. I'm sorry for all the trouble I've caused you.' He spoke with no regional inflection whatsoever.

'No trouble at all. I simply don't see of what use I could be to your mother.'

'That's what I said to her, too, but she insisted. And she wouldn't give me any hint as to why she wished to inconvenience you.'

He looked at the fingertips of his right hand as if

seeing them for the first time, then discreetly cleared his throat.

'Please try to understand, Inspector.'

'I don't understand.'

'For Mama's sake. It's been a very trying time for her.'

The young man turned to leave, then suddenly stopped.

'Ah, Inspector, I wanted to inform you so you wouldn't find yourself in an embarrassing situation that Mama knows how my father died and where he died. How she found out, I have no idea. She already knew two hours after the body was found. Please excuse me.'

Montalbano felt relieved. If the widow knew, he wouldn't be forced to concoct any pious fictions to hide the indecency of her husband's death from her. He went back to enjoying the paintings. At his house in Vigàta he had only drawings and prints by Carmassi, Attardi, Guida, Cordio and Angelo Canevari, to which he had been able to treat himself by docking his meagre salary. More than that he couldn't afford; he could never pay for a painting on the level of these.

'Do you like them?'

He turned about abruptly. He hadn't heard the signora enter. She was a woman past fifty, not tall, with an air of determination; the tiny wrinkles lining her face had not yet succeeded in destroying the beauty of her features. On the contrary, they highlighted the radiance of her penetrating green eyes.

'Please make yourself comfortable,' she said, then went and sat on the sofa as the inspector took a seat in an armchair. 'Such beautiful pictures. I don't know much about painting, but I do like them. There are about thirty scattered around the house. My husband bought them. Painting was his secret vice, he loved to say. Unfortunately, it wasn't his only one.'

We're off to a good start, Montalbano thought, then asked, 'Are you feeling better, signora?'

'Compared to when?'

The inspector stammered, as if he were in front of a teacher asking him difficult questions.

'Well, I – I don't know, compared to this morning . . . I heard you were unwell today – in the cathedral.'

'Unwell? I was fine, as good as one might feel in such circumstances. No, my friend, I merely pretended to faint. I'm a good actress. Actually, a thought had come into my mind: if a terrorist, I said to myself, were to blow up this church with all of us inside, at least one-tenth of all the hypocrisy in the world would disappear with us. So I had myself escorted out.'

Impressed by the woman's candour, Montalbano didn't know what to say, so he waited for her to resume speaking.

'When I was told where my husband had been found, I called the police commissioner and asked him who was in charge of the investigation – if there *was* any investigation. The commissioner gave me your name, adding that you were a decent man. I had my doubts: *are* there still any decent men? And so I had my son phone you.'

'I can only thank you, signora.'

'But we're not here to exchange compliments. I don't want to waste your time. Are you absolutely certain it wasn't a homicide?'

'Absolutely.'

'Then what are your misgivings?'

'Misgivings?'

'Yes, my dear, you must have some. There is no other way to explain your reluctance to close the investigation.'

'I'll be frank, signora. They're only impressions,

impressions I really can't and shouldn't allow myself, in the sense that, since we are dealing with a death by natural causes, my duty should lie elsewhere. If you have nothing new to tell me, I shall inform the judge this very evening—'

'But I do have something new to tell you.'

Montalbano was struck dumb.

'I don't know what your impressions may be,' the signora continued, 'but I'll tell you what mine are. Silvio was, of course, a shrewd, ambitious man. If he stayed in the shadows all those years, it was with a specific purpose in mind: to come into the limelight at the right moment and stay there. Now, do you really believe that this man, after all that time spent on patient manoeuvres to get where he did, would decide, one fine evening, to go with a woman, surely of ill repute, to a shady place where anyone could recognize him and possibly blackmail him?'

'That, signora, is one of the things that has perplexed me the most.'

'Do you want to be even more perplexed? I said "woman of ill repute", and I would like to clarify that I didn't mean a prostitute or any sort of woman for whom one pays. I'm not sure if I'm explaining myself clearly. Let me tell you something: right after we got married, Silvio confided in me that he had never been with a prostitute or gone to a licensed brothel when they still existed. Something prevented him. So this leads one to wonder what sort of woman it was who convinced him to have relations with her in that hideous place.'

Montalbano had never been with a prostitute either, and he hoped that no new revelations about Luparello would reveal other points of similarity between him and a man with whom he would not have wanted to break bread.

'You see, my husband quite comfortably gave in to his vices, but he was never tempted by self-destruction, by that "ecstasy for baseness", as one French writer put it. He consummated his affairs discreetly, in a little house he had built, though not in his name, at the tip of Capo Massaria. I found out about it from the customary compassionate friend.'

She stood up, went over to the desk, rummaged through a drawer, then sat back down holding a large yellow envelope, a metal ring with two keys, and a magnifying glass. She handed the keys to the inspector.

'Incidentally, he had a mania for keys. He had two

copies of each set, one of which he would keep in that drawer; the other he always carried on his person. Well, the second copy was never found.'

'They weren't in your husband's pockets?'

'No. And they weren't in his engineering studio either. Nor were they found in his other office, the so-called political office. Vanished, evaporated.'

'He could have lost them on the street. We don't necessarily know that they were removed from him.'

'It's not possible. You see, my husband had six sets of keys. One for this house, one for the country house, one for the house by the sea, one for the office, one for the studio, one for his little house. He kept them all in the glove compartment of his car. From time to time he would take out the set he needed.'

'And none of these sets was found?'

'No. I gave orders to have all the locks changed. With the exception of the little house, of whose existence I am officially unaware. If you wish, you may visit the place. I'm sure you'll find some revealing vestiges of his affairs.'

Twice she had said 'his affairs', and Montalbano wished he could console her in some way.

'Aside from the fact that Mr Luparello's affairs do

not fall within the scope of my investigation, I have nevertheless questioned some people, and I must say in all sincerity that the answers I've received have been rather generic, applicable to anyone.'

The woman looked at him with the faint hint of a smile.

'I never did reproach him for it, you know. Practically speaking, two years after the birth of our son, my husband and I ceased to be a couple. And so I was able to observe him calmly and quietly for thirty years, without having my vision clouded by the agitation of the senses. You seem not to understand, please forgive me: in speaking of his "affairs", my intention was to avoid specifying the sex.'

Montalbano hunched his shoulders, sinking farther down into the armchair. He felt as if he'd just taken a blow to the head from a crowbar.

'On the other hand,' the woman continued, 'to get back to the subject of greatest interest to me, I am convinced that we are dealing with a criminal act – let me finish – not a homicide, not a physical elimination, but a political crime. An act of extreme violence was done, and it led to his death.'

'Please explain, signora.'

'I am convinced that my husband was forced, under the threat of violence or blackmail, to go to that disgraceful place where he was found. They had a plan, but they were unable to execute it in full because his heart gave out under the stress or – why not? – out of fear. He was very ill, you know. He had just been through a very difficult operation.'

'But how would they have forced him?'

'I don't know. Perhaps you can help me find out. They probably lured him into a trap. He was unable to resist. I don't know, maybe they photographed him at that place or had him recognized by someone. And from that moment on they had my husband in the palm of their hands; he became their puppet.'

'Who are "they"?'

'His political adversaries, I think, or some business associates.'

'You see, signora, your reasoning, or rather your conjecture, has one serious flaw: you have no proof to support it.'

The woman opened the yellow envelope she'd been holding in her hand all this time and pulled out some photographs, the ones the lab had taken of the corpse at the Pasture.

'Oh, God,' Montalbano murmured, shuddering. The woman, for her part, showed no emotion as she studied them.

'How did you get these?'

'I have good friends. Have you looked at them?'

'No.'

'You were wrong not to.' She chose a photo and handed it to Montalbano along with the magnifying glass. 'Now, take a good look at this one. His trousers are pulled down, and you can just get a glimpse of the white of his underpants.'

Montalbano was covered in sweat; the discomfort he felt irritated him, but there was nothing he could do about it.

'I don't see anything strange about that.'

'Oh, no? What about the label of the underpants?'

'Yes, I can see it. So?'

'You shouldn't be able to see it. This kind of brief – and if you come into my husband's bedroom, I'll show you others – has the label on the back and on the inside. If you can see them, as you can, it means they were put on backwards. And you can't tell me that Silvio when getting dressed that morning put them on that way and never noticed. He took a diuretic, you see, and had to go to the bathroom many times a day and could have easily put them properly back on at any point of the day. And this can mean only one thing.'

'What's that?' the inspector asked, stunned by the woman's lucid, pitiless analysis, which she made without shedding a tear, as though the deceased were a casual acquaintance.

'That he was naked when they surprised him, and that they forced him to get dressed in a hurry. And the only place he could have been naked was in the little house at Capo Massaria. That is why I gave you the keys. I repeat, it was a criminal act against my husband's public image, but only half successful. They wanted to make him out to be a pig, so they could feed him to the pigs at any moment. It would have been better if he hadn't died; forced to cover himself, he would have done whatever they asked. The plan did, however, succeed in part: all my husband's men have been excluded from the new leadership. Rizzo alone escaped; actually, he gained by it.'

'And why did he?'

'That is up to you to discover, if you so desire.

Or else you can stop at the shape they've given the water.'

'I'm sorry, I don't understand.'

'I'm not Sicilian; I was born in Grosseto and came to Montelusa when my father was made prefect here. We owned a small piece of land and a house on the slopes of the Amiata and used to spend our summers there. I had a little friend, a peasant boy, who was younger than me. I was about ten. One day I saw that my friend had put a bowl, a cup, a teapot and a square milk carton on the edge of a well, had filled them all with water, and was looking at them attentively.

' "What are you doing?" I asked him. And he answered me with a question in turn.

' "What shape is water?"

' "Water doesn't have any shape!" I said, laughing. "It takes the shape you give it." '

At that moment the door to the library opened, and an angel appeared.

ELEVEN

The angel – Montalbano at that moment didn't know how else to define him – was a young man of about twenty, tall, blond, very tanned, with a perfect body and an ephebic aura. A pandering ray of sun had taken care to bathe him in light in the doorway, accentuating the Apollonian features of his face.

'May I come in, *zia*?'

'Come in, Giorgio, come in.'

While the youth moved toward the sofa, weightlessly, his feet seeming not to touch the ground but merely to glide across the floor, navigating a sinuous, almost spiral path, brushing past objects within reach or, more than brushing, lightly caressing them, Montalbano caught a glance from the signora that told him to put the photograph he was holding in his pocket. He obeyed, while the widow quickly put the other photos back in the yellow envelope, which she placed beside her on the sofa. When the young man came near, the inspector noticed that his blue eyes were streaked with red, puffy from tears, and ringed with dark circles.

'How do you feel, *zia*?' he asked in an almost singing voice, then knelt elegantly beside the woman, resting his head in her lap. In Montalbano's mind flashed the memory, bright as if under a floodlight, of a painting he had seen once – he couldn't remember where – a portrait of an English lady with a greyhound in the exact same position as the one the young man had assumed.

'This is Giorgio,' the woman said. 'Giorgio Zìcari, son of my sister Elisabetta and Ernesto Zìcari, the criminal lawyer. Perhaps you know him.'

As she spoke, the woman caressed his hair. Giorgio gave no indication of having understood what was said. Visibly absorbed in his devastating grief, he didn't even bother to turn toward the inspector. The woman, moreover, had taken care not to tell her nephew who Montalbano was and what he was doing in their house.

'Were you able to sleep last night?'

Giorgio's only reply was to shake his head.

'I'll tell you what you should do. Did you notice that Dr Capuano's here? Go talk to him, have him prescribe you a strong sedative, then go back to bed.'

Without a word, Giorgio stood up fluidly, levitated over the floor with his curious, spiral manner of movement, and disappeared beyond the door.

'You must forgive him,' the lady said. 'Giorgio is without doubt the one who has suffered most, and who suffers most, from the death of my husband. You see, I wanted my own son to study and find himself a position independently of his father, far from Sicily. You can perhaps imagine my reasons for this. As a result, in Stefano's absence my husband poured all his affection on our nephew, and his love was returned to the point of idolatry. The boy even came to live with us, to the great displeasure of my sister and her husband, who felt abandoned.'

She stood up, and Montalbano did likewise.

'I've told you everything I thought I should tell you, Inspector. I know I'm in honest hands. You may call me whenever you see fit, at any hour of the day or night. And don't bother to spare my feelings; I'm what they call "a strong woman". In any event, act as your conscience dictates.'

'One question, signora, which has been troubling me for some time. Why weren't you concerned to make it known that your husband hadn't returned . . .? What I mean is, wasn't it disturbing that your husband didn't come home that night? Had it happened before?'

'Yes, it had. But, you see, he phoned me on Sunday night.'

'From where?'

'I couldn't say. He said he would be home very late. He had an important meeting and might even be forced to spend the night away.'

She extended her hand to him, and the inspector, without knowing why, squeezed it in his own and then kissed it.

*

Once outside, having exited by the same rear door of the villa, he noticed Giorgio sitting on a stone bench nearby, bent over, shuddering convulsively.

Concerned, Montalbano approached and saw the youth's hands open and drop the yellow envelope and the photos, which scattered about on the ground. Apparently, spurred by a catlike curiosity, he had got hold of them when crouching beside his aunt.

'Are you unwell?'

'Not like that, oh, God, not like that!'

Giorgio spoke in a clotted voice, his eyes glassy, and hadn't even noticed the inspector standing there. It took a second, then suddenly he stiffened, falling backwards from the bench, which had no back. Montalbano knelt beside him, trying in some way to immobilize that spasm-racked body; a white froth was beginning to form at the corners of the boy's mouth.

Stefano Luparello appeared at the door to the villa, looked around, saw the scene, and came running.

'I was coming after you to say hello. What's happening?'

'An epileptic fit, I think.'

They did their best to prevent Giorgio, at the height of the crisis, from biting off his tongue or striking his head violently against the ground. Then the youth calmed down, his shudders diminishing in fury.

'Help me carry him inside,' said Stefano.

The same maid who had opened the door for the inspector came running at Stefano's first call.

'I don't want Mama to see him in this state.'

'My room,' said the girl.

They walked with difficulty down a different corridor from the one the inspector had taken upon entering. Montalbano held Giorgio by the armpits, with Stefano grabbing the feet. When they arrived in the servants' wing, the maid opened a door. Panting, they laid the boy down on the bed. Giorgio had plunged into a leaden sleep.

'Help me to undress him,' said Stefano.

Only when the youth was stripped down to his boxers and T-shirt did Montalbano notice that from the base of the neck up to the bottom of his chin, the skin was extremely white, diaphanous, in sharp contrast to the face and the chest, which were bronzed by the sun.

'Do you know why he's not tanned there?' he asked Stefano.

'I don't know,' he said. 'I got back to Montelusa just last Monday afternoon, after being away for months.'

'I know why,' said the maid. 'Master Giorgio hurt himself in a car accident. He took the collar off less than a week ago.'

'When he comes to and can understand,' Montalbano said to Stefano, 'tell him to drop by my office in Vigàta tomorrow morning, around ten.'

He went back to the bench, bent down to the ground to pick up the envelope and photos, which Stefano had not noticed, and put them in his pocket.

*

Capo Massaria was about a hundred yards past the San Filippo bend, but the inspector couldn't see the little house that supposedly stood right on the point, at least according to what Signora Luparello had told him. He started to back the car up, proceeding very slowly. When he was exactly opposite the cape, he espied, amid dense, low trees, a path forking off the main road. He took this and shortly afterwards found the small road blocked by a gate, the sole opening in a long dry-stone wall that sealed off the part of the cape that jutted out over the sea.

The keys were the right ones. Leaving the car outside the gate, Montalbano headed up a garden path made of blocks of tufa set in the ground. At the end of this he went down a small staircase, also made of tufa, which led to a sort of landing where he found the house's front door, invisible from the landward side because it was built like an eagle's nest, right into the rock, similar to a mountain refuge.

Entering, he found himself inside a vast room facing the sea, indeed suspended over the sea, and the impression of being on a ship's deck was reinforced by an entire wall of glass. The place was in perfect order. There was a dining table with four chairs in one corner, a sofa and two armchairs turned toward the window, a nineteenth-century sideboard full of glasses, dishes, bottles of wine and liqueur, and a television with a VCR. On top of a low table beside it was a row of video cassettes, some pornographic, others not. The large room had three doors, the first of which opened onto an immaculate kitchenette with shelves packed with foodstuffs and a refrigerator almost empty except for a few bottles of champagne and vodka. The bathroom, which was quite spacious, smelled of disinfectant. On the shelf under the mirror were an electric razor, deodorants and a flask of eau de cologne. In the bedroom, which also had a large window looking onto the sea, there was a double bed covered with a freshly laundered sheet; two bedside tables, one with a telephone; and a wardrobe with three doors. On the wall at the head of the bed, a drawing by Emilio Greco, a very sensual nude. Montalbano opened the drawer of the bedside table with the telephone, no doubt the side of the bed Luparello usually slept on. Three condoms, a pen, a white notepad. He gave a start when he saw the pistol, a 7.65, at the very back of the drawer, loaded. The drawer to the other bedside table was empty. Opening the left-hand door of the wardrobe, he saw two men's suits. In the top drawer, a shirt, three sets of underpants, some handkerchiefs, a T-shirt. He checked the underpants: the signora was right, the label was inside and in the back. In the bottom drawer, a pair of loafers and a pair of slippers. The wardrobe's middle door was covered by a mirror that reflected the bed. That section was divided into three shelves: the topmost and middle shelves contained, jumbled together, hats, Italian and foreign magazines whose common denominator was pornography, a vibrator, sheets and pillowcases. On the bottom shelf were three female wigs on their respective stands – one brown, one blonde, one red. Maybe they were part of the engineer's erotic games. The biggest surprise, however, came when he opened the right-hand door: two women's dresses, very elegant, on coat hangers. There were also two pairs of jeans and some blouses. In a drawer, minuscule panties but no bras. The other was empty. As he leaned forward to better inspect this second drawer, Montalbano understood what it was that had so surprised him: not the sight of the feminine apparel but the scent that emanated from them, the very same he had smelled, only more vaguely, at the old factory, the moment he'd opened the leather handbag.

There was nothing else to see. Just to be thorough, he bent down to look under the furniture. A tie had been wrapped around one of the rear legs of the bed. He picked it up, remembering that Luparello had been found with his shirt collar unbuttoned. He took the photographs out of his pocket and decided that the tie, for its colour, would have gone quite well with the suit the engineer was wearing at the time of his death.

*

At headquarters he found Germanà and Galluzzo in a state of agitation.

'Where's the sergeant?'

'Fazio's with the others at a petrol station, the one on the way to Marinella. There was some shooting there.'

'I'll go there at once. Did anything come for me?'

'Yes, a package from Jacomuzzi.'

He opened it. It was the necklace. He wrapped it back up.

'Germanà, you come with me to this petrol station. You'll drop me off there and continue on to Montelusa in my car. I'll tell you what road to take.'

He went into his office, phoned Rizzo, told him the necklace was on its way with one of his men, and added that he should hand over the cheque for ten million lire to the agent.

As they were heading toward the site of the shooting, the inspector explained to Germanà that he must not turn the package over to Rizzo before he had the cheque in his pocket and that he was to take this cheque – he gave him the address – to Saro Montaperto, advising him to cash it as soon as the bank opened, at eight o'clock the following morning. He couldn't say why, and this bothered him a great deal, but he sensed that the Luparello affair was quickly drawing to a conclusion.

'Should I come back and pick you up at the petrol station?'

'No, stop at headquarters. I'll return in a squad car.'

*

The police car and a private vehicle were blocking the entrances to the petrol station. As soon as he stepped out of his car, with Germanà taking the road for Montelusa, the inspector was overwhelmed by the strong odour of petrol.

'Watch where you step!' Fazio shouted at him.

The gasoline had formed a kind of bog, the fumes of which made Montalbano feel nauseous and mildly faint. Stopped in front of the station was a car with a Palermo licence plate, its windscreen shattered.

'One person was injured, the guy at the wheel,' said the sergeant. 'He was taken away by ambulance.'

'Seriously injured?'

'No, just a scratch. But it scared him to death.'

'What happened, exactly?'

'If you want to speak to the station attendant yourself . . .'

The man answered Montalbano's questions in a voice so high pitched that it had the same effect on him as fingernails on glass. Things had happened more or less as follows: a car had stopped, the only person inside had asked him to fill it up, the attendant had stuck the nozzle into the car and left it there to do its work, setting it on automatic stop because meanwhile another car had pulled in and its driver had asked for thirty thousand in gas and a quick oil check. As the attendant was about to serve the second client, a car on the road had fired a burst from a sub-machine gun and sped off, disappearing in traffic. The man at the wheel of the first car had set off immediately in pursuit, the nozzle had slipped out and continued to pump gasoline. The driver of the second vehicle was shouting like a madman; his shoulder had been grazed by a bullet. Once the initial moment of panic had passed and he realized there was no more danger, the attendant had assisted the injured man, while the pump continued to spread gasoline all over the ground.

'Did you get a good look at the face of the man in the first car, the one that drove off in pursuit?'

'No, sir.'

'Are you really sure?'

'As sure as there's a God in heaven.'

Meanwhile, the firemen summoned by Fazio arrived.

'Here's what we'll do,' Montalbano said to the sergeant. 'As soon as the firemen are done, pick up the attendant, who hasn't convinced me one bit, and take him down to the station. Put some pressure on him: the guy knows perfectly well who the man they shot at was.'

'I think so, too.'

'How much do you want to bet it's one of the Cuffaro gang? I think this month it's their turn to get it.'

'What, you want to take the money right out of my pocket?' the sergeant asked, laughing. 'That's a bet you've already won.'

'See you later.'

'Where are you going? I thought you wanted me to give you a lift in the squad car.'

'I'm going home to change my clothes. It's only about twenty minutes from here on foot. A little breath of air will do me good.'

He headed off. He didn't feel like meeting Ingrid Sjostrom dressed in his Sunday best.

TWELVE

He plonked down in front of the television right out of the shower, still naked and dripping. The images were from Luparello's funeral that morning, and the cameraman had apparently realized that the only people capable of lending a sense of drama to the ceremony – in every other way so like countless other tedious official events – were the trio of the widow, Stefano the son, and Giorgio the nephew. From time to time Signora Luparello, without realizing it, would jerk her head backwards, as if repeatedly saying no. This 'no' was interpreted by the commentator, in a low, sorrowful voice, as the obvious gesture of a creature irrationally rejecting the concrete fact of death; but as the cameraman was zooming in on her to catch the expression in her gaze, Montalbano found confirmation of what the widow had already confessed to him: there was only disdain and boredom in those eyes. Beside her sat her son, 'numb with grief', according to the announcer, and he called him 'numb' only because the composure the young engineer showed seemed to border on indifference. Giorgio instead teetered like a tree in the wind, livid as he swayed, continually twisting a tear-soaked handkerchief in his hands.

The telephone rang, and Montalbano went to answer it without taking his eyes off the television screen.

'Inspector, this is Germanà. Everything's been taken care of. Counsellor Rizzo expressed his thanks and said he'd find a way to repay you.'

Some of Rizzo's ways of repaying debts, he whispered to himself, his creditors would have gladly done without.

'Then I went to see Saro and gave him the cheque. It took some effort to convince them – they thought it was some kind of practical joke – and then they started kissing my hands. I'll spare you all the things they said the Lord should do for you. The car's at headquarters. You want me to bring it to you?'

The inspector glanced at his watch; there was still

a little more than an hour before his rendezvous with Ingrid.

'All right, but there's no hurry. Let's say nine-thirty. Then I'll give you a ride back into town.'

He didn't want to miss the moment when she pretended to faint. He felt like a spectator to whom the magician had revealed his secret: the pleasure would be in appreciating not the surprise but the skill. The one who missed it, however, was the cameraman, who was unable to capture that moment even though he had quickly panned from his close-up of the minister back to the group of family members, where Stefano and two volunteers were already carrying the signora out while Giorgio remained in place, still swaying.

*

Instead of dropping Germanà off in front of police headquarters and continuing on, Montalbano got out with him. Fazio was back from Montelusa, and he had spoken with the wounded man, who had finally calmed down. The man, the sergeant recounted, was a household-appliance salesman from Milan who every three months would catch a plane, land in Palermo, rent a car and drive around. Having stopped at the petrol station, he was looking at a piece of paper to check the address of the next store on his list of clients when he suddenly heard the shots and felt a sharp pain in his shoulder. Fazio believed his story.

'Chief, when this guy goes back to Milan, he's going to join up with the people who want to separate Sicily from the rest of Italy.'

'What about the attendant?'

'The attendant's another matter. Giallombardo's talking to him now, and you know what he's like: someone spends a couple of hours with him, talking like he's known him for a hundred years, and afterward he realizes he's told him secrets he wouldn't even tell the priest at confession.'

*

The lights were off, the glass entrance door barred shut. Montalbano had chosen the Marinella Bar on the one day it was closed. He parked the car and waited. A few minutes later a two-seater arrived, red and flat as a fillet of sole. The door opened, and Ingrid emerged. Even by the dim light of a street lamp, the inspector saw that she was even better than he had imagined her: tight jeans wrapping very long legs, white shirt open at the collar with the sleeves rolled up, sandals, hair gathered in a bun. A real cover girl. Ingrid looked around, noticed the darkness inside the bar, walked lazily but surely over to the inspector's car, then leaned forward to speak to him through the open window.

'See, I was right. So where do we go now? Your place?'

'No,' Montalbano said angrily. 'Get in.' The woman obeyed, and at once the car was filled with the scent that Montalbano already knew well.

'Where do we go now?' Ingrid repeated. She wasn't joking any more; utter female that she was, she had noticed the man's agitation.

'Do you have much time?'

'As much as I want.'

'We're going somewhere you'll feel comfortable, since you've already been there. You'll see.'

'What about my car?'

'We'll come back for it later.'

They set off, and after a few minutes of silence Ingrid asked him a question she should have asked from the start.

'Why did you want to see me?'

The inspector was mulling over the idea that had come to him as he told her to get in the car: it was a real cop's sort of idea, but he was, after all, a cop.

'I wanted to see you, Mrs Cardamone, because I need to ask you some questions.'

'Mrs Cardamone? Listen, Inspector, I'm very familiar with everyone I meet, and if you're too formal with me I'll only feel uncomfortable. What's your first name?'

'Salvo. Did Counsellor Rizzo tell you we found the necklace?'

'What necklace?'

'What do you mean, what necklace? The one with the diamond-studded heart.'

'No, he didn't tell me. Anyway, I have no dealings with him. He certainly must have told my husband.'

'Tell me something, I'm curious: are you in the habit of losing jewellery and then finding it again?'

'Why do you ask?'

'Come on, I tell you we found your necklace, which is worth about a hundred million lire, and you don't bat an eyelash?'

Ingrid gave a subdued laugh, confined to her throat.

'The fact is, I don't like jewellery. See?'

She showed him her hands.

'I don't wear rings, not even a wedding band.'

'Where did you lose the necklace?'

Ingrid didn't answer at once.

She's reviewing her lesson, thought Montalbano.

Then the woman began speaking, mechanically. Being a foreigner didn't help her to lie.

'I was curious about this place called the Pastor—'

'Pasture,' Montalbano corrected.

'I'd heard so much about it. I talked my husband into taking me there. Once there I got out, walked a little, and was almost attacked. I got scared and was afraid my husband would get in a fight. We left. Back at home I realized I no longer had the necklace on.'

'How did you happen to put it on that evening, since you don't like jewellery? It doesn't really seem appropriate for going to the Pasture.'

Ingrid hesitated.

'I had it on because that afternoon I'd been with a friend who wanted to see it.'

'Listen,' said Montalbano, 'I should preface all this by saying that even though I am, of course, talking to you as a police inspector, I'm doing so in an unofficial capacity.'

'What do you mean? I don't understand.'

'What I mean is, anything you tell me will remain between you and me. How did your husband happen to choose Rizzo as his lawyer?'

'Was he not supposed to?'

'No, at least not logically. Rizzo was the right-hand man of Silvio Luparello, who was your father-in-law's biggest political adversary. By the way, did you know Luparello?'

'I knew who he was. Rizzo's always been Giacomo's lawyer. And I don't know a bloody thing about politics.' She stretched, arching her arms behind her head. 'I'm getting bored. Too bad. I thought an encounter with a cop would be more exciting. Could you tell me where we're going? Is there still far to go?'

'We're almost there.'

*

After they passed the San Filippo bend, the woman grew nervous, looking at the inspector two or three times out of the corner of her eye. She muttered, 'Look, there aren't any bars or cafés around here.'

'I know,' said Montalbano, and, slowing the car down, he reached for the leather bag that he had placed behind the seat Ingrid was in. 'I want you to see something.'

He put it on her lap. The woman looked at it and seemed truly surprised.

'How did you get this?'

'Is it yours?'

'Of course it's mine. It has my initials on it.'

When she saw that the two letters of the alphabet were missing, she became even more confused.

'They must have fallen off,' she said in a low voice, but she was unconvinced. She was losing her way in a labyrinth of questions without answer, and clearly something was beginning to trouble her now.

'Your initials are still there, you just can't see them because it's dark. Somebody tore them off, but their imprints are there in the leather.'

'But who tore them off? And why?'

A note of anxiety sounded in her voice. The inspector didn't answer. He knew perfectly well why they had done it: to make it look as if Ingrid had wanted to make the bag anonymous. When they came to the little dirt road that led to Capo Massaria,

Montalbano, who had accelerated as if intending to go straight, suddenly spun the wheel violently, turning onto the path. All at once, without a word, Ingrid threw open the car door, nimbly exited the moving vehicle, and started running through the trees. Cursing, the inspector braked, jumped out, and gave chase. After a few seconds he realized he would never catch her and stopped, undecided. At that exact moment he saw her fall. When he was beside her, Ingrid, who had been unable to get back up, interrupted her Swedish monologue, incomprehensible but clearly expressing fear and rage.

'Fuck off!' she said, and continued massaging her ankle.

'Get up, and no more bullshit.'

With effort, she obeyed and leaned against Montalbano, who remained motionless, not helping her.

*

The gate opened easily; it was the front door that put up resistance.

'Let me do it,' said Ingrid. She had followed him without making a move, as though resigned. But she had been preparing her plan of defence.

'You won't find anything inside, you know,' she said in the doorway, her tone defiant.

She turned on the light, confident, but when she looked inside and saw the video cassettes and the perfectly furnished room, she reacted with visible surprise, a wrinkle creasing her brow.

'They told me—'

She checked herself at once and fell silent, shrugging her shoulders. She eyed Montalbano, waiting for his next move.

'Into the bedroom,' said the inspector.

Ingrid opened her mouth, about to make an easy quip, but lost heart. Turning her back, she limped into the other room, turned on the light, and this time showed no surprise; she had expected it to be all in order. She sat down at the foot of the bed. Montalbano opened the left-hand door of the wardrobe.

'Do you know whose clothes these are?'

'They must belong to Silvio, to Mr Luparello.'

He opened the middle door.

'Are these wigs yours?'

'I've never worn a wig.'

When he opened the right-hand door, Ingrid closed her eyes.

'Look, that's not going to solve anything. Are these yours?'

'Yes, but—'

'But they weren't supposed to be there any more,' Montalbano finished her sentence.

Ingrid gave a start.

'How did you know? Who told you?'

'Nobody told me. I figured it out. I'm a cop, remember? Was the bag also in the wardrobe?'

Ingrid nodded yes.

'And the necklace you said you lost, where was that?'

'Inside the bag. I had to wear it once, then I came here and left it here.'

She paused a moment and looked the inspector long in the eye.

'What does this all mean?' she asked.

'Let's go back in the other room.'

*

Ingrid took a glass from the sideboard, half filled it with straight whisky, drank almost all of it in a single draft, then refilled it.

'You want any?'

Montalbano said no. He had sat down on the couch and was looking out at the sea. The light was dim enough to allow him to see beyond the glass. Ingrid came and sat down beside him.

'I've sat here looking at the sea in better times.'

She slid a little closer on the sofa and rested her head on the inspector's shoulder. He didn't move; he immediately understood that her gesture was not an attempt at seduction.

'Ingrid, remember what I told you in the car? That our conversation was an unofficial one?'

'Yes.'

'Now answer me truthfully. Those clothes in the wardrobe, did you bring them here yourself or were they put there?'

'I brought them myself. I thought I might need them.'

'Were you Luparello's mistress?'

'No.'

'No? You seem quite at home here.'

'I slept with Luparello only once, six months after arriving in Montelusa. But never again. He brought me here. But we did become friends, true friends, like I had never had before with a man, not even in my country. I could tell him anything, anything at all. If I got into trouble, he would manage to get me out of it, without asking any questions.'

'Are you trying to make me believe that the one time you were here you brought all those dresses, jeans, and panties, not to mention the bag and the necklace?'

Ingrid pulled away, irritated.

'I'm not trying to make you believe anything. I'm just telling you. After a while I asked Silvio if I could use this house now and then, and he said yes. He asked me only one thing: to be very discreet and never tell anyone who it belonged to.'

'And when you wanted to come, how did you know if the place was empty and available?'

'We had agreed on a code of telephone rings. I kept my word with Silvio. I used to bring only one man here, always the same one.'

She took a long sip, and sort of hunched her shoulders forward.

'A man who forced his way into my life two years ago. Because I – afterwards, I didn't want to anymore.'

'After what?'

'After the first time. I was afraid, of the whole situation. But he was . . . sort of blinded, sort of obsessed with me. Only physically, though. He would want to see me every day. Then, when I brought him here, he would jump all over me, turn violent, tear my clothes off. That was why I had those changes of clothes in the wardrobe.'

'Did this man know whose house this was?'

'I never told him, and he never asked. He's not jealous, you see, he just wants me. He never gets tired of being inside me. He's ready to take me at any moment.'

'I see. And for his part did Luparello know who you were bringing here?'

'Same thing – he didn't ask, and I didn't tell.'

Ingrid stood up.

'Couldn't we go somewhere else to talk? This place depresses me now. Are you married?'

'No,' said Montalbano, surprised.

'Let's go to your place.' She smiled cheerlessly. 'I told you it would end up this way, didn't I?'

THIRTEEN

Neither of them felt like talking, and fifteen minutes passed in silence. But once again the inspector surrendered to the cop in him. In fact, once they had reached the bridge that spanned the Canneto, he pulled up to the side, put on the brakes, and got out of the car, telling Ingrid to do the same. From the summit of the bridge Montalbano showed the woman the river's dry bed, which one could make out in the moonlight.

'See,' he said, 'the riverbed leads straight to the beach. It's on a steep incline and full of big rocks and stones. Think you could drive a car down there?'

'I don't know. It'd be different if it was daylight. But I could try, if you want me to.'

She stared at the inspector and smiled, her eyes half shut.

'You found out about me, eh? So what should I do?'

'Do it.'

'All right. You wait here.'

She got in the car and drove off. It took only a few seconds for the headlights to disappear from view.

'Well, that's that. She took me for a sucker,' said Montalbano, resigning himself.

As he was getting ready for the long walk back to Vigàta, he heard her return with the motor roaring.

'I think I can do it. Do you have a torch?'

'In the glove compartment.'

The woman knelt down, illuminated the car's underside, then stood back up.

'Got a handkerchief?'

Montalbano gave her one, and Ingrid used it to wrap her sore ankle tightly.

'Get in.'

Driving in reverse, she reached a dirt road that led from the provincial road to the area under the bridge.

'I'm going to give it a try, Inspector. Bear in mind that one of my feet isn't working. Fasten your seat belt. Should I drive fast?'

'Yes, but it's important that we get to the beach in one piece.'

Ingrid put the car in gear and took off like a shot. It was ten minutes of continuous, ferocious jolts. At one point Montalbano felt as if his head were dying to detach itself from the rest of his body and fly out of the window. Ingrid, however, was calm, determined, driving with her tongue sticking out between her lips. The inspector wanted to tell her not to do that – she might inadvertently bite it off.

When they had reached the beach, Ingrid asked, 'Did I pass the test?'

Her eyes glistened in the darkness. She was excited and pleased.

'Yes.'

'Let's do it again, going uphill this time.'

'You're insane! That's quite enough.'

She was right to call it a test except that it was a test that didn't solve anything. Ingrid was able to drive down that road easily, which was a point against her; on the other hand, when the inspector had asked her to do so, she had not seemed nervous, only surprised, and this was a point in her favour. But the fact that she hadn't broken anything on the car, how was he to interpret that? Negatively or positively?

'So, shall we do it again? Come on, this was the only time this evening I've had any fun.'

'No, I already said no.'

'All right, then you drive. I'm in too much pain.'

The inspector drove along the shore, confirming in his mind that the car was in working order. Nothing broken.

'You're really good, you know.'

'Well,' said Ingrid, assuming a serious, professional tone, 'anyone could drive down that stretch. The skill is in bringing the car through it in the same condition it started out in. Because afterwards you might find yourself on a paved road, not a beach like this, and you have to speed up to recover lost time. I don't know if that's clear.'

'Perfectly clear. Somebody who, for example, after driving down there, comes to the beach with broken suspension is somebody who doesn't know what he's doing.'

They arrived at the Pasture. Montalbano turned right.

'See that large bush? That's where Luparello was found.'

Ingrid said nothing and didn't even seem very curious. They drove down the path; not much was happening that evening. When they were beside the wall of the old factory, Montalbano said, 'This is where the woman who was with Luparello lost her necklace and threw the leather bag over the wall.'

'My bag?'

'Yes.'

'Well, it wasn't me,' Ingrid murmured, 'and I swear I don't understand a damned thing about any of this.'

*

When they got to Montalbano's house, Ingrid was unable to step out of the car, so the inspector had to wrap one arm around her waist while she leaned her weight against his shoulder. Once inside, the young woman dropped into the first chair that came within reach.

'Christ! Now it really hurts.'

'Go into the other room and take off your jeans so I can wrap it up for you.'

Ingrid stood up with a whimper and limped along, steadying herself against the furniture and walls.

Montalbano called headquarters. Fazio informed him that the petrol-station attendant had remembered everything and had precisely identified the man at the wheel, the one the assailants had tried to kill: Turi Gambardella, of the Cuffaro gang. QED.

'So Galluzzo went to Gambardella's house,' Fazio went on, 'but his wife said she hadn't seen him for two days.'

'I would have won the bet,' said the inspector.

'Why? You think I would have been stupid enough to make it?'

He heard the water running in the bath. Ingrid apparently belonged to that category of women who cannot resist the sight of a bathtub. He dialled Gegè's number, the one for his cell phone.

'Are you alone? Can you talk?'

'As for being alone, I'm alone. As for talking, that depends.'

'I just need a name from you. There's no risk to you in giving me this information, I promise. But I want a precise answer.'

'Whose name?'

Montalbano explained, and Gegè had no trouble giving him the name, and for good measure he even threw in a nickname.

*

Ingrid had lain down on the bed, wearing a large towel that covered very little of her.

'Sorry, but I can't stand up.'

Montalbano took a small tube of salve and a roll of gauze from a shelf in the bathroom.

'Give me your leg.'

When she moved, her minuscule panties peeped out and so did one breast, which looked as if it had been painted by a painter who understood women. The nipple seemed to be looking around, curious about the unfamiliar surroundings. Once again Montalbano understood that Ingrid had no seductive intentions, and he was grateful to her for it.

'You'll see, in a little while it'll feel better,' he said after spreading the salve on her ankle, which he then wrapped tightly in gauze. The whole time Ingrid did not take her eyes off him.

'Have you got any whisky? Let me have half a glass, no ice.'

It was as though they had known each other all their lives. After bringing her the whisky, Montalbano pulled up a chair and sat down beside the bed.

'You know something, Inspector?' said Ingrid, looking at him with green, sparkling eyes. 'You're the first real man I've met around here in five years.'

'Better than Luparello?'

'Yes.'

'Thanks. Now listen to my questions.'

'Fire away.'

As Montalbano was about to open his mouth, the doorbell rang. He wasn't expecting anyone and went in confusion to answer the door. There in the doorway was Anna, in civilian clothing, smiling at him.

'Surprise!'

She walked round him and into the house.

'Thanks for the enthusiasm,' she said. 'Where've you been all evening? At headquarters they said you were here, so I came, but it was all dark. I phoned five more times, to no avail. Then I finally saw the lights on.'

She eyed Montalbano, who hadn't opened his mouth.

'What's with you? Have you lost your voice? OK, listen—'

She fell silent. Past the bedroom door, which had been left open, she had caught a glimpse of Ingrid, half naked, glass in hand. First she turned pale, then blushed violently.

'Excuse me,' she whispered, rushing out of the house.

'Run after her!' Ingrid shouted to him. 'Explain everything! I'm going home.'

In a rage, Montalbano kicked the front door shut, making the wall shake as he heard Anna's car leave, burning rubber as furiously as he had just slammed the door.

'I don't have to explain a goddamn thing to her!'

'Should I go?' Ingrid had half risen from the bed, her breasts now triumphantly outside the towel.

'No, but cover yourself.'

'Sorry.'

Montalbano took off his jacket and shirt, stuck his head in the sink, and ran cold water over it for a while. Then he returned to his chair beside the bed.

'I want to know the real story of the necklace.'

'Well, last Monday, Giacomo, my husband, was

woken up by a phone call. I didn't catch much of it – I was too sleepy. He got dressed in a hurry and went out. He came back two hours later and asked me where the necklace was, since he hadn't seen it around the house for some time. I couldn't very well tell him it was inside the bag at Silvio's house. If he had asked to see it, I wouldn't have known what to answer. So I told him I'd lost it at least a year before and that I hadn't told him sooner because I was afraid he'd get angry. The necklace was worth a lot of money; it was a present he gave me in Sweden. Then Giacomo had me sign my name at the bottom of a blank sheet of paper. He said he needed it for the insurance.'

'So where did this story about the Pasture come from?'

'That happened later, when he came home for lunch. He explained to me that Rizzo, his lawyer, had told him the insurance company needed a more convincing story about how I lost the necklace and had suggested the story about the Pastor to him.'

'Pasture,' Montalbano patiently corrected her. The mispronunciation bothered him.

'Pasture, Pasture,' Ingrid repeated. 'Frankly, I didn't find that story very convincing either. It seemed screwy, made up. That's when Giacomo told me that everyone saw me as a whore, and so it would seem believable that I might get an idea like the one about having him take me to the Pasture.'

'I understand.'

'Well, I don't!'

'They were trying to frame you.'

'Frame me? What does that mean?'

'Look, Luparello died at the Pasture in the arms of a woman who persuaded him to go there, right?'

'Right.'

'Well, they want to make it look like you were that woman. The bag is yours, the necklace is yours, the clothes at Luparello's house are yours, you're capable of driving down the Canneto – I'm supposed to arrive at only one conclusion: that the woman is Ingrid Sjostrom.'

'Now I understand,' she said, falling silent, eyes staring at the glass in her hand. Then she roused herself. 'It's not possible.'

'What's not possible?'

'That Giacomo would go along with these people who want to . . . to frame me.'

'Maybe they forced him to go along with them.

Your husband's financial situation's not too good, you know.'

'He never talks to me about it, but I can see that. Still, I'm sure that if he did it, it wasn't for money.'

'I'm pretty sure of that myself.'

'Then why?'

'There must be another explanation, which could be that your husband was forced to get involved to save someone who is more important to him than you. Wait.'

He went into the other room, where there was a small desk covered with papers. He picked up the fax that Nicolò Zito had sent to him.

'But to save someone else from what?' Ingrid asked as soon as he returned. 'If Silvio died when he was making love, it's not anybody's fault. He wasn't killed.'

'To protect someone not from the law, Ingrid, but from a scandal.'

The young woman began reading the fax first with surprise, then with growing amusement; she laughed openly at the polo-club episode. But immediately afterwards she darkened, let the sheet fall on the bed, and leaned her head to one side.

'Was he, your father-in-law, the man you used to take to Luparello's pied-à-terre?'

Answering the question visibly cost Ingrid some effort.

'Yes. And I can see that people are talking about it, even though I did everything I could so they wouldn't. It's the worst thing that's happened to me the whole time I've been in Sicily.'

'You don't have to tell me the details.'

'But I want to explain that it wasn't me who started it. Two years ago my father-in-law was supposed to take part in a conference in Rome, and he invited Giacomo and me to join him. At the last minute my husband couldn't come, but he insisted on my going anyway, since I had never been to Rome. It all went well, except that the very first night my father-in-law entered my room. He seemed insane, so I went along with him just to calm him down, because he was yelling and threatening me. On the aeroplane, on the way back, he was crying at times, and he said it would never happen again. You know that we live in the same palazzo, right? Well, one afternoon when my husband was out and I was lying in bed, he came in again, like that night, trembling all over. And again I felt afraid;

the maid was in the kitchen . . . . The next day I told Giacomo I wanted to move out. He became upset, I became insistent, we quarrelled. I brought up the subject a few times after that, but he said no every time. He was right, in his opinion. Meanwhile my father-in-law kept at it – kissing me, touching me whenever he had the chance, even risking being seen by his wife or Giacomo. That was why I begged Silvio to let me use his house on occasion.'

'Does your husband have any suspicions?'

'I don't know, I've wondered myself. Sometimes it seems like he does, other times I'm convinced he doesn't.'

'One more question, Ingrid. When we got to Capo Massaria, as you were opening the door you told me I wouldn't find anything inside. And when you saw instead that everything was still there, just as it had always been, you were very surprised. Had someone assured you that everything had been taken out of Luparello's house?'

'Yes, Giacomo told me.'

'So your husband did know?'

'Wait, don't confuse me. When Giacomo told me what I was supposed to say in case I was questioned by the insurance people – that is, that I had been to the Pasture with him – I became worried about something else: that with Silvio dead, sooner or later someone would discover his little house, with my clothes, my bag, and everything else inside.'

'Who would have found them, in your opinion?'

'Well, I don't know, the police, his family . . . I told Giacomo everything, but I told him a lie. I didn't say anything about his father; I made him think I was going there with Silvio. That evening he told me everything was all right, that a friend of his would take care of it, and that if anyone discovered the little house, they would find only whitewashed walls inside. And I believed him. What's wrong?'

Montalbano was taken aback by the question.

'What do you mean, what's wrong?'

'You keep touching the back of your neck.'

'Oh. It hurts. Must have happened when we drove down the Canneto. How's your ankle?'

'Better, thanks.'

Ingrid started laughing. She was changing moods from one moment to the next, like a child.

'What's so funny?'

'Your neck, my ankle – we're like two hospital patients.'

'Feel up to getting out of bed?'

'If it was up to me, I'd stay here till morning.'

'We've still got some things to do. Get dressed. Can you drive?'

FOURTEEN

Ingrid's red fillet-of-sole car was still parked in its spot by the Marinella Bar. Apparently it was judged too much trouble to steal; there weren't many like it in Montelusa and its environs.

'Take your car and follow me,' said Montalbano. 'We're going back to Capo Massaria.'

'Oh, God! To do what?' Ingrid pouted. She really didn't feel like it, and the inspector realized this.

'It's in your own interests.'

*

By the glare of the headlights, which he quickly turned off, Montalbano realized that the entrance gate to the house was open. He got out and walked over to Ingrid's car.

'Wait for me here. Turn off your headlights. Do

you remember whether we closed the gate when we left?'

'I don't really remember, but I'm pretty sure we did.'

'Turn your car round and make as little noise as possible.'

She did as he said and the car's nose pointed toward the main road.

'Now listen to what I say. I'm going down there. You keep your ears pricked, and if you hear me shout or notice anything suspicious, don't think twice, just push off and go home.'

'Do you think there's someone inside?'

'I don't know. Just do as I said.'

From his car he took the bag and his pistol. He headed off, trying to step as lightly as possible, and descended the staircase. This time the front door opened without any resistance or sound. He passed through the doorway, pistol in hand. The large room was somehow dimly illuminated by reflections off the water. He kicked open the bathroom door and then the others one by one, feeling ridiculously like the hero of an American TV programme. There was nobody in the house, nor was there any sign that anyone else had been there. It didn't take much to convince him that he himself had left the gate open. He slid open the picture window and looked below. At that point Capo Massaria jutted out over the sea like a ship's prow. The water below must have been quite deep. He ballasted Ingrid's bag with some silverware and a heavy crystal ashtray, spun it around over his head and hurled it out to sea. It wouldn't be so easily found again. Then he took everything that belonged to Ingrid from the wardrobe in the bedroom and went outside, making sure the front door was well shut. As soon as he appeared at the top of the stairs, he was bathed in the glare of Ingrid's headlights.

'I told you to keep your lights *off.* And why did you turn the car back around?'

'I didn't want to leave you here alone. If there was trouble . . .'

'Here are your clothes.'

She took them and put them on the passenger seat.

'Where's the bag?'

'I threw it into the sea. Now go back home. They have nothing left to frame you with.'

Ingrid got out of the car, walked up to Montalbano, and embraced him. She stayed that way awhile, her head leaning on his chest. Then, without looking back at him, she got back into her car, put it in gear, and left.

*

Right at the entrance to the bridge over the Canneto a car was stopped, blocking most of the road. A man was standing there, elbows propped against the roof of the car, hands covering his face, lightly rocking back and forth.

'Anything wrong?' asked Montalbano, pulling up.

The man turned round. His face was covered with blood, which poured out of a broad gash in the middle of his forehead.

'Some bastard,' he said.

'I don't understand. Please explain.' Montalbano got out of the car and approached him.

'I was breezing quietly along when this son of a bitch passes me, practically running me off the road. So I got pissed off and started chasing after him, honking the horn and flashing my lights. Suddenly the guy puts on his brakes and turns the car sideways. He gets out of the car, and he's got something in his hand that I can't make out, and I get scared, thinking he's got a weapon. He comes toward me – my window was down – and without saying a word he bashes me with that thing, which I realized was a monkey wrench.'

'Do you need assistance?'

'No, I think the bleeding's gonna stop.'

'Do you want to file a police report?'

'Don't make me laugh. My head hurts.'

'Do you want me to take you to the hospital?'

'Would you please mind your own fucking business?'

*

How long had it been since he'd had a proper night of God-given sleep? Now he had this bloody pain at the back of his head that wouldn't give him a moment's peace. It continued unabated, and even if he lay still, belly up or belly down, it made no difference, the pain persisted, silent, insidious, without any sharp pangs, which possibly made it worse. He turned on the light. It was four o'clock. On the bedside table were still the salve and roll of gauze he'd used on Ingrid. He grabbed them and, in front of the bathroom mirror, rubbed a little of the salve on the nape of his neck – maybe it would give him some relief – then wrapped his neck in the gauze, securing it with a piece of adhesive tape. But perhaps he put the wrap on too tight; he had trouble moving his head. He looked at himself in the mirror, and at that moment a blinding flash exploded in his brain, drowning out even the bathroom light. He felt like a comic-book character with X-ray vision who could see all the way inside of things.

In grammar school he'd had an old priest as his teacher of religion. 'Truth is light,' the priest had said one day.

Montalbano, never very studious, had been a mischievous pupil, always sitting in the last row.

'So that must mean that if everyone in the family tells the truth, they save on the electric bill.'

He had made this comment aloud which had got him kicked out of the classroom.

Now, some thirty-odd years after the fact, he silently asked the old priest to forgive him.

*

'Boy, do you look ugly today!' exclaimed Fazio as soon as he saw the inspector come in to work. 'Not feeling well?'

'Leave me alone,' was Montalbano's reply. 'Any news of Gambardella? Did you find him?'

'Nothing. Vanished. I've decided we'll end up finding him back in the woods somewhere, eaten by dogs.'

There was something, however, in the sergeant's tone of voice that he found suspicious; he had known him for too many years.

'Anything wrong?'

'It's Gallo. He's gone to the emergency room. Hurt his arm. Nothing serious.'

'How'd it happen?'

'With the squad car.'

'Did he crash it speeding?'

'Yes.'

'Are you going to spit it out or do you need a midwife to pull the words out of your mouth?'

'Well, I'd sent him to the town market on an emergency, some kind of brawl, and he took off in a hurry – you know how he is – and he skidded and crashed into a telephone pole. The car got towed to our depot in Montelusa and they gave us another.'

'Tell me the truth, Fazio: had the tyres been slashed?'

'Yes.'

'And did Gallo check, as I had told him a hundred times to do? Can't you clowns understand that slashing tyres is the national sport in this goddamned country? Tell him he'd better not show his face at the office or I'll bust his arse.'

He slammed the door to his room, furious. Searching inside a tin can in which he kept almost everything from postage stamps to buttons, he found the key to the old factory and went out without saying goodbye.

*

Sitting on the rotten beam near where he'd found Ingrid's bag, he was staring at what had previously looked like an unidentifiable object, a kind of coupling sleeve for pipes, but which he now easily identified: it was a neck brace, brand-new, though it had clearly been used. As if by power of suggestion, his neck started hurting again. He got up, grabbed the brace, left the old factory, and returned to headquarters.

*

'Inspector? This is Stefano Luparello.'

'What can I do for you?'

'Yesterday I told my cousin Giorgio you wanted to see him this morning at ten. Just ten minutes ago, however, my aunt, Giorgio's mother, called me. I don't think Giorgio can come to see you, though he had intended to do so.'

'What happened?'

'I'm not exactly sure, but apparently he was out all night, my aunt said. He got back just a little while ago, around nine o'clock, in a pitiful state.'

'Excuse me, Mr Luparello, but I believe your mother told me he sleeps at your house.'

'He did, but only until my father died, then he moved back home. At our house, without Father around, he felt uneasy. Anyway, my aunt called the doctor, who gave him a shot of sedative. He's in a deep sleep right now. I'm very sorry for him, you know. He was probably too attached to Father.'

'I understand. But if you see your cousin, tell him I really do need to talk to him. No hurry, though, nothing important, at his convenience.'

'Of course. Ah, Mama, who's right next to me, tells me to give you her regards.'

'And I send mine. Tell her I – Your mother is an

extraordinary woman, Mr Luparello. Tell her I respect her immensely.'

'I certainly shall, thank you.'

*

Montalbano spent one hour signing papers and a few more hours writing. They were complicated and useless questionnaires for the public prosecutor's office. Suddenly Galluzzo, without knocking, threw open the door with such violence that it crashed against the wall. He was clearly upset.

'What the fuck! What is it?'

'Montelusa headquarters just called. Counsellor Rizzo's been murdered. Shot. They found him next to his car, in the San Giusippuzzu district. If you want, I'll find out more.'

'Forget it, I'm going there myself.'

Montalbano looked at his watch – eleven o'clock – and rushed out of the door.

*

Nobody answered at Saro's flat. Montalbano knocked at the next-door apartment, and a little old lady with a belligerent face opened up.

'What is it? What you doin', botherin' people like this?' she said in thick dialect.

'Excuse me, signora, I was looking for Mr and Mrs Montaperto.'

'The mister and the missus! Some mister and missus! Them's garbage people. Scum!'

Relations apparently were not good between the two families.

'And who are you?'

'I'm a police inspector.'

The woman's face lit up, and she started yelling in a tone of extreme contentedness.

'Turiddru! Turiddru! Come here, quick!'

'What is it?' asked a very skinny old man, appearing.

'This man's a police inspector! Doncha see I was right! D'ya see who the cops are lookin' for? D'ya see they were nasty folk! D'ya see they ran away so they wouldn't end up in jail?'

'When did they leave, signora?'

'Not half an hour ago. With the li'l brat. You go after 'em right now, you might still catch 'em along the road.'

'Thank you, signora. I'm going after them right now.'

Saro, his wife, and their little son had made it.

*

Along the road to Montelusa the inspector was stopped twice, first by an army patrol of Alpinists and then by another patrol of carabinieri. The worst came on the way to San Giusippuzzu, where between barricades and checkpoints it took him forty-five minutes to go less than three miles. At the scene he found the commissioner, the colonel of the carabinieri, and the entire Montelusa police department on a full day. Even Anna was there, though she pretended not to see him. Jacomuzzi was looking around, trying to find someone to tell him the whole story in minute detail. As soon as he saw Montalbano, he came running up to him.

'A textbook execution, utterly ruthless.'

'How many were there?'

'Just one, or at least only one fired the gun. The poor counsellor left his study at six-thirty this morning. He'd picked up some documents and headed toward Tabbìta, where he had an appointment with a client. He left the study alone – this much is certain – but along the way he picked up someone he knew in the car.'

'Maybe it was someone who thumbed a ride.'

Jacomuzzi burst into laughter so loud that a few people nearby turned and stared at him. 'Can you picture Rizzo, with all the responsibilities he has on his shoulders, blithely giving a ride to a total stranger? The guy had to beware of his own shadow! You know better than I that behind Luparello there was Rizzo. No, no, it was definitely someone he knew, a Mafioso.'

'A Mafioso, you think?'

'I'd bet my life on it. The Mafia raised the price – they always ask for more – and the politicians aren't always in a position to satisfy their demands. But there's another hypothesis. He may have made a mistake, now that he felt stronger after his recent appointment. And they made him pay for it.'

'Jacomuzzi, my congratulations, this morning you're particularly lucid – apparently you had a good shit. How can you be so sure of what you're saying?'

'By the way the guy killed him. First he kicked him in the balls, then had him kneel down, placed his gun against the back of his neck, and fired.'

Immediately a pang shot through Montalbano's neck.

'What kind of gun?'

'Pasquano says that at a glance, considering the entrance and exit wounds and the fact that the barrel was practically pressed against his skin, it must have been a 7.65.'

'Inspector Montalbano!'

'The commissioner's calling you,' said Jacomuzzi, and he stole away.

The commissioner held his hand out to Montalbano, and they exchanged smiles.

'What are you doing here?'

'Actually, Mr Commissioner, I was just leaving. I happened to be in Montelusa when I heard the news, and I came out of curiosity, pure and simple.'

'See you this evening, then. Don't forget! My wife is expecting you.'

*

It was a conjecture, only a conjecture, and so fragile that if he had stopped a moment to consider it well, it would have quickly evaporated. And yet he kept the accelerator pressed to the floor and even risked being shot at as he drove through a roadblock. When he got to Capo Massaria, he bolted out of the car without even bothering to turn off the engine, leaving the door wide open, easily opened the gate and the front door of the house, and raced into the bedroom. The pistol in the drawer of the bedside table was gone. He cursed himself violently. He'd been an idiot: after discovering the weapon on his first visit, he had been back to the house twice with Ingrid and hadn't bothered to check if the gun was still in its place, not once, not even when he'd found the gate open and had set his own mind at rest, convinced that it was he who'd forgotten to shut it.

*

And now I'm going to dawdle a bit, he thought as soon as he got home. He liked the verb 'dawdle', *tambasiare* in Sicilian, which meant poking about from room to room without a precise goal, preferably doing pointless things. Which he did: he rearranged his books, put his desk in order, straightened a drawing on the wall, cleaned the gas burners on the stove. He was dawdling. He had no appetite, had not gone to the restaurant, hadn't even opened the refrigerator to see what Adelina had prepared for him.

Upon entering, he had as usual turned on the television. The first item on the Televigàta news gave the details surrounding the murder of Counsellor Rizzo. Only the details, because the initial announcement of the event had already been given in an emergency broadcast. The newsman had no doubt about it, Rizzo had been ruthlessly murdered by the Mafia, which became frightened when the deceased had recently risen to a position of great political responsibility from which he could better carry on the struggle against organized crime. For this was the watchword of the political renewal: all-out war against the Mafia. Even Nicolò Zito, having rushed back from Palermo, spoke of the Mafia on the Free Channel, but he did so in such contorted fashion that it was impossible to understand anything he said. Between the lines – indeed, between the words – Montalbano sensed that Zito thought it had actually been a brutal settling of scores but wouldn't say so openly, fearing yet another lawsuit among the hundreds he already had pending against him. Finally Montalbano got tired of all the empty chatter, turned off the television, closed the shutters to keep the daylight out, threw himself down on the bed, still dressed, and curled up. What he wanted to do now was *accuttufarsi* – another verb he liked, which meant at once to be beaten up and to withdraw from human society. At that moment, for Montalbano, both meanings were more than applicable.

FIFTEEN

More than a new recipe for baby octopus, the dish invented by Signora Elisa, the commissioner's wife, seemed to Montalbano's palate a truly divine inspiration. He served himself an abundant second helping, but when he saw that this one, too, was coming to an end, he slowed down the rhythm of his chewing, to prolong, however briefly, the pleasure that delicacy afforded him. Signora Elisa watched him happily; like all good cooks, she took delight in the expressions that formed on the faces of her table companions as they tasted one of her creations. And Montalbano, because he had such an expressive face, was one of her favourite dinner guests.

'Thank you very, very much,' the inspector said to her at the end of the meal, sighing. The *purpiteddri* had worked a sort of partial miracle – partial because while it was true that Montalbano now felt at peace with man and God, it was also true that he still did not feel very pacified in his own regard.

When the meal was over, the signora cleared the table and understandingly put a bottle of Chivas on the table for the inspector and a bottle of bitters for her husband.

'I'll let you two talk about your murder victims, the real ones; I'm going into the living room to watch the pretend murders, which I prefer.'

It was a ritual they repeated at least twice a month. Montalbano was fond of the commissioner and his wife, and that fondness was amply repaid in kind by both. The commissioner was a refined, cultured, reserved man, almost a figure from another age.

They talked about the disastrous political situation, the unknown dangers the growing unemployment held in store for the country, the shaky, crumbling state of law and order. Then the commissioner asked a direct question.

'Can you tell me why you haven't yet closed the Luparello investigation? I got a worried phone call from Lo Bianco today.'

'Was he angry?'

'No, only worried, as I said. Perplexed, rather. He can't understand why you're dragging things out so much. And I can't either, to tell you the truth. Look, Montalbano, you know me and you know that I would never presume to pressure one of my officers to settle something one way or another.'

'Of course.'

'So if I'm here asking you this, it's out of personal curiosity, understood? I'm speaking to my friend Montalbano, mind you. To a friend whom I know to possess an intelligence, an acumen, and, most important, a courtesy in human relations quite rare nowadays.'

'Thank you, sir, I'll be honest with you. I think you deserve as much. What seemed suspicious to me from the start of the whole affair was the place where the body was found. It was inconsistent, blatantly inconsistent, with the personality and lifestyle of Luparello, a sensible, prudent, ambitious man. I asked myself: why did he do it? Why did he go all the way to the Pasture for a sexual encounter, putting his life and his public image in danger? I couldn't come up with an answer. You see, sir, it was as if, in all due proportion, the president of the Republic had died of a heart attack while dancing to rock music at a third-rate disco.'

The commissioner raised a hand to stop him.

'Your comparison doesn't really work,' he observed with a smile that wasn't a smile. 'We recently had a minister go wild on the dance floor of third- and worse-rate nightclubs, and he didn't die . . .'

The 'unfortunately' he was clearly about to add disappeared on the tip of his tongue.

'But the fact remains,' Montalbano insisted. 'And this first impression was abundantly confirmed for me by the engineer's widow.'

'So you've met her? Quite a mind, that lady.'

'It was she who sought me out, after you had spoken well of me. In our conversation yesterday she told me her husband had a pied-à-terre at Capo Massaria and gave me the keys. So what reason would he have to risk exposure at a place like the Pasture?'

'I have asked myself the same question.'

'Let us assume for a moment, for the sake of argument, that he did go there, that he let himself be talked into it by a woman with tremendous powers of persuasion. A woman not from the place, who took an absolutely impassable route to get him there. Bear in mind that it's the woman who's driving.'

'The road was impassable, you say?'

'Yes. And not only do I have exact testimony to back this up, but I also had my sergeant take that route, and I took it myself. So the car is actually driven down the dry bed of the Canneto, ruining the suspension. When it comes to a stop, almost inside a big shrub in the Pasture, the woman immediately mounts the man beside her, and they begin making love. And it is during this act that Luparello suffers the misfortune that kills him. The woman, however, does not scream, does not call for help. Cool as a cucumber, she walks slowly down the path that leads to the provincial road, gets into a car that has pulled up, and disappears.'

'It's all very strange, you're right. Did the woman ask for a ride?'

'Apparently not, and you've hit the nail on the head. And I have yet another testimony to this effect. The car that pulled up did so in a hurry, with its door actually open. In other words, the driver knew whom he was supposed to encounter and pick up without wasting any time.'

'Excuse me, Inspector, but did you get sworn statements for all these testimonies?'

'No, there wasn't any reason. You see, one thing is certain: Luparello died of natural causes. Officially speaking, I have no reason to be investigating.'

'Well, if things are as you say, there is, for example, the failure to assist a person in danger.'

'Do you agree with me that that's nonsense?'

'Yes.'

'Well, that's as far as I'd gone when Signora Luparello pointed out something very essential to me, that is, that her husband, when he died, had his underwear on backwards.'

'Wait a minute,' said the commissioner, 'let's slow down. How did the signora know that her husband's underwear was on backwards, if indeed it was? As far as I know, she wasn't there at the scene, and she wasn't present at the crime lab's examinations.'

Montalbano became worried. He had spoken impulsively, not realizing he had to avoid implicating Jacomuzzi, who he was sure had given the widow the photos. But there was no turning back.

'The signora got hold of the crime-lab photos. I don't know how.'

'I think I do,' said the commissioner, frowning.

'She examined them carefully with a magnifying glass and showed them to me. She was right.'

'And based on this detail she formed an opinion?'

'Of course. It's based on the assumption that although her husband, when getting dressed in the morning, might by chance have put them on backwards, inevitably over the course of the day he would have noticed, since he took diuretics and had to urinate frequently. Therefore, on the basis of this hypothesis, the signora believes that Luparello must have been caught in some sort of embarrassing situation, to say the least, at which point he was forced to put his clothes back on in a hurry and go to the Pasture, where – in the signora's opinion, of course – he was to be compromised in some irreparable way, so that he would have to retire from political life. But there's more.'

'Don't spare me any details.'

'The two street cleaners who found the body, before calling the police, felt duty-bound to inform Counsellor Rizzo, who they knew was Luparello's alter ego. Well, Rizzo not only showed no surprise, dismay, shock, alarm, or worry, he actually told the two to report the incident at once.'

'How do you know this? Had you tapped the phone line?' the commissioner asked, aghast.

'No, no phone taps. One of the street cleaners faithfully transcribed the brief exchange. He did it for reasons too complicated to go into here.'

'Was he contemplating blackmail?'

'No, he was contemplating the way a play is written. Believe me, he had no intention whatsoever of committing a crime. And this is where we come to the heart of the matter: Rizzo.'

'Wait a minute. I was determined to find a way this evening to scold you again. For wanting always to complicate simple matters. Surely you've read Sciascia's *Candida.* Do you remember that at a certain point the protagonist asserts that it is possible that things are almost always simple? I merely wanted to remind you of this.'

'Yes, but, you see, Candido says "almost always", he doesn't say "always". He allows for exceptions. And Luparello's case is one of those where things were set up to appear simple.'

'When in fact they are complicated?'

'Very complicated. And speaking of *Candida,* do you remember the subtitle?'

'Of course: *A Dream Dreamed in Sicily.*'

'Exactly, whereas we are dealing with a nightmare of sorts. Let me venture a hypothesis that will be very difficult to confirm now that Rizzo has been murdered. On Sunday evening, around seven, Luparello phones his wife to tell her he'll be home very late – he has an important political meeting. In fact, he goes to his little house on Capo Massaria for a lovers' tryst. And I'll tell you right away that any eventual investigation as to the person who was with Luparello would prove rather difficult, because the engineer was ambidextrous.'

'What do you mean? Where I come from, ambidextrous means someone can use both hands, right or left, without distinction.'

'In a less correct sense, it's also used to describe someone who goes with men as well as women, without distinction.'

Both very serious, they seemed like two professors compiling a new dictionary.

'What are you saying?' wondered the commissioner.

'It was Signora Luparello herself who intimated

this to me, and all too clearly. And she certainly had no interest in making things up, especially in this regard.'

'Did you go to the little house?'

'Yes. Cleaned up to perfection. Inside were a few of Luparello's belongings, nothing else.'

'Continue with your hypothesis.'

'During the sex act, or most probably right after, given the traces of semen that were recovered, Luparello dies. The woman who is with him—'

'Stop,' the commissioner ordered. 'How can you say with such assurance that it was a woman? You've just finished describing the engineer's rather broad sexual horizons.'

'I can say it because I'm certain of it. So, as soon as the woman realizes her lover is dead, she loses her head, she doesn't know what to do, she gets all upset, and she even loses the necklace she was wearing, but doesn't realize it. When she finally calms down, she sees that the only thing she can do is to phone Rizzo, Luparello's shadow man, and ask for help. Rizzo tells her to get out of the house at once and suggests that she leave the key somewhere so he can enter. He reassures her, saying he'll take care of everything;

nobody will ever know about the tryst that led to such a tragic end. Relieved, the woman steps out of the picture.'

'What do you mean, "steps out of the picture"? Wasn't it a woman who took Luparello to the Pasture?'

'Yes and no. Let me continue. Rizzo races to Capo Massaria and dresses the corpse in a big hurry. He intends to get him out of there and have him found somewhere less compromising. At this point, however, he sees the necklace on the floor and inside the wardrobe finds the clothes of the woman who just phoned him. And he realizes that this may just be his lucky day.'

'In what sense?'

'In the sense that he's now in a position to put everyone's back to the wall, political friends as well as enemies. He can become the top gun in the party. The woman who called him is Ingrid Sjostrom, the Swedish daughter-in-law of Dr Cardamone, Luparello's natural successor and a man who certainly will want to have nothing to do with Rizzo. Now, you see, a phone call is one thing, but proving that La Sjostrom was Luparello's mistress is something else. Besides, there's still more to be done. Rizzo knows that Luparello's party cronies are the ones who will pounce on his political inheritance, so in order to eliminate them he must make things such that they will be ashamed to wave Luparello's banner. For this to happen, the engineer must be utterly disgraced, dragged through the mud. He gets the brilliant idea of having the body found at the Pasture. And since she's already involved, why not make it look as though the woman who wanted to go to the Pasture with Luparello was Ingrid Sjostrom herself, who's a foreigner and certainly not nunnish in her habits, and who might have been seeking a kinky thrill? If the set-up works, Cardamone will be in Rizzo's hands. Rizzo phones his men, whom we know, without being able to prove it, to be underhanded butcher boys. One of these is Angelo Nicotra, a homosexual better known in their circles as Marilyn.'

'How were you able to learn even his name?'

'An informer told me, someone in whom I have absolute faith. In a way, we're friends.'

'You mean Gegè, your old schoolmate?' Montalbano eyed the commissioner, mouth agape. 'Why are you looking at me that way? I'm a cop, too. Go on.'

'When his men get there, Rizzo has Marilyn dress

up as a woman, has him put on the necklace, and tells him to take the body to the Pasture, but by way of an impassable route, actually by way of a dry riverbed.'

'To what end?'

'Further proof against La Sjostrom, who is a racing champion and knows how to travel a route like that.'

'Are you sure?'

'Yes. I was in the car with her when I had her drive down the riverbed.'

'Oh, God!' The commissioner groaned. 'You forced her to do that?'

'Not at all! She did it quite willingly.'

'But how many people have you dragged into this? Do you realize you're playing with dynamite?'

'It all goes up in smoke, believe me. So while his two men leave with the corpse, Rizzo, who has taken the keys Luparello had on him, returns to Montelusa and has no trouble getting his hands on documents belonging to Luparello and of greatest interest to him. Marilyn, meanwhile, executes to perfection the orders he's been given: he gets out of the car after going through the motions of sex, walks away, and, near an old, abandoned factory, hides the necklace behind a bush and throws the bag over the factory wall.'

'What bag are you talking about?'

'Ingrid Sjostrom's bag. It's even got her initials on it. Rizzo found it in the little house and decided to use it.'

'Explain to me how you arrived at these conclusions.'

'Rizzo, you see, is showing one card, the necklace, and hiding another, the bag. The discovery of the necklace, however it occurs, will prove that Ingrid was at the Pasture at the time of Luparello's death. If somebody happens to pocket the necklace and not say anything, he can still play the bag card. But he actually has a lucky break, in his opinion: the necklace is found by one of the sanitation men, who turned it in to me. Rizzo gives a plausible explanation for the discovery of the necklace, but in the meantime he has established the Sjostrom–Luparello–Pasture triangle of connection. It was I, on the other hand, who found the bag, based on the discrepancy between the two testimonies: the woman, when she got out of Luparello's car, was holding a bag that she no longer had when a car picked her up along the provincial road. Finally, to cut a long story short, Rizzo's two men return to the little house and put everything in order. At the first light of dawn, Rizzo phones Cardamone and begins playing his cards.'

'All right, fine, but he also begins playing with his life.'

'That's another matter, if that is indeed the case,' said Montalbano.

The commissioner gave him a look of alarm.

'What do you mean? What the hell are you thinking?'

'Quite simply that the only person who comes out of this story unscathed is Cardamone. Don't you think Rizzo's murder was providentially fortunate for him?'

The commissioner gave a start, and it wasn't clear whether he was speaking seriously or joking. 'Listen, Montalbano, don't get any more brilliant ideas. Leave Cardamone in peace. He's an honourable man who wouldn't hurt a fly!'

'I was just kidding, Commissioner. But allow me to ask, are there any new developments in the investigation?'

'What new developments would you expect? You know the kind of person Rizzo was. Out of every ten people he knew, respectable or otherwise, eight, respectable or otherwise, would have liked to see him dead. A veritable forest, my friend, a jungle of potential murderers, by their own hand or through intermediaries. I must say your story has a certain plausibility, but only for someone who knows what kind of stuff Rizzo was made of.'

He sipped a dram of bitters slowly.

'You certainly had me fascinated. What you've told me is an exercise of the highest intelligence; at moments you seemed like an acrobat on a tightrope, with no net underneath. Because, to be brutally frank, underneath your argument, there's nothing. You have no proof of anything you've said. It could all be interpreted in another way, and any good lawyer could pick apart your deductions without breaking sweat.'

'I know.'

'What do you intend to do?'

'Tomorrow morning I'm going to tell Lo Bianco that I've no objection if he wants to close the case.'

SIXTEEN

'Hello, Montalbano? It's Mimi Augello. Sorry to disturb you, but I called to reassure you. I've come back to home base. When are you leaving?'

'The flight from Palermo's at three, so I have to leave Vigàta around twelve-thirty, right after lunch.'

'Then we won't be seeing each other, since I think I have to stay a little late at the office. Any news?'

'Fazio will fill you in.'

'How long will you be gone?'

'Up to and including Thursday.'

'Have fun and get some rest. Fazio has your number in Genoa, doesn't he? If anything big comes up, I'll give you a ring.'

His assistant inspector, Mimi Augello, had returned punctually from his holidays, and thus Montalbano could now leave without problems. Augello was a capable person. Montalbano phoned Livia to tell her his time of arrival, and Livia, pleased by the news, said she would meet him at the airport.

When he got to the office, Fazio informed him that the workers from the salt factory, who had all been 'made mobile' – a pious euphemism for being fired – had occupied the train station. Their wives, by lying down on the tracks, were preventing all trains from passing. The carabinieri were already on the scene. Should they go down there, too?

'To do what?'

'I don't know, to give them a hand.'

'Give whom a hand?'

'What do you mean, Chief? The carabinieri, the forces of order, which would be us, until proved to the contrary.'

'If you're really dying to help somebody, help the ones occupying the station.'

'Chief, I've always suspected it: you're a communist.'

*

'Inspector? This is Stefano Luparello. Please excuse me. Has my cousin Giorgio been to see you?'

'No, I don't have any news.'

'We're very worried here at home. As soon as he recovered from his sedative, he went out and vanished again. Mama would like some advice: shouldn't we ask the police to conduct a search?'

'No. Please tell your mother I don't think that's necessary. Giorgio will turn up. Tell her not to worry.'

'In any case, if you hear any news, please let us know.'

'That will be very difficult, because I'm going away on holiday. I'll be back on Friday.'

*

The first three days spent with Livia at her house in Boccadasse made him forget Sicily almost entirely, thanks to a few nights of leaden, restorative sleep, with Livia in his arms. *Almost* entirely, though, because two or three times, by surprise, the smell, the speech, the things of his island picked him up and carried him weightless through the air, for a few seconds, back to Vigàta. And each time he was sure that Livia had noticed his momentary absence, his wavering, and she had looked at him without saying anything.

*

On Thursday evening he got an entirely unexpected phone call from Fazio.

'Nothing important, Chief. I just wanted to hear your voice and confirm that you'll be back tomorrow.'

Montalbano was well aware that relations between the sergeant and Augello were not the easiest.

'Do you need comforting? Has that mean Augello been spanking your little behind?'

'He criticizes everything I do.'

'Be patient, I'll be back tomorrow. Any news?'

'Yesterday they arrested the mayor and three town councillors for graft and accepting bribes.'

'They finally succeeded.'

'Yeah, but don't get your hopes too high, Chief. They're trying to copy the Milanese judges here, but Milan is very far away.'

'Anything else?'

'We found Gambardella, remember him? The guy who was shot at when he was trying to fill his tank? He wasn't laid out in the countryside, but goat-tied in the trunk of his own car, which was later set on fire and completely burnt up.'

'If it was completely burnt up, how did you know Gambardella was goat-tied?'

'They used metal wire, Chief.'

'See you tomorrow, Fazio.'

This time it wasn't the smell and speech of his island that sucked him back there but the stupidity, the ferocity, the horror.

*

After making love, Livia fell silent for a while, then took his hand.

'What's wrong? What did your sergeant tell you?'

'Nothing important, I assure you.'

'Then why are you suddenly so gloomy?' Montalbano felt confirmed in his conviction: if there was one person in all the world to whom he could sing the whole High Mass, it was Livia. To the commissioner he'd sung only half the Mass, skipping some parts. He sat up in bed, fluffed up the pillow. 'Listen.'

*

He told her about the Pasture, about Luparello, about the affection a nephew of his, Giorgio, had for him, about how at some point this affection turned (degenerated?) into love, into passion, about the final tryst in the bachelor pad at Capo Massaria, about

Luparello's death and how young Giorgio, driven mad by the fear of scandal – not for himself but for his uncle's image and memory – had dressed him back up as best he could, then dragged him to the car to drive him away and leave the body to be found somewhere else . . . He told her about Giorgio's despair when he realized that this fiction wouldn't work, that everyone would see he was carrying a dead man in the car, about how he got the idea to put the neck brace he'd been wearing until that very day – and which he still had in the car – on the corpse, about how he had tried to hide the brace with a piece of black cloth, how he became suddenly afraid he might have an epileptic fit, which he suffered from, about how he had phoned Rizzo – Montalbano explained to her who the lawyer was – and how Rizzo had realized that this death, with a few arrangements, could be his lucky break.

He told her about Ingrid, about her husband Giacomo, about Dr Cardamone, about the violence – he couldn't think of a better word – to which the doctor customarily resorted with his daughter-in-law ('That's disgusting,' Livia commented), about how

Rizzo had suspicions as to their relationship and tried to implicate Ingrid, getting Cardamone but not himself to swallow the bait; he told her about Marilyn and his accomplice, about the phantasmagorical ride in the car, about the horrific pantomime acted out inside the parked car at the Pasture (Livia: 'Excuse me a minute, I need a strong drink'). And when she returned, he told her still other sordid details – the necklace, the bag, the clothes – he told her about Giorgio's heartrending despair when he saw the photographs, having understood Rizzo's double betrayal, of him and of Luparello's memory, which he had wanted to save at all costs.

'Wait a minute,' said Livia. 'Is this Ingrid beautiful?'

'Very beautiful. And since I know exactly what you're thinking, I'll tell you even more: I destroyed all the false evidence against her.'

'That's not like you,' she said resentfully.

'I did even worse things, just listen. Rizzo, who now had Cardamone in the palm of his hand, achieved his political objective, but he made a mistake: he underestimated Giorgio's reaction. Giorgio's an extremely beautiful boy.'

'Oh, come on! Him, too!' said Livia, trying to make light.

'But with a very fragile personality,' the inspector continued. 'Riding the wave of his emotions, devastated, he ran to the house at Capo Massaria, grabbed Luparello's pistol, tracked down Rizzo, beat him to a pulp, and shot him at the base of the skull.'

'Did you arrest him?'

'No, I just said I did worse than destroy evidence. You see, my colleagues in Montelusa think – and the hypothesis is not just hot air – that Rizzo was killed by the Mafia. And I never told them what I thought the truth was.'

'Why not?'

Montalbano didn't answer, throwing his hands up in the air. Livia went into the bathroom, and the inspector heard the water running in the tub. A little later, after asking permission to enter, he found her in the full tub, her chin resting on her raised knees.

'Did you know there was a pistol in that house?'

'Yes.'

'And you left it there?'

'Yes.'

'So you gave yourself a promotion, eh?' asked Livia after a long silence. 'From inspector to god – a fourth-rate god, but still a god.'

*

After getting off the aeroplane, he headed straight for the airport café. He was in dire need of a real espresso after the vile, dark dishwater they had forced on him in flight. He heard someone calling him: it was Stefano Luparello.

'Where are you going, Mr Luparello, back to Milan?'

'Yes, back to work. I've been away too long. I'm also going to look for a larger apartment; as soon as I find one, my mother will come to live with me. I don't want to leave her alone.'

'That's a very good idea, even though she has her sister and nephew in Montelusa—'

The young man stiffened.

'So you don't know?'

'Don't know what?'

'Giorgio is dead.'

Montalbano put down his espresso; the shock had made him spill the coffee.

'How did that happen?'

'Do you remember, the day of your departure I called you to find out if you'd heard from him?'

'Of course.'

'The following morning he still hadn't returned, so I felt compelled to alert the police and the carabinieri. They conducted some extremely superficial searches – I'm sorry, perhaps they were too busy investigating Rizzo's murder. On Sunday afternoon a fisherman, from his boat, saw that a car had fallen onto the rocks, right below the San Filippo bend. Do you know the area? It's just before Capo Massaria.'

'Yes, I know the place.'

'Well, the fisherman rowed in the direction of the car, saw that there was a body in the driver's seat and raced off to report it.'

'Did they manage to establish the cause of the accident?'

'Yes. My cousin, as you know, from the moment Father died, lived in a state of almost constant derangement: too many tranquillizers, too many sedatives. Instead of taking the curve, he continued straight – he was going very fast at that moment – and crashed through the little guard wall. He never got over my father's death. He had a real passion for him. He loved him.'

He uttered the two words, 'passion' and 'love', in a firm, precise tone, as if to eliminate, with crisp outlines, any possible blurring of their meaning. The voice over the loudspeaker called for passengers taking the Milan flight.

As soon as he was outside the airport car park, where he had left his car, Montalbano pressed the accelerator to the floor. He didn't want to think about anything, only to concentrate on driving. After some sixty miles he stopped at the shore of an artificial lake, got out of the car, opened the trunk, took out the neck brace, threw it into the water and waited for it to sink. Only then did he smile. He had wanted to act like a god; what Livia said was true. But that fourth-rate god, in his first and, he hoped, last experience, had guessed right.

*

To reach Vigàta he had no choice but to pass in front of the Montelusa police headquarters, and it was at that exact moment that his car decided suddenly to die on him. He got out and was about to go to ask for help at the station when a policeman who knew him and had witnessed his useless manoeuvres approached him. The officer lifted up the bonnet, fiddled around a bit, then closed it.

'That should do it. But you ought to have it looked at.'

Montalbano got back in the car, turned on the ignition, then bent over to pick up some newspapers that had fallen to the floor. When he sat back up, Anna was leaning into the open window.

'Anna, how are you?'

The girl didn't answer; she simply glared at him.

'Well?'

'And you're supposed to be an honest man?'

Montalbano realized she was referring to the night when she saw Ingrid lying half naked on his bed.

'No, I'm not,' he said. 'But not for the reasons you think.'

Author's Note

I believe it essential to state that this story was not taken from the crime news and does not involve any real events. It is, in short, to be ascribed entirely to my imagination. But since in recent years reality has seemed bent on surpassing the imagination, if not entirely abolishing it, there may be a few unpleasant coincidences of name and situation. As we know, however, one cannot be held responsible for the whims of chance.

Notes

page 5 – **face worthy of a Lombroso diagram** – Cesare Lombroso (1836–1909) was an Italian physician and criminologist who theorized a relationship between criminal behaviour and certain physical traits and anomalies, maintaining that such characteristics were due in part to degeneration and atavism. Lombroso's theories were disproved in the early twentieth century by British researcher Charles Goring, who reported finding as many instances of Lombroso's criminal physical traits among English university students as among English convicts.

page 15 – **The thought of going to the carabinieri . . . under the command of a Milanese lieutenant** – The Italian carabinieri are a national police force, bureaucratically separate from local police forces and actually a function of the military (like the Guardia Civil in Spain and the Gendarmerie in France). Their officers are often not native to the regions they serve, and this geographic estrangement, coupled with the procedural separateness from the local police, has been known to create confusion in the execution of their duties. The carabinieri are frequently the butt of jokes, being commonly perceived as less than sharp-witted. This stereotype lurks wryly behind many of Inspector Montalbano's dealings with them.

page 18 – **'phone the Montelusa department, have them send someone from the lab'** – Montelusa, in Camilleri's imagined topography, is the capital of the province in which the smaller town of Vigàta is situated. In the Italian law-enforcement hierarchy, the *Questum* – the central police department of a major city or provincial capital – is at the top of the local chain of command and, as the procedural nucleus, has the forensic laboratory used by the police departments of the various satellite towns or, in the case of a large metropolis, of the various urban zones. The carabinieri use their own crime labs.

page 20 – **'what's new in the chicken coop?'** – The name 'Gallo' means 'rooster' in Italian, and Galluzzo is a diminutive of same.

page 30 – **'Twenty million lire'** – At the time of this novel's writing, about £9,000. Eleven thousand lire was worth about £5.

page 35 – **Don Luigi Sturzo** – Luigi Sturzo (1871–1959) was a priest and founder of the Partito Popolare Italiano, a reform-oriented, Catholic coalition that became the Christian Democratic Party after the Second World War.

Persecuted by the Fascist regime, Don Luigi took refuge in the United States and never sought public office.

page 37 – **Not even the earthquake unleashed . . . had touched him** – This is a reference to what came to be known as *Operazione mani pulite* (Operation Clean Hands), a campaign, led in the early 1990s by a handful of Milanese investigating magistrates, to uproot the corruption endemic in the Italian political system. Their efforts helped to bring about the collapse of the Christian Democratic and Socialist parties but, as this and other such allusions in this novel indicate, the new code of ethics had trouble taking hold, especially in the south. Indeed the whole story of Luparello's career is typical of the Christian Democratic politician reconstituted to conform to the new political landscape while remaining essentially unreconstructed.

page 47 – **'the prefect'** – In Italy, the *prefetti* are representatives of the central government, assigned each to one province. They are part of the national, not local, bureaucracy.

page 97 – **corso** – A central, usually broad and commercially important, street in Italian cities and towns.

page 107 – **the prince of Salina** – Prince Fabrizio Corbera di Salina is the protagonist of Giuseppe Tomasi di Lampedusa's historical novel about Sicily at the time of the Italian Wars of Unification, *Il Gattopardo (The Leopard)*. In a famous passage, it is actually the prince's nephew Tancredi who says, 'If we want things to stay as they are, things will have to change.'

page 124 – **'Sicilchim'** – The name of the abandoned chemical factory. It's shorthand for Sicilia Chimica, or Sicilian Chemicals.

page 169 – **would jerk her head backwards, as if repeatedly saying no** – In Sicily, this gesture expresses a negative response.

page 211 – **an army patrol of Alpinists** – The *Alpini* are a division of the Italian army trained in mountain warfare and tactics. Sporting quaint Tyrolean feathered caps as part of their uniform, their sudden appearance at this point in the story, though perfectly plausible and consistent with the government policy (mentioned on page 5) of dispatching army units to Sicily for the maintenance of order, is sort of a sight-gag, one that inevitably calls attention to the endlessly complicated and criss-crossing chains of command between the military and the local police forces in Italy.

page 236 – **goat-tied** – The Sicilian word is *incaprettato* (containing the word for goat, *capra*), and it refers to a particularly cruel method of execution used by the Mafia, where the victim, face-down, has a rope (in this case, a wire) looped around his neck and then tied to his feet, which are raised behind his back as in hog-tying. Fatigue eventually forces him to lower his feet, strangling him in the process.

Notes compiled by Stephen Sartarelli

THE TERRACOTTA DOG

ONE

To judge from the entrance the dawn was making, it promised to be a very iffy day – that is, blasts of angry sunlight one minute, fits of freezing rain the next, all of it seasoned with sudden gusts of wind – one of those days when someone who is sensitive to abrupt shifts in weather and suffers them in his blood and brain is likely to change opinion and direction continuously, like those sheets of tin, cut in the shape of banners and roosters, that spin every which way on rooftops with each new puff of wind.

Inspector Salvo Montalbano had always belonged to this unhappy category of humanity. It was something passed on to him by his mother, a sickly woman who used to shut herself up in her bedroom, in the dark, whenever she had a headache, and when this happened one could make no noise about the house and had to tread lightly. His father, on the other hand, on stormy seas and smooth, always maintained an even keel, always the same unchanging state of mind, rain or shine.

This time, too, the inspector did not fail to live up to

his inborn nature. No sooner had he stopped his car at the ten-kilometre marker along the Vigàta–Fela highway, as he had been told to do, than he felt like putting it back in gear and returning to town, bagging the whole operation. He managed to control himself, brought the car closer to the edge of the road, opened the glove compartment, and reached for the pistol he normally did not carry on his person. His hand, however, remained poised in mid-air: immobile, spellbound, he stared at the weapon.

Good God! It's real! he thought.

The previous evening, a few hours before Gegè Gullotta called to set up the whole mess – Gegè being a small-time dealer of soft drugs and the manager of an open-air bordello known as 'the Pasture' – the inspector had been reading a detective novel by a writer from Barcelona who greatly intrigued him and had the same surname as he, though hispanicized: Montalbán. One sentence in particular had struck him: 'The pistol slept, looking like a cold lizard.' He withdrew his hand with a slight feeling of disgust and closed the glove compartment, leaving the lizard to its slumber. After all, if the whole business that was about to unfold turned out to be a trap, an ambush, he could carry all the pistols he wanted, and still they would fill him with holes with their Kalashnikovs however and whenever they so desired, thank you and good night. He could only hope that Gegè, remembering the years they'd spent together on the same bench in elementary school and the friendship they'd carried over into adulthood, had not decided, out of self-interest, to sell him like pork at the market, feeding him any old bullshit just to lead him to the slaughter. No, not just any old bullshit: this business, if for real, could be really big, make a lot of noise.

He sighed deeply and began to make his way slowly, step by step, up a narrow, rocky path between broad expanses of vineyard. The vines bore table grapes, with round, firm seeds, the kind called, who knows why, 'Italian grapes', the only kind that would take in this soil. As for trying to grow vines for making wine, you were better off sparing yourself the labour and expense.

The two-storey cottage, one room on top of another, was at the summit of the hill, half hidden by four large Saracen olive trees that nearly surrounded it. It was just as Gegè had described it. Faded, shuttered windows and door, a huge caper bush in front, with some smaller shrubs of touch-me-not – the small, wild cucumber that squirts seeds into the air if you touch it with the tip of a stick – a collapsed wicker chair turned upside down, an old zinc bucket eaten up by rust and now useless. Grass had overgrown everything else. It all conspired to give the impression that the place had been uninhabited for years, but this appearance was deceptive, and experience had made Montalbano too savvy to be fooled. In fact, he was convinced somebody was eyeing him from inside the cottage, trying to guess his intentions from the moves he would make. He stopped three steps away from the front of the house, took off his jacket, and hung it from a branch of the olive tree so they could see he wasn't armed. Then he called out without raising his voice much, like a friend come to visit a friend.

'Hey! Anybody home?'

No answer, not a sound. Montalbano pulled a lighter and a packet of cigarettes from his trouser pocket, put a cigarette in his mouth, and lit it, turning round halfway to shelter himself from the wind. That way whoever was inside the house could examine him from behind, having already examined him from the front. He took two puffs, then went to the door and knocked with his fist, hard enough to hurt his knuckles on the crusts of paint on the wood.

'Is there anyone here?' he asked again.

He was ready for anything, except the calm, ironic voice that surprised him from behind.

'Sure there is. Over here.'

*

It had all started with a phone call.

'Hello? Hello? Montalbano! Salvuzzo! It's me, Gegè.'

'I know it's you. Calm down. How are you, my little honey-eyed orange blossom?'

'I'm fine.'

'Working the mouth hard these days? Been perfecting your blow-job techniques?'

'Come on, Salvù, don't start with your usual faggot stuff. You know damn well that I don't work myself. I only make other mouths work for me.'

'But aren't you the instructor? Aren't you the one who

teaches your multicoloured assortment of whores how to hold their lips and how hard to suck?'

'Salvù, even if what you're saying was true, they'd be the ones teaching me. They come to me at age ten already well trained, and at fifteen they're top-of-the-line professionals. I've got a little Albanian fourteen-year-old—'

'You trying to sell me your merchandise now?'

'Listen, I got no time to fuck around. I have something I'm supposed to give you, a package.'

'At this hour? Can't you get it to me tomorrow morning?'

'I won't be in town tomorrow.'

'Do you know what's in the package?'

'Of course. *Mostaccioli* with mulled wine, the way you like 'em. My sister Mariannina made them just for you.'

'How's Mariannina doing with her eyes?'

'Much better. They work miracles in Barcelona.'

'They also write good books in Barcelona.'

'What's that?'

'Never mind. Just talking to myself. Where do you want to meet?'

'The usual place, in an hour.'

*

The usual place was the little beach of Puntasecca, a short tongue of sand beneath a white marl hill, almost inaccessible by land, or rather, accessible only to Montalbano and Gegè, who back in grade school had discovered a trail that was difficult enough on foot and downright foolhardy to attempt by car. Puntasecca was only a few kilometres from Montalbano's little house by the sea just outside of Vigàta, and that was why he took his time. But the moment he opened the door to go to his rendezvous, the telephone rang.

'Hi, darling. It's me, right on time. How did things go today?'

'Business as usual. And you?'

'Ditto. Listen, Salvo, I've been thinking long and hard about what—'

'Livia, sorry to interrupt, but I haven't got much time. Actually I don't have any time at all. You caught me just as I was going out of the door.'

'All right then, goodnight.'

Livia hung up and Montalbano was left standing with the receiver in his hand. Then he remembered that the night before, he had told her to call him at midnight on the dot, because they would certainly have as much time as they wanted to talk at that hour. He couldn't decide whether to call Livia back right then or when he returned, after his meeting with Gegè. With a pang of remorse, he put the receiver down and went out.

*

When he arrived a few minutes late, Gegè was already waiting for him, pacing back and forth the length of his car. They exchanged an embrace and kissed; it had been a while since they'd seen each other.

'Let's go sit in my car,' said the inspector, 'it's a little chilly tonight.'

'They put me up to this,' Gegè broke in as soon as he sat down.

'Who did?'

'Some people I can't say no to. You know, Salvù, like every businessman, I gotta pay my dues so I can work in peace and keep the Pasture, or they'd put me out to pasture in a hurry. Every month the good Lord sends our way, somebody comes by to collect.'

'For whom? Can you tell me?'

'For Tano the Greek.'

Montalbano shuddered, but didn't let his friend notice. Gaetano 'the Greek' Bennici had never so much as seen Greece, not even through a telescope, and knew as much about things Hellenic as a cast-iron pipe, but he came by his nickname owing to a certain vice thought in the popular imagination to be greatly appreciated in the vicinity of the Acropolis. He had three certain murders under his belt, and in his circles held a position one step below the top bosses. But he was not known to operate in or around Vigàta; it was the Cuffaro and Sinagra families who competed for that territory. Tano belonged to another parish.

'So what's Tano the Greek's business in these parts?'

'What kind of stupid question is that? What kind of fucking cop are you? Don't you know that for Tano the Greek there's no such thing as "these parts" and "those parts" when it comes to women? He was given control and a piece of every whore on the island.'

'I didn't know. Go on.'

'Around eight o'clock this evening the usual guy came by to collect; today was the appointed day for paying dues. He took the money, but then, instead of leaving, he opens his car door and tells me to get in.'

'So what'd you do?'

'I got scared and broke out in a cold sweat. What could I do? I got in, and we drove off. To make a long story short, he took the road for Fela, and stopped after barely half an hour's drive . . .'

'Did you ask him where you were going?'

'Of course.'

'And what did he say?'

'Nothing, as if I hadn't spoken. After half an hour, he makes me get out in some deserted spot without a soul around, and gestures to me to follow some dirt road. There wasn't even a dog around. At a certain point, and I have no idea where he popped out from, Tano the Greek suddenly appears in front of me. I nearly had a stroke, my knees turned to butter. Don't get me wrong, I'm no coward, but the guy's killed five people.'

'Five?'

'Why, how many do you think he's killed?'

'Three.'

'No way. It's five, I guarantee it.'

'Okay, go on.'

'I got to thinking. Since I always pay on time, I figured

Tano wanted to raise the price. Business is good, I got no complaints, and they know it. But I was wrong, it wasn't about money.'

'What did he want?'

'Without even saying hello, he asked me if I knew you.'

Montalbano thought he hadn't heard right.

'If you knew who?'

'You, Salvù, you.'

'And what did you tell him?'

'Well, I was shitting my pants, so I said, yeah, I knew you, but just casually, by sight – you know, hello, how ya doin'. And he looked at me, you gotta believe me, with a pair of eyes that looked like a statue's eyes, motionless, dead, then he leaned his head back and gave this little laugh and asked me if I wanted to know how many hairs I had on my arse 'cause he could tell me within two. What he meant was that he knew everything about me from the cradle to the grave, and I hope that won't be too soon. And so I just looked at the ground and didn't open my mouth. That's when he told me he wanted to see you.'

'When and where?'

'Tonight, at dawn. I'll tell you where in a second.'

'Do you know what he wants from me?'

'I don't know and I don't want to know. He said to rest assured you could trust him like a brother.'

Like a brother. Those words, instead of reassuring Montalbano, sent a shiver down his spine. It was well known that foremost among Tano's three – or five – murder victims was his older brother Nicolino, whom he first strangled and then, in accordance with some mysterious semiological rule, meticulously flayed. The inspector started thinking dark thoughts, which became even darker, if that was possible, at the words that Gegè, putting his hand on his shoulder, then whispered in his ear.

'Be careful, Salvù, the guy's an evil beast.'

*

He was driving slowly back home when the headlights of Gegè's car behind him started flashing repeatedly. He pulled over and Gegè, pulling up, leaned all the way across the seat towards the window on the side closest to Montalbano and handed him a package.

'I forgot the *mostaccioli.*'

'Thanks. I thought it was just an excuse.'

'What do you think I am? Somebody who says something and means something else?'

He accelerated away, offended.

*

The inspector spent the kind of night one tells the doctor about. His first thought was to phone the commissioner, wake him up, and fill him in, to protect himself in the event the affair took any unexpected turns. But Tano the Greek had been explicit, according to Gegè: Montalbano must not say anything to anyone and must come to the appointment alone. This was not, however, a game of cops and robbers: his duty was his duty. That is, he must inform his superiors and plan, down to the smallest details, how to surround and capture the criminal, perhaps with the help of considerable reinforcements. Tano had been a fugitive for nearly ten years, and he, Montalbano, was supposed to go and visit him as if he were some pal just back from America? There was no getting around it, the commissioner must by all means be informed of the matter. He dialed the number of his superior's home in Montelusa, the provincial capital.

'Is that you, love?' murmured the voice of Livia from Boccadasse, Genoa.

Montalbano remained speechless for a moment. Apparently his instinct was leading him away from speaking to the commissioner, making him dial the wrong number.

'Sorry about before. I had just received an unexpected phone call and had to go out.'

'Never mind, Salvo, I know what your work is like. Actually, I'm sorry I got upset. I was just feeling disappointed.'

Montalbano looked at his watch: he had at least three hours before he was supposed to meet Tano.

'If you want, we could talk now.'

'Now? Look, Salvo, it's not to get back at you, but I'd rather not. I took a sleeping pill and can barely keep my eyes open.'

'All right, all right. Till tomorrow, then. I love you, Livia.'

Livia's tone of voice suddenly changed, becoming more awake and agitated.

'Huh? What's wrong? Eh, what's wrong, Salvo?'

'Nothing's wrong. What could be wrong?'

'Oh, no you don't, you're hiding something. Are you about to do something dangerous? Don't make me worry, Salvo.'

'Where do you get such ideas?'

'Tell me the truth, Salvo.'

'I'm not doing anything dangerous.'

'I don't believe you.'

'Why not, for Christ's sake?'

'Because you said "I love you", and since I've known you, you've said it only three times. I've counted them, and every time it was for something out of the ordinary.'

The only hope was to cut the conversation short; with Livia, one could easily end up talking till morning.

'Ciao, my love. Sleep well. Don't be silly. I have to go out again.'

*

So how was he going to pass the time now? He took a shower, read a few pages of the book by Montalbán, understood little, shuffled from one room to the other, straightening a picture, re-reading a letter, a bill, a note, touching everything that came within his reach. He took another shower and shaved, managing to cut himself right on the chin. He turned on the television and immediately shut it off. It made him feel nauseated. Finally, it was time. As he was on his way out, he decided he needed a *mostacciolo.*

With sincere astonishment, he saw that the box on the table had been opened and not a single pastry was left in the cardboard tray. He had eaten them all, too nervous to notice. And what was worse, he hadn't even enjoyed them.

TWO

Montalbano turned around slowly, as if to offset the dull, sudden anger he felt at having let himself be caught unawares from behind like a beginner. For all that he'd been on his guard, he hadn't heard the slightest sound.

One to nothing in your favour, bastard! he thought.

Though he'd never seen him in person, he recognized him at once: as compared with the mugshots from a few years back, Tano had grown his moustache and beard, but the eyes remained the same, expressionless, 'like a statue's', as Gegè had accurately described them.

Tano the Greek gave a short bow, and there wasn't the slightest hint of provocation or mockery in the gesture. Montalbano automatically returned the greeting. Tano threw his head back and laughed.

'We're like two Japanese warriors, the kind with swords and breastplates. What do you call them?'

'Samurai.'

Tano opened his arms, as if wanting to embrace the man standing before him.

'What a pleasure to meet the famous Inspector Montalbano, personally in person.'

Montalbano decided to dispense with the ceremonies and get straight to the point, just to put the encounter on the right footing.

'I'm not sure how much pleasure you'll get from meeting me, sir.'

'Well, you've already given me one.'

'Explain.'

'You called me "sir". That's no small thing. No cop, not a single one – and I've met a lot – has ever called me "sir".'

'You realize, I hope, that I'm a representative of the law, while you are a dangerous fugitive charged with several murders. And here we are, face to face.'

'I'm unarmed. How about you?'

'Me too.'

Tano threw his head back again and gave a full-throated laugh.

'I'm never wrong about people, never!'

'Unarmed or not, I have to arrest you just the same.'

'And I am here, Inspector, to let you arrest me. That's why I wanted to see you.'

He was sincere, no doubt about it. But it was this very sincerity that put Montalbano on his guard, since he couldn't tell where Tano wanted to go with this.

'You could have come to police headquarters and turned yourself in. Here or in Vigàta, it's the same thing.'

'Ah, no, dear Inspector, it is not the same thing. You

surprise me, you who know how to read and write. The words are not the same. I am letting myself be arrested, I am not turning myself in. Go and get your jacket and we'll talk inside. I'll open the door in the meantime.'

Montalbano took his jacket from the olive tree, draped it over his arm, and entered the house behind Tano. It was completely dark inside. The Greek lit an oil lamp and gestured to the inspector to sit down in one of two chairs beside a small table. In the room there was a cot with only a bare mattress, no pillow or sheets, and a glass-fronted cupboard with bottles, glasses, biscuits, plates, packets of pasta, jars of tomato sauce and assorted tin cans. There was also a wood-burning stove with pots and pans hanging over it. But the inspector's eyes came to rest on a far more dangerous animal than the lizard sleeping in the glove compartment of his car: this was a veritable poisonous snake, a machine gun sleeping on its feet, propped against the wall beside the cot.

'I've got some good wine,' said Tano, like a true host.

'All right. Thanks,' replied Montalbano.

What with the cold, the night, the tension, and the two-plus pounds of *mostaccioli* he had wolfed down, he felt he could use some wine.

The Greek poured and then raised his glass.

'To your health.'

The inspector raised his own and returned the toast.

'To yours.'

The wine was something special; it went down beautifully, and on its way gave comfort and heat.

'This is truly good,' Montalbano complimented him.

'Another glass?'

To avoid the temptation, the inspector gruffly pushed the glass away.

'Let's talk.'

'Let's. As I was saying, I decided to let myself be arrested—'

'Why?'

Montalbano's question, fired point-blank, left the other momentarily confused. After a pause, Tano collected himself.

'I need medical care. I'm sick.'

'May I say something? Since you think you know me well, you probably also know that I'm not someone you can fuck with.'

'I'm sure of it.'

'Then why not show me some respect and stop feeding me bullshit?'

'You don't believe I'm sick?'

'I do. But don't try to make me swallow this bullshit that you need to be arrested to get medical help. I'll explain, if you like. You spent a month and a half at Our Lady of Lourdes Clinic in Palermo, then three months at the Gethsemane Clinic of Trapani, where Dr Amerigo Guarnera even operated on you. And although things today are a little different from a few years ago, if you want, you can find plenty of hospitals willing to look the other way and say nothing to the police if you stay there. So it's not because you're sick that you want to be arrested.'

'What if I told you that times are changing and that the wheel is turning fast?'

'That would be a little more convincing.'

'You see, when I was a little kid, my father – who was a man of honour when the word "honour" still meant something – my father, rest his soul, used to tell me that the cart that men of honour travelled on needed a lot of grease to make the wheels turn, to make them go fast. When my father's generation passed on and it was my turn to climb aboard the cart, some of our men said: "Why should we keep on buying the grease we need from the politicians, mayors, bankers and the rest of their kind? Let's make it ourselves! We'll make our own grease!" Great! Bravo! Everyone agreed. Sure, there was still the guy who stole his friend's horse, the guy who blocked the road for some associate of his, the guy who would start shooting blindly at some other gang's cart, horse, and horseman . . . But these were all things we could settle among ourselves. The carts multiplied in number, there were more and more roads to travel. Then some genius had a big idea, he asked himself: "What's it mean that we're still travelling by cart? We're too slow," he explained, "we're getting screwed, left behind, everybody else is travelling by car, you can't stop progress!" Great! Bravo! And so everybody ran and traded in their cart for a car and got a driver's licence. Some of them, though, didn't pass the driving-school test and went out, or were pushed out. Then we didn't even have the time to get comfortable with our new cars before the younger guys, the ones who'd been riding in cars since they were born and who'd studied law or economics in the States or Germany, told us our cars were too slow. Now you were supposed to hop in a racing car, a Ferrari, a Maserati equipped with radiophone and fax, so you could take off like a flash of lightning. These kids are new, brand-new, they talk to cellphones instead of people, they don't even know you, don't know who you used to be and if they do, they don't give a fuck. Half the time they don't even know each other, they just talk over the computer. To cut it short, these kids don't ever look anyone in the eye. As soon as they see you in trouble with a slow car, they run you off the road without a second thought and you end up in the ditch with a broken neck.'

'And you don't know how to drive a Ferrari.'

'Exactly. That's why, before I end up dead in a ditch, it's better for me to step aside.'

'But you don't seem to me the type who steps aside of his own choosing.'

'It's my own choosing, Inspector, all my own, I assure you. Of course, there are ways to make someone act freely of his own choosing. Once a friend of mine who was educated and read a lot told me a story which I'm going to repeat to you exactly the way he told it, something he read in a German book. A man says to his friend: "Want to bet my cat will eat hot mustard, the kind that's so hot it makes a hole in your stomach?" "But cats don't like mustard," says his friend. "Well, I can make my cat eat it anyway," says the man. "Do you make him eat it with your fist or with a stick?" asks the friend. "No sirree," says the man, "he eats it freely, of his own choosing." So they make the bet, the man takes a nice spoonful of mustard, the kind that makes your stomach burn just to look at it, picks up the cat and wham! shoves it right up the animal's ass. Poor cat, feeling his asshole burn like that, he starts licking it. And so, licking it up little by little, he eats all the mustard, of his own choosing. And that, my friend, says it all.'

'I see what you mean. Now let's go back to where we started.'

'I was saying I want to be arrested, but I'm going to need some theatricals to save face.'

'I don't understand.'

'Let me explain.'

He explained at great length, drinking a glass of wine from time to time. In the end Montalbano was satisfied with Tano's reasons. But could he trust him? That was the question. In his youth, Montalbano had a great passion for card-playing, which he had luckily grown out of; for this reason he now sensed that Tano was playing him straight, with unmarked cards. He had no choice but to put his faith in this intuition and hope he was not mistaken. And so they meticulously, painstakingly worked out the details of the arrest to ensure that nothing could go wrong. When they had finished talking, the sun was already high in the sky. Before leaving the house and letting the performance begin, the inspector gave Tano a long look, eye to eye.

'Tell me the truth.'

'At your command, Inspector.'

'Why did you choose me?'

'Because you, as you are showing me even now, are someone who understands things.'

*

As he raced headlong down the little path between the vineyards, Montalbano remembered that Agatino Catarella would now be on duty at the station, and that therefore the phone conversation he was about to engage in promised at the very least to be problematic, if not the source of unfortunate and even dangerous misunderstandings. This Catarella was frankly hopeless. Slow to think and slow to act, he had been hired by the police because he was a distant relative of the formerly all-powerful Chamber Deputy Cusumano, who, after spending a summer cooling off in Ucciardone prison, had managed to re-establish solid enough connections with the new people in power to win himself a large slice of the cake, the very same cake that from time to time was miraculously renewed by merely sticking in a few new candied fruits or putting new candles in the place of the ones already melted.

With Catarella, things would get most muddled whenever he got it in his head – which happened often – to speak in what he called Talian.

One day he had shown up with a troubled look.

'Chief, could you by any chance be able to give me the name of one of those doctors called specialists?'

'Specialist in what, Cat?'

'Gonorrhea.'

Montalbano had looked at him open-mouthed.

'Gonorrhea? You? When did you get that?'

'As I remember, I got it first when I was still a li'l thing, not yet six or seven years old.'

'What the hell are you saying, Cat? Are you sure you mean gonorrhea?'

'Absolutely. Had it all my life, on and off. It's here and gone, here and gone. Gonorrhea.'

*

In the car, on his way to a telephone booth that was supposed to be near the Torresanta crossroads (supposed to be, that is, unless the receiver had been torn off, the entire telephone had been stolen, or the booth itself had disappeared), Montalbano decided not to call even his second-in-command, Mimì Augello, because he was the type – he couldn't help it – who before anything else would inform the newsmen and then pretend to be surprised when they showed up at the scene. That left only Fazio and Tortorella, the two sergeants or whatever the hell they were called nowadays. He chose Fazio, since Tortorella had been shot in the belly not long before and hadn't yet fully recovered, feeling pain now and then in the wound.

The booth was miraculously still there, the phone miraculously worked, and Fazio picked up before the second ring had finished.

'Fazio, are you already awake at this hour?'

'Sure am, Chief. Less than a minute ago I got a call from Catarella.'

'What did he want?'

'He was speaking Talian so I couldn't make much sense of it. But if I had to guess, I'd say that last night somebody cleaned out Carmelo Ingrassia's supermarket, the great big one just outside of town. They used a large truck or tractor-trailer at the very least.'

'Wasn't there a night watchman?'

'There was, but nobody can find him.'

'Were you on your way there now?'

'Yes.'

'Forget it. Phone Tortorella immediately and tell him to fill Augello in. Let those two take care of it. Tell them you can't go, make up whatever bullshit you can think of, say you fell out of bed and hit your head. No: tell them the carabinieri came and arrested you. Better yet, call them and tell them to notify the carabinieri – it's small potatoes, after all, just some shitty little robbery, and they're always happy when we bring them into our cases. Now listen, here's what I want you to do: notify Tortorella, Augello, and the carabinieri about the theft, then round up Gallo, Galluzzo – Jesus Christ, I feel like I'm running a chicken farm here – and Germanà, and bring them all where I tell you to go. And arm yourselves with sub-machine guns.'

'Shit!'

'Shit is right. This is a big deal and we have to handle it carefully. No one is to whisper even half a word about this, especially Galluzzo with his newsman brother-in-law. And tell that chickenhead Gallo not to drive like he's at Monza. No sirens, no flashing lights. When you splash and muddy the waters, the fish escapes. Now pay attention and I'll explain where you're to meet me.'

*

They arrived very quietly, not half an hour after the phone call, looking like a routine patrol. Getting out of the car, they went up to Montalbano, who signalled them to follow him. They met back up behind a half-ruined house, so they could not be seen from the main road.

'There's a machine gun in the car for you,' said Fazio.

'Stick it up your arse. Now listen: if we play our cards right, we just might bring Tano the Greek home with us.'

Montalbano palpably felt that his men had ceased to breathe for a moment.

'Tano the Greek is around here?' Fazio wondered aloud, being the first to recover.

'I got a good look at him, and it's him. He's grown a moustache and a beard, but you can still recognize him.'

'How did you find him?'

'Never mind, Fazio, I'll explain everything later. Tano's in a little house at the top of that hill. You can't see it from here. There are olive trees all around it. It's a two-room house, one room on top of the other. It's got a door and a window in front; there's another window to the top room, but that's in back. Is that clear? Did you take that all in? Tano's only way out is through the front, unless he decides in desperation to throw himself out of the rear window, though he'd risk breaking his legs. So here's what we'll do: Fazio and Gallo go in the back; me, Germanà, and Galluzzo will break in the door and go inside.'

Fazio looked doubtful.

'What's wrong? Don't you agree?'

'Wouldn't it be better to surround the house and tell him to surrender? It's five against one, he'd never get away.'

'How do you know there's nobody inside the house with Tano?'

Fazio shut up.

'Listen to me,' said Montalbano, concluding his brief war council, 'it's better if we bring him an Easter egg with a surprise inside.'

THREE

Montalbano calculated that Fazio and Gallo must have been in position behind the cottage for at least five minutes. As for him, sprawled belly down on the grass, pistol in hand, with a rock pushing irksomely straight into the pit of his stomach, he felt profoundly ridiculous, like a character in a gangster film, and therefore could not wait to give the signal to raise the curtain. He looked at Galluzzo, who was beside him – Germanà was farther away, to the right – and asked him in a whisper, 'Are you ready?'

'Yessir,' answered the policeman, who was a visible bundle of nerves and sweating. Montalbano felt sorry for him, but couldn't very well come out and tell him that it was all a put-on – of dubious outcome, it was true, but still humbug.

'Go!' he ordered him.

As though launched by a tightly compressed spring and almost not touching the ground, in three bounds Galluzzo reached the house and flattened himself against the wall to the left of the door. He seemed to have done so without effort, though Montalbano could see his chest heaving up and down, breathless. Galluzzo got a firm grip on his sub-machine gun and gestured to the inspector that he was ready for phase two. Montalbano then looked over at Germanà, who seemed not only serene, but actually relaxed.

'I'm going now,' he said to him without a sound, exaggeratedly moving his lips and forming the syllables.

'I'll cover you,' Germanà answered back in the same manner, gesturing with his head towards the machine gun in his hands.

Montalbano's first leap forward was one for the books, or at the very least a training manual: a decisive, balanced ascent from the ground, worthy of a high-jump specialist, a weightless, aerial suspension, and a clean, dignified landing that would have amazed a ballerina. Galluzzo and Germanà, who were watching him from different perspectives, took equal delight in their chief's bodily grace. The start of the second leap was even better calibrated than the first, but something happened in mid-air that caused Montalbano, from his upright posture, to tilt suddenly sideways like the tower of Pisa, then plunge earthward in what looked truly like a clown's routine. After tottering with arms outstretched in search of a non-existent handle to grab onto, he crashed heavily to one side. Instinctively, Galluzzo made a move as if to help him, but stopped himself in time, plastering himself back against the wall. Germanà also stood up a moment, but quickly got back down.

A good thing this was all a sham, the inspector thought. Otherwise Tano could have cut them down like ninepins then and there. Muttering some of the pithiest curses in his vast repertoire, Montalbano began to crawl around in search of the pistol that had slipped from his hand during the fall. At last he spotted it under a touch-me-not bush, but as soon as he stuck his arm in there to retrieve it, all the little cucumbers burst and sprayed his face with seeds. With a certain melancholy rage the inspector realized he'd been demoted from gangster-film hero to a character in an Abbott and Costello movie. No longer in the mood to play the athlete or dancer, he covered the last few yards between him and the house with a few quick steps, merely hunching forward a little.

Montalbano and Galluzzo looked one another in the eye without speaking and agreed on the plan. They positioned themselves three steps from the door, which did not look very resistant, took a deep breath and flung themselves against it with their full weight. The door turned out to be made of tissue paper, or almost – a swat of the hand would have sufficed to push it open – and thus they both found themselves hurtling inside. The inspector managed by some miracle to come to a stop, whereas Galluzzo, carried forward by the violence of his thrust, flew all the way across the room and slammed his face against the wall, crushing his nose and ending up choking on the blood that started to gush violently forth. By the dim light of the oil lamp that Tano had left burning, the inspector was able to appreciate the Greek's consummate acting skills. Pretending to have been surprised awake, he leapt to his feet cursing and hurled himself towards the Kalashnikov, which was now leaning against the table and therefore far from the cot. Montalbano was ready to recite his lines as the foil, as they say in the theatre.

'Stop in the name of the law! Stop or I'll shoot!' he shouted at the top of his lungs, then fired four shots into the ceiling. Tano froze, hands raised. Convinced that someone must be hiding upstairs, Galluzzo fired a burst from his machine gun at the wooden staircase. Outside, Fazio and Gallo, upon hearing all the shooting, opened fire on the little window to discourage anyone from trying that route. With everyone inside the cottage still deaf from the roar of the gunshots, Germanà burst in with the final flourish.

'Don't anybody move or I'll shoot!'

He barely had time to finish uttering his threat when he was bumped from behind by Fazio and Gallo and pushed directly between Montalbano and Galluzzo, who, having set down his weapon, was dabbing his nose with a handkerchief he had taken out of his pocket, the blood having already dripped onto his shirt, tie and jacket. At the sight of him, Gallo became agitated.

'Did he shoot you? The bastard shot you, didn't he?' he yelled in rage, turning towards Tano, who was still standing as patient as a saint in the middle of the room, hands raised, waiting for the forces of order to put some order to the great confusion they were creating.

'No, he didn't shoot me. I ran into the wall,' Galluzzo managed to say with some difficulty. Tano avoided their eyes, looking down at his shoes.

He thinks it's funny, thought Montalbano, then he brusquely ordered Galluzzo, 'Handcuff him.'

'Is it him?' asked Fazio in a soft voice.

'Sure it's him. Don't you recognize him?' said Montalbano.

'What do we do now?'

'Put him in the car and take him to police headquarters in Montelusa. On the way, ring up the commissioner and explain everything. Make sure nobody sees or recognizes the prisoner. The arrest, for the moment, has to remain top secret. Now go.'

'What about you?'

'I'm going to have a look around, search the house. You never know.'

Fazio and the officers, holding the handcuffed Tano between them, started moving towards the door, with Germanà holding the prisoner's Kalishnikov in his hand. Only then did Tano the Greek raise his head and look momentarily at Montalbano. The inspector noticed that the statue-like gaze was gone; now those eyes were animated, almost smiling.

When the group of five had vanished from sight at the bottom of the path, Montalbano went back inside the cottage to begin his search. In fact, he opened the cupboard, grabbed the bottle of wine, which was still half full, and went and sat in the shade of an olive tree, to drink it down in peace. The capture of a dangerous fugitive had been brought to a successful conclusion.

*

As soon as he saw Montalbano come into the office, Mimì Augello, looking possessed by the devil, put him through the meat grinder.

'Where the hell have you been?! Where've you been hiding? What happened to everybody else? What the fuck is going on here, anyway?'

He must have been really angry to speak so frankly. In the three years they had been working together, the inspector had never heard his assistant use obscenities. Actually, no: the time some arsehole shot Tortorella in the stomach, Augello had reacted the same way.

'Mimì, what's got into you?'

'What's got into me? I got scared, that's what!'

'Scared? Of what?'

'At least six people have phoned here. Their stories all differed as to the details, but they were all in agreement as to the substance: a gunfight with dead and wounded. One of them even called it a bloodbath. You weren't at home. Fazio and the others had gone out with the car without saying a word to anyone . . . So I just put two and two together. Was I wrong?'

'No, you weren't wrong. But you shouldn't blame me, you should blame the telephone. It's the telephone's fault.'

'What's the telephone got to do with it?'

'It's got everything to do with it! Nowadays you've got telephones even in the most godforsaken country haylofts. So what do people do, when there's a phone within reach? They phone. And they say things. True things, imagined things, possible things, impossible things, dreamed-up things like in that Eduardo de Filippo comedy, what's it called, oh yes, *The Voices Inside* – they inflate things and deflate things but never give you their name and surname. They dial emergency numbers where anyone can say the craziest bullshit in the world without ever assuming any responsibility for it! And meanwhile the Mafia experts get all excited because they think *omertà* is on the decline in Sicily! No more complicity! No more fear! Hah! I'll tell you what's on the decline: my arse is on the decline, and meanwhile the phone bill is on the rise.'

'Montalbano! Stop confusing me with your chatter! Were there any dead and wounded or not?'

'Of course not. There was no gunfight. We just fired a few shots into the air, Galluzzo smashed his nose all by himself, and the guy surrendered.'

'What guy?'

'A fugitive.'

'Yeah, but who?'

Catarella arrived breathless and spared him the embarrassment of answering.

'Chief, that would be his honour the commissioner on the phone.'

'I'll tell you later,' said Montalbano, fleeing into his office.

*

'My dear friend, I want to give you my most heartfelt congratulations.'

'Thank you.'

'You really hit the bullseye this time.'

'We got lucky.'

'Apparently the man in question is even more important than he himself let on.'

'Where is he now?'

'On his way to Palermo. The Anti-Mafia Commission insisted; they wouldn't take no for an answer. Your men weren't even allowed to stop in Montelusa; they had to drive on. I sent along an escort car with four of my men to keep them company.'

'So you didn't speak with Fazio?'

'I didn't have the time or the chance. I know almost nothing about this case. So, actually, I'd appreciate it if you could pass by my office this afternoon and fill me in on the details.'

Ay, there's the hitch, thought Montalbano, remembering a nineteenth-century translation of Hamlet's monologue. But he merely asked, 'At what time?'

'Let's say around five. Ah, also, Palermo wants absolute secrecy about the operation, at least for now.'

'If it was only up to me . . .'

'I wasn't referring to you, since I know you well and can say that compared to you, even fish are a talkative species. Listen, by the way . . .'

There was a pause. The commissioner had broken off and Montalbano didn't feel like saying anything: a troubling alarm bell had gone off in his head at the sound of that laudatory 'I know you well.'

'Listen, Montalbano,' the commissioner hesitantly started over, and with that hesitation the alarm began to ring more loudly.

'Yes, Commissioner?'

'I'm afraid that this time there's no way I can prevent your promotion to assistant commissioner.'

'*Madunnuzza biniditta!* Why not?'

'Don't be silly, Montalbano.'

'Well, I'm sorry, but why should I be promoted?'

'What a question! Because of what you did this morning.'

Montalbano felt simultaneously hot and cold: he had sweat on his forehead and chills down his spine. The prospect terrorized him.

'I didn't do anything different from what my colleagues do every day, Commissioner.'

'I don't doubt it. But this particular arrest, when it comes to be known, will cause quite a stir.'

'So there's no hope?'

'Come on, don't be childish.'

The inspector felt like a tuna caught in the net, the chamber of death. He began to feel short of breath, mouth opening and closing on emptiness. Then he tried a desperate suggestion:

'Couldn't we blame Fazio?'

'Blame?'

'I'm sorry, I meant couldn't we give him the credit?'

'See you later, Montalbano.'

*

Augello, who was lurking behind the door, made a questioning face.

'What'd the commissioner say?'

'We spoke about the situation.'

'Oh, right! You should see the look on your face!'

'What look?'

'Like you've been to a funeral.'

'I had trouble digesting what I ate last night.'

'Anything interesting?'

'Three pounds of *mostaccioli*.'

Augello looked at him in dismay. Montalbano, sensing that he was about to ask him the name of the arrested fugitive, used the opportunity to change the subject and put him on another track.

'Did you guys ever find the night watchman?'

'The one in the supermarket? Yeah, I found him myself. The thieves bashed him in the head, then bound and gagged him and threw him in a great big freezer.'

'Is he dead?'

'No, but I don't think he's feeling very alive either. When we pulled him out, he looked like a giant frozen stockfish.'

'Any idea which way they went?'

'I've got half an idea myself and the carabinieri lieutenant has another. But one thing is certain: to haul all that stuff, they had to use a heavy truck. And there must have been a team of at least six people to load it, under the command of some professional.'

'Listen, Mimì, I have to run home and change my clothes. I'll be right back.'

*

Near Marinella he noticed that the reserve light for the gas tank was flashing. He stopped at the same filling station where there'd been a drive-by shooting a while back, when he'd had to bring in the attendant to get him to talk. Upon seeing the inspector, the attendant, who bore him no grudge, greeted him in his usual high-pitched voice, which made Montalbano shudder. After filling the tank, the attendant counted the money and eyed the inspector.

'What's wrong? Didn't I give you enough?'

'No sir. There's enough money here, all right. I just wanted to tell you something.'

'Let's have it,' Montalbano said impatiently. If the guy went on talking, even a little, his nerves would give out.

'Look at that truck over there.'

And he pointed at a large tractor-trailer parked in the lot behind the filling station, tarps pulled down tight to hide the cargo.

'It was already here early this morning,' he continued, 'when I opened up. Now it's been four hours and still nobody's come to get it.'

'Did you look to see if anyone's sleeping in the cab?'

'Yessir, I looked, there's nobody. And another weird

thing: the keys are still in the ignition. The first soul to come along could start it up and drive it away.'

'Show me,' said Montalbano, suddenly interested.

FOUR

A tiny man with rat-tail moustaches, an unpleasant smile, gold-framed glasses, brown shoes, brown socks, brown suit, brown shirt, brown tie, a veritable nightmare in brown, Carmelo Ingrassia, owner of the supermarket, pressed the crease in his trousers with his fingers, right leg crossed over the left, and repeated his succinct interpretation of events for the third time.

'It was a joke, Inspector, a practical joke that somebody, I guess, wanted to play on me.'

Montalbano was lost in contemplation of the ballpoint pen he held in his hand. Concentrating his attention on the cap, he removed it, examined it inside and out as though he had never seen so strange a gizmo, blew into it as if to cleanse it of some invisible speck of dust, looked at it again, remained unsatisfied, blew into it again, put it down on the desk, unscrewed the pen's metal tip, thought about this for a moment, set it down alongside the cap, carefully considered the piece remaining in his hand, lined this up near the other two pieces, and sighed deeply. This allowed him to calm down and check the impulse – which for a second had nearly overwhelmed him – to get up, go over to Ingrassia, punch him in the face, and ask, 'Now tell me truthfully: in your opinion, am I joking or am I serious?'

Tortorella, who was present for the interview and knew his chief's reactions well, visibly relaxed.

'Let me try and understand,' said Montalbano, in full control of himself.

'What's to understand, Inspector? It's all clear as day. The stolen goods were all in the truck that you found. Not one toothpick was missing, not a single lollipop. So, if they didn't do it to rob me, they must have done it as a joke, for fun.'

'You'll have to be patient with me, Mr Ingrassia, I'm a little slow in the head. So: eight days ago, from a depot in Catania – that is, on the other side of the island – two people steal a truck with a trailer belonging to the Sferlazza company. At that moment the truck is empty. For eight days they keep this truck out of sight, hiding it somewhere between Catania and Vigàta, since it wasn't seen in circulation. Logically speaking, therefore, the only reason that truck was stolen and hidden was to take it out of circulation, when the time was right, to play a joke on you. Let me continue. Last night the truck rematerializes and around one a.m., when there's almost nobody on the streets, it stops in front of your supermarket. The night watchman thinks it's there to bring in new stocks, even at that odd hour. We don't know exactly how things went, the watchman still can't talk, but we do know that they put him out of commission, took his keys, and went inside. One of the thieves stripped the watchman and put on his uniform. This, I must say, was a brilliant move. The next brilliant move was that the others turned on the lights and got down to work in plain sight, taking no precautions – in broad daylight, one might say, if it wasn't night. Ingenious, no doubt about it. Because a stranger passing through the neighbourhood, noticing the watchman in uniform overseeing a few people loading a truck, would never dream that he was actually witnessing a robbery. This is the reconstruction of events offered by my colleague Augello; it was confirmed by the testimony of Cavaliere Misuraca, who was on his way home at the time.'

At the mention of that name, Ingrassia, who had seemed to be losing interest as the inspector went on, sat up in his chair as if stung by a wasp.

'Misuraca?!'

'Yes, the one who used to work at the Records Office.'

'But he's a Fascist!'

'I don't see what the cavaliere's political beliefs have to do with the case we're discussing.'

'They have everything to do with it! Because when I used to be involved in politics, he was my enemy.'

'You're no longer involved in politics?'

'What's to be involved in any more! With that handful of Milanese judges who've decided to ruin politics, commerce and industry, all at the same time!'

'Listen, the cavaliere merely gave a testimonial establishing the modus operandi of the thieves.'

'I don't give a shit what the cavaliere was establishing. He's an old geezer who can't even remember when he turned eighty. He's so senile he's liable to see a cat and say it's an elephant. What was he doing out at that time of the night anyway?'

'I don't know, I'll ask him. Shall we get back to the subject?'

'Fine.'

'Once it was loaded, at your supermarket, after at least two hours of labour, the truck leaves. It drives three or four miles, turns around, parks in the lot behind the filling station, and remains there until I find it. And, in your opinion, someone went through this whole elaborate set-up, committed half a dozen crimes, risking years in jail, just so he, or you, could have a good laugh?'

'Inspector, we could stay here all day arguing, but I swear to you that I can't imagine how it could have been anything but a joke.'

*

In the refrigerator Montalbano found a plate of cold pasta with tomatoes, basil, and black *passuluna* olives that gave off an aroma to wake the dead, and a second course of fresh anchovies with onions and vinegar. Montalbano was in the habit of trusting entirely in the simple but zestful culinary imagination of Adelina, the housekeeper who came once a day to see to his needs, a mother of two irremediably delinquent sons, one of whom was still in jail, put there by Montalbano. And this day, too, she did not disappoint him. Every time he was about to open the oven or fridge, he still felt the same trepidation he used to feel as a little boy when, on the second of November, he would look for the wicker basket in which the dead had left their gifts during the night – a celebration now lost, obliterated by the banality of presents under the Christmas tree, obliterated like the memory of the dead themselves. The only ones who did not forget their dead, and who indeed tenaciously kept their memory burning, were the mafiosi; but the presents they sent in remembrance were certainly not little tin trains or marzipan fruits.

Surprise, in short, was an indispensable spice in Adelina's dishes.

He took his two courses, a bottle of wine, and some bread to the table, turned on the television, and sat down to dinner. He loved to eat alone, relishing every bite in silence. This was yet another bond that tied him to Livia, who never opened her mouth when she ate. It occurred to him that in matters of taste he was closer to Maigret than to Pepe Carvalho, the protagonist of Montalbán's novels, who stuffed himself with dishes that would have set a shark's belly on fire.

On the national television stations, an ill wind of malaise was blowing. The governing majority found itself split over a law that would deny early prison release to those who had eaten up half the country; the magistrates who had laid bare the dirty secrets of political corruption were resigning in protest; and there was a faint breeze of revolt animating the interviews with people in the street.

He switched to the first of the two local TV stations. TeleVigàta was pro-government by congenital faith, whether the government was red, black, or sky blue. The news reporter made no mention of the capture of Tano the Greek, stating only that a few conscientious citizens had alerted the Vigàta police of a lively but mysterious shoot-out at dawn in the rural area known as 'the Walnut', and that investigators, after arriving promptly at the scene, had found nothing unusual. The newscaster for the Free Channel, Nicolò Zito, who did not hide his Communist sympathies, likewise failed to mention Tano's arrest. Which seemed to indicate that the news, fortunately, had not leaked out. But then, out of the blue, Zito started talking about the bizarre robbery at the Ingrassia supermarket and the inexplicable rediscovery of the truck with all the stolen merchandise. The common opinion, reported Zito, was that the vehicle must have been abandoned following an argument between the robbers over how to divide up the loot. Zito, however, did not agree. In his opinion, things had gone differently; the real explanation was surely far more complicated.

'And so I appeal directly to you, Inspector Montalbano. Is it not true that there must be more to this story than meets the eye?' the newsman asked, closing his report.

Hearing himself personally addressed and seeing Zito's eyes looking out at him from the screen as he was eating,

Montalbano let the wine he was drinking go down the wrong way and started coughing and cursing.

After finishing his meal, he put on his bathing suit and dived into the sea. It was freezing cold, but the swim brought him back to life.

*

'Now tell me exactly how it all happened,' said the commissioner.

After admitting the inspector into his office, he had stood up and gone right over to him, embracing him warmly.

One thing about Montalbano was that he was incapable of deceiving or stringing along people he knew were honest or who inspired his admiration. With crooks and people he didn't like, he could spin out the flimflam with the straightest of faces and was capable of swearing he'd seen the moon trimmed in lace. The fact that he not only admired his superior, but had actually at times spoken to him as to a father, now put him, after the other's command, in a state of agitation: he blushed, began to sweat, kept squirming in his chair as if he were under cross-examination. The commissioner noticed his uneasiness but attributed it to the discomfort that Montalbano genuinely felt whenever he had to talk about a particularly successful operation. The commissioner had not forgotten that at the last press conference, in front of the TV cameras, the inspector had expressed himself – if you could call it that – in long, painful stammerings at times devoid of common meaning, eyes bulging, pupils dancing as if he were drunk.

'I'd like some advice, before I begin.'

'At your service.'

'What should I write in the report?'

'What kind of question is that? Have you never written a report before? In reports you write down what happened,' the commissioner replied curtly, a bit astonished. And since Montalbano hadn't yet made up his mind to speak, he continued. 'In other words, you say you were able to take advantage of a chance encounter and turn it into a successful police operation, skilfully, courageously, it's true, but—'

'Look, I just wanted to say—'

'Let me finish. I can't help but notice that you took a big risk, and exposed your men to grave danger – you should have asked for substantial reinforcements, taken due precaution. Luckily, it all went well. But it was a gamble. That's what I'm trying to tell you, in all sincerity. Now let's hear your side.'

Montalbano studied the fingers on his left hand as if they had just sprouted spontaneously and he didn't know what they were there for.

'What's wrong?' the commissioner asked.

'What's wrong is that it's all untrue!' Montalbano burst out. 'There wasn't any chance encounter. I went to talk with Tano because he had asked to see me. And at that meeting we made an agreement.'

The commissioner ran his hand over his eyes.

'An agreement?'

'Yes, on everything.'

And while he was at it, he told him the whole story, from Gegè's phone call to the farce of the arrest.

'Is there anything else?' the commissioner asked when it was over.

'Yes. Things being what they are, in no way do I deserve to be promoted to assistant commissioner. If I were promoted, it would be for a lie, a deception.'

'Let me be the judge of that,' the commissioner said brusquely.

He got up, put his hands behind his back, and stood there thinking a moment. Then he made up his mind and turned around.

'Here's what we'll do. Write me two reports.'

'Two?' said Montalbano, mindful of the effort it normally cost him to apply ink to paper.

'Don't argue. The fake report I'll leave lying around for the inevitable mole who will make sure to leak it to the press or to the Mafia. The real one I'll put in the safe.'

He smiled.

'And as for this promotion business, which seems to be what terrifies you most, come to my house on Friday evening and we'll talk it over a little more calmly. My wife has invented a fabulous new sauce for sea bream.'

*

Cavaliere Gerlando Misuraca, who carried his eighty-four years belligerently, was true to form, going immediately on the offensive as soon as the inspector said, 'Hello?'

'Who is that imbecile who transferred my call?'

'Why, what did he do?'

'He couldn't understand my surname! He couldn't get it into that thick head of his! "Bizugaga", he called me!' He paused warily, then changed his tone. 'Can you assure me, on your word of honour, that he's just some poor bastard who doesn't know any better?'

Realizing that it was Catarella who had answered the phone, Montalbano could reply with conviction.

'I can assure you. But why, may I ask, do you need my assurance?'

'Because if he meant to make fun of me or what I represent, I'll be down there at the station in five minutes and will give him such a thrashing, by God, he won't be able to walk!'

And just what did Cavaliere Misuraca represent? Montalbano wondered while the other continued to threaten to do terrible things. Nothing, absolutely nothing from a, so to speak, official point of view. A municipal employee long since retired, he did not hold nor had he ever held any public office, being merely a card-carrying member of his party. A man of unassailable honesty, he lived a life of dignified quasi-poverty. Even in the days of Mussolini, he had refused to seek personal gain, having always been a 'faithful follower', as one used to say back then. In return, from 1935 onwards, he had fought in every war and been in the thick of the worst battles. He hadn't missed a single one, and indeed seemed to have a gift for being everywhere at once, from Guadalajara, Spain, to Bir el Gobi in North

Africa by way of Axum, Ethiopia. Followed by imprisonment, his refusal to cooperate, and an even harsher imprisonment as a result, on nothing but bread and water. He therefore represented, Montalbano concluded, the historical memory of what were, of course, historic mistakes, but he had lived them with a naive faith and paid for them with his own skin: among several serious injuries, one had left him lame in his left leg.

'Tell me,' Montalbano had mischievously asked him one day face to face, 'if you'd been able, would you have gone to fight at Salò, alongside the Germans and the *repubblichini*?' In his way, the inspector was sort of fond of the old Fascist. How could he not be? In that circus of corrupters and corrupted, extortionists and grafters, bribe-takers, liars, thieves and perjurers – turning up each day in new combinations – Montalbano had begun to feel a kind of affection for people he knew to be incurably honest.

At this question, the old man had seemed to deflate from within, the wrinkles on his face multiplying as his eyes began to fog over. Montalbano then understood that Misuraca had asked himself the same question a thousand times and had never been able to come up with an answer. So he did not insist.

'Hello? Are you still there?' Misuraca's peevish voice asked.

'At your service, Cavaliere.'

'I just remembered something. Which is why I didn't mention it when I gave my testimony.'

'I have no reason to doubt you, Cavaliere. I'm all ears.'

'A strange thing happened to me when I was almost in front of the supermarket, but at the time I didn't pay it much mind. I was nervous and upset because these days there are certain bastards about who—'

'Please come to the point, Cavaliere.'

If one let him speak, Misuraca was capable of taking his story back to the foundation of the first Fascist militias.

'Actually, I can't tell you over the phone. I need to see you in person. It's something really big, if I saw right.'

The old man was considered someone who always told things straight, without overstating or understating the case.

'Is it about the robbery at the supermarket?'

'Of course.'

'Have you already discussed it with anybody?'

'Nobody.'

'Don't forget: not a word to anyone.'

'Are you trying to insult me? Silent as the grave, I am. I'll be at your office early tomorrow morning.'

'Just out of curiosity, Cavaliere, what were you doing, alone and upset, in your car at that hour of the night? You know, after a certain age, one must be careful.'

'I was on my way back from Montelusa, from a meeting of the local party leaders. I'm not one of them, of course, but I wanted to be present. Nobody shuts his door on Gerlando Misuraca. Someone has to save our party's honour. They can't continue to govern alongside those bastard sons of bastard politicians and agree to an ordinance allowing all the sons of bitches who devoured our country out of jail! You must understand, Inspector—'

'Did the meeting end late?'

'It went on till one o'clock in the morning. I wanted to continue, but everyone else was against it. They were all falling asleep. They've got no balls, those people.'

'And how long did it take you to get back to Vigàta?'

'Half an hour. I drive slowly. But as I was saying—'

'Excuse me, Cavaliere, I'm wanted on another line,' Montalbano cut him off. 'See you tomorrow.'

FIVE

'Worse than criminals! Worse than murderers! That's how those dirty sons of bitches treated us! Who do they think they are? The fuckers!'

There was no calming down Fazio, who had just returned from Palermo. Germanà, Gallo and Galluzzo served as his psalmodizing chorus, wildly gesticulating to convey the exceptional nature of the event.

'Total insanity! Total insanity!'

'Simmer down, boys. Let's proceed in an orderly fashion,' Montalbano ordered, imposing his authority.

Then, noticing that Galluzzo's shirt and jacket no longer bore traces of the blood from his crushed nose, the inspector asked him, 'Did you go home and change before coming here?'

'Home? Home? Didn't you hear what Fazio said? We've just come from Palermo, we came straight back! When we got to the Anti-Mafia Commission and turned over Tano the Greek, they took us one by one and put us in separate rooms. Since my nose was still hurting, I wanted to put a wet handkerchief over it. I'd been sitting there for half an hour, and still nobody'd shown up, so I opened the door and found an officer standing in front of me. Where you going? he says. I'm going to get a little water for my nose. You can't leave, he says, go back inside. Get that, Inspector? I was under guard! Like *I* was Tano the Greek!'

'Don't mention that name and lower your voice!' Montalbano scolded him. 'Nobody is supposed to know that we caught him! The first one who talks gets his arse kicked all the way to Asinara.'

'We were all under guard,' Fazio cut in, indignant.

Galluzzo continued his story: 'An hour later some guy I know entered the room, a colleague of yours who was kicked upstairs to the Anti-Mafia Commission. I think his name is Sciacchitano.'

A perfect arsehole, the inspector thought, but said nothing.

'He looked at me as if I smelt bad or something, like some beggar. Then he kept on staring at me, and finally he said: "You know, you can't very well present yourself to the Prefect looking like that."'

Still feeling hurt by the absurd treatment, he had trouble keeping his voice down.

'The amazing thing was that he had this pissed-off look in his eye, like it was all my fault! Then he left, muttering to himself. Later a cop came in with a clean shirt and jacket.'

'Now let me talk,' Fazio butted in, pulling rank. 'To make a long story short, from three o'clock in the afternoon to midnight yesterday, every one of us was interrogated eight times by eight different people.'

'What did they want to know?'

'How the arrest came about.'

'Actually, I was interrogated ten times,' said Germanà with a certain pride. 'I guess I tell a good story, and for them it was like being at the movies.'

'Around one o'clock in the morning they gathered us together,' Fazio continued, 'and put us in a great big room, a kind of large office, with two sofas, eight chairs and four tables. They unplugged the telephones and took them away. Then they sent in four stale sandwiches and four warm beers that tasted like piss. We got as comfortable as we could, and at eight the next morning some guy came in and said we could go back to Vigàta. No good morning, no goodbye, not even "get outta here" like you say to get rid of the dog. Nothing.'

'All right,' said Montalbano. 'What can you do? Go on home now, rest up, and come back here in the late afternoon. I promise you I'll take this whole business up with the commissioner.'

*

'Hello? This is Inspector Salvo Montalbano from Vigàta. I'd like to speak with Inspector Arturo Sciacchitano.'

'Please hold.'

Montalbano grabbed a sheet of paper and a pen. He

started doodling without paying attention and only later noticed he had drawn a pair of buttocks on a toilet seat.

'I'm sorry, the inspector's in a meeting.'

'Listen, please tell him I'm also in a meeting, that way we're even. He can interrupt his for five minutes, I'll do the same with mine, and we'll both be happy as babies.'

He appended a few turds to the shitting buttocks.

'Montalbano? What is it? Sorry, but I haven't got much time.'

'Me neither. Listen, Sciacchitanov—'

'Eh? Sciacchitanov? What the hell are you saying?'

'Isn't that your real name? You mean you don't belong to the KGB?'

'I'm not in the mood for jokes, Montalbano.'

'Who's joking? I'm calling you from the commissioner's office, and he's very upset over the KGB-style treatment you gave my men. He promised me he'd write to the interior minister this very day.'

The phenomenon cannot be explained, and yet it happened: Montalbano actually saw Sciacchitano, universally known as a pusillanimous arse-lick, turn pale over the telephone line. His lie had the same effect on the man as a baton to the head.

'What are you saying? You have to understand that I, as defender of public safety—'

Montalbano interrupted him.

'Safety doesn't preclude politeness,' he said pithily, sounding like one of those road signs that say: BE POLITE, FOR SAFETY'S SAKE.

'But I was extremely polite! I even gave them beer and sandwiches!'

'I'm sorry to say, despite the beer and sandwiches, there will be consequences higher up. But cheer up, Sciacchitano, it's not your fault. You can't fit a square peg into a round hole.'

'What do you mean?'

'I mean that you, being a born arsehole, will never be a decent, intelligent person. Now, I demand that you write a letter, addressed to me, praising my men to the skies. And I want it by tomorrow. Goodbye.'

'Do you think if I write the letter, the commissioner will let it drop?'

'To be perfectly honest, I don't know. But if I were you, I'd write that letter. And I might even date it yesterday. Got that?'

*

He felt better now, having let off some steam. He called Catarella.

'Is Inspector Augello in his office?'

'No sir, but he just now phoned. He said that, figuring he was about ten minutes away, he'd be here in about ten minutes.'

Montalbano took advantage of the time to start writing the fake report. The real one he'd written at home the night before. At a certain point Augello knocked and entered.

'You were looking for me?'

'Is it really so hard for you to come to work a little earlier?'

'Sorry, but in fact I was busy till five o'clock in the morning. Then I went home and drifted off to sleep, and that was that.'

'Busy with one of those whores you like so much? The kind that pack two hundred and fifty pounds of flesh into a tight little dress?'

'Didn't Catarella tell you?'

'He told me you'd be coming in late.'

'Last night, around two, there was a fatal car accident. I went to the scene myself, thinking I'd let you sleep, since the thing was of no importance to us.'

'To the people who died, it was certainly important.'

'There was only one victim. He took the downhill stretch of the Catena at high speed – apparently his brakes weren't working – and ended up wedged under a truck that had started coming up the slope in the opposite direction. The poor guy died instantly.'

'Did you know him?'

'I sure did. So did you. Cavaliere Misuraca.'

*

'Montalbano? I just got a call from Palermo. They want us to hold a press conference. And that's not all: they want it to make some noise. That's very important. It's part of their strategy. Journalists from other cities will be there, and it will be reported on the national news. It's going to be a big deal.

'They want to show that the new government is not letting up in the fight against the Mafia, and that, on the contrary, they will be more resolute, more relentless than ever—

'Is something wrong, Montalbano?'

'No. I was just imagining the next day's headlines.'

'The press conference is scheduled for noon tomorrow. I just wanted to give you advance warning.'

'Thank you, sir, but what have I got to do with any of it?'

'Montalbano, I am a nice man, a kind man, but only up to a point. You have everything to do with it! Stop being so childish!'

'What am I supposed to say?'

'Good God, Montalbano! Say what you wrote in the report.'

'Which one?'

'I'm sorry, what did you say?'

'Nothing.'

'Just try to speak clearly, don't mumble, and keep your head up. And – Oh, yes, your hands. Decide once and for all where you're going to put them and keep them there. Don't do like last time, where the correspondent of the *Corriere* offered aloud to cut them off for you, to make you feel more comfortable.'

'And what if they question me?'

'Of course they'll "question" you, to use your odd phrasing. They're journalists, aren't they? Good-day.'

*

Too agitated by everything that was happening and was going to happen the following day, Montalbano had to leave the office. He went out, stopped at the usual shop, bought a small bag of *càlia e simenza,* and headed towards the jetty. When he was at the foot of the lighthouse and about to turn back, he found himself face to face with Ernesto Bonfiglio, the owner of a travel agency and a very good friend of the recently deceased Cavaliere Misuraca.

'Isn't there anything we can do?' Bonfiglio blurted out at him aggressively.

Montalbano, who was trying to dislodge a small fragment of peanut stuck between two teeth, merely looked at him, befuddled.

'I'm asking if there's anything we can do,' Bonfiglio repeated resentfully, giving him a hostile look in return.

'Do about what?'

'About my poor dead friend.'

'Would you like some?' asked the inspector, holding out the bag.

'Thanks,' said the other, taking a handful of *càlia e simenza.*

The pause allowed Montalbano to put the man he was speaking to in better perspective: Bonfiglio, aside from being like a brother to the late cavaliere, was a man who held extreme right-wing ideas and was not all there in the head.

'You mean Misuraca?'

'No, I mean my grandfather.'

'And what am I supposed to do?'

'Arrest the murderers. It's your duty.'

'And who would these murderers be?'

'Who they *are,* not "would be". I'm referring to the local party leaders, who were unworthy to have him in their ranks. *They* killed him.'

'I beg your pardon. Wasn't it an accident?'

'Oh, I suppose you think accidents just happen accidentally?'

'I would say so.'

'You would be wrong. If someone's looking for an accident, there's always somebody else ready to send one his way. Let me cite an example to illustrate my point. This last February Mimì Crapanzano drowned when he went for a swim. An accidental death, they said. But here I ask you: how old was Mimì when he died? Fifty-five years old. Why, at that age, did he get this brilliant idea to go for a swim in the cold, like he used to do when he was a kid? The answer is because less than three months before, he had got married to a Milanese girl twenty-four years younger than him, and one day, when they were out strolling on the beach, she asked him: "Is it true, darling, that you used to swim in this sea in February?" "It sure is," replied Crapanzano. The girl, who apparently was already tired of the old man, sighed. "What's wrong?" Crapanzano asked, like an idiot. "I'm sorry I won't ever have a chance to see you do it again," said the slut. Without saying a word, Crapanzano took off his clothes and jumped into the water. Does that clarify my point?'

'Perfectly.'

'Now, to get back to the party leaders of Montelusa province. After a first meeting ended with harsh words, they held another last night. The cavaliere, along with a few other people, wanted the chapter to issue a press release protesting against the government's ordinance granting amnesty to crooks. Others saw things differently. At a certain point, some guy called Misuraca a geezer, another said he looked like something out of the puppet theatre, a third man called him a senile wreck. I learned all these things from a friend who was there. Finally, the secretary, some jerk who's not even Sicilian and goes by the name of Biraghìn, asked him please to vacate the premises, since he had no authorization whatsoever to attend the meeting. Which was true, but no one had ever dared say this before. So Gerlando got in his little Fiat and headed back home to Vigàta. His blood was boiling, no doubt about it, but the others had made him lose his head on purpose. And you're going to tell me it was an accident?'

The only way to reason with Bonfiglio was to put oneself squarely on his level. The inspector knew this from experience.

'Is there one television personality you find particularly obnoxious?' he asked him.

'There are a hundred thousand, but Mike Bongiorno is

the worst. Whenever I see him, my stomach gets all queasy and I feel like smashing the screen.'

'Good. And if, after watching this particular MC, you get in your car, drive into a wall, and kill yourself, what am I supposed to do, in your opinion?'

'Arrest Mike Bongiorno,' the other said firmly.

*

He went back to the office feeling calmer. His encounter with the logic of Ernesto Bonfiglio had distracted and amused him.

'Any news?' he asked as he walked in.

'There's a personal letter for you that came just now in the mail,' said Catarella, repeating, for emphasis, 'Per-son-al.'

On his desk he found a postcard from his father and some office memos.

'Hey, Cat! Where'd you put the letter?'

'I said it was personal!' Catarella said defensively.

'What's that supposed to mean?'

'It means that you have to receive it in person, it being personal and all.'

'Okay. The person is here in front of you. Where's the letter?'

'It's gone where it was supposed to go. Where the person personally lives. I told the postman to deliver it to your house, Chief, your personal residence, in Marinella.'

*

Standing in front of the Trattoria San Calogero, catching a breath of air, was the cook and owner.

'Where you going, Inspector? Not coming in?'

'I'm eating at home today.'

'Whatever you say. But I've got some rock lobster ready for the grill that'll seem like you're not eating them, but dreaming them.'

Montalbano went inside, won over by the image more than the desire. Then, after finishing his meal, he pushed the dishes away, crossed his arms on the table, and fell asleep. He always ate in a small room with three tables, and so it was easy for Serafino, the waiter, to steer customers towards the big dining room and leave the inspector in peace. Around four o'clock, with the restaurant already closed, the proprietor, noticing that Montalbano was showing no signs of life, made him a cup of coffee, then gently woke him up.

SIX

As for the personally personal letter earlier announced by Catarella, he'd completely forgotten about it. It came back to him only when he stepped right on it upon entering his home: the postman had slipped it under the door. The address made it look like an anonymous letter: MONTALBANO – POLICE HEADQUARTERS – CITY. Then, on the upper left, the inscription: *PERSONAL*. Which had then set Catarella's earthquake-damaged wits in motion.

Anonymous it was not, however. On the contrary. The signature that Montalbano immediately looked for at the end went off in his brain like a gunshot.

Esteemed Inspector,

It occurred to me that in all probability I won't be able to come to see you tomorrow morning as planned. If the meeting of the Party leadership of Montelusa, which I shall attend upon completing this letter, were by chance – as appears quite likely – to spell failure for my positions, I believe it would be my duty to go to Palermo to try and awaken the souls and consciences of those comrades who make the decisions within the Party. I am even ready to fly to Rome to request an audience with the National Secretary. These intentions, if realized, would necessitate the postponement of our meeting, and thus I beg you please to excuse me for putting in writing what I ought properly to have told you in person.

As you will surely recall, the day after the strange robbery/non-robbery at the supermarket, I came of my own accord to police headquarters to report what I had happened to see – that is, a group of men quietly at work, however odd the hour, with lights on and under the supervision of a uniformed man who looked to me like the night watchman. No passer-by would have seen anything unusual in this scene; had I noticed anything out of the ordinary, I would have made sure to alert the police myself.

The night following my testimony, I was too upset from the arguments I'd had with my Party colleagues to fall asleep, and thus I had occasion to review the scene of the robbery in my mind. Only then did I remember a detail that could prove to be very important. On my way back from Montelusa, agitated as I was, I took the wrong approach route for Vigàta, one that has been recently made very complicated by a series of incomprehensible one-way streets. Instead of taking the Via Granet, I turned onto the old Via Lincoln and found myself going against the flow of traffic. After realizing my mistake about fifty yards down the street, I decided to retrace my path in reverse, completing my manoeuvre at the corner of Vicolo Trupìa, thinking I would back into this street, so that I could then point my car in the right direction. I was unable to do this, however, because the vicolo was entirely blocked by a large car, a model heavily advertised these days but available only in very limited quantities, the 'Ulysses', licence plate Montelusa 328280. At this point I had no choice but to proceed in my directional violation. A few yards down the street, I came out into the Piazza Chiesa Vecchia, where the supermarket is.

To spare you further investigation: that car, the only one of its kind in town, belongs to Mr Carmelo Ingrassia. Now, since Ingrassia lives in Monte Ducale, what was his car doing a short distance away from the supermarket, also belonging to Mr Ingrassia, at the very moment when it was being burgled? I leave the answer to you.

Yours very sincerely,

Cav. Gerlando Misuraca

'You've fucked me royally this time, Cavaliere!' was Montalbano's only comment as he glared at the letter he had set down on the dining table. And dining, of course, was now out of the question. He opened the refrigerator only to pay glum homage to the culinary mastery of his housekeeper, a deserved homage, for an enveloping fragrance of poached baby octopus immediately assailed his senses. But he closed the fridge. He wasn't up to it; his stomach was tight as a fist. He undressed and, fully naked, went for a walk along the beach; at that hour there was nobody around anyway. Couldn't eat, couldn't sleep. Around four o'clock in the morning he dived into the icy water, swam a long time, then returned home. He noticed, laughing, that he had an erection. He started talking to it, trying to reason with it.

'It's no use deluding yourself.'

The erection told him a phone call to Livia might be just the thing. To Livia lying naked and warm with sleep in her bed.

'You're just a dickhead telling me dickheaded things. Teenage jerk-off stuff.'

Offended, the erection withdrew. Montalbano put on a pair of briefs, threw a dry towel over his shoulder, grabbed a chair and sat down on the veranda, which gave onto the beach.

He remained there watching the sea as it began to lighten slowly, then take on colour, streaked with yellow sunbeams. It promised to be a beautiful day, and the inspector felt reassured and ready to act. He'd had a few ideas, after reading the cavaliere's letter; the swim had helped him to organize them.

*

'You can't show up at the press conference looking like that,' pronounced Fazio, looking him over severely.

'What, are you taking lessons from the Anti-Mafia Commission now?' Montalbano opened the padded nylon bag he was holding. 'In here I've got trousers, jacket, shirt and tie. I'll change before I go to Montelusa. Actually, do me a favour. Take them out and put them on a chair; otherwise they'll get wrinkled.'

'They're already wrinkled, Chief. But I wasn't talking about your clothes; I meant your face. Like it or not, you've got to go to the barber.'

Fazio had said 'like it or not' because he knew him well and realized how much effort it cost the inspector to go to the barber. Running a hand behind his head, Montalbano agreed that his hair could use a little trim, too. His face darkened.

'Not one fucking thing's going to go right today!' he predicted.

Before exiting, he left orders that, while he was out beautifying himself, someone should go and pick up Carmelo Ingrassia and bring him to headquarters.

'If he asks why, what should I tell him?' asked Fazio.

'Don't tell him anything.'

'What if he insists?'

'If he insists, tell him I want to know how long it's been since he last had an enema. Good enough?'

'There's no need to get upset.'

*

The barber, his young helper and a client who was sitting in one of the two rotating chairs that barely fitted into the shop – which was actually only a recess under a staircase – were in the midst of an animated discussion, but fell silent as soon as the inspector appeared. Montalbano had entered with what he himself called his 'barber-shop face', that is, mouth shrunken to a slit, eyes half-closed in suspicion, eyebrows furrowed, expression at once scornful and severe.

'Good morning. Is there a wait?'

Even his voice came out deep and gravelly.

'No sir. Have a seat, Inspector.'

As Montalbano took his place in the vacant chair, the barber, in accelerated, Chaplinesque movements, held a mirror behind the client's head to let him admire the finished product, freed him of the towel round his neck, tossed it into a bin, took out a clean one and put it over the inspector's shoulders. The client, denied even the customary brush-down by the assistant, literally fled from the shop after muttering 'Good-day.'

The ritual of the haircut and shave, performed in

absolute silence, was swift and funereal. A new client appeared, parting the beaded curtain, but he quickly sniffed the atmosphere and, recognizing the inspector, said, 'I'll pass by later.' Then he disappeared.

On the street, as he headed back to his office, Montalbano noticed an indefinable yet disgusting odour wafting around him, something between turpentine and a certain kind of face powder prostitutes used to wear some thirty years back. The stink was coming from his own hair.

*

'Ingrassia's in your office,' Tortorella said in a low voice, sounding conspiratorial.

'Where'd Fazio go?'

'Home to change. The commissioner's office called. They said Fazio, Gallo, Galluzzo and Germanà should also take part in the press conference.'

I guess my phone call to that arsehole Sciacchitano had an effect, thought Montalbano.

Ingrassia, who this time was dressed entirely in pastel green, started to rise.

'Don't get up,' said the inspector, sitting down behind his desk. He distractedly ran a hand through his hair, and immediately the smell of turpentine and face powder grew stronger. Alarmed, he brought his fingers to his nose and sniffed them, confirming his suspicion. But there was nothing to be done; there was no shampoo in the office bathroom. Without warning, he resumed his 'barber-shop face'. Seeing him suddenly transformed, Ingrassia became worried and started squirming in his chair.

'Is something wrong?' he asked.

'In what sense do you mean?'

'Well . . . in every sense, I suppose,' said Ingrassia, flustered.

Montalbano shrugged evasively and went back to sniffing his fingers. The conversation stalled.

'Have you heard about poor Cavaliere Misuraca?' the inspector asked, as if chatting among friends in his living room.

'Ah! Such is life!' The other sighed sorrowfully.

'Imagine that, Mr Ingrassia. I'd asked him if he could give me some more details about what he'd seen the night of the robbery, we'd agreed to meet again, and now this . . .'

Ingrassia threw his hands up in the air, inviting Montalbano, with this gesture, to resign himself to fate. He allowed a respectful pause to elapse, then, 'I'm sorry,' he said, 'but what other details could the poor cavaliere have given you? He'd already told you everything he saw.'

Montalbano wagged his forefinger, signalling 'no'.

'You don't think he told you everything he saw?' asked Ingrassia, intrigued.

Montalbano wagged his finger again.

Stew in your own juices, scumbag, he was thinking.

The green Ingrassia started to tremble like a leafy branch in the breeze.

'Well, then, what did you want him to tell you?'

'What he thought he didn't see.'

The breeze turned into a gale, the branch began to lurch.

'I don't understand.'

'Let me explain. You're familiar, are you not, with a painting by Pieter Brueghel called *Children's Games*?'

'Who? Me? No,' said Ingrassia, worried.

'Doesn't matter. But you must be familiar with the works of Hieronymus Bosch?'

'No sir,' said Ingrassia, starting to sweat. Now he was really getting scared, his face starting to match the colour of his outfit – green.

'Never mind, then, don't worry about it,' Montalbano said magnanimously. 'What I meant was that when someone sees a scene, he usually remembers the first general impression he has of it. Right?'

'Right,' said Ingrassia, prepared for the worst.

'Then, little by little, a few other details may start coming back to him, things that registered in his memory but were discarded as unimportant. An open or closed window, for example, or a noise, a whistle, a song – what else? – a chair out of place, a car where it's not supposed to be, a light . . . That sort of thing. You know, little details that can later turn out to be extremely important.'

Ingrassia took a white handkerchief with a green border out of his pocket and wiped the sweat from his face.

'You had me brought here just to tell me that?'

'No. That would be inconveniencing you for no reason. I would never do a thing like that. I was wondering if you'd heard from the people who, in your opinion, played that joke on you, you know, the phony robbery.'

'Not a word from anyone.'

'That's odd.'

'Why?'

'Because the best part of any practical joke is enjoying it afterward with the person it was played on. Well, if you do hear from anybody, please let me know. Good-day.'

'Good-day,' muttered Ingrassia, standing up. He was dripping wet, his trousers sticking to his bottom.

*

Fazio showed up all decked out in a shiny new uniform.

'I'm here,' he said.

'And the pope is in Rome.'

'I know, Inspector, I know: today is not your day.'

He started to leave but stopped in the doorway.

'Inspector Augello called, said he had a terrible toothache. He says he's not coming unless he has to.'

'Listen, do you have any idea where the wreck of Cavaliere Misuraca's Fiat ended up?'

'It's still here, in our garage. If you ask me, it's just envy.'

'What are you talking about?'

'Inspector Augello's toothache. It's just a bout of envy.'

'Who's he envious of?'

'You. Because it's your press conference and not his. And he's probably also pissed off because you wouldn't tell him who you'd arrested.'

'Would you do me a favour?'

'All right, all right, I'm going.'

When Fazio had closed the door, Montalbano dialed a number. The voice of the woman who answered sounded like a parody of an African in a dubbed film.

'Hallo? Who dare? Who you callin' dare?'

Where did the Cardamones find these housekeepers?

'Is Signora Ingrid there?'

'Ya, but who callin?'

'This is Salvo Montalbano.'

'You wait dare.'

Ingrid's voice, on the other hand, was the very same as the voice the Italian dubber had given to Greta Garbo, who was herself Swedish.

'Ciao, Salvo. How are you? Long time no see.'

'I need your help, Ingrid. Are you free tonight?'

'Actually, no. But if it's really important I can drop everything.'

'It's important.'

'Tell me where and when.'

'Nine o'clock tonight, at the Marinella Bar.'

*

For Montalbano, the press conference proved, as of course he knew it would, to be a long, painful embarrassment. Anti-Mafia Vice-Commissioner De Dominicis came from Palermo and sat on the Montelusa police commissioner's right. Imperious gestures and angry glances prevailed upon

Montalbano, who had wanted to remain in the audience, to sit on his superior's left. Behind him, standing, were Fazio, Germanà, Gallo and Galluzzo. The commissioner spoke first and began by naming the man they had arrested, the number one of the number twos: Gaetano Bennici, known as 'Tano the Greek', wanted for multiple murders and long a fugitive from justice. It was literally a bombshell. The journalists, who were there in great numbers – there were even four TV cameras – jumped out of their chairs and started talking to one another, making such a racket that the commissioner had difficulty re-establishing silence. He stated that credit for the arrest went to Inspector Montalbano who, with the assistance of his men – and here he named and introduced them one by one – had been able to exploit a golden opportunity with skill and courage. Then De Dominicis spoke, explaining Tano the Greek's role within his criminal organization, certainly a prominent one, though not of the utmost prominence. As the Anti-Mafia Vice-Commissioner sat back down, Montalbano realized he was being thrown to the dogs.

The questions came in rapid-fire bursts, worse than a Kalashnikov. Had there been a gunfight? Was Tano alone? Were any law enforcement personnel injured? What did Tano say when they handcuffed him? Had he been sleeping or awake? Was there a woman with him? A dog? Was it true he took drugs? How many murders had he committed? How was he dressed? Was he naked? Was it true he rooted for the Milan soccer team? Did he have a photo of

Ornella Muti on his person? Could the inspector explain a little better the golden opportunity the commissioner had alluded to?

Montalbano struggled to answer the questions as best he could, seeming to understand less and less what he was saying.

It's a good thing the TV's here, he thought. *That way, at least, I can watch and make some sense of the bullshit I've been telling them.*

And just to make things even harder, there were the adoring eyes of Corporal Anna Ferrara, staring at him from the crowd.

Nicolò Zito, newsman from the Free Channel and a true friend, tried to rescue him from the quicksand in which he was drowning.

'Inspector, with your permission,' said Zito. 'You said you met Tano on your way back from Fiacca, where you'd been invited to eat a *tabisca* with friends. Is that correct?'

'Yes.'

'What is a *tabisca*?'

They'd eaten *tabisca* many times together. Zito was simply tossing him a life preserver. Montalbano seized it. Suddenly confident and precise, the inspector went into a detailed description of that extraordinary, multi-flavoured pizza.

SEVEN

In the alternately desperate, stammering, hesitant, bewildered, flabbergasted, lost but always wild-eyed man framed pitilessly in the foreground by the Free Channel's videocamera, Montalbano scarcely recognized himself under the storm of questions from vile snake-in-the-grass journalists. And the part where he'd explained how *tabisca* was made – the part in which he came off best – had been cut out. Maybe it wasn't strictly in keeping with the principal subject, the capture of Tano the Greek.

The aubergine Parmesan his housekeeper had left for him in the oven suddenly tasted flavourless. But that was impossible, it couldn't be right. It must have been some sort of psychological effect from seeing himself look like such a stupid shit on television.

All at once he felt like crying, like throwing himself down on his bed and wrapping himself up in the sheet like a mummy.

*

'Inspector Montalbano? This is Luciano Acquasanta from the newspaper *Il Mezzogiorno*. Would you be so kind as to grant me an interview?'

'No.'

'I won't waste your time, I promise.'

'No.'

*

'Is this Inspector Montalbano? Spingardi here, Attilio Spingardi, from the RAI office in Palermo. We're putting together a round table to discuss—'

'No.'

'At least let me finish!'

'No.'

*

'Darling? It's Livia. How are you feeling?'

'Fine. Why?'

'I just saw you on TV.'

'Oh, Christ! You mean they showed that all over Italy?'

'I think so. But it was very brief, you know.'

'Could you hear what I was saying?'

'No, one could only hear the commentator speaking. But I could clearly see your face, and that's what got me worried. You were yellow as a lemon.'

'It was even in colour?'

'Of course it was in colour. You kept putting your hand over your eyes and rubbing your forehead.'

'I had a headache and the lights were bothering me.'

'Are you better now?'

'Yes.'

*

'Inspector Montalbano? My name is Stefania Quattrini, from the magazine *Essere Donna.* We'd like to do a telephone interview with you. Could you remain on the line?'

'No.'

'It'll only take a few seconds.'

'No.'

*

'Do I have the honour of actually speaking with the famous Inspector Montalbano who holds press conferences?'

'Don't break my balls.'

'No, don't worry about your balls, we won't break them. It's your arse we're after.'

'Who is this?'

'It's your death, that's who. You're not gonna wiggle out of this one so easy, you lousy fucking actor. Who'd you think you were fooling with that little song and dance you put on with your pal Tano? You're gonna pay for trying to fuck with us.'

'Hello? Hello?'

*

The line had gone dead. But Montalbano didn't have a chance to take in those threatening words and mull them over, because he realized that the insistent noise he'd been hearing for some time amid the flurry of phone calls was the doorbell ringing. For some reason he was convinced it must be a journalist more clever than the rest who'd decided to show up at his house. Exasperated, he ran to the entrance and without opening, yelled, 'Who the hell is it?'

'It's the commissioner.'

What could *he* want from him, at home, at that hour, without even having called to alert him? He released the bolt with a swat of the hand and yanked the door wide open.

'Hello, come on in, make yourself comfortable,' he said, standing aside to let him in.

'We haven't got any time. Get yourself in order, I'll wait for you in the car.'

He turned around and walked away. Passing in front of the large mirror on the armoire, Montalbano realized what the commissioner had meant by 'Get yourself in order'. He was completely naked.

*

The car had none of the usual police markings; it looked, rather, like a rental car. At the wheel, in civilian clothing, was an officer from the Montelusa station whom he knew. As soon as he sat down, the commissioner began to speak.

'I apologize for not calling beforehand, but your phone was always busy.'

'I know.'

The commissioner could have cut into the line, of course, but that wasn't in keeping with his polite, gentlemanly way of doing things. Montalbano didn't explain why the telephone had given him no peace. It didn't matter. His boss was gloomier than he'd ever seen him before, face drawn, mouth half twisted in a kind of grimace.

*

After they'd been driving on the highway to Palermo for some forty-five minutes with the driver going full tilt, Montalbano started looking out on that part of his island's landscape which charmed him most.

'You like it? Really?' an astonished Livia had asked him once, a few years earlier, when he brought her to this area.

Arid hills like giant tumuli, covered only by a yellow stubble of dry grass and abandoned by the hand of man after sudden failures owing to drought, extreme heat, or more simply to the weariness of a battle lost from the outset, were interrupted here and there by a group of rocky peaks rising absurdly out of nothing or perhaps fallen from above, stalactites or stalagmites of the deep, open-air cave that is Sicily. The few houses one saw, all single-storey, domed structures, cubes of dry stone, stood askew, as if by chance alone they'd survived the violent bucking of an earth that didn't want them on its back. Still there was the rare spot of green, not of trees or cultivation, but of agaves, sword grass, buckthorn and sorghum, beleaguered and dusty, they too on the verge of surrender.

As if he had been waiting for the appropriate scenery, the commissioner finally began to speak, though Montalbano realized the words were addressed not to him but to the commissioner himself, in a kind of painful, furious monologue.

'Why did they do it? Who decided to decide? If an investigation were held – an impossible conjecture – it would turn out that either nobody took the first step, or they were acting on orders from above. So let's see who these superiors who gave the orders are. The head of the Anti-Mafia Commission would deny all knowledge, as would the minister of the interior and the prime minister, the head of state. Which leaves the pope, Jesus Christ, the Virgin Mary, and God the Father, in that order. All would cry in outrage: how could anyone think it was *they* who gave the order? That leaves only the Devil, notorious for being the cause of all evil. He's the guilty one! Satan! . . . Anyway, to make a long story short, they decided to transfer him to another prison.'

'Tano?' Montalbano ventured to ask. The commissioner didn't even answer.

'Why? We'll never know, that much is certain. And while we were holding our press conference, they were putting him in an ordinary car with two plainclothes men as escort – ah! how clever! – so as not to attract attention, of course! And so, when the requisite high-powered motorcycle appeared from an alley with two men aboard, rendered utterly unrecognizable by their helmets . . . Final tally: two policemen dead, Tano in the hospital, on death's doorstep. And there you have it.'

Montalbano absorbed it all, thinking cynically that if only they'd killed Tano a few hours earlier, he would have been spared the torture of the press conference. He started asking questions only because he sensed that the commissioner had calmed down a little after his outburst.

'But how did they know—'

The commissioner slammed the seat in front of him, making the driver start and the car veer slightly.

'What do you think, Montalbano? A mole, no? That's what's driving me so crazy!'

The inspector let a minute or two pass before asking another question.

'Where do we come in?'

'He wants to talk to you. He knows he's dying, and he wants to tell you something.'

'I see. So why did you go to all this trouble? I could have gone by myself.'

'I came along to prevent any snags or delays. In their sublime intelligence, these guys are capable of denying you access to him.'

*

In front of the hospital gate there was an armoured car, as well as some ten guards scattered about the yard, submachine guns in hand.

'Idiots,' said the commissioner.

They passed through at least five checkpoints, growing more irritated each time, then finally reached the ward where Tano's room was. All the other patients had been cleared out, transferred elsewhere amid curses and obscenities. At each end of the corridor were four armed policemen, plus two outside the door of the room Tano was obviously in. The commissioner showed them his pass.

'Congratulations,' he said to the corporal.

'For what, Mr Commissioner?'

'For maintaining order.'

'Thank you,' said the corporal, brightening, the commissioner's irony sailing far over his head.

'You go in alone,' the commissioner said to Montalbano, 'I'll wait outside.'

Only then did he notice how ashen the inspector was, his forehead bathed in sweat.

'My God, Montalbano, what's wrong? Do you feel ill?'

'I'm perfectly fine,' the inspector replied through clenched teeth.

He was lying. In fact, he felt terrible. The dead left him utterly indifferent. He could sleep with them, pretend to break bread with them, play hearts or spades with them. They didn't bother him in the least. The dying, on the other hand, made him break into a sweat: his hands would start to tremble, he would go cold all over, a hole would open up in his stomach.

*

Under the sheet that covered him, Tano's body looked shrunken, smaller than the inspector remembered it. His arms lay stretched along his sides, the right arm wrapped in thick bandages. Oxygen tubes sprouted from his nose, which had turned almost transparent, and his face looked unreal, as if it belonged to a wax doll. Overcoming the desire to run away, Montalbano pulled up a metal chair and sat down beside the dying man, who kept his eyes shut, as if asleep.

'Tano? Tano? It's Inspector Montalbano.'

The other reacted immediately, opening his eyes and making as if to sit up in bed, a violent start surely triggered by the animal instinct of one who has long been hunted. Then his eyes brought the inspector into focus, and the tension in his body visibly relaxed.

'You wanted to talk to me?'

Tano nodded yes, and gave a hint of a smile. He spoke very slowly, with great effort.

'They ran me off the road anyway.'

He was referring to the discussion they'd had in the cottage. Montalbano didn't know what to say.

'Come closer,' the old man said.

Montalbano rose from his chair and leaned over.

'Closer.'

The inspector bent down so far forward, his ear actually touched Tano's lip. The man's burning breath made him feel disgusted. Tano then told him what he had to tell, lucidly and precisely. But the talking had worn him out, and he closed his eyes again. Montalbano didn't know what to do, whether to leave or stay a little while longer. He decided to sit down, and Tano said something again, in a gurgly voice. The inspector stood back up and leaned over the dying man.

'What did you say?'

'I'm spooked.'

Tano was afraid, and in his present state he didn't hesitate to admit it. Was it pity, this sudden wave of heat, this flutter of the heart, this agonizing surge of emotion? He put a hand on Tano's forehead, and the intimate words came out spontaneously.

'You needn't be ashamed to say so. It's one more thing that makes you a man. We'll all be scared when our time comes. Goodbye, Tano.'

He walked out quickly, closing the door behind him. In the hallway, together with the commissioner and policemen, were De Dominicis and Sciacchitano. He ran up to them.

'What did he say?' De Dominicis asked anxiously.

'Nothing. He didn't manage to say anything. He wanted to, but couldn't. He's dying.'

'Hah!' said Sciacchitano, doubtful.

Very calmly, Montalbano placed his open hand on Sciacchitano's chest and gave him a violent push. The man reeled three steps backward, stunned.

'Stay right where you are and don't come any closer,' the inspector said through clenched teeth.

'That's enough, Montalbano,' the commissioner intervened.

De Dominicis seemed to pay no mind to the two men's differences.

'Who knows what he wanted to tell you,' he persisted, eyeing Montalbano inquisitively, as if to say: you're not talking straight.

'If you'd like, I can try and guess,' Montalbano retorted insolently.

*

Before leaving the hospital, Montalbano knocked back a double J&B, neat, at the bar. Then they headed back to Montelusa. He figured he'd be back in Vigàta by 7.30, and therefore could keep his appointment with Ingrid.

'He talked, didn't he?'

'Yes.'

'Anything important?'

'Yes, in my opinion.'

'Why did he choose you?'

'He said he wanted to give me a present, for playing fair with him throughout this whole business.'

'I'm listening.'

Montalbano told him everything, and when he had finished, the commissioner looked pensive. Then he sighed.

'You work it all out yourself, with your men. It's better if this remains a secret. Nobody else should know about it, not even in my office. As you've just seen, there are moles everywhere.'

He visibly sank back into the bad mood he'd been in during the drive to the hospital.

'So it's come to this!' he said angrily.

Halfway home, the cellphone rang.

'Yes?' answered the commissioner.

Somebody spoke briefly at the other end.

'Thank you,' said the commissioner. He turned to Montalbano. 'That was De Dominicis. He kindly informed me that Tano died virtually as we were leaving the hospital.'

'They'd better be careful,' said Montalbano.

'Careful?'

'Not to let anyone steal the body,' the inspector said with bitter irony.

They rode another while in silence.

'Why did De Dominicis bother to inform you that Tano was dead?'

'That call, for all practical purposes, was meant for you, my friend. Obviously De Dominicis, who's no fool, correctly believes that Tano managed to tell you something. And he would like a share of the pie, if not the whole thing.'

*

Back at headquarters, he found only Catarella and Fazio. It was better this way; he preferred talking to Fazio with nobody around. Out of a sense of duty more than curiosity, he asked: 'Where are the others?'

'They went chasing after four kids who were racing each other on two motorbikes.'

'Jesus! The whole squad is gone chasing after a pair of racing motorbikes?'

'It's a special kind of race,' Fazio explained. 'One motorbike is green, the other yellow. The yellow one starts out first and races the whole length of a street, snatching whatever's there to be snatched. An hour or two later, after the people have calmed down, the green one takes off and swipes whatever's still there to be swiped. Then they change street and neighbourhood, but this time the green one goes first. It's a race to see who can steal the most.'

'I see. Listen, Fazio, this evening I want you to drop by the Vinti warehouse and ask the manager, in my name, to lend us some shovels, pickaxes, mattocks and spades, ten or so. We'll all meet here tomorrow morning at six. Inspector Augello and Catarella will stay behind at headquarters. I want two cars – no, make that one car, 'cause you're going to ask Vinti's to give you a Jeep, too. By the way, who has the key to our garage?'

'Whoever's on duty always has it. At the moment, that would be Catarella.'

'Get it from him and give it to me.'

'Right away. But if you don't mind my asking, what do we need shovels and pickaxes for?'

'We're changing profession. As of tomorrow, we're going into farming, the healthy life, working in the fields. What do you say?'

'You know, Inspector, for the last few days there's just no reasoning with you. Maybe you could tell us what's got into you? You're always obnoxious and rude.'

EIGHT

He first met Ingrid in the course of an investigation in which, through a series of false leads, she'd been offered up to him, though completely innocent, as the scapegoat. Since then a strange sort of friendship had developed between the inspector and that splendid woman. From time to time Ingrid would call him up and they would spend the evening chatting. The young woman would talk about her problems, confiding in Montalbano, and he would dispense wise, brotherly advice. He was a kind of spiritual father – a role he'd had to impose on himself by force, since Ingrid didn't exactly arouse spiritual feelings – and his recommendations were always studiously ignored. At none of their meetings – there'd been six or seven – had Montalbano ever shown up before she did. Ingrid had a mania for punctuality.

This time too, after parking in the Marinella Bar's car park, he noticed her car was already there, beside a Porsche convertible that looked like a rocket and was painted a tasteless shade of yellow that offended the eyes.

When he entered the bar, Ingrid was standing at the

counter drinking a whisky. Beside her was a man aged fortyish dressed in a fancy canary-yellow suit, sporting a Rolex and ponytail, and talking to her confidentially.

When he has to change clothes, thought the inspector, does he also change cars?

As soon as she saw him, Ingrid came running and embraced him, kissing him lightly on the lips. She was obviously happy to see him. Montalbano, too, was pleased: Ingrid looked like a gift from God, with her jeans painted on her very long legs, her sandals, her light-blue see-through blouse affording a glimpse of her round breasts, her blonde hair hanging loose around her shoulders.

'Sorry,' he said to the canary who was with her. 'See you around.'

They went and sat down at a table. Montalbano didn't feel like drinking anything. The man with the Rolex and ponytail took his whisky out to the seaside terrace. Ingrid and the inspector smiled at each other.

'You're looking well,' she said. 'A lot better than you did on TV today.'

'Yeah,' said Montalbano, then changed the subject. 'You look like you're doing all right yourself.'

'Did you want to see me to exchange compliments?'

'I wanted to ask a favour of you.'

'Here I am.'

The man with the ponytail was eyeing them from the terrace.

'Who's that?'

'Somebody I know. I passed him on my way here. He followed and offered me a drink.'

'In what sense do you know him?'

Ingrid turned serious, a line creasing her forehead.

'Are you jealous?'

'No, you know better than that. Anyway, there'd be no reason, with him. It's just that he got on my nerves from the minute I saw him. What's his name?'

'Come on, Salvo. What do you care?'

'Tell me his name.'

'Beppe . . . Beppe De Vito.'

'And what does he do to earn his Rolex, Porsche and everything else?'

'Trades in leather goods.'

'Ever slept with him?'

'Yes, about a year ago, only once. And he was just suggesting we do it again. But I don't have a very pleasant memory of it.'

'Some kind of degenerate?'

Ingrid eyed him for a moment, then let out a laugh that made the bartender jump.

'What's so funny?'

'The face you just made: the good cop full of indignation. No, Salvo, he's just the opposite. Totally lacking in imagination. All I can remember is that it seemed suffocating and pointless.'

Montalbano gestured for the man with the ponytail to come over to their table, and as he approached, smiling, Ingrid gave the inspector a worried look.

'Hello. Don't I know you? You're Inspector Montalbano, aren't you?'

'Unfortunately for you, you're going to get to know me even better.'

The other became flustered, his whisky trembling in his glass, ice cubes tinkling.

'Why "unfortunately"?'

'Your name is Giuseppe De Vito and you deal in leather goods, am I correct?'

'Yes, but . . . I don't understand.'

'You'll understand in due time. One of these days you're going to be called in to Montelusa police headquarters. I'll be there, too. I think we'll have a lot to talk about.'

The man with the ponytail, face suddenly pale, set his glass down on the table, unable to hold it any longer.

'Couldn't you . . . at least give me a hint . . . some explanation . . .?'

Montalbano assumed the expression of someone just overcome by an irresistible wave of generosity.

'All right, but only because you're a friend of the lady. Do you know a German man by the name of Kurt Suckert?'

'Never heard of him, I swear,' the man said, digging a canary-coloured handkerchief out of his pocket and mopping his brow with it.

'Well, if that's your answer, I have nothing more to say to you,' the inspector said icily. He looked him up and down, then gestured for him to come closer. 'I'll give you my advice: don't try to be too clever. Goodbye.'

'Goodbye,' De Vito replied mechanically. And without even looking back at Ingrid, he raced out of the bar.

'You're a shit,' Ingrid said calmly, 'and an arsehole.'

'Yes, you're right. Every now and then something comes over me, and I get that way.'

'Does this Suckert really exist?'

'He used to. But he called himself Curzio Malaparte. He was a writer.'

They heard the roar of the Porsche, burning rubber as it pulled out.

'So did you get it out of your system?' Ingrid asked.

'I think so.'

'I could tell right away, you know, that you were in a bad mood. What is it? Can you tell me?'

'I could, but it's not worth going into. Problems at work.'

*

Montalbano suggested that Ingrid leave her car in the bar's car park; they would come back later to get it. Ingrid didn't ask him where they were going, nor what they were going to do. All of a sudden Montalbano asked her, 'How's it going with your father-in-law?'

'Fine!' Ingrid said cheerfully. 'I'm sorry, I should have mentioned it sooner. Things are fine with my father-in-law. He's left me in peace for two months now. He's no longer after me.'

'What happened?'

'I don't know. He hasn't told me anything. The last time was on our way back from Fela, where we'd been to a wedding. My husband couldn't make it and my mother-in-law wasn't feeling well, so the two of us were left alone again. At some point he turned off onto a side road, continued for a mile or two, then stopped in a wooded area. He made me get out of the car, tore off my clothes, threw me to the ground, and fucked me with his usual brutality. The next day I left for Palermo with my husband, and when I got back a week later, my father-in-law seemed like he'd aged. He was trembling. Since then, he's sort of been avoiding me. Now when I find myself face to face with him in some corridor of the house, I'm no longer afraid he's going to push me up against the wall with one hand on my tits and the other on my cunt.'

'It's better this way, isn't it?'

*

The story Ingrid had just told him Montalbano knew better than she did. The inspector had learned of Ingrid's relations with her father-in-law the very first time he met her. Then one night, as they were talking, without warning, Ingrid had burst into convulsive sobs; she could no longer bear the situation with her husband's father. An absolutely liberated woman, she felt soiled, demeaned by this quasi-incestuous relationship that was being forced on her. She thought of leaving her husband and returning to Sweden.

Being an excellent mechanic, she would manage to earn a living.

That was when Montalbano had made up his mind to help get her out of that mess. The following day, he'd invited Corporal Anna Ferrara to his house for dinner. Young Anna was in love with him and convinced that he and Ingrid were lovers.

'I'm desperate,' he had told her, opening the evening with a face worthy of a great tragic actor.

'Oh my God, what's wrong?' asked Anna, squeezing one of his hands in hers.

'Ingrid is cheating on me.'

He let his head fall to her breast and by some miracle managed to make his eyes grow moist.

Anna suppressed an exclamation of triumph. She'd been right all along! Meanwhile the inspector was hiding his face in his hands, and the girl felt overwhelmed by this exhibition of despair.

'You know, I never told you anything because I didn't want to upset you, but I did a little investigation about Ingrid. You're not the only man.'

'But I knew that!' said the inspector, his hands still over his face.

'What is it, then?'

'It's different this time! It's not some little fling like all the rest, which I could even forgive. She's in love, and he feels the same way!'

'Do you know who she's in love with?'

'Yes, her father-in-law.'

'Oh, Christ!' said Anna, giving a start. 'She told you herself?'

'No, I found out on my own. Actually, she denies it. She denies everything. I need some kind of irrefutable proof, something to throw in her face. Do you know what I mean?'

Anna had offered to provide him with this irrefutable proof. And she'd gone to such lengths that she even managed to take some pictures of that rustic episode in the woods. She'd had them enlarged by a trusted girlfriend of hers in the crime lab and then turned them over to the inspector. Ingrid's father-in-law, aside from being chief physician at Montelusa Hospital, was also a prominent local politician. And so Montalbano sent the man some eloquent initial documentation at his provincial party office, the hospital, and to his home. On the back of each photo were only the words: *We've got you now.* The barrage of images had apparently scared him to death: in a flash he'd seen his career and family jeopardized. In case of need, the inspector had another twenty or so photographs. He'd said nothing about this to Ingrid. The woman might throw a fit if she knew her Swedish sense of privacy had been violated.

Montalbano accelerated, now satisfied that the complex machinations he'd set in motion had achieved their desired goal.

*

'You bring the car inside,' said Montalbano, getting out and starting to raise the metal grille of the police garage.

Once she'd pulled in, he turned on the lights and lowered the grille.

'What do you want me to do?' Ingrid asked.

'See that wrecked Fiat 500 over there? I want to know if its brakes have been tampered with.'

'I don't know if I'll be able to tell.'

'Try.'

'There goes my blouse.'

'No, wait. I brought something.'

He reached into the back seat of his car and pulled out a shirt and pair of jeans that belonged to him.

'Here. Put these on.'

While Ingrid was changing, he went to look for a portable mechanic's lamp, found one on the counter, and plugged it in. Without saying a word, Ingrid took the lamp, a monkey wrench and a screwdriver and slid under the little Fiat's twisted chassis. It took her only about ten minutes. She came out from under the car covered with dust and grease.

'I was lucky. The brake cable was partly cut, I'm sure of it.'

'What do you mean "partly"?'

'I mean, it wasn't cut all the way through. They left just enough so the car wouldn't crash right away. But with the first hard pull, the cable would certainly have snapped.'

'Are you positive it didn't break all by itself? It was a very old car.'

'The cut is too clean. There's no shredding. Or very little.'

'Now listen closely,' said Montalbano. 'The man who was at the wheel drove from Vigàta to Montelusa, stopped there a little while, then headed back to Vigàta. The accident occurred on the steep descent right before you come into town, the Catena hillside. He slammed straight into a truck, and that was that. Clear so far?'

'Yes.'

'What I want to know is this: in your opinion, was this slick little job done in Vigàta or in Montelusa?'

'In Montelusa,' said Ingrid. 'If they'd done it in Vigàta, he would definitely have crashed much sooner. Anything else?'

'No. Thanks.'

Ingrid didn't change her clothes, and didn't even wash her hands.

'I'll do it at your house.'

*

Ingrid got out in the bar's car park, took her car, and followed the inspector. It was a warm evening, not yet midnight.

'You want to take a shower?' he asked her when they got to his place.

'No, I'd rather go for a swim. I'll shower later, if I feel like it.'

She took off the grease-stained clothes of Montalbano's that she was wearing and slipped out of her panties. The inspector meanwhile had to make some effort to reassume his much-suffered guise as spiritual adviser.

'Come on. Take your clothes off and join me,' she said.

'No. I like watching you from the veranda.'

The full moon was actually too bright. Montalbano remained in his deck chair, enjoying the sight of Ingrid's silhouette as she reached the water's edge and began a dance of little hops in the water, arms extended. He saw her dive in, following awhile the small black dot that was her head, and then, suddenly, he fell asleep.

*

When he awoke, day was already dawning. He got up, slightly chilled, made coffee and drank three cups in a row. Before leaving, Ingrid had cleaned the house: there was no trace of her having been there. Ingrid was worth her weight in gold: she'd done everything he'd asked of her and hadn't even wanted an explanation. As far as curiosity was concerned, she was certainly not female. But only as far as curiosity was concerned.

Feeling a pang of hunger, he opened the refrigerator. The aubergine Parmesan he hadn't eaten at lunchtime was gone, dispatched by Ingrid. He had to content himself with a piece of bread and some processed cheese. Better than nothing. He took a shower and put on the clothes he had lent to Ingrid. They still bore a trace of her scent.

As was his habit, he arrived at headquarters about ten minutes late. His men were all ready with one squad car and the Jeep on loan from Vinti's, which was loaded up with shovels, mattocks, pickaxes and spades. They looked like labourers on their way to earn a day's pay working the land.

*

The Crasto mountain, which for its part would never have dreamed of calling itself a mountain, was a rather bald little hill that rose up west of Vigàta barely five hundred yards from the sea. It had been carefully pierced by a tunnel, now boarded up, that was supposed to have been an integral part of a road that started nowhere and led nowhere, a very useful bypass route for diverting funds into bottomless pockets. It was, in fact, called 'the bypass'. Legend had it that deep in the mountain's bowels was a *crasto,* a ram, made of solid gold. The tunnel-diggers never found it, but those who won the bid for the government contract certainly did. Attached to the mountain, on the landward side, was a kind of stronghold of rock called the Crasticeddru, the 'little Crasto'. The earthmovers and trucks had never reached this area, and it preserved an untamed beauty.

Having come down some virtually impassable roads to avoid attracting attention, the two cars headed straight for the Crasticeddru. In the absence of any further path or trail, it was very hard to go on, but the inspector insisted that the cars pull right up to the foot of the rocky spur.

Montalbano ordered everyone out of the cars. The air was cool, the morning bright.

'What do you want us to do?' asked Fazio.

'Search the Crasticeddru, all of you, very carefully. Look everywhere, and look hard. There's supposed to be an entrance to a cave somewhere. It's been covered up, camouflaged by rocks or vegetation. Keep your eyes peeled. We have to find it. I assure you it's there.'

They fanned out.

*

Two hours later, discouraged, they met back up beside the cars. The sun was beating down, they were sweating, but far-sighted Fazio had brought along thermoses of coffee and tea.

'Let's try again,' said Montalbano. 'But don't look only around the rock; search also along the ground, you might see something that looks fishy.'

They resumed their hunt, and half an hour later Montalbano heard Galluzzo call from afar.

'Inspector! Inspector! Come here!'

The inspector went over to the policeman, who had assigned himself the side of the spur closest to the highway that went to Fela.

'Look.'

Someone had tried to make them disappear, but at a certain point along the ground, there were clearly visible tracks left behind by a large truck.

'They lead over there,' said Galluzzo, pointing to the rock face. As he was saying this, he suddenly stopped, mouth agape.

'Jesus God!' said Montalbano.

How had they managed not to see it before? There was a huge boulder placed in an odd position, with shoots of withered grass sticking out from behind. As Galluzzo was calling to his mates, the inspector ran towards the boulder, grabbed a tuft of sword grass and tugged hard. He almost fell backward: the clump had no roots. It had merely been stuck there with bunches of sorghum to camouflage the entrance to the cave.

NINE

The boulder was a great stone slab, roughly rectangular in shape, that appeared to be of a piece with the rock around it and rested on a sort of giant step, also rock. At a glance Montalbano determined that it was about six feet tall and four and a half feet wide; moving it by hand was out of the question. And yet there had to be a way. Halfway up its right side, about four inches from the edge, was a perfectly natural-looking hole.

'If this was an actual wooden door,' the inspector reasoned, 'that opening would be at the right height for inserting a doorknob.'

He took a pen out of his pocket and stuck it in the hole. The pen fitted all the way inside, but when Montalbano was about to put it back in his pocket, he noticed that the pen had soiled his hand. He looked at his fingers, then smelled them.

'That's grease,' he said to Fazio, the only person remaining beside him.

The other policemen had taken shelter in the shade.

Gallo had found a clump of sheep's sorrel and offered some to the others.

'Suck the stalk,' he said, 'it's delicious and quenches your thirst.'

Montalbano thought of the only possible solution.

'Do we have a steel cable?'

'Sure do, inside the Jeep.'

'All right, then pull the car up here as close as you can.'

As Fazio was walking away, the inspector, now convinced he'd found the proper expedient for moving the big slab, looked at the surrounding landscape with different eyes. If this was indeed the place that Tano the Greek had revealed to him on his deathbed, there must be some spot nearby from which one could keep it under surveillance. The area seemed deserted and remote; one would never have imagined that right behind the bluff, a few hundred yards away, was the highway with all its traffic. Not far from there, on a rise of dry, rocky terrain, was a minuscule cottage, a cube consisting of a single room. He called for some binoculars. The little structure's wooden door, which was closed, looked solid. Next to the door, at the height of a man's head, was a small window without shutters, protected by two crisscrossing iron bars. The cottage appeared uninhabited, and it was the only possible observation point in the vicinity. All the other houses were too far away. Still doubtful, he called to Galluzzo.

'Go have a look at that little house. Do what you can to open the door, but don't break it in. Be careful, we may need to use it. See if there are any recent signs of life inside, if anyone's been living there in the last few days. But leave everything exactly as it was, as if you'd never been there.'

The Jeep had meanwhile backed almost all the way up to the base of the boulder. The inspector took the end of the steel cable, inserted it easily into the hole and started pushing it inside. This required little effort, for the cable slid into the boulder as if following a well-greased, unobstructed groove. In fact, a few seconds later, the cable end popped out on the other side of the slab, looking like the head of a snake.

'Take this end,' Montalbano told Fazio, 'fix it to the Jeep, put the engine in gear and pull away, but very, very gently.'

As the Jeep began to move, so did the boulder, its right side starting to come detached from the rock face as if turning on invisible hinges.

'Open sesame . . .' Germanà murmured in amazement, recalling the children's formula that magically served to open all doors.

*

'I assure you, Commissioner, that stone slab was turned into a door by a superb master craftsman. Just imagine, the iron hinges were totally invisible from the outside. Closing the door was as easy as opening it. We went in with flashlights. Inside, the cave was very carefully and intelligently fitted out. They'd made a floor, for example, out of a dozen or so puncheons nailed together and set down on the bare earth.'

'What's a puncheon?'

'I can't think of the proper word. Let's just say they're very thick planks. They built a floor to keep the crates of weapons from coming into direct contact with the damp ground. The walls are covered with lighter boards. The whole inside of the cave is a sort of giant wooden box without a top. They obviously worked a long time on it.'

'What about the weapons?'

'A veritable arsenal. About thirty machine guns and sub-machine guns, a hundred or so pistols and revolvers, two bazookas, thousands of ammunition rounds, cases of every kind of explosive, from TNT to Semtex. And a large quantity of police and carabinieri uniforms, bullet-proof vests, and various other things. All in perfect order, with each item wrapped in cellophane.'

'We've really dealt them a serious blow, eh?'

'Absolutely. Tano avenged himself well, just enough to avoid looking like a traitor or repenter. I want you to know that I didn't sequester the weapons; I left them in the cave. I've arranged for my men to stand guard, in two shifts, round the clock. They're in an uninhabited cottage a few hundred yards away from the arms depot.'

'You're hoping someone will come for supplies?'

'That's the idea.'

'Good, I agree with that. We'll wait a week, keep everything under close watch, and if nothing happens, we'll go ahead with the seizure. Ah, Montalbano, do you remember my dinner invitation for the day after tomorrow?'

'How could I forget?'

'I'm afraid we'll have to postpone it a few days. My wife has the flu . . .'

*

There was no need to wait a week. The third day after they had discovered the weapons, Catarella, having completed his midnight-to-midday shift on guard, went to report to Montalbano, asleep on his feet. The inspector had asked them all to do the same as soon as they went off duty.

'Any news?'

'Nothing, Chief. All peacefulness and quietude.'

'Good. Actually, bad. Go get some sleep.'

'Uh, wait. Now that I put my head to it, there was something, nothing, really, I just thought I'd tell you more out of consciousness than duty, but it's nothing.'

'What kind of nothing?'

'A tourist came by.'

'Explain a little better, Cat.'

'It looked to be around twenty-one hundred hours in the morning.'

'If it was morning, it was nine, Cat.'

'Whatever you say. Then right then and there I heard the roar of a motorcycle. So I grabbed the binoculars around my neck and precautiously looked out the window for confirmation. The motorcycle was red.'

'The colour is of no importance. Then what?'

'Then a tourist of the male sex descended from off said motorcycle.'

'What made you think he was a tourist?'

'He was wearing a camera around his neck, a really big camera, so big it looked like a cannon.'

'Must have been a telephoto lens.'

'Yessir, that it was. Then he started taking telephotos.'

'Of what?'

'Everything, Chief, everything. The countryside, the Crasticeddru, even the location I was located in.'

'Did he get close to the Crasticeddru?'

'Never, sir. But when he climbed back on his motorcycle to leave, he waved at me with his hands.'

'He saw you?'

'No. I stayed inside the whole time. But as I was saying, once he started up, he waved goodbye to the little house.'

*

'Commissioner? I've got some news, and it's not good. Looks like they somehow got wind of our discovery and sent somebody on reconnaissance to confirm.'

'And how do you know this?'

'This morning the man on duty in the cottage saw some guy arrive on a motorcycle and take photographs of the whole area with a powerful telephoto. They must have set up a very specific marker around the boulder blocking the entrance, like, say, a stick pointing in a certain direction, a rock placed a certain distance away . . . It simply would not have been possible for us to put everything back exactly the way it was.'

'Excuse me, but had you given precise instructions to the officer on duty?'

'Of course. The man on duty should have stopped the motorcyclist, identified him, confiscated the camera, and brought him to the station . . .'

'So why didn't he?'

'For one very simple reason: the officer was Catarella, whom we both know well.'

'Ah,' was the commissioner's laconic reply.

'What do we do now?'

'We'll go ahead and sequester the arms immediately, today. Palermo has ordered me to give it maximum coverage.'

Montalbano felt his armpits getting soaked in sweat.

'Another press conference?'

'I'm afraid so. Sorry.'

*

As he was about to leave for the Crasticeddru with two cars and a van, Montalbano noticed Galluzzo imploring him with his eyes, like a battered dog. He called him aside.

'What's the problem?'

'Think I could invite my brother-in-law, the newsman?'

'No,' Montalbano said at once, but he immediately reconsidered. Another idea had come into his mind, and he felt very pleased with himself for having thought of it. 'Listen,' he said, 'okay, as a favour to you. Give him a call and tell him to come.'

The idea was that if Galluzzo's brother-in-law was there on the spot and gave the discovery sufficient publicity, the need for the press conference might just go up in smoke.

*

Montalbano not only allowed Galluzzo's brother-in-law and his TeleVigàta cameraman a free hand, he actually helped them stage their scoop by acting as director. He had his men assemble a bazooka, which Fazio then mounted on his shoulder as if to fire, then had the cave brightly illuminated so that every cartridge clip, every magazine, could be filmed or photographed.

After two hours of serious work, the cave was completely emptied of its cargo. The news reporter and his cameraman raced off to Montelusa to edit their feature, and Montalbano called the commissioner on a cellphone.

'It's all loaded up.'

'Good. Send it here to me, in Montelusa. And one more thing: leave a man on duty. Jacomuzzi will soon be there with the crime lab team. Congratulations.'

*

It was Jacomuzzi, in the end, who took care of setting the idea of the press conference definitively to rest. Wholly involuntarily, of course, since Jacomuzzi was blissfully in his element at press conferences and interviews. In fact, before coming to the cave to gather evidence, the crime lab chief had taken the trouble to alert some twenty journalists from the press and television. Thus, while the report put together by Galluzzo's brother-in-law quickly reverberated in the local news, the commotion unleashed by the stories on Jacomuzzi and his men had national resonance. The commissioner – as Montalbano had correctly foreseen – decided to call off the press conference, since everyone already knew everything, and settled for issuing a detailed press release instead.

At home in his underpants, and with a large bottle of beer in his hand, Montalbano relished the sight of Jacomuzzi's face on TV, the whole time in close-up, as the head of the crime lab explained how his men were dismantling the wooden construction inside the cave, piece by piece, searching for the slightest clue, any hint of a fingerprint, any trace of a footprint. When the cave was stripped bare, restored to its primordial state, the Free Channel cameraman did a long, slow pan of the whole interior. And in the course of this shot, the inspector saw something that didn't look right to him. It was just an impression, nothing more. But he might as well check it out. He phoned the Free Channel and asked for Nicolò Zito, the Communist journalist and his friend.

'No problem, I'll have it sent over to you.'

'But I haven't got one of those thingamajigs, whatever the hell they're called.'

'Then come and watch it here.'

'Would tomorrow morning around eleven be all right?'

'That's fine. I won't be here, but I'll leave word.'

*

At nine o'clock the next morning, Montalbano went to Montelusa, to the headquarters of the party that Cavaliere Misuraca had served. The plaque next to the main door indicated that the offices were on the fifth floor. But the treacherous sign did not specify that the only way to get there was on foot, since the building was not equipped with a lift. After climbing at least ten flights of stairs, and a little out of breath, Montalbano knocked and knocked on a door that remained stubbornly closed. He went back down the stairs and out into the street. Right next door was a greengrocer; inside, an elderly man was serving a customer. The inspector waited until the greengrocer was alone.

'Did you know Cavaliere Misuraca?'

'And who, may I ask, gives a fuck who I know and who I don't?'

'I give a fuck. I'm with the police.'

'All right. And I'm Lenin.'

'Are you trying to be funny?'

'Not at all. That's really my name. My father named me Lenin and I'm proud of it. But maybe you're of the same stripe as the people next door?'

'No, I'm not. Anyway, I'm only here on a case. So I'll repeat my question: did you know Cavaliere Misuraca?'

'I certainly did. He spent his whole life going in and out of that door and busting my balls with his rattletrap Fiat 500.'

'Did the car bother you?'

'Did it bother me? He always parked it in front of my store! Even on the day he smashed into that truck!'

'He parked it right here?'

'Do I speak Turkish or something? Right here, he parked it. And I asked him to move it, but he went nuts and started yelling and said he didn't have any time to waste on me. So I got really mad and gave him hell. Anyway, to make a long story short, we were about to go at it when luckily some kid passed by and told the late cavaliere he'd be happy to move the car for him. So Misuraca gave him the keys.'

'Do you know where he parked it?'

'No sir.'

'You think you could recognize this kid? Had you ever seen him before?'

'I seen him sometimes going in next door. Must be a member of their fancy club.'

'The party chief's name is Biraghìn, isn't it?'

'Something like that. He's from around Venice somewhere. Works at the Public Housing Office; he's probably there now. This place here won't re-open till after six; right now it's too early.'

*

'Mr Biraghìn?' he shouted into the public phone. 'This is Inspector Montalbano of Vigàta Police. Sorry to disturb you at work.'

'Not at all. What can I do for you?'

'I need you to remember something for me. The last party meeting attended by Cavaliere Misuraca, what kind of meeting was it?'

'I don't understand the question.'

'No need to get touchy, sir, this is just a routine investigation to clarify the circumstances of the cavaliere's death.'

'Why, was there something unclear about it?'

A real pain in the arse, this Ferdinando Biraghìn.

'It's all clear as day, I assure you.'

'So what's the problem?'

'I have to close the file, understand? I can't leave a dossier incomplete.'

Upon hearing the words 'file' and 'dossier', Biraghìn, a bureaucrat from the Public Housing Office, changed his tune at once.

'Yes, of course, I know how it is. Well, it was a meeting of the local party leadership, which the cavaliere was not entitled to attend. But we stretched the rules a little.'

'So it was a rather small meeting.'

'About ten people.'

'Did anyone come looking for the cavaliere?'

'No. We'd locked the door. I would remember something like that. Actually, he did get a phone call.'

'Pardon my asking, but I assume you're unfamiliar with the tenor of that conversation?'

'I'm not only familiar with the tenor, I also know the bass, the baritone and the soprano!' He laughed.

Such a wit, this Ferdinando Biraghìn.

'You know how the cavaliere spoke, of course,' Biraghìn continued. 'As if everyone else were deaf. It was hard not to overhear when he was talking. Just imagine, on one occasion—'

'I'm sorry, sir, I haven't got much time. So you were able to grasp the—' he stopped, discarding the word 'tenor' to spare himself another dose of Biraghìn's tragic sense of humour – 'the gist of that phone call?'

'Of course. Somebody had done the cavaliere the favour of moving his car. And by way of thanks, the cavaliere only scolded him for parking it too far away.'

'Were you able to tell who it was that called?'

'No. Why do you ask?'

'Because,' said Montalbano. And he hung up.

So the kid, having completed his deadly little service in the shelter of some complicitous garage, had also decided, just for fun, to make the cavaliere get a little exercise.

*

At the Free Channel studios, Montalbano explained to a polite young woman that he was utterly hopeless when it came to anything electronic. Turning on a television, yes, flipping the channels, turning it off, no problem. As for the rest, utter darkness. With patience and grace, the girl put in the cassette, then started to rewind it, stopping the image every time Montalbano asked. By the time he left the Free Channel offices, the inspector was convinced he'd seen exactly what had aroused his interest. But what had aroused his interest seemed not to make any sense.

TEN

He stood outside the Trattoria San Calogero, undecided. It was indeed time to eat, and his stomach certainly felt empty; and yet an idea that had come to him while watching the videotape and which demanded to be verified was pushing him to continue on to the Crasticeddru. The scent of fried mullet coming from the restaurant won the duel. He ate a special appetizer of shellfish, then had them bring him two sea perches so fresh they seemed to be still swimming in the sea.

'You're eating without conviction, Inspector.'

'It's true. The fact is, I've got something on my mind.'

'The mind should be forgotten when the Lord in His grace puts such perches in front of you,' Calogero said solemnly, walking away.

*

He passed by the office to see if there was any news.

'Jacomuzzi called several times for you,' Germanà informed him.

'If he calls again, tell him I'll get back to him later. Do we have a very powerful flashlight?'

After turning off the main road and stopping near the Crasticeddru, he abandoned the car and decided to proceed on foot. It was a beautiful day, with a light breath of wind that cooled the air and lifted Montalbano's spirits. The ground around the rocky spur was marked by tyre tracks apparently left by people who had come up there out of curiosity. The boulder that served as the door had been pulled open several yards, the cave entrance now entirely exposed. As he was about to enter, he stopped, pricking up his ears. From inside came a low murmur occasionally interrupted by some stifled moans. He became alarmed: want to bet they're torturing someone in there? There wasn't time to run back to the car to get his pistol. He bounded inside, simultaneously turning on the powerful flashlight.

'Everybody freeze! Police!'

The two people inside the cave froze, but the greatest chill was felt by Montalbano himself. They were a very young couple, completely nude, making love: she with her hands braced against the wall, arms extended, he glued to her from behind. In the glare of the flashlight they looked like statues, beautiful. The inspector felt his face burning with shame. Turning off the flashlight, he started to withdraw, awkwardly muttering:

'I'm sorry . . . It was a mistake . . . Don't let me bother you.'

They came out less than a minute later. (It doesn't take long to put one's jeans and T-shirt back on.) Montalbano was truly sorry for having interrupted them. In their way, the two youngsters had been reconsecrating the cave, now that it was no longer a depository of death. The boy passed in front of him, head bowed and hands in his pockets; the girl instead glanced at him a moment, smiling faintly, an amused glint in her eye.

A simple, superficial reconnaissance of the site was all the inspector needed to confirm that what he had noticed in the videotape corresponded to what he was seeing in reality: that while the sides of the cave were relatively smooth and solid, the lower part of the rear wall, that is, the surface opposite the entrance, was quite uneven in texture, with protuberances and recesses, and might at first glance appear sloppily chiselled. But there was nothing chiselled about it. In fact, it consisted of stones stacked one atop and beside the other. Time had since taken care of binding and cementing them, camouflaging them with dust, earth, seeping water and saltpetre, finally transforming the rough surface into an almost natural wall.

He continued looking very closely, exploring inch by inch, and in the end he no longer had any doubt: at the back of the cave, there must be an opening at least three feet square that had been covered over quite a few years ago.

*

'Jacomuzzi? Montalbano here. I absolutely need you to—'

'Do you mind telling me where you've been hiding your arse? I spent the whole morning looking for you!'

'Well, I'm here now.'

'I found a piece of cardboard, from a parcel or, rather, from a large box, the kind used for shipping.'

'You tell a secret, I tell a secret: I once found a red button.'

'What an arsehole you are! I'm not going to say any more.'

'Oh, come on, honeybuns, don't be offended.'

'On this piece of cardboard are some printed letters. I found it under the wooden underframe of the cave; it must have slipped through one of the interstices between the planks.'

'What was that word you said?'

'Underframe?'

'No, after that.'

'Interstices?'

'Yes. My, my, aren't we educated? And so well spoken! Did you find anything else under this whatever-it-was you called it?'

'Yes. Rusted nails, a button, in fact – but this one was black – a pencil stub and some scraps of paper, but the dampness had turned them all to mush. That piece of cardboard is still in good condition because it had apparently been there only a few days.'

'Send it down to me. Listen, have you got an echo sounder and anyone who might know how to use it?'

'Yes. We used it at Misilmesi just last week to look for three dead bodies, which we eventually found.'

'Could you have it here to me in Vigàta by five o'clock?'

'Are you insane? It's four-thirty! Let's say in two hours. I'll bring it myself, along with the cardboard. But what do you need it for?'

'To sound your little behind.'

*

'Headmaster Burgio is here for you. Says if you'll see him, he has something to tell you. It won't take more than five minutes.'

'Show him in.'

Headmaster Burgio had already been retired for ten years or so, but everyone still called him by that title because he'd been headmaster of the Vigàta Business School. He and Montalbano were well acquainted. The headmaster was a very cultured, energetic man, with a keen interest in life despite his age, and he sometimes accompanied the inspector on his restful walks along the jetty. The inspector stood up to greet him.

'How nice to see you! Please sit down.'

'Since I was in the neighbourhood, I thought I'd ask if I could talk to you. If I hadn't found you in the office, I would have phoned.'

'What can I do for you?'

'I wanted to let you know a few things about the cave where you found those weapons. I'm not sure it'll be of any interest, but—'

'Are you kidding? Tell me everything you know.'

'Well, let me state first that what I'm about to say is

based on what I've heard on the local TV and read in the newspapers. It's possible they got a few things wrong. In any case, somebody said that the boulder covering the cave entrance had been made into a door by mafiosi or by whoever was trafficking in weapons. It's not true. This work of . . . let's call it adjustment, was done by the grandfather of a very dear friend of mine, Lillo Rizzitano.'

'How long ago? Do you know?'

'Of course I know. It was in about 1941, when oil, flour and wheat were growing scarce because of the war. At that time, all the land around the Crasto and the Crasticeddru belonged to Giacomo Rizzitano, Lillo's grandfather, who had made a lot of money in America by less than legitimate means, or at least that's what people in town said. Anyway, it was Giacomo Rizzitano's idea to seal off the cave by turning that boulder into a door. Inside it they kept all sorts of good things, selling them on the black market with the help of his son Pietro, Lillo's father. They were unscrupulous men, who'd been implicated in other affairs which decent people at the time never talked about, including, apparently, some acts of violence. Lillo, on the other hand, had turned out differently. He was sort of literary, he wrote nice poems and read a lot. It was he who first introduced me to Pavese's *Paesi tuoi*, Vittorini's *Conversazione in Sicilia*, and so on. I used to go to visit him, usually when his parents weren't there, in a small house right at the foot of the Crasto, on the seaward side.'

'Was it demolished to build the tunnel?'

'Yes. Or, more precisely, the earthmovers working on the tunnel merely got rid of the ruins and foundations, since the house was literally pulverized during the bombings that preceded the Allied landing in 1943.'

'Think you could track down this Lillo friend of yours?'

'I don't even know whether he's dead or alive, or where he's lived since then. I say this because you should bear in mind that Lillo was, or is, four years older than me.'

'Tell me, Mr Burgio, have you ever been inside that cave?'

'No. I once asked Lillo, but he said no. He had strict orders from his father and grandfather. He was very afraid of them; the fact that he'd even told me the secret of the cave was already a lot.'

*

Officer Balassone, despite his Piedmontese name, spoke Milanese dialect and always wore a haggard face worthy of the Day of the Dead.

'*L'è el dì di mort, alegher!*' Montalbano thought upon seeing him, reminded of the title of a poem by Delio Tessa.

After half an hour of fussing about with his instrument at the back of the cave, Balassone removed his headset and gave the inspector an even more disconsolate look than usual, if that was possible.

I was wrong, thought Montalbano, *and now I'm going to look like a stupid shit in Jacomuzzi's eyes.*

Jacomuzzi, for his part, after ten minutes inside the

cave, had made it known he suffered from claustrophobia and gone outside.

Maybe because now there aren't any TV cameras pointed at you? Montalbano thought maliciously.

'So?' the inspector finally asked Balassone, to confirm his failure.

'It's there, behind the wall,' Balassone said mysteriously. He was not only a melancholic, but also a man of few words.

'Would you please tell me – if it's not asking too much – exactly *what* is there behind the wall?' asked Montalbano, who was becoming dangerously polite.

'*On sit voeuij.*'

'Would you please have the courtesy to speak Italian?'

The appearance and tone seemed those of an eighteenth-century gentleman of the court. Baldassone had no idea that, if he went on at this rate, he was in line to have his nose rearranged. Luckily for him, he obeyed.

'There's a hollow,' he said, 'and it's as big as this cave here.'

The inspector took comfort. He'd seen right. At that moment Jacomuzzi came in.

'Find anything?'

With his immediate superior, Baldassone's tongue suddenly loosened. Montalbano gave him a dirty look.

'Yessir,' said the Piedmontese. 'There apparently is another cave behind this one. It's like something I saw once on television. There was this Eskimo's house – what do you call them? – oh, yes, this igloo, and right next to it was another igloo. And the two igloos were connected by a kind of passageway, a short, low corridor. It's the same here.'

'At a rough glance,' said Jacomuzzi, 'I'd say the passage between the two caves must date from a good number of years ago.'

'Yessir,' said Baldassone, looking more and more weary. 'If any weapons were hidden in the other cave, they'd have to go back as least as far as the Second World War.'

*

The first thing Montalbano noticed about the piece of cardboard, which the crime lab had dutifully inserted in a little transparent plastic bag, was that it had the same shape as Sicily. In the middle of it were some letters printed in black: ATO-CAT.

'Fazio!'

'At your service!'

'Get Vinti's to lend you the Jeep and shovels and pick axes again. We're going back to the Crasticeddru tomorrow, you, me, Germanà and Galluzzo.'

'This is becoming a bad habit!' Fazio cried out.

*

Montalbano felt tired. In the fridge he found some boiled squid and a slice of nicely aged caciocavallo cheese. He set himself up on the veranda. When he had finished eating, he went to look in the freezer, and there he found a tub of lemon ice, which the housekeeper made regularly for him by following a one-two-four formula: one glass of lemon juice, two of sugar, and four of water. A finger-licking delight. Then he decided to stretch out on the bed and finish the novel by Montalbán. He was unable to read even a chapter. Despite his interest, sleep got the better of him. He woke up with a start less than two hours later. He looked at his watch: barely eleven o'clock. As he was putting the watch back on the bedside table, his eye fell on the piece of cardboard, which he'd brought with him. He picked it up and went into the bathroom. Sitting on the toilet in the cold fluorescent light, he studied it closely. Suddenly an idea flashed in his brain. For a moment it seemed as if the bathroom light were growing steadily in intensity, until it exploded in a luminescent burst. He started laughing.

Is it possible ideas only come to me when I'm on the loo?

He studied the piece of cardboard again and again.

I'll try again tomorrow morning, with a cooler head.

But it was not to be. After fifteen minutes of tossing and turning in bed, he got up, grabbed the phonebook, and looked up the number of Captain Aliotta of the Customs Police in Montelusa, who was a friend of his.

'Sorry to call so late, but I urgently need some information. Have you ever done any inspections at the supermarket of a certain Carmelo Ingrassia in Vigàta?'

'The name doesn't ring a bell. And if I can't remember, it probably means that there was an inspection, but it turned up nothing irregular.'

'Thanks.'

'Wait. The person responsible for these kinds of procedures is Sergeant Laganà. If you want, I'll have him phone you at home. You're at home, right?'

'Yes.'

'Give me ten minutes.'

He had enough time to go into the kitchen and drink a glass of cold water before the telephone rang.

'Laganà speaking. The captain filled me in. The last inspection check at that supermarket was two months ago. Everything was in order.'

'Was it done at your own instigation?'

'Just a routine check. Nothing out of order. In fact, it's not that often we come across a store owner with his papers in such good order. If somebody wanted to screw him, they'd have nothing to grab on to.'

'And you checked everything? Accounts, invoices, receipts?'

'Excuse me, Inspector, but how do you think we do our checks?' asked the sergeant, starting to sound a little testy.

'For heaven's sake, Sergeant, I didn't mean to cast any doubt . . . That wasn't the reason for my question. You see, I'm unfamiliar with certain procedures, and that's why I'm asking for your help. How do these supermarkets get their stocks?'

'From wholesalers. They might use five or ten different ones, depending on what they need.'

'I see. Would you be able to tell me who the suppliers of the Ingrassia supermarket are?'

'I think so. I should have some notes around here somewhere.'

'I really appreciate this. I'll call you tomorrow at the barracks.'

'But I'm at the barracks right now! Stay on the line.'

Montalbano heard some whistling.

'Hello, Inspector? Here we are. The wholesalers that stock Ingrassia . . . there's three from Milan, one from Bergamo, one in Taranto, one in Catania. Take this down. In Milan—'

'Wait. Excuse me for interrupting. Start with Catania.'

'The corporate name of the Catanian company is "Pan", you know, like "frying pan". Owned by Salvatore Nicosia, who resides at—'

It didn't add up.

'Thanks, that's enough.'

'Wait, here's something else I'd forgotten about. The supermarket is also supplied by another wholesaler, also in Catania, for its household goods. That one's called Brancato.'

ATO-CAT, the piece of cardboard said. Brancato-Catania: it added up, and how! Montalbano's cry of joy thundered in the sergeant's earpiece, frightening him.

'Inspector? Inspector! Oh, my God, what happened? Are you all right, Inspector?'

ELEVEN

Fresh and smiling, in jacket and tie and enveloped in a haze of cologne, Montalbano showed up at the home of Francesco Lacommare, manager of the Ingrassia supermarket, at seven o'clock in the morning. The manager greeted him not only with legitimate astonishment, but also in his underwear, with a glass of milk in his hand.

'What is it?' he asked, turning pale upon recognizing the inspector.

'Two simple little questions and I'll get out of your hair. But, first, one very serious stipulation: this meeting must remain between you and me. If you speak to anyone at all about it, even your boss, I'll find an excuse to throw your arse in jail, and you can bank on that.'

As Lacommare was struggling to recover his breath, a shrill, annoying female voice exploded inside the apartment:

'Ciccino! Who's that at this hour?'

'It's nothing, Carmelina, go back to sleep,' Lacommare reassured her, pulling the door shut behind him.

'Do you mind, Inspector, if we talk over here on the

landing? The top floor, the one right above us, is vacant, so there's no danger anyone will bother us.'

'Who do you buy from in Catania?'

'From Pan and Brancato.'

'Do they have fixed delivery schedules?'

'Once a week for Pan, once a month for Brancato. We've coordinated it with the other supermarkets that use the same wholesalers.'

'Very good. So, as I understand it, Brancato will load up a truck with merchandise and send it out to make the rounds of the supermarkets. Now, where on these rounds is your store situated? Let me explain better—'

'I understand, Inspector. The truck leaves Catania, services the Caltanissetta area first, then Trapani, then Montelusa. The Vigàta markets are the last ones the truck visits before heading back to Catania.'

'One last question. The merchandise those thieves took and then left behind—'

'You're very intelligent, Inspector.'

'You are, too, if you can answer me before I've asked you a question.'

'The fact is, this whole story's been keeping me up at night. Here's the problem: the Brancato merchandise was delivered early. We were expecting it first thing the next morning, but it arrived the evening before, just as we were closing. The driver told us one of his supermarkets in Trapani had been suddenly closed for mourning, so he was ahead of schedule. Mr Ingrassia, to free up the truck, had it unloaded, checked the list, and counted the crates. But he didn't have anyone open them up. Said it was too late. He didn't want to pay anybody overtime and said we could do everything the next day. A few hours later, the store was robbed. So, my question is: who told the robbers the merchandise had arrived early?'

Lacommare was putting some passion into his reasoning. Montalbano decided to play devil's advocate. After all, the manager must not be allowed to get too close to the truth; that might cause trouble. Most of all, it was obvious he was unaware of Ingrassia's trafficking.

'The two things aren't necessarily connected,' the inspector said. 'The thieves could have come to rob what you already had in storage and ended up finding the freshly delivered merchandise instead.'

'Yes, but then why leave it all behind?'

That was indeed the question. Montalbano was hesitant to give an answer that might satisfy Lacommare's curiosity.

'But who the fuck is that anyway?' asked the now enraged female voice from within.

She must have been a woman of delicate sentiment, this Signora Lacommare. Montalbano took advantage of the interruption to leave. He'd found out what he wanted to know.

'My respects to your lovely wife,' he said, starting back down the stairs.

When he reached the front door, however, he sprang back upstairs like a tethered ball and rang the doorbell.

'You again?' Lacommare had drunk his milk but was still in his underwear.

'I'm sorry, I forgot something. Are you sure the truck was completely empty after you unloaded it?'

'No, I didn't say that. There were still about fifteen large crates. The driver said they belonged to that supermarket in Trapani that he'd found closed.'

'But what is all this fucking commotion so early in the morning?' Signora Carmelina shrieked from within, and Montalbano fled without even saying goodbye.

*

'I think I've determined, with reasonable accuracy, the route the weapons travelled before reaching the cave. Bear with me, Mr Commissioner. Here goes: in some way that we have yet to discover, the weapons come to the Brancato firm in Catania from some other part of the world. Brancato warehouses them and puts them in big boxes with the company name on them, so they look like they contain normal electrical appliances to be sold in supermarkets. When they receive the order to deliver, the Brancato people load the boxes with the weapons onto the truck, along with the rest. As a precaution, along some stretch of road between Catania and Caltanissetta, they replace the company truck with a stolen one. That way, if anybody finds the weapons, Brancato's can claim they had nothing to do with it, they know nothing about it, the truck isn't theirs, and, in fact, they themselves were robbed. The stolen truck begins its circuit, dropping off the . . . uh . . . "clean" crates at the various supermarkets it supplies, then heads off to Vigàta. Before arriving, however, it stops in the middle of the night at the Crasticeddru and unloads the weapons in the cave. Early that morning – according to Lacommare, the store manager – they deliver their final packages to the Ingrassia supermarket and then leave. On the way back to Catania, the stolen truck is then replaced by the company's actual truck, which returns home as if it has made its full journey. Maybe they take care to tinker with the odometer each time. And they've been playing this little game for at least three years, since Jacomuzzi said that the outfitting of the cave in fact goes back three years.'

'Your explanation makes excellent logical sense,' said the commissioner. 'But I still don't understand the whole charade of the phony robbery.'

'They acted out of necessity. Do you remember that gunfight between a patrol of carabinieri and three thugs in the Santa Lucia countryside, where one carabiniere was wounded?'

'Yes, I do remember it, but what's that got to do with this?'

'The local radio stations broadcast the news around nine p.m., right when the truck was on its way to the Crasticeddru. Santa Lucia is only about a mile and a half away from the cave. The traffickers must have heard the news on the radio. It would have been stupid to let themselves be spotted in a deserted place by some patrol – of which there were many that night, racing to the site of the shoot-out. So they decided to push on to Vigàta. They were certain to run into a roadblock, but that was the lesser evil at this point, since they stood a good chance of slipping through. And that's what happened. So, they arrive well ahead of schedule and make up the story about the supermarket closed for mourning in Trapani. Ingrassia, who's been alerted of the hitch, has his employees unload the truck, which then pretends to head back to Catania. It's still carrying the weapons, those same crates which they told Lacommare, the manager, were supposed to have gone to the supermarket in Trapani. The truck is then hidden somewhere around Vigàta, on Ingrassia's or some accomplice's property.'

'I ask you again: why fake the heist? From where they'd hidden it, the truck could have easily gone back to the Crasticeddru without having to pass through Vigàta.'

'But it did have to pass through Vigàta. If they'd been stopped by the carabinieri, the Customs Police, or whomever, with those fifteen crates aboard, unaccompanied by any delivery note, they would have aroused suspicion. They'd have been forced to open one, and that would have been the end of that. They absolutely did have to take back the packages that Ingrassia had unloaded, and which he had every reason not to open.'

'I'm beginning to understand.'

'So, at a certain hour of the night, the truck returns to the supermarket. The night watchman is in no position to recognize either the delivery men or the truck because he wasn't yet on duty when they came the previous evening. They load the still-sealed packages, head off to the Crasticeddru, unload the weapons crates, turn back round, ditch the truck in the car park behind the filling station, and their work is done.'

'But can you tell me why they didn't simply get rid of the stolen merchandise and head back to Catania?'

'That's the stroke of genius. By leaving the truck behind with all the stolen merchandise inside, they throw us off their trail. We're automatically forced to assume some kind of flap – a threat, a warning for not paying one's protection dues. In short, they force us to investigate at a lower level, the kind of stuff that is unfortunately an everyday matter in this part of Italy. And Ingrassia plays his part very well, absurdly calling it all a practical joke.'

'A real stroke of genius,' said the commissioner.

'Yes, but if you look closely enough, you can always uncover a mistake. In our case, they didn't realize that a piece of cardboard had slipped under the planks that served as the cave's floor.'

'Right, right,' the commissioner said pensively. Then, as if to himself 'Who knows where the empty boxes ended up?' he queried.

Now and then the commissioner would pause in idiotic wonder over meaningless details.

'They probably loaded them into some car and burned them out in the country. Because some accomplices brought at least two cars to the Crasticeddru, perhaps to take the driver away after he'd ditched the truck behind the petrol station.'

'So without that piece of cardboard we would never have discovered anything,' the commissioner concluded.

'Well, not exactly,' said Montalbano. 'I was following another path that would eventually have led me to the same conclusions. They were forced, you see, to kill a poor old man.'

The commissioner gave a start, darkening.

'A murder? Why was I not informed of this?'

'Because it was made to look like an accident. I only ascertained a couple of nights ago that the brakes on his car had been tampered with.'

'Was it Jacomuzzi who told you?'

'For the love of God! Jacomuzzi, bless his soul, is certainly competent, but mixing him up in this would have been like issuing a press release.'

'One of these days I'm going to give that Jacomuzzi a good dressing down . . . I'm going to skin him alive,' said the commissioner, sighing. 'Now tell me the whole story, but slowly, and in chronological order.'

Montalbano told him about Misuraca and the letter the cavaliere had sent him.

'He was murdered needlessly,' he concluded. 'His killers didn't know he'd already written to me and told me everything.'

'Listen, explain to me what reason Ingrassia had for being near his supermarket while the phony robbery was taking place, if we're to believe Misuraca.'

'If there were any other snags – an untimely visit, for example – he could jump out and readily explain that everything was all right and they were sending the merchandise back because the people at Brancato's had got the order wrong.'

'And what about the night watchman in the freezer?'

'He was no longer a problem. They would have bumped him off.'

'How should we proceed?' the commissioner asked after a pause.

'Tano the Greek has given us a tremendous gift, even without naming any names,' Montalbano began, 'and we shouldn't waste it. If we go about this carefully, we could get our hands on a network the size of which we can't even imagine. But we've got to be cautious. If we immediately arrest Ingrassia or someone from the Brancato firm, we'll come up empty for all our effort. We need to aim for the bigger fish.'

'I agree,' said the commissioner. 'I'll call Catania and tell them to put a tail on—'

He broke off with a grimace, painfully remembering the mole who'd talked in Palermo and brought about Tano's death. There might well be another in Catania.

'Let's start at the bottom,' he decided. 'We'll put only Ingrassia under surveillance.'

'All right. I'll get the court order from the judge,' said the inspector.

As he was heading out the door, the commissioner called him back inside.

'By the way, my wife is feeling much better. How would Saturday evening do for you? We have a lot to discuss.'

*

He found Judge Lo Bianco in an unusually good mood, his eyes sparkling.

'You look well,' the inspector couldn't help saying.

'Yes, yes, I'm quite well, in fact.' He then looked around, assumed a conspiratorial air, leaned towards Montalbano, and said in a low voice: 'Did you know that Rinaldo had six fingers on his right hand?'

Montalbano faltered a moment, befuddled. Then he remembered that the judge had been working devotedly for years on a ponderous book entitled *The Life and Deeds of Rinaldo and Antonio Lo Bianco, Masters of Law at the University of Girgenti at the time of King Martin the Younger (1402–1409)*. Lo Bianco had got it into his head that the two ancient barristers were his ancestors.

'Oh, really?' Montalbano asked with jovial surprise. It was best to humour him.

'Yes, indeed. Six fingers, on his right hand.'

Jerking off must have been heaven, Montalbano was about to say sacrilegiously, but managed to restrain himself.

He told the judge everything about the weapons traffic and Misuraca's murder. He even detailed the strategy he wanted to follow and asked him for a court order to tap Ingrassia's phone lines.

Normally, Lo Bianco would have raised objections,

created obstacles, imagined problems. This time, delighted with his discovery of Rinaldo's six-fingered hand, he would have granted Montalbano an order to torture, impale, or burn someone at the stake.

*

He went home, put on his bathing suit, went for a long, long swim, came back inside, dried himself off, but did not get dressed again. There was nothing in the refrigerator, but in the oven sat, as on a throne, a casserole with four huge servings of *pasta 'ncasciata,* a dish worthy of Olympus. He ate two portions, put the casserole back in the oven, set his alarm clock, slept like a rock for one hour, got back up, took a shower, put his already dirty jeans and shirt back on, and went to the station.

Fazio, Germanà and Galluzzo were waiting for him in their work clothes. As soon as they saw him, they grabbed their shovels, pickaxes and mattocks and struck up the old day labourers' chorus, shaking their tools in the air, 'Give land to those who work! Give land to those who work!'

'Fucking idiots,' was Montalbano's only comment.

*

Prestìa, Galluzzo's newsman brother-in-law, was already there, at the entrance of the Crasticeddru cave, along with a camera man who had brought along two large battery-powered floodlights.

Montalbano gave Galluzzo a dirty look.

'Well,' the latter said, blushing, 'I just thought that since you allowed him last time—'

'All right, all right,' the inspector cut him off.

They entered the weapons cave, and when Montalbano gave the order, Fazio, Germanà and Galluzzo started working on removing the stones that had fused together over the years. They laboured for a good three hours, and even Prestìa, the cameraman, and the inspector joined in, periodically relieving the three men. In the end the wall came down. They could clearly see the little passageway, just as Balassone had said. The rest was lost in darkness.

'You go in first,' Montalbano said to Fazio.

The sergeant took a flashlight, started crawling on his belly, and disappeared. A few seconds later, they heard an astonished voice from the other side.

'Oh, my God! Inspector! You have to see this.'

'The rest of you come in when I call you,' said Montalbano to the others, looking especially at the newsman, who upon hearing Fazio had started forward and was about to throw himself to the ground and start crawling.

The little tunnel was roughly the same length as the inspector's body. An instant later he was on the other side, and he turned on his flashlight. The second cave was smaller than the first and immediately gave the impression of being perfectly dry. In the very middle was a rug still in good condition. In the far left corner of the rug, a bowl. To the right, in the symmetrically corresponding position, a jug. Forming the vertex of this upside-down triangle, at the near end of the rug, was a life-size shepherd dog, made of terracotta. And on the rug were two dead bodies, all shrivelled up as in a horror film, embracing.

Montalbano felt short of breath; he couldn't open his mouth. He remembered the two youngsters he had surprised in the act of making love in the other cave. The men took advantage of his silence and, unable to resist, came in one after the other. The cameraman turned on his floods and began frantically filming. Nobody spoke. The first to recover was Montalbano.

'Call the crime lab, the judge and Dr Pasquano,' he said.

He didn't even turn around towards Fazio to give the order. He just stood there, in a trance, staring at that scene, afraid that his slightest gesture might wake him from the dream he was living.

TWELVE

Rousing himself from the spell that had paralysed him, Montalbano started shouting to everyone to stand with their backs to the wall and not to move, not to tread on the floor of the cave, which was covered with a very fine, reddish sand. Where it had filtered in from was anyone's guess. Maybe it was on the walls. There was no trace of this sand whatsoever in the other cave; perhaps it had somehow halted the decomposition of the corpses. These were a man and a woman, their ages impossible to determine by sight. That they were of different sex the inspector could tell by the shapes of their bodies and not, of course, by any sexual attributes, which had been obliterated by natural process. The man was lying on his side, arm extended across the breast of the woman, who was supine. They were therefore embracing, and would remain in that embrace forever. In fact, what had once been the flesh of the man's arm had sort of stuck to and fused with the flesh of the woman's breast. No, they would be separated soon enough, by the hand of Dr Pasquano. Standing out under the wizened, shrivelled flesh was the white of their bones. The lovers had been dried out, reduced to pure form. They looked as if they were laughing, the lips pulled back, stretched about the mouth and showing the teeth. Next to the dead man's head was the bowl, with some round objects inside; next to the woman was the earthenware jug, the kind in which peasants used to carry cool water around with them as they worked. At the couple's feet, the terracotta dog. It was about three feet long, its colours, grey and white, still intact. The craftsman who made it had portrayed it with front legs extended, hind legs folded, mouth half-open with the pink tongue hanging out, eyes watchful. Lying down, in short, but on guard. The rug had a few holes through which one could see the sand of the cave floor, but these may well have been already there when the rug was put in the cave.

'Everybody out!' Montalbano ordered. Then, turning to Prestìa and the cameraman 'And turn off those lamps. Now.'

He had suddenly realized how much damage the heat of the floodlights and their own mere presence must be causing. He was left alone in the cave. By the beam of the flashlight, he carefully examined the contents of the bowl: those round objects were metal coins, oxydized and covered with verdigris. Gently, with two fingers, he picked one up, seemingly the best preserved: it was a twenty-centesimo piece, minted in 1941, with a portrait of King Victor Emmanuel on one side and a female profile with the Roman fasces on the other. When he aimed the light at the dead man's head, he noticed a hole in his temple. He was too well versed in such matters not to realize that it had been made by a firearm. The man had either committed suicide or been killed. But if it had been a suicide, where was the weapon? The woman's body, on the other hand, bore no trace of violent, induced death. Montalbano remained pensive. The two were naked, yet there was no clothing in the cave. What did it mean? Without growing first yellow and dim, the flashlight suddenly went out. The battery had died. He was momentarily blinded and couldn't get his bearings. To avoid damaging anything, he crouched down on the sand, waiting for his eyes to adjust to the dark; in a minute he would surely start to glimpse the faint glow of the passageway. Yet those few seconds of total darkness and silence were enough for him to notice an unusual odour that he was certain he had smelt before. He tried to remember where, even if it was of no importance. Ever since childhood he had always associated a colour with every smell that caught his attention; this smell, he decided, was dark green. From this association he was able to remember where he had first noticed it. It was in Cairo, inside the pyramid of Cheops, in a corridor off-limits to tourists which he had been able to visit courtesy of an Egyptian friend. And all at once he felt like a *quaquaraquà*, a worthless man, with no respect for anything. That morning, by surprising the two kids making love, he had desecrated life; and now, by exposing the two bodies that should have remained forever unknown to the world in their embrace, he had desecrated death.

*

Perhaps because of this feeling of guilt, Montalbano did not wish to take part in the evidence-gathering, which Jacomuzzi and his crime lab team, along with Dr Pasquano, began at once. He had already smoked five cigarettes, seated on the boulder that served as a door to the weapons cave, when he heard Pasquano call to him in an agitated, irritated voice.

'Where the hell is the judge?'

'You're asking me?'

'If he doesn't get here soon, things are going to turn nasty. I've got to get these corpses to Montelusa and put them in the fridge. They're practically decomposing before our eyes. What am I supposed to do?'

'Have a cigarette with me,' Montalbano said, trying to pacify him.

Judge Lo Bianco arrived fifteen minutes later, after the inspector had smoked another two cigarettes.

Lo Bianco glanced distractedly at the scene and, since the dead were not from the time of King Martin the Younger, said hastily to the coroner, 'Do whatever you want with them. It's ancient history, in any case.'

*

TeleVigàta had immediately discovered the proper angle from which to present the story. The first thing one saw on the evening news at 8.30 was Prestìa's excited face announcing an extraordinary scoop for which, he said, they were indebted to 'one of those ingenious intuitions that make Inspector Salvo Montalbano of Vigàta a figure perhaps unique among crime investigators across the island of Sicily and – why not? – in all of Italy.' He went on to recount the inspector's dramatic arrest of the fugitive Tano the Greek, the bloodthirsty Mafia boss, and his discovery of the weapons cache inside the Crasticeddru cave. Then they played some footage of the press conference held after Tano's arrest, in which an insane-looking, stammering man who answered to the name and title of Inspector Montalbano was having trouble putting together four consecutive words. Prestìa resumed his account of how this exceptional detective had become convinced that behind the cave of weapons there must be another cave connected to it.

'Trusting in the inspector's intuition,' said Prestìa, 'I followed him, assisted by my cameraman, Gerlando Schirirò.'

At this point Prestìa, adopting a tone of mystery, raised a few questions: what sort of secret, paranormal powers did the inspector possess? What was it made him think that an ancient tragedy lay hidden behind a few rocks blackened by time? Did the inspector have X-ray vision, like Superman?

Upon hearing this last question, Montalbano – who was watching the broadcast from his home and for the last half-hour had been unsuccessfully searching for a clean pair of underpants, which he knew must be around somewhere – told the newsman to go fuck himself.

As the chilling images of the bodies in the cave started rolling, Prestìa expounded his thesis with conviction. Since he didn't know about the hole in the man's head, he spoke of two people who had died for love. In his opinion, the lovers, their passion opposed by their families, had shut themselves up in the cave, sealing off the passageway and letting themselves starve to death. They had furnished their final refuge with an old rug and a jug full of water, and had waited for death in each other's arms. Of the bowl full of coins he said nothing: it would have clashed with the scene he was painting. The two – Prestìa went on – had not been identified; their story had taken place at least fifty years ago. Then another newscaster started talking about the day's events: a six-year-old girl raped and bludgeoned to death with a stone by a paternal uncle; a corpse discovered in a well; a shoot-out at Merfi resulting in three dead and four injured; a labourer killed in an industrial accident; the disappearance of a dentist; the suicide of a businessman who had been squeezed by loan sharks; the arrest of a town councillor in Montevergine for graft and corruption; the suicide of the provincial president, who had been indicted for receiving stolen goods; a dead body washed ashore . . .

Montalbano fell into a deep sleep in front of the television.

*

'Hello, Salvo? Gegè here. Let me talk, and don't interrupt with your usual bullshit. I need to see you. I need to tell you something.'

'Okay, Gegè. Even tonight's okay, if you want.'

'I'm not in Vigàta, I'm in Trapani.'

'So when?'

'What day is today?'

'Thursday.'

'How about Saturday midnight at the usual place?'

'Listen, Gegè, Saturday night I'm having dinner with someone, but I can come anyway. If I'm a little late, wait for me.'

*

The phone call from Gegè, who from his tone of voice sounded worried – enough not to tolerate any joking – had woken him up just in time. It was ten o'clock, and he tuned in to the Free Channel. Nicolò Zito, with his intelligent face, red hair, and red ideas, opened the news broadcast with the story of a labourer who died at his workplace in Fela, roasted alive in a gas explosion. He listed a series of examples to demonstrate how, in at least 90 per cent of the cases, management was blithely indifferent to safety standards. He then moved on to the arrest of some public officials charged with various forms of embezzlement and used this instance to remind viewers of how several different elected governments had tried in vain to pass laws that might prevent the clean-up operation currently under way.

His third item was the suicide of the businessman strangled by debts to a loan shark, and here he criticized the government's provisions against usury as utterly inadequate. Why, he asked, were those investigating this scourge so careful to keep loan-sharking and the Mafia separate? How many different ways were there to launder dirty money?

Finally, he came to the news of the two bodies found in the cave, but he approached it from a peculiar perspective, indirectly challenging the angle that Prestìa and TeleVigàta had taken on the story. Somebody, he said, once asserted that religion is the opium of the people; today, instead, one would have to say that the real opium is television. For example: why had certain people presented this case as a story of two lovers thwarted in their love? What facts authorized anyone to advance such a hypothesis? The two were found nude: what had happened to their clothes? No trace of any weapon was found in the cave. How would they have killed themselves? By starving to death? Come on! Why did the man have a bowl beside him containing coins no longer current today but still valid at the time of their deaths? To pay Charon's toll? The truth, claimed the newsman, is that they want to turn a probable crime into a certain suicide, a romantic suicide. And in our dark days, with so many threatening clouds on the horizon, he concluded, we puff up a story like this to drug people, to distract their attention from the serious problems and divert them with a Romeo and Juliet story, one scripted, however, by a soap-opera writer.

*

'Darling, it's Livia. I wanted to tell you I've booked our tickets. The flight leaves from Rome, so you'll have to buy a ticket from Palermo to Fiumicino; I'll do the same from Genoa. We'll meet at the airport and board together.'

'Mm-hmm.'

'I've also reserved our hotel. A friend of mine has stayed there and said it's really nice without being too fancy. I think you'll like it.'

'Mm-hmm.'

'We leave in two weeks and a day. I'm so happy. I'm counting the days and the hours.'

'Mm-hmm.'

'Salvo, what's wrong?'

'Nothing. Why should there be anything wrong?'

'You don't sound very enthusiastic.'

'Of course I am, what do you mean?'

'Look, Salvo, if you wiggle out of this at the last minute, I'll go anyway, by myself.'

'Come on.'

'But what's wrong with you?'

'Nothing. I was sleeping.'

*

'Inspector Montalbano? Good evening. This is Headmaster Burgio.'

'Good evening. What can I do for you?'

'I'm very sorry to disturb you at home. I just heard on television about the two bodies that were found.'

'Could you identify them?'

'No. I'm calling about something that was said in passing on TV, but which might be of interest to you. I'm talking about the terracotta dog. If you have no objection, I thought I'd come to your office tomorrow morning with Burruano, the accountant. Do you know him?'

'I know who he is. Ten o'clock all right?'

*

'Here,' said Livia. 'I want to do it here, right away.'

They were in a kind of park, dense with trees. Crawling about at their feet were hundreds of snails of every variety, garden snails, tree snails, escargots, slugs, periwinkles.

'Why right here? Let's get back in the car and in five minutes we'll be home. Around here, somebody might see us.'

'Don't argue, jerk!' Livia shot back, grabbing his belt and trying awkwardly to unbuckle it.

'I'll do it,' he said.

In an instant Livia was naked, while he was still struggling with his trousers, then his underpants.

She's accustomed to stripping in a hurry, he thought, in a surge of Sicilian jealousy.

As Livia threw herself down on the wet grass, legs spread, caressing her breasts with her hands, he heard, to his disgust, the sound of dozens of snails being crushed under the weight of her body.

'Come on, hurry up,' she said.

Montalbano finally managed to strip down naked, shuddering in the chill air. Meanwhile, a few snails had started slithering over Livia's body.

'And what do you expect to do with that?' she asked critically, eyeing his cock. With a look of compassion, she got up on her knees, took it in her hands, caressed it, and put her lips around it. When she felt he was ready, she resumed her prior position.

'Fuck me to kingdom come,' she said.

When did she become so vulgar? he wondered, bewildered.

As he was about to enter her, he saw the dog a few steps away, a white dog with its pink tongue sticking out, growling menacingly, teeth bared, a string of slobber dribbling from its mouth. When did it get there?

'What are you doing? Has it gone soft again?'

'There's a dog.'

'What the hell do you care? Give it to me.'

At that exact moment the dog sprang into the air and he froze, terrified. The dog landed a few inches from his head, turned stiff, its colour lightly fading, then lay down, its front legs extended, hind legs folded. It became fake, turned into terracotta. It was the dog in the cave, the one guarding the dead couple.

Then all at once the sky, trees, and grass disappeared, walls of rock formed around them and overhead, and in horror he realized that the dead couple in the cave were not two strangers, but Livia and himself.

He awoke from the nightmare breathless and sweating,

and immediately in his mind he begged Livia's forgiveness for having imagined her as so obscene in the dream. But what was the meaning of that dog? And those disgusting snails slithering all over the place?

That dog had to have a meaning, he was sure of it.

*

Before going to the office, he stopped at a kiosk and bought Sicily's two newspapers. Both of them prominently featured the story of the bodies found in the cave; as for the discovery of the weapons, they had prominently forgotten about that. The paper published in Palermo was certain that it had been a love suicide, whereas the one published in Catania was also open to the possibility of murder, while not, of course, discounting suicide, and indeed its headline read: DOUBLE SUICIDE OR DUAL HOMICIDE? – implying some vague, mysterious distinction between 'double' and 'dual'. On the other hand, no matter what the issue, this newspaper customarily never took a position. Whether the subject was a war or an earthquake, it always liked to play both sides of the fence, and for this had gained a reputation as an independent, freethinking daily. Neither of the two dwelt on the jug, the bowl, or the terracotta dog.

The instant Montalbano appeared in the doorway, Catarella asked him what he should say to the hundreds of journalists who were certain to phone, wanting to speak with the inspector.

'Tell them I've gone on a mission.'

'What, you've become a missionary?' quipped the policeman, lightning-quick, chuckling noisily to himself.

Montalbano concluded that he'd been right, the previous evening, to unplug the telephone before going to bed.

THIRTEEN

'Dr Pasquano? Montalbano here. Just wondering if there's any news.'

'Yes, there certainly is. My wife has a cold and my granddaughter lost a baby tooth.'

'Are you angry, Doctor?'

'I certainly am!'

'With whom?'

'You ask me if there's any news! Well, let me ask you how you can have the gall to ask me anything at nine o'clock in the morning! What do you think, that I've just spent the night opening up those two corpses' bellies like some kind of vulture? I happen to sleep at night! And, at the moment, I'm working on that guy who drowned around Torre Spaccata. Who didn't drown at all, since before being tossed into the sea he'd been stabbed three times in the chest.'

'Shall we make a bet, Doctor?'

'On what?'

'On whether or not you spent the night with those two corpses.'

'All right, all right. You win.'

'What did you find out?'

'Right now I can't tell you much; I still have to look at a few other things. One sure thing is that they were killed by gunshot wounds. He to the head, she to the heart. You couldn't see the woman's wound because his hand was covering it. A textbook execution, while they were sleeping.'

'Inside the cave?'

'I don't think so. They were probably already dead when they were brought there, then were rearranged, still naked and all.'

'Have you managed to establish their ages?'

'I wouldn't want to be wrong, but I'd say they were young, very young.'

'And when did the crime take place, in your opinion?'

'I could venture a guess, which you can take with a pinch of salt. About fifty years ago, more or less.'

*

'I'm not here for anyone. No phone calls for the next fifteen minutes,' Montalbano told Catarella. Then he locked the door to his office, returned to his desk, and sat down. Mimì Augello was also sitting there, but stiff as a poker, bolt upright.

'Who goes first?' asked Montalbano.

'I do,' said Augello, 'since it was I who asked to talk to you. Because I think it's time I said something.'

'Well, I'm here to listen.'

'Could you please tell me what I've done to you?'

'You? To me? Nothing at all. Why do you ask?'

'Because I feel like I've become a stranger in this place. You don't tell me what you're doing, you keep me at a distance, and I feel insulted. For example, was it right, in your opinion, to keep me in the dark about Tano the Greek? I'm not Jacomuzzi, who shouts these things from the rooftops. I can keep a secret. I didn't find out what happened at my own police station until I heard it at the press conference. Does that seem like the right way to treat someone who's your second-in-command until proved otherwise?'

'But do you realize how sensitive this matter was?'

'It's precisely because I realize it that I'm so pissed off. Because it must mean that for you, I'm not the right person for sensitive matters.'

'I've never thought that.'

'You've never thought it, but you've always done just that. Like with the weapons, which I found out about by accident.'

'Come on, Mimì, I was overwhelmed by the pressure and anxiety. It didn't occur to me to inform you.'

'That's bullshit, Salvo. That's not the real story.'

'Oh, yeah? What's the real story?'

'I'll tell you. You've created a police station in your own image and likeness. Fazio, Germanà, Galluzzo, take anyone you want, they're all just limbs that obey one single head: yours. They never contradict you, never ask questions: they just follow orders. There are two foreign bodies here: Catarella and me. Catarella, because he's too stupid, and me—'

'Because you're too intelligent.'

'See? That's not what I was going to say. You make me out to be arrogant, which I'm not, and you do it maliciously.'

Montalbano looked at him, stood up, put his hands in his pockets, circled round the chair in which Augello was sitting, then stopped.

'It wasn't malicious, Mimì. You really are intelligent.'

'If you seriously believe that, then why do you cut me out? I could be at least as useful to you as the others.'

'That's just it, Mimì. Not *as* useful, but more so. I'm speaking to you quite frankly, since you're making me think seriously about my attitude towards you. And maybe this is what bothers me most.'

'So, just to please you, I ought to dumb myself down a little?'

'Listen, if you want to have it out with me, let's go. That's not what I meant. The fact is that over the course of time, I've realized I'm sort of a solitary hunter – I'm sorry if that sounds idiotic, maybe it's not the right term. Because I do like to go hunting with others, but I want to be the only one to organize the hunt. That's the one necessary precondition for making my brain function properly. An intelligent observation made by someone else merely upsets me – it throws me off, sometimes for a whole day, and can even prevent me from following my own train of thought.'

'I get it,' said Augello. 'Actually, I got it some time ago, but I wanted to hear you say it yourself. So I'm telling you now, without any hostility or hard feelings: I'm going to write to the commissioner today and request a transfer.'

Montalbano looked him over, drew near, and leaned forward, putting his hands on Augello's shoulders.

'Will you believe me if I tell you that would hurt me very deeply?'

'So fucking what!' Mimì exploded. 'Do you expect everyone to give you everything? What kind of man are you? First you treat me like shit, then you try the affectionate approach? Do you realize how monstrously egotistical you are?'

'Yes, I do,' said Montalbano.

*

'Allow me to introduce Mr Burruano, the accountant who so kindly consented to come here with me today,' said Headmaster Burgio with stuffed-shirt ceremoniousness.

'Please sit down,' said Montalbano, gesturing towards two small, old armchairs in a corner of the room, which were reserved for distinguished guests. For himself he pulled up one of the two straight-back chairs in front of his desk, normally reserved for people who were decidedly undistinguished.

'These last few days I feel it's been up to me to correct

or at least clarify what gets said on television,' Burgio began.

'Then correct and clarify,' Montalbano said, smiling.

'Mr Burruano and I are almost the same age. He's four years older, but we remember the same things.'

Montalbano heard a note of pride in the headmaster's voice. There was good reason for it: the twitchy Burruano, who was a bit milky-eyed to boot, looked at least ten years older than his friend.

'You see, right after the TeleVigàta news, which showed the inside of the cave in which they found th—'

'Excuse me for interrupting, but the last time we spoke you mentioned the weapons cave, but said nothing about this other cave. Why?'

'Because I simply didn't know it existed. Lillo never said anything about it to me. Anyway, right after the news, I called Mr Burruano because I'd seen that statue of the dog before, and I wanted confirmation.'

The dog! That was why it appeared in his nightmare, because the headmaster had alluded to it on the phone. Montalbano felt overcome by a childish feeling of gratitude.

'Would you gentlemen like some coffee? Eh? A cup of coffee? They make it so well at the corner cafe.'

The two men shook their heads in unison.

'An orangeade? Coca-Cola? Beer?'

If they didn't stop him, he would soon be offering them ten thousand lire each.

'No, no, thank you, we can't drink anything. Old age, you know,' said Burgio.

'All right, then, tell me your story.'

'It's better if Mr Burruano tells it.'

'From February 1941 to July 1943,' the accountant began, 'though still very young, I was *podestà* of Vigàta. Either because Fascism claimed to like the young – in fact it liked them so much it ate them all, roasted or frozen, made no difference – or because the only people left in town were women, children and the elderly. Everybody else was at the front. I couldn't go because I was consumptive. I really was.'

'I was too young to be sent to the front,' Burgio interjected, to avoid any misunderstanding.

'Those were terrible times. The British and Americans were bombing us every day. In one thirty-six-hour period I counted ten bombing raids. Very few people were left in town, most had been evacuated, and we were living in the shelters that had been dug into the hill of marl above the city. Actually, they were tunnels with two exits, very safe. We even took our beds in there. Vigàta's grown a lot over the years. It's no longer the way it was back then, a handful of houses around the port and a strip of buildings between the foot of the mountain and the sea. Up on the hill, the Piano Lanterna, which today looks like New York with its highrises, had just four structures along a single road, which led to the cemetery and then disappeared into the countryside. The enemy aircraft had three targets: the power station, the port with its warships and merchant ships, and the anti-aircraft and naval batteries along the ridge of the hill. When it was the British overhead, things went better than with the Americans.'

Montalbano was impatient. He wanted the man to get to the point – the dog, that is – but didn't feel like interrupting his digressions.

'Went better in what sense, Mr Burruano? It was still bombs they were dropping.'

Lost within some memory, Burruano had fallen silent, and so Headmaster Burgio spoke for him.

'The British, how shall I say, played more fairly. When they dropped their bombs they tried to hit only military targets, whereas the Americans dropped them helter-skelter, come what may.'

'Towards the end of 1942,' Burruano resumed, 'the situation got even worse. We had nothing: no bread, no medicine, no water, no clothing. So for Christmas I decided to make a nativity scene that we could all pray to. We had nothing else left. I wanted it to be a very special nativity. That way, I thought, for a few days at least, I could take people's minds off their worries – there were so many – and distract them from the terror of the bombings. There wasn't a single family that didn't have at least one man fighting far from home, in the ice of Russia or the hell of Africa. We'd all become edgy, difficult, quarrelsome – the slightest thing would set people off; our nerves were frayed. Between the anti-aircraft machine guns, the exploding bombs, the roar of the low-flying planes, and the cannon-blasts from the ships at sea, we couldn't get a wink of sleep at night. And everyone would come to me or to the priest to ask one thing or another and I didn't know which way to turn. I didn't feel so young any more. I felt then the way I feel now.'

He stopped to catch his breath. Neither Montalbano nor Burgio felt like filling that pause.

'Anyway, to make a long story short, I mentioned my idea to Ballassaro Chiarenza, who was a real artist with terracotta. He did it for pleasure, since he was a carter by trade. It was his idea to make the statues all life-size. Baby Jesus, the Virgin Mary, Saint Joseph, the ox, the donkey, the shepherd with the lamb over his shoulders, a sheep, a dog and the other shepherd, the one who's always portrayed with his arms raised in a gesture of wonder. So he made the whole thing, and it came out really beautiful. We even decided not to put it in the church, but to set it up under the arch of a bombed-out house, so it would look like Jesus had been born amid the suffering of our people.'

He put a hand in his pocket and pulled out a photograph, which he passed to the inspector. The nativity really was beautiful; Mr Burruano was right. It seemed so ephemeral, so perishable, and at the same time conveyed a comforting warmth, a superhuman serenity.

'It's astonishing,' Montalbano complimented him, his emotions welling up. But only for an instant, as the cop in him got the upper hand and began carefully examining the dog. There was no doubt about it: that was the same dog he had found in the cave. Burruano put the photo back in his pocket.

'The nativity performed a miracle, you know. For a few days we were considerate towards one another.'

'What became of the statues?'

This was where Montalbano's real interest lay. The old man smiled.

'I sold them at auction, all of them. I made enough to pay Chiarenza, who wanted only to be reimbursed for his expenses, and to give alms to those who needed them most. And there were many.'

'Who bought the statues?'

'Well, that's the problem. I don't remember. I had the receipts and all, but they were lost when the town hall caught fire during the American invasion.'

'During the period you're talking about, had you heard any news about a young couple disappearing?'

Burruano smiled, but Headmaster Burgio actually laughed out loud.

'Was that a stupid question?'

'I'm sorry, Inspector, but it really was,' remarked the headmaster.

'You see, in 1939, the population of Vigàta was fourteen thousand,' Burruano explained. 'I know my numbers. By 1942, we were down to eight thousand. The people who could leave, did, finding temporary refuge in the inland towns, the tiny little villages of no importance to the Americans. Then, between May and July of 1943, our numbers dropped, give or take a few, to four thousand, without counting the Italian and German soldiers, and the sailors. Everyone else had scattered across the countryside, living in caves, in barns, in any hole they could find. How could we have known about one disappearance or another? Everybody disappeared!'

They laughed again. Montalbano thanked them for the information.

*

Good, at least he'd managed to find a few things out. The moment the headmaster and accountant left, the surge of gratitude the inspector had felt towards them turned into an uncontrollable attack of generosity which he knew he would sooner or later regret. He called Mimì Augello into his office, made a full apology for his misdeeds towards his friend and collaborator, put his arm around the young man's shoulders, walked around the room with him, expressed his 'unconditional faith' in him, spoke at great length of the investigation he was conducting in weapons trafficking, told him about the murder of Misuraca, and informed him he'd requested a court order to tap Ingrassia's telephone lines.

'So what do you want me to do?' asked Augello, overcome with enthusiasm.

'Nothing. You must only listen to me,' said Montalbano, suddenly himself again. 'Because if you do the slightest thing on your own initiative, I'll break your neck.'

*

The telephone rang. Picking up the receiver, Montalbano heard the voice of Catarella, who served as phone operator.

'Hullo, Chief? There's – what's he called? – Chief Jacomuzzi to talk to you.'

'Put him on the line.'

'Talk with the chief, Chief, over the phone,' he heard Catarella say.

'Montalbano? Since I was passing by here on the way back from the Crasticeddru—'

'But where are you?'

'What do you mean where am I? I'm in the room next to yours.'

Montalbano cursed the saints. Was it possible to be stupider than Catarella?

'Come on in.'

The door opened and Jacomuzzi entered, covered with red sand and dust, dishevelled and rumpled.

'Why would your officer only let me talk to you by phone?'

'Jacomù, what's more idiotic, Carnival or the people who celebrate it? Don't you know what Catarella's like? You should have just given him a kick in the pants and come in.'

'I've finished my examination of the cave. I had the sand sifted. Worse than the gold-seekers in American movies! We found absolutely nothing. And that can mean only one thing, since Pasquano told me they both had entrance and exit wounds.'

'That the two were shot somewhere else.'

'Right. If they'd been killed in the cave, we would have found the bullets. Oh, and another thing, rather odd. The sand inside the cave was mixed together with very tiny fragments of snail shells. There must have been thousands of the creatures in there.'

'Jesus!' Montalbano muttered. The dream, the nightmare, Livia's naked body with the slimy things crawling over her . . . What could it mean? He brought a hand to his forehead and found it drenched in sweat.

'Are you ill?' asked Jacomuzzi, concerned.

'It's nothing, a little dizziness. I'm tired, that's all.'

'Call Catarella and have him bring you a cordial from the cafe.'

'Catarella? Are you joking? Once, when I asked him to bring me an espresso, he brought me a postal envelope.'

Jacomuzzi put three coins on the desk.

'These were from the bowl. I sent the rest to the lab. They won't be of any use to you. You can keep 'em as souvenirs.'

FOURTEEN

With Adelina, it was possible for an entire season to go by without the two of them ever seeing each other. Every week Montalbano would leave shopping money for her on the kitchen table, and every thirty days her monthly wages. Between them, however, a tacit system of communication had developed: when Adelina needed more shopping money, she would leave the *caruso* – the little clay money box he had bought at a fair and kept because it looked nice – on the table for him to see; when new supplies of socks or underwear were needed, she would leave a pair on the bed. Naturally the system did not work in one direction only; Montalbano, too, would tell her things by the strangest means, which she, however, understood. For some time now, the inspector had noticed that, when he was tense, troubled, and nervous, Adelina would somehow know it from the way he left the house in the morning, and in these instances she would make special dishes for him to find on his return, to lift his spirits. That day, Adelina had been back in action: in the fridge Montalbano found a squid sauce, dense and black, just the way he liked it. Was there or wasn't there a hint of oregano? He inhaled the aroma deeply before putting it on the heat, but this investigation, too, came to nothing. Once he'd finished eating, he donned his bathing suit with the intention of taking a brief stroll on the beach. After walking only a little while, he felt tired, the balls of his feet sore.

> Sex standing up and walking on sand
> will bring any man to a bad end.

He'd once had sex standing up and afterward did not feel so destroyed as the proverb implied; whereas it was true that if you walked on sand, even the firm sand nearest the sea, you tired quickly. He glanced at his watch and was amazed: some little while! He'd been walking for two hours. He collapsed on the beach.

'Inspector! Inspector!'

The voice came from far away. He struggled to his feet and looked out at the sea, convinced that someone must be calling him from a boat or dinghy. But the sea was deserted all the way to the horizon.

'Inspector, over here! Inspector!'

He turned around. It was Tortorella, waving his arms from the highway that for a long stretch ran parallel to the beach.

*

As Montalbano quickly washed and dressed, Tortorella told him they'd received an anonymous telephone call at the station.

'Who took the call?' asked Montalbano.

If it was Catarella, who knows what harebrained idiocies he might have understood or reported?

'Don't worry,' said Tortorella smiling, having guessed what his chief was thinking. 'He'd gone out to the bathroom for a minute, and I was manning the switchboard for him. The voice had a Palermo accent, putting *i*'s in the place of *r*'s, but he might have been doing it on purpose. He said we would find some bastard's corpse at the Pasture, inside a green car.'

'Who went to check it out?'

'Fazio and Galluzzo did, and I raced over here to get you. I'm not sure that was the right thing; maybe the phone call was only a joke.'

'What a bunch of jokers we Sicilians are!'

*

Montalbano arrived at the Pasture at five o'clock, the hour of what Gegè called the 'changing of the guard', the time of day when the unpaid couples – that is, lovers, adulterers, boyfriends and girlfriends – got off (*in every sense,* thought Montalbano), giving way to Gegè's flock, bitchin' blondes from Eastern Europe, Bulgarian transvestites, ebony Nigerian nymphs, Brazilian *viados,* Moroccan queens, and so on in procession, a veritable UN of cock, arse and cunt. And there indeed was the green car, trunk open, surrounded by three carabinieri vehicles. Fazio's car was stopped a short distance away. Montalbano got out and Galluzzo came up to him.

'We got here late.'

They had an unwritten understanding with the National Police. Whoever arrived first at the scene of a crime would shout 'Bingo!' and take the case. This prevented meddling, polemics, elbowing and long faces. But Fazio was gloomy.

'They got here first.'

'So what? What do you care? We're not paid by the corpse, on a job-by-job basis.'

By a strange coincidence, the green car was right next to the same bush beside which an 'outstanding corpse' had been found a year earlier, a case in which Montalbano had become very involved. The lieutenant of the carabinieri, who was from Bergamo and went by the name of Donizetti, approached, and they shook hands.

'We were tipped off by a phone call,' said the lieutenant.

Someone had really wanted to make sure the body was found. The inspector studied the curled-up corpse in the trunk. The man appeared to have been shot only once, with the bullet entering his mouth, shattering his teeth and lips, and exiting through the back of the neck, opening a wound the size of a fist. Montalbano didn't recognize the face.

'I'm told you know the manager of this open-air whorehouse,' the lieutenant enquired with some disdain.

'Yes, he's a friend of mine,' Montalbano replied in a tone of obvious defiance.

'Do you know where I could find him?'

'At home, I would imagine.'

'He's not there.'

'Excuse me, but why do you think I can tell you where he is?'

'You're his friend, you said so yourself.'

'Oh, and I suppose you can tell me, at this exact moment, where all your friends from Bergamo are and what they're doing?'

Cars were continually arriving from the main road, turning onto the Pasture's small byways, noticing the swarm of carabinieri squad cars, shifting into reverse, and quickly returning to the road they'd come from. The blondes from the East, Brazilian *viados,* Nigerian nymphs, and the rest of the gang were coming to work, smelling something fishy, and scattering in every direction. It promised to be a miserable night for Gegè's business.

The lieutenant walked back towards the green car. Montalbano turned his back to him and without saying a word returned to his own vehicle. He said to Fazio, 'You and Galluzzo stay here. See what they're doing and what they find out. I'm going to the station.'

*

Montalbano stopped in front of Sarcuto's Stationery and Book Shop, the only one in Vigàta that was true to its sign; the other two sold not books but satchels, notebooks and pens. He remembered he'd finished the Vasquez Montalbán novel and had nothing else to read.

'We've got the new book on Falcone and Borsellino!' Signora Sarcuto announced as soon as she saw him enter.

She still hadn't understood that Montalbano hated books that talked about the Mafia, murder and Mafia victims. He didn't know why she couldn't grasp this, since he never bought them and didn't even read their jacket copy. He bought a book by Luigi Consolo, who'd won an important literary prize some time before. After he'd taken a few steps outside, the book slid out from under his arm and fell onto the pavement. He bent down to pick it up, then got back in his car.

At headquarters Catarella told him there was no news. Montalbano obsessively wrote his name in every book he bought. As he reached for one of the pens on his desk, his eye fell on the coins that Jacomuzzi had left him. The first one, a copper coin dated 1934, had the king's profile and the words 'Victor Emmanuel III, King of Italy' on one side, and a spike of wheat and 'C. 5', five centesimi, on the other. The second coin, dated 1936 and also copper, was a little bigger and had the same king's head with the same words on one side, and a bee resting on a flower with the letter 'C' and the number '10', ten centesimi, on the other. The third was made of a light metal alloy, with the inevitable king's head and accompanying words on one side, on the other an eagle displayed, with a Roman fasces partially visible behind it. This side also had four inscriptions: 'L. 1', which meant one lira; 'ITALIA', which meant Italy; '1942', which was the date of minting; and 'XX', which meant year twenty of the Fascist era. As he was staring at this last coin, Montalbano remembered what it was he had seen when bending down to pick up the book he'd dropped in front of the bookshop. He'd seen the front window of the shop next door, which featured a display of antique coins.

He got up from his desk, informed Catarella he was going out and would be back in half an hour at the most, and headed off to the shop on foot. It was called Things, and things were what it sold: desert roses, stamps, candlesticks, rings, brooches, coins, semi-precious stones. He went inside, and a neat, pretty girl welcomed him with a smile. Sorry to disappoint her, the inspector explained that he wasn't there to buy anything, but since he'd seen some ancient coins displayed in the window, he wanted to know if there was anyone, there in the shop or in Vigàta, with expertise in numismatics.

'Of course there is,' said the girl, still smiling delightfully. 'There's my grandfather.'

'Where might I disturb him?'

'You wouldn't be disturbing him at all. Actually, he'd be happy to help you. He's in the back room. Just wait a moment while I go tell him.'

He hadn't even had time to look at a hammerless late-nineteenth-century pistol when the girl reappeared.

'You can go inside.'

The back room was a glorious jumble of old phonographs with horns, prehistoric sewing machines, copying presses, paintings, prints, chamber pots and pipes. And it was entirely lined with bookshelves on which sat, higgledy-piggledy, an assortment of incunabula, parchment-bound tomes, lampshades, umbrellas and opera hats. In the middle of it all was a desk with an old man sitting behind it, an art nouveau lamp shedding light on his labours. He was holding a stamp with a pair of tweezers and examining it under a magnifying glass.

'What is it?' he asked gruffly, without looking up.

Montalbano laid the three coins down in front of him. The old man took his eyes momentarily off the stamp and glanced distractedly at them.

'Worthless,' he said.

Of the various old men he'd been encountering in his investigation of the Crasticeddru deaths, this one was the grumpiest.

I ought to gather them all together at an old people's home, the inspector thought. *That'd make it easier to question them.*

'I know they're worthless.'

'So what is it you want to know?'

'When they went out of circulation.'

'Use your brain a little.'

'When the Republic was proclaimed?' Montalbano hesitantly guessed.

He felt like a student who hadn't studied for the exam. The old man laughed, and his laugh sounded like the noise of two empty tin cans rubbing together.

'Am I wrong?'

'Very wrong. The Americans landed here the night of July 9–10, 1943. In October of that same year, these coins went out of use. They were replaced by Amlire, the paper money printed up by Amgot, the Allied military administration of the occupied territories. And since these bills were for one, five and ten lire, the centesimo coins disappeared from circulation.'

*

By the time Fazio and Galluzzo returned, it was already dark. The inspector scolded them.

'Damn you both! You certainly took your time!'

'Who, us?' Fazio shot back. 'You know what the lieutenant's like! Before he could touch the body, he had to wait for Pasquano and the judge to arrive. And *they* certainly did take their time!'

'And so?'

'A new-laid corpse if I ever saw one, fresh as can be. Pasquano said less than an hour had passed between the killing and the phone calls. The guy had an ID card on him. Pietro Gullo's his name, forty-two years old, blue eyes, blond hair, fair complexion, born in Merfi, resident of Fela, Via Matteotti 32, married, no distinguishing features.'

'You ought to get a job at the Records Office.'

Fazio nobly ignored the provocation and continued.

'I went to Montelusa and checked the archives. This Gullo had an uneventful youth, two robberies and a brawl. Then he straightened himself out, at least apparently. He dealt in grain.'

*

'I really appreciate you seeing me right away,' Montalbano said to Headmaster Burgio, who had answered the door.

'What are you saying? The pleasure's all mine.'

He let the inspector in, led him into the living room, and asked him to sit down.

'Angelina!' the headmaster called.

A tiny old woman appeared, curious about the unexpected visit, looking smart and well groomed, her lively, attentive eyes sparkling behind thick glasses.

The old peoples home! thought Montalbano.

'Allow me to introduce my wife, Angelina.'

Montalbano gave her an admiring bow. He sincerely liked elderly ladies who kept up appearances, even at home.

'Please forgive me for bothering you at supper time.'

'No bother at all. On the contrary, Inspector, are you busy this evening?'

'Not at all.'

'Why don't you stay and have supper with us? We're just having some old-people fare, since we're supposed to eat lightly: soft vegetables and striped mullet with oil and lemon.'

'Sounds like a feast to me.'

Mrs Burgio exited, content.

'What can I do for you?' asked the headmaster.

'I've managed to discover the time frame in which the double homicide of the Crasticeddru took place.'

'Oh. So when did it happen?'

'Definitely between early 1943 and October of the same year.'

'How did you come to that conclusion?'

'Easy. The terracotta dog, as Mr Burruano told us, was sold after Christmas of 1942, which reasonably means after the Epiphany of 1943. The coins found inside the bowl went out of circulation in October that same year.' He paused. 'And this can mean only one thing,' he added.

But what that one thing was, he didn't say. He patiently waited while Burgio collected his thoughts, stood up, and took a few steps around the room.

'I get it,' said the old man. 'You're saying that during this period, the Crasticeddru cave belonged to the Rizzitanos.'

'Exactly. And as you told me, the cave was already sealed off by the boulder at the time, because the Rizzitanos kept merchandise to be sold on the black market in it. They must have known about the other cave, the one where the dead couple were brought.'

The headmaster gave him a confused look.

'Why do you say they were 'brought' there?'

'Because they were killed somewhere else. Of that I am absolutely certain.'

'But it doesn't make any sense. Why put them there and set them up as if they were asleep, with the jug, the bowl of money and the dog?'

'I've been asking myself the same question. And maybe the only person who could tell us something is your friend Lillo Rizzitano.'

Signora Angelina came in.

'It's ready.'

The soft vegetables, which consisted of the leaves and

flowers of Sicilian courgettes – the long, smooth kind, which are white, lightly speckled with green – had come out so tender, so delicate, that Montalbano actually felt deeply moved. With each bite he could feel his stomach purifying itself, turning clean and shiny the way he'd seen happen with certain fakirs on television.

'How do you find them?' asked Signora Angelina.

'Beautiful,' said Montalbano. Seeing the couple's surprise, he blushed and explained himself. 'I'm sorry. Sometimes I abuse my adjectives.'

The striped mullet, boiled and dressed in olive oil, lemon, and parsley, was every bit as light as the vegetables. Only when the fruit was brought to the table did the headmaster come back to the question Montalbano had asked him – but not before he'd had his say on the problem of the schools and the reform the new minister of education had decided to carry out, which would abolish mandatory secondary-school attendance.

'In Russia at the time of the tsars,' said Burgio, 'they had secondary schools, though they called them whatever they're called in Russian. In Italy it was Gentile who called them lyceums when he instituted his own reform, which placed humanistic studies above all others. Well, Lenin's Communists, being the kind of Communists they were, didn't have the courage to abolish secondary schools. Only an upstart, a semi-illiterate nonentity like our minister, could conceive of such a thing. What's he called, Guastella?'

'Vastella,' said Signora Angelina.

Actually, he was called something else as well, but the inspector refrained from pointing this out.

'Lillo and I were friends in everything, but not in school, since he was a few years ahead of me. When I entered my third year of lyceum, he had just graduated. On the night of the American landing, Lillo's house, which was at the foot of the Crasto, was destroyed. From what I was able to find out once the storm had passed, Lillo had been at home alone and was seriously injured. A peasant saw some Italian soldiers putting him on a truck; he was bleeding profusely. That was the last I heard of Lillo. I haven't had any news since, though God knows I've searched far and wide!'

'Is it possible nobody from his family survived?'

'I don't know.'

The headmaster noticed that his wife looked lost in thought, absent, her eyes half-closed.

'Angelina!' Burgio called.

The old woman roused herself, then smiled at Montalbano.

'Forgive me. My husband says I've always been a "woman of fantasy", but he doesn't mean it as a compliment. He means I sometimes let my fantasies run away with me.'

FIFTEEN

When he returned home after supper with the Burgios, it wasn't even ten o'clock. Too early to go to bed. On TV there was a debate on the Mafia, another on Italian foreign policy, still another on the economic situation, a round table on conditions in the Montelusa insane asylum, a discussion about freedom of information, a documentary on juvenile delinquency in Moscow, another documentary on seals, still another on tobacco farming, a gangster film set in thirties Chicago, a nightly programme in which a former art critic, now a parliamentary deputy and political opinion-maker, was raving against magistrates, leftist politicians and various adversaries, making himself into a little Saint-Just when his rightful place was among the ranks of carpet salesman, wart-healers, magicians and strippers who were appearing with increasing frequency on the small screen. Turning off the television, Montalbano switched on the outdoor light, went out on the veranda, and sat down on the little bench with a magazine to which he subscribed. It was nicely printed, with interesting articles, and edited by a group of young environmentalists in the province. Scanning the table of contents, he found nothing of interest and thus started looking at the photographs, which occasionally realized their ambition of illustrating news events in emblematic fashion.

The ring of the doorbell caught him by surprise. He wasn't expecting anyone, he said to himself, but a second later he remembered that Anna had called in the afternoon. When she had suggested coming by to see him, he couldn't say no. He felt indebted to the girl for having used her – contemptibly, he had to admit – in that whole story he'd concocted to save Ingrid from persecution by her father-in-law.

Anna kissed him on each cheek and handed him a package.

'I brought you a *petrafèrnula*.'

This was a cake now very hard to find, which Montalbano loved, but it was anyone's guess why the pastry shops had stopped making it.

'I had to go to Mittica for work and saw it in a window, so I bought it for you. Careful with your teeth.'

The harder the cake was, the tastier.

'What were you doing?'

'Nothing, just reading a magazine. Why don't you come outside?'

They sat down on the bench. Montalbano went back to looking at the photographs, while Anna rested her head on her hands and gazed out at the sea.

'It's so beautiful here!'

'Yes.'

'All you hear are the waves.'

'Yes.'

'Does it bother you if I talk?'

'No.'

Anna fell silent. After a brief pause, she spoke again.

'I'm going inside to watch TV. I feel a little chilly.'

'Mm-hmm.'

The inspector didn't want to encourage her. Anna clearly wanted to abandon herself to a solitary pleasure, that of pretending she was his partner, imagining they were spending a quiet evening together like so many others. On the very last page of the magazine, he saw a photo that showed the inside of a cave, the 'grotto of Fragapane', which was actually a necropolis, a network of Christian tombs dug out of ancient cisterns. The picture served in its way to illustrate the review of a recent book by one Alcide Maraventano entitled *Funerary Rites in the Montelusa Region*. The publication of this richly documented essay by Maraventano, the reviewer claimed, filled a void, giving us a work of great scholarly value that investigated, with keen intelligence, a subject spanning the period from prehistory to the Byzantine–Christian era.

He sat there a long time meditating on what he had just read. The idea that the jug, the bowl with coins and the dog might be part of some burial rite had never even crossed his mind. And perhaps he'd been wrong not to think of this; in fact, the investigation should probably have started from this very premise. He suddenly felt uncontrollably pressed. He went inside, unplugged the phone, then picked up the whole apparatus.

'What are you doing?' asked Anna, who was watching the gangster movie.

'I'm going into the bedroom to make some phone calls. I don't want to disturb you out here.'

He dialled the Free Channel's number and asked for his friend Nicolò Zito.

'Quick, Montalbà, I go on the air in a few seconds.'

'Do you know someone by the name of Maraventano who wrote—'

'Alcide? Sure, I know him. What do want from him?'

'I'd like to talk to him. Do you have his phone number?'

'He hasn't got a phone. Are you at home? I'll track him down myself and let you know.'

'I need to talk to him by tomorrow.'

'I'll call you back in an hour at the latest and tell you what to do.'

He turned off the bedside lamp. In the dark it was easier to think about the idea that had just come to him. He tried to imagine the Crasticeddru's cave the way it had looked when he first entered. If you removed the two bodies from the picture, that left the rug, a bowl, a jug and a terracotta dog. If you drew lines between the three objects, they formed a perfect triangle, though upside down with respect to the cave's entrance. At the centre of the triangle lay the two corpses. Did it mean anything? Maybe he needed to study the triangle's orientation?

Between thinking, musing and fantasizing, he ended up dozing off. After a spell of indeterminate length, he was awakened by the ring of the telephone. He answered in a thick voice.

'Did you fall asleep?'

'Yeah, nodded off.'

'And here I am putting myself out for you. So, Alcide is expecting you tomorrow afternoon at five-thirty. He lives in Gallotta.'

Gallotta was a village a few miles outside Montelusa, a handful of peasant houses once famous for being inaccessible in winter, when the rains were heavy.

'Give me the address.'

'What address? If you're coming from Montelusa, it's the first house on the left, a big tumbledown villa that would delight any horror-film director. You can't miss it.'

*

He fell back asleep as soon as he put down the receiver. Then he woke with a start, feeling something moving on his chest. It was Anna, whom he'd completely forgotten about, lying down beside him on the bed and unbuttoning his shirt. On every piece of skin she uncovered, she planted her lips and held them there a long time. When she reached his navel, the girl raised her head, slipped one hand under his shirt to caress his nipple, then plastered her mouth against Montalbano's. Since he made no sign of reacting to her passionate kiss, Anna let her hand slide farther down his body. She caressed him there as well.

Montalbano decided to speak.

'See, Anna? It's hopeless. Nothing happens.'

In a single bound Anna sprang out of bed and locked herself in the bathroom. Montalbano didn't move, not even when he heard her sobbing – a childish wail, like that of a little girl denied a toy or some sweets. Against the light of the bathroom, whose door she left open on her way out, Montalbano saw her fully dressed.

'A wild animal has more feelings than you,' she said, leaving.

Sleep then abandoned Montalbano. At four in the morning, he was still up, trying to finish even one game of solitaire, though it was clear he would never succeed.

*

He arrived at work grumpy and troubled, the encounter with Anna weighing on his mind. He felt remorseful for treating her the way he did. On top of this, that morning he'd started wondering: had it been Ingrid instead of Anna, would he have behaved the same way?

'I need to speak to you urgently,' said Mimì Augello, standing in his doorway looking agitated.

'What do you want?'

'To bring you up to date on the investigation.'

'What investigation?'

'Okay, I get the message. I'll come by later.'

'No, you stay right here and tell me what fucking investigation you're talking about.'

'What do you mean? The one into the weapons traffic!'

'And I, in your opinion, put you in charge?'

'In my opinion? We talked about it! Remember? It seemed implicit to me.'

'Mimì, the only implicit thing around here is that you're a goddamned son of a bitch, no offense to your mother, of course.'

'Let's do this: I'll tell you what I've done, and you can decide if I should continue.'

'All right, let's hear what you've done.'

'First of all, I thought Ingrassia should be kept on a leash, so I assigned two of our men to tail him day and night. He can't even take a piss without me knowing about it.'

'Two of our men? You put two of ours on his tail? Don't you know that that guy knows everything about our men down to the hairs on their arse?'

'I'm not stupid. They're not actually ours, not from the Vigàta force, I mean. They're two officers from Ragòna that the commissioner transferred to my service after I spoke to him.'

Montalbano looked at him in admiration.

'Ah, so you spoke to the commissioner. Well done, Mimì, you really do know how to get around!'

Augello did not respond in kind, preferring to continue his explanation.

'We also listened in on a phone conversation that might mean something. I've got the transcript in my room, I'll go and get it.'

'Do you know it by heart?'

'Yes, but if you hear it, you might be able to discover—'

'Mimì, at this point I think you've discovered everything there was to discover. Don't make me waste time. Now tell me what they said.'

'Well, from his supermarket, Ingrassia phones the Brancato company in Catania. He asks for Brancato himself, who comes to the phone. Ingrassia complains about the snags that occurred during the last delivery, he says you can't send the truck so far ahead of schedule, that this caused him a lot of problems. He wants them to meet so they can study different, safer means of delivery. Here Brancato's answer is shocking, to say the least. He raises his voice in anger and asks Ingrassia, "How dare you call me here?" Ingrassia, now stammering, asks for an explanation. Which Brancato provides, saying that Ingrassia is insolvent, and that the banks have advised him to cease doing business with him.'

'And how did Ingrassia react?'

'He didn't. He didn't even make a peep. He just hung up.'

'Do you realize what that phone call means?'

'Of course. Ingrassia was asking for help, and they cut him loose.'

'Stay on top of Ingrassia.'

'I already am, as I told you.'

There was a pause.

'What should I do?' continued Mimì. 'Continue the investigation?'

Montalbano wouldn't answer.

'You're such a fucking jerk!' commented Augello.

*

'Salvo? Are you alone in your office? Can I speak openly?'

'Yes. Where are you calling from?'

'From home. I'm in bed with a bit of fever.'

'I'm sorry.'

'Well, you shouldn't be. It's one of those growing fevers.'

'I don't understand. What do you mean?'

'It's one of those fevers little children get. They last two or three days, around one hundred and one or one hundred and two degrees, no cause for alarm. It's natural, it's a growing fever. When it passes, the child has grown an inch or so. And I'm sure that when my fever is over, I too will have grown. In my head, not my body. What I mean is, never, as a woman, have I been so offended as with you.'

'Anna—'

'Let me finish. You really did offend me. You're mean, Salvo, wicked. I didn't deserve that kind of treatment.'

'Be reasonable, Anna. What happened last night was for your own good—'

Anna hung up. Even though he had made her understand a hundred different ways that what she wanted was out of the question, Montalbano, realizing that the girl at that moment was suffering terribly, felt like considerably less than a pig, since pork, at least, can be eaten.

*

Montalbano easily found the villa upon entering Gallotta, but it did not seem possible to him that anyone could live in that ruin. Half the roof was visibly caved in, which must surely have let in the rain on the third floor. The faint wind in the air was enough to rattle a shutter that remained attached by means not immediately apparent. The outer wall on the upper part of the facade had cracks the width of a fist. The second, first and ground floors looked in better shape. The surface plaster had long disappeared; the shutters were all broken and flaking, but at least they closed, however askew. There was a wrought-iron gate, half open and leaning outward, apparently in this position since time immemorial, amid weeds and peaty soil. The yard was an amorphous mass of contorted trees and dense shrubbery, a thick, closely knit tangle. He proceeded up the path of disconnected stones and stopped when he reached the peeling front door. Darkness was already falling. The switch from daylight time to standard time really did shorten the days. There was a doorbell, and he rang it. Or, rather, he pushed it, since he heard no sound whatsoever, not even far away. He tried again before realizing that the doorbell hadn't worked since the discovery of electricity. He rapped on the door with the horse-head knocker, and finally, after the third rap, he heard some shuffling footsteps. The door opened, without any noise from a lock or bolt, only a long wail as of a soul in purgatory.

'It was open. You needed only to push, come inside and call me.'

It was a skeleton speaking to him. Never in his life had Montalbano seen anyone so thin. Or, rather, he had seen a few such people, on their deathbeds, dried up, shrivelled by illness. This man, however, was standing, though bent over in two, and appeared to be alive. He was wearing a priest's cassock whose original black now tended towards green, the once-stiff white collar now a dense grey. On his feet, two hobnailed peasant boots of the kind you couldn't buy any more. He was completely bald, and his face looked like a death's head on which somebody, as a joke, had placed a pair of gold eyeglasses with extremely thick lenses, behind which the eyes foundered. Montalbano thought the couple in the cave, who'd been dead for fifty years, had more flesh on their bones than this priest. Needless to say, he was very old.

In ceremonious fashion, the man invited him inside and led him into an enormous room literally crammed with books, not only on the shelves but stacked on the floor in piles that stretched nearly to the lofty ceiling and remained standing by means of some impossible equilibrium. No light entered through the windows; the books amassed on their ledges covered them completely. The furniture consisted of a desk, a chair and an armchair. The lamp on the desk looked to Montalbano like an authentic oil lantern. The old priest cleared the armchair of books and told the inspector to sit down.

'I cannot imagine how I could be of any use to you, but go ahead and talk.'

'As you were probably told, I'm a police inspector and I—'

'No, nobody told me anything, and I didn't ask. Late last night somebody from the village came and said a man from Vigàta wanted to see me, and I said to have him come at five-thirty. If you're an inspector, you've come to the wrong place. You're wasting your time.'

'Why am I wasting my time?'

'Because I haven't set foot outside this house for at least thirty years. What would I go out for? The old faces have all disappeared and I don't care much for the new ones. Somebody does my shopping every day, and in any case I only drink milk, and chicken broth once a week.'

'You probably heard on television—'

He had barely started the sentence when he interrupted himself; the word 'television' had sounded incongruous to him.

'There's no electricity in this house.'

'Well, you've probably read in the papers—'

'I don't read newspapers.'

Why did he keep setting off on the wrong foot? Taking a deep breath, he got a kind of running start and told him everything, from the arms traffic to the discovery of the dead couple in the Crasticeddru.

'Let me light the lamp,' said the old man, 'we'll talk better that way.'

He rummaged through some papers on the desktop, found a box of kitchen matches, and lit one with a trembling hand. Montalbano felt a chill come over him.

If he drops it, he thought, *we'll be roasted alive in three seconds.*

The operation, however, was a success, except that it made matters worse, in that the lamp shed a feeble light over half of the desktop and plunged the side on which the old man sat into total darkness. In amazement Montalbano saw the old man reach out with one hand and seize a small bottle with an odd sort of cork. There were three other such bottles on the desk, two empty and the other full with a white liquid. They weren't regular bottles, actually, but baby bottles, each furnished with a nipple. The inspector felt himself growing stupidly irritated as the old man started sucking.

'You'll have to forgive me. I haven't any teeth.'

'But why don't you drink the milk from a mug or a cup or, I don't know, a glass?'

'Because it gives me more pleasure this way. It's as if I were smoking a pipe.'

Montalbano decided to leave as quickly as possible. Standing up, he took from his jacket pocket two of the photos taken by Jacomuzzi and handed them to the priest.

'Might this have been some sort of burial rite?'

The old man looked at the photos, growing animated and groaning.

'What was inside the bowl?'

'Coins from the 1940s.'

'And in the jug?'

'Nothing . . . There was no trace of anything . . . It must have contained only water.'

The old man sat there sucking a good while, engrossed in thought. Montalbano sat back down.

'It makes no sense,' said the priest, setting the photos down on the desk.

SIXTEEN

Montalbano was at the end of his rope. Bombarded with questions by the priest, he felt his thoughts growing confused and, what was worse, every time he was unable to answer, Alcide Maraventano made a kind of whining sound and in protest began sucking louder than usual. He was already working on his second baby bottle.

In what directions were the heads of the dead pointed?

Was the jug made of absolutely normal clay or some other material?

How many coins were there inside the bowl?

Exactly how far from the two bodies were the jug, bowl and terracotta dog?

At last the third degree ended.

'It makes no sense.'

The interrogation's conclusion confirmed precisely what the priest had immediately surmised at the start. The inspector, with a certain, not very well-concealed relief, thought he could now get up, take his leave and go.

'Wait. What's the hurry?'

Montalbano sat back down, resigned.

'It's not a funerary rite, but maybe it's something else.'

All at once, the inspector roused himself from his lethargy and regained full possession of his mental faculties. This Maraventano was a thinking mind.

'Tell me, I'd much appreciate your opinion.'

'Have you read Umberto Eco?'

Montalbano began to sweat.

Jesus, now he's giving me a literature exam, he thought, but he managed to say: 'I've read his first novel and the two small diaries, which seemed to me—'

'Well, I haven't. I don't know the novels. I was referring to the *Treatise of General Semiotics,* a few of whose passages might be of use to us.'

'I'm embarrassed to say, I haven't read it.'

'And I suppose you haven't read Kristeva's *Semeiotiké* either?'

'No, and I have no desire to,' said Montalbano, starting to feel angry. He was beginning to suspect that the old man was pulling his leg.

'All right, then,' said Alcide Maraventano, sighing, 'I'll give you a down-to-earth example.'

'Something on my level,' Montalbano muttered to himself.

'If you, then, are a police inspector, and you find a man who's been shot and killed, and in whose mouth the killers have placed a stone, what conclusion might you draw?'

'That's old stuff, you know,' said Montalbano, bent on

regaining the upper hand. 'Nowadays they murder without giving any explanations.'

'I see. So for you that stone in the mouth is a kind of explanation.'

'Of course.'

'And what does it mean?'

'It means the dead man talked too much, said things he wasn't supposed to say, or was an informer.'

'Exactly. You, therefore, understood the explanation because you possessed the code of that language, which in this case was a metaphorical language. But if you'd been ignorant of the code, what would you have understood? Nothing. To you, that man would have been a murder victim in whose mouth the killers had in-ex-pli-ca-bly placed a stone.'

'I'm beginning to understand.'

'Now, to return to our discussion: somebody kills two young people for reasons we don't know. He could make the bodies disappear in many different ways, in the sea, underground, under the sand. But, no, he puts them in a cave instead. Not only that, but he arranges a bowl, a jug and a terracotta dog around them. What, therefore, has he done?'

'He's made a statement, sent a message,' said Montalbano in a soft voice.

'That's right, a message, which you, however, can't read because you don't possess the code,' concluded the priest.

'Let me think,' said Montalbano. 'But the message must

have been directed at someone, just not at us, fifty years after the fact.'

'And why not?'

Montalbano thought about this a moment, then stood up.

'I'm going to go, I don't want to take up any more of your time. What you've told me has been very valuable to me.'

'I'd like to be even more useful to you.'

'How so?'

'You just said that nowadays they kill without providing any explanations. There is always an explanation and it is always provided, otherwise you wouldn't be in the line of work you're in. It's just that the codes have multiplied and diversified.'

'Thank you,' said Montalbano.

*

For dinner they'd eaten fresh anchovies *all'agretto,* which Signora Elisa, the commissioner's wife, had cooked with art and skill, the secret of success lying in correctly determining the infinitesimal length of time to keep the pan in the oven. Then, after the meal, the signora had retired to the living room to watch television, but not before having arranged, on the desk in her husband's study, a bottle of Chivas, another of bitters, and two glasses.

While they were eating, Montalbano had spoken enthusiastically of Alcide Maraventano and his peculiar way of life, his erudition, his intelligence. The commissioner, however, had shown only lukewarm curiosity, more out of politeness to his guest than out of real interest.

'Listen, Montalbano,' he broke in as soon as they were alone, 'I can easily understand the sense of urgency you might feel about the two murder victims you found in the cave. I daresay I've known you too long not to expect you to become fascinated by a case like this, because it defies explanation, but also – and I think this is the real reason – because even if you were to find the solution, it would prove utterly useless. Just the sort of uselessness that you would find amusing and – excuse me for saying so – almost congenial.'

'Useless in what way?'

'Useless, useless, don't play innocent. To be generous – since fifty or more years have since passed – the murderer, or murderers, are either dead or, in the best of cases, little old men at least seventy years old. Right?'

'Right,' Montalbano reluctantly agreed.

'Therefore – forgive me, because what I'm about to say is not normally part of my vocabulary – but what you're engaged in is not an investigation, but an act of mental masturbation.'

Montalbano, lacking the strength or arguments to rebut him, took it all in.

'Now, I could allow you this little exercise,' the commissioner continued, 'if I wasn't afraid you'd end up devoting the best of your brainpower to it, and neglecting other investigations of greater significance and reach.'

'No! That's not true!' the inspector bridled.

'But it is. Look, none of this is intended, in any way, as a reproach. We're here talking, at my home, between friends. Why, for example, did you assign the weapons trafficking case – an extremely delicate case – to your deputy, who is a very capable officer but certainly not on your level?'

'But I haven't assigned him anything! It's he who—'

'Don't be childish, Montalbano. You've been throwing the better part of the investigation on his shoulders. Because you're well aware that you can't devote all your energies to it, since three-fourths of your brain are tied up with the other case. Tell me, quite honestly, if you think I'm wrong.'

'You're right,' Montalbano honestly admitted, after a pause.

'So let's leave it at that, and move on to other matters. Why the hell don't you want me to recommend you for a promotion?'

'You really want to keep crucifying me.'

*

He left the commissioner's house pleased – with the anchovies *all'agretto*, but also because he'd managed to obtain a postponement of the recommendation of promotion. There was no rhyme or reason to the arguments he'd cited, but his superior politely pretended to accept them. Could Montalbano very well have told him that the mere idea of a transfer, of a change of habits, gave him a fever?

It was still early. His appointment with Gegè wasn't for another two hours. He dropped by the Free Channel studios, wanting to learn more about Alcide Maraventano.

'Extraordinary, isn't he?' said Nicolò Zito. 'Did he suck milk from a baby bottle in front of you?'

'And how.'

'It's all a put-on, you know. He's just play acting.'

'What do you mean? He has no teeth.'

'You have heard of an invention called dentures, I presume? He owns a set, and they work perfectly well. I'm told he sometimes wolfs down a quarter of veal or a roast suckling goat when nobody's looking.'

'So why does he do it?'

'Because he's a born tragedian. Or comedian, if you prefer.'

'Is he really a priest?'

'He quit the priesthood.'

'And the things he says, are they true or made up?'

'You don't have to worry about that. His knowledge is limitless, and when he says something, it's better than gospel. Did you know he shot somebody about ten years ago?'

'Come on.'

'Really. Some thief broke into his house, on the ground floor. He bumped into a pile of books and they came crashing down, making an infernal racket. Maraventano, who'd been asleep upstairs, woke up, came down, and shot him with a muzzle-loading rifle, a kind of household cannon. The blast made half the village jump out of bed.

When the smoke cleared, the robber was wounded in the leg, a dozen or so books were ruined, and the old man had a fractured shoulder from the gun's tremendous kick. The robber, however, maintained he'd entered the house not with any criminal intent, but because he'd been invited there by the priest, who at a certain point, for no apparent reason, picked up a rifle and shot him. And I believe him.'

'Whom?'

'The supposed thief.'

'But why would he shoot him?'

'I suppose you know what goes on inside the head of Alcide Maraventano? Maybe it was to see if the rifle still worked. Or just to make a scene, which is more likely.'

'Listen, before I forget, do you have Umberto Eco's *Treatise of General Semiotics*?'

'Me? Are you crazy?'

*

On his way to the car, which he'd left in the Free Channel's car park, Montalbano got soaked. It had started raining without warning, very fine drops but very dense. He got home with time to spare before the appointment. He changed clothes and sat down in the armchair in front of the TV, but then immediately got up again and went to his desk to fetch a postcard that had arrived that morning.

It was from Livia. As she'd informed him by telephone, she had gone to visit a cousin in Milan for ten days or so. On the glossy side, which showed the inevitable view of the cathedral, there was a luminescent trail of slime cutting the image in half. Montalbano touched it with the tip of his index finger: it was very fresh, and slightly sticky. He examined the desk more closely. A *scataddrizzo,* a large, dark brown snail, was slithering across the cover of the Consolo book. Montalbano did not hesitate. The horror he'd felt after the dream, which he was still carrying around with him, was too strong. Grabbing the Vasquez Montalbán novel, which he'd already read, he slammed it violently down on the one by Consolo. Caught in between, the *scataddrizzo* made such a noise as it was being crushed that Montalbano felt nauseated. He then tossed the two novels into the rubbish bin. He would buy new copies tomorrow.

*

Gegè wasn't there, but the inspector knew he wouldn't be long. His friend was never late by much. The rain had stopped, but there must have been quite a storm at sea: large puddles had formed along the beach, and the sand gave off a strong smell of wet wood. He lit a cigarette. All at once, by the faint light of the moon that had suddenly appeared, he saw the dark shape of a car approaching very slowly, lights extinguished, from the opposite direction to where he'd come in, which was the same direction Gegè should have come from. Alarmed, he opened the glove compartment, took out his pistol, cocked it and disengaged the car door, ready to jump out. When the other car came within range, he turned on his high beam all at once. The car was Gegè's, no doubt about that, but it might easily be somebody else at the wheel.

'Turn off your lights!' he heard someone shout from the car.

It was definitely Gegè's voice, and the inspector obeyed. They spoke one to the other, each in his own car, through their lowered windows.

'What the fuck are you doing? I nearly fired at you,' Montalbano said angrily.

'I wanted to see if they'd followed you.'

'If who'd followed me?'

'I'll tell you in a second. I got here half an hour ago and was hiding behind the jetty at Punta Rossa.'

'Come over here,' said the inspector.

Gegè got out of his car and into Montalbano's, almost huddling against him.

'What's wrong, you cold?'

'No, but I'm shivering anyway.'

He stank of fear. As Montalbano knew from experience, fear had a smell all its own, sour, yellow-green in colour.

'Do you know who that was who got killed?'

'Gegè, a lot of people get killed. Who are you talking about?'

'Pietro Gullo, that's who, the one they drove to the Pasture after they killed him.'

'Was he a client of yours?'

'A client? If anything, I was *his* client. He was Tano the Greek's man, his collector. The same guy who told me Tano wanted to meet you.'

'Why so surprised, Gegè? It's the usual story: winner take all. They use the same system in politics. Tano's businesses are changing hands, so they're liquidating everybody who worked with him. You were neither an associate nor a dependent of Tano's. So what are you worried about?'

'No,' Gegè said firmly, 'that's not how it is. That's not what they told me in Trapani.'

'So how is it, then?'

'They said there was an agreement.'

'An agreement?'

'Oh, yes. An agreement between you and Tano. They said the shoot-out was bogus, a sham, a masquerade. And they're convinced that the people who staged this masquerade were me, Pietro Gullo, and somebody else they're sure to kill one of these days.'

Montalbano remembered the telephone call he'd received after the press conference, when an anonymous voice had called him a 'lousy fucking actor'.

'They feel offended,' Gegè continued. 'They can't bear the thought that you and Tano spat in their faces, made them look like chumps. It means more to them than the weapons. Now you tell me: what am I supposed to do?'

'Are you sure they have it in for you too?'

'I swear to God. Why else did they bring Gullo all the way to the Pasture, which is my turf? You can't get any clearer than that!'

The inspector thought of Alcide Maraventano and what he'd said about codes.

It must have been a change in the density of the

darkness, or a split-second glimmer seen out of the corner of one eye, but the fact is that an instant before the explosion of gunfire, Montalbano's body obeyed a series of impulses frantically transmitted by his brain: he bent over, opening the car door with his left hand, and hurled himself out while all around him was a thunder of gunshots, shattering glass, plates of metal flying apart, quick red flashes brightening the dark. Montalbano remained motionless, wedged between Gegè's car and his own, and only then did he realize he had his pistol in his hand. When Gegè had come inside his car, he'd set it on the dashboard. He must have grabbed it by instinct. After the pandemonium, a leaden silence reigned. Nothing moved. There was only the sound of the agitated sea. Then, about twenty yards away, to the side where the beach ended and the hill of marl began, there was a voice, 'Everything okay?'

'Everything okay,' said another voice, this one very close.

'Make sure they're both finished, then we can go.'

Montalbano tried to picture the movements the man would have to make to verify that they were dead: *chuff, chuff* went his footsteps in the sodden sand. Now the man must be right beside the car; in a moment he would bend down to look inside.

Montalbano leapt to his feet and fired. A single shot. He clearly heard the thud of a body collapsing on the sand, then a gasping, a kind of gurgling, then nothing.

'Jujù, everything all right?' asked the distant voice.

Without getting back in his car, Montalbano, through the open door, put his hand on the high-beam switch and waited. He could hear nothing. He decided to try his luck and started counting in his head. When he got to fifty, he turned on the lights bright and stood straight up. Swathed in light, about ten yards away, appeared a man with a submachine gun in hand, frozen in surprise. Montalbano fired, the man immediately reacted, firing blindly into the dark. Feeling something like a tremendous punch in his left side, the inspector staggered, leaned his left hand against the car, then fired again, three shots in a row. The man sort of jumped in the air, turned around, and started running, as Montalbano saw the white beam of the headlights begin to turn yellow, his eyes clouding over, head spinning. He sat down on the sand, realizing that his legs could no longer support him, and leaned back against the side of the car.

He waited for the pain, and when it came it was so intense he started howling and crying like a child.

SEVENTEEN

As soon as he awoke, he realized he was in a hospital room, and he remembered everything in minute detail: the meeting with Gegè, the words they exchanged, the shooting. Memory failed him only from the moment he found himself between the two cars, lying on the wet sand with an unbearable pain in his side. But it did not fail him completely. He remembered, for example, Mimì Augello's contorted face, his cracking voice.

'How do you feel? How do you feel? The ambulance is coming now, it's nothing, just stay calm.'

How had Mimì managed to find him?

Then, already in the hospital, someone in a white smock, 'He's lost too much blood.'

After that, nothing. He tried to look around. The room was clean and white. There was a large window, the daylight pouring through. He couldn't move; his arms were stuck full of IVs. His side didn't hurt any more, however; it felt instead like a dead part of his body. He tried to move his legs but couldn't. He slipped slowly away into sleep.

He awoke again towards what must have been evening, since the lights were on. He closed his eyes at once when he saw that there were people in the room. He didn't feel like talking. Then, out of curiosity, he raised his eyelids just enough to see a little. Livia was there, sitting beside the bed in the only metal chair; behind her, standing, was Anna. On the other side of the bed, also standing, was Ingrid. Livia's eyes were wet with tears, Anna was crying without restraint, and Ingrid was pale, her face drawn.

Good God! Montalbano said to himself in terror.

He closed his eyes and escaped into sleep.

*

At 6.30 on what he thought was the next morning, two nurses washed him and changed his dressings. At seven the chief physician appeared, accompanied by five assistants, all of them in white smocks. The chief physician examined the chart at the foot of the bed, pulled the sheet aside, and began to touch him on his injured side.

'Seems to be coming along very nicely,' he declared. 'The operation was a complete success.'

Operation? What operation was he talking about? Ah, maybe to remove the bullet that had wounded him. But it's not often a machine-gun bullet stays inside the body instead of slicing right through it. He would have liked to ask questions, demand explanations, but the words wouldn't come out. The doctor, however, seeing his eyes, guessed what questions the inspector was formulating.

'We had to perform an emergency operation on you. The bullet passed through your colon.'

Colon? And what the hell was his colon doing in his side? The colon had nothing to do with one's sides, it was supposed to be in the belly. But if it had to do with the belly, did this mean – and here he gave such a start that the doctors noticed – that from this moment on, for the rest of his life, he could eat only mush?

'. . . mush?' Montalbano finally managed to mutter, the horror of that prospect reactivating his vocal cords.

'What did he say?' the chief physician asked, turning to his assistants.

'I think he said brush,' said one.

'No, no, he said ambush,' interjected another.

They left arguing over the question.

*

At 8.30 the door opened and Catarella appeared.

'Chief, how goes it? How you feeling?'

If there was one person in the entire world with whom Montalbano felt dialogue was useless, it was Catarella. He didn't answer, but merely moved his head as if to say that things were a little less bad.

'I'm on guard here, over you, I mean. This hospital's a revolving door, people come, people go, back and forth and back and forth. Somebody could maybe come in immotivated with bad intentions, trying to finish the job they didn't finish. You know what I mean?'

The inspector knew exactly what he meant.

'Know what, Chief? I gave blood for the transfusal.'

And he went back on guard against the badly immotivated. Montalbano thought bitterly of the dark years that lay ahead of him, surviving on Catarella's blood and eating semolina mush.

*

The first in the long series of kisses he would receive over the course of the day were from Fazio.

'Did you know, Chief, that you shoot like a god? You got one guy in the throat with a single shot, and you wounded the other.'

'I also wounded the other guy?'

'You certainly did. We don't know in what part of the body, but you wounded him all right. It was Jacomuzzi who noticed a red puddle about ten yards from the cars. Blood.'

'Have you identified the one who died?'

'Of course.'

Fazio pulled a piece of paper from his pocket.

'Munafò, first name Gerlando, born in Montelusa on the sixth of September, 1971, unmarried, resident of Montelusa, Via Crispi 43, no distinguishing features.'

He still hasn't given up his Records Office fetish, thought Montalbano.

'And how did he stand with the law?'

'Not a thing. Clean record.' Fazio put the sheet of

paper back in his pocket. 'For a job like that, they get half a million lire maximum.'

He paused. He obviously had something to say but didn't have the courage to say it. Montalbano decided to help him out.

'Did Gegè die on the spot?'

'Didn't suffer at all. The volley took half his head off.'

The others came in, and there was an orgy of kisses and embraces.

*

Jacomuzzi and Dr Pasquano came from Montelusa to see him.

'All the papers are talking about you,' said Jacomuzzi. He seemed moved but a little envious.

'I was truly sorry I didn't get to do your autopsy,' said Pasquano. 'I'd really like to know how you're put together inside.'

*

'I was the first on the scene,' said Mimì Augello, 'and when I saw you in that condition, in that situation, I got so scared I nearly shit my pants.'

'How did you find out?'

'There was an anonymous call to headquarters saying there'd been some shooting at the foot of the Scala dei Turchi. Galluzzo was on duty and phoned me right away. He also said something I didn't know. He said you were in the habit of meeting Gegè at the place where the shooting was heard.'

'He knew that?!'

'Apparently everybody knew! Half the town knew! So, anyway, I didn't even get dressed, I went right outside in my pyjamas—'

Montalbano raised a tired hand, interrupting him.

'You sleep in pyjamas?'

'Yes,' said Augello, confused. 'Why?'

'Never mind. Go on.'

'As I was racing there in my car, I called an ambulance with my cellphone. Which was a good thing, because you were losing a lot of blood.'

'Thanks,' Montalbano said gratefully.

'What do you mean, "thanks"? Wouldn't you have done the same for me?'

Montalbano did a little rapid soul-searching and decided not to answer.

'Oh, I also wanted to mention something strange,' Augello continued. 'The first thing you asked me, when you were still lying on the sand, groaning, was to remove the snails that were crawling on you. You were sort of delirious, so I said yes, I'd remove them, but there wasn't a single snail on you.'

*

Livia came and gave him a long hug, started crying, and lay down on the bed beside him as best she could.

'Stay like that,' said Montalbano.

He liked the scent of her hair as she rested her head on his chest.

'How did you find out?'

'From the radio. Actually, it was my cousin who heard the news. What a way to wake up!'

'What did you do?'

'First I called Alitalia and booked a flight to Palermo, then I called your office in Vigàta. They put Augello on, and he was very nice. He reassured me and even offered to come and get me at the airport. He told me the whole story in the car.'

'Livia, how am I?'

'You're doing well, considering what happened.'

'Am I ruined forever?'

'What are you talking about?!'

'Will I have to eat bland food for the rest of my life?'

*

'But you leave me no choice,' the commissioner said, smiling.

'Why?'

'Because you've been going about things like a sheriff, or, if you prefer, like some kind of nocturnal avenger, and it's going to end up all over the television and newspapers.'

'That's not *my* fault.'

'No, it's not, but neither will it be my fault if I'm forced to promote you. You're just going to have to behave for a little while. Fortunately you won't be able to leave this place for another twenty days.'

'Twenty days?!'

'By the way, Under Secretary Licalzi's in Montelusa at the moment. He says he's here to sensitize public opinion to the struggle against the Mafia. He's made it known he intends to pay you a visit this afternoon.'

'I don't want to see him!' Montalbano shouted, upset.

The under secretary was someone who had been up to his ears in sweetheart deals with the Mafia and was now recycling himself, as always with the Mafia's consent.

At that exact moment the head physician came in. Seeing there were six people in the room with Montalbano, he frowned.

'Don't take this the wrong way, but I beg you please to leave him alone. He needs to rest.'

They were starting to say their goodbyes when the doctor said to the nurse, in a loud voice, 'And no more visitors for the rest of the day.'

'The under secretary is supposed to leave this afternoon at five,' the commissioner whispered to Montalbano. 'Unfortunately, I suppose he won't be able to see you. Doctor's orders.'

They exchanged smiles.

*

A few days later they removed the IV from his arm and put a telephone on his bedside table. That same morning, he received a visit from Nicolò Zito, who came in like Santa Claus.

'I've brought you a TV, a VCR and a cassette. I've even brought the newspaper articles that talk about you.'

'What's on the cassette?'

'I taped and spliced together all the idiocies that I, TeleVigàta, and all the other TV stations said about the incident.'

*

'Hello, Salvo? It's Mimì. How are you feeling today?'

'Better, thanks.'

'I'm calling to let you know they killed our friend Ingrassia.'

'I expected as much. When did it happen?'

'This morning. They shot him as he was driving into town. Two guys on a high-powered motorcycle. The officer who was tailing him couldn't do anything but try to give him first aid, but it was too late. Listen, Salvo, I'm coming to see you tomorrow morning. You're going to have to tell me, for the record, every detail of your shoot-out.'

*

He told Livia to put in the cassette. Not that he was so curious; it was just to pass the time. On TeleVigàta, Galluzzo's brother-in-law indulged in a fantasy worthy of a scriptwriter for films like *Raiders of the Lost Ark*. In his opinion, the shooting was a direct consequence of the discovery of the two mummified bodies in the cave. What terrible, indecipherable secret lay behind that distant crime? The newsman did not blush to recall, however briefly, the sad end to which the discoverers of the pharaohs' tombs had come, and likened this to the ambush of the inspector.

Montalbano laughed so hard he felt a stab of pain in his side. Next appeared the face of Pippo Ragonese, the same station's political commentator, a former Communist, former Christian Democrat, and now a representative of the Renewal Party. Mincing no words, Ragonese asked himself: what was Montalbano doing in that place with a pimp and drug dealer who was rumoured to be his friend? Were such associations consistent with the rigorous moral standards that every public servant should abide by? Times have changed, the commentator noted sternly; thanks to the new government, an atmosphere of renewal was shaking up the country, and we must all march in step. The old attitudes, the old collusions, must end, once and for all.

Montalbano felt another stab of pain in his side, from rage this time, and he cried out. Livia got up at once and turned off the video.

'You're getting upset over what that arsehole says?'

*

After half an hour of insistence and entreaties, Livia gave in and turned the video back on. Nicolò Zito's commentary was affectionate, indignant and rational. Affectionate towards his friend, the inspector, to whom he sent his sincerest good wishes; indignant because, despite all the politicians' promises, the Mafia had a free hand across the island; and rational because it connected Tano the Greek's arrest with the discovery of the weapons. As the man responsible for these two powerful blows against organized crime, Salvo Montalbano had become a dangerous adversary, one who must be liquidated at all costs. Zito ridiculed the conjecture that the ambush might be an act of revenge for desecrating the dead. With what money would the assassins have been paid? With the obsolete coins that were found in the bowl?

The picture then switched back to the TeleVigàta newsman, who was now interviewing Alcide Maraventano, presented to the viewing public as a 'specialist in the occult'. The defrocked priest was wearing a cassock sewn with multicoloured patches and sucking from a baby's bottle. In response to a series of insistent questions intended to make him acknowledge a possible connection between the ambush of the inspector and the supposed desecration, Maraventano, like a masterly, consummate actor, both did and did not acknowledge the possibility, leaving everyone in nebulous suspense.

Zito's cassette concluded with the logo of Ragonese's editorial segment. But then an unknown newsman appeared, saying that his colleague was prevented from airing his commentary that evening because he'd been the victim of a brutal assault. A group of hoodlums, still unidentified, had roughed him up and robbed him the night before, as he was returning home from his job at TeleVigàta. The newsman then launched into a violent attack on the police, accusing them of no longer being able to guarantee the safety of the citizenry.

'Why did Zito want you to see that report, which has nothing to do with you?' naively asked Livia, who was from the North and didn't understand certain insinuations.

*

Augello interrogated him, and Tortorella took it all down. He explained that he'd been schoolmates and friends with Gegè, and that their friendship had endured over the years, even though they found themselves on opposite sides of the barricade. He had them write in the report that Gegè, that evening, had asked to see him, but they'd managed to exchange only a few words, barely more than a greeting.

'He started to mention the weapons traffic, said he'd heard talk of something that might interest me, but he didn't get a chance to tell me what it was.'

Augello pretended to believe this, and Montalbano went on to recount the various stages of the gunfight.

'Now it's your turn to tell me,' he said to Mimì.

'First sign the statement,' said Augello.

Montalbano signed, and Tortorella said goodbye and headed back to headquarters. There wasn't much to tell, said Augello. Ingrassia's car was overtaken by the motorcycle; the guy on the back turned round, opened fire, and that was that. Ingrassia's car ended up in a ditch.

'They were pruning a dead branch,' Montalbano commented. Then, with a touch of melancholy because he felt left out of the game. 'What do you think you'll do?'

'The people in Catania, whom I've informed, promised not to let Brancato get away.'

'We can always hope.'

Augello didn't realize it, but by informing his colleagues in Catania, he may have signed Brancato's death warrant.

'So who was it?' Montalbano asked bluntly after a pause.

'Who was what?'

'Take a look at this.'

He pressed the remote and showed him the segment reporting the news of the assault on Ragonese. Mimì played the part of someone in the dark to perfection.

'You're asking me? Anyway, it doesn't concern us; Ragonese lives in Montelusa.'

'You're such an innocent, Mimì! Here, bite my pinky.'

And he held out his little finger to him, as one does to teething babies.

EIGHTEEN

After a week, the visits, embraces, phone calls and congratulations gave way to loneliness and boredom. He had persuaded Livia to go back to her cousin in Milan; there was no point in wasting her holidays. The planned trip to Cairo, for the moment, was out of the question. They agreed that Livia would fly back down as soon as Montalbano got out of the hospital. Only then would she decide how and where to spend her two remaining weeks of vacation.

And little by little, the uproar surrounding the inspector and what had happened likewise died down to a mere echo, before disappearing entirely. Every day, however, Augello or Fazio would come to keep him company. But they didn't stay long, just enough to tell him the latest news and the state of certain investigations.

Every morning when he opened his eyes, Montalbano made a point of devoting his thoughts and speculations to the dead couple of the Crasticeddru. He wondered when he would again have the chance to be alone, in precious silence, with no disturbance of any kind, so he could develop a sustained line of reasoning from which he might receive a flash, a spark. He needed to take advantage of this situation, he would say to himself, and he'd begin to replay the whole affair in his mind with the speed of a galloping horse. Soon, however, he would find himself moving at a lazy trot, then at a walk, and finally a kind of torpor would ever-so-slowly overwhelm him, body and mind.

'Must be my convalescence,' he told himself.

He would sit down in the armchair, pick up a newspaper or magazine, and halfway through an article just a little longer than the rest, he would get fed up, his eyes would start to droop, and he would sink into a sweaty sleep.

*

Sargint Fasio said you was comin home today. I am hapy and releved. The sargint also said for me to feed you lite foods. Adelina

The housekeeper's note was on the kitchen table. Montalbano rushed to the fridge to see exactly what she meant by 'lite'. There were two fresh hakes to be served with oil and lemon. He unplugged the phone; he wanted to reaccustom himself at an easy pace to living at home. There was a lot of mail, but he didn't open a single letter or read a single postcard. He ate and went to bed.

Before falling asleep, he asked himself a question: if the doctors reassured him that he would recover all his strength, why did he have that lump of sadness in his throat?

*

For the first ten minutes he drove apprehensively, paying closer attention to the reactions of his side than to the road. Then, seeing that he was weathering the bumps without difficulty, he accelerated, passed through Vigàta, took the road to Montelusa, turned left at the Montaperto crossroads, drove another few miles, turned onto an unpaved trail, and pulled up at a small clearing in front of a farmhouse. He got out of the car. Mariannina, Gegè's sister, who had been his teacher at school, was sitting in a wicker chair beside the front door, mending a basket. The moment she saw the inspector, she ran up to meet him.

'Salvù! I knew you'd come.'

'You're the first person I'm visiting since leaving the hospital,' said Montalbano, embracing her.

Mariannina began weeping very softly, without a sound, only tears, and Montalbano's eyes welled up.

'Pull up a chair,' said Mariannina.

Montalbano sat down beside her. She took his hand and began to stroke it.

'Did he suffer?'

'No. I realized while they were still shooting that they'd snuffed out Gegè on the spot. This was later confirmed. I don't even think he ever realized what was happening.'

'Is it true you killed the one who killed Gegè?'

'Yeah.'

'Gegè will be happy, wherever he is.'

Mariannina sighed and squeezed the inspector's hand a little harder.

'Gegè loved you with all his soul.'

Meu amigo de alma, the title of a book, came to Montalbano's mind.

'I loved him, too,' he said.

'Do you remember how naughty he was?'

And a naughty boy he was, mischievous, bad. Clearly Mariannina was not referring to recent years, when Gegè had his run-ins with the law, but to a distant time when her younger brother was a restless little scamp. Montalbano smiled.

'Do you remember the time he threw a firecracker into a copper cauldron that someone was repairing, and the blast made the poor guy faint?'

'And the time he emptied his inkwell into Mrs Longo's purse?'

They talked about Gegè and his exploits for nearly two hours, recounting episodes that never went beyond his adolescence.

'It's getting late,' said Montalbano. 'I should go.'

'I'd like to tell you to stay for dinner, but what I made is probably too heavy for you.'

'What did you make?'

'*Attuppateddri* in tomato sauce.'

Attuppateddri were small light brown snails which, when they went into hibernation, would secrete a fluid that solidified into a white sheet, which served to close – *attuppari* in Sicilian – the entrance to the shell. Montalbano's first impulse was to decline in disgust. How long would this obsession continue to torment him? In the end, he coolly decided to accept, as a twofold challenge to his stomach and his psyche. With the plate in front of him giving off an exquisite, ochre-coloured scent, he had to steel himself, but after extracting the first *attuppateddru* with a pin and tasting it, he suddenly felt liberated: with the obsession gone and the melancholy banished, there was no doubt the belly, too, would adjust.

*

At headquarters he was smothered by embraces. Tortorella even wiped away a tear.

'I know what it means to come back after being shot!' said the officer.

'Where's Augello?'

'In his office, your office,' said Catarella.

He opened the door without knocking and Mimì leapt out of the chair behind the desk as if he'd been caught stealing. He blushed.

'I haven't touched anything. It's just that from here, the phone calls—'

'Mimì, you did absolutely the right thing,' Montalbano cut him short, repressing the urge to kick him in the arse for having dared to sit in his place.

'I was planning to come to your house today,' said Augello.

'To do what?'

'To arrange protection.'

'Protection? For whom?'

'For whom? For you, of course. There's no saying they won't try again, after coming up empty the first time.'

'You're wrong. Nothing more's going to happen to me. Because, you see, Mimì, it was you who had me shot.'

Augello turned so red, he looked as though someone had inserted a high-voltage plug up his bum. He started trembling. Then all his blood disappeared God knows where, leaving him pale as a corpse.

'Where do you get these ideas?' he managed to mutter awkwardly.

Montalbano reckoned he'd sufficiently avenged himself for the expropriation of his desk.

'Calm down, Mimì. That's not what I meant to say. What I meant was: it was you who set the mechanism in motion that led to my shooting.'

'Explain yourself,' said Augello, collapsing into the chair and dabbing all around his mouth and forehead with his handkerchief.

'You, my good friend, without consulting me, without asking if I agreed or not, put two officers on Ingrassia's tail. Did you really think he was so stupid he wouldn't notice? It took him maybe half a day to find out he was being shadowed. And he understandably thought it was me who gave the order. He knew he'd fucked up a couple of times and that I had him in my sights, and so, to brush up his image for Brancato, who was planning to get rid of him – it was you who related their phone conversation to me – he hired two arseholes to eliminate me. Except that his scheme turned into a fiasco. By this time Brancato, or somebody else, had got fed up with Ingrassia and his brilliant ideas – don't forget the pointless little murder of poor Cavaliere Misuraca – and so they took matters in hand and made him vanish from the face of the earth. If you hadn't put Ingrassia on his guard, Gegè would still be alive and I wouldn't have this pain in my side. And there you have it.'

'If that's how things went . . . I guess you're right,' said Mimì, annihilated.

'That's how things went, you can bet your arse on it.'

*

The plane pulled up very near to the gate, so the passengers didn't need to be shuttled by bus to the terminal. Montalbano saw Livia descend the ramp and walk towards the entrance with her head down. Hiding in the crowd, he watched Livia as she waited interminably for her baggage, collected it, loaded it onto a cart, and then headed towards the taxi stand. They had agreed the night before that she would take the train from Palermo to Montelusa and that he would limit himself to picking her up at the station. At the last minute, however, he had decided to surprise her and show up at Punta Ràisi airport.

'Are you alone? Need a lift?'

Livia, who was making her way towards the first cab in line, stopped in her tracks and shouted.

'Salvo!'

They embraced happily.

'But you look fantastic!' she commented.

'So do you,' said Montalbano. 'I've been watching you for over half an hour, ever since you got off the plane.'

'Why didn't you say something sooner?'

'I like seeing how you exist without me.'

They got in the car and immediately Montalbano, instead of starting the ignition, hugged and kissed her, put a hand on her breast and lowered his head, caressing her knees and stomach with his cheek.

'Let's get out of here,' said Livia, breathing heavily, 'or we'll get arrested for lewd behaviour in public.'

On the road to Palermo, the inspector had an idea and made a suggestion.

'Shall we stop in town? I want to show you La Vuccirìa.'

'I've already seen it. In the Guttuso painting.'

'That's a shitty painting, believe me. We'll book a hotel room, hang out a little, walk around, go to La Vuccirià, get some sleep, and head back to Vigàta tomorrow morning. I don't have any work to do, in any case, so I can consider myself a tourist.'

*

Once inside the hotel, they failed in their intention to freshen up quickly and go out. They did not go out. They made love and fell asleep. Then they woke up and made love again. When they finally left the hotel it was already getting dark.

They went to La Vuccirìa. Livia was shocked and overwhelmed by the shouts, the exhortations, the cries of the merchants calling out their wares, the speech, the arguments, the sudden brawls, the colours so bright they seemed unreal, painted. The smell of fresh fish mingled with that of tangerines, boiled lamb entrails sprinkled with caciocavallo cheese, a dish called *mèusa,* and fritters, all of them fusing into a unique, almost magical whole.

Montalbano stopped in front of a second-hand clothes shop.

'In my university days, when I used to come here to eat *mèusa* and bread, which today would only make my liver burst, this shop was the only one of its kind in the world. Now they sell second-hand clothes, but back then the shelves were empty, all of them. The owner, Don Cesarino, used to sit there behind the counter – which was also completely bare – and receive clients.'

'Clients? But the shelves were all empty.'

'They weren't exactly empty. They were, well, full of purpose, full of requests. The man sold stolen goods to order. You'd go to Don Cesarino and say: I need a certain kind of watch; or, I want a painting, say, a nineteenth-century dock scene; or, I need this or that sort of ring. He'd take your order, write it down on a piece of pasta paper, the rough, yellow kind we used to have, he'd negotiate the price and then tell you when to come back. On the appointed date, and not one day later, he would pull the requested merchandise out from under the counter and hand it over to you. All sales were final.'

'But what need was there for him to have a shop? I

mean, he could have done that sort of business anywhere, in a cafe, on a street corner . . .'

'You know what his friends in La Vuccirìa used to call him? Don Cesarino *u putiàru,* "the shop-owner". Because Don Cesarino didn't see himself as a front man, as they might call him today, nor as a "receiver of stolen goods". He was a shopkeeper like any other, and his shop – for which he paid rent and electricity – was proof of this. It wasn't a facade.'

'You're all insane.'

*

'Like a son! Let me hug you like a son!' said the headmaster's wife, squeezing him to her breast and holding him there.

'You have no idea how worried you had us!' said her husband, echoing her sentiments.

Headmaster Burgio had phoned him that morning to invite him to dinner. Montalbano had declined, suggesting he drop by in the afternoon instead. They showed him into the living room.

'Let's get right to the point,' Burgio began, 'we don't want to take up too much of your time.'

'I have all the time in the world, being unemployed for the moment.'

'My wife told you, when you were here that time for dinner, that I call her a woman of fantasy. Well, right after you left, she started fantasizing again. We had wanted to call you sooner, but then what happened happened.'

'Suppose we let the inspector decide whether or not they're fantasies?' the signora said, slightly piqued, before continuing in a polemical tone: 'Shall you speak, or shall I?'

'Fantasies are your domain.'

'I don't know if you still remember, but when you asked my husband where you could find Lillo Rizzitano, he answered that he hadn't had any news of him since July 1943. Then something came back to me: that a girlfriend of mine also disappeared during that period. Except that I actually heard from her a while later, but in the strangest way . . .'

Montalbano felt a chill run down his spine. The two lovers of the Crasticeddru had been murdered very young.

'How old was this friend of yours?'

'Seventeen. But she was a lot more mature than me. I was still a little girl. We went to school together.'

She opened an envelope that was on the coffee table, took out a photograph, and showed it to Montalbano.

'This was taken on our last day of school, our final year. She's the first one on the left in the back row, and that's me next to her.'

All smiling and wearing the Fascist uniforms of the Giovani Italiane. The teacher was giving the Roman salute.

'Since the situation in Sicily was becoming too dangerous with all the bombing, schools closed on the last day in April, and we were spared the dreaded final exam. We passed or failed solely on the basis of our grades. Lisetta – that was my friend's name, Lisetta Moscato – moved to a little inland village with her family. She wrote to me every other day, and I still have all her letters, at least the ones that arrived. The mail in those days, you know . . . My family also moved out; we went all the way to the mainland, to live with one of my father's brothers. When the war was over, I wrote to my friend at both addresses, the one in the inland village and the one in Vigàta. But she never wrote back, and this worried me. Finally, in late 1946, we returned to Vigàta, and I looked up Lisetta's parents. Her mother had died, and at first her father didn't want to see me. Then he was rude to me and said Lisetta had fallen in love with an American soldier and gone away with him, against her family's wishes. And he added that as far as he was concerned, his daughter might as well be dead.'

'That does seem plausible, frankly,' said Montalbano.

'What did I tell you?' the headmaster cut in triumphantly.

'But you see, Inspector, the whole thing was strange just the same, even without counting what happened later. It's strange because, first of all, if Lisetta had fallen in love with an American soldier, she would have let me know in any way possible. And second, because in the letters she sent me from Serradifalco – that was the name of the village where they'd taken refuge – she kept harping on the same theme: the torment she suffered being separated from a mysterious young man with whom she was terribly in love, whose name she would never tell me.'

'Are you sure this mysterious lover really existed? Might he not have been some girlish fantasy?'

'Lisetta wasn't the type to indulge in fantasies.'

'You know,' said Montalbano, 'at age seventeen, and even later, you can never swear by matters of the heart.'

'Put that in your pipe and smoke it,' said the headmaster.

Without saying a word, the signora extracted another photo from the envelope. It showed a young woman in bridal dress, giving her arm to a good-looking boy in a US army uniform.

'This came to me from New York in early 1947, according to the postmark.'

'And this, in my opinion, dispels all doubt,' the headmaster concluded.

'Not at all. If anything, it raises doubt.'

'In what sense, signora?'

'Because it was the only thing that came in the envelope – only this photograph of Lisetta and the soldier, nothing else, no note, nothing. Not even any writing on the back of the photo; you can see for yourself. So, can you explain to me why a true, intimate friend would send me only a photograph without writing a single word?'

'Did you recognize your friend's handwriting on the envelope?'

'The address was typed.'

'Ah,' said Montalbano.

'And one last thing: Lisetta Moscato and Lillo Rizzitano were first cousins. And Lillo really loved her, like a little sister.'

Montalbano looked at the headmaster.

'He adored her,' Burgio admitted.

NINETEEN

The more he mulled it over, circled round it, snuck up beside it, the more convinced he became that he was on the right track. He hadn't even needed his customary meditative walk to the end of the jetty. Upon leaving the Burgio house with the wedding photo in his pocket, he'd raced off directly to Montelusa.

'Is the doctor in?'

'Yes, but he's busy. I'll let him know you're here,' said the receptionist.

Pasquano and his two assistants were standing around the marble table, on top of which lay a naked corpse with eyes agape. And the dead man had good reason to look so wide-eyed, as if in surprise, since the three were drinking a toast with paper cups. The doctor had a bottle of spumante in his hand.

'Come on in, we're celebrating.'

Montalbano thanked the assistant, who handed him a cup, and Pasquano poured him a finger or two of the sparkling wine.

'To whose health?' asked the inspector.

'To mine. With this guy here, I've just performed my thousandth autopsy.'

Montalbano drank up, called the doctor aside, and showed him the photograph.

'Do you think the dead girl from the Crasticeddru could have had a face like this one?'

'Would you please go fuck yourself?' Pasquano gently asked.

'Sorry,' said the inspector.

He turned on his heels and left. He was the arsehole, not the doctor. He'd let himself get carried away by his enthusiasm and had gone and asked Pasquano the most idiotic question imaginable.

He had no better luck at the crime lab.

'Is Jacomuzzi in?'

'No, he's at the commissioner's office.'

'Who's in charge of the photography lab?'

'De Francesco, in the basement.'

De Francesco eyed the photo as if he hadn't yet learned that one could reproduce images on light-sensitive film.

'What do you want me to do?'

'Tell me if you think it's a photomontage.'

'Ah, that's not my game. I only know about taking pictures and developing them. The more difficult stuff we send to Palermo.'

*

Then the wheel turned in the right direction, and things started falling into place. Montalbano phoned the photographer of the magazine that had published the review of Maraventano's book, whose name he remembered.

'Sorry to trouble you. Is this Mr Contino?'

'Yes, it is. Who's speaking?'

'This is Inspector Montalbano. I need to talk to you about something.'

'Pleased to make your acquaintance. You can come right now, if you like.'

The photographer lived in the old part of Montelusa, in one of the few houses to survive a landslide that had done away with an entire quarter, one that bore an Arab name.

'Actually, I'm not a photographer by profession. I teach history at the lyceum, and I love it. How can I be of help to you?'

'Do you think you could tell me if this photograph is a montage?'

'I could try,' said Contino, examining the photo. 'When was it taken, do you know?'

'Around 1946, I'm told.'

'Come by again tomorrow.'

Montalbano hung his head and said nothing.

'Is it very urgent? I'll tell you what, I can give you a preliminary answer in, say, two hours, but I'll need more time to confirm it.'

'It's a deal.'

*

The inspector spent the two hours in an art gallery that was featuring a show by a seventy-year-old Sicilian painter still caught up in a sort of populist rhetoric, but felicitous in his intense and lively use of colour. Yet he lent only a distracted eye to the paintings, as he was impatient for Contino's answer. Every five minutes he looked at his watch.

'So, what did you find?'

'I've just finished. In my opinion, it is definitely a photomontage. Rather well done.'

'What makes you think so?'

'The background shadows. The girl's head has been mounted in place of the real bride's head.'

Montalbano had not told him this. In no way had Contino been alerted to this fact or been led to this conclusion by the inspector.

'I'll say even more: the girl's face has been retouched.'

'In what way?'

'She's been, well, made to look a little older.'

'Could I have it back?'

'Sure, I don't have any more use for it. I thought it was going to be more difficult, but there's no need for any further confirmation.'

'You've been extremely helpful.'

'Listen, Inspector, the opinion I gave you is just between us, okay? It has no legal value whatsoever.'

*

The commissioner greeted him at once, with arms joyfully open.

'What a wonderful surprise! Do you have a little time? Come along with me, we'll go to my house. I'm expecting a phone call from my son. My wife will be so happy to see you.'

The commissioner's son, Massimo, was a doctor who belonged to a volunteer organization that defined itself as 'without borders'. Its members went to work in war-torn countries, lending their skills as best they could.

'My son's a pediatrician, you know. He's in Rwanda at the moment. I'm very worried about him.'

'Is there still fighting?'

'I wasn't referring to the fighting. Every time he manages to call us, he sounds more and more overwhelmed by the horror and anguish.'

The commissioner fell silent. To distract him from his preoccupations, Montalbano told him the news.

'I'm ninety-nine per cent certain I know the first and last name of the dead girl we found in the Crasticeddru.'

The commissioner said nothing, but only gaped at him.

'Her name was Lisetta Moscato, aged seventeen.'

'How the devil did you find that out?'

Montalbano recounted the whole story.

The commissioner's wife took his hand as if he were a little boy, and had him sit down on the sofa. They spoke for a short while, and then the inspector stood up and said he had an engagement and had to go. It wasn't true, but he didn't want to be there when the call came. The commissioner and his wife should be allowed to enjoy their faraway son's voice in peace and by themselves, however full of sorrow and pain his words might be. As he was leaving the house, he heard the telephone ring.

*

'I've kept my word, as you can see. I brought you back the photograph.'

'Come in, come in.'

Signora Burgio stepped aside to let him in.

'Who is it?' her husband called loudly from the dining room.

'It's the inspector.'

'Well, invite him inside!' the headmaster roared as if his wife had somehow refused to let him in.

They were eating supper.

'Shall I set a place for you?' the signora asked pleasantly. And without waiting for an answer, she put a soup dish on the table for him. Montalbano sat down, and the signora served him some fish broth, reduced to a divine density and enlivened with parsley.

'Were you able to find anything out about the photo?' she asked, without noticing the disapproving look her husband was giving her for being, in his opinion, too forward.

'Unfortunately, yes, signora. I think it's a photomontage.'

'My God! So whoever sent it to me wanted me to believe something that wasn't true!'

'Yes, I do think that was the purpose. To try to put an end to your enquiries about Lisetta.'

'See? I was right!' the woman practically yelled at her husband, and then she started to weep.

'Come on, why are you crying?' Burgio asked.

'Because Lisetta is dead, and they wanted me to think she was alive and happily married!'

'Well, it might have been Lisetta herself who—'

'Don't be ridiculous!' said the signora, throwing her napkin on the table.

There was an awkward silence. Then Mrs Burgio spoke again.

'She's dead, isn't she, Inspector?'

'I'm afraid she is.'

The headmaster's wife got up and left the dining room, covering her face with her hands. As soon as she was out of the room they heard her give in to a kind of plaintive whimpering.

'I'm sorry,' said the inspector.

'She got what she was looking for,' Burgio said without pity, keeping to the logic of his own side of the marital quarrel.

'Let me ask you one question. Are you sure that the feelings Lillo and Lisetta had for each other were only the kind that you and your wife mentioned?'

'What do you mean?'

Montalbano decided to speak plainly.

'Couldn't Lillo and Lisetta have been lovers?'

The headmaster started laughing, swatting the idea away with a swipe of the hand.

'Look, Lillo was madly in love with a Montelusa girl he'd stopped hearing from after July 1943. Besides, the corpse in the Crasticeddru couldn't be him, for the simple reason that the farmer who saw him bleeding and being loaded onto the truck by the soldiers, and then carried away who knows where, was a sensible, serious person.'

'Then,' said Montalbano, 'this can mean only one thing: that it's not true that Lisetta ran away with an American soldier. Therefore Lisetta's father told your wife a big fat lie. Who was Lisetta's father, anyway?'

'I vaguely remember his name was Stefano.'

'Is he still alive?'

'No, he died at least five years ago.'

'What did he do for a living?'

'I think he dealt in timber. But Stefano Moscato was not someone we talked about in my house.'

'Why not?'

'Because he, too, wasn't our kind of person. He was in cahoots with his relatives, the Rizzitanos, need I say more? He'd had trouble with the law, I don't know exactly what sort. In those days, in good, respectable families, you simply didn't talk about people like that. It was like talking about shit, if you'll excuse my language.'

Signora Burgio came back, eyes red, an old letter in her hand.

'This is the last letter I received from Lisetta when I

was staying in Acquapendente, where I'd moved with my family.'

Serradifalco, June 10, 1943

My dear Angelina,

How are you? How is everyone in your family? You have no idea how much I envy you, since your life in a northern town can't be even remotely comparable to the prison in which I spend my days. And don't think I'm exaggerating by using the word 'prison'. Aside from Papa's asphyxiating surveillance, there's also the monotonous, stupid life of a village with only a handful of houses. Just imagine, last Sunday, as we were coming out of church, a local boy whom I don't even know said hi to me. Papa noticed, called him aside, and started slapping him. Sheer madness! My only recreation is reading. And I have a friend: Andreuccio, a ten-year-old boy, my cousins' son. He's very smart. Have you ever noticed that little children are sometimes more clever than we are?

For several days now, Angelina, I've been living in despair. I received – by means so adventurous it would take me too long to explain here – a little note, four lines, from Him Him Him. He says he's desperate, he can no longer stand not seeing me, and now, after staying put all this time in Vigàta, they've just received orders to leave in the next few days. I feel like I'm dying without him. Before he leaves, before he goes away, I must must must spend a few hours with him, even if it means doing something crazy. I'll keep you informed. Meanwhile I send you a great big hug. Yours truly,

Lisetta

'So you never did find out who this "Him" was,' said the inspector.

'No. She never wanted to tell me.'

'Did you receive any other letters after this one?'

'Are you joking? It was already a miracle I got this

one. At the time you couldn't cross the Strait of Messina; they were bombing it non-stop. Then, on July 9, the Americans landed and all communications were cut.'

'Excuse me, signora, but do you remember your friend's address at Serradifalco?'

'Of course. It was care of the Sorrentino family, Via Crispi 18.'

*

He was about to put the key in the lock, but stopped in alarm. Voices and noises were coming from inside the house. He thought of going back to the car and getting his pistol, but did nothing. He opened the door cautiously, without making the slightest noise.

Then all at once he remembered that he'd completely forgotten about Livia, who had been waiting for him for God knows how long.

It took him half the night to make peace.

*

At seven in the morning he tiptoed out of bed and dialled a phone number.

'Fazio?' he said very softly. 'I need you to do me a favour. You have to call in sick.'

'No problem.'

'By this evening, I want to know everything – from the cradle to the grave – about a certain Stefano Moscato, who died here in Vigàta about five years ago. Ask around town, check the records office and anywhere else you can think of. It's very important.'

'Don't worry, I'll take care of it.'

He hung up the phone, grabbed a pen and a sheet of paper, and wrote:

> *Darling, I have to run out for something urgent and didn't want to wake you. I'll be back by early afternoon, promise. Why don't you get a cab and go to see the temples again? They're as splendid as ever. All my love.*

He stole out of the house like a thief. Had Livia opened her eyes, there would have been hell to pay.

*

It took him an hour and a half to get to Serradifalco. It was a clear day, and he even started whistling. He felt happy. It made him think of Caifas, his father's dog, who used to mope about the house, lethargic and melancholy, until he saw his master start getting his cartridges ready, and immediately he would turn frisky and spry, before transforming into a mass of sheer energy when he was finally out in the fields for the hunt.

Montalbano found Via Crispi right away; number 18 was a small nineteenth-century building of two storeys. There was one doorbell, with the name SORRENTINO inscribed beside it. A pleasant girl of about twenty asked him what he wanted.

'I'd like to speak with Andrea Sorrentino.'

'That's my father. He's not at home. You can find him at the town hall.'

'Does he work there?'

'Sort of. He's the mayor.'

*

'Of course I remember Lisetta,' said Andrea Sorrentino. He wore his sixty-odd years quite well, only a few white hairs. A handsome man. 'But why do you ask?'

'I'm conducting a rather confidential investigation. I'm sorry I can't tell you more. But you must believe me: it's very important that I get some information about her.'

'All right, Inspector. I have very beautiful memories of Lisetta, you know. We used to take long walks in the country. With her at my side, I felt so proud, like a grown-up man. She used to treat me as if we were the same age. But after her family left Serradifalco and she returned to Vigàta, I never heard from her again.'

'Why's that?'

The mayor hesitated a moment.

'Well, I'll tell you because it's all in the past now. I think my father and Lisetta's father had a terrible row. Around the end of August 1943, my father came home in an awful state. He'd been to Vigàta, to see Uncle Stefano – *u zu Stefano*, as I called him – I don't remember what for. He was pale and had a fever. I remember my mother got very scared, and so I, too, got scared. I don't know what transpired between the two of them, but the next day, at the dinner table, my father said that in our house, the Moscatos' name must never be mentioned again. I obeyed, even though I really wished I could ask him about Lisetta. You know how it is, with these horrible feuds between relatives . . .'

'Do you remember the American soldier Lisetta met here?'

'Here? An American soldier?'

'Yes. Or so I've been led to believe. She met an American soldier in Serradifalco, they fell in love, she followed him, and a little while later they got married in the United States.'

'I heard some vague talk of this marriage business, when an aunt of mine, my father's sister, was sent a photo of Lisetta in bridal dress with an American soldier.'

'So why were you surprised when I mentioned it?'

'I was surprised that you said Lisetta met the American here. You see, Lisetta disappeared from our house at least ten days before the Americans occupied Serradifalco.'

'What?'

'Oh, yes. One afternoon, it must have been around three or four o'clock, I saw Lisetta getting ready to leave. I asked her where we were going on our walk that day, and she told me I shouldn't feel hurt, but she wanted to take her walk by herself. Of course I felt deeply hurt. That evening, at supper time, Lisetta still hadn't returned. Uncle Stefano, my father and some local peasants went out looking for her but never found her. Those were terrible hours for us. There were Italian and German soldiers about, and the grown-ups were worried she'd come to harm . . . The following afternoon, Uncle Stefano said goodbye, telling us he wouldn't be back until he found his daughter. Lisetta's mother stayed behind with us; poor thing, she was devastated. Then the Americans landed, and we were cut off by the front. The very day the front moved on, Stefano Moscato came back to get his wife and said he'd found Lisetta in Vigàta and that her escape had been a childish prank. Now, if you've been following me, you will have understood why Lisetta could not have met her future husband here in Serradifalco, but must have met him in her own town, in Vigàta.'

TWENTY

I know the temples are splendid. Since I've known you I've been forced to see them about fifty times. You can therefore stick them, column by column, you know where. I'm going off by myself and don't know when I'll be back.

Livia's note oozed with rage, and Montalbano took it in. But since a wolf-like hunger had seized hold of him on his way back from Serradifalco, he opened the fridge: nothing. He opened the oven: nothing. Livia, who didn't want the housekeeper about for the time of her stay in Vigàta, had taken her sadism to the point of cleaning everything utterly. Not the tiniest piece of bread was to be found. He got back in his car and drove to the Trattoria San Calogero, where they were already rolling down their shutters.

'We're always open for you, Inspector.'

To quell his hunger and to spite Livia, he ate so much he nearly had to call the doctor.

*

'There's one statement here that's got me thinking,' said Montalbano.

'You mean where she says she might do something crazy?'

They were sitting in the living room having coffee, the inspector, the headmaster and Signora Angelina.

Montalbano was holding young Lisetta's letter, which he'd just finished rereading aloud.

'No, signora, we know she eventually did that. Mr Sorrentino told me so, and he would have no reason to lie to me. A few days before the landing, therefore, Lisetta got it in her head to flee Serradifalco and come here, to Vigàta, to see the one she loved.'

'But how would she have done that?'

'She probably asked some military vehicle for a lift. In those days the German and Italian troops must have been constantly on the move. A pretty girl like her, she wouldn't have had to try very hard,' interjected Headmaster Burgio, who'd decided to cooperate, having resigned himself to the fact that once in a while, his wife's fantasies might have some connection to reality.

'But what about the bombing? And the machine-gun fire? My God, what courage,' said the signora.

'So, which statement do you mean?' the headmaster asked impatiently.

'The one where Lisetta writes that her lover has told her that, after all this time in Vigàta, they've now received the order to leave.'

'I don't understand.'

'You see, signora, that statement tells us he'd been in Vigàta for a long time, which implies that he was not from the town. Second, it also informs Lisetta that he was about to be compelled, forced, to leave town. Third, she says "they", and therefore he's not the only one who has to leave Vigàta; it's a whole group of people. All this leads me to think he's a soldier. I could be wrong, but it seems like the most logical conclusion.'

'Yes, logical,' echoed the headmaster.

'Tell me, signora, when did Lisetta first tell you she was in love? Do you remember?'

'Yes, because in the last few days I've done nothing but try to recall every last detail of my meetings with Lisetta. It was definitely around May or June 1942. I refreshed my memory with an old diary I dug up.'

'She turned the whole house upside down,' grumbled her husband.

'We need to find out what troops were stationed here between early 1942, or even earlier, and July 1943.'

'You think that's easy, Inspector?' Burgio commented. 'I, for example, can remember a whole slew of different troops. There were the anti-aircraft batteries, the naval batteries, there was a train armed with cannon that remained hidden inside a tunnel, there were soldiers in barracks, soldiers in bunkers . . . Sailors, no; they would come and go. It'd be practically impossible to find out.'

They became discouraged. Then the headmaster stood up.

'I'm going to phone Burruano. He stayed in Vigàta the whole time, before, during and after the war. Whereas I was evacuated at a certain point.'

His wife resumed speaking.

'It was probably an infatuation – at that age it's hard to distinguish, you know – but it certainly was something serious, serious enough to make her run away from home, to make her go against her father, who was like her jailer, or so she used to tell me, at least.'

A question came to Montalbano's lips. He didn't want to ask it, but the hunter's instinct got the better of him.

'Excuse me for interrupting, but could you be more precise – I mean, could you tell me exactly what Lisetta meant by that word, "jailer"? Was it a Sicilian father's jealousy of the female child? Was it obsessive?'

Signora Angelina looked at him a moment, then lowered her eyes.

'Well, as I said, Lisetta was much more mature than me; I was still a little girl. Since my father forbade me to go to the Moscatos' house, we used to meet up at school or in church, where we would spend a few quiet hours together. And we would talk. Lately, I've been going over and over in my mind what she said or hinted at back then. I think there were a lot of things I didn't understand at the time . . .'

'Such as?'

'For example, up until a certain point, Lisetta referred to her father as "my father"; after that, however, she always called him "that man". But this might not mean anything. Another time she said to me, "One day that man's going to hurt me, he's going to hurt me very badly." And at the time I imagined a beating, a whipping. Now I'm starting to have a terrible feeling about the true meaning of that statement.'

She stopped, took a sip of coffee, and continued.

'She was brave, very brave. In the shelter, when the bombs were falling and we were trembling and crying with fear, it was she who gave us courage and consoled us. But to do what she did, she needed twice that much courage, to defy her father and run out under a hail of bullets, to come all the way here and make love to someone who wasn't even her official lover. Back then we were different from today's seventeen-year-olds.'

Signora Angelina's monologue was interrupted by the return of her husband, who seemed restless.

'I couldn't find Burruano, he wasn't home. Come, Inspector, let's go.'

'To look for Burruano?'

'No, no, I've just had an idea. If we're lucky, and I've guessed right, I'll donate fifty thousand lire to San Calogero on his next feast day.'

San Calogero was a black saint revered by the townsfolk.

'If you've guessed right, I'll throw in another fifty myself,' said Montalbano, caught up in the old man's enthusiasm.

'Think you could tell me where you're going?'

'I'll tell you later,' the headmaster said to his wife.

'And leave me here in the lurch?' the woman insisted.

Burgio, frantic, was already out of the door. Montalbano bent down to her. 'I'll keep you informed of everything.'

*

'How the hell did I forget *La Pacinotti*?' the headmaster muttered to himself as soon as they were in the street.

'Who's she?' Montalbano asked. He imagined her fiftyish and stubby. Burgio didn't answer. Montalbano asked another question.

'Should we take the car? Are we going far?'

'Far? It's right round the corner.'

'Would you explain to me who this Pacinotti woman is?'

'Woman? She was a ship, a mother ship that would repair any damage the warships sustained. She anchored in the port towards the end of 1940 and never moved. Her crew was made up of sailors who were also mechanics, carpenters, electricians, plumbers . . . They were all kids. And because the ship was there for so long, many of them became like family and ended up seeming like towns folk. They made friends, and they also took girlfriends. Two of them married local girls. One of them has since died, name was Tripcovich; the other's name is Marin and he owns the repair garage in Piazza Garibaldi. You know him?'

'He's my mechanic,' the inspector said, bitterly thinking he was about to resume his journey through the old people's memories.

*

A fiftyish-year-old man in filthy overalls, fat and surly, said nothing to the inspector and attacked Headmaster Burgio.

'Why are you wasting your time coming here? It's not ready yet. I told you the work would take a long time.'

'I didn't come for the car. Is your father here?'

'Of course he's here. Where else would he be? He's here busting my balls, telling me I don't know how to work, that the mechanical geniuses in his family are him and his grandson.'

A lad of twenty or so, also in overalls, who'd been looking under a car bonnet, stood up and greeted the two men with a smile. Montalbano and Burgio walked across the garage, which must have originally been a warehouse, and came to a kind of partition made of wooden boards.

Inside, behind a desk, was Antonio Marin.

'I overheard everything,' he said. 'And if arthritis hadn't messed me up, I could teach that one a thing or two.'

'We need some information.'

'What do you need to know, Inspector?'

'It's better if I let Headmaster Burgio tell you.'

'Do you remember how many crew members of the *Pacinotti* were killed or wounded or declared missing in combat?'

'We were lucky,' the old man said, growing animated. Apparently he liked talking about that heroic time; at home they probably told him to shut up whenever he started in on the subject. 'We had one dead from bomb shrapnel, name was Arturo Rebellato; and one wounded, also from shrapnel, and his name was Silvio Destefano; and one missing, Mario Cunich. We were all very close, you know; most of us hailed from up north, Venice, Trieste . . .'

'Missing at sea?' asked the inspector.

'What sea? We were moored in the harbour the whole time. We practically became an extension of the wharf.'

'Then why was he declared missing?'

'Because on the evening of July the seventh, 1943, he never returned to ship. The bombing had been heavy that afternoon, and he was out on a pass. Cunich was from Monfalcone, and he had a friend from the same town who was also my friend, Stefano Premuda. Well, the next morning Premuda forced the whole crew to go looking for Cunich. We spent the entire day going from house to house asking after him, to no avail. We went to the military hospital, the civilian hospital, we went to the place where they collected all the dead bodies found under the rubble . . . Nothing. Even the officers joined in the search, since some time before that they'd been given advance notice, a kind of warning, that in the coming days we were going to have to weigh anchor . . . We never did, though; the Americans arrived first.'

'Couldn't he have simply deserted?'

'Cunich? Never! He believed in the war. He was a Fascist. A good kid, but a Fascist. And he was smitten.'

'What do you mean?'

'Smitten, in love. With a girl from here. Like me, actually. He said that as soon as the war was over, he was going to get married.'

'And you never had any news of him again?'

'Well, when the Americans landed, they decided that a repair ship like ours, which was a jewel, suited them just fine. So they kept us in service, in Italian uniform, but they gave us an armband to wear on our sleeves to avoid any misunderstandings. So Cunich had all the time in the world to return to the ship, but he never did. He just disappeared. I stayed in touch with Premuda afterward, and now and then I'd ask him if he'd heard from Cunich or had any news of him . . . Nothing, not a word.'

'You said you knew Cunich had a girlfriend here. Did you ever meet her?'

'Never.'

One more thing needed to be asked, but Montalbano stopped, and with a glance he let Burgio have the honour.

'Did he at least tell you her name?' the headmaster asked, accepting Montalbano's generous offer.

'Well, Cunich was very reserved. But he did tell me once that her name was Lisetta.'

What happened? Did an angel pass, did time stop? Montalbano and Burgio froze, and the inspector grabbed his side. He felt a violent pain, while the headmaster brought his hand to his heart and leaned against a car to keep from falling. Marin became terrified.

'What did I say? My God, what did I say?'

*

Immediately outside the garage, the headmaster started shouting cheerfully, 'We guessed right!'

And he traced a few dance steps. Two passers-by, who knew him as a pensive, sombre man, stopped in shock. Having got it out of his system, Burgio turned serious again.

'Don't forget we promised San Calogero fifty thousand lire a head.'

'I won't forget.'

'Do you know San Calogero?'

'I haven't missed the annual celebration since I moved to Vigàta.'

'That doesn't mean you know him. San Calogero is someone who – how shall I say? – who doesn't let things slide. I'm telling you this for your own good.'

'Are you joking?'

'Absolutely not. He's a vengeful saint, and it doesn't take much to get his dander up. If you make him a promise, you have to keep it. If you, for example, get in a car crash and narrowly escape with your life, and you make a promise to the saint which you don't keep, you can bet your last lira you're going to get in another accident and lose your legs at the very least. Get the idea?'

'Perfectly.'

'Let's go home now, so you can tell my wife the whole story.'

'So *I* can tell her?'

'Yes, because I don't want to give her the satisfaction of hearing me say she was right.'

*

'To summarize,' said Montalbano, 'things may have gone as follows.'

He was enjoying this investigation in slippers, in a home from another age, over a cup of coffee.

'The sailor Mario Cunich, who became a kind of local boy around Vigàta, fell in love with Lisetta Moscato, who loved him too. How they managed to meet and talk to each other, God only knows.'

'I've given it a lot of thought,' said Signora Angelina. 'There was a period – I think it was from 1942 until March or April 1943 – when her father had to go far away from Vigàta on business. They could have fallen in love then, and they would certainly have had plenty of opportunities to spend time together in secret.'

'They did fall in love, that much we know,' resumed Montalbano. 'Then her father's return again prevented them from seeing each other. Soon the evacuation also came between them. So when news came of his imminent departure . . . Lisetta escaped, she came here, she met Cunich, but we don't know where. The sailor, so he could have as much time as possible with Lisetta, didn't return to ship. And at some point, they were murdered in their sleep. So far, everything clicks.'

'Clicks?' asked Angelina, taken aback.

'I'm sorry, I merely meant that thus far, our reconstruction makes sense. The person who killed them may have been a jilted lover, or even Lisetta's father, who may have caught them together and felt dishonoured. We may never know.'

'What do you mean, we may never know?' said Angelina. 'Aren't you interested in finding out who murdered those two poor kids?'

He didn't have the heart to tell her that he didn't care that much about the killer himself. What really intrigued him was why someone, perhaps even the killer, had taken it upon himself to move the bodies into the cave and set up that scene with the bowl, the jug and the terracotta dog.

*

Before going back home he stopped at a grocery store and bought two hundred grammes of peppered cheese and a loaf of durum-wheat bread. He got these provisions because he was sure he wouldn't find Livia at the house. And indeed she wasn't there; everything was the same as when he'd left to see the Burgios.

He didn't have time to set the bag of groceries on the table when the phone rang. It was the commissioner.

'Montalbano, I thought I should tell you that Under Secretary Licalzi called me today, wanting to know why I hadn't yet put in a request for your promotion.'

'But what the hell does that man want from me, anyway?'

'I took the liberty of inventing a story of love, something mysterious, I said, left unstated, between the lines . . . He took the bait; apparently he's a passionate reader of pulp romances. But he did settle the matter. He told me to write to him and ask that you be given a substantial bonus. So I wrote the request and sent it. You want to hear it?'

'Spare me.'

'Too bad. I thought I'd written a little masterpiece.'

Montalbano set the table and cut a thick slice of bread before the telephone rang again. It wasn't Livia, as he had hoped, but Fazio.

'Chief, I've been working all bleeding day for you. This Stefano Moscato wasn't the kind of guy you'd want to sit down to dinner with.'

'A mafioso?'

'Really and truly mafioso, I don't think so. But he was certainly violent. Various convictions for brawling, violence and assault. They don't seem like Mafia offences to me; a mafioso doesn't get himself convicted for stupid shit.'

'What's the date of the last conviction?'

'Nineteen eighty-one, if I'm not mistaken. With one foot in the grave he still busted some guy's head with a chair.'

'Do you know if he did any time in jail in 1942 and 1943?'

'Sure did. Assault and battery. From March 1942 to April 1943 he was in Palermo, at Ucciardone prison.'

The news from Fazio greatly enhanced the flavour of the peppered cheese, which was already no joking matter all by itself.

TWENTY-ONE

Galluzzo's brother-in-law opened his news programme with the story of a grisly bombing, clearly bearing the Mafia's signature, on the outskirts of Catania. A well-known and respected businessman from that city, Corrado Brancato, owner of a large warehouse that supplied supermarkets around the island, had decided to treat himself to an afternoon of rest in a small house he owned just outside town. After turning the key in the lock, he had, for all intents and purposes, opened the door onto nothingness: a horrific explosion, triggered by an ingenious device linking the door to an explosive charge, literally pulverized the house, the businessman and his wife, Giuseppa née Tagliafico. Investigations, the newsman added, were proving difficult, since Mr Brancato had a clean record and did not appear to be in any way involved with the Mafia.

Montalbano turned off the television and started whistling Schubert's Eighth, the 'Unfinished'. It came out splendidly, he didn't miss a note.

He dialed Mimì Augello's number. Surely his second-in-command would know more about this most recent development. There was no answer.

When he'd finally finished eating, Montalbano made every trace of the meal disappear, carefully washing even the glass from which he'd drunk three gulps of wine. He undressed and was about to get into bed when he heard a vehicle pull up, followed by some voices, a car door shutting, and the car driving away. Very quickly, he slipped under the covers, turned off the light, and pretended to be sleeping deeply. He heard the front door open and close, then Livia's footsteps, which came to a sudden halt. Montalbano realized she'd stopped in the bedroom doorway and was staring at him.

'Stop clowning around.'

Montalbano gave in and turned on the light.

'How did you know I was faking?'

'From your breathing. Do you know how you breathe when you're asleep? No. I do.'

'Where've you been?'

'To Eraclea Minoa and Selinunte.'

'By yourself?'

'Mr Inspector, I'll tell you everything, I'll confess, just drop this third degree, for Christ's sake! I went with Mimì Augello.'

Montalbano's face turned ugly, and he pointed a threatening finger.

'I'm warning you, Livia; Augello already moved into my desk once. I don't want him moving into anything else of mine.'

Livia stiffened.

'I'm pretending I don't understand. It's better for both of us. But, in any case, I'm not some piece of property of yours, you arsehole of a Sicilian.'

'All right, I'm sorry.'

They kept arguing a good while, even after Livia got undressed and came to bed. As for Mimì, however, Montalbano was determined not to let him get away with this. He got up.

'Now where are you going?'

'To give Mimì a ring.'

'Leave the guy in peace. He would never dream of doing anything that might offend you.'

'Hello, Mimì? Montalbano here. Oh, you just got in? Good. No, no, don't worry, Livia's just fine. She thanks you for the wonderful time she had with you today. And I, too, want to thank you. Oh, by the way, Mimì, did you know that Corrado Brancato was blown up today in Catania? No, I'm not kidding, they said so on TV. You haven't heard anything? What do you mean, you haven't heard anything? Oh, of course, you were out all day. And our colleagues in Catania were probably looking for you over land and sea. And no doubt the commissioner, too, was wondering what had become of you. Well, what can you do? Try to patch it up, I guess. Good night, Mimì. Sleep tight.'

'To say you're a real piece of shit is putting it mildly,' said Livia.

*

'All right,' said Montalbano. It was three o'clock in the morning. 'I admit it's all my fault, that when I'm here I get all wrapped up in my thoughts and act as if you didn't exist. I'm too accustomed to being alone. Let's go away.'

'And where will you leave your head?' asked Livia.

'What does that mean?'

'It means you're going to have to bring your head with you, along with everything inside it. And therefore, inevitably, you'll keep thinking about your own concerns even if we're a thousand miles away.'

'I promise I'll empty my head out before we leave.'

'And where will we go?'

Since Livia had clearly caught the archaeological-touristic bug, he thought it wise to play along.

'You've never seen the island of Mozia, have you? Tell you what: this very morning, around eleven, we'll leave for Mazara del Vallo. I've got a friend there, Assistant Commissioner Valente, whom I haven't seen in a long time. From there we'll head on to Marsala and eventually to Mozia. Then, when we get back to Vigàta, we'll plan another tour.'

They made peace.

*

Giulia, Assistant Commissioner Valente's wife, was not only the same age as Livia, but also a native of the Genoa suburb of Sestri. The two women took an immediate liking to each other. Montalbano took a bit less of a liking to Giulia, owing to the shamefully overcooked pasta, a beef stew conceived by an obviously deranged mind, and dishwater coffee of a sort that even airline crews wouldn't foist on anyone. At the end of this so-called lunch, Giulia suggested to Livia that the two of them stay at home and go out later; Montalbano accompanied his friend to the office. There, awaiting the assistant commissioner, was a man of about forty with long sideburns and a sun-baked Sicilian face.

'Every day, it's something else! I'm sorry, Mr Commissioner, but I need to talk to you. It's very important.'

'Inspector, let me introduce Farid Rahman, a friend of mine from Tunis,' said Valente. Then, turning to Rahman, 'Will it take long?'

'Fifteen minutes at the most.'

'I'll go and visit the Arab quarter,' said Montalbano.

'If you'll wait for me,' Farid Rahman interjected, 'I'd be delighted to be your guide.'

'I have an idea,' suggested Valente. 'I know my wife doesn't know how to make coffee. Piazza Mokarta is three blocks from here. Go and sit in the cafe there and have yourself a decent cup. Farid will come and pick you up.'

*

He didn't order the coffee immediately. First he went to work on a hefty, fragrant dish of *pasta al forno* that lifted him out of the gloom into which the culinary art of Signora Giulia had plunged him. By the time Rahman arrived,

Montalbano had already done away with all trace of the pasta and had only an innocent, empty demitasse of coffee in front of him. They headed off to the Arab quarter.

'How many of you are there in Mazara?'

'We're now more than a third of the local population.'

'Have there been many incidents between the Arabs and the Mazarese?'

'No, very few, practically nothing compared to other cities. I think we're sort of a historical memory for the Mazarese, almost a genetic fact. We're family. Al-Imam al-Mazari, the founder of the Maghrebin juridical school, was born in Mazara, as was the philologist Ibn al-Birr, who was expelled from the city in 1068 because he liked wine too much. But the basic fact is that the Mazarese are seafaring people. And the man of the sea has a great deal of common sense; he understands what it means to have one's feet on the ground. And speaking of the sea – did you know that the motor trawlers around here have mixed crews, half Sicilian, half Tunisian?'

'Do you have an official position here?'

'No, God save us from officialdom. Here everything works out for the best because it's all done unofficially. I'm an elementary-school teacher, but I also act as a liaison between my people and the local authorities. Here's another example of good, common sense: when a school principal gave our community some classrooms to use, we instructors came over from Tunis and created our school. But the superintendency is officially unaware of this situation.'

*

The Arab quarter was a piece of Tunis that had been picked up and carried, unaltered, to Sicily. The shops were closed because it was Friday, the day of rest, but life in the narrow little streets was still colourful and animated. First, Rahman showed Montalbano the large public baths, the social meeting place for Arabs from time immemorial; then he took him to a smoking den, a cafe with hookahs. They passed by a sort of empty storefront, inside of which an old man with a grave expression sat on the floor, legs folded under him, reading from a book and offering commentary. In front of him, sitting the same way, were some twenty boys listening attentively.

'That's one of our imams, explaining the Koran,' said Rahman, who made as if to keep walking.

Montalbano stopped him, resting a hand on his arm. He was struck by the truly religious absorption of those kids, who once outside of the empty store would again let loose, shouting and scuffling as always.

'What's he reading to them?'

'The eighteenth sura, the one about the cave.'

Montalbano, without knowing the cause, felt a slight tremor in his backbone.

'The cave?'

'Yes, *al-kahf*, the cave. The sura says that when some young people prayed to God not to let them be corrupted and led astray from the path of the true religion, He made them fall into a deep sleep inside a cave. And so that there would always be total darkness inside the cave, God reversed the course of the sun. They slept for about three hundred and nine years. Also with them was a dog, who slept in front of the entrance, but on guard, with his front legs extended—'

He broke off, having noticed that Montalbano had turned very pale and was opening and closing his mouth as if gasping for air.

'What's wrong, signore? Do you feel ill, signore? Do you want me to call a doctor? Signore!'

Frightened by his own reaction, Montalbano felt faint, his head spinning, legs buckling. Apparently he was still feeling the effects of the wound and the operation. A small crowd, meanwhile, had gathered around Rahman and the inspector. The teacher gave a few orders, and an Arab ran off and quickly returned with a glass of water. Another arrived with a wicker chair in which he forced Montalbano, who felt ridiculous, to sit. The water revived him.

'How do you say in your language: God is great and merciful?'

Rahman told him, and Montalbano did his best to imitate the sounds of the words. The small crowd laughed at his pronunciation, but repeated them in chorus.

*

Rahman shared an apartment with an older colleague named El Madani, who was at home at that moment. Rahman made tea while Montalbano explained the reasons for his malaise. Rahman was entirely unaware of the discovery of the two young murder victims in the Crasticeddru, whereas El Madani had heard mention of it.

'What I'd like to know, if you'd be so kind,' said the inspector, 'is to what extent the objects placed inside the cave correspond to what the sura says. As far as the dog is concerned, there's no doubt whatsoever.'

'The dog's name is Kytmyr,' said El Madani, 'but he's also called Quotmour. Among the Persians, you know, that dog, the one in the cave, became the guardian of written communication.'

'Does the sura say anything about a bowl with money inside?'

'No, there's no bowl, for the simple reason that the sleepers have money in their pockets. When they awake, one of them will be given money to go and buy the best food there is. They're hungry. But the one sent on this mission is betrayed by the fact that the coins are not only no longer current, but are now worth a fortune. People follow him back to the cave, hoping to find a treasure, and that is how the sleepers come to be discovered.'

'But in the case that concerns me,' Montalbano said to Rahman, 'the bowl can be explained by the fact that the boy and girl were naked when placed inside the cave, and therefore the money had to be put somewhere.'

'Agreed,' said El Madani, 'but it is not written in the Koran that they were thirsty. The water receptacle has no connection to the sura.'

'I know many legends about sleepers,' Rahman added, 'but none of them says anything about water.'

'How many sleepers were there in the cave?'

'The sura is vague about this – the number is probably

not important – three, four, five, six, not counting the dog. But it has become common belief that there were seven sleepers, eight with the dog.'

'If it's of any use to you,' said El Madani, 'you should know that the sura is a retelling of an old Christian legend, the Seven Sleepers of Ephesus.'

'There's also a modern Egyptian drama, *Ahl al-kahf*, which means "The People of the Cave", by the writer Taufik al-Hakim. In it the young Christians, persecuted by the emperor Decius, fall into a deep sleep and reawaken in the time of Theodosius the Second. There are three of them, as well as the dog.'

'Therefore,' Montalbano concluded, 'whoever put the bodies in the cave must have known the Koran, and perhaps even the play by this Egyptian.'

*

'Mr Burgio? Montalbano here. I'm calling you from Mazara del Vallo. I'm about to leave for Marsala. Sorry to be in such a rush, but I have to ask you something very important. Did Lillo Rizzitano know Arabic?'

'Lillo? Not a chance.'

'He couldn't perhaps have studied it at university?'

'Impossible.'

'What was his degree in?'

'In Italian, with Professor Aurelio Cotroneo. He may have even told me what his thesis was about, but I can't remember.'

'Did he have any Arab friends?'

'Not that I know of.'

'Were there any Arabs in Vigàta around 1942 to 1943?'

'Inspector, the Arabs were here at the time of their domination, and now they've returned, poor things, but not as dominators. No, during that period there weren't any. But what are the Arabs to you?'

*

It was already dark outside when they left for Marsala. Livia was cheerful and animated. She was very happy to have met Valente's wife. At the first intersection, instead of turning right, Montalbano turned left. Livia noticed immediately, and the inspector was forced to make a difficult U-turn. At the second intersection, Montalbano did the exact opposite: instead of going left, he turned right, and this time Livia was too engrossed in what she was saying to realize it. To their great astonishment, they found themselves back in Mazara. Livia exploded.

'You really try a woman's patience!'

'But you could have kept an eye out yourself!'

'Your word is worth nothing! You promised me before leaving Vigàta that you'd empty your head of all your concerns, and instead you keep getting lost in your own thoughts.'

'I'm sorry, I'm sorry.'

He paid very close attention for the first half hour of road, but then, treacherously, the thought returned: the dog made sense, as did the bowl with the money, but not the jug. Why?

He hadn't even begun to venture a hypothesis when he was blinded by a truck's headlights and realized he had drifted left of centre and was heading straight into what would have been a ghastly collision. He jerked the wheel wildly, deafened by Livia's scream and the angry blast of the truck's horn, and they bounced their way across a newly ploughed field before the car came to a halt, stuck in a furrow. Neither of them said a word; there was nothing to say. Livia was panting heavily. Montalbano dreaded what lay in store for him the moment the woman he loved caught her breath. Like a coward he took cover and sought her compassion.

'You know, I didn't tell you earlier because I didn't want to alarm you, but this afternoon, after lunch, I was unwell . . .'

✡

Then the whole incident turned into something between tragedy and a Laurel and Hardy film. The car would not budge, were they even to fire cannons at it. Livia withdrew into a scornful silence. At a certain point, Montalbano abandoned his efforts to get out of the rut, for fear of overheating the engine. He slung their bags over his shoulder, Livia following a few steps behind. A passing motorist took pity on the wretched pair at the edge of the road and drove them to Marsala. After leaving Livia at a hotel, Montalbano went to the local police station, identified himself, and with the help of an officer woke up someone with a tow truck. Between one thing and the next, when he lay down beside Livia, who was tossing in her sleep, it was four o'clock in the morning.

TWENTY-TWO

To win forgiveness, Montalbano made up his mind to be affectionate, patient, pleasant and obedient. It worked, and Livia soon cheered up. She was enchanted by Mozia, amazed by the road just under the water's surface, which linked the island with the coast, and charmed by the mosaic flooring of white and black river pebbles in an ancient villa.

'This is the *tophet*,' said their guide, 'the sacred area of the Phoenicians. There were no buildings; the rites were performed out in the open.'

'The usual sacrifices to the gods?' asked Livia.

'To god,' the guide corrected her, 'the god Baal Hammon. They would sacrifice a first-born son, strangle him, burn him, and put his remains in a vase that they would bury in the ground, and beside it they would erect a stela. Over seven hundred of these stelae have been found here.'

'Good God!' exclaimed Livia.

'It was not a very nice place for children, signora. When Dionysius of Syracuse sent the admiral Leptines to conquer the island, the Mozians, before surrendering, slit their children's throats. However you roll the dice, fate was never kind to the little ones of Mozia.'

'Let's get out of here,' said Livia. 'I don't want to hear any more about these people.'

*

They decided to leave for the island of Pantelleria. They stayed there for six days, finally without quarrels or arguments. It was the right place for Livia to ask one night, 'Why don't we get married?'

'Why not?'

They wisely decided to think it over calmly. The one who stood to lose the most was Livia, since she would have to move far from her home in Boccadasse and adapt to a new rhythm of life.

*

As soon as the aircraft took off, carrying Livia away with it, Montalbano rushed to the nearest public telephone and called his friend Zito in Montelusa. He asked him for a name and got his answer, along with a Palermo phone number, which he dialled at once.

'Professor Riccardo Lovecchio?'

'That's me.'

'A mutual friend, Nicolò Zito, gave me your name.'

'How is the old carrot top? I haven't heard from him for a long time.'

The loudspeaker requested that passengers for the

Rome flight go to the gate. This gave him an idea as to how he might see the man immediately.

'Nicolò's doing well and sends his regards. Listen, Professor, my name's Montalbano. I'm here at Punta Ràisi airport and have roughly four hours before I have to catch another flight. I need to speak with you.' The loud-speaker repeated the request on cue, as if in cahoots with the inspector, who needed answers, and fast.

'Listen, are you Inspector Montalbano of Vigàta, the one who found the two young murder victims in the cave? Yes? What a coincidence! You know, I was going to look you up one of these days! Come see me at home, I'll wait for you. Here's the address.'

*

'I, for example, once slept for four days and four nights in a row, without eating or drinking. Of course, contributing to my sleep were some twenty-odd joints, five rounds of sex, and a billy club to the head from the police. It was 1968. My mother got very worried and wanted to call a doctor. She thought I was in a deep coma.'

Professor Lovecchio had the look of a bank clerk. He didn't show his age of forty-five; a faint glint of madness sparkled in his eye. He was fuelling himself on straight whisky at eleven in the morning.

'There was nothing miraculous about my sleep,' Lovecchio went on. 'To achieve a miracle you have to be out for at least twenty years. In the Koran, again – I think it's in the second sura – it's written that a man, whom the commentators identify as Ezra, slept for a hundred years. The prophet Salih, on the other hand, slept for twenty years, he, too, in a cave, which isn't the most comfortable place for getting a good sleep. Not to be outdone, the Jews, in the Jerusalem Talmud, boast of a certain Hammaagel, who, in the inevitable cave, slept for seventy years. And let's not forget the Greeks. Epimenides woke up after fifty years – in a cave. In those days, in short, all you needed was a cave and somebody who was dead tired, and you had a miracle. The two youngsters you found had been sleeping for how long?'

'From 1943 to 1994. Fifty years.'

'The perfect time to be woken up. Would it complicate your deductions if I told you that in Arabic one uses the same verb for sleeping and dying? And that a single verb is also used for waking up and coming back to life?'

'What you're saying is absolutely spellbinding, but I've got a flight to catch and have very little time. Why were you thinking of contacting me?'

'To tell you not to be fooled by the dog. And that the dog seems to contradict the jug and vice versa. Do you understand why?'

'Not a bit.'

'You see, the legend of the sleepers is not oriental in origin, but Christian. In Europe, it was Gregory of Tours who first introduced it. It tells of seven youths of Ephesus who, to escape the anti-Christian persecutions of Decius, took refuge in a cave, where the Lord put them to sleep. The cave of Ephesus exists; you can even find it in the *Italian Encyclopedia*. They built a sanctuary over it, which was later destroyed. The Christian legend says there's a spring inside the cave. Thus the sleepers, as soon as they awoke, drank first, then sent one of their own in search of food. But at no time in the Christian legend, or in any of its endless European variants, is there any mention of a dog. The dog, whose name is Kytmyr, is purely and simply the poetic invention of Mohammed, who loved animals so much he once cut off a sleeve so as not to wake up the cat that was sleeping on it.'

'You're losing me.'

'But there's no reason to get lost, Inspector. I was merely trying to say that the jug was put there as a symbol of the spring that was in the Ephesian cave. So, to conclude: the jug, which thus belongs to the Christian legend, can only co-exist with the dog, which is a poetic invention of the Koran, if one has an overview of all the variants that the different cultures have contributed to the story . . . In my opinion, the person who staged that scene in the cave can only be someone who, in his studies . . .'

As in a comic book, Montalbano saw the lightbulb flash in his brain.

*

He screeched to a halt in front of the Anti-Mafia Commission offices. The guard on duty raised his sub-machine gun in alarm.

'I'm Inspector Montalbano!' he shouted, holding up his driver's licence, the first thing he'd happened to grab. Short of breath, he ran past another officer acting as usher and yelled, 'Please inform Mr De Dominicis that Inspector Montalbano's on his way up, quick!'

In the lift, taking advantage of being alone, Montalbano mussed up his hair, loosened his tie, and unbuttoned his top button. He thought of pulling his shirt a bit out of his trousers, but decided that would be excessive.

'De Dominicis, I've got it!' he said, panting slightly, closing the door behind him.

'You've got what?' asked De Dominicis, alarmed by the inspector's appearance and rising from his gilded armchair in his gilded office.

'If you're willing to give me a hand, I'll let you in on an investigation that—'

He stopped, putting a hand over his mouth as if to prevent himself from saying anything more.

'What's it about? Give me a hint, at least.'

'I can't, believe me, I really can't.'

'What am I supposed to do?'

'By this evening at the latest, I want to know what the subject of the university thesis of someone named Calogero Rizzitano was. His academic adviser was a certain Professor Cotroneo, I think. He must have graduated in late 1942. The subject of this thesis is the key to everything. We could deal a mortal blow to—'

Again he interrupted himself, became bug-eyed, and said to himself dementedly, 'I haven't said anything, you know.'

Montalbano's agitation infected De Dominicis.

'What can we do? The students . . . at the time . . . why, there must have been thousands! Assuming the records still exist.'

'What are you saying? A few dozen, not thousands. At the time, all the young men were in the service. It should be easy to find out.'

'Then why don't you look into it yourself?'

'They would be sure to waste a great deal of my time with their red tape, whereas for you they would open every door.'

'Where can I reach you?'

'I'm heading back to Vigàta in a hurry; I don't want to lose track of certain developments. Phone me as soon as you've got any news. Call me at home, don't forget. Not at the office; there may be a mole there.'

He waited until evening for De Dominicis's call, which never came. This did not worry him, however; he was sure that De Domenicis had swallowed the bait. Apparently, even for him, the going had not been easy.

*

The next morning he had the pleasure of seeing Adelina the housekeeper again.

'Why haven't you been around these days?'

'Whattaya mean, why? 'Cause the young lady don't like seein' me 'bout the house when she's here, that's why.'

'How did you know Livia was gone?'

'I found out in town.'

Everybody, in Vigàta, knew everything about everyone.

'What'd you buy for me?'

'I'm gonna make you *pasta con le sarde,* and *purpi alla carrettera* for after.'

Exquisite, but deadly. Montalbano gave her a hug.

*

Around midday the telephone rang and Adelina, who was cleaning the house top to bottom to get rid of every trace of Livia's presence, went to answer.

'Signuri, Dr Didumminici wants you.'

Montalbano, who'd been sitting on the veranda re-reading Faulkner's *Pylon* for the fifth time, rushed inside. Before picking up the receiver, however, he quickly established a plan of action for getting De Dominicis out of his hair once he'd obtained the information.

'Yes? Hello? Who's this?' he said in a tired voice full of disappointment.

'You were right, it was easy. Calogero Rizzitano graduated on November 13, 1942. You'd better write this down, because the title is a long one.'

'Wait while I look for a pen. For what it's worth . . .'

De Dominicis noticed the flatness in Montalbano's voice.

'Are you all right?'

Complicity had made De Dominicis more concerned and personal.

'Am I all right? Need you ask? I told you I needed an

answer by last night! I'm no longer interested! You're too late. Everything's fucked now, fizzled out.'

'I couldn't have done it any sooner, believe me.'

'All right, all right. Let's have the title.'

'*The Use of Macaronic Latin in the Mystery Play of the Seven Sleepers by an Anonymous Sixteenth-Century Author*. Now you tell me what the Mafia could have to do with a title—'

'It has a lot to do with it! It has everything to do with it! Except that now, because of you, I don't need it any more and I certainly can't thank you for it.'

He hung up and burst into a high-pitched whinny of joy. Immediately a sound of breaking glass could be heard in the kitchen: in terror, Adelina must have dropped something. Taking a running start, he leapt from the veranda onto the sand, executed a somersault, then a cartwheel, then a second somersault and a second cartwheel. The third somersault failed, and he collapsed on the sand, out of breath. Adelina ran towards him from the veranda screaming:

'*Madunnuzza beddra!* He's gone crazy! He's broke 'is neck!'

*

To set his own mind at rest, Montalbano got in his car and drove to the Montelusa public library.

'I'm looking for a mystery play,' he said to the chief librarian.

The chief librarian, who knew him as a police inspector, was mildly astonished but said nothing.

'All we've got,' she said, 'are the two volumes of D'Ancona and two more by De Bartholomaeis. But these books can't be taken out. You'll have to consult them here.'

He found the *Mystery Play of the Seven Sleepers* in the second tome of the D'Ancona anthology. It was a short, very naive text. Lillo's thesis must have centred around the dialogue between two heretical scholars who expressed themselves in an amusing macaronic Latin. But what most interested the inspector was the long preface by D'Ancona. It contained everything: the quotation from the Koranic sura, the legend's itinerary through various European and African countries, in all its different variants and mutations. Professor Lovecchio had been correct: sura number eighteen of the Koran, taken by itself, would have proved a very tough nut to crack. It had to be complemented with the contributions of other cultures.

*

'I'm going to venture a hypothesis, and I'd like to have your approval,' said Montalbano, who had brought the Burgios up to date on his latest discoveries. 'You both told me, with a great deal of conviction, that Lillo saw Lisetta as a little sister and was crazy about her. Right?'

'Yes,' the two said in chorus.

'Good. Now, let me ask you a question. Do you think Lillo would have been capable of killing Lisetta and her young lover?'

'No,' said the old couple without a moment's hesitation.

'I'm of the same opinion,' said Montalbano, 'precisely because it was Lillo who put the two bodies in a position – so to speak – to be hypothetically resurrected. No killer wants his victims to come back to life.'

'And so?' asked the headmaster.

'If, in an emergency, Lisetta had asked him to put them up, she and her boyfriend, at the Rizzitano house on the Crasto, how do you think Lillo would have responded?'

Signora Angelina didn't pause to think twice.

'He would have done whatever Lisetta asked of him.'

'Let's try, then, to imagine what happened during those days in July. Lisetta runs away from Serradifalco, with luck she makes it to Vigàta, meets up with Mario Cunich, and the boyfriend deserts his post – or strays from his ship, let's say. The two now have nowhere to hide. Going to Lisetta's house would be like walking into the wolf's den; it's the first place her father would look. So she asks Lillo Rizzitano for help; she knows he won't say no. Lillo puts the couple up at his house at the foot of the Crasto, where he's been living alone since the rest of his family was evacuated. Who killed the two lovers, and why, we don't know, and perhaps we never will. But there can be no doubt that it was Lillo who buried them in the cave, because he followed, step by step, both the Christian and the Koranic versions of the story. In both cases, the sleepers will one day awake. But what did he mean, what was he trying to say by staging that scene? Was he trying to tell us that the two lovers are asleep and will one day awake or be awakened? Or was he hoping, in fact, that someone in the future would find them and wake them up? Purely by chance, it was I who found them and woke them up. But, believe me, I really wish I had never discovered that cave.'

He was telling the truth, and the old couple realized this.

'I could stop here,' he continued. 'I've managed to satisfy my own personal curiosity. I'm still missing some answers, it's true, but the ones I've found are probably enough for me. As I said, I could stop here.'

'They may be enough for you,' said Signora Angelina, 'but I would like to see Lisetta's killer before me.'

'If you see him, it'll be in a photograph,' her husband said wryly, 'because by now it's ninety-nine per cent certain that the killer is dead and buried.'

'I'll leave it up to you two,' said Montalbano. 'You tell me: what should I do? Should I continue? Should I stop? It's your decision, since these murders are no longer of any interest to anyone. You are perhaps the only link the two dead lovers still have to this world.'

'I say you should go ahead,' said Mrs Burgio, bold as ever.

'Me too,' said the headmaster, seconding her after a pause.

*

When he arrived at the exit for Marinella, instead of turning and heading home, he let the car continue along the coastal highway as if of its own will. There was little traffic, and in just a few minutes he was at the foot of the

Crasto mountain. He got out of the car and climbed up the slope that led to the Crasticeddru. A stone's throw from the weapons cave, he sat down on the grass and lit a cigarette. He remained seated, watching the sunset while his brain was whirring: he had an obscure feeling that Lillo was still alive. But how would he ever flush him out? As darkness began to fall, he headed back to the car, and at that moment his eye fell on the gaping hole in the side of the mountain, the entrance to the unused tunnel, boarded up since time immemorial. Right near the mouth, there was a pile of sheet metal and, beside it, a sign on two stakes. His legs took off in that direction before his brain had even given the order. He arrived out of breath, his side smarting from the dash. The sign said: GAETANO NICOLOSI & SON CONSTRUCTION CO. – PALERMO – VIA LAMARMORA, 33 – PROJECT FOR THE EXCAVATION OF A HIGHWAY TUNNEL – WORKS MANAGER, COSIMO ZIRRETTA, ENG. – ASST. MANAGER, SALVATORE PERRICONE. This was followed by some other information of no interest to Montalbano.

He made another dash to his car and sped like a bullet back to Vigàta.

TWENTY-THREE

At the Gaetano Nicolosi & Son Construction Co. of Palermo, whose number Montalbano had got from directory enquiries, nobody was answering the phone. It was too late in the day; the company's offices must have been deserted. Montalbano tried and tried again, eventually losing hope. Having cursed a few times to let off steam, he then requested the number of the engineer Cosimo Zirretta, assuming that he, too, was from Palermo. He'd guessed right.

'Hello, this is Inspector Montalbano from Vigàta. How did you manage the expropriation?'

'What expropriation?'

'The land that the road and tunnel you were building cuts through, outside of Vigàta.'

'Look, that's not my domain, I'm only responsible for the construction. That is, I *was* responsible until an ordinance put a halt to the whole project.'

'So who should I talk to?'

'Somebody from the company.'

'I phoned there but nobody answered.'

'Then try Commendatore Gaetano or his son Arturo. When they get out of Ucciardone.'

'Oh, really?'

'Yes. Extortion and bribery.'

'So there's no hope?'

'Well, you can hope that the judges will be lenient and let them out in five years. Just kidding. Actually, you could try the company's lawyer, Di Bartolomeo.'

*

'Listen, Inspector, it's not the company's job to deal with expropriation procedures. That's up to the city council of the district in which the expropriated land is located.'

'Then what are you people doing there?'

'That's none of your business.'

And the lawyer hung up. A little touchy, this Di Bartolomeo. Maybe his job was to cover the arses of Nicolosi father and son from the repercussions of their frauds, except that this time he hadn't succeeded.

*

The office hadn't been open five minutes before the company land surveyor Tumminello saw Inspector Montalbano standing in front of him, looking somewhat agitated. And, in fact, it had been a restless night for Montalbano; he'd been unable to fall asleep and so had stayed up reading Faulkner. The surveyor, whose troubled son – who was mixed up with hoodlums, brawls, and motorcycles – once again hadn't come home that night, turned pale, and his hands began to shake. Montalbano, noticing the other's reaction upon seeing him, imagined the worst.

This guy's trying to hide something.

He was still a cop, no matter how well read.

'Is anything wrong?' asked Tumminello, expecting to hear that his son had been arrested. Which, in fact, would have been a stroke of luck, or the least of all evils, since he might as easily have had his throat slit by his little friends.

'I need some information. About an expropriation.'

Tumminello visibly relaxed.

'You over your scare now?' Montalbano couldn't resist asking him.

'Yes,' the surveyor admitted frankly. 'I'm worried about my son. He didn't come home last night.'

'Does he do that often?'

'Yes, actually. You see, he's mixed up with—'

'Then you shouldn't worry,' Montalbano cut him off. He didn't have time for the problems of youth. 'I need to see the bill of sale or expropriation for the land used to build the Crasto tunnel. That's your area, isn't it?'

'Yes, it is. But there's no point in taking out the documents; I know all the information. Tell me specifically what it is you want to know.'

'I want to know about the land that belonged to the Rizzitano family.'

'As I expected,' said the surveyor. 'When I heard about the weapons being discovered, and then about the two dead bodies, I thought: didn't those places belong to the Rizzitanos? And so I went and looked at the documents.'

'And what do the documents say?'

'First, there's something you should know. There were a lot of proprietors whose land stood to be damaged, so to speak, by the construction of the road and tunnel. Forty-five, to be exact.'

'Jesus!'

'There's even a little postage stamp of land, two thousand square metres, which, because it was divided up in an inheritance, has five owners. The note of transfer can't be made out collectively to the heirs; it must be made out individually to each one. Once our order was granted by the prefect, we offered the proprietors a modest sum, since most of the land in question was farmland. For Calogero Rizzitano, who was a presumed proprietor, since there's no piece of paper confirming his ownership – I mean there's no deed of inheritance, since his father died without leaving a will – for Calogero Rizzitano we had to resort to Article 143 of the Code of Civil Procedure, which concerns rightful claimants who cannot be found. As you probably know, Article 143 states—'

'I'm not interested. How long ago did you make out this note of transfer?'

'Ten years ago?'

'Therefore, ten years ago, Calogero Rizzitano could not be found.'

'Nor after that, either. Because out of the forty-five

landowners, forty-four appealed for a higher figure than the sum we were offering. And they got it.'

'And the forty-fifth, the one who did not, was Calogero Rizzitano.'

'Exactly. And we put the money due to him in escrow. Since for us, to all intents and purposes, he's still alive. Nobody asked for a declaration of presumed death. So when he reappears, he can pick up his money.'

*

When he reappears, the land surveyor had said. But everything pointed to the conclusion that Lillo Rizzitano was in no mood to reappear. Or, more likely, was no longer in any condition to reappear. Headmaster Burgio and Montalbano had taken for granted that the wounded Lillo, carried on board a military truck and driven who knows where on the night of July 9, had survived. But they had no idea how serious his wounds might have been. He could well have died in transit or in hospital, if they'd even brought him to a hospital. Why keep conjuring visions out of nothing? It was very possible that, at the moment of their discovery, the two corpses in the Crasticeddru were in better shape than Lillo Rizzitano had been in for some time. For fifty years and more, not a word, not a line. Nothing. Not even when they requisitioned his land and demolished the remains of his house and everything else that belonged to him. The meanders of the labyrinth the inspector had willingly entered led him straight into a wall. But perhaps the labyrinth was being kind to him by preventing him from going any further, stopping him in front of the most logical, most natural solution.

*

Supper was light, yet cooked, in every regard, with a touch the Lord grants only very rarely to the Chosen. But Montalbano did not thank the commissioner's wife; he merely looked at her with the eyes of a stray dog awarded a caress. The two men then retired to the study to chat. For Montalbano the commissioner's dinner invitation had been like a life preserver thrown to a man drowning not in a stormy sea, but in the flat, unrippled calm of boredom.

The first thing they discussed was Catania, and they concurred that informing the Catania police of their investigation of Brancato had led, as its first result, to the elimination of the very same Brancato.

'We're like a sieve,' the commissioner said bitterly. 'We can't take one step without our enemies' knowing about it. Brancato had Ingrassia killed because he was getting too nervous, but when the people pulling the strings learned that we had Brancato in our sights, they took care of him as well. And so the trail we were so painstakingly following was conveniently obliterated.'

He was gloomy. The idea that moles were planted everywhere offended him; it embittered him more than a betrayal by a family member.

Then, after a long pause during which Montalbano

did not open his mouth, the commissioner asked 'How's your investigation of the Crasticeddru murders coming along?'

From the commissioner's tone of voice, Montalbano could tell that his superior viewed this investigation as mere recreation for the inspector, a pastime he was being allowed to pursue before he returned to more serious matters.

'I've managed to find out the man's name, too,' he said, feeling vindicated in the eyes of the commissioner, who gave a start, astonished and now interested.

'You are extraordinary! Tell me how.'

Montalbano told him everything, even mentioning the theatricals he'd performed for De Dominicis, and the commissioner was quite amused. The inspector concluded with an admission of failure of sorts. It made no sense to continue the search, he said, since, among other things, nobody could prove that Lillo Rizzitano wasn't dead.

'All the same,' the commissioner said after a moment's reflection, 'if somebody really wants to disappear, it can be done. How many cases have we seen where people apparently vanish into thin air and then, suddenly, there they are? I don't want to cite Pirandello, but let's take Sciascia at least. Have you read the little book about the disappearance of Majorana, the physicist?'

'Of course.'

'I am convinced, as was Sciascia himself, that in the end Majorana wanted to disappear, and succeeded. He did not commit suicide. He was too religious.'

'I agree.'

'And what about that very recent case of the Roman university professor who stepped out of his home one day and was never seen again? Everybody looked for him – police, carabinieri, even his students, who loved him. It was a planned disappearance, and he also succeeded.'

'True,' Montalbano concurred. Then he thought about what they were saying and looked at his superior. 'It sounds to me as if you're encouraging me to continue the investigation, though on another occasion you reproached me for getting too involved in this case.'

'So what? Now you're convalescing, whereas the other time you were on the job. There's quite a difference, I think,' the commissioner replied.

*

Montalbano returned home and paced from room to room. After his meeting with the surveyor, he had decided to screw the whole investigation, convinced that Rizzitano was good and dead. Now the commissioner had gone and resurrected him, so to speak. Didn't the early Christians use the word *dormitio* to mean death? It was quite possible Rizzitano had put himself 'in sleep', as the Freemasons used to say. Fine, but if that was the case, Montalbano would have to find a way to bring him out of the deep well in which he was hiding. That would require something big, something that would make a lot of noise, something the newspapers and television stations all over Italy would talk about. He had to unleash a bombshell. But what? He needed to forget about logic and dream up something fantastic.

It was eleven o'clock, too early to turn in. He lay down on the bed, fully dressed, and read *Pylon*.

> 'At midnight last night the search for the body of Roger Shumann, racing pilot who plunged into the lake on Saturday p.m., was finally abandoned by a three-seater biplane of about eighty horsepower which managed to fly out over the water and return without falling to pieces and dropping a wreath of flowers into the water approximately three quarters of a mile away from the spot where Shumann's body is generally supposed to be . . .'

There were only a few lines left until the end of the novel, but the inspector sat up in bed with a wild look in his eyes.

'It's insane,' he said, 'but I'm going to do it.'

✡

'Is Signora Ingrid there? I know it's late, but I need to speak to her.'

'Signora no home. You say, I write.'

The Cardamones specialized in finding housekeepers in places where not even Tristão da Cunha would have dared set foot.

'*Manau tupapau,*' said the inspector.

'No understand.'

He'd cited the title of a Gauguin painting. That eliminated Polynesia and environs from the housekeeper's possible land of origin.

'You ready write? Signora Ingrid phone Signor Montalbano when she come home.'

*

When Ingrid got to Marinella, wearing an evening dress with a slit all the way up to her arse, it was already past two in the morning. She hadn't batted an eyelash at the inspector's request to see her right away.

'Sorry, but I didn't have time to change. I was at the most boring party.'

'What's wrong? You don't look right to me. Is it simply because you were bored at the party?'

'No, your intuition's right. It's my father-in-law. He's started pestering me again. The other morning he pounced on me when I was still in bed. He wanted me right away. I convinced him to leave by threatening to scream.'

'Then we'll have to take care of it.'

'How?'

'We'll give him another massive dose.'

At Ingrid's questioning glance, he opened a desk drawer that had been locked, took out an envelope, and handed it to her. Ingrid, seeing the photos portraying her getting fucked by her father-in-law, first turned pale, then blushed.

'Did you take these?'

Montalbano weighed the pros and cons; if he told her

it was a woman who took them, Ingrid might knife him then and there.

'Yeah, it was me.'

The Swedish woman's mighty slap thundered in his skull, but he was expecting it.

'I'd already sent three to your father-in-law. He got scared and stopped bothering you for a while. Now I'll send him another three.'

Ingrid sprang forward, her body pressing against Montalbano's, her lips forcing his open, her tongue seeking and caressing his. Montalbano felt his legs giving out, and luckily Ingrid withdrew.

'Calm down,' she said, 'it's over. It was just to say thank you.'

On the backs of three photos personally chosen by Ingrid, Montalbano wrote: RESIGN FROM ALL YOUR POSTS, OR NEXT TIME YOU'LL BE ON TV.

'I'm going to keep the rest here,' said the inspector. 'When you need them, let me know.'

'I hope it won't be for a long time.'

'I'll send them tomorrow morning, and then I'll make an anonymous phone call that'll give him a heart attack. Now listen, because I have a long story to tell you. And when I'm done, I'm going to ask you to lend me a hand.'

*

He got up at the crack of dawn, having been unable to sleep even a wink after Ingrid had left. He looked in the mirror: his face was a wreck, maybe even worse than after he'd been shot. He went to the hospital for a check-up, and they pronounced him perfect. The five medicines they'd been giving him were reduced to just one. Then he went to the Montelusa Savings Bank, where he kept the little money he was able to put aside. He asked to meet privately with the manager.

'I need ten million lire.'

'Do you need a loan, or have you got enough in your account?'

'I've got it.'

'I don't understand, then. What's the problem?'

'The problem is that it's for a police operation I want to pay for myself, without risking the State's money. If I go to the cashier now and ask for ten million in bills of one hundred thousand, it'll seem strange. That's why I need your help.'

Understanding, and proud to take part in a police operation, the manager bent over backwards for Montalbano.

*

Ingrid pulled her car up alongside the inspector's, right in front of the road sign indicating the superhighway for Palermo, just outside of Montelusa. Montalbano gave her a bulging envelope with the ten million lire inside, and she put it in her shoulder bag.

'Call me at home as soon as you're done. And be careful not to get your purse snatched.'

She smiled, waved him a kiss from her fingertips, and put her car in gear.

*

In Vigàta he got a new supply of cigarettes. On his way out of the tobacco shop, he noticed a big green poster with black lettering, freshly pasted up, inviting the townspeople to attend a cross-country motorbike race the following Sunday, starting at three in the afternoon, in the place called the 'Crasticeddru flats'.

He could never have hoped for such a coincidence. Perhaps the labyrinth had been moved to pity and was opening another path for him?

TWENTY-FOUR

The 'Crasticeddru flats', which stretched out behind the rocky spur, weren't close to being flat, not even in dreams. But the vales, jags and marshes made it an ideal place for a cross-country motorcycle race. The weather that day was a definite foretaste of summer, and people didn't wait for three o'clock to go out to the flats. Actually, they began to gather in the morning – grandmothers, grandfathers, tots and teens and everyone else determined not so much to watch a race, as to enjoy a day in the country.

That morning, Montalbano phoned Nicolò Zito.

'Are you coming to the cross-country motorbike race this afternoon?'

'Me? Why should I? We've sent one of our sports reporters and a cameraman over there.'

'Actually, I was suggesting that we go together, the two of us, just for fun.'

*

They got to the flats at about 3.30, but there was no sign the race would be starting any time soon. There already was, however, a deafening racket, produced mostly by fifty or so motorcycles being tested and revved up, and by loudspeakers blasting raucous music.

'Since when are you interested in sport?' Zito asked in amazement.

'Now and then I get the urge.'

Although they were outside, they had to shout to converse. As a result, when a little touring plane trailing its publicity banner appeared high in the sky over the ridge of the Crasticeddru, few in the crowd noticed, since the noise of the plane – which is what usually makes people look up – couldn't reach their ears. The pilot must have noticed he would never get their attention in this fashion since, after flying three tight circles round the crest of the Crasticeddru, he headed straight for the flats and the crowd, going into an elegant dive and flying extremely low over everyone's head. He practically forced people to read his banner and then to follow it with their eyes as he pulled up slightly, flew over the ridge three more times, descended to the point of almost touching the ground in front of the cave's gaping entrance, and then dropped a shower of rose petals from the aircraft. The crowd fell silent. They were all thinking of the two young lovers found dead in the Crasticeddru as the small plane turned round and came back, skimming the ground, this time dropping countless little strips of paper. It then headed westward toward the horizon and disappeared. And while the banner had aroused a lot of curiosity

– since it wasn't advertising a soft drink or a furniture factory, but displayed only the two names Lisetta and Mario – and the rain of rose petals had given the crowd a kind of thrill, the words on the strips of paper, all identical, set them all guessing, sending them on a lively merry-go-round of speculation and conjecture. What indeed was the meaning of: LISETTA AND MARIO ANNOUNCE THEIR REAWAKENING? It couldn't be a wedding or christening announcement. So what was it? Among the swirl of questions, only one thing seemed certain: that the plane, the petals, the pieces of paper and the banner had something to do with the dead lovers found in the Crasticeddru.

Then the races began, and the people watched and amused themselves. Nicolò Zito, upon seeing the rose petals fall from the plane, had told Montalbano not to move from where he stood and had then disappeared into the crowd.

He returned fifteen minutes later, followed by a Free Channel cameraman.

'Will you grant me an interview?'

'Of course.'

This unexpected compliance on Montalbano's part convinced the newsman of his suspicion, which was that the inspector was involved up to his neck in this business with the aircraft.

'Just a few minutes ago, during the preliminaries for the cross-country motorcycle race currently taking place here in Vigàta, we were all witness to an extraordinary event. A small advertising plane . . .' And here he followed with a description of what had just occurred. 'Since, by a fortunate coincidence, we have Inspector Salvo Montalbano here with us among the crowd, we would like to ask him a few questions. In your opinion, Inspector, who are Lisetta and Mario?'

'I could dodge the question,' the inspector said bluntly, 'and say I don't know anything about this and that it might be the work of some newly-weds who wished to celebrate their marriage in an original way. But I would be contradicted by what is written on that piece of paper, which speaks not of marriage but of reawakening. I shall therefore answer honestly and say that Lisetta and Mario were the names of the two young people found murdered inside the cave of the Crasticeddru, that spur of rock right here in front of us.'

'But what does all this mean?'

'I can't really say. You'd have to ask whoever it was that organized the plane stunt.'

'How were you able to identify the two?'

'By chance.'

'Could you tell us their last names?'

'No. I could, but I won't. I can disclose that she was a young woman from these parts, and he was a sailor from the North. I should add that the person who wanted, in such manifest fashion, to remind us of their rediscovery – which this person calls "reawakening" – forgot about the dog, which, poor thing, also had a name: he was called Kytmyr, and was an Arab dog.'

'But why would the murderer have wanted to stage such a scene?'

'Wait a second. Who said that the murderer and the person behind this spectacle are one and the same? I, for one, don't believe they are.'

'I've got to run and edit the report,' said Nicolò Zito, giving Montalbano a strange look.

Soon the crews from TeleVigàta, the RAI regional news and the other private stations arrived. Montalbano answered all their questions politely and with, for him, unnatural ease.

*

Prey to violent hunger pangs, he stuffed himself with seafood appetizers at the Trattoria San Calogero and then raced home, turned on the television, and tuned into the Free Channel. In his report on the mysterious aeroplane, Nicolò Zito piled it on thick, pumping up the story in every way possible. What crowned it all, however, was not his own interview, which was aired in its entirety, but another interview – which Montalbano hadn't expected – with the manager of the Publi-2000 agency of Palermo, which Zito had tracked down easily, since it was the only advertising agency in western Sicily that had an aeroplane available for publicity.

The manager, still visibly excited, recounted that a beautiful young woman – 'Jesus, what a woman! She looked unreal, she really did, like a model in a magazine. Jesus, was she beautiful!' – an obvious foreigner because she spoke bad Italian – 'Did I say bad? I'm wrong, actually, on her lips our words were like honey' – no, he couldn't be sure as to her nationality, maybe German or English – had come to the agency four days earlier – 'God! An apparition!' – and had asked about the plane. She'd explained in great detail what she wanted written on the banner and the strips of paper. Yes, the rose petals were also her doing. And, oh yes, as for the place, was she ever particular! Very precise. Then the pilot, on his own, the manager explained, had a brilliant idea: instead of releasing the pieces of paper at random along the coastal road, he thought it would be better to drop them on a large crowd that had gathered to watch a race. The lady – 'For the love of God, let's stop talking about her or my wife will kill me!' – paid in advance, cash, and had the invoice made out to a certain Rosemarie Antwerpen at a Brussels address. He had asked nothing more of the lovely stranger – 'God!' – but then, why should he have? She certainly wasn't asking them to drop a bomb! And she was so beautiful! And refined! And polite! And what a smile! A dream.

Montalbano relished it all. He had advised Ingrid: 'You must make yourself even more beautiful than usual. That way, when they see you, they won't know what's what any more.'

TeleVigàta went wild with the story of the mysterious beauty, calling her 'Nefertiti resurrected' and cooking up a fanciful story intertwining the pyramids with the Crasticeddru; but it was clear they were following the lead set by

Nicolò Zito's story on their competitor's news programme. Even the regional RAI news gave the matter extensive coverage.

Montalbano was getting the uproar, the commotion, the resonance he had sought. His idea had turned out to be right.

*

'Montalbano? It's the commissioner. I just heard about the plane. Congratulations. A stroke of genius.'

'The credit goes to you. It was you who told me to carry on, remember? I'm trying to flush our man out. If he doesn't turn up reasonably soon, it means he's no longer among us.'

'Good luck. Keep me posted. Oh, it was you, of course, who paid for the plane?'

'Of course. I'm counting on my promised bonus.'

*

'Inspector? This is Headmaster Burgio. My wife and I are speechless with admiration. What an idea.'

'Let's hope for the best.'

'Don't forget, Inspector: if Lillo should turn up, please let us know.'

*

On the midnight edition of the news, Nicolò Zito devoted more time to the story and showed photos of the two corpses in the Crasticeddru, zooming in on the images in detail.

Provided courtesy of the ever-eager Jacomuzzi, thought Montalbano.

Zito isolated the body of the young man, whom he called Mario, then that of the young woman, whom he called Lisetta. Then he showed the aeroplane dropping rose petals and gave a close-up of the words on the strips of paper. From here he went on to weave a tale that was part mystery, part tear-jerker, and decidedly not in the Free Channel style, but rather more like TeleVigàta fare. Why were the two young lovers killed? What sad fate led them to that end? Who was it that took pity on them and set them up in the cave? Had the beautiful woman who showed up at the advertising agency perhaps returned from the past to demand revenge on the victims' behalf? And what connection was there between this beauty and the two kids from fifty years ago? How were we to understand the word 'reawakened'? And how did Inspector Montalbano happen to know even the name of the terracotta dog? How much did he know about this mystery?

*

'Salvo? Hi, it's Ingrid. I hope you didn't think I ran off with your money.'

'Come on! Why, was there some left?'

'Yes. The whole thing cost less than half the amount you gave me. I've got the rest with me. I'll give it back to you as soon as I return to Montelusa.'

'Where are you calling from?'

'Taormina. I met someone. I'll be back in four or five days. Did I do a good job? Did it go they way you wanted?'

'You did a fantastic job. Have fun.'

*

'Montalbano? It's Nicolò. Did you like the reports? I think I deserve some thanks, no?'

'For what?'

'For doing exactly what you wanted.'

'But I didn't ask you to do anything.'

'That's true – not directly, at least. Except that I'm not stupid, and so I gathered that you wanted the story to get as much publicity as possible and to be presented in a way that would touch people's hearts. I said things I will never live down for the rest of my life.'

'Well, thanks – even though, I repeat, I still don't know why you want me to thank you.'

'You know, our switchboard has been overwhelmed with phone calls. The RAI, Fininvest, Ansa and all the national newspapers have asked for a videotape of the report. You've made quite a splash. Can I ask you a question?'

'Sure.'

'How much did the aeroplane cost you?'

*

He slept splendidly, as gods pleased with their handiwork are said to sleep. He'd done everything possible, and even something impossible. Now there was nothing to do but wait for an answer. The message had been sent out, in such a way as to allow somebody to decipher the code, as Alcide Maraventano would say. The first phone call came in at seven in the morning. It was Luciano Acquasanta of *Il Mezzogiorno,* who wanted to corroborate one of his opinions. Was it not possible the two young people were sacrificed in the course of some Satanic rite?

'Why not?' said Montalbano, polite and open to anything.

The second call came fifteen minutes later. It was Stefania Quattrini, from the magazine *Essere Donna.* Her theory was that Mario was caught making love to Lisetta by another, jealous woman – we know what sailors are like – who did away with both of them. She probably then skipped the country, but on her deathbed confided in her daughter, who in turn told her own daughter of the grandmother's crime. This girl, to make good in some way, had gone to Palermo – she spoke with a foreign accent, didn't she? – and arranged the whole business with the aeroplane.

'Why not?' said Montalbano, polite and open to anything.

Cosimo Zappalà of the weekly magazine *Vivere!* communicated his hypothesis to Montalbano at 7.25. Lisetta and Mario, drunk on love and youth, were in the habit of strolling through the countryside hand in hand, naked as Adam and Eve. Surprised one unlucky day by a contingent of retreating German soldiers, also drunk, but on fear and ferocity, they were raped and murdered. On his deathbed, one of the Germans . . . And here this version linked up curiously with Stefania Quattrini's.

'Why not?' said Montalbano, polite and open to anything.

At eight, Fazio knocked on the door and brought him all the dailies available in Vigàta, as he'd been ordered to do the night before. The inspector leafed through them while repeatedly answering the phone. All of them, with greater or lesser degrees of emphasis, reported the story. The headline that most amused him was the one in the *Corriere,* which read: POLICE INSPECTOR IDENTIFIES TERRACOTTA DOG DEAD FOR FIFTY YEARS. All of it, even the irony, was grist for his mill.

✲

Adelina was amazed to find him at home and not out, as was usually the case.

'Adelina, I'm going to be staying home for a few days. I'm waiting for an important phone call, so I want you to make my siege comfortable.'

'I din't unnastand a word you said.'

Montalbano then explained that her task was to alleviate his voluntary seclusion by putting a little extra imagination in her lunch and dinner dishes.

✲

Around ten, Livia called.

'What's going on? Your phone is always busy!'

'I'm sorry. It's just that I've been getting all these calls in reference to—'

'I know what they're in reference to. I saw you on TV. You were so unselfconscious and glib, you didn't seem yourself. It's obvious you're better off when I'm not around.'

*

He rang Fazio at headquarters and asked him to bring all mail home to him and to buy an extension cord for the phone. The mail, he added, should be brought to him at home each day, as soon as it arrived. And Fazio should pass the word on: anyone who asked for him at the office must be given his private number by the switchboard operator, with no questions asked.

Less than an hour passed before Fazio arrived with two unimportant postcards and the extension cord.

'What's new at the office?'

'What's new? Nothing. You're the one who attracts the big stuff. Inspector Augello only gets the little shit: purse snatchings, petty theft, a mugging here and there.'

'I attract the big stuff? What's that supposed to mean?'

'It means what I said. My wife, for instance, is scared of rats. Well, I swear, she draws them to her like a magnet. Wherever she goes, the rats soon arrive.'

For forty-eight hours he'd been like a dog on a chain. His field of action was only as large as the extension cord would allow, and therefore he could neither walk on the beach nor go out for a run. He carried the phone with him everywhere, even when he went to the bathroom, and every now and then – the mania took hold of him after twenty-four hours – he would pick up the receiver and bring it to his ear to see if it was working. On the morning of the third day a thought came into his mind, *Why bother to wash if you can't go outside?* This was followed by another, closely related thought, *So what need is there to shave?*

On the morning of the fourth day, filthy and bristly, wearing slippers and the same shirt since the first day, he gave Adelina a fright.

'*Maria santissima, signuri!* Whata happen to you? Are you sick?'

'Yes.'

'Why don' you call a doctor?'

'It's not the sort of thing for a doctor.'

✡

He was a very great tenor, acclaimed in all the world. That evening he was to sing at the Cairo Opera, at the old theatre which hadn't yet burned down, though he knew well that it would soon be devoured by flames. He'd asked an attendant to inform him the moment Signor Gegè sat down in his box, the fifth from the right on the second level. He was in costume, the last touches having been applied to his make-up. He heard the call, 'Who's on next?' He didn't move. The attendant arrived, out of breath, and told him that Signor Gegè – who hadn't died, this was well known, he'd escaped to Egypt – hadn't shown up yet. He dashed onto the stage, looking out into the theatre through a small opening in the curtain: it was full. The only empty box was the fifth from the right, second level. He made a split-second decision: he returned to his dressing room, took off his costume and put his regular clothes back on, leaving the make-up, including the long, grey beard and thick, white eyebrows, untouched. Nobody would ever recognize him again, and therefore he would never sing again. He well understood that his career was over and he would have to scramble to survive, but he didn't know what to do about it. Without Gegè he couldn't sing.

He woke up bathed in sweat. In his own fashion, he had produced a classic Freudian dream, that of the empty theatre box. What did it mean? That the pointless wait for Lillo Rizzitano would ruin his life?

*

'Inspector? It's Headmaster Burgio. It's been a while since we last spoke. Have you any news of our mutual friend?'

'No.'

Monosyllabic, hasty, at the risk of seeming impolite, he had to discourage long or pointless phone conversations. If Rizzitano were to make up his mind, he might think twice if he found the line busy.

'I'm afraid the only way we'll ever get to talk to Lillo, if you'll forgive my saying so, is to hire a medium.'

*

He had a big squabble with Adelina. The housekeeper had just gone into the kitchen when he heard her start yelling. Then she appeared in the bedroom.

'Signuri, you din't eat nothin yesterday for lunch or dinner!'

'I wasn't hungry, Adelì.'

'I work m'self to death cookin' d'licious things and you jes turn up ya nose at 'em.'

'I don't turn up my nose at them, I'm just not hungry, as I said.'

'An' this house's become a pigsty! You don' want me to wash the floor, you don' want me to wash ya clothes! For five days you been wearin the same shirt anna same shorts! You stink, signuri!'

'I'm sorry, Adelina. I'll snap out of it, you'll see.'

'Well, lemme know when you snap out of it, and I'll come back. 'Cause I ain't settin' foot back in 'ere. Call me when ya feelin' better.'

*

He went out onto the veranda, sat down on the bench, put the telephone beside him, and stared at the sea. He couldn't do anything else – read, think, write – nothing. Only stare at the sea. He was losing himself in the bottomless well of an obsession, and he knew it. He remembered a film he'd seen, perhaps based on a novel by Dürrenmatt, in which a police inspector stubbornly kept waiting for a killer who was supposed to pass through a certain place in the mountains, when in fact the guy would never come through there again. But the inspector didn't know this, and so he waited and waited, and meanwhile days, months, years went by . . .

*

Around eleven o'clock that same morning, the telephone rang. Nobody had called since Headmaster Burgio, several hours before. Montalbano didn't pick up the receiver; he froze as though paralysed. He knew, with utter certainty – though he couldn't have explained why – who would be there at the other end.

He made an effort, and picked up.

'Hello? Inspector Montalbano?'

A fine, deep voice, even though it belonged to an old man.

'Yes, this is he,' said Montalbano. And he couldn't refrain from adding 'Finally!'

'Finally,' the other repeated.

They both remained silent a moment, listening to their breathing.

'I've just landed at Palermo. I could be at your place in Vigàta by one-thirty this afternoon at the latest. If that's all right with you, perhaps you could tell me exactly how to find you. I've been away a long time. Fifty-one years.'

TWENTY-FIVE

He dusted, swept and scrubbed the floors with the speed of a slapstick silent movie. Then he went into the bathroom and washed as he had done only once before in his life, when, at age sixteen, he'd gone on his first date. He took an interminable shower, sniffing his armpits and the skin on his arms, then doused himself, for good measure, with eau de cologne. He knew he was being ridiculous, but he chose his best suit, his most serious tie, and polished his shoes until they looked as if they had their own internal light source. Then he got the idea to set the table, but only for one. He was, it was true, in the throes of a canine hunger, but he was sure he would not be able to swallow.

He waited, endlessly. One-thirty came and went, and he felt sick and had something like a fainting spell. He poured himself a double shot of whisky and gulped it down. Finally, liberation: the sound of a car coming up the driveway. He quickly threw the front door wide open. There was a taxi with a Palermo licence plate, and a very well-dressed old man got out, holding a cane in one hand

and an overnight bag in the other. The man paid the driver, and while the car was manoeuvring to leave, he looked around. He stood erect, head high, and cut an impressive figure. Immediately Montalbano felt he had seen him somewhere before. He went out to meet him.

'Is it all houses around here?' the old man asked.

'Yes.'

'There used to be nothing, only brush and sand and sea.'

They hadn't greeted each other or introduced themselves. They already knew one another.

*

'I'm almost blind, I see very poorly,' said the old man, seated on the bench on the veranda. 'But it seems very beautiful here, very peaceful.'

Only then did the inspector realize where he had seen the old man. Actually, it wasn't exactly him, but a perfect double, a jacket-flap photo of Jorge Luis Borges.

'Would you like something to eat?'

'You're very kind,' said the old man after a moment's hesitation. 'But just a small salad, perhaps some lean cheese, and a glass of wine.'

'Let's go inside, I've set the table.'

'Will you eat with me?'

Montalbano had a knot in the pit of his stomach, but above all he felt strangely moved.

'I've already eaten,' he lied.

'Then, if you don't mind, could you set me a place out here?'

Rizzitano had used the Sicilian verb *conzare,* meaning 'to set the table' – like an outsider trying his best to speak the local language.

'What made me realize you'd figured almost everything out,' Rizzitano said while eating slowly, 'was an article in the *Corriere.* I can't watch television any more, you know; all I see are shadows that hurt my eyes.'

'TV hurts my eyes, too, and my vision is excellent,' said Montalbano.

'But I already knew you had found Lisetta and Mario. I have two sons; one's an engineer, the other's a teacher like me, both married. One of my daughters-in-law is a rabid *leghista,* an insufferable imbecile. Actually, she's very fond of me, but she considers me an exception, since she thinks all southerners are criminals or, in the best of cases, lazy. She never misses an opportunity to say to me, "You know, Papa, down in your parts" – for her, "my parts" extend from Sicily up to and including Rome – "in your parts so-and-so was murdered, so-and-so was kidnapped, so-and-so was arrested, so-and-so planted a bomb . . ." Well, one day she said, "In your own town, inside a cave, they found two young people murdered fifty years ago . . ."'

'How's that?' Montalbano interjected. 'Does your family know you're from Vigàta?'

'Of course they know. However, I never told anyone, not even my wife, rest her soul, that I still owned property in Vigàta. I said my parents and most of my relatives had been wiped out during the bombing. In no way could anybody connect me with the corpses in the Crasticeddru; they didn't know that it was on a piece of my land. But when I heard the news, I got sick, with a high fever. Everything started coming violently back to me. But I was telling you about the article in the *Corriere*. It said that a police inspector in Vigàta, the same one who'd found the bodies, had not only succeeded in identifying the two young victims, but had also learned that the terracotta dog's name was Kytmyr. Well, that made me certain you'd managed to find my university thesis. And so I knew you were sending me a message. I lost some time persuading my sons to let me come here alone; I told them I wanted to revisit, one last time before I die, the place where I was born and lived as a boy.'

Montalbano was still not convinced on this point, so he went back to it.

'So everybody, in your home, knew that you were from Vigàta?'

'Why should I have hidden it? I never changed my name, either, and have never had false documents.'

'You mean you were able to disappear without ever wanting to disappear?'

'Exactly. A person is found when somebody really needs to find him, or really sets his mind to it . . . In any case, you must believe me when I say that I've lived my life with my real first and last names; I entered competitions and even won, I taught, I got married, had children, and I have grandchildren who bear my name. Now I'm retired, and my pension is made out to Calogero Rizzitano, birthplace Vigàta.'

'But you must at least have written to, say, the town hall, or the university, to request the necessary documents?'

'Of course. I did write to them, and they sent me what I needed. You mustn't make a mistake of historical perspective, Inspector. At the time, nobody was looking for me.'

'But you didn't even claim the money the city government owed you for the expropriation of your land.'

'That was precisely the point. I'd had no contact with Vigàta for thirty years, since the older you get, the less you need documents from your birthplace. But the documents required for the expropriation money, those were a little risky. Somebody might have remembered me then. Whereas I had turned my back on Sicily long before that. I didn't want – I still don't want – to have anything to do with it. If there existed some kind of special device that could remove the blood circulating in my veins, I'd be happy.'

'Would you like to go for a walk along the beach?' Montalbano asked when his guest had finished eating.

They'd been walking for five minutes, the old man leaning on his cane but holding onto Montalbano with his other he arm, when he asked, 'Would you tell me how you were able to identify Lisetta and Mario? And how did you figure out that I was involved? Forgive me, but walking and talking at the same time is very taxing for me.'

As Montalbano was telling him the whole story, now

and then the old man would twist his mouth as if to say that was not how it went.

Montalbano then felt Rizzitano's arm weighing heavier on his. Wrapped up in his own words, he hadn't noticed that the old man was tired from the walk.

'Shall we go back?'

They sat down again on the bench on the veranda.

'Well,' said Montalbano. 'Why don't you tell me how things really went?'

'Yes, of course, that's why I'm here. But it costs me a great deal of effort.'

'I'll try to spare you the effort. Tell you what: I'll say what I think happened, and you correct me if I'm wrong.'

'All right.'

'Well, one day in early July, 1943, Lisetta and Mario came to your house at the foot of the Crasto, where at that moment you were living alone. Lisetta had run away from Serradifalco to rejoin her boyfriend, Mario Cunich, a sailor from the *Pacinotti,* a mother ship that was supposed to leave a few days later—'

The old man raised his hand and the inspector stopped.

'Excuse me, but that's not what happened. And I remember everything, down to the smallest details. The memory of the aged becomes clearer and clearer with time. It has no pity. On the evening of the sixth of July, around nine o'clock, I heard someone knocking desperately at the door. I went to see who it was, and there was Lisetta, who had run away. She'd been raped.'

'On her way from Serradifalco to Vigàta?'

'No. By her father, the night before.'

Montalbano didn't feel like opening his mouth.

'And that was only the beginning,' said the old man. 'The worst was yet to come. Lisetta had confided to me that, now and then, her father – Uncle Stefano, as I used to call him, since we were related – used to take certain liberties with her. One day, Stefano Moscato, who, not long before, had come out of prison and been evacuated to Serradifalco with the rest of the family, discovered the letters that Mario had sent to his daughter. He told her he wanted to talk to her about something important, then took her out to the country, threw the letters in her face, beat her and raped her. Lisetta was . . . she'd never been with a man before. But she didn't create a scandal; she had very strong nerves. The next day she simply ran away and came to see me. I was like a brother to her, more than a brother. The following morning I went into town to tell Mario that Lisetta had come. Mario showed up early that afternoon. I left them alone and went for a walk in the country. When I got back home around seven that evening, Lisetta was alone. Mario had returned to his ship. We made some supper, and then we went to the window to watch the fireworks – that's what they looked like – of the Allied strike on Vigàta. Lisetta finally went upstairs to sleep, in my bedroom. I stayed downstairs and read a book by the light of an oil lamp. That was when . . .'

Rizzitano broke off, exhausted, and heaved a long sigh.

'Would you like a glass of water?'

The old man seemed not to have heard him.

'. . . that was when I heard someone shouting in the distance. Actually, at first it sounded to me like a wailing animal, a howling dog. But in fact it was Uncle Stefano, calling his daughter. The sound of that voice made my hair stand on end, because it was the agonized, agonizing cry of a cruelly abandoned lover who was suffering and screaming out his pain like an animal; it was not the voice of a father looking for his daughter. It upset me terribly. I opened the door. Outside was total darkness. I shouted that I was alone in the house. I said, "Why come looking for your daughter at my house?" Then suddenly there he was in front of me, as though catapulted. He ran inside like a madman, trembling, insulting me and Lisetta. I tried to calm him and approached him. He punched me in the face and I fell backward, stunned. Finally I noticed he had a pistol in his hand. He said he was going to kill me. Then I made a mistake. I retorted that he only wanted his daughter so he could rape her again. He shot at me but missed; he was too agitated. Then he took better aim, but another shot exploded in the room. I used to keep a loaded shotgun in my room, near the bed. Lisetta had taken it and fired at her father from the top of the stairs. Struck in the shoulder, Uncle Stefano staggered, and his weapon fell from his hand. Coldly, Lisetta ordered him to get out or she would finish him off. I have no doubt she would have done so without hesitation. Uncle Stefano looked his daughter long in the eye, then began to whimper with his mouth closed, and not only, I suspect, because of his wound. Then he turned his back and left. I bolted all the doors and windows. I was terrified, and it was Lisetta who gave me back my courage and strength. We remained barricaded inside the next morning as well. Around three o'clock Mario arrived, we told him what had happened, and he decided to spend the night with us. He didn't want to leave us alone there, since Lisetta's father would surely be back. Around midnight a horrific bombing raid was launched over Vigàta, but Lisetta remained calm because her Mario was with her. On the morning of July ninth, I went to Vigàta to see if the house we owned in town was still standing. I strongly advised Mario not to open the door for anyone and to keep the shotgun within reach.'

He stopped.

'My throat is dry.'

Montalbano ran into the kitchen and returned with a glass and a pitcher of cold water. The old man took the glass in both hands; his whole body was shaking. The inspector felt keenly sorry.

'If you'd like to rest awhile, we can resume later.'

The old man shook his head.

'If I stop now, I'll never resume. I stayed in Vigàta until late afternoon. The house hadn't been destroyed, but it was a tremendous mess: doors and windows blown out by the shock waves, upended furniture, broken glass. I cleaned up as best I could, and that kept me busy till evening. My bicycle was gone from the entrance hall, stolen. So I headed back to the Crasto on foot. It was an hour's walk. Actually I had to walk by the side of the main road because there were so many military vehicles, Italian and German, moving in both directions. The moment I arrived at the top of the dirt road that led to my house, two American fighter-bombers appeared overhead and started machine-gunning and dropping fragmentation bombs. The planes were flying very low to the ground and roaring like thunder. I threw myself into a ditch and almost immediately was struck very hard in the back by something that I first thought was a large stone sent flying by an exploding bomb. In fact it was a military boot, with the foot still inside, severed just above the ankle. I sprang to my feet and started running up the driveway, but I had to stop to vomit. My legs were giving out, and I fell two or three times, as behind me the noise of the aircraft began to fade and I could hear the cries and screams and prayers more clearly, and the orders being shouted between the burning trucks. The instant I set foot in my house, I heard two shots ring out upstairs, quickly, one right after the other. Uncle Stefano, I thought, had managed to get inside the house and carry out his revenge. Near the door there was a big iron bar that was used to bolt it shut. I grabbed it and went upstairs without a sound. My bedroom door was open; a man was standing just inside with his back to me, still holding the revolver in his hand.'

The old man, who until this point hadn't once looked up at the inspector, now stared him straight in the eye.

'In your opinion, do I have the face of a murderer?'

'No,' said Montalbano. 'And if you're referring to the man in the room with the gun in his hand, you can set your mind at rest. You acted out of necessity, in self-defence.'

'Someone who kills a man is still someone who kills a man. The legal formulas come later. What counts is the will of the moment. And I wanted to kill that man, no matter what he had done to Lisetta and Mario. So I raised the rod and dealt him a blow to the nape of the neck with all my might, hoping to shatter his skull. He fell forward, revealing the scene on the bed. There were Mario and Lisetta, naked, clutching one another, in a sea of blood. They must have been making love when they were surprised by the bombs falling so close to the house, and then embraced each other like that out of fear. There was nothing more to be done for them. Something perhaps could still have been done for the man on the floor behind me, who was gasping his last. With a kick I turned him face up. He was some flunky of Uncle Stefano's, a cheap thug. Systematically, with the iron bar, I began to beat his head to a pulp. And then I went crazy. I started running from room to room, singing. Have you ever killed anyone?'

'Yes, unfortunately.'

'You say "unfortunately", which means you felt no satisfaction. What I felt was not so much satisfaction as joy. I felt happy; I sang, as I said. Then I collapsed in a chair, overwhelmed by the horror, horrified with myself. I hated myself. They had managed to turn me into a murderer, and I hadn't been able to resist. On the contrary, I was pleased to have done it. The blood inside me was infected, no matter how hard I might try to cleanse it with reason, education, culture, and whatever else you want. It was the blood of the Rizzitanos, of my grandfather and my father, of men the honest people in town preferred not to mention. Men like them, even worse than them. Then, in my delirium, a possible solution appeared. If Mario and Lisetta were to go on sleeping, then all this horror had never happened. It was a nightmare, a bad dream. And so . . .'

The old man couldn't go on. Montalbano was afraid he would pass out.

'Let me tell the rest. You took the two kids' bodies, transported them to the cave, and set them up there.'

'Yes, but that's easy to say. I had to carry them inside one by one. I was exhausted, and literally soaked with blood.'

'The second cave, the one you put the bodies in, was it also used to store black-market goods?'

'No. My father had closed up the entrance to it with a dry wall of stones. I removed the stones and later put them back in place when I was done. I used flashlights to help me see; we had quite a few at our country house. Now I had to find the symbols of sleep, the ones from the legend. The jug and the bowl with coins were easy enough, but what about the dog? Well, the previous Christmas in Vigàta—'

'I know the whole story,' said Montalbano. 'When the dog was sold at auction, somebody in your family bought it.'

'My father did. But since Mama didn't like it, we put it in a storeroom in the cellar. I remembered it. When I had done everything and closed up the cave with the great hinged boulder, it was pitch dark outside and I felt almost at peace. Lisetta and Mario really were asleep. Nothing had happened. And so the corpse I found upstairs on my return no longer frightened me. It didn't exist; it was the fruit of my war-ravaged imagination. Then utter pandemonium broke out. The house began to shake from bombs exploding just a few yards away, but I couldn't hear any aeroplanes. They were shelling from the ships at sea. I raced outside, afraid I might get buried under the rubble if the house were hit. On the horizon it looked as if day were breaking. What was all that light? I wondered. Suddenly, behind me the house exploded, literally, and I was struck on the head with a piece of debris and passed out. When I opened my eyes, the light on the horizon was even brighter, and I could hear a continuous, distant rumble. I managed to drag myself to the road and started waving and gesturing, but none of the passing vehicles would stop. They were all fleeing. I was in danger of being run over by a truck. Finally, one stopped, and an Italian soldier hoisted me aboard. From what they were saying, I gathered that the American invasion had begun. I begged them to take me with them, wherever they were going. And they did. What happened to me after that I doubt is of any interest to you. I'm very tired.'

'Would you like to lie down awhile?'

Montalbano had to carry him bodily, then helped him to undress.

'Please forgive me,' he said, 'for awakening the sleepers and bringing you back to reality.'

'It had to happen.'

'Your friend Burgio, who was a big help to me, would love to see you again.'

'No, not me. And if you have no objection, you should act as if I never came.'

'No, of course not, I've no objection.'

'Do you want anything else from me?'

'Nothing. Only to say that I'm deeply grateful to you for answering my call.'

They had nothing more to say to each other. The old man looked at his watch so closely he appeared to be sticking it in his eye.

'Let's do this. Let me sleep for an hour or so, then wake me up, call me a taxi, and I'll go back to Punta Ràisi.'

Montalbano drew the blinds over the window and headed for the door.

'Just a minute, Inspector.'

From the wallet he had laid on the night table the old man took out a photograph and handed it to Montalbano.

'This is my youngest granddaughter, seventeen years old. Her name's Lisetta.'

Montalbano went over to a shaft of light. Except for the jeans she was wearing and the motor scooter she was leaning against, this Lisetta was identical to the other, a perfect likeness. He handed the photo back to Rizzitano.

'Excuse me again, but could you bring me another glass of water?'

*

Seated on the veranda, Montalbano answered the questions his policeman's mind was asking. The assassin's body, assuming they'd found it under the rubble, certainly could never have been identified. Lillo's parents had either believed that those remains belonged to their son, or that, according to the peasant's story, he'd been picked up by the soldiers as he was dying. And since they never heard from him again, he must surely have died somewhere. For Stefano Moscato, however, those remains belonged to his trig-german, who after finishing his work – that is, after killing Lisetta, Mario and Lillo and disposing of their bodies – had returned to the house to steal a few things but was crushed under the bombs. Assured that Lisetta was dead, he had come out with the story of the American soldier. But a relative of his from Serradifalco, when he came to Vigàta, had refused to believe it and severed relations with him. The photomontage recalled to mind the photograph the old man had shown him. Montalbano smiled. Elective affinities were a clumsy game compared to the unfathomable convolutions of the blood, which could give weight, form and breath to memory. He glanced at his watch and gave a start. Well over an hour had passed. He went into the bedroom. The old man was enjoying a peaceful sleep, his breathing untroubled, his expression calm and relaxed. He was travelling through the land of dreams, no longer burdened with baggage. He could sleep a long time, since he had a wallet with money and a glass of water on the night table. Montalbano remembered the stuffed dog he'd bought for Livia in Pantelleria. He found it on top of the dresser, hidden behind a box. He put it on the floor, at the foot of the bed, then closed the door softly behind him.

Author's Note

The idea for writing this story came to me when, as a courtesy to two Egyptian student stage directors, we studied *The People of the Cave*, by Taufik al-Hakim, in a class of mine.

It seems therefore appropriate to dedicate this book to my students at the Silvio d'Amico National Academy of the Dramatic Arts, where I have been teaching stage direction for over twenty-three years.

It is boring to repeat, with each new published book, that the events, characters and situations are purely fictional. Still, it is necessary. So while I'm at it, I would like to add that the names of my characters come to me by virtue of their amusing assonances, with no malice intended.

Notes

page 5 – **four large Saracen olive trees** – Very ancient olive trees with gnarled trunks, tangling branches, and very long roots. The name suggests that they date from the time of the Arab conquest of Sicily, which began in earnest in the late ninth century, after more than a century of isolated raids, and lasted until the Norman conquest, which began in 1060.

page 20 – **'a man of honour'** – An epithet that stands for 'mafioso', used mostly by the mafiosi themselves. Tano the Greek's regret for the decline of honour among them is a common refrain among mobsters of the older generation, such as the 'repentant' Tommaso Buscetta.

page 23 – **to speak in what he called Talian** – Many uneducated Sicilians, even in this day of mass media and standardized speech, can only speak the local dialect and tend to struggle with proper Italian. Often what comes out when they attempt to use the national language is a linguistic jumble that is neither fish nor fowl. In such speech the first syllable of the word 'italiano' is often dropped to 'taliano', especially when the preceding word ends in a vowel, as in '*parlare taliano*'.

page 25 – **notify the carabinieri** – The Italian carabinieri are a national police force, bureaucratically separate from local police forces and actually a branch of the military.

page 25 – **'like I'm running a chicken farm here'** – Gallo and Galluzzo both mean 'rooster', the second being a diminutive of the first.

page 34 – **'they think *omertà* is on the decline'** – *Omertà* is the traditional Sicilian 'law of silence', in force particularly among members of the Mafia.

page 36 – ***'madunnuzza biniditta!'*** – 'Blessèd little Madonna!' (Sicilian dialect).

page 36 – **caught in the net, the chamber of death** – A reference to traditional Sicilian tuna- and sword-fishing and the *mattanza,* when the fish are slaughtered. Schools of the fish are caught in nets which are then gradually closed until the space holding them, the *cammara della morte,* becomes very small, like a death chamber.

page 42 – **'the testimony of Cavaliere Misuraca'** – The honorific title of *cavaliere,* bestowed on members of various orders of knighthood (e.g. Cavaliere di Malta, Cavaliere della Repubblica) and often awarded in the modern age to successful men in different areas of business and industry (such as *il cavaliere* Silvio Berlusconi), was given out wholesale during the Fascist period. Cavaliere Misuraca, as the unfolding episode implies, was probably a beneficiary of this Fascist largesse or earned his title for his efforts in war.

page 45 – **government was red, black, or sky blue** – Red refers to the Communist and Socialist parties, black to the Fascist (or now 'Post-Fascist') Party, sky blue to the now-defunct Christian Democratic Party.

page 50 – **'the *repubblichini*?'** – These were the members and supporters of the so-called Republic of Salò, the puppet government instituted in 1943 under the Nazi occupation in the North Italian town of the same name, after German parachutists boldly snatched Mussolini away from the anti-Fascist partisans who had captured him. The 'government' was made up of die-hard Fascists under the recently deposed and now resurrected Duce.

page 51 – **the first Fascist militias** – These were the *fasci di combattimento,* an association of private militias that engaged in strike-breaking, street violence and other forms of political action and intimidation. The Fascist movement was born from these groups.

page 54 – **'Asinara'** – A high-security prison on the island of the same name.

page 60 – ***càlia e simenza*** – A mix of roasted chickpeas and pumpkin seeds; sometimes peanuts are added.

page 78 – **'*Il Mezzogiorno*'** – This is an actual newspaper. Its name means 'The South' (or, literally, 'Midday').

page 79 – **'*Essere Donna*'** – The magazine is purely fictional; its name means 'To Be a Woman'.

page 108 – **'a traitor or repenter'** – In Italy, Mafia turncoats who turn state's witness are called *pentiti,* or 'repenters'.

page 125 – **'*L'è el dì di mort, alegher!*'** – 'It's the Day of the Dead, oh joy!' (Milanese dialect). Delio Tessa (1886–1939) is a well-known Milanese dialect poet. The Day of the Dead, November 2, is commonly called All Souls' Day in English.

page 128 – **Customs Police** – This is the Guardia di Finanza, a police force subordinate to the Ministry of Finance and responsible for overseeing customs, state monopolies and taxes. Their duties include serving as the national coastguard.

page 141 – ***pasta 'ncasciata*** – A casserole of *pasta corta* – that is, elbow macaroni, penne, ziti, mezzi ziti, or something similar – tomato sauce, minced beef, Parmesan cheese and béchamel.

page 141 – **'Give land to those who work!'** – In Italian, '*La terra a chi lavora!*' This was the rallying cry of the land-reform movement that, in the late 1940s, demanded the break-up of the large landed estates, much of whose vast territories (*latifondi*) lay fallow while the peasantry went hungry.

page 163 – **'*podestà*'** – The head of the municipal government, equivalent to the mayor, in the Fascist period. It was an appointed, not elected, office.

page 171 – **Sex standing up . . . to a bad end.** – '*Fùttiri addritta e caminari na rina / portanu l'omu a la ruvina*' (Sicilian proverb).

page 173 – **National Police** – The carabinieri.

page 173 – **'outstanding corpse'** – The term *cadavere eccellente* – is Italian jargon for the dead body of an important personage, especially when the death has occurred in shady circumstances.

page 174 – **'Falcone and Borsellino!'** – Giovanni Falcone and Paolo Borsellino were prominent investigating magistrates in the struggle against the Mafia in Sicily, both murdered by the mob in 1992.

page 180 – **'Epiphany of 1943'** – In Italy the Christmas holiday lasts until the first day after the Epiphany (January 6).

page 181 – **'Gentile'** – Giovanni Gentile (1875–1944) was a prominent Italian philosopher and politician of Sicilian birth (Castelvetrano, province of Trapani), author of many important works of philosophy from the turn of the century onwards and editor and organizer of the *Enciclopedia Italiana* – (1925–1943). As minister of education under the Fascist government from 1922 to 1924, he instituted sweeping reforms of the national educational system; as president of two commissions for the reform of the Italian constitution, he also contributed to laying the institutional foundations of the Fascist corporate state in 1925. Though his political influence steadily declined thereafter, he remained loyal to the regime until the bitter end, even serving as president of the Accademia d'Italia under the Nazi collaborationist Republic of Salò, established after the armistice of September 8, 1943. He was killed by anti-Fascist partisans in Florence on April 15, 1944.

page 181 – **'lyceums'** – The Italian word is *liceo* (sing.), which, like the French *lycée*, harks back to the ancient Greek *Lykeion*, the Gymnasium near Athens where Aristotle taught.

page 200 – **fresh anchovies *all'agretto*** – Baked in a sauce of lemon juice.

page 230 – **La Vuccirìa** – The large, old market district in Palermo.

page 231 – ***mèusa*** – Calf's spleen sliced into thin strips and cooked in fat.

page 233 – **Giovani Italiane** – This was the compulsory Fascist youth organization (the 'Young Italians') for adolescents aged sixteen and seventeen. The groups for younger children were the Figli della Lupa (Children of the She-Wolf) and the Balilla (named after the boy who incited the Genoese to rebel against the Austrian occupation in 1746). The girls' uniform of the Giovani Italiane consisted of a black pleated skirt, a white blouse with an M (for Mussolini) on the front, and a black beret.

page 267 – ***pasta al forno*** – A casserole of pasta and a variety of other ingredients that may include meat, eggs, vegetables, tomato, or cream sauces, and so on. It is a typically southern Italian dish.

page 276 – **sacred area of the Phoenicians** – Early Phoenician settlements existed in coastal Sicily and its surrounding islands before the Greek era. The most important Phoenician centres were Panormos (modern Palermo), Soloeis and Motya (modern Mozia). Later Carthaginian settlement (fifth and fourth centuries BC) in the southern and western regions of the island reinforced this Sicilian link to Phoenician civilization, opposing these regions to the Greek culture fast gaining prominence in much of the rest of the island. Following the Punic Wars, when Rome defeated Carthage, all of Sicily became Roman (after 210 BC). In the Middle Ages, the Arab rule of the island from the late ninth to the mid-eleventh century again revived Sicily's historic links to the cultures of North Africa and the Middle East.

page 283 – **'*pasta con le sarde,* and *purpi alla carrettera*'** – *Pasta con le sarde* is a classic Sicilian dish served usually with bucatini, broad spaghetti-like strings that are hollow in the middle. The sauce consists of fresh sardines, tops of wild fennel, pine nuts, raisins, garlic and saffron. *Purpi alla carrettera* is octopus served in a sauce of olive oil, lemon and a great deal of hot pepper.

page 306 – **RAI regional news** – The RAI (Radiotelevisione Italiana) is the government-owned national television network, which also has regional news broadcasts.

page 310 – **'Fininvest, Ansa'** – Fininvest is the financial and media conglomerate owned by Silvio Berlusconi; Ansa is an acronym for Azienda Nazionale Stampa Associata, the national news agency.

page 312 – ***Corriere*** – *Corriere della Sera,* the Milan daily and the premier newspaper of Italy.

page 320 – **'leghista'** – A member or supporter of the formerly secessionist Northern League (Lega Nord), a right-wing political party known for its prejudice against foreign immigrants and southern Italians.

Notes compiled by Stephen Sartarelli

THE SNACK THIEF

ONE

He woke up in a bad way. The sheets, during the sweaty, restless sleep that had followed his wolfing down three pounds of sardines *a beccafico* the previous evening, had wound themselves tightly round his body, making him feel like a mummy. He got up, went into the kitchen, opened the refrigerator, and guzzled half a bottle of cold water. As he was drinking, he glanced out of the wide-open window. The dawn light promised a good day. The sea was as flat as a table, the sky clear and cloudless. Sensitive as he was to the weather, Montalbano felt reassured as to his mood in the hours to come. Because it was still too early to get up, he went back to bed and readied himself for two more hours of slumber, pulling the sheet over his head. He thought, as he always did before falling asleep, of Livia lying in her bed in Boccadasse, outside Genoa. She was a soothing presence, propitious to any journey, long or short, 'in country sleep', as Dylan Thomas had put it in a poem he liked very much.

No sooner had the journey begun when it was interrupted by the ringing of the telephone. Like a drill, the sound seemed to enter one ear and come out of the other, boring through his brain.

'Hello!'

'Whoozis I'm speaking with?'

'Tell me first who you are.'

'This is Catarella.'

'What's the matter?'

'Sorry, Chief, I din't rec'nize your voice as yours. You mighta been sleeping.'

'I certainly might have, at five in the morning! Would you please tell me what the hell is the matter without busting my balls any further?'

'Somebody was killed in Mazàra del Vallo.'

'What the fuck is that to me? I'm in Vigàta.'

'But, Chief, the dead guy—'

Montalbano hung up and unplugged the phone. Before shutting his eyes he thought that perhaps his friend Valente, vice-commissioner of Mazàra, was looking for him. He would call him later, from his office.

*

The shutter slammed hard against the wall. Montalbano sat bolt upright in bed, eyes agape with fright, convinced, in the haze of sleep still enveloping him, that he'd been shot at. In the twinkling of an eye, the weather had changed: a cold, humid wind was kicking up waves with a yellowish froth, the sky was now entirely covered with clouds that threatened rain.

Cursing the saints, he got up, went into the bathroom, turned on the shower and lathered himself. All at once the water ran out. In Vigàta, and therefore also in Marinella, where he lived, water was distributed roughly every three days. Roughly, because there was no way of knowing whether you would have water the very next day or the following week. For this reason Montalbano had taken the precaution of having several large tanks installed on the roof of his house, which would fill up when water was available. This time, however, there had apparently been no new water for eight days, for that was the maximum autonomy granted him by his reserves. He ran into the kitchen, put a pot under the tap to collect the meagre trickle that came out, and did the same in the bathroom sink. With the bit of water thus collected, he somehow managed to rinse the soap off his body, but the whole procedure certainly didn't help his mood.

While driving to Vigàta, yelling obscenities at all the motorists to cross his path – whose only use for the Highway Code, in his opinion, was to wipe their arses with it, one way or another – he remembered Catarella's phone call and the explanation he'd come up with for it, which didn't make sense. If Valente had needed him for some homicide that took place in Mazàra, he would have called him at home, not at headquarters. He had concocted that explanation for convenience's sake, to unburden his conscience and sleep for another two hours in peace.

*

'There's absolutely nobody here!' Catarella told him as soon as he saw him, respectfully rising from his chair at the switchboard. Montalbano had decided, with Sergeant Fazio's agreement, that this was the best place for him. Even with his habit of passing on the wildest, most unlikely phone calls, he would surely do less damage there than anywhere else.

'What is it, a holiday?'

'No, Chief, it's not a holiday. They're all down at the port because of that dead guy in Mazàra I called you about, if you remember, sometime early this morning or thereabouts.'

'But if the dead guy's in Mazàra, what are they all doing at the port?'

'No, Chief, the dead guy's here.'

'But, Jesus Christ, if the dead guy's here, why the hell are you telling me he's in Mazàra?'

'Because he was from Mazàra. That's where he worked.'

'Cat, think for a minute, so to speak . . . or whatever it is that you do: if a tourist from Bergamo was killed here in Vigàta, what would you tell me? That somebody was killed in Bergamo?'

'Chief, the point is, this dead guy was just passing through. I mean, they shot him when he was on a fishing boat from Mazàra.'

'Who shot him?'

'The Tunisians did, Chief.'

Montalbano gave up, demoralized.

'Did Augello also go down to the port?'

'Yessir.'

His second-in-command, Mimì Augello, would be delighted if he didn't show up at the port.

'Listen, Cat I have to write a report. I'm not in for anyone.'

*

'Hello, Chief? I got Signorina Livia on the line here from Genoa. What do I do, Chief? Should I put her on or not?'

'Put her on.'

'Since you said, not ten minutes ago, that you wasn't in for nobody—'

'I said put her on, Cat . . . Hello, Livia? Hi.'

'Hi, my eye. I've been trying to call you all morning. The phone at your house just rings and rings.'

'Really? I suppose I forgot to plug it back in. You want to hear something funny? At five o'clock this morning, I got a phone call about—'

'I don't want to hear anything funny. I tried ringing at seven-thirty, at eight-fifteen, I tried again at—'

'Livia, I already told you I forgot—'

'You forgot *me*, that's what you forgot. I told you yesterday I was going to phone you at seven-thirty this morning to decide whether—'

'Livia, I'm warning you. It's windy outside and about to rain.'

'So what?'

'You know what. This kind of weather puts me in a bad mood. I wouldn't want my words to be—'

'I get the picture. I just won't phone you any more. You phone me, if you feel like it.'

*

'Montalbano! How are you? Officer Augello told me everything. This is a very big deal, one that will certainly have international repercussions. Don't you think?'

Montalbano felt at sea. He had no idea what the commissioner was talking about. He decided to be generically affirmative.

'Oh, yes, yes.'

International repercussions?

'Anyway, I've arranged for Augello to confer with the prefect. The matter is, how shall I say, beyond my competence.'

'Yes, yes.'

'Are you feeling all right, Montalbano?'

'Yes, fine. Why?'

'Nothing, it just seemed . . .'

'Just a slight headache, that's all.'

'What day is today?'

'Thursday, sir.'

'Listen, why don't you come to dinner at our house on Saturday? My wife'll make you her black spaghetti in squid ink. It's delicious.'

Pasta with squid ink. His mood was black enough to dress a hundred pounds of spaghetti. International repercussions?

*

Fazio came in and Montalbano immediately laid into him.

'Would somebody please be so kind as to tell me what the fuck is going on?'

'C'mon, Chief, don't take it out on me just because it's windy outside. For my part, early this morning, before contacting Inspector Augello, I had somebody phone you.'

'You mean Catarella? If you have Catarella phoning me about something important, then you really must be a shit-head, since you know damn well that nobody can ever understand a fucking thing the guy says. What happened, anyway?'

'A motor trawler from Mazàra, which according to the ship's captain was fishing in international waters, was attacked by a Tunisian patrol boat and sprayed with machine-gun fire. The fishing boat signalled its position to one of our patrols, the *Fulmine,* then managed to escape.'

'Good going,' said Montalbano.

'On whose part?' asked Fazio.

'On the part of the captain of the fishing boat, who instead of surrendering had the courage to run away. What else?'

'The shots killed one of the crew.'

'Somebody from Mazàra?'

'Sort of.'

'Would you please explain?'

'He was Tunisian. They say his working papers were in order. Down around Mazàra all the crews are mixed. First of all because they're good workers, and secondly because, if they're ever stopped, they can talk to the patrols from the other side.'

'Do you believe the trawler was fishing in international waters?'

'Me? Do I look like a moron or something?'

*

'Hello, Inspector Montalbano? This is Major Marniti of the Harbour Office.'

'What can I do for you, Major?'

'I'm calling about that unfortunate incident on the Mazarese fishing boat, where the Tunisian was killed. I'm questioning the captain, trying to determine exactly where they were at the moment they were attacked, and to establish the sequence of events. Afterwards, he's going to drop into your office.'

'Why? Hasn't my assistant already questioned him?'

'Yes.'

'Then there's really no need for him to come here. Thanks for calling.'

They were trying to drag him into this mess by the ear.

*

The door flew open with such force that the inspector jumped out of his chair. Catarella appeared, looking very agitated.

'Sorry 'bout that, Chief. Door slipped outa my hand.'

'If you ever come in like that again, I'll shoot you. What is it?'

'Somebody just now phoned that somebody's inside a lift.'

The inkwell, made of finely wrought bronze, missed Catarella's forehead but made such a noise when it struck the wooden door that it could have been a cannon shot. Catarella cringed, covering his head with his arms. Montalbano started kicking his desk. In rushed Fazio, his hand on his open holster.

'What was that? What happened?'

'Get this arsehole to explain to you this business about somebody stuck in a lift. Let 'em call the damn fire department! But get him out of here, I don't want to hear his voice.'

Fazio returned in a flash.

'Somebody got killed in a lift,' he said, brief and to the point, to pre-empt any further flying inkwells.

*

'Giuseppe Cosentino, security guard,' said the man standing near the open lift door, introducing himself. 'I was the one who found Mr Lapècora.'

'How come there's nobody around? Where are all the nosy neighbours?' Fazio asked in amazement.

'I sent them all home. They do what I say around here. I live on the sixth floor,' the security guard said proudly, adjusting the jacket of his uniform.

Montalbano wondered how much authority Giuseppe Cosentino would have if he lived in the basement.

The dead Mr Lapècora was sitting on the floor of the

lift, with his shoulders propped against the rear wall. Next to his right hand was a bottle of Corvo white, still corked and sealed. Next to his left hand, a light grey hat. Dressed to the nines, tie and all, the late Mr Lapècora was a distinguished-looking man of about sixty, with eyes open in a look of astonishment, perhaps for having wet his trousers. Montalbano bent down and with the tip of his forefinger touched the dark stain between the dead man's legs. It wasn't piss, but blood. The lift was one of those set inside the wall, so there was no way to look behind the corpse to see if the man had been stabbed or shot. He took a deep breath and didn't smell any gunpowder, though it was possible it had already dissipated.

They needed to alert the coroner.

'You think Dr Pasquano is still at the port or would he already be back in Montelusa by now?'

'Probably still at the port.'

'Go and give him a ring. And if Jacomuzzi and the forensics gang are there, tell them to come too.'

Fazio raced out. Montalbano turned to the security guard, who, sensing he was about to be addressed, came to attention.

'At ease,' Montalbano said wearily.

The inspector learned that the building had six floors, with three apartments per floor, all inhabited.

'I live on the sixth floor, the top floor,' Giuseppe Cosentino felt compelled to reaffirm.

'Was Mr Lapècora married?'

'Yessir. To Antonietta Palmisano.'

'Did you send the widow home too?'

'No sir. She doesn't know she's a widow yet, sir. She went out early this morning to visit her sister in Fiacca, seeing as how this sister's not in good health. She took the six-thirty bus.'

'Excuse me, but how do you know all these things?'

Did living on the sixth floor grant him that power too? Did they all have to tell him what they were doing and why?

'Mrs Palmisano Lapècora told my wife yesterday,' the security guard explained. 'Seeing as how the two women talk to each other and everything.'

'Do the Lapècoras have any children?'

'One son. He's a doctor. But he lives a long way from Vigàta.'

'What was Lapècora's profession?'

'Businessman. Had his office in Salita Granet, number twenty-eight. But in the last few years, he only went there three times a week: Monday, Wednesday and Friday, seeing as how he didn't feel much like working any more. He had some money stashed away, didn't have to depend on anyone.'

'You are a gold mine, Mr Cosentino.'

The security guard sprang back to attention.

At that moment, a woman of about fifty appeared, with legs like tree trunks. Her hands were loaded with plastic bags filled to bursting.

'I went shopping!' she declared with a surly glance at the inspector and the security guard.

'I'm glad,' said Montalbano.

'Well I'm not, all right? Because now I have to climb up six flights of stairs. When are you going to take the body away?'

And, glaring again at the two men, she began her difficult ascent, snorting like an enraged bull.

'A terrible woman, Mr Inspector. Her name is Gaetana Pinna. She lives in the apartment next to mine, and not a day goes by without her trying to start an argument with my wife, who, since she's a real lady, won't give her the satisfaction. And so the woman gets even by making a horrible racket, especially when I'm trying to catch up on my sleep after my long shift.'

*

The handle of the knife stuck between Mr Lapècora's shoulder blades was worn. A common kitchen utensil.

'When did they kill him, in your opinion?' the inspector asked Dr Pasquano.

'To make a rough guess, I'd say between seven and eight o'clock this morning. I'll be able to tell you more precisely a little later.'

Jacomuzzi arrived with his men from the crime lab, and they began their intricate search.

Montalbano stepped out of the building's main door. It was windy, the sky still overcast. The street was a very short one, with only two shops, one opposite the other. On the left-hand side of the street was a greengrocer, behind whose counter sat a very thin man with thick glasses. One of the lenses was cracked.

'Hello, I'm Inspector Montalbano. This morning, did you by any chance see Mr Lapècora come in or go out of the front door of his building?'

The thin man chuckled and said nothing.

'Did you hear my question?' asked the inspector, slightly miffed.

'Oh, I heard you all right,' the greengrocer said. 'But as for seeing, I can't help you much there. I couldn't even see a tank if one came through that door.'

On the right-hand side of the street was a fishmonger's shop, with two customers inside. The inspector waited for them to come out, then entered.

'Hello, Lollo.'

'Hello, Inspector. I've got some really fresh striped bream today.'

'I'm not here to buy fish, Lollo.'

'You're here about the death.'

'Yeah.'

'How'd Lapècora die?'

'A knife in the back.'

Lollo looked at him open mouthed.

'Lapècora was murdered?!'

'Why so surprised?'

'Who would have wished Mr Lapècora any harm? He was a good man, Mr Lapècora. Unbelievable!'

'Did you see him this morning?'

'No.'

'What time did you open up?'

'Six-thirty. Ah, but I did run into his wife, Antonietta, on the corner. She was in a rush.'

'She was running to catch the bus for Fiacca.'

In all likelihood, Montalbano concluded, Lapècora was killed in the lift, as he was about to go out. He lived on the fourth floor.

*

Dr Pasquano took the body to Montelusa for the autopsy. Meanwhile, Jacomuzzi wasted a little more time filling three small plastic bags with a cigarette butt, a bit of dust and a tiny piece of wood.

'I'll keep you posted.'

Montalbano went into the lift and signalled to the security guard, who had not moved an inch all the while, to come along with him. Cosentino seemed hesitant.

'What's wrong?'

'There's still blood on the floor.'

'So what? Just be careful not to get it on your shoes. Would you rather climb six flights of stairs?'

TWO

'Come in, come in,' said a cheerful Signora Cosentino, an irresistibly likeable balloon with a moustache.

Montalbano entered a living room with the dining room attached. The housewife turned to her husband with a look of concern.

'You weren't able to rest, Pepè.'

'Duty. And when duty calls, duty calls.'

'Did you go out this morning, signora?'

'I never go out before Pepè comes home.'

'Do you know Mrs Lapècora?'

'Yes. We chat a little, now and then, when we're waiting for the lift together.'

'Did you also chat with the husband?'

'No, I didn't care much for him. A good man, no doubt about that, but I just didn't like him. If you'll excuse me a minute . . .'

She left the room. Montalbano turned to the security guard.

'Where do you work?'

'At the salt depot. From eight in the evening to eight in the morning.'

'It was you who discovered the body, correct?'

'Yes, sir. It must've been about ten past eight at the latest. The depot's just around the corner. I called the lift—'

'It wasn't on the ground floor?'

'No, it wasn't. I distinctly remember calling it.'

'And of course you don't know what floor it was on.'

'I've thought about that, Inspector. Based on the amount of time it took to arrive, I'd say it was on the fifth floor. I think I calculated right.'

It didn't add up. All decked out, Mr Lapècora . . .

'What was his first name, by the way?'

'Aurelio, but he went by Arelio.'

. . . instead of taking the lift down, took it up one floor. The grey hat meant he was about to go outside, not to visit someone inside the building.

'What did you do next?'

'Nothing. Seeing that the lift had arrived, I opened the door and saw the dead body.'

'Did you touch it?'

'Are you kidding? I've got experience with that sort of thing.'

'How did you know the man was dead?'

'As I said, I have experience. So I ran to the greengrocer's and called you, the police. Then I went and stood guard in front of the lift.'

Mrs Cosentino came in with a steaming cup.

'Would you like a little coffee?'

Montalbano accepted and emptied the demitasse. Then he rose to leave.

'Wait a minute,' said the security guard, opening a drawer and handing him a writing pad and ballpoint pen.

'You'll probably want to take notes,' he said in response to the inspector's questioning glance.

'What, are we in school or something?' he replied rudely.

He couldn't stand policemen who took notes. Whenever he saw one doing so on television, he changed the channel.

*

In the apartment next door, Signora Gaetana Pinna, with the tree-trunk legs, was waiting. As soon as she saw Montalbano, she pounced.

'Did you finally take the body away?'

'Yes, signora. You can use the lift now. No, don't close your door. I need to ask you a few questions.'

'Me? I've got nothin' to say.'

He heard a voice from inside the flat, but it wasn't so much a voice as a kind of deep rumble.

'Tanina! Don't be so rude! Invite the gentleman inside!'

The inspector entered another typical living-dining room. Sitting in an armchair, in an undershirt, with a sheet pulled over his legs, was an elephant, a man of gigantic proportions. His bare feet, sticking out from under the sheet, looked like elephant feet; even his long, pendulous nose resembled a trunk.

'Please sit down,' the man said, apparently in a talkative mood, motioning towards a chair. 'You know, when my wife gets bad-tempered like that, I feel like . . . like . . .'

'Trumpeting?' Montalbano couldn't help saying.

Luckily the man didn't understand.

'. . . like breaking her neck. What can I do for you?'

'Did you know Mr Lapècora?'

'I don't know nobody in this building. I been livin' here five years and don't even know a friggin' dog. In five years I ain't even made it as far as the landing. I can't move my legs, takes too much effort. Took three stevedores to get me up here, since I couldn't fit in the lift. They put a sling around me and hoisted me up, like a piano.'

He laughed, rather like a roll of thunder.

'I knew that Mr Lapècora,' the wife cut in. 'Nasty man. He couldn't be bothered to say hello, like it caused him pain.'

'You, signora, how did you find out he was dead?'

'How'd I find out? I had to go out shopping and so I called the elevator, but nothing happened. It wouldn't come. I guessed somebody must've left the door open, which these rude people's always doing 'round here. So I went down on foot and saw the security man standing guard over the body. And after I went shopping, I had to climb back up the stairs and I still haven't caught my breath!'

'So much the better. That way you'll talk less,' said the elephant.

*

THE CRISTOFOLETTI FAMILY said the plaque on the door of the third apartment, but no matter how hard the inspector knocked, nobody opened up. He went back to the Cosentino flat and rang the doorbell.

'What can I do for you, Inspector?'

'Do you know if the Cristofoletti family—'

Cosentino slapped himself noisily on the forehead.

'I forgot to tell you! With all this business about the dead body, it completely slipped my mind. Mr and Mrs Cristofoletti are both in Montelusa. She, Signora Romilda, that is, had an operation – woman stuff. They should be back tomorrow.'

'Thanks.'

'Don't mention it.'

Montalbano took two steps on the landing, turned around and knocked again.

'What can I do for you, Inspector?'

'Earlier you said you had experience dealing with dead people. What did you mean?'

'I worked as a nurse for a few years.'

'Thanks.'

'Don't mention it.'

*

He went down to the fifth floor, where according to Cosentino the lift had been waiting with the already murdered Aurelio Lapècora inside. Had he perhaps gone up one flight to meet someone who then knifed him?

'Excuse me, signora, I'm Inspector Montalbano.'

The young housewife who had come to the door – about thirty, very attractive but unkempt – put a finger to her lips, her expression complicit, enjoining him to be quiet.

Montalbano fell silent. What did that gesture mean? Damn his habit of always going about unarmed! Gingerly the young woman stood aside from the door, and the inspector, on his guard and looking all around him, entered a small study full of books.

'Please speak very softly. If the baby wakes up, that's the end, we won't be able to talk. He cries like there's no tomorrow.'

Montalbano heaved a sigh of relief.

'You already know everything, signora, don't you?'

'Yes, Mrs Gullotta, the lady next door, told me,' the woman said, breathing the words in his ear. The inspector found the situation very arousing.

'So you didn't see Mr Lapècora this morning?'

'I haven't been out of the house yet.'

'Where is your husband?'

'In Fela. He teaches at the middle school there. He leaves every morning at six-fifteen sharp.'

He was sorry their encounter had to be so brief. The more he looked at Signora Gulisano – that was the surname on the plaque – the more he liked her. In feminine fashion, she sensed this and smiled.

'Will you stay for a cup of coffee?'

'With pleasure.'

*

The little boy who answered the door to the next apartment couldn't have been more than four years old and was fiercely cock-eyed.

'Who are you, stranger?' he asked.

'I'm a policeman,' Montalbano said, smiling, forcing himself to play along.

'You'll never take me alive,' said the kid, and he shot his water pistol at the inspector, hitting him squarely in the forehead.

The scuffle that followed was brief, and as the disarmed child started to cry, Montalbano cold-bloodedly squirted him in the face, drenching him.

'What is this? What's going on here?'

The little angel's mother, Signora Gullotta, had nothing in common with the young mother next door. As a preliminary measure she slapped her son hard, then she grabbed the water pistol the inspector had let fall to the floor and hurled it out of the window.

'There! That'll put an end to all this aggravation!'

With a heart-rending wail, the little boy ran into another room.

'It's his father's fault, always buying him these toys! He's out of the house all day long, doesn't give a damn, and I'm stuck here to look after that little demon! And what do you want?'

'I'm Inspector Montalbano. Did Mr Lapècora by any chance come up to your apartment this morning?'

'Mr Lapècora? To our apartment? Why would he do that?'

'That's what I'm asking you.'

'I guess I knew the man, but it was never anything more than good morning, good evening . . . Not a word more.'

'Perhaps your husband—'

'My husband never spoke to Lapècora. Anyway, when could he have? The guy's always out. He just doesn't give a damn.'

'Where is your husband?'

'He's out, as you can see.'

'Yes, but where does he work?'

'At the port, at the fish market. He's up at four-thirty in the morning and back at eight in the evening. I'm lucky I ever see him at all.'

An understanding woman, this Mrs Gullotta.

*

On the door to the third and last apartment on the fifth floor was the name PICCIRILLO. The woman who answered the door, a distinguished-looking fifty-year-old, was clearly upset and nervous.

'What do you want?'

'I'm Inspector Montalbano.'

The woman looked away.

'We don't know anything.'

Montalbano immediately smelled a rat. Could this woman have been the reason Lapècora went one flight up?

'Let me in. I still have to ask you some questions.'

Signora Piccirillo gruffly stepped aside to let him in, then led him into a small but pleasant sitting room.

'Is your husband at home?'

'I'm a widow. I live with my daughter, Luigina, who's unmarried.'

'Call her in here, if she's at home.'

'Luigina!'

A jeans-clad girl in her early twenties appeared. Cute but very pale, and literally terrified.

The rat smell grew even stronger, and the inspector decided to go on the attack.

'This morning Mr Lapècora came to see you here. What did he want?'

'No!' said Luigina, almost yelling.

'He didn't, I swear it!' the mother proclaimed.

'What was your relation to Mr Lapècora?'

'We knew him by sight,' said Mrs Piccirillo.

'We haven't done anything wrong,' Luigina whined.

'Well, listen closely: if you haven't done anything wrong, you shouldn't be afraid. We have a witness who claims that Mr Lapècora was on the fifth floor when—'

'But why hold that against us? There are two other families living on this floor who—'

'Stop it!' Luigina exploded, in the throes of an hysterical fit. 'Stop it, Mama! Tell him everything! Tell him!'

'Oh, all right. This morning, my daughter, on her way out for an appointment at the hairdresser's, called the lift, which arrived at once. It must have been stopped at the floor below us, the fourth floor.'

'What time was it?'

'Eight o'clock, five past . . . She opened the door and

saw Mr Lapècora sitting on the floor. When I looked inside the lift – I'd gone out with her to wait for it – the man seemed drunk. He had a bottle of wine, unopened, and, uh . . . it looked like he'd soiled himself. My daughter felt disgusted. She closed the lift door. At that moment it left, somebody downstairs had called it. Well, my daughter has a delicate stomach, and that sight made us both a little queasy. So Luigina came back inside to freshen up, and so did I. Not five minutes later, Mrs Gullotta came and told us that poor Mr Lapècora wasn't drunk at all, but dead! And that's the whole story.'

'No,' said Montalbano. 'That's not the whole story.'

'What did you say? I told you the truth!' the woman said, upset and offended.

'The truth is slightly different and more unpleasant. You both immediately realized the man was dead. But you didn't say anything; you acted as if you'd never seen him at all. Why?'

'We didn't want our names ending up on everyone's lips,' Signora Piccirillo admitted in defeat. Then in a sudden burst of energy, she shouted hysterically: 'We're honest people!'

So these two honest people had left the corpse to be discovered by someone else, perhaps someone less honest. And what if Lapècora hadn't been dead yet? They'd left him there to rot, to save . . . to save what?

He went out, slamming the door behind him, and found Fazio, who was on his way to keep him company, standing before him.

'Here I am, Inspector. If you need anything—'

An idea flashed in his brain.

'Yes, I do need something. Knock on this door. There are two women inside, mother and daughter. Failure to offer assistance. Haul 'em in, and make as much racket as possible. I want everyone in the building to think they've been arrested. Then, when I get back to headquarters, we'll let 'em go.'

*

Upon opening the door, Mr Culicchia, an accountant who lived in the first apartment on the fourth floor, gave the inspector a little push backwards.

'We can't let my wife hear us,' he said, standing outside the doorway.

'I'm Inspector—'

'I know, I know. Did you bring me back my bottle?'

'What bottle?' Montalbano asked in shock, staring at the skinny seventy-year-old, who had assumed a conspiratorial air.

'The one that was next to the dead man, the bottle of Corvo white.'

'Wasn't it Mr Lapècora's?'

'Absolutely not! It's mine!'

'I'm sorry, I don't quite understand. Explain.'

'I went out this morning to go shopping, and when I got back, I opened the lift door, and there was Mr Lapècora inside, dead. I realized it at once.'

'Did you call the lift?'

'Why would I do that? It was already on the ground floor.'

'And what did you do?'

'What could I have done, my boy? I've got injuries to my left leg and right arm. Got shot by the Americans. I had four bags in each hand. I couldn't very well have taken the stairs now, could I?'

'Are you telling me you came up in the lift with the body inside?'

'I had no choice! But then, when the lift stopped at my floor, which was also the deceased's floor, the bottle of wine rolled out of one of my bags. So I opened the door to my apartment, took all the bags inside, and then came back out to get the bottle. But I didn't get back in time; somebody'd called the lift to the next floor up.'

'How is that possible if the door was open?'

'But it wasn't! I'd closed it without thinking! Ah, the mind! At my age one doesn't think so clearly any more. I didn't know what to do. If my wife found out I'd lost a bottle of wine she'd skin me alive. You must believe me, Inspector. She's capable of anything, that woman.'

'Tell me what happened next.'

'The lift passed by in front of me again and went down to the ground floor. So I started going down the stairs. When I finally arrived, bum leg and all, I found the security guard there, who wasn't letting anyone get near. I told him about the wine and he promised he'd mention it to the authorities. Are you the authorities?'

'In a sense.'

'Did the guard mention the bottle of wine to you?'

'No.'

'So what am I supposed to do now? Eh? What am I supposed to do? That woman counts the money I spend!' he complained, wringing his hands.

Upstairs they could hear the desperate voices of the Piccirillo women, and Fazio's imperious commands:

'Down the stairs! On foot! And keep quiet!'

Doors opened, questions were asked aloud from floor to floor.

'Who's been arrested? The Piccirillo girls? Are they being taken away? Are they going to jail?'

When Fazio came within reach, Montalbano handed him ten thousand lire.

'After you've taken them to headquarters, go and buy a bottle of Corvo white and bring it to this gentleman here.'

*

Montalbano's interrogation of the other tenants did not yield any important new information. The only one who said anything of interest was the elementary-school teacher Bonavia, who lived on the third floor. He explained to the inspector that his eight-year-old son Matteo had fallen down and bloodied his nose when getting ready for school. As it wouldn't stop bleeding, he had taken him to Casualty. This was around seven-thirty, and there was no trace of Mr Lapècora, dead or alive, in the lift.

Aside from the lift rides he'd taken as a corpse, two things about the deceased seemed clear to Montalbano:

one, he was a decent man, but decidedly unpleasant; and two, he was killed in the lift, between seven thirty-five and eight o'clock.

Since the murderer had run the risk of being surprised with the corpse in the lift by a tenant, this meant the crime had not been premeditated, but committed on impulse.

It wasn't much to go on. Back at headquarters, the inspector thought about this a little, then glanced at his watch. Two o'clock! No wonder he felt so famished. He called Fazio.

'I'm going to Calogero's for some lunch. If Augello arrives in the meantime, send him to me. And one more thing: post a guard in front of the deceased's apartment. Don't let her in before I get there.'

'Don't let who in?'

'The victim's wife, Mrs Lapècora. Are the Piccirillos still here?'

'Yessir.'

'Send 'em home.'

'What'll I tell them?'

'Tell 'em the investigation is continuing. Let those honest people shit their pants a little.'

THREE

'What can I serve you today?'

'What've you got?'

'For the first course, whatever you like.'

'No first course for me today, I'd rather keep it light.'

'For the main course, I've prepared *alalonga all'agrodolce*, and hake in a sauce of anchovies.'

'Going in for haute cuisine, eh, Calò?'

'Now and then I get the urge.'

'Bring me a generous serving of the hake. Ah, and, while I'm waiting, make me a nice plate of seafood antipasto.'

He was overcome by doubt. Was that a light meal? He left the question unanswered and opened the newspaper. It turned out that the little economic measure the government had promised would not be for fifteen billion lire, but twenty. There were sure to be price increases, petrol and cigarettes among them. The unemployment rate in the south had reached a figure that was better left unmentioned. The Northern League, after their tax revolt, had decided to expel the local prefects, a first step towards secession.

Thirty youths in a town near Naples had gang-raped an Ethiopian girl. The town was defending them: the black girl was not only black, but a whore. An eight-year-old boy had hung himself. Three pushers were arrested, average age twelve. A twenty-year-old man had blown his brains out playing Russian roulette. A jealous old man of eighty—

'Here's your appetizer.'

And a good thing too. A few more news items and his appetite would have been gone. Then eight pieces of hake arrived, enough to feed four people. They were crying out their joy – the pieces of hake, that is – at having been cooked the way God had meant them to be. One whiff was enough to convey the dish's perfection, achieved by the right amount of breadcrumbs and the delicate balance between the anchovies and the whisked egg.

He brought the first bite to his mouth, but did not swallow it immediately. He let the flavour spread sweetly and uniformly over his tongue and palate, allowing both to fully appreciate the gift they'd just been given. Then he swallowed, and Mimì Augello appeared in front of the table.

'Sit down.'

Mimì Augello sat down.

'I wouldn't mind a bite myself,' he said.

'Do whatever you want, but don't talk. I'm telling you as a brother, for your own good. Don't talk for any reason in the world. If you interrupt me while I'm eating this hake, I'm liable to wring your neck.'

'Could I have some spaghetti with clams?' Mimì, unfazed, asked Calogero as he was passing by.

'White sauce or red?'

'White.'

While waiting, Augello appropriated the inspector's newspaper and started reading. When the spaghetti arrived, Montalbano had fortunately finished his hake. Fortunately, because Mimì proceeded to sprinkle a generous helping of Parmesan cheese over his plate. Christ! Even a hyena, which, being a hyena, feeds on carrion, would have been sickened to see a dish of pasta with clam sauce covered with Parmesan!

'How did you act with the commissioner?'

'What do you mean?'

'I just want to know if you licked his ass or his balls.'

'What on earth are you thinking?'

'C'mon, Mimì, I know you. You pounced on the case of the machine-gunned Tunisian just to make a good impression.'

'I merely did my duty, since you were nowhere to be found.'

Apparently the Parmesan was not enough, as he added two more spoonfuls, then ground a bit of pepper on top.

'And how did you enter the prefect's office, on your hands and knees?'

'Knock it off, Salvo.'

'Why should I? Since you never miss a single opportunity to stab me in the back!'

'Me? Stab you in the back? Listen, Salvo, if after working for four years with you I had really wanted to stab you in the back, you'd now be running the most godforsaken police station in the most godforsaken backwater in Sardinia, while I would be vice-commissioner at the very least. You know what you are, Salvo? You're a colander that leaks water out of a thousand holes, and all I'm ever doing is trying to plug as many holes as possible.'

He was absolutely right, and Montalbano, having let off some steam, changed his tone. 'Tell me at least what happened.'

'I wrote a report, it's all in there. A large motor trawler from Mazàra del Vallo, the *Santopadre,* with a crew of six including one Tunisian. It was his first time on board, poor guy. The usual scenario, what can I say? A Tunisian patrol boat orders them to stop, the fishing boat refuses, the patrol boat fires. Except that things went a bit differently this time. This time, somebody got killed, and I'm sure the Tunisians are sorrier than anybody about it. Because all they care about is seizing the boat and squeezing a ton of money out of the owner, who then has to negotiate with the Tunisian government.'

'What about ours?'

'Our what?'

'Our government. Don't they come into the picture somewhere?'

'God forbid! They'd make everybody waste an endless amount of time trying to resolve the problem through diplomatic channels. You see, the longer the fishing boat is detained, the less the owner earns.'

'But what do the Tunisian coast guards get out of it?'

'They get a cut, just like the municipal police in some of our towns. Not officially, of course. The captain of the *Santopadre,* who's also the owner, says it was the *Rameh* that attacked them.'

'And what's that?'

'That's the name of a Tunisian motor patrol boat whose commanding officer is notorious for behaving exactly like a pirate. But since somebody got killed this time, our government will be forced to intervene. The prefect asked for a very detailed report.'

'So why did they come and bust our balls instead of dealing directly with Mazàra?'

'The Tunisian didn't die immediately, and Vigàta was the nearest port. At any rate, the poor bastard didn't make it.'

'Did they radio for help?'

'Yes, they hailed the *Fulmine,* a patrol boat that's always riding at anchor in our port.'

'How did you put that?'

'Why, what did I say?'

'You said, "riding at anchor". And you probably wrote that in your report to the prefect. A nitpicker like that, I can already imagine his reaction! You're fucked, Mimì, by your very own hand.'

'And what should I have written?'

' "Moored", Mimì, or "docked". "Riding at anchor" means anchored on the open sea. There's a fundamental difference.'

'Oh, God!'

It was well known that the prefect, who went by the name of Dieterich and hailed from Bolzano, didn't know a caïque from a cruiser, but Augello had swallowed the bait and Montalbano relished his small victory.

'Don't worry about it. So what was the upshot?'

'The *Fulmine* arrived at the scene in less than half an hour, but once there, they didn't find anything. They cruised around a bit in the area, with no results. This is what the Harbour Office learned by radio. When our patrol boat comes back in we'll know a few more details.'

'Bah!' said the inspector, doubtful.

'What's wrong?'

'I don't see why it should be of any concern to us or our government if some Tunisians kill a Tunisian.'

Mimì, mouth agape, just stared at him.

'You know, Salvo, I'm sure I say my share of stupid things, but when you come out with one, it's always a whopper.'

'Bah!' repeated Montalbano, unconvinced he'd said anything stupid.

'So, what about our dead man, the one in the lift? What can you tell me about him?'

'I'm not going to tell you anything. That dead man's mine. You took the Tunisian, I'm taking the guy from Vigàta.'

Let's hope the weather improves, thought Augello. *Otherwise, how's anyone going to put up with this guy?*

*

'Hello, Inspector Montalbano? This is Marniti.'

'What can I do for you, Major?'

'I wanted to let you know that our command has decided – and I agree with them – that the fishing-boat incident should be handled by the Harbour Office of Mazàra. The *Santopadre* should therefore weigh anchor at once. Do your people need to do any further searches on the vessel?'

'I don't think so. But I'm thinking that we, too, ought to abide by the wise decision of your command.'

'I didn't dare ask.'

*

'Montalbano here, Mr Commissioner. Please excuse me if—'

'Any news?'

'No, nothing. I was just having some, uh, procedural doubts. Major Marniti of the Harbour Office phoned me just now to tell me their command has decided that the investigation of the Tunisian who was machine-gunned should be transferred to Mazàra. So I was wondering if we, too—'

'Yes, I see, Montalbano. I think you're right. I'll call my counterpart in Trapani at once and tell him we're stopping the investigation. They've got a vice-commissioner in Mazàra who's really on the ball, if I remember correctly. We'll let them take over everything. Were you handling the case directly yourself?'

'No, my deputy, Inspector Augello, was taking care of it.'

'Tell him we'll be sending the autopsy and ballistics reports to Mazàra. We'll have copies sent to Inspector Augello to keep him informed.'

*

He kicked open the door to Mimì Augello's office, held out his right arm, clenching the fist and grabbing the forearm with his left hand.

'Here, Mimì.'

'What's that supposed to mean?'

'It means the investigation of the killing on the fishing boat has been transferred to Mazàra. You're left empty-handed, while I've still got my lift murder. One to nothing.'

He felt in a better mood now. In fact, the wind had dropped and the sky was clearing.

*

Around three in the afternoon, Officer Gallo, guarding the late Lapècora's apartment and awaiting his widow's return, saw the door to the Culicchia flat open up. The accountant approached the policeman and said in a whisper, 'My wife has fallen asleep.'

Informed of this, Gallo didn't know what to say.

'The name's Culicchia, the inspector knows me. Have you eaten?'

Gallo, whose insides were tied in knots from hunger, shook his head 'no'.

Culicchia went back into his apartment and soon returned with a platter on which there was a bread roll, a sizable slice of caciocavallo cheese, five slices of salami, and a glass of wine.

'That's Corvo white. The inspector bought it for me.'

He returned again half an hour later.

'I brought you the newspaper, to help you pass the time.'

*

At seven-thirty that evening, as if on cue, every single balcony or window on the same side of the building as the main entrance was full of people looking out for the return of Signora Antonietta, who still didn't know she'd become a widow. The show was going to be in two parts.

Part one: Signora Antonietta, stepping off the bus from Fiacca, the seven twenty-five, would appear at the top of the street five minutes later, with her usual unsociability and self-possession in full view, and with no idea whatsoever that a bomb was about to explode over her head. This first part was indispensable to a full appreciation of the second (for which the spectators would move quickly away from balconies and windows and onto landings and stairwells): upon hearing from the officer on duty why she couldn't enter her apartment, the widow, now apprised of her widowhood, would begin behaving like the Virgin Mary, tearing out her hair, crying out, beating her breast while being ineffectually restrained by fellow mourners who in the meantime would have promptly come to her aid.

The show never took place.

It wasn't right, the security guard and his wife decided,

for Signora Antonietta to learn of her husband's murder from a stranger's mouth. Dressed for the occasion – he in a charcoal-grey suit, she completely in black – they lay in wait for her near the bus stop. When Signora Antonietta got off, they came forward, their faces now matching the colours of their clothing: he grey, she black.

'What's wrong?' Signora Antonietta asked in alarm.

There is no Sicilian woman alive, of any class, aristocrat or peasant, who, after her fiftieth birthday, isn't always expecting the worst. What kind of worst? Any, so long as it's the worst. Signora Antonietta conformed to the rule.

'Did something happen to my husband?' she asked.

Since she was doing it all herself, the only thing left for Cosentino and his wife was to play supporting roles. They spread their hands apart, looking sorrowful.

And here Signora Antonietta said something that, logically speaking, she shouldn't have said.

'Was he murdered?'

The Cosentinos spread their hands apart again. The widow teetered, but kept her footing.

The people at their windows and balconies therefore witnessed a scene that could only have been a disappointment: Mrs Lapècora walking between Mr and Mrs Cosentino and speaking calmly. She was explaining in great detail the operation that her sister had just undergone in Fiacca.

In the dark as to these developments, Officer Gallo, upon hearing the lift stop at his floor at seven thirty-five, stood up from the stair on which he'd been sitting, reviewing what he was supposed to say to the unhappy woman, and took a step forward. The lift door opened and a man got out.

'Giuseppe Cosentino's the name. Seeing as how Mrs Lapècora is going to have to wait, I'm putting her up at my place. Please inform the inspector. I live on the sixth floor.'

*

The Lapècora apartment was in perfect order. Living-dining room, bedroom, study, kitchen and bath, nothing out of place. On the desk in the study lay the wallet of the deceased, with all his documents and one hundred thousand lire. Therefore – Montalbano said to himself – Aurelio Lapècora had got dressed to go somewhere he wouldn't need identification, credit or money. He sat down in the chair behind the desk and opened the drawers, one after the other. In the first drawer on the left he found stamps, old envelopes with AURELIO LAPÈCORA INC. / IMPORTAZIONE–ESPORTAZIONE printed on the back, pencils, ballpoint pens, erasers, outdated stamps and two sets of keys. The widow explained that one set was for the house and the other for the office. In the drawer below this one, there were only some yellowed letters bound together with string. The first drawer on the right held a surprise: a brand-new Beretta with two reserve cartridge clips and five boxes of ammunition. Mr Lapècora, if he'd wanted to, could have carried out a massacre. The last drawer contained lightbulbs, razor blades, rolls of string and rubber bands.

The inspector told Galluzzo, who had replaced Gallo, to bring the weapon and ammunition to headquarters.

'Then check to see if the pistol was registered.'

A smell of stale perfume, burnt straw in colour, hung aggressively in the air of the study, even though the inspector, upon entering, had thrown the window wide open.

The widow had gone and sat in an armchair in the living room. She seemed utterly indifferent, as if sitting in a railway station waiting room, awaiting her train.

Montalbano also sat down in an armchair, and at that moment the doorbell rang. Signora Antonietta instinctively started to get up, but the inspector stopped her with a gesture.

'Galluzzo, go see who it is.'

The door was opened, they heard some whispering, and the policeman returned.

'There's somebody who lives on the sixth floor says he wants to talk to you. Says he's a security guard.'

Cosentino had put on his uniform; he was on his way to work.

'Sorry to disturb you, but seeing as how something just occurred to me—'

'What is it?'

'You see, after she got off the bus, Signora Antonietta, when she found out her husband was dead, asked us if he'd been murdered. Now, if somebody came to me and told me my wife was dead, I might think of the different ways she could have died, but I would never imagine she'd been murdered. Unless I'd considered the possibility beforehand. I'm not sure if that's clear . . .'

'It's perfectly clear. Thank you,' said Montalbano.

He went back in the living room. Mrs Lapècora looked as if she'd been embalmed.

'Do you have any children, signora?'

'Yes.'

'How many?'

'One son.'

'Does he live here?'

'No.'

'What does he do?'

'He's a doctor.'

'How old is he?'

'Thirty-two.'

'He should be informed.'

'I'll tell him.'

Gong. End of the first round. When they resumed, the widow took the initiative.

'Was he shot?'

'No.'

'Strangled?'

'No.'

'Then how did they manage to kill him in a lift?'

'With a knife.'

'A kitchen knife?'

'Probably.'

The woman got up and went into the kitchen. The

inspector heard her open and close a drawer. She returned and sat back down.

'Nothing missing here.'

The inspector went on the counter attack.

'Why did you think the knife might be yours?'

'Just a thought.'

'What did your husband do yesterday?'

'He did what he did every Wednesday. He went to his office. He used to go there Mondays, Wednesdays and Fridays.'

'What was his schedule?'

'He'd go from ten in the morning to one in the afternoon, then he'd come home for lunch, take a little nap, go back to work at three-thirty and stay there till six-thirty.'

'What would he do at home?'

'He'd sit down in front of the television and not move.'

'And on the days when he didn't go to the office?'

'Same thing, he'd sit in front of the TV.'

'So this morning, today being a Thursday, your husband should have stayed at home.'

'That's right.'

'Instead he got dressed to go out.'

'That's right.'

'Do you have any idea where he was going?'

'He didn't tell me anything.'

'When you left the house, was your husband awake or asleep?'

'Asleep.'

'Don't you think it's strange that, as soon as you went

out, your husband suddenly woke up, got dressed in a hurry, and—'

'He might have got a phone call.'

A clear point in the widow's favour.

'Did your husband still have many business relationships?'

'Business? He shut down the business years ago.'

'So why did he keep going regularly to the office?'

'Whenever I asked him, he'd say he went to watch the flies. That's what he'd say.'

'Would you say that after your husband came home from the office yesterday, nothing out of the ordinary happened?'

'Nothing. At least till nine o'clock in the evening.'

'What happened at nine o'clock in the evening?'

'I took two Tavors. And I slept so soundly that the building could have collapsed on top of me and I still wouldn't have woken up.'

'So if Mr Lapècora had received a phone call or visitor after nine o'clock, you wouldn't have known.'

'Of course not.'

'Did your husband have any enemies?'

'No.'

'Are you sure?'

'Yes.'

'Any friends?'

'One. Cavaliere Pandolfo. They used to phone each other on Tuesdays and then go and chat at the Caffè Albanese.'

'Have you any suspicions as to who might have—'

She interrupted him.

'Suspicions, no. Certainty, yes.'

Montalbano leapt out of the armchair. Galluzzo said 'Shit!' but in a soft voice.

'And who would that be?'

'Who would that be, Inspector? His mistress, that's who. Her name's Karima, with a *K*. She's Tunisian. They used to meet at the office on Mondays, Wednesdays and Fridays. The slut would go there pretending she was the cleaning woman.'

FOUR

The first Sunday of the previous year had fallen on the fifth, the widow said, and that fateful date remained forever etched in her mind.

Anyway, upon coming out of church, where she'd attended Holy Mass at midday, she was approached by Signora Collura, who owned a furniture store.

'Signora, tell your husband that the item he was waiting for arrived yesterday.'

'What item?'

'The sofa bed.'

Signora Antonietta thanked her and went home with a drill boring a hole in her head. What did her husband need a sofa bed for? Although her curiosity was eating her alive, she said nothing to Arelio. To make a long story short, that piece of furniture never arrived at their home. Two Sundays later, Signora Antonietta approached the furniture lady.

'You know, the colour of the sofa bed clashes with the shade of the wall.'

A shot in the dark, but right on target.

'I'm sorry, signora, but he told me he wanted dark green, the same as the wallpaper.'

The back room of the office was dark green. So that's where he had the sofa bed delivered, the shameless pig!

On the thirtieth of June that same year – this date, too, forever etched in her memory – she got her first anonymous letter. She had received three in all, between June and September.

'Could I see them?' Montalbano asked.

'I burned them. I don't keep filth.'

The three anonymous notes, written with letters cut out from newspapers in keeping with the finest tradition, all said the same thing: your husband Arelio is seeing a Tunisian jade named Karima, known by all to be a whore, three times a week, Mondays, Wednesdays and Fridays. The woman went there either in the morning or afternoon on those days. Occasionally she would buy cleaning supplies at a shop on the same street, but everyone knew she was meeting Signor Arelio to do lewd things.

'Were you ever able to . . . verify any of this?' the inspector asked tactfully.

'Do you mean did I ever spy on them to see when the trollop was going in and out of my husband's office?'

'Well, that too.'

'I don't stoop to such things,' the woman said proudly. 'But I managed just the same. A soiled handkerchief.'

'Lipstick?'

'No,' the widow said with some effort, turning slightly red in the face.

'And a pair of underpants,' she added after a pause, turning even redder.

*

When Montalbano and Galluzzo got to Salita Granet, the three shops on that short, sloping street were already closed. Number 28 was a small building, the ground floor raised three steps up from street level, with two more floors above that. To the side of the main door were three nameplates. The first said: AURELIO LAPÈCORA, IMPORT–EXPORT, GROUND FLOOR; the second: ORAZIO CANNATELLO, NOTARY; the third: ANGELO BELLINO, BUSINESS CONSULTANT, TOP FLOOR. Using the keys Montalbano had taken from Lapècora's study, they went inside. The front room was a proper office, with a big nineteenth-century desk made of black mahogany, a small secretarial table with a 1940s Olivetti typewriter on it, and four large metal bookcases overflowing with old files. On the desk was a functioning telephone. There were five chairs in the office, but one was broken and overturned in the corner. In the back room . . . The back room, with its now familiar dark green walls, seemed not to belong to the same apartment. It was sparkling clean, with a large sofa bed, television, telephone extension, stereo system, cocktail trolley with a variety of liqueurs, mini-fridge, and a horrendous female nude, buttocks to the wind, over the couch. Next to the sofa was a small end table with a faux art nouveau lamp on top, its drawer stuffed with condoms of every kind.

'How old was the guy?' Galluzzo asked.

'Sixty-three.'

'Jesus!' said the policeman, giving a whistle of admiration. The bathroom, like the back room, was dark green and glistening, equipped with built-in hairdryer, bath with shower-hose extension, and full-length mirror.

They returned to the front room, rummaged through the desk's drawers, opened a few of the files. The most recent correspondence was more than three years old.

They heard some footsteps upstairs, in the office of the notary, Cannatello. The notary wasn't in, they were told by the secretary, a reed-thin thirtyish young man with a disconsolate expression. He said the late Mr Lapècora used to come to the office just to pass the time. On the days when he was there, a good-looking Tunisian girl would come to do the cleaning. Oh, and, he almost forgot, over the last few months Mr Lapècora had received fairly frequent visits from a nephew, or at least that's how Mr Lapècora introduced him the one time the three had met at the front door. He was about thirty, tall, dark, well-dressed, and he drove a metallic-grey BMW. He must have spent a lot of time abroad, this nephew, because he spoke with an odd sort of accent. No, he couldn't remember anything about the BMW's number plate, hadn't paid any notice.

Suddenly the thin young man assumed the expression of somebody looking at the ruins of his home after an earthquake. He said he had a precise opinion about this crime.

'And what would that be?' asked Montalbano.

It could only have been the usual young lowlife looking for money to feed his drug habit.

They went back downstairs, where Montalbano called Mrs Lapècora from the office phone.

'Excuse me, but why didn't you tell me you have a nephew?'

'Because we don't.'

*

'Let's go back to the office,' Montalbano said when they were just around the corner from headquarters. Galluzzo didn't dare ask why. In the bathroom of the dark green room, the inspector buried his nose in the towel, breathed deeply, then started riffling through the little cupboard beside the sink. He found a small bottle of perfume, called Volupté, and handed it to Galluzzo.

'Here, put some of this on.'

'Where?'

'Up your arse,' came the inevitable reply.

Galluzzo dabbed a drop of Volupté on his cheek, and Montalbano stuck his nose next to it and inhaled. That was it: the very same scent, the colour of burnt straw, that he'd smelled in Lapècora's study. Wanting to be absolutely certain, he repeated the gesture.

Galluzzo smiled.

'Uh, Chief, if anybody saw us . . . who knows what they'd think?'

The inspector didn't answer, but walked over to the phone.

'Hello, signora? Sorry to disturb you again. Did your husband use any kind of perfume or cologne? No? Okay, thanks.'

*

Galluzzo came into Montalbano's office.

'Lapècora's Beretta was registered on the eighth of December of last year. Since he didn't have a licence to carry a gun, he was only allowed to keep it at home.'

Something, the inspector thought, must have been troubling him about that time, if he decided to buy a gun.

'What are we going to do with the pistol?'

'We'll keep it here. Listen, Gallù, here are the keys to the office. I want you to go there early tomorrow morning, let yourself in, and wait there. Try not to let anyone see you. If the Tunisian girl hasn't found out what happened, she should show up tomorrow according to schedule, since it's Friday.'

Galluzzo grimaced.

'It's unlikely she hasn't heard.'

'Why? Who would have told her?'

It looked to the inspector as if Galluzzo was desperately trying to back out.

'I don't know . . . Word gets out . . .'

'Ah, and I don't suppose you said anything to your brother-in-law the reporter? Because if you did—'

'Inspector, I swear, I haven't told him anything.'

Montalbano believed him. Galluzzo wasn't the type to tell a bare-faced lie.

'Well, you're going to Lapècora's office anyway.'

*

'Montalbano? This is Jacomuzzi. I wanted to notify you of our test results.'

'Oh God, Jacomù, wait a second, my heart is racing. God, what excitement! . . . There, I'm a little calmer now. Please "notify" me, as you put it in your peerless bureaucratese.'

'Aside from the fact that you're an incurable arsehole, the cigarette butt was a common stub of Nazionale without filter; there was nothing abnormal in the dust we collected from the floor of the lift, and as for the little piece of wood—'

'It was only a kitchen match.'

'Exactly.'

'I'm speechless, breathless – in fact, I think I'm about to have a heart attack! You've delivered the murderer to me!'

'Go fuck yourself, Montalbano.'

'It'd still be better than listening to you. What did he have in his pockets?'

'A handkerchief and a set of keys.'

'And what can you tell me about the knife?'

'A kitchen knife, very used. Between the blade and the handle we found a fish scale.'

'Didn't you pursue that any further? Was it a mullet scale or a cod scale? Keep investigating, don't leave me hanging!'

'What is wrong with you anyway?'

'Jacomù, try to use your brains a little. If we were in the Sahara desert and you came to me and said you'd found a fish scale on a knife that had been used to kill a tourist, then the thing might, I say might, mean something. But what the fuck could it possibly mean in a town like Vigàta, where out of twenty thousand inhabitants, nineteen thousand nine hundred and seventy eat fish all the time?'

'And why don't the other thirty?' asked Jacomuzzi, stunned and curious.

'Because they're newborn babies.'

*

'Hello? Montalbano here. Could I please speak with Dr Pasquano?'

'Please hold.'

He had just enough time to start singing: *E te lo vojo dì / che sò stato io . . .*

'Hello, Inspector? The doctor's very sorry, but he's performing an autopsy on the two men found goat-tied in Costabianca. But he said to tell you that as far as your murder victim is concerned, the man was bursting with health and would have lived to be a hundred if somebody hadn't killed him first. A single stab wound, dealt with a firm hand. The incident occurred between seven and eight o'clock this morning. D'you need anything else?'

*

In the fridge he found some pasta with broccoli, which he put in the oven to warm up. As a second course, Adelina had made him some roulades of tuna. Thinking he'd had a light lunch, he felt obliged to eat everything. Then he turned on the television and tuned in to the Free Channel, a good local station where his red-haired, Red-sympathizing friend Nicolò Zito worked. Zito was commenting on the killing of the Tunisian aboard the *Santopadre* as the camera zoomed in on the bullet-riddled wheelhouse and on a dark stain in the wood that was probably blood. All of a sudden Jacomuzzi appeared, kneeling down and looking at something through a magnifying glass.

'Buffoon!' Montalbano shouted, then switched the channel to TeleVigàta, the station where Galluzzo's brother-in-law Prestìa worked. Here, too, Jacomuzzi made an appearance, except that he was no longer on the fishing boat; now he was pretending to take fingerprints inside the lift where Lapècora had been murdered. Montalbano cursed the saints, stood up, threw a book against the wall. That was why Galluzzo had been so reticent! He knew that the news had spread but didn't have the courage to tell him. Without a doubt it was Jacomuzzi who'd notified the journalists, so he could show off as usual. He couldn't live without it. The man's exhibitionism reached heights comparable only to what one might find in a mediocre actor or some writer with print runs of a hundred and fifty copies.

Now Pippo Ragonese, the station's political commentator, appeared on the screen. He wanted to talk, he said, about the cowardly Tunisian attack on one of our motor trawlers that had been peacefully fishing in our own territorial waters, which was the same as saying on the sacred soil of our homeland. It wasn't literally soil, of course, being the sea, but it was still our homeland. A less faint-hearted government than the current one in the hands of the extreme left would certainly have reacted more severely to a provocation that—

Montalbano turned off the television.

*

The agitation he felt at Jacomuzzi's brilliant move showed no signs of passing. Sitting on the small veranda that gave onto the beach and staring at the sea in the moonlight, he smoked three cigarettes in a row. Maybe Livia's voice would calm him down enough so he could go to bed and fall asleep.

'Hi, Livia. How are you?'

'So-so.'

'I've had a rough day.'

'Oh, really?'

What the hell was wrong with Livia? Then he remembered their phone call that morning, which had ended on a sour note.

'I called to ask you to forgive me for my boorishness.

But that's not the only reason. If you only knew how much I missed you . . .'

It occurred to him that he might be overdoing it.

'Do you miss me, really?'

'Yes, a lot, really.'

'Listen, Salvo, why don't I catch a plane on Saturday morning? I'll be in Vigàta just before lunchtime.'

He became terrified. Livia was the last thing he needed at the moment.

'No, no, darling, it's such a bother for you . . .'

When Livia got something in her head, she was worse than a Calabrian. She'd said Saturday morning, and Saturday morning it would be. Montalbano realized he'd have to call the commissioner the next day. Goodbye, pasta in squid ink!

*

At about eleven o'clock the next morning, since nothing was happening at headquarters, the inspector headed lazily off to Salita Granet. The first shop on that street was a bakery; it had been there for six years. The baker and his helper had indeed heard that a man who owned an office at number 28 had been murdered, but they didn't know him and had never seen him. As this was impossible, Montalbano became more insistent in his questioning, acting more and more the policeman until he realized that to get to his office from his home, Mr Lapècora would have come up the opposite end of the street. And in fact, at the grocer's at number 26, they did know the late lamented Mr Lapècora, and how! They also knew the Tunisian girl, what's-her-name, Karima, good-looking woman – and here a few sly glances and grins were exchanged between the grocer and his customers. They couldn't swear by it, of course, but the inspector could surely understand, a pretty girl like that, all alone indoors with a man like the late Mr Lapècora, who carried himself awfully well for his age . . . Yes, he did have a nephew, an arrogant punk who sometimes used to park his car right up against the door to the shop, so that once Signora Micciché, who tipped the scales at a good three hundred pounds, got stuck between the car and the door to the shop . . . No, the number plate? No. If it had been one of the old kinds, with PA for Palermo or MI for Milan, that would have been a different story.

The third and last shop on Salita Granet sold electrical appliances. The proprietor, a certain Angelo Zircone (as the sign said outside), was standing behind the counter, reading the newspaper. Of course he knew the deceased; the shop had been there for ten years. Whenever Mr Lapècora passed by – in recent years it was only on Mondays, Wednesdays and Fridays – he always said hello. Such a nice man. Yes, the appliance man also used to see the Tunisian girl, and a fine-looking girl she was. Yes, the nephew, too, now and then. The nephew and his friend.

'What friend?' asked Montalbano, taken by surprise.

It turned out that Mr Zircone had seen this friend at least three times. He would come with the nephew, and the two of them would go to number 28. About thirty, blondish, sort of fat. That was about all he could tell him. The number plate? Was he kidding? With these number plates nowadays you couldn't even tell if someone was a Turk or a Christian . . . A metallic grey BMW. If he said any more, he'd be making it up.

The inspector rang the doorbell to Lapècora's office. No answer. Galluzzo, behind the door, was apparently trying to decide how to react.

'It's Montalbano.'

The door opened at once.

'The Tunisian girl hasn't shown up yet,' said Galluzzo.

'And she's not going to. You were right, Gallù.'

The policeman lowered his eyes, confused.

'Who leaked the news?'

'Jacomuzzi.'

To pass the time during his stake-out, Galluzzo had organized himself. Having seized a pile of old issues of *Il Venerdì di Repubblica,* the glossy Friday magazine supplement of the Rome daily that Mr Lapècora kept in orderly stacks on a shelf with fewer files, he had scattered them across the desktop in search of photos of more or less naked women. After tiring of looking at these, he had applied himself to solving a crossword puzzle in a yellowed old magazine.

'Do I have to stay here all frigging day?' he asked dejectedly.

'I'm afraid so. You'll have to make the best of it. Listen, I'm going out the back, to take advantage of Mr Lapècora's bathroom.'

It wasn't often that nature called so far off schedule for him. Perhaps the rage he'd felt the previous evening upon seeing Jacomuzzi playing the fool on television had altered his digestive rhythms.

He sat down on the toilet seat, heaving his customary sigh of satisfaction, and at that exact moment his mind brought into focus something he'd seen a few minutes earlier but had paid absolutely no attention to.

He leapt to his feet and raced into the next room, holding his trousers and underpants at half-mast in one hand.

'Stop!' he ordered Galluzzo, who, in fright, turned pale as death and instinctively put his hands up.

There it was, right next to Galluzzo's elbow: a black **R** in boldface, carefully cut out of some newspaper. No, not some newspaper, but a magazine: the paper was glossy.

'What is going on?' Galluzzo managed to articulate.

'It might be everything and it might be nothing,' replied the inspector, sounding like the Cumaean sibyl.

He pulled up his trousers, fastened his belt, leaving the zipper down, and picked up the telephone.

'Sorry to disturb you, signora. On what date did you say you received the first anonymous letter?'

'On the thirteenth of June last year.'

He thanked her and hung up.

'Gimme a hand, Gallù. We're going to put all these issues of this magazine in order and see if any pages are missing.'

They found what they were looking for: the 7 June

issue was the only one from which two pages had been torn out.

'Let's keep going,' said the inspector.

The 30 July issue was also missing two pages; the same for 1 September.

The three anonymous letters had been composed right there, in the office.

'Now, if you'll excuse me,' Montalbano said politely.

Galluzzo heard him singing in the bathroom.

FIVE

'Mr Commissioner? Montalbano here. I'm calling to say I'm very sorry, but I can't make it to dinner at your house tomorrow evening.'

'Are you sorry because you won't be able to see us, or because you'll miss the pasta in squid ink?'

'Both.'

'Well, if it's something to do with work, I can't really—'

'No, it's got nothing to do with work . . . It's that I'm about to receive an impromptu twenty-four-hour visit from my . . .'

Fiancée? That sounded downright nineteenth century to the inspector's ear. Girlfriend? At their age?

'Companion?' the commissioner suggested.

'Right.'

'Miss Livia Burlando must be very fond of you to undertake such a long and tedious journey to see you for just twenty-four hours.'

Never had he so much as mentioned Livia to his superior, who – officially, at least – should have been unaware of her existence. Not even when he was in the hospital, that time he'd been shot, had the two ever met.

'Listen,' said the commissioner, 'why don't you introduce her to us? My wife would love that. Bring her along with you tomorrow evening.'

Saturday's feast was safe.

*

'Is this the inspector I'm speaking to? In person?'

'Yes, signora, this is he.'

'I wanted to tell you something about the gentleman who was murdered yesterday morning.'

'Did you know him?'

'Yes and no. I never spoke to him. Actually, I only found out his name yesterday, on the TV news.'

'Tell me, signora, do you consider what you have to tell me truly important?'

'I think so.'

'All right. Come to my office this afternoon, around five.'

'I can't.'

'Well, tomorrow, then.'

'I can't tomorrow, either. I'm paralyzed.'

'I see. Then I'll come to you, right away, if you wish.'

'I'm always at home.'

'Where do you live, signora?'

'Salita Granet 23. My name is Clementina Vasile Cozzo.'

*

Walking down the Corso on his way to the appointment, he heard someone call him. It was Major Marniti, sitting at the Caffè Albanese with a younger officer.

'Let me introduce to you Lieutenant Piovesan, commander of the *Fulmine,* the patrol boat that—'

'Montalbano's the name, pleased to meet you,' said the inspector. But he wasn't pleased at all. He had managed to dump that case. Why did they keep dragging him back in?

'Have a coffee with us.'

'Actually, I'm busy.'

'Just five minutes.'

'All right, but no coffee.'

He sat down.

'You tell him,' Marniti said to Piovesan.

'In my opinion, none of it's true.'

'What's not true?'

'I find the whole story of the fishing boat hard to swallow. We received the *Santopadre*'s Mayday signal at one in the morning; they gave us their position and said they were being pursued by the patrol boat *Rameh*.'

'What was their position?' the inspector enquired in spite of himself.

'Just outside our territorial waters.'

'And you raced to the scene.'

'Actually it should have been up to the *Lampo* patrol boat, which was closer.'

'So why didn't the *Lampo* go?'

'Because an hour earlier, an SOS was sent out by a fishing boat that was taking in water from a leak. The

Lampo radioed the *Tuono* for back-up, and so a big stretch of sea was left unguarded.'

Fulmine, Lampo, Tuono: lightning, flash, thunder. *It's always bad weather for the coastguard,* thought Montalbano. But he said, 'Naturally, they didn't find any fishing boat in trouble.'

'Naturally. And me, too, when I arrived at the scene, I found no trace of the *Santopadre* or the *Rameh,* which, by the way, was certainly not on duty that night. I don't know what to think, but the whole thing stinks to me.'

'Of what?'

'Of smuggling.'

The inspector stood up, threw up his hands and shrugged.

'Well, what can we do? The people in Trapani and Mazàra have taken over the investigation.'

A consummate actor, Montalbano.

*

'Inspector! Inspector Montalbano!' Somebody was calling him again. Was he ever going to get to see Signora, or Signorina, Clementina before nightfall? He turned around; it was Gallo who was chasing after him.

'What's wrong?'

'Nothing's wrong. I saw you walking by so I called you.'

'Where are you going?'

'Galluzzo phoned me from Lapècora's office. I'm going to buy some sandwiches and keep him company.'

Number 23, Salita Granet, was directly opposite number 28. The two buildings were identical.

*

Clementina Vasile Cozzo was a very well-dressed seventy-year-old lady. She was in a wheelchair. Her apartment was so clean it glistened. With Montalbano following behind, she rolled herself over to a curtained window. She gestured to the inspector to pull up a chair and sit down in front of her.

'I'm a widow,' she began, 'but my son Giulio sees to all my needs. I'm retired; I used to teach at primary school. My son pays for a housekeeper to look after me and my flat. She comes three times a day, in the morning, at midday, and in the evening, when I go to bed. My daughter-in-law, who loves me like a daughter, drops by at least once a day, as does Giulio. I can't complain, except for this one misfortune, which befell me six years ago. I listen to the radio, watch television, but most of the time I read. You see?'

She waved her hand toward two bookcases full of books.

So when was the signora – not signorina, that much was clear – going to get to the point?

'I've just given you this preamble to let you know I'm not some old gossip who spends all her time spying on what others are up to. Still, now and then I do see things I would rather not have seen.'

A cordless phone rang on the shelf below the woman's armrest.

'Giulio? Yes, the inspector's here. No, I don't need anything. See you later. Bye.'

She looked at Montalbano and smiled.

'Giulio was against our meeting. He didn't want me getting mixed up in things that, in his opinion, were no concern of mine. For decades the respectable people here did nothing but repeat that the Mafia was no concern of theirs but only involved the people involved in it. But I used to teach my pupils that the "see-nothing, know-nothing" attitude is the most mortal of sins. So now that it's my turn to tell what I saw, I'm supposed to take a step back?'

She fell silent, sighing. Montalbano was starting to like Clementina Vasile Cozzo more and more.

'You'll have to forgive me for rambling. In my forty years as a schoolteacher, I did nothing but talk and talk. I never lost the habit. Please stand.'

Montalbano obeyed, like a good schoolboy.

'Come here behind me and lean forward; bring your head next to mine.'

When the inspector was close enough to whisper in her ear, the signora raised the curtain.

They were practically inside the front room of Mr Lapècora's office, since the white muslin lying directly against the windowpanes was too light to act as a screen. Gallo and Galluzzo were eating their sandwiches, which were actually more like half-loaves, with a bottle of wine and two paper cups between them. Signora Clementina's window was slightly higher than the one across the street, and by some strange effect of perspective, the two policemen and the various objects in the room looked slightly enlarged.

'In winter, when they had the light on, you could see better,' the woman commented, letting the curtain drop.

Montalbano returned to his chair.

'So, signora, what did you see?' he asked.

Clementina Vasile Cozzo told him.

*

When she'd finished her story and he was already taking his leave, the inspector heard the front door open and close.

'The housekeeper's here,' said Signora Clementina.

A girl of about twenty, short, stocky, and stern-looking, cast a stern glance at the intruder.

'Everything all right?' she asked suspiciously.

'Oh yes, everything's fine.'

'Then I'll go in the kitchen and put the water on,' she said. And she exited, in no way reassured.

'Well, signora, thank you so much . . .' the inspector began, standing up.

'Why don't you stay and eat with me?'

Montalbano felt his stomach blanch. Signora Clementina was sweet and nice, but she probably lived on semolina and boiled potatoes.

'Actually, I have so much to—'

'Pina, the housekeeper, is an excellent cook, believe me. For today she's made *pasta alla Norma,* you know, with fried aubergine and *ricotta salata.*'

'Jesus!' said Montalbano, sitting back down.

'And braised beef for the second course.'

'Jesus!' repeated Montalbano.

'Why are you so surprised?'

'Aren't those dishes a little heavy for you?'

'Why? I've got a stronger stomach than any of these twenty-year-old girls who can happily go a whole day on half an apple and some carrot juice. Or perhaps you're of the same opinion as my son Giulio?'

'I don't have the pleasure of knowing what that is.'

'He says it's undignified to eat such things at my age. He considers me a bit shameless. He thinks I should live on porridge. So what will it be? Are you staying?'

'I'm staying,' the inspector replied decisively.

*

Crossing the street, he climbed three steps and knocked at the door to the office. Gallo came and opened up.

'I relieved Galluzzo,' he explained. Then, 'Did you come from the office, Chief?'

'No, why?'

'Fazio phoned here asking if we'd seen you. He's looking for you. Says he's got something important to tell you.'

The inspector ran to the phone.

'Sorry to bother you, Inspector, but it seems we have a serious new development. Do you remember, yesterday, you told me to put out an all-points bulletin for this Karima? Well, about half an hour ago, Mancuso of the Immigration

Bureau called me from Montelusa. He says he's managed to find out, purely by chance, where the girl lives.'

'Let's have it.'

'She lives in Villaseta, at 70 Via Garibaldi.'

'I'll be right over, we'll go together.'

*

At the main entrance to headquarters he was stopped by a well-dressed man of about forty.

'Are you Inspector Montalbano?'

'Yes, but I'm in a rush.'

'I've been waiting for you for two hours. Your colleagues didn't know if you were coming back or not. I'm Antonino Lapècora.'

'The son? The doctor?'

'Yes.'

'My condolences. Come inside. But I can only give you five minutes.'

Fazio appeared.

'Car's ready.'

'We'll leave in five minutes. I have to talk to this gentleman first.'

They went into his office. The inspector asked the doctor to sit down, then sat down himself, behind the desk.

'I'm listening.'

'Well, Inspector, I've been living in Valledolmo, where I practise my profession, for about fifteen years. I'm a paediatrician. I got married in Valledolmo. I mention this merely to let you know that I haven't had a close relationship with my parents for some time. Actually, we've never been very intimate. We always spent the obligatory holidays together, of course, and we used to phone each other twice a month. That was why I was so surprised to receive a letter from my father early last October. Here it is.'

He reached into his jacket pocket, took out the letter, and handed it to the inspector.

My dear Nino,

I know this letter will surprise you. I have tried to keep you from knowing anything about some business I'm involved in which is threatening to turn very serious. But now I realize I can't go on like this. I absolutely need your help. Please come at once. And don't say anything to Mama about this note. Kisses.

Papa

'And what did you do?'

'Well, you see I had to leave for New York two days later . . . I was away for a month. When I got back, I phoned Papa and asked him if he still needed my help, and he said no. Then we saw each other in person, but he never brought up the subject again.'

'Did you have any idea what this dangerous business was that your father was referring to?'

'At the time I thought it had to do with the business he'd wanted to reopen in spite of the fact that I was strongly against it. We even quarrelled over it. On top of that, Mama had mentioned he was involved with another woman and was being forced to spend a lot of money—'

'Stop right there. So you were convinced that the help

your father was asking you for was actually some sort of loan?'

'To be perfectly frank, yes.'

'And you refused to get involved, despite the desperate, disturbing tone of the letter.'

'Well, you see—'

'Do you make a good living, Doctor?'

'I can't complain.'

'Tell me something: why did you want me to see the letter?'

'Because the murder put everything in a whole new light. I thought it might be useful to the investigation.'

'Well, it's not,' Montalbano said calmly. 'Take it back and treasure it always. Do you have any children, Doctor?'

'A son, Calogerino. Four years old.'

'I hope you never need him for anything.'

'Why?' asked Dr Antonino Lapècora, bewildered.

'Because, if he's his father's son, you're screwed, sir.'

'How dare you!'

'If you're not out of my sight in ten seconds, I'll have you arrested for the first thing I can think of.'

The doctor fled so quickly he knocked over the chair he'd been sitting on.

Aurelio Lapècora had desperately asked his son for help, and the man decided to put an ocean between them.

*

Until thirty years ago, Villaseta consisted of some twenty houses, or rather cottages, arranged ten on each side of the provincial road between Vigàta and Montelusa. In the boom years, however, the frenzy of construction (which seemed to be the constitutional foundation of our country: 'Italy is a Republic founded on construction work') was accompanied by a road-building fever, and Villaseta thus found itself at the intersection of three high-speed routes, one superhighway, one so-called link, two provincial roads, and two inter-provincial roads. Several of these roads, after a few kilometres of picturesque landscape with guard rails appropriately painted red where judges, policemen, carabinieri, financiers and even prison guards had been killed, often surprised the unwary traveller by suddenly ending inexplicably (or all too explicably) against a hillside so desolate as to feed the suspicion that it had never been trod by human foot. Others instead came to an abrupt halt at the seashore, on beaches of fine blond sand with not a single house as far as the eye could see, not a single boat on the horizon, promptly plunging the unwary traveller into the Robinson Crusoe syndrome.

Having always followed its primary instinct to build houses along any road that might appear, Villaseta thus rapidly turned into a sprawling, labyrinthine town.

'We'll never find this Via Garibaldi!' complained Fazio, who was at the wheel.

'What's the most outlying area of Villaseta?' enquired the inspector.

'The one along the road to Butera.'

'Let's go there.'

'How do you know Via Garibaldi is that way?'

'Trust me.'

He knew he wasn't wrong. He had learned from personal experience that in the years immediately preceding the aforementioned economic miracle, the central area of every town or city had streets named, as dutiful reminders, after the founding fathers of the country (such as Mazzini, Garibaldi, Cavour), the old politicians (Orlando, Sonnino, Crispi), and the classic authors (Dante, Petrarch, Carducci; Leopardi less often). After the boom, the street names changed. The fathers of the country were banished to the outskirts, while the town centres now featured Pasolini, Pirandello, De Filippo, Togliatti, De Gasperi, and the ever-present Kennedy (John, not Bobby, although Montalbano, in a lost village in the Nebrodi Mountains, once ended up in a 'Piazza Elli Kennedy,' that is, a 'Kennedy Brothers Square').

*

In reality, the inspector had guessed right on the one hand and wrong on the other. Right insofar as the centrifugal shift of street names had indeed occurred along the road to Butera; wrong insofar as the streets of that neighbourhood, if you could call it a neighbourhood, were named not after the fathers of the country, but, for reasons unknown, after Verdi, Bellini, Rossini and Donizetti. Discouraged, Fazio decided to ask for directions from an old peasant astride a donkey laden with dried branches. Except that the donkey decided not to stop, and Fazio was forced to coast alongside him in neutral.

'Excuse me, can you tell me the way to Via Garibaldi?'

The old man seemed not to have heard.

'The way to Garibaldi!' Fazio repeated more loudly.

The old man turned round and looked angrily at the stranger.

'Away to Garibaldi? You say, "Away to Garibaldi" with the mess we got on this island? Away? Garibaldi should come back, and fast, and break all these sons of bitches' necks!'

SIX

Via Garibaldi, which they finally found, bordered on a yellow, uncultivated countryside interrupted here and there by the small green patches of stunted kitchen gardens. Number 70 was a little house of unwhitewashed sandstone consisting of two rooms, one above the other. The bottom room had a rather small door with a window beside it; the top room, which featured a balcony, was reached by an external staircase. Fazio knocked on the door. It was soon answered by an old woman wearing a threadbare but clean jellaba. Seeing the two men, she unleashed a stream of Arabic words, frequently punctuated by short, shrill cries.

'Well, so much for that idea!' Montalbano commented in irritation, immediately losing heart (the sky had clouded over a little).

'Wait, wait,' Fazio told the old woman, thrusting his hands palms forward in that international gesture that means 'stop'. The woman understood and fell silent at once.

'Ka-ri-ma?' Fazio asked and, afraid he might not have

pronounced the name correctly, he swayed his hips, stroking a mane of long, imaginary hair. The old woman laughed.

'Karima!' she said, then pointed her index finger towards the room upstairs.

With Fazio in front, Montalbano behind him, and the old woman bringing up the rear and yelling incomprehensibly, they climbed the outside staircase. Fazio knocked, but nobody answered. The old woman started to scream even louder. Fazio knocked again. The woman pushed the inspector firmly aside, walked past him, moved Fazio away as well, planted herself with her back to the door, imitated Fazio's swaying of the hips and stroking of the hair, made a gesture that meant 'gone away', then lowered her right hand, palm down, raised it again, spread her fingers, then repeated the 'gone away' gesture.

'She had a son?' the inspector asked in amazement.

'She left with her five-year-old boy, if I've understood correctly,' Fazio confirmed.

'I want to know more,' said Montalbano. 'Call the Immigration Bureau and have them send us someone who speaks Arabic. On the double.'

Fazio walked away, followed by the old woman, who kept on talking to him. The inspector sat down on a stair, fired up a cigarette, and entered an immobility contest with a lizard.

*

Buscaìno, the officer who knew Arabic because he was born and raised in Tunisia up to the age of fifteen, was there in less than forty-five minutes. Hearing the new arrival speak her tongue, the old woman became anxious to cooperate.

'She says she'd like to tell her uncle the whole story,' Buscaìno translated for them.

First the kid, now an uncle?

'And who the fuck is that?' asked Montalbano, befuddled.

'Uh, the uncle, that would be you, Inspector,' the policeman explained. 'It's a title of respect. She says Karima came back here around nine yesterday morning, but went out again in a hurry. She says she seemed very upset, frightened.'

'Has she got a key to the upstairs room?'

'Yes,' said the policeman, after asking her.

'Get it from her and we'll have a look.'

As they were climbing the stairs, the woman spoke without interruption, with Buscaìno rapidly translating. Karima's son was five years old; she would leave him with the old woman every day on her way to work; the little boy's name was François; he was the son of a Frenchman who had met Karima when passing through Tunisia.

Karima's room was a model of cleanliness and had a double bed, a cot for the boy behind a curtain, a small table with a telephone and television, a bigger table with four chairs, a dressing table with four small drawers, and an armoire. Two of the drawers were full of photographs. In one corner was a cubbyhole sealed off by a plastic sliding door, behind which they found a toilet, bidet and sink. Here the scent of the perfume the inspector had smelled in Lapècora's study, Volupté, was very strong. Aside from the little balcony, there was also a window on the back wall, overlooking a well-tended garden.

Montalbano picked out a photograph of a pretty, dark-skinned woman of about thirty, with big, intense eyes, holding a little boy's hand.

'Ask her if this is Karima and François.'

'Yes, that's them,' said Buscaìno.

'Where did they eat? I don't see any stove or hot plate here.'

The old woman and the policeman murmured animatedly to each other. Buscaìno then said the little boy always ate with the old woman, even when Karima was at home, which she was, sometimes, in the evening.

Did she receive men?

As soon as she heard the question translated, the old woman grew visibly indignant. Karima was practically a djinn, a holy woman halfway between the human race and the angels. Never would she have done *haram*, illicit things. She sweated out a living as a housemaid, cleaning the filth of men. She was good and generous; for shopping expenses, looking after the boy, and keeping the house in order, she used to give the old woman far more than she ever spent, and never once did she ask for change. As the uncle – Montalbano, that is – was clearly a man of honourable sentiment and behaviour, how could he ever think such a thing about Karima?

'Tell her,' the inspector said while looking at the photographs from the drawer, 'that Allah is great and merciful, but if she's bullshitting me, Allah is going to be very upset, because she'll be cheating justice, and then she'll really be fucked.'

Buscaìno carefully translated, and the old woman shut up as if her spring had come unwound. But then a little key inside her wound her back up, and she resumed speaking uncontrollably. The uncle, who was very wise, was right; he'd seen things clearly. Several times in the last two years, Karima had received visits from a young man who came in a large automobile.

'Ask her what colour.'

The exchange between Buscaìno and the old woman was long and laboured.

'I believe she said metallic grey.'

'And what did Karima and this young man do?'

What a man and woman do, uncle. The woman heard the bed creaking over her head.

Did he sleep with Karima?

Only once, and the next morning he drove her to work in his automobile. But he was a bad man. One night there was a lot of commotion. Karima was shouting and crying, and then the bad man left.

She had come running and found Karima sobbing, her naked body bearing signs of having been hit. Fortunately, François hadn't woken up.

Did the bad man by any chance come to see her last Wednesday evening?

How had the uncle guessed? Yes, he did come, but

didn't do anything with Karima. He only took her away in his car.

What time was it?

It might have been ten in the evening. Karima brought François down to her, saying she'd be spending the night out. And in fact she came back the next morning about nine, then disappeared with the boy.

Was the bad man with her then?

No, she'd taken the bus. The bad man arrived a little later, about fifteen minutes after Karima had left with her son. As soon as he learned the woman wasn't there, he got back in his car and sped away to look for her.

Had Karima told her where she was going?

No, she hadn't said anything. The old woman had only seen them heading on foot towards the old quarter of Villaseta, where the buses stop.

Did she have a suitcase with her?

Yes, a very small one.

He told the old woman to look around. Was there anything missing from the room?

She threw open the doors of the armoire, and the scent of Volupté exploded in the room. She opened a few drawers and rummaged around in them.

When she'd finished, she said that Karima had packed the suitcase with a pair of slacks, a blouse and some panties. She didn't wear bras. She'd also thrown in a change of clothes and some underwear for the boy.

The inspector asked the woman to look very carefully. Was anything else missing?

Yes, the large book she kept next to the telephone.

The book turned out to be some sort of diary or ledger. Karima must certainly have taken it with her.

'She's not planning to stay away very long,' Fazio commented.

'Ask her,' the inspector told Buscaìno, 'if Karima spent the night out often.'

Now and then, not often. But she always let her know.

Montalbano thanked Buscaìno and asked him, 'Could you give Fazio a ride to Vigàta?'

Fazio gave his superior a perplexed look.

'Why, what are you going to do?'

'I'm going to hang around a little longer.'

*

Among the many photographs the inspector began to examine were those in a large yellow envelope, some twenty-odd photos of Karima in the nude, in various poses from provocative to downright obscene, a kind of sampling of the merchandise, which was obviously of the highest quality. How was it a woman like that hadn't succeeded in finding a husband or rich lover to take care of her so she wouldn't have to prostitute herself? There was a shot of a pregnant Karima some time before, gazing lovingly at a tall, blond man and literally hanging from him. Probably François's father, the Frenchman passing through Tunisia. Other photos showed Karima as a little girl with a boy slightly older than her. They bore a strong resemblance, had the same eyes. Brother and sister, no doubt. Actually there were a great many photos of her with her brother, taken over the years. The last must have been the one in which Karima, with her infant son, a few months old, in her arms, stood next to her brother, who was wearing some sort of uniform and holding a sub-machine gun. He took this photograph and went downstairs.

The woman was crushing minced meat in a mortar, folding in grains of cooked wheat. On a platter beside her, all ready to be roasted, were some skewers of meat, with each morsel wrapped in a vine leaf. Montalbano brought his fingertips together, pointing upwards, artichoke-like – *a cacòcciola,* in Sicilian – and shook his hand up and down. The old woman understood the question and, pointing to the mortar, said:

'*Kubba.*'

Then she picked up one of the skewers.

'Kebab,' she said.

The inspector showed her the photo and pointed at the man. The woman answered something incomprehensible. Montalbano felt pissed off at himself. Why had he been in such a hurry to send Buscaìno away? Then he remembered that for years and years the Tunisians had been mixed up with the French. He gave it a try.

'*Frère?*'

The old woman's eyes lit up.

'*Oui. Son frère Ahmed.*'

'*Où est-il?*'

'*Je ne sais pas,*' said the woman, throwing up her hands.

After this exchange straight out of a French conversation

manual, Montalbano went back upstairs and grabbed the photo of the pregnant Karima with the blond man.

'*Son mari?*'

The old woman made a gesture of scorn.

'*Simplement le père de François. Un mauvais homme.*'

She'd met too many of them – bad men, that is – had the beautiful Karima, and was apparently still meeting them.

'*Je m'appelle Aisha,*' the old woman said out of the blue.

'*Mon nom est Salvo,*' said Montalbano.

*

He got in the car, found the pastry shop he'd caught a glimpse of on the way, bought twelve cannoli, and drove back to the house. Aisha had set a table under a tiny pergola behind the cottage, at the front of the garden. The countryside was deserted. Before doing anything else, Montalbano unwrapped the pastry tray, and the old woman immediately ate two cannoli as an appetizer. Montalbano wasn't too thrilled with the *kubba,* but the kebabs had a tart, herbal flavour that made them a little more sprightly, or so, at least, he defined them according to his imperfect use of adjectives.

During the meal Aisha probably told him the story of her life, but she'd forgotten her French and was speaking only Arabic. Nevertheless, the inspector actively participated: when the old woman laughed, he laughed too; when she grew sad, he put on a face fit for a funeral.

When supper was over, Aisha cleared the table, while Montalbano, at peace with himself and the world, smoked a cigarette. When the old woman returned, she was wearing a mysterious, conspiratorial expression. In her hand was a narrow, flat black box that probably once held a necklace or something similar. Aisha opened it, and inside was a savings-account passbook for the Banca Popolare di Montelusa.

'Karima,' the old woman said, bringing her forefinger to her lips, meaning that this was a secret and should remain so.

Montalbano took the booklet from the box and opened it.

An even five hundred million lire.

*

The previous year – Signora Clementina Vasile Cozzo told him – she'd suffered a terrible spell of insomnia she could do nothing about. Luckily it lasted only a few months. She would spend most of the night watching television or listening to the radio. Reading, no. She couldn't read for very long, because after a while her eyes would start to flutter. Once – it must have been around four in the morning, perhaps earlier – she heard the shouts of two drunkards quarrelling right under her window. She opened the curtain, just out of curiosity, and noticed that the light was on in Mr Lapècora's office. What could Mr Lapècora be doing there at that hour of the night? But Mr Lapècora was not there, in fact. Nobody was there; the front room of the office was empty. So Signora Vasile Cozzo concluded that somebody had left the light on.

Suddenly, however, from the other room, which she knew existed but couldn't see from her window, there emerged a young man who used to come to the office now and then, even when Lapècora wasn't there. Stark naked, the man ran to the telephone, picked up the receiver, and started talking. Apparently the telephone had been ringing, though the signora hadn't heard it. Moments later, Karima emerged, also from the back room, and also naked. She stood there listening to the young man, who was growing animated as he spoke. When the telephone call was over, the young man grabbed Karima and they went back into the other room to finish what they'd been doing when they were interrupted by the telephone. They later reappeared fully dressed, turned off the light, and left in the man's large metallic grey car.

Over the course of the previous year this scenario had repeated itself four or five times. For the most part they would stay there for hours not doing or saying anything. If he grabbed her by the arm and took her into the other room, it was only to pass the time. Sometimes he would write or read, and she would doze in the chair, head resting on the table, waiting for the phone to ring. Sometimes, after the call came in, the man would make a call or two himself.

On Mondays, Wednesdays and Fridays, the woman, Karima, would clean the office – but what was there to clean, for Christ's sake? And sometimes she would answer the phone, but she never passed the call on to Mr Lapècora, even when he was right next to her. He would only sit there, listening to her talk, head down and looking at the floor, as if none of it was his concern, or as if he felt offended.

In the opinion of Clementina Vasile Cozzo, the maid, the Tunisian girl, was a bad, evil woman.

Not only did she do what she did with the dark young man, but now and then she would go and wheedle poor old Lapècora, who inevitably would give in, letting himself be led into the back room. One time, when Lapècora was sitting at the little secretarial table reading the newspaper, she kneeled in front of him, unzipped his trousers, and, still kneeling . . .

At this point Signora Vasile Cozzo, blushing, interrupted her narrative.

It was clear that Karima and the young man had keys to the office, whether they had been given them by Lapècora or had copies made themselves. It was also clear, even though there were no insomniac witnesses, that the night before Lapècora was murdered, Karima had spent a few hours in the victim's home. This was proved by the scent of Volupté. Did she also own a set of keys to the flat, or had Lapècora himself let her in, taking advantage of the fact that his wife had taken a generous dose of sleeping pills? In any case, the whole thing seemed not to make sense. Why risk being caught in the act by Mrs Lapècora when they could easily have met at the office? For the hell of it? Just to season an otherwise predictable relationship with the thrill of danger?

And then there was the matter of the three anonymous

letters, unquestionably pieced together in that office. Why had Karima and the dark young man done it? To put Lapècora in a difficult bind? It didn't tally. They had nothing to gain by it. On the contrary, they risked jeopardizing the availability of their telephone number and whatever it was the company had become.

For a better understanding of all this, Montalbano would have to wait for Karima to return. Fazio was right: she must have slipped away to avoid answering dangerous questions and would come back on the sly. The inspector was positive that Aisha would keep the promise she'd made to him. In his unlikely French, he'd explained to her that Karima had got mixed up with a nasty crowd, and that sooner or later that bad man and his friends would surely kill not only her but also François and Aisha herself. He had the impression he'd sufficiently convinced and frightened her.

They agreed that as soon as Karima reappeared, the old woman would phone him; she had only to ask for Salvo and say only her name, Aisha. He left her the telephone numbers to his office and home, telling her to make sure she hid them well, as she had done with the passbook.

Naturally the argument held water on one condition: that Karima was not the killer. But no matter how much he turned it over in his head, the inspector could not picture her with a knife in her hand.

*

He glanced at his watch by the flame of his lighter. Almost midnight. For more than two hours now he'd been sitting on the veranda, in darkness to avoid getting eaten alive by mosquitoes and sand flies, hashing and rehashing what he'd learned from Signora Clementina and Aisha.

Yet he needed one further clarification. Could he possibly call Mrs Vasile Cozzo at that hour? She had told him that every evening the housekeeper, after giving her dinner, would help her undress and put her in the wheelchair. But even if she was ready for bed, she didn't turn in immediately; she would watch television late into the night. She could move from the wheelchair to the bed, and vice versa, by herself.

'Signora, it's unforgivable, I know.'

'Not at all, Inspector, not at all! I was awake, watching a movie.'

'Well, signora. You told me the dark young man sometimes used to read or write. Do you know what it was he read? Or wrote? Could you tell?'

'He used to read newspapers and letters. And he would write letters. But he didn't use the typewriter that was there in the office. He'd bring his own, a portable. Anything else?'

*

'Hi, darling. Were you asleep? No? Are you sure? I'll be at your place tomorrow around one in the afternoon. Don't go out of your way for me, please. I'll just come, and if you're not there, I'll wait. I have the keys, after all.'

SEVEN

Apparently, in his sleep, one part of his brain had kept working on the Lapècora case. Around four o'clock in the morning, in fact, a memory came back to him, and he got up and started searching frantically among his books. Suddenly he remembered that he'd lent the book he was looking for to Augello, after his deputy had seen the film made from it on television. He'd now had it for six months and still hadn't given it back. Montalbano got upset.

'Hello, Mimì? Montalbano here.'

'Ohmygod! What's going on? What happened?'

'Do you still have that novel by Le Carré entitled *Call for the Dead*? I'm sure I lent it to you.'

'What the fuck?! It's four in the morning!'

'So what? I want it back.'

'Salvo, I'm telling you this as a loving brother: why don't you have yourself committed?'

'I want it back immediately.'

'But I was asleep! Calm down. I'll bring it to the office

in the morning. Otherwise I would have to put on my underwear, start looking, get dressed—'

'I don't give a shit. You're going to look for it, find it, get in your car, even in your underwear, and bring it to me.'

He dragged himself about the house for half an hour, doing pointless things like trying to understand the phone bill or reading the label on a bottle of mineral water. Then he heard a car screech to a halt, a dull thud against the door, and the car leaving. He opened the door: the book was on the ground, the lights of Augello's car already far away. He had a mind to make an anonymous phone call to the carabinieri.

Hello, this is a concerned citizen. There's some madman driving around in his underwear . . .

He let it drop. He started leafing through the novel.

The story went exactly as he'd remembered it. Page 8:

> 'Smiley, Maston speaking. You interviewed Samuel Arthur Fennan at the Foreign Office on Monday, am I right?'
>
> 'Yes . . . yes I did.'
>
> 'What was the case?'
>
> 'Anonymous letter alleging Party membership at Oxford . . .'

And there, on page 139, was the beginning of the conclusion that Smiley would arrive at in his report:

> 'It was, however, possible that he had lost his heart for his work, and that his luncheon invitation to me was

a first step to confession. With this in mind he might also have written the anonymous letter which could have been designed to put him in touch with the Department.'

Following Smiley's logic, it was therefore possible that Lapècora had written the anonymous letters exposing himself. But if he was their author, why hadn't he sent them to the police or carabinieri under some other pretext?

No sooner had he formulated this question than he smiled at himself for being so naive. In the hands of the police or carabinieri, an anonymous letter might have triggered an investigation and have led to far graver consequences for Lapècora. By sending them to his wife, Lapècora was hoping to provoke a reaction of the more domestic variety, but one that would nevertheless rescue him from a situation that was becoming either too dangerous or unbearable. He wanted to pull out, and those were cries for help. But his wife had taken them at face value, that is, as anonymous letters denouncing a tawdry, common liaison. Offended, she had not reacted, but only withdrawn into a scornful silence. And so Lapècora, in despair, had written to his son, this time without hiding behind a veil of anonymity. But the son, blinded by egotism and the fear of losing a few lire, fled to New York.

Thanks to Smiley, it all made sense. He went back to sleep.

*

Commendatore Baldassare Marzachì, director of the Vigàta post office, was notorious for being a presumptuous imbecile. And he didn't fail to live up to his reputation this time, either.

'I cannot grant your request.'

'And why not, if I may ask?'

'Because you don't have a judge's authorization.'

'And why should I need that? Any other employee of your office would have given me the information I asked for. It's of no consequence whatsoever.'

'That's your opinion. Had they given you this information, my employees would have committed a punishable infraction.'

'Commendatore, let's be reasonable. I am merely asking you for the name of the postman who services the neighbourhood in which Salita Granet is located. Nothing more.'

'And I'm not going to tell you, okay? Supposing I did tell you, what would you do?'

'I would ask the postman a few questions.'

'See? You want to violate the postal code of secrecy.'

'What on earth are you talking about?'

An utter nitwit. Which isn't so easy to find these days, now that nitwits disguise themselves as intelligent people. The inspector decided to resort to a bit of high drama that would annihilate his adversary. Without warning, he let his body fall backwards, shoulders planted firmly against the back of the chair, and began shaking his hands and legs, trying desperately to open his shirt collar.

'Oh God,' he gasped.

'Oh God!' echoed Commendator Marzachì, standing up and rushing to the inspector. 'Are you ill?'

'Please help me,' wheezed Montalbano.

The post-office manager bent down, tried to loosen the inspector's collar, and at that moment Montalbano started shouting.

'Let me go! For God's sake, let me go!'

All at once he grabbed Marzachì's hands, and as the commendatore was instinctively struggling to break free, he held them up around his own neck.

'What are you doing?' muttered Marzachì, totally confused, not understanding what was happening. Montalbano yelled again.

'Let me go! How dare you!' he bawled, still clutching the commendatore's hands.

The door flew open, and two terrorized postal employees appeared, a man and a woman, who unmistakably saw their boss trying to strangle the inspector.

'Get out of here!' Montalbano yelled at the two. 'Out! It's nothing! Everything's fine!'

The employees withdrew, closing the door behind them. Montalbano calmly readjusted his collar and glared at Marzachì, who, as soon as he'd released him, had backed up against a wall.

'You're fucked, Marzachì. They saw you, those two. And since they hate you like the rest of your staff, I'm sure they'd be happy to testify. Assaulting a police officer. What shall we do? Do you want to be reported or not?'

'Why do you want to ruin me?'

'Because I hold you responsible.'

'For what, for God's sake?'

'For the worst things imaginable. For letters that take two months to go from one part of Vigàta to another, for packages that arrive torn apart with half the contents missing – and you talk to me of the postal code of secrecy, which you can stick straight up your arse – for books that I wait and wait for and that never come . . . You're a piece of shit that dresses up in dignity to cover this cesspool. Is that enough?'

'Yes,' said Marzachì, shattered.

*

'Yes, of course he used to receive mail. Not a lot, but some. There was one company outside of Italy that used to write to him, but nobody else, really.'

'Where were they from?'

'I never noticed. But the stamps were foreign. I can tell you what the company was called, though, because its name was on the envelope. Aslanidis was the name. I remember it because my dad, rest his soul, who'd fought in Greece, met a girl from those parts whose name was Galatea Aslanidis. Used to talk about her all the time.'

'Did the envelopes say what this company sold?'

'Yes. *Dattes,* they said. Dates.'

*

'Thanks for coming so quickly,' said Signora Antonietta Palmisano, lately become the widow Lapècora, as soon as she opened the door for Montalbano.

'Why? Did you want to see me?'

'Yes. Didn't they tell you I phoned your office?'

'I haven't been there yet today. I came here on my own.'

'Then it's a case of kleptomania,' the woman concluded.

For a moment the inspector felt confused; then he understood that she'd intended to say 'clairvoyance'.

One of these days I'll introduce her to Catarella, he thought, *then I'll transcribe the dialogue. Better than Ionesco!*

'What did you want to see me about, signora?'

Antonietta Palmisano Lapècora mischievously wagged a small forefinger.

'No, no, no. You have to talk first, since you thought to come on your own.'

'Signora, I would like you to show me exactly what you did the other morning when you were getting ready to go out to see your sister.'

The widow was dumbfounded, opening and closing her mouth.

'Is this some kind of joke?'

'Hardly.'

'Are you asking me to put on my nightgown?' said Signora Antonietta, blushing.

'I wouldn't dream of it.'

'Well, let me think. I got out of bed as soon as the alarm went off. Then I took—'

'No, signora, perhaps I didn't make myself clear enough.

I don't want you to *tell* me what you did, I want you to *show* me. Let's go in the other room.'

They went into the bedroom. The armoire was wide open, a suitcase full of women's dresses on the bed. On one of the bedside tables was a red alarm clock.

'Do you sleep on this side of the bed?' asked Montalbano.

'Yes. What should I do, lie down?'

'No need. Just sit on the edge.'

The widow obeyed, but then:

'What's any of this got to do with Arelio's murder?' she asked.

'Please do as I say, it's important. Just five minutes and I'll be out of your hair. Tell me: did your husband also wake up when the alarm went off?'

'Normally he slept lightly. His eyes would pop open if I made the slightest noise. But now that you've made me think back on it, that morning he didn't hear the alarm. In fact, he must have had a bit of a cold, a stuffed-up nose, because he started snoring, which he hardly ever did.'

A terrible actor, poor old Lapècora. But it worked, at least that time.

'Go on.'

'I got up, picked up the clothes I'd put on that chair over there, and went into the bathroom.'

'Let's move.'

Embarrassed, the woman led the way. When they were in the bathroom, Signora Antonietta, looking at the floor, asked, 'Do I have to do everything?'

'Of course not. You were dressed when you came out of the bathroom, correct?'

'Yes, fully dressed, that's how I always do it.'

'Then what did you do?'

'I went into the dining room.'

Having learned her lesson by now, she walked towards the dining room, followed by the inspector.

'I picked up my purse, which I'd prepared on this couch the night before, then I opened the door and went out on the landing.'

'Are you sure you locked the door behind you when you went out?'

'Absolutely certain. I called the lift—'

'That'll be enough, thank you. What time was it, do you remember?'

'Six twenty-five. I was late, actually, so late that I started running.'

'What was the snag?'

The woman gave him a questioning look.

'For what reason were you running late? Let me put it another way. If someone knows he has to go somewhere the next morning, he usually sets the alarm clock, calculating the amount of time it will take to—'

Signora Antonietta smiled.

'A callus on my foot was hurting,' she said. 'I put on some ointment, wrapped it up, and lost some time I hadn't allowed for.'

'Thanks again, and sorry for the disturbance. Goodbye.'

'Wait! Where are you going? Are you leaving?'

'Oh, yes, of course. You had something to tell me.'

'Sit down a minute.'

Montalbano did as she said. In any case, he'd found out what he wanted to know: that is, the widow Lapècora had not entered the study, where Karima almost certainly had been hiding.

'As you can see,' the woman began, 'I'm getting ready to leave. As soon as I can give Arelio a proper funeral, I'm going away.'

'Where will you go, signora?'

'To stay with my sister. She has a big house, and she's sick, as you know. I'll never set foot in Vigàta again, even after I'm dead.'

'Why not go and live with your son?'

'I don't want to inconvenience him. And I don't get along with his wife, who spends money like water while my poor son is always complaining that he can't make ends meet. Anyway, what I wanted to tell you was that, when I was going through some old stuff I don't need anymore and want to throw away, I found the envelope the first anonymous letter came in. I thought I'd burned it, but I must have destroyed only the letter. And since you seemed particularly interested . . .'

The address had been typed.

'May I keep this?'

'Of course. Well, that's all.'

She stood up, as did the inspector, but then she went over to the sideboard, picked up a letter that was lying on it, and shook it at Montalbano.

'Look at this, Inspector. Arelio's been dead barely two days and already I have to start paying the debts he ran up with his filthy little arrangements. Just yesterday I received – apparently the post office already knows he was killed – I received two bills from the office. One for electricity: two hundred and twenty thousand lire! And one for the phone: three hundred and eighty thousand! But he wasn't the one using the phone, you know. Who would he ever call anyway? It was that Tunisian whore who was phoning, that's for sure, probably calling her family in Tunisia. Then this morning, this came. God only knows what kinds of ideas that dirty slut put into my idiot husband's head!'

So compassionate, the widow Antonietta Lapècora, née Palmisano. The envelope had no stamp on it; it had been hand-delivered. Montalbano decided not to show too much curiosity, only as much as was necessary.

'When was this brought here?'

'This morning, as I said. A bill for one hundred and seventy-seven thousand lire, from the Mulone printing works. Incidentally, Inspector, could you give me back the keys to the office?'

'Do you need them right away?'

'Not right this instant. But I'd like to start showing it to people who might be interested in buying it. I want to sell the apartment too. I've already worked out that the funeral alone is going to cost me over five million lire between one thing and the next.'

Like mother, like son.

'With the proceeds from the office and the apartment,' said Montalbano in a fit of malice, 'you could pay for twenty funerals.'

*

Empedocle Mulone, owner of the print shop, said yes, the late Mr Lapècora had indeed ordered some stationery with slightly different letterhead from the old one. Signor Arelio had been coming to him for twenty years, and they were friends.

'How was it different?'

'It said "Import-Export" instead of "Importazione-Esportazione." But I advised him against it.'

'He shouldn't have made the change?'

'I didn't mean the letterhead, but the idea of restarting the business. He'd already been retired about five years, but things are different now. Businesses are failing. It's a bad time. And you know what he did, instead of thanking me for the advice? He got pissed off. He said he read the newspapers and watched TV, and so he knew what the situation was.'

'Did you send the parcel with the printed matter to his home or his office?'

'He asked me to send it to the office, and that's what I did, on one of the weekdays when he was there. I don't remember the exact date, but if you want—'

'Never mind.'

'The bill, on the other hand, I sent to the missus, since

I guess Mr Lapècora can't very well make it to the office now, can he?'

And he laughed.

*

'Here's your espresso, Inspector,' said the barman at the Caffè Albanese.

'Totò, listen. Did Mr Lapècora sometimes come here with his friends?'

'Sure! Every Tuesday. They'd talk and play cards. Always the same group.'

'Give me their names.'

'All right. Let's see: Pandolfo, the accountant—'

'Wait. Give me the phone book.'

'No need to call him on the phone. He's the elderly gentleman sitting at that table over there, eating an ice.'

Montalbano took his demitasse and went over to the accountant.

'May I sit down?'

'Absolutely, Inspector.'

'Thanks. Do we know each other?'

'You don't know me, sir, but I know you.'

'Mr Pandolfo, did you play cards with the deceased very often?'

'Often? We played every Tuesday. Because, you see, every Monday, Wednesday, and—'

'Friday he was at the office,' said Montalbano, completing the now familiar refrain.

'What would you like to know?'

'Why did Mr Lapècora decide to go back into business?'

Pandolfo looked sincerely surprised.

'Go back into business? When did he ever do that? He never talked about it with us. But we all knew he went to the office out of habit, just to pass the time.'

'Did he ever mention the maid, a certain Karima, who used to come and clean the office?'

There was a darting of the eyes, an imperceptible hesitation that would have gone unnoticed had Montalbano not been keeping the man squarely in his sights.

'The man had no reason to tell me about his cleaning woman.'

'Did you know Lapècora well?'

'Whom can you say you know well? Some thirty years ago when I lived in Montelusa, I had a friend, a smart man, bright, witty, sharp, sensible. He had it all. And he was generous, too, a real angel. If anyone was in need, they could have anything he owned. Then one evening his sister left her baby boy with him, not six months old. He was supposed to look after him for two hours or so, maximum. As soon as the sister left, the guy picked up a knife, chopped the baby up and boiled him in a pot with a sprig of parsley and a clove of garlic. I'm not kidding, you know. I'd been with the man that same day, and he'd been the same as always, smart, polite. So, to get back to poor old Lapècora, yeah, I knew him, all right, enough to see that he'd really changed over the last two years.'

'In what way?'

'Well, he became nervous, never laughed. In fact, he'd pick a fight and make a big to-do over the smallest things.'

'Any idea what might have been the cause?'

'One day I asked him about it. It was a health problem, he said. The first stages of arteriosclerosis, that's what his doctor told him.'

*

The first thing he did in Lapècora's office was sit down at the typewriter. He opened the drawer to the little secretarial table and found some stationery printed with the old letterhead and yellowed with age. He took out a sheet, reached into his coat pocket, and removed the envelope that Signora Antonietta had given him. He copied its address on the typewriter. A foolproof test if there ever was one. The *r*'s jumped above the line, the *a*'s dropped below, and the *o* was a little black ball. The address on the anonymous letter's envelope had been written on this same typewriter.

He looked outside. Signora Vasile Cozzo's housekeeper, standing on a stepladder, was cleaning the windows. He opened the window and called out.

'Hello! Is the signora there?'

'Wait,' said the girl, giving him a dirty look. Clearly she wasn't very fond of the inspector.

She stepped down from the ladder, disappeared, and a short while later Signora Clementina's head appeared just above the sill. There was no need for them to raise their voices so much, as they were less than ten yards away from each other.

'Excuse me, signora, but if I'm not mistaken, you told me that, sometimes, the young man, do you remember . . .?'

'Yes, the young man.'

'You said he used to type sometimes. Is that right?'

'Yes, but he didn't use the office typewriter. He would bring his own portable.'

'Are you sure? Might it have been a computer?'

'No, it was a portable typewriter.'

What kind of idiotic way to conduct an investigation was this? He suddenly realized the two of them must look like a couple of old housewives gossiping across their balconies.

After saying goodbye to Clementina, to regain some semblance of dignity in his own eyes he began a detailed search of the office like a true professional, looking for the parcel the printer had sent. But he never found it; nor did he find a single envelope or sheet of paper with the new letterhead in English.

They'd removed everything.

As for the portable typewriter Lapècora's bogus nephew used to bring along instead of using the office machine, he thought he'd come up with a plausible explanation for this. The young man had no use for the keyboard of the old Olivetti. Apparently, he needed one with a different alphabet.

EIGHT

He left the office, got in his car, and drove to Montelusa. At Customs Police headquarters, he asked for Captain Aliotta, who was his friend. They let him in immediately.

'It's been so long since we spent an evening together! I'm not blaming you. It's my fault, too,' said Aliotta, embracing Montalbano.

'Let's forgive each other and try to rectify the situation soon.'

'Okay. What can I do for you?'

'I need the name of that sergeant of yours I spoke to on the phone last year, the one who gave me that precious information about the supermarket in Vigàta. The case of the weapons traffic, remember?'

'Of course. His name's Laganà.'

'Could I speak with him?'

'What's it about?'

'He would have to come to Vigàta for half a day at the most, I think. I'd like him to examine the files of a business owned by that guy who was murdered in a lift.'

'I'll call him for you.'

Sergeant Laganà was a burly fifty-year-old with a crew cut and gold-rimmed glasses. Montalbano took an immediate liking to him.

He explained in great detail what he wanted from him and gave him the keys to Lapècora's office. The sergeant looked at his watch.

'I can be in Vigàta at three o'clock this afternoon, if the captain has no objection.'

*

Just to be thorough, once the inspector had finished chatting with Aliotta, he asked if he could use his phone and phoned headquarters, where he hadn't shown his face since the previous evening.

'Chief, is that really you yourself?'

'Cat, it's really me myself. Been any calls?'

'Yessir, Chief. Two for Inspector Augello, one for—'

'Cat, I don't give a fuck about other people's phone calls!'

'But you asked me yourself just now!'

'All right, Cat: have there been any phone calls personally for me myself?'

By making the necessary linguistic adjustments, maybe he would get a sane answer.

'Yessir, Chief. There was one. But it didn't make sense.'

'What do you mean, it didn't make sense?'

'I couldn't understand anything. But I think they were relatives.'

'Whose relatives?'

'Yours, Chief. They called you by your first name: Salvo, Salvo.'

'Then what?'

'Then they sounded like they were in pain, or sneezing or something. They said: 'Aiee . . . sha! Aiee . . . sha!'

'Wait, who was "they"? Was it a man or a woman?'

'An old woman, Chief.'

Aisha! He dashed out the door, forgetting to say goodbye to Aliotta.

*

Aisha was sitting in front of her house, upset and weeping. No, Karima and François had not shown up; she'd called him for another reason. She stood up and led him inside. The room had been turned upside down; they'd even gutted the mattress. Want to bet they'd taken the bank book? No, that they didn't find, Aisha said reassuringly.

Upstairs, where Karima lived, it was even worse. Some flagstones had been torn out of the floor; one of François's toys, a little plastic truck, was in pieces. The photographs were all gone, including the ones advertising Karima's charms. *A good thing I took a few myself,* the inspector thought. But they must have made a tremendous racket. Where had Aisha run off to in the meantime? She hadn't run off, the old woman explained. The previous day she'd gone to see a friend in Montelusa. It got late, and so she slept over. A stroke of luck: if they'd found her at home, they would certainly have cut her throat. They must have had keys;

neither of the doors, in fact, had been forced. Surely they'd come for the photos; they wanted to erase the very memory of what Karima looked like.

Montalbano told the old woman to gather her things together. He was going to take her himself to her friend's house in Montelusa. She would have to remain there for a few days, just to be safe. Aisha glumly agreed to go. The inspector explained that while she was getting ready, he was going out to the nearest tobacco shop and would be back in ten minutes at most.

*

A short distance before the tobacco shop, in front of the Villaseta primary school, there was a noisy gathering of gesticulating mothers and weepy children. They were laying siege to two municipal policemen from Vigàta who'd been seconded to Villaseta and whom Montalbano knew. He drove on, bought his cigarettes, but on the way back, curiosity got the better of him. He pushed through the crowd, invoking his authority, deafened by the shouting.

'They bothered you about this bullshit too?' asked one of the policemen in amazement.

'No, I just happened to be passing by. What's going on?'

The mothers, who heard his question, answered all at once, with the result that the inspector understood nothing.

'Quiet!' he yelled.

The mothers fell silent, but the children, now terrified, started wailing even louder.

'The whole thing's ridiculous, Inspector,' said the same policeman as before. 'Apparently, since yesterday morning, there's been some little kid attacking the other kids on their way to school. He steals their food and then runs away. He did the same thing this morning.'

'Looka here, looka here,' one mother butted in, showing Montalbano a little boy with eyes puffy from being punched. 'My son din't wanna give 'im 'is omelette, and so 'e 'it 'im! An' 'e really 'urt 'im!'

The inspector bent down and stroked the little boy's head.

'What's your name?'

''Ntonio,' said the little boy, proud to have been the one chosen from the crowd.

'Do you know this boy who stole your omelette?'

'No sir.'

'Is there anyone here who recognized him?' the inspector asked in a loud voice. There was a chorus of 'No.'

Montalbano leaned back down to 'Ntonio.

'What did he say to you? How did you know he wanted your omelette?'

'He spoke foreign. I din't unnastand. So he pulled off my backpack and opened it. I tried to take it back, but he punched me, twice, and he grabbed my omelette sandwich and ran away.'

'Continue the investigation,' Montalbano ordered the two police officers, managing by some miracle to keep a straight face.

*

At the time of the Muslim domination of Sicily, when Montelusa was called Kerkent, the Arabs built a district, on the outskirts of town, where they lived by themselves. When the Muslims later fled in defeat, the Montelusians moved into their homes and the name of the district was Sicilianized into Rabàtu. In the second half of the twentieth century, a tremendous landslide swallowed it up. The few houses left standing were damaged and lopsided, remaining upright by absurd feats of equilibrium. When they returned, this time as paupers, the Arabs moved back into that part of town, replacing the roof tiles with sheet metal and using partitions of heavy cardboard for walls.

It was to this quarter that Montalbano accompanied Aisha with her paltry bundle of belongings. The old woman, still calling him 'uncle', wanted to kiss and embrace him.

*

It was three o'clock in the afternoon and Montalbano, who hadn't had time to eat, was in the throes of a gut-twisting hunger. He went to the Trattoria San Calogero and sat down.

'Is there anything left to eat?'

'For you, sir, there's always something.'

At that exact moment he remembered about Livia. She'd completely slipped his mind. He rushed to the phone, trying feverishly to think of an excuse. Livia had said she'd be there by lunchtime. She was probably furious.

'Livia, darling.'

'I just got here, Salvo. The flight left two hours late, with no explanation. Were you worried, darling?'

'Of course I was worried,' Montalbano lied shamelessly, realizing the winds were favourable. 'I've been phoning home every fifteen minutes without any answer. A little while ago I decided to call the airport, and they told me the flight was two hours late. That finally set my mind at rest.'

'Sorry, love, but it wasn't my fault. When are you coming home?'

'Unfortunately I can't right now. I'm in the middle of a meeting in Montelusa; I'll be at least another hour I'm sure. Then I'll come running. Oh, and listen: tonight we're going to the commissioner's for dinner.'

'But I didn't bring anything to wear!'

'You can go in jeans. Have a look in the fridge, Adelina must have cooked something.'

'No, that's all right. I'll wait for you, we can eat together.'

'I've already made do with a sandwich. I'm not hungry. See you soon.'

He sat back down at his table, where a pound of mullet awaited him, fried to a delicate crisp.

*

A little weary from her journey, Livia had gone to bed. Montalbano got undressed and lay down beside her. They kissed. Suddenly Livia pulled away and started sniffing him.

'You smell like fried food.'

'Of course I do. I just spent an hour interrogating some guy in a fried-food shop.'

They made love calmly, knowing they had all the time in the world. Then they sat up in bed, pillows behind their heads, and Montalbano told her the story of Lapècora's murder. Thinking he was amusing her, he told her how he'd had Mrs Piccirillo and her daughter, who set such great store by their honour, brought in to the station. He also told her he'd had Fazio buy a bottle of wine for Mr Culicchia, who'd lost his when it rolled next to the corpse. Instead of laughing, as Montalbano expected, Livia looked at him coldly.

'Arsehole,' she said.

'I beg your pardon?' Montalbano asked with the aplomb of an English lord.

'You're an arsehole and a sexist. First you disgrace those two wretched women, and then you buy a bottle of wine for the guy who had no qualms about riding up and down in the lift with a corpse. Now tell me that's not acting like a jerk.'

'Come on, Livia, don't look at it that way.'

Unfortunately Livia insisted on looking at it that way. It was six o'clock before he managed to appease her. To distract her he told her the story of the little boy who was stealing other children's late-morning snacks.

But Livia didn't laugh this time, either. In fact, she seemed to turn melancholy.

'What's wrong? What did I say? Did I do something wrong again?'

'No, I was just thinking of that poor little boy.'

'The one who got beaten up?'

'No, the other one. He must be really famished and desperate. You say he didn't speak Italian? He's probably the child of some immigrants who can't even put food on the table. Or maybe he was abandoned.'

'Jesus Christ!' cried Montalbano, thunderstruck by the revelation, yelling so loudly that Livia gave a start.

'What's got into you?'

'Jesus Christ!' the inspector repeated, eyes bulging out of his head.

'What on earth did I say?' Livia asked, concerned.

Without answering, Montalbano dashed to the phone, completely naked.

'Catarella, get the fuck off the line and get me Fazio at the double. Fazio? In one hour, at the latest, I want you all at the office. Got that? All of you. If anybody's missing, I'll be furious.'

He hung up, then dialled another number.

'Commissioner? Montalbano here. I'm embarrassed to say, but I can't make it to dinner tonight. No, it's not because of Livia. It's got to do with work. I'll explain everything. Lunch tomorrow? By all means. And please give your wife my apologies.'

Livia had got out of bed, trying to understand how her words could have provoked such a frantic reaction.

Montalbano's only answer was to throw himself on the bed, dragging her along with him. His intentions were perfectly clear.

'But didn't you say you'd be at the office in an hour?'

'Fifteen minutes more or less, what's the difference?'

*

Crammed into Montalbano's office, which was certainly not spacious, were Augello, Fazio, Tortorella, Gallo, Germanà, Galluzzo and Grasso, who had begun working at the station less than a month ago. Catarella stood leaning against the door frame, an ear to the switchboard. Montalbano had brought along a reluctant Livia.

'But what am I going to do there?'

'Believe me, you might be very useful.'

But he hadn't given her a single word of explanation.

In utter silence, he drew a rough but sufficiently precise street map of Villaseta, which he then showed to all present.

'This is a little house on Via Garibaldi in Villaseta. No one is living there at the moment. Here behind it is a garden . . .'

He went on to illustrate every detail, the neighbouring houses, the main junctions, the smaller crossroads. He had committed everything to memory the previous afternoon, when alone in Karima's room. With the exception of Catarella, who would remain on duty at headquarters, they were all to have a part in the operation. Using the map, the inspector pointed out the position that each was to take up. He ordered them to arrive at the scene one by one: no sirens, no uniforms – in fact, no police cars at all. They were to remain absolutely inconspicuous. If anybody wanted to bring his own car, he must leave it at least half a kilometre away from the house. They could bring along whatever they wanted, sandwiches, coffee, beer, because it was probably going to take a long time. They might have to lie in wait all night, and there wasn't even any guarantee of success. Most likely the person they were looking for wouldn't show up. When the street lights came on, that would signal the start of the operation.

'Weapons?' asked Augello.

'Weapons? What weapons?' Montalbano muttered, momentarily bewildered.

'I don't know, but since it seemed like something serious, I thought—'

'Who is it we're looking to capture?' Fazio cut in.

'A snack thief.'

Everyone in the room seemed to stop breathing. Beads of sweat appeared on Augello's forehead.

I've been telling him for the last year he should have his head examined, he thought.

*

It was a clear, moonlit night, windless and still. It had only one flaw, in Montalbano's eyes. It seemed as if time didn't want to pass. Every minute was mysteriously expanding, dilating into five more.

By the light of a cigarette lighter, Livia had put the gutted mattress back on the bed frame, lain down, and gradually fallen asleep. She was now sleeping in earnest.

The inspector, seated in a chair beside the window that looked over the back, had a clear view of the garden and the surrounding countryside. Fazio and Grasso were supposed to be in that area, but no matter how hard he squinted, he could see no trace of them. They were probably hidden among the almond trees. He felt pleased with his men's professionalism; they'd embraced the assignment wholeheartedly after he told them the little boy was probably François, Karima's son. He took a drag on his fortieth cigarette and glanced at his watch by the faint glow. He decided to wait another half hour, after which he would tell his men to go back home. At this exact moment he noticed a very slight movement at the point where the garden ended and the countryside began; but, more than a movement, it was a momentary break in the reflection of the moon on the straw and yellow scrub. It couldn't have been Fazio or Grasso. He had purposely wanted to leave that area unguarded, as if to favour, even suggest, that approach. The movement, or whatever it was, repeated itself, and this time Montalbano could make out a small, dark shape coming slowly forward. It was the kid, no doubt about it.

He moved slowly toward Livia, guided by her breath.

'Wake up, he's coming.'

He returned to the window and was joined at once by Livia. Montalbano spoke into her ear:

'As soon as they catch him, I want you to go immediately downstairs. He's going to be terrified, but when he sees a woman he might feel reassured. Stroke him, kiss him, tell him whatever you can think of.'

The little boy was right next to the house now. They

could see him clearly as he raised his head and looked up towards the window. Suddenly a man's shape appeared, descended on the boy and grabbed him. It was Fazio.

Livia flew down the stairs. François, kicking, let out a long, heart-rending wail, like an animal caught in a trap. Montalbano turned on the light and leaned out of the window.

'Bring him upstairs. You, Grasso, go and round up the others.'

Meanwhile the child's wailing had stopped and turned into sobbing. Livia was holding him in her arms, talking to him.

*

He was still very tense but had stopped crying. Eyes glistening and ardent, he studied the faces around him, slowly regaining confidence. He was sitting at the same table where, only a few days before, he had sat with his mother beside him. This, perhaps, was why he clung to Livia's hand and didn't want her to leave him.

Mimì Augello, who had briefly absented himself, returned with a bag in his hand. Everyone immediately realized he'd been the only one with the right idea. Inside were some ham sandwiches, bananas, cookies and two cans of Coca-Cola. As a reward, Mimì received an emotional glance from Livia, which naturally irritated Montalbano. The deputy inspector stammered, 'I had somebody prepare it last night . . . I thought that, if we were dealing with a hungry little boy . . .'

As he was eating, François gave in to fatigue and fell asleep. He didn't manage to finish the cookies. All at once his head fell forward onto the table, as if someone had turned off a switch inside him.

'So where do we take him now?' asked Fazio.

'To our house,' Livia said decisively.

Montalbano was struck by that 'our'. And as he was gathering up a pair of jeans and a T-shirt for the little boy, he couldn't tell whether he should be pleased or upset.

The child didn't open his eyes once during the ride back to Marinella, or when Livia undressed him after making up a bed for him on the living-room sofa.

'What if he wakes up and runs away while we're asleep?' asked the inspector.

'I don't think he will,' Livia reassured him.

Montalbano, in any case, wasn't taking any chances. He closed the window, lowered the shutters, and gave the front-door key two turns.

They too went to bed. But despite how tired they were, it took them a long time to fall asleep. The presence of François, whom they could hear breathing in the next room, made them both inexplicably uneasy.

*

Around nine o'clock the next morning, very late for him, the inspector woke up, got quietly out of bed so as not to disturb Livia, and went to check on François. The boy wasn't there. Not on the couch, nor in the bathroom. He'd escaped, just as the inspector had feared. But how the hell did he do it, with the front door locked and the shutters still down? He started looking everywhere the child might be hiding. Nothing. Vanished. He had to wake Livia and tell her what had happened, get her advice. He reached out and at that moment saw the child's head resting against his woman's breast. They were sleeping in each other's arms.

NINE

'Inspector? Sorry to bother you at home. Could we meet this morning? I'd like to give you my report.'

'Certainly. I'll come to Montelusa.'

'No, that's all right. I'll come down to Vigàta. Shall we meet in an hour at the office in Salita Granet?'

'Yes, thanks, Laganà.'

*

He went into the bathroom, trying to make as little noise as possible. Also to avoid disturbing Livia and François, he put on his clothes from the previous day, which were additionally rumpled from the night-long stake-out. He left a note: there was a lot of stuff in the fridge, he'd be back by lunchtime. As soon as he'd written it, he remembered that the commissioner had invited them for lunch. That was out of the question now, with François there. He decided to phone at once, otherwise he might forget. He knew that the commissioner spent Sunday mornings at home, except in extraordinary circumstances.

'Montalbano? Don't tell me you're not coming for lunch!'

'Unfortunately I can't, Mr Commissioner, I'm sorry.'

'Is it something serious?'

'Quite. The fact is, early this morning, I became – I don't know how to put this – sort of a father.'

'Congratulations!' was the commissioner's reply. 'So, Miss Livia . . . I can't wait to tell my wife, she'll be so happy. But I don't understand how this would prevent you from coming. Ah, I get it: the event is imminent.'

Flummoxed by his superior's misapprehension, Montalbano recklessly proceeded to entangle himself in a long, tortuous, stammering explanation that jumbled together murder victims and children's snacks, Volupté perfume and the Mulone printing works. The commissioner gave up.

'All right, all right, you can explain it all later. Listen, when is Miss Livia leaving?'

'Tonight.'

'So we won't have the pleasure of meeting her. Too bad. It'll have to wait till next time. Tell you what, Montalbano: when you think you'll have a couple of free hours, give me a ring.'

Before going out, he went to take a last look at Livia and François, who were still asleep. Who would ever break their embrace? He frowned, gripped by a dark premonition.

*

The inspector was astonished to find everything in Lapècora's office exactly as he had left it. Not one sheet of paper out of place, not a single clip where he hadn't seen it last time. Laganà had understood.

'It wasn't a search, Inspector. There was no need to turn the place upside down.'

'So, what can you tell me?'

'Well, the business was founded by Aurelio Lapècora in 1965. He'd worked as a clerk before that. The business was involved in importing tropical fruit and had a warehouse in Via Vittorio Emanuele Orlando, near the port, equipped with cold-storage rooms. They exported cereals, chickpeas, broad beans, pistachios, things of that sort. The volume of business was decent, at least until the second half of the eighties. Then things went steadily downhill. To make a long story short, in January of 1990, Lapècora was forced to liquidate, but it was all above board. He even sold the warehouse and made a tidy profit. His papers are all on file. An orderly man, this Lapècora. If I'd had to do an inspection here, I wouldn't have found anything wrong. Four years later, also in January, he obtained authorization to reopen the business, which was still incorporated. But he never bought another depository or warehouse, nothing whatsoever. And you know what?'

'I think I already know. You found no trace of any business transaction from 1994 to the present.'

'Right. If Lapècora only wanted to come and spend a few hours at the office – I'm referring to what I saw in the next room – what need was there to reconstitute the business?'

'Find any recent post?'

'No, sir. All the post's at least four years old.'

Montalbano picked up a yellowed envelope that had been lying on the desk and showed it to the sergeant.

'Did you find any envelopes like this, but new, with the words "Import-Export" in the return address?'

'Not a single one.'

'Listen, Sergeant. Last month a local print shop sent Lapècora a parcel of stationery to this office. Since you found no trace of it, do you think it's possible the whole stock got used up in four weeks?'

'I wouldn't think so. Even when things were going well, he couldn't have written that many letters.'

'Did you find any letters from a foreign firm called Aslanidis, which exports dates?'

'Nothing.'

'And yet, according to the postman, some were delivered here.'

'Did you search Lapècora's home, Inspector?'

'Yes. There's nothing related to his new business there. You want to know something else? According to a very reliable witness, on certain nights, when Lapècora wasn't here, this place was buzzing with activity.'

He proceeded to tell him about Karima and the dark young man posing as a nephew, who used to make and receive phone calls and write letters, but only on his own portable typewriter.

'I get it,' said Laganà. 'Don't you?'

'I do, but I'd like to hear your idea first.'

'The business was a cover, a front, the receiving end of

some kind of illegal trafficking. It certainly wasn't used to import dates.'

'I agree,' said Montalbano. 'And when they killed Lapècora, or the night before, they came here and got rid of everything.'

*

He dropped in at headquarters. Catarella was at the switchboard, working on a crossword puzzle.

'Tell me something, Cat. How long does it take you to solve a puzzle?'

'Ah, they're hard, Chief, really hard. I been workin' on this one for a month and I still can't get it.'

'Any news?'

'Nothing serious, Chief. Somebody arsoned Sebastiano Lo Monaco's parking garage by setting fire to it. The firemen went and put it out. Five motor vehicles got roasted. Then somebody shot at somebody by the name of Filippo Quarantino but they missed and got the window of the house where Mrs Saveria Pizzuto lives and she got so scared she had to go to casualty. Then there was another fire, an arson fire for sure. But just little shit, Chief, kid stuff, nothin' important.'

'Who's in the office?'

'Nobody, Chief. They're all out taking care of these things.'

Montalbano went into his office. On the desk was a parcel wrapped in the paper of the Pipitone pastry shop. He opened it: cannoli, cream puffs, *torroncini.*

'Catarella!'

'At your orders, Chief.'

'Who put these pastries here?'

'Inspector Augello did. He says he bought 'em for the little boy from last night.'

How thoughtful and attentive to abandoned children Mr Mimì Augello had suddenly become! Was he hoping for another glance from Livia?

The telephone rang.

'Chief? It's His Honour Judge Lo Bianco. He says he wants to speak personally with you.'

'Put him on.'

A couple of weeks earlier, Judge Lo Bianco had sent the inspector a complimentary copy of the first tome, all seven hundred pages, of a work to which he'd been devoting himself for years: *The Life and Exploits of Rinaldo and Antonio Lo Bianco, Masters of Jurisprudence at the University of Girgenti at the Time of King Martin the Younger (1402–1409)*. He'd got it in his head that these Lo Biancos were his ancestors. Montalbano had leafed through the book one sleepless night.

'Hey, Cat, are you going to put the judge on the line or not?'

'The fact is, Chief, I can't put him on the line, seeing as he's already here personally in person.'

Cursing, Montalbano rushed to the door, showed the judge into his office, and expressed his apologies. He already felt guilty towards the judge for having phoned him only once about the Lapècora murder, after which he'd completely forgotten he existed. No doubt he'd come to give him a tongue-lashing.

'Just a quick hello, my dear Inspector. Thought I'd drop in, since I was passing by on my way to see my mother who's staying with friends at Durrueli. Let's give it a try, I said to myself. And I was lucky: here you are.'

And what the hell do you want from me? Montalbano said to himself. Given the solicitous glance the judge cast his way, it didn't take him long to figure it out.

'You know, Judge, lately I've been losing sleep.'

'Really? Why's that?'

'I spend the nights reading your book. It's more gripping than a mystery novel, and so rich in detail.'

A lethal bore: dates upon dates, names upon names. By comparison, the train timetable had more surprises and plot twists.

He remembered one episode recounted by the judge in which Antonio Lo Bianco, on his way to Castrogiovanni on a diplomatic mission, fell from his horse and broke a leg. To this insignificant event the judge devoted twenty-two maniacally detailed pages. To show he'd actually read the book, Montalbano foolishly quoted from it.

And so Judge Lo Bianco engaged him for two hours, adding other details as useless as they were minute. When he finally said goodbye, the inspector felt a headache coming on.

'Oh, and listen, dear boy, don't forget to keep me posted on the Lacapra case.'

*

When he got to Marinella, neither Livia nor François were there. They were down by the water, Livia in her bathing suit and the boy in his underpants. They'd built an enormous sandcastle and were laughing and talking. In French, of course, which Livia spoke as well as Italian. Along with English. Not to mention German, truth be told. The house ignoramus was he, who barely knew three or four words of French he'd learned in school.

He set the table, then looked in the fridge and found the *pasta 'ncasciata* and veal roulade from the day before. He put them in the oven at low heat, then quickly got undressed, put on his swimming trunks, and joined the other two. The first things he noticed were a little bucket, a shovel, a sand-sifter and some moulds in the shapes of fish and stars. He, of course, didn't have such things about the house, and Livia certainly hadn't bought them, since it was Sunday. And there wasn't a soul on the beach aside from the three of them.

'What are those?'

'What are what?'

'The shovel, the bucket—'

'Augello brought them this morning. He's so sweet! They belong to his little nephew, who last year . . .'

He didn't want to hear any more. He dived into the sea, infuriated.

When they returned to the house, Livia noticed the cardboard tray full of pastries.

'Why did you buy those? Don't you know sweets are bad for children?'

'Yes I do, it's your friend Augello who doesn't know it. *He* bought them. And now you're going to eat them, you and François.'

'While we're at it, your friend Ingrid called, the Swedish woman.'

Thrust, parry, counterthrust. And what was the meaning of that 'while we're at it'?

Those two liked each other, that was clear. It had started the previous year, when Mimì had driven Livia around in his car for an entire day. And now they were picking up where they'd left off. What did they do when he wasn't there? Trade cute little glances, smiles, compliments?

They began eating, with Livia and François murmuring to each other from time to time, enclosed inside an invisible bubble of complicity from which Montalbano was utterly excluded. The delicious meal, however, prevented him from getting as angry as he would have liked.

'Excellent, this *brusciuluni*,' he said.

'What did you call it?'

'*Brusciuluni*. The roulade.'

'You nearly frightened me. Some of your Sicilian words . . .'

'You Ligurians don't kid around either. Speaking of which, what time does your flight leave? I think I can drive you to Palermo.'

'Oh, I forgot to tell you. I cancelled my reservation and called Adriana, a colleague of mine, and asked her to fill in for me. I'm going to stay a few more days. It suddenly dawned on me that if I'm not here, who are you going to leave François with?'

The dark premonition he'd had that morning, when he saw them sleeping in each other's arms, was beginning to take shape. Who would ever pry those two apart?

'You seem displeased . . . I don't know . . . irritated.'

'Me? Come on, Livia!'

*

As soon as they'd finished eating, the little boy's eyelids started to droop; he was sleepy and must still have been quite worn out. Livia took him into the bedroom, undressed him, and put him to bed.

'He told me something,' she said, leaving the door ajar.

'Tell me.'

'When we were building the sandcastle, at a certain point he asked me if I thought his mother would ever return. I told him I didn't know anything about what had happened, but I was sure that one day his mother would come back for him. He twisted up his face, and I didn't say any more. A little while later, he brought it up again and said he didn't think she was coming back. Then he dropped the subject. That child is darkly aware of something terrible. Then all of a sudden he started talking again. He told me that that morning, his mother had come home in a rush and seemed frightened. She told him they had to go away. They ran to the centre of Villaseta; his mother told him they had to catch a bus.'

'A bus for where?'

'He doesn't know. While they were waiting, a car drove up. He knew it well; it belonged to a bad man who would sometimes beat his mother. Fahrid.'

'What's the name?'

'Fahrid.'

'Are you sure?'

'Absolutely. He even told me that, when you write it, there's an *h* between the *a* and the *r*.'

So Mr Lapècora's dear young nephew, the owner of the metallic grey BMW, had an Arab name.

'Go on.'

'This Fahrid then got out of the car, grabbed Karima's arm, and tried to force her to get in. She resisted and shouted to François to run away. The boy fled; Fahrid was too busy with Karima and had to choose. François found a hiding place and was too terrified to come out. He didn't dare go back to a woman he called his grandma.'

'Aisha.'

'He got so hungry he had to rob other children of their schooltime snacks to survive. At night he would go up to the house, but he found it all dark and was afraid that Fahrid was lying in wait for him there. He slept outside. He felt hunted like an animal. The other night he couldn't stand it any longer; he had to go back home at all costs. That's why he came so close to the house.'

Montalbano remained silent.

'Well, what do you think?' she asked.

'I think we've got an orphan on our hands.'

Livia blanched; her voice began to tremble.

'Why do you think that?'

'Let me explain the opinion I've formed of the whole affair thus far, also based on what you've just told me. Five years ago, more or less, this attractive, beautiful Tunisian woman comes to our country with her baby boy. She looks for work as a cleaner and has no trouble finding it, because, among other things, she grants favours, upon request, to older men. That's how she meets Lapècora. But at a certain point this Fahrid enters her life. He's probably a pimp or something similar. Fahrid then comes up with a scheme to force Lapècora to reopen his old import-export business as a front for some sort of shady dealings, probably drugs or prostitution. Lapècora, who's basically an honest man, senses that something's not right and gets scared. He tries to wiggle out of a nasty situation by rather ingenuous means. Just imagine, he writes anonymous letters to his wife denouncing himself. Things go on this way for a while, but at a certain point, and I don't know why, Fahrid is forced to clear out. At this point, however, he has to eliminate Lapècora. He arranges for Karima to spend a night at Lapècora's house, hiding in his study. Lapècora's wife has to go to Fiacca the following day, to visit her sister who's sick. Karima had probably filled Lapècora's brain with visions of wild sex in the marriage bed when the wife was away. Who knows? Early the next morning, after Mrs Lapècora has left, Karima opens the front door and lets in Fahrid, who then kills the old man. Lapècora may have attempted to escape; perhaps that was why he was found in the lift. Except that, based on what you just told me, Karima must not have known that Fahrid intended to kill him. When she sees that her accomplice has stabbed Lapècora, she flees. But she doesn't get very far; Fahrid tracks her down and kidnaps her. In all probability, he later kills her, to keep her from talking. And the proof of this is that he went back to Karima's place to remove all the photos of her. He didn't want her to be identified.'

Silently, Livia started crying.

*

He was alone. Livia had gone to lie down next to François. Montalbano, not knowing what to do, went and sat on the veranda. In the sky, two seagulls were engaged in some sort of duel; on the beach, a young couple were strolling, exchanging a kiss from time to time, but wearily, as if following a script. He went back inside, picked up the last novel written by the late Gesualdo Bufalino, the one about a blind photographer, and went back out on the veranda. He glanced at the cover, the jacket flaps, then closed it. He was unable to concentrate. He could feel an acute malaise slowly growing inside him. And suddenly he understood the reason.

It was merely a foretaste, an advance instalment, of the quiet, familial Sunday afternoons that awaited him, perhaps not even in Vigàta but in Boccadasse. With a little boy who, upon awakening, would call him Papa and ask him to play . . .

Panic seized him by the throat.

TEN

He had to run away at once, to flee the familial ambushes awaiting him in that house. As he got in his car, he couldn't help but smile at the schizophrenic attack he was suffering. His rational side told him he could easily control the new situation, which in any case existed only in his imagination; his irrational side was spurring him to flee, just like that, without a thought.

He arrived in Vigàta and went to his office.

'Any news?'

Instead of answering, Fazio asked another question:

'How's the kid?'

'Fine,' he replied, slightly annoyed. 'Well?'

'Nothing serious. An unemployed man went into a supermarket with a big stick and started smashing up the shelves—'

'Unemployed? You mean there are still people without work in our country?'

Fazio looked stunned.

'Of course there are, Chief. Didn't you know?'

'Frankly, I didn't. I thought everyone had work these days.'

Fazio was clearly at sea.

'And how are they supposed to find this work?'

'By repenting, Fazio. Turning state's witness against the Mafia. This unemployed bloke smashing up supermarket shelves, he's not out of work, he's an arsehole. Did you arrest him?'

'Yes.'

'Go and tell him, on my behalf, that he should turn state's witness.'

'For what case?'

'Anything! Tell him to make something up. But he has to say he's repented. Any bullshit he feels like saying. Maybe you can suggest something to him. But as soon as he turns state's witness, he's set for life. They'll pay him, find him a house, send his kids to school. Tell him.'

Fazio eyed him in silence. Then he said, 'Chief, it's a beautiful day, and still you're in a filthy mood. What gives?'

'None of your goddamn business.'

*

The owner of the shop where Montalbano usually supplied himself with *càlia e simenza* had devised an ingenious system for getting around the obligatory Sunday closing. He would set up a well-stocked booth in front of the lowered shutter.

'Got fresh-roasted peanuts here, nice and hot,' the shopkeeper informed him.

The inspector had him add twenty or so to his *coppo*, the paper cornet already half-full of chickpeas and pumpkin seeds.

His solitary, ruminating stroll to the tip of the eastern jetty lasted longer than usual this time, until after sunset.

*

'This child is extremely intelligent!' Livia said excitedly as soon as she saw Montalbano enter the house. 'I taught him how to play draughts just three hours ago, and now look: he's already beat me once and is about to win again.'

The inspector remained standing beside them, watching the final moves of the game. Livia made a devastating mistake and François gobbled up her two remaining chips. Consciously or unconsciously, Livia had wanted the kid to win; if she'd been playing him instead of François, she would have fought tooth and nail to deny him the satisfaction of victory. Once she even stooped to pretending she'd fainted, letting all the pieces fall to the floor.

'Are you hungry?'

'I can wait, if you want,' the inspector replied, complying with her implicit request to delay supper.

'We'd love to go for a little walk.'

She and François, naturally. The idea that he might wish to tag along never even crossed her mind.

Montalbano set the table grandly, and when he finished he went into the kitchen to see what Livia had made. Nothing. An arctic desolation. The dishes and cutlery sparkled, uncontaminated. Lost in her preoccupation with

François, she hadn't even thought to make dinner. He drew up a rapid, unhappy inventory: as a first course, he could make a little pasta with garlic and oil; as a second course, he could throw something together using sardines in brine, olives, caciocavallo cheese and canned tuna. The worst, in any case, would come the following day, when Adelina, showing up to clean the house and cook, found Livia there with a little boy. The two women didn't take to each other. Once, because of certain comments Livia had made, Adelina had abruptly dropped everything, half finished, to return only after she was certain her rival was gone and already hundreds of miles away.

It was time for the evening news. He turned on the television and tuned into TeleVigàta. On the screen appeared the chicken-arse mug of Pippo Ragonese, their editor. Montalbano was about to change the channel when Ragonese's first words paralysed him.

'What is going on at Vigàta police headquarters?' the newsman asked himself and the entire universe in a tone that would have made Torquemada, in his best moments, seem like he was telling jokes.

He went on to say that in his opinion, Vigàta these days could be compared to the Chicago of the Prohibition era, with all its shoot-outs, robberies and arson. The life and liberty of the common, honest citizen were in constant danger. And did the viewers know what that overrated Police Inspector Montalbano, in the midst of this tragic situation, was working on? The question mark was so emphatically underscored that the inspector thought he could actually see it superimposed on the man's chicken-arse face. Having caught his breath, the better to express due wonder and indignation, Ragonese then stressed every syllable 'On-chas-ing-af-ter-a-snack-thief!'

But he wasn't working on this alone, our inspector. He'd dragged all his men along with him, leaving police headquarters unprotected, with only a sorry switchboard operator on duty. How did he, Ragonese, come to learn of this seemingly comical but surely tragic situation? Needing to speak with Assistant Inspector Augello to get some information, he had telephoned the central police station, only to receive the extraordinary answer given him by the switchboard operator. At first, he'd thought it must be a joke, a tasteless one to be sure, and so he'd insisted. Yet in the end he understood that it was not a prank, but the incredible truth. Did the viewers of Vigàta realize what sort of hands they were in?

'What have I ever done to deserve Catarella?' the inspector asked himself bitterly as he changed channel.

On the Free Channel's news programme, they were broadcasting images of the funeral, in Mazàra, of the Tunisian fisherman machine-gunned to death aboard the trawler *Santopadre*. At the end of the report, the speaker commented on the Tunisian's misfortune to have died so tragically his first time out on the fishing boat. Indeed, he had only just arrived in town, and hardly anyone knew him. He had no family, or at least hadn't had the time to bring them to Mazàra. He was born thirty-two years ago in Sfax, and his name was Ben Dhahab. They showed a photo of him, and at that moment Livia and the little boy walked in, back from their stroll. Seeing the face on the television screen, François smiled and pointed a small finger.

'*Mon oncle*' he said.

Livia was about to tell Salvo to turn off the television because it bothered her when she was eating; for his part, Montalbano was about to reproach her for not having prepared anything for supper. Instead they just stood there dumbstruck, forefingers pointing at each other, while a third forefinger, the little boy's, still pointed at the screen. It was as if an angel had passed, the one who says 'Amen', and everyone remains just as they were. The inspector pulled himself up and sought confirmation, doubting his scant understanding of French.

'What'd he say?'

'He said: "my uncle"', replied a very pale Livia.

When the image vanished from the screen, François took his place at the table, anxious to start eating and in no way disturbed by having seen his uncle on TV.

'Ask him if the man he just saw is his uncle uncle.'

'What kind of idiotic question is that?'

'It's not idiotic. They called me "uncle," too, even though I'm nobody's uncle.'

François answered that the man he'd just seen was his uncle uncle, his mother's brother.

'He has to come with me, right away.'

'Where do you want to take him?'

'To headquarters. I want to show him a photograph.'

'Forget it. Nobody's going to steal your photograph.

François has to eat first. Afterwards, I'm going to come with you; you're liable to lose the boy along the way.'

The pasta came out overcooked, practically inedible.

*

At headquarters there was only Catarella, who, upon seeing the makeshift little family and the look on his superior's face, took fright.

'All peaceable and quiet-like here, Chief.'

'But not in Chechnya.'

The inspector opened a drawer and took out the photos he'd lifted from Karima's house. He selected one and showed it to François. The boy, without a word, brought it to his lips and kissed his mother's image.

Livia barely suppressed a sob. There was no need to ask any questions; the resemblance between the man shown on television and the uniformed man with Karima in the photo was obvious. But the inspector asked anyway.

'Is this *ton oncle?*'

'*Oui.*'

'*Comment s'appelle-t-il?*'

Montalbano felt pleased with his French, like a tourist at the Eiffel Tower or the Moulin Rouge.

'Ahmed,' said the little boy.

'*Seulement* Ahmed?'

'Oh, *non.* Ahmed Moussa.'

'*Et ta mère? Comment s'appelle?*'

'Karima Moussa,' said François, shrugging his shoulders at the obviousness of the question.

Montalbano poured out his anger at Livia, who was not expecting the violent assault.

'What the fuck! You're with the child day and night, you play with him, teach him draughts, but it never occurs to you to find out his name! All you had to do was ask! And that fucking arsehole Mimì! The big investigator! He brings the little bucket, the little shovel, the little sand moulds, the little pastries, and instead of talking to the kid he only talks to you!'

Livia didn't react. Montalbano immediately felt ashamed of his outburst.

'Forgive me, Livia. I'm on edge.'

'I can see.'

'Ask him if he's ever met this uncle in person, even recently.'

Livia and the boy spoke to each other softly. Livia then explained that he had not seen him recently, but that when François was three, his mother had taken him to Tunisia, and there he'd met his uncle along with some other men. But his memory of all this wasn't very clear; he'd mentioned it only because his mother had spoken to him about it.

Therefore, Montalbano concluded, there had been a sort of summit two years earlier, in which, in some way, the fate of poor Mr Lapècora had been decided.

'Listen. Take François to see a movie. There's still time to make the last showing. Then come back here. I've got some work to do.'

*

'Hello, Buscaìno! Montalbano here. I've just found out the full name of the Tunisian woman who lives in Villaseta. Remember?'

'Of course. Karima.'

'Her name is Karima Moussa. Could you do a check there at your own office, at the Immigration Bureau?'

'Are you joking, Inspector?'

'No, I'm not. Why?'

'What? How can you ask me such a thing, with all your experience?'

'Explain yourself.'

'Look, Inspector, even if you were to tell me her parents' names, her grandparents' names on both sides, and her date and place of birth—'

'Pea soup?'

'What else would you expect? They can pass all the laws they want in Rome, but here Tunisians, Moroccans, Libyans, Cape Verdians, Senegalese, Nigerians, Rwandans, Albanians, Serbs and Croats come and go as they please. We're in the blasted Colosseum here: there aren't any doors. The fact that we found this Karima's address the other day is not in the normal order of things. It belongs to the realm of the miraculous.'

'Well, try anyway.'

*

'Montalbano? What's this business about you chasing after somebody who steals snacks from children? Is he some kind of maniac?'

'No, no, Mr Commissioner. He was a little boy who was starving and so he started robbing schoolchildren of their morning snacks. That's all.'

'What do you mean, that's all? I'm well aware that every now and then you, how shall I say, go off on a tangent. But this time, frankly, I think—'

'Mr Commissioner, I assure you it won't happen again. It was absolutely necessary that we catch him.'

'Did you?'

'Yes.'

'And what did you do with him?'

'I brought him home with me. Livia's looking after him.'

'Are you mad, Montalbano? You must give him back to his parents at once!'

'He hasn't got any. He may be an orphan.'

'What do you mean, "may be"? Do a search, for God's sake!'

'I am. But François—'

'Who on earth is that?'

'The little boy; that's his name.'

'He's not Italian?'

'No, he's Tunisian.'

'Listen, Montalbano, let's drop it for the moment, I'm too confused. But I want you to come to my office tomorrow morning and explain everything to me.'

'I can't, I have to go out of Vigàta. It's very important, believe me. I'm not trying to slip away.'

'Then we'll see each other in the afternoon. I'm serious;

don't let me down. I need you to provide me with a line of defence; Chamber Deputy Pennacchio is here . . .'

'The one charged with criminal association with mafiosi?'

'The very same. He's preparing a motion to be sent to the Minister of the Interior. He wants your head.'

Indeed. It was Montalbano himself who had initiated the investigation of the honourable deputy.

*

'Nicolò? Montalbano here. I need to ask a favour of you.'

'So what else is new? Fire away.'

'Are you going to be much longer at the Free Channel?'

'I have to do the midnight report and then I'm going home.'

'It's ten o'clock now. If I come to the studio in half an hour and bring you a photo, do you think you could still get it on the air for the midnight report?'

'Sure. I'll wait for you.'

*

He had sensed immediately, at first whiff, that the story of the *Santopadre* fishing boat was bad news. In fact, he'd done everything he could to steer clear of it. But now chance had grabbed him by the hair and ground his face in it, as one does with cats to teach them not to pee in certain places. Livia and François would have needed only to return a few moments later, and the kid would never have seen his uncle's picture on TV, the dinner would have proceeded peacefully, and everything would have gone just fine. He cursed himself for being such an incurable cop. Anyone else in his place would have said, 'Oh yeah? The kid recognized his uncle, did he? How about that!'

And he would have brought the first forkful to his mouth. But he couldn't. He had to dive in and knock his head against it. The instinct of the hunt, it was once called by Dashiell Hammett, who understood these things well.

'Where's the photo?' asked Nicolò as soon as Montalbano walked in.

It was the one of Karima and her son.

'Do you want me to frame the whole thing? Or just a detail?'

'As is.'

Nicolò Zito left the room, then soon returned without the photograph and sat himself comfortably down.

'Tell me everything. But most of all, tell me about the snack thief, which Pippo Ragonese thinks is bullshit but I don't.'

'I haven't got the time, Nicolò, believe me.'

'No, I don't believe you. Question: was the boy stealing snacks the one in the photo you just gave me?'

He was dangerously intelligent, this Nicolò. Better play along.

'Yes, that's him.'

'And who's the mother?'

'She's someone who was definitely involved in the murder the other day – you know, the guy found in the lift.

But no more questions. As soon as I manage to make some sense of this, you'll be the first to know, I promise.'

'Could you tell me at least what I'm supposed to say about the photo?'

'Right, of course. Your tone should be that of somebody telling a sad, sorrowful story.'

'So you're a director now?'

'You should say that an elderly Tunisian woman came to you in tears, begging you to show that photo on TV. She's had no news of either mother or child for three days. Their names are Karima and François. Anyone who's seen them, etcetera, anonymity guaranteed, etcetera, should call Vigàta police headquarters, etcetera.'

'Up yours, etcetera,' said Nicolò Zito.

*

Back at home, Livia went to bed immediately, taking the kid along with her. Montalbano, on the other hand, stayed up, waiting for the midnight news report. Nicolò did what he was supposed to do, keeping the photo on screen as long as possible. When the programme was over, the inspector called to thank him.

'Could you do me another favour?'

'I've half a mind to charge you a fee. What do you want?'

'Could you run the segment again tomorrow on the one p.m. news? I don't think too many people saw it at this hour.'

'Yes, sir!'

He went into the bedroom, released François from

Livia's embrace, picked the child up, took him into the living room and put him down to sleep on the sofa that Livia had already made up. He then took a shower and got into bed. Livia, though asleep, felt him beside her and nudged closer with her back to him, pressing her whole body against him. She had always liked to do it this way, half-asleep, in that pleasant no-man's-land between the country of sleep and the city of consciousness. This time, however, as soon as Montalbano began to caress her, she moved away.

'No. François might wake up.'

For a moment, Montalbano stiffened, petrified. He hadn't considered this other aspect of familial bliss.

*

He got up. Sleep, in any case, had abandoned him. On their way back to Marinella, he'd had something in mind that he wanted to do, and now he remembered what it was.

'Valente? Montalbano here. Sorry to bother you at home, especially at this hour. I need to see you at once, it's extremely urgent. Would it be all right if I came to Mazàra tomorrow morning, around ten?'

'Sure. Could you give me some—'

'It's a complicated, confusing story. I'm going purely on a hunch. It's about that Tunisian who was killed.'

'Ben Dhahab.'

'Just for starters, his name was Ahmed Moussa.'

'Holy shit.'

'Exactly.'

ELEVEN

'There's not necessarily any connection,' observed Vice-Commissioner Valente after Montalbano had finished telling his story.

'If that's your opinion, then do me a big favour. We'll keep each to his own side: you go ahead and investigate why the Tunisian used an assumed name, and I'll look for the reasons for Lapècora's murder and Karima's disappearance. And if we happen to cross paths along the way, we'll pretend we don't know each other and won't even say hello. Okay?'

'Jesus! Why don't you fly straight off the handle!'

Inspector Angelo Tomasino, a thirty-year-old with the look of a bank teller, the kind who hand counts five hundred thousand lire in small bills ten times before handing them over to you, threw down his ace, in support of his boss, 'Anyway, it's not necessarily true.'

'What's not necessarily true?'

'That Ben Dhahab is an assumed name. His full name

might have been Ben Ahmed Dhahab Moussa. Who knows, with these Arab names?'

'I won't bother you any longer,' said Montalbano, standing up.

His blood was boiling, and Valente, who had known him a long time, realized this.

'What should we do, in your opinion?' he asked simply.

The inspector sat back down.

'Find out, for example, who knew him here in Mazàra. How he managed to sign on to that fishing boat. If his papers were in order. Go and search his living quarters. Do I have to tell you to do these things?'

'No,' said Valente. 'I just like to hear you say them.'

He picked up a sheet of paper from his desk and handed it to Montalbano. It was a search warrant for the home of Ben Dhahab, complete with stamp and signature.

'This morning I woke up the judge at the crack of dawn,' Valente said, smiling. 'Care to come along for the ride?'

*

The widow Ernestina Locìcero, née Pipìa, was keen to point out that she wasn't a landlady by profession. She did own, by the grace of her dear departed, a *catojo*, that is, a little ground floor room that in its day had been a barber shop or, as they say now, a hair salon, though whatever they say, it was certainly not a salon. The gentlemen would see it soon enough, and anyway, what need was there for that whatdoyoucallit, that search warren? They had only to come and say, Signora Pipìa, this is how it is, and she wouldn't have made any trouble. The only people who make trouble are the ones who got something to hide, whereas she, well, as anyone in Mazàra could testify – anyone except for the sons of bitches and bastards – she'd always led, and continued to lead, a clean life, squeaky clean. What was the late Tunisian man like? Look, gentlemen, on no account would she ever have rented a room to an African – not to one who was black as ink nor to one whose skin din't look no different than a Mazarese's. Nothing doing. She was scared of those Africans. So why did she rent the room to Ben Dhahab? He was so well bred, gentlemen! A real man of distinction, the likes of which you don't find anymore, not even in Mazàra. Yes, sir, he spoke 'Talian, or least managed to get his point across most of the time. He even showed her his passport—

'Just a second,' said Montalbano.

'Just a minute,' said Valente at the same time.

Yessirs, his passport. All in order. Written the way the Arabs write, and there were even words written in a foreign language. Ingrish? Frinch? Dunno. The photograph matched. And if the gentlemen really, really wanted to know, she'd even filed an official rental statement, as required by law.

'When did he arrive, exactly?' Valente asked.

'Exactly ten days ago.'

And in ten days he'd had enough time to settle in, find work, and get killed.

'Did he tell you how long he planned to stay?' Montalbano asked.

'Another ten days. But . . .'

'But?'

'Well, he wanted to pay me for a whole month in advance.'

'And how much did you ask of him?'

'I asked him straightaway for nine hundred thousand. But you know what Arabs are like, they bargain and bargain, and so I was ready to come down to, I dunno, six hundred, five hundred thousand . . . But the man didn't even let me finish. He just put his hand in his pocket, pulled out a roll of bills as fat as the belly of a bottle, took off the rubber band holding 'em together, and counted out nine one-hundred-thousand-lire bills.'

'Give us the key and explain a little better where this place is,' Montalbano cut in. The Tunisian's good breeding and distinction, in the eyes of the widow Locìcero, were concentrated in that roll of bills as fat as the belly of a bottle.

'Gimme a minute to get ready and I'll come with you.'

'No, signora, you stay here. We'll bring the key back to you.'

*

A rusty iron bed, a wobbly table, an armoire with a piece of plywood in place of the mirror, three wicker chairs. A small bathroom with toilet and sink, and a dirty towel; and on a shelf, a razor, a tin of shaving cream and a comb.

They went back into the single room. There was a blue canvas suitcase on a chair. They opened it: empty.

Inside the armoire, a new pair of trousers, a dark, very clean jacket, four pairs of socks, four pairs of briefs, six handkerchiefs, two undershirts: all brand new, not yet worn. In one corner of the armoire was a pair of sandals in good condition; in the opposite corner, a small plastic bag of dirty laundry. They emptied it onto the floor: nothing unusual. They stayed about an hour, searching everywhere. When they'd lost all hope, Valente got lucky. Not hidden, but clearly dropped and left wedged between the iron headboard and the bed, was a Rome-Palermo plane ticket, issued ten days earlier and made out to Mr Dhahab. So Ahmed had arrived in Palermo at ten o'clock in the morning, and two hours later, at the most, he was in Mazàra. To whom had he turned to find a place to rent?

'Did Montelusa send you the personal effects along with the body?'

'Of course,' replied Valente. 'Ten thousand lire.'

'Passport?'

'No.'

'What about all that money he had?'

'If he left it here, I'm sure the signora took care of it. The one who leads a squeaky-clean life.'

'He didn't even have his house keys in his pocket?'

'Not even. How do I have to say it? Should I sing it? He had ten thousand lire and nothing else.'

*

Summoned by Valente, Master Rahman, an elementary-school teacher who looked like a pure Sicilian and served as an unofficial liaison between his people and the Mazarese authorities, arrived in ten minutes.

Montalbano had met him the year before, when involved in the case later dubbed 'the terracotta dog'.

'Were you in the middle of a lesson?' asked Valente.

In an uncommon show of good sense, a school principal in Mazàra, without involving the superintendency, had allowed some classrooms to be used to create a school for the local Tunisian children.

'Yes, but I called in a substitute. Is there a problem?'

'Perhaps you could help clarify something for us.'

'About what?'

'About whom, rather. Ben Dhahab.'

They had decided, Valente and Montalbano, to sing only half the Mass to the schoolteacher. Afterwards, depending on his reactions, they would determine whether or not to tell him the whole story.

Upon hearing that name, Rahman made no effort to hide his uneasiness.

'What would you like to know?'

It was up to Valente to make the first move; Montalbano was only a guest.

'Did you know him?'

'He came and introduced himself to me about ten days ago. He knew who I was and what I represent. You see, last January or thereabouts, a Tunis newspaper published an article on our school.'

'And what did he say to you?'

'He said he was a journalist.'

Valente and Montalbano exchanged a very quick glance.

'He wanted to do a feature on the lives of our countrymen in Mazàra. But he intended to present himself to everyone as somebody looking for a job. He also wanted to sign on with a fishing boat. I introduced him to my colleague El Madani. And he put him in touch with Signora Pipìa about renting a room.'

'Did you ever see him again?'

'Of course. We ran into each other a few times by chance. We also were both at the same festival. He had become, well, perfectly integrated.'

'Was it you who set him up with the fishing boat?'

'No. It wasn't El Madani, either.'

'Who paid for his funeral?'

'We did. We have a small emergency fund that we set up for such things.'

'And who gave the TV reporters the photos and information on Ben Dhahab?'

'I did. You see, at that festival I mentioned, there was a photographer. Ben Dhahab objected; he said he didn't want anyone taking his picture. But the man had already taken one. And so, when the TV reporter showed up, I got hold of that photo and gave it to him, along with the bit of information Ben Dhahab had told me about himself.'

Rahman wiped away his sweat. His uneasiness had increased. And Valente, who was a good policeman, let him stew in his juices.

'But there's something strange in all this,' Rahman decided.

Montalbano and Valente seemed not even to have heard him, looking as if their minds were elsewhere. But in fact they were paying very close attention, like cats that, keeping their eyes closed as if asleep, are actually counting the stars.

'Yesterday I called the newspaper in Tunis to tell them about the incident and to make arrangements for the body. As soon as I told the editor that Ben Dhahab was dead, he started laughing and said my joke wasn't very funny: Ben Dhahab was in the room right next to his at that very moment, on the telephone. And then he hung up.'

'Couldn't it simply be a case of two men with the same name?' Valente asked provocatively.

'Absolutely not! He was very clear with me! He specifically said he'd been sent by that newspaper. He therefore lied to me.'

'Do you know if he had any relatives in Sicily?' Montalbano stepped in for the first time.

'I don't know, we never talked about that. If he'd had any in Mazàra, he certainly wouldn't have turned to me for help.'

Valente and Montalbano again consulted each other with a glance, and Montalbano, without speaking, gave his friend the go-ahead to fire the shot.

'Does the name Ahmed Moussa mean anything to you?'

It was not a shot, but an out-and-out cannon blast. Rahman jumped out of his chair, fell back down in it, then wilted.

'What . . . what . . . has . . . Ahmed Moussa got to do with this?' the schoolmaster stammered, breathless.

'Pardon my ignorance,' Valente continued implacably, 'but who is this man you find so frightening?'

'He's a terrorist. Somebody who . . . a murderer. A blood-thirsty killer. But what has he got to do with any of this?'

'We have reason to believe that Ben Dhahab was really Ahmed Moussa.'

'I feel ill,' Schoolmaster Rahman said in a feeble voice.

*

From the earth-shaken words of the devastated Rahman, they learned that Ahmed Moussa, whose real name was more often whispered than stated aloud and whose face was practically unknown, had formed a paramilitary cell of desperadoes some time before. He had introduced himself to the world three years earlier with an unequivocal calling card, blowing up a small cinema that was showing French cartoons for children. The luckiest among the audience were the ones who died; dozens of others were left blinded, maimed, or disabled for life. The cell espoused, in its communiqués at least, a nationalism so absolute as to be almost abstract. Moussa and his people were viewed with suspicion by even the most intransigent of fundamentalists. They had access to almost unlimited amounts of money, the source of which remained unknown. A large bounty had been placed on Ahmed Moussa's head by the Tunisian government. This was all that Master Rahman knew. The idea that he had somehow helped the terrorist so troubled him that he trembled and teetered as if suffering a violent attack of malaria.

'But you were deceived,' said Montalbano, trying to console him.

'If you're worried about the consequences,' Valente added, 'we can vouch for your absolute good faith.'

Rahman shook his head. He explained that it wasn't fear he was feeling, but horror. Horror at the fact that his own life, however briefly, had intersected with that of a cold-blooded killer of innocent children.

They comforted him as best they could, and as they were leaving they warned him not to repeat a word of their conversation to anyone, not even to his colleague and friend El Madani. They would call him if they needed him for anything else.

'Even at night, you call, no disturb,' said the schoolteacher, who suddenly had difficulty speaking Italian.

*

Before discussing everything they'd just learned, they ordered some coffee and drank it slowly, in silence.

'Obviously the guy didn't sign on to learn how to fish,' Valente began.

'Or to get killed.'

'We'll have to see how the captain of the fishing boat tells the story.'

'You want to summon him here?'

'Why not?'

'He'll end up repeating what he already told Augello. It might be better first to try and find out what people down on the docks think. A word here, a word there, and we might end up learning a lot more.'

'I'll put Tomasino on it.'

Montalbano grimaced. He really couldn't stand Valente's second-in-command, but this wasn't a very good reason, and it especially wasn't something he could say.

'You don't like that idea?'

'Me? It's you who have to like the idea. Your men are yours. You know them better than I do.'

'C'mon, Montalbano, don't be a shit.'

'Okay, I don't think he's right for the job. The guy acts like a tax collector, and nobody's going to feel like confiding in him when he comes knocking.'

'Yeah, you're right. I'll put Tripodi on it. He's a smart kid, fearless. And his father's a fisherman.'

'The important thing is to find out exactly what happened on the night the trawler crossed paths with the motor patrol. There's something about the whole story that doesn't add up, no matter which way you look at it.'

'And what would that be?'

'Let's forget, for the moment, how he managed to sign on with the boat. Ahmed set out with specific intentions, which are unknown to us. Here I ask myself: did he reveal these intentions to the captain and the crew? And did he reveal them before they put out or when they were already at sea? In my opinion, he did state his intentions – though I don't know exactly when – and everyone agreed to go along with him. Otherwise they would have turned around and put him ashore.'

'He could have forced them at gun point.'

'But in that case, once they put in at Vigàta or Mazàra, the captain and crew would have said what happened. They had nothing to lose.'

'Right.'

'To continue. Unless Ahmed's intention was to get killed off the shores of his native land, I can come up with only two hypotheses. The first is that he wanted to be put ashore at night, at an isolated spot along the coast, so he could steal back into his country undercover. The second is that he'd arranged some sort of meeting at sea, some secret conversation, which he absolutely had to attend in person.'

'The second seems more convincing to me.'

'Me too. And then something unexpected happened.'

'They were intercepted.'

'Right. But here that hypothesis becomes more of a stretch. Let's assume the Tunisian motor patrol doesn't know that Ahmed's aboard the fishing boat. They intercept a vessel fishing in their territorial waters, they order it to stop, the fishing vessel takes off, a machine gun is fired from the patrol boat, and purely by accident it happens to kill Ahmed Moussa. This, in any case, is the story we were told.'

This time it was Valente who grimaced.

'Unconvinced?'

'It reminds me of the Warren Commission's reconstruction of the Kennedy assassination.'

'Here's another version. In place of the man he's supposed to meet, Ahmed finds someone else, who then shoots him.'

'Or else it is in fact the man he's supposed to meet, but they have a difference of opinion, an altercation, and it ends badly, with the guy shooting him.'

'With the ship's machine gun?'

He immediately realized what he'd just said. Without even asking Valente's permission, and cursing under his breath, he grabbed the phone and asked for Jacomuzzi in Montelusa. While waiting for the connection, he asked Valente, 'In the reports you were sent, did they specify the calibre of the bullets?'

'They spoke generically of firearms.'

'Hello? Who's this?' asked Jacomuzzi at the other end of the line.

'Listen, Baudo—'

'Baudo? This is Jacomuzzi.'

'But you wish you were Pippo Baudo. Would you tell me what the fuck they used to kill that Tunisian on the fishing boat?'

'Firearms.'

'How odd! I thought he'd been suffocated with a pillow!'

'Your jokes make me puke.'

'Tell me exactly what kind of firearm.'

'A sub-machine gun, probably a Skorpion. Didn't I write that in the report?'

'No. Are you sure it wasn't the ship's machine gun?'

'Of course I'm sure. Those patrol boats, you know, are equipped with weapons that can shoot down a plane.'

'Really? Your scientific precision simply amazes me, Jacomù.'

'How do you expect me to talk to an ignoramus like you?'

*

After Montalbano related the contents of the phone call, they sat awhile in silence. When Valente finally spoke, he said exactly what the inspector was thinking.

'Are we sure the patrol boat was Tunisian?'

*

Since it was getting late, Valente invited the inspector to his house for lunch. But as Montalbano already had first-hand experience of the vice-commissioner's wife's ghastly cooking, he declined, saying he had to leave for Vigàta at once.

He got in his car and, after a few miles, saw a trattoria right on the beach. He stopped, got out, and sat down at a table. He did not regret it.

TWELVE

It had been hours since he last spoke to Livia. He felt guilty about this; she was probably worried about him. While waiting for them to bring him a *digestivo* of anisette (the double serving of bass was beginning to weigh on his stomach), he decided to phone her.

'Everything okay there?'

'Your phone call woke us up.'

So much for being worried about him.

'You were asleep?'

'Yes. We had a very long swim. The water was warm.'

They were living it up, without him.

'Have you eaten?' asked Livia, purely out of politeness.

'I had a sandwich. I'm on the road. I'll be back in Vigàta in an hour at the most.'

'Are you coming home?'

'No, I have to go to the office. I'll see you this evening.'

It was surely his imagination, but he thought he heard something like a sigh of relief at the other end.

*

But it took him more than an hour to get back to Vigàta. Just outside of town, five minutes away from the office, the car suddenly decided to go on strike. There was no way to get it started again. Montalbano got out, opened the bonnet, looked at the motor. It was a purely symbolic gesture, a sort of rite of exorcism, since he didn't know a thing about cars. If someone had told him the motor consisted of a string or a twisted rubber band as on certain toy vehicles, he might well have believed it. A carabinieri squad car with two men inside passed by, then stopped and backed up. They'd had second thoughts. One was a corporal, the other a ranking officer at the wheel. The inspector had never seen them before, and they didn't know Montalbano.

'Anything we can do?' the corporal asked politely.

'Thanks. I don't understand why the engine suddenly died.'

They pulled up to the edge of the road and got out. The afternoon Vigàta–Fiacca bus stopped a short distance away, and an elderly couple got on.

'Motor looks fine to me,' was the officer's diagnosis. Then he added with a smile, 'Shall we have a look at the petrol tank?'

There wasn't a drop.

'Tell you what, Mr . . .'

'Martinez, Claudio Martinez. I'm an accountant,' said Montalbano.

No one must ever know that Inspector Montalbano was rescued by the carabinieri.

'All right, Mr Martinez, you wait here. We'll go to the nearest petrol station and bring back enough petrol to get you back to Vigàta.'

'You're very kind.'

He got back in the car, fired up a cigarette, and immediately heard an ear-splitting horn blast behind him. It was the Fiacca–Vigàta bus wanting him to get out of the way. He got out and used gestures to indicate that his car had broken down. The bus driver steered around him with a great show of effort and, once past the inspector's car, stopped at the same point where the other bus, going in the other direction, had stopped. Four people got off.

Montalbano sat there staring at the bus as it headed towards Vigàta. Then the carabinieri returned.

*

By the time he got to the office it was already four o'clock. Augello wasn't in. Fazio said he'd lost track of him since morning; Mimì'd stuck his head in at nine and then disappeared. Montalbano flew into a rage.

'Everybody does whatever they please around here! Anything goes! Ragonese will turn out to have been right, just wait and see!'

News? Nothing. Oh yes, the widow Lapècora phoned to inform the inspector that her husband's funeral would be held on Wednesday morning. And there was a land surveyor by the name of Finocchiaro who'd been waiting since two to speak to him.

'Do you know him?'

'By sight. He's retired, an old guy.'

'What's he want?'

'He wouldn't tell me. But he seems a tad upset.'

'Let him in.'

Fazio was right. The man looked shaken. The inspector asked him to sit down.

'Could I have some water, please?' asked the land surveyor, whose throat was obviously dry.

After drinking his water, he said his name was Giuseppe Finocchiaro, seventy-five years old, unmarried, former land surveyor, now retired, residing at Via Marconi 38. Clean record, not even a parking fine.

He stopped and drank the last gulp of water remaining in the glass.

'On TV today, on the afternoon news, they showed a photograph. A woman and child. You know how they said to inform you if we recognized them?'

'Yes.'

Yes. One more syllable, at that moment, might have sparked a doubt, a change of mind.

'I know the woman. Her name's Karima. The kid I've never seen before. In fact I never knew she had a son.'

'How do you know her?'

'She comes to clean my house once a week.'

'What day?'

'Tuesday mornings. She stays for four hours.'

'Tell me something. How much did you pay her?'

'Fifty thousand. But . . .'

'But?'

'Sometimes as much as two hundred thousand for extras.'

'Like blow jobs?'

The calculated brutality of the question made the surveyor first turn pale, then red.

'Yes.'

'So, let me get this straight. She would come to your house four times a month. How often did she perform these "extras"?'

'Once a month, twice at the most.'

'How did you meet her?'

'A friend of mine, retired like me, told me about her. Professor Mandrino, who lives with his daughter.'

'So no extras for the professor?'

'There were extras just the same. The daughter's a teacher, so she's out of the house every morning.'

'What day did Karima go to the professor's house?'

'On Saturday.'

'If you haven't anything else to tell me, you can go, Mr Finocchiaro.'

'Thank you for being so understanding.'

The man stood up awkwardly and eyed the inspector.

'Tomorrow is Tuesday,' he said.

'So?'

'Do you think she'll come?'

He didn't have the heart to disappoint him.

'Maybe. If she does, let me know.'

*

Then the procession began. Preceded by his howling mother, 'Ntonio, the little boy Montalbano had met at Villaseta, who'd been punched because he wouldn't hand over his food, walked in. He'd recognized the thief in the photo they showed on TV. That was him, no doubt about it. 'Ntonio's mother, shouting loud enough to wake the dead and hurling curses and expletives, presented her demands to the horrified inspector: thirty years for the thief, life imprisonment for the mother. And in case earthly justice did not agree, from divine justice she demanded galloping consumption for the mother and a long, debilitating illness for the boy.

The son, however, unfazed by his mother's hysteria, shook his head.

'Do you also want him to die in jail?' the inspector asked him.

'No,' the boy said decisively. 'Now that I seen him calm, he looks nice.'

*

The 'extras' granted Paolo Guido Mandrino, a seventy-year-old professor of history and geography, now retired, consisted of a little bath Karima would give him. On one of the four Saturday mornings when she came, the professor would wait for her under the bedclothes, naked. When Karima ordered him to go and take his bath, Paolo Guido would pretend to be very reluctant. And so Karima, yanking down the sheets, would force the professor to turn over and would proceed to spank him. When he finally got in the bath, Karima would carefully cover him with soap and then wash him. That was all. Price of the extras: one hundred and fifty thousand lire; price of the house cleaning: fifty thousand lire.

*

'Montalbano? Listen, contrary to what I told you, I can't see you today. I have a meeting with the prefect.'

'Just say when, Mr Commissioner.'

'Well, it's really not very urgent. Anyway, after what Inspector Augello said on TV—'

'Mimì?' he yelled, as if he were singing *La Bohème*.

'Yes. Didn't you know?'

'No. I was in Mazàra.'

'He appeared on the one o'clock news. He issued a firm, blunt denial. He said Ragonese hadn't heard correctly. The man being sought wasn't a snack thief, but a sneak thief, a dangerous drug addict who went around with dirty syringes for protection in case he got caught. Augello offered apologies for the entire police department. It was very effective. I think maybe Deputy Pennacchio will calm down now.'

*

'We've already met,' said Vittorio Pandolfo, accountant, as he entered the office.

'Yes,' said Montalbano. 'What do you want?'

Rude, and he wasn't just play acting. If Pandolfo was

there to talk about Karima, it meant he'd been lying when he said he didn't know her.

'I came because on TV they showed—'

'A photograph of Karima, the woman you said you knew nothing about. Why didn't you tell me anything sooner?'

'Inspector, these are delicate matters, and sometimes one feels a little embarrassed. You see, at my age—'

'You're the Thursday-morning client?'

'Yes.'

'How much do you pay her to clean your house?'

'Fifty thousand.'

'And for extras?'

'One hundred and fifty.'

Fixed rate. Except that Pandolfo got extras twice a month. But the person being bathed, in this case, was Karima. Afterwards, the accountant would lay her down on the bed and sniff her all over. And now and then, a little lick.

'Tell me something, Mr Pandolfo. Were you, Lapècora, Mandrino and Finocchiaro her regular playmates?'

'Yes.'

'And who was it that first mentioned Karima?'

'Poor old Lapècora.'

'And what was his financial situation?'

'Awfully good. He had almost a billion lire in Treasury bonds, and he also owned his flat and office.'

*

The three afternoon clients on Tuesdays, Thursdays and Saturdays lived in Villaseta, all widowers or bachelors getting on in years. The price was the same as in Vigàta. The extra granted Martino Zaccarìa, greengrocer, consisted of having her kiss the soles of his feet; with Luigi Pignataro, retired middle-school headmaster, Karima would play blindman's buff. The headmaster would strip her naked, blindfold her, then go and hide somewhere. Karima would then look for him and find him, after which she would sit down in a chair, take him in her lap and suckle him. When Montalbano asked Calogero Pipitone, an expert agronomist, what his extras were, the man looked at him, dumbfounded.

'What do you think they were, Inspector? Me on top and her on the bottom.'

Montalbano felt like embracing him.

*

Since on Mondays, Wednesdays and Fridays Karima was employed full-time at Lapècora's, there wouldn't be any more clients. Oddly enough, Karima rested on Sundays, not Fridays. Apparently she'd adapted to local customs. Montalbano was curious to know how much she earned per month; but since he was hopeless with numbers, he opened the door to his office and asked in a loud voice, 'Anybody got a calculator?'

'Me, Chief.'

Catarella came in and pulled a calculator not much bigger than a calling card out of his pocket.

'What do you calculate on that, Cat?'

'The days,' was his enigmatic reply.

'Come back for it in a little bit.'

'I should warrant you the machine works by *ammuttuna*.'

'What do you mean?'

Catarella mistakenly thought his superior didn't understand the last word. He stepped toward the door and called out, 'How you say *ammuttuna* in Italian?'

'Shove,' somebody translated.

'And how am I supposed to shove this calculator?'

'Same way you shove a watch when it don't run.'

Anyway, calculating Lapècora separately, Karima earned one million two hundred thousand lire per month as a housekeeper, to which was added another million two hundred thousand lire for extras. At the very least, for full-time service, Lapècora slipped her another million lire. Which came to three million four hundred thousand lire monthly, tax free. Forty-four million two hundred thousand lire annually.

Karima, from what they could gather, had been working in the area for at least four years, so that made one hundred and seventy-six million eight hundred thousand lire.

What about the other three hundred and twenty-four million that was in the bank book? Where had that come from?

The calculator had worked fine; there was no need for *ammuttuna*.

*

A burst of applause rang out from the other rooms. What was going on? He opened his door and discovered that the man of the hour was Mimì Augello. He started foaming at the mouth.

'Knock it off! Clowns!'

They looked at him in shock and horror. Only Fazio attempted to explain the situation.

'Maybe you don't know, Chief, but Inspector Augello—'

'I already know! The commissioner called me personally, demanding an explanation. Mr Augello, of his own initiative, without my authorization – as I made certain to emphasize to the commissioner – went on TV and spoke a pile of bullshit!'

'Uh, if I may,' Augello ventured.

'No, you may not! You told a pack of lies!'

'I did it to protect all of us here, who—'

'You can't defend yourself by lying to someone who spoke the truth!'

And he went back into his office, slamming the door behind him. Montalbano, man of ironclad morals, was in a murderous rage at the sight of Augello basking in applause.

*

'May I come in?' asked Fazio, opening the door and cautiously sticking his head inside. 'Father Jannuzzo's here and wants to talk to you.'

'Let him in.'

Don Alfio Jannuzzo, who never dressed like a priest,

was well known in Vigàta for his charitable initiatives. A tall, robust man, he was about forty years old.

'I like to cycle,' he began.

'I don't,' said Montalbano, terrified at the thought that the priest might want him to participate in some sort of charity race.

'I saw that woman's photo on television.'

The two things seemed in no way connected, and the inspector began to feel uncomfortable. Might this mean that Karima did work on Sundays after all, and that her client was none other than Don Jannuzzo?

'Last Thursday, about nine o'clock in the morning, give or take fifteen minutes, I was near Villaseta, cycling down from Montelusa to Vigàta. On the other side of the road, a car was stopped.'

'Do you remember the make?'

'Yes, it was a BMW, metallic grey in colour.'

Montalbano pricked up his ears.

'A man and a woman were inside the car. It looked like they were kissing, but when I passed right beside them, the woman broke free sort of violently, then looked at me and opened her mouth as if to say something. But the man pulled her back by force and embraced her again. I didn't like the look of it.'

'Why?'

'Because it wasn't just a lovers' quarrel. The woman's eyes, when she looked at me, were full of fear. It seemed as if she was asking for help.'

'And what did you do?'

'Nothing, because the car left almost immediately. But when I saw the photograph on television today, I knew it was the woman I'd seen in the car, I could swear to it. I'm very good with faces, Inspector, and when I see a face, even for only a second, it's forever etched in my memory.'

Fahrid, pseudo-nephew of Lapècora, and Karima.

'I'm very grateful to you, Father . . .'

The priest raised a hand to stop him.

'I haven't finished yet. I took down the number plate. As I said, I didn't like what I'd seen.'

'Do you have the number with you?'

'Of course.'

From his pocket he extracted a notebook page neatly folded in four and held it out to the inspector.

'It's written down here.'

Montalbano took it between two fingers, delicately, as one does with the wings of a butterfly.

AM 237 GW.

*

In American films, the policeman had only to tell somebody the licence-plate number, and in less than two minutes, he would know the owner's name, how many children he had, the colour of his hair, and the number of hairs on his arse.

In Italy, things were different. Once they made Montalbano wait twenty-eight days, in the course of which the owner of the vehicle (as they later wrote to him) was goat-tied and burnt to a crisp. By the time the answer arrived, it had all come to nothing.

His only choice was to turn to the commissioner, who by now had perhaps ended his meeting with the prefect.

'Montalbano here, Commissioner.'

'I just got back in the office. What is it?'

'I'm calling about that woman who was kidnapped—'

'What woman who was kidnapped?'

'You know, Karima.'

'Who's that?'

To his horror he realized he was talking to the wind. He hadn't yet said an intelligible word to the commissioner about the case.

'Mr Commissioner, I'm simply mortified—'

'Never mind. What did you want?'

'I need to have a number plate traced as quickly as possible, and I want the owner's name and address.'

'Give me the number.'

'AM 237 GW.'

'I'll have something for you by tomorrow morning.'

THIRTEEN

'I set a place for you in the kitchen. The dining-room table is being used. We've already eaten.'

He wasn't blind. He couldn't help but see that the table was covered by a giant jigsaw puzzle of the Statue of Liberty, practically life-size.

'And you know what, Salvo? It took him only two hours to solve it.'

She didn't say whom, but it was clear she was talking about François, former snack thief, now family genius.

'Did you buy it for him yourself?'

Livia dodged the question.

'Want to come down to the beach with me?'

'Right now or after I've eaten?'

'Right now.'

There was a sliver of moon shedding its light. They walked in silence. In front of a little pile of sand, Livia sighed sadly.

'You should have seen the castle he made! It was fantastic! It looked like Gaudì!'

'He'll have time to make another.'

He was determined not to give up. Like a policeman, and a jealous one at that.

'What shop did you find the puzzle in?'

'I didn't buy it myself. Mimì came round this afternoon, just for a second. The puzzle belongs to a nephew of his who—'

He turned his back to Livia, thrust his hands in his pockets, and walked away, imagining dozens of Mimì's nephews and nieces in tears, systematically despoiled of their toys by their uncle.

'Come on, Salvo, stop acting like a fool!' said Livia, running up to him.

She tried to slip her arm in his; Montalbano pulled away.

'Fuck you,' Livia said calmly, and she went back to the house.

What was he going to do now? Livia had avoided the quarrel, and he would have to get it out of his system on his own. He walked irritably along the water's edge, soaking his shoes and smoking ten cigarettes.

I'm such a fucking idiot! he said to himself at a certain point. *It's obvious that Mimì likes Livia and Livia's fond of Mimì. But, this aside, I'm only giving Mimì grist for his mill. It's clear he enjoys pissing me off. He's waging a war of attrition against me, as I do against him. I have to plan a counter-offensive.*

He went home. Livia was sitting in front of the television, which she had turned down very low in order not to wake François, who was sleeping in their bed.

'I'm sorry – seriously,' he said to her as he walked past her on his way to the kitchen.

In the oven he found a casserole of mullet and potatoes that smelled inviting. He sat down and tasted his first bite: exquisite. Livia came up behind him and stroked his hair.

'Do you like it?'

'Excellent. I must tell Adelina—'

'Adelina came this morning, saw me, said "I don' wanna disturb," turned around, and left.'

'Are you telling me you made this casserole yourself?'

'Of course.'

For an instant, but only an instant, the casserole went down the wrong way when a thought popped into his head: that she'd made it only to win forgiveness for this business with Mimì. But then the deliciousness of the dish prevailed.

*

Before sitting down beside Montalbano to watch television, Livia stopped a moment to admire the jigsaw puzzle. Now that Salvo had calmed down, she could freely talk about it.

'You should have seen how fast he put it together. It was stunning. You or I would have taken longer.'

'Or we would have got bored first.'

'But that's just it. François also thinks puzzles are boring, because they have fixed rules. Every little piece, he says, is cut so that it will fit with another. Whereas it would be more fun if there were a puzzle with many different solutions!'

'He said that?'

'Yes. And he explained it better, since I was drawing it out of him.'

'And what did he say?'

'I think I understood what he meant. He was already familiar with the Statue of Liberty and therefore when he put the head together he already knew what to do; but he was forced to do it that way because the puzzle's designer had cut out the pieces in a way that obliged the player to follow his design. Is that clear so far?'

'Clear enough.'

'It would be fun, he said, if the player could actually create his own alternative puzzle with the same pieces. Don't you think that's an extraordinary thought for so small a child?'

'They're precocious nowadays,' said Montalbano, immediately cursing himself for the banality of the expression. He'd never talked about children before, and couldn't help but resort to clichés.

*

Nicolò Zito gave a summary of the Tunisian government's official statement on the fishing-boat incident. Having conducted the necessary investigations, they had no choice but to reject the protest of the Italian government, since the Italians were powerless to prevent their own fishing boats from invading Tunisian territorial waters. That night, a Tunisian military patrol boat had sighted a trawler a few miles from Sfax. They gave the order to halt, but the fishing boat tried to flee. The patrol then fired a burst of warning from the ship's machine gun that unfortunately struck and killed a Tunisian fisherman, Ben Dhahab, whose family had already been granted substantial aid by the government in Tunis. The tragic incident should serve as a lesson.

'Have you managed to find out anything about François's mother?'

'Yeah, I have a lead, but don't get your hopes up,' replied the inspector.

'If . . . if Karima were never to come back . . . what . . . would happen to François?'

'I honestly don't know.'

'I'm going to bed,' said Livia, abruptly standing up.

Montalbano took her hand and brought it to his lips.

'Don't get too attached to him.'

*

He delicately freed François from Livia's embrace and laid him down to sleep on the sofa, which had already been made up. When he got into bed, Livia pressed her back against him, and this time did not resist his caresses. On the contrary.

'And what if the boy wakes up?' Montalbano asked at the crucial moment, still acting the swine.

'If he wakes up, I'll go and console him,' Livia said, breathing heavily.

*

At seven o'clock in the morning, he slipped softly out of bed and locked himself in the bathroom. As always, the first thing he did was look at himself in the mirror and twist up his mouth. He didn't like his own face. So why the hell was he looking at it?

He heard Livia scream sharply, rushed to the door, and opened it. Livia was in the living room; the sofa was empty.

'He's run away!' she said, trembling.

In one bound, the inspector was on the veranda. He could see him: a tiny little dot at the edge of the water, walking towards Vigàta. Dressed as he was, in only his underpants, he dashed off in pursuit. François was not running, but walking with determination. When he heard footsteps coming up behind him, he stopped in his tracks, without turning round. Montalbano, gasping for air, crouched down before him but said nothing.

The little boy wasn't crying. His eyes were staring into space, past Montalbano.

'*Je veux maman,*' he said. I want Mama.

Montalbano saw Livia approaching at a run, wearing one of his shirts; he stopped her with a single gesture, giving her to understand she should go back to the house. Livia obeyed. The inspector took the boy by the hand, and they began to walk very, very slowly. For fifteen minutes neither of them said a word. When they came to a beached boat, Montalbano sat down on the sand, François sat beside him, and the inspector put his arm around him.

'*Iu persi a me matri ch'era macari cchiù nicu di tia,*' he began, telling the child he'd lost his own mother when he was even smaller than François.

They started talking, the inspector in Sicilian and the boy in Arabic, and they understood each other perfectly.

Montalbano confided things he'd never told anyone before, not even Livia.

He told him about the nights when he used to cry his heart out, head under the pillow so that his father wouldn't hear him, and the despair he would feel every morning, knowing his mother wasn't in the kitchen to make him breakfast, or, a few years later, to make him a snack to take to school. It's an emptiness that can never be filled again; you carry it with you to the grave. The child asked him if he had the power to bring his mother back. No, replied Montalbano, nobody has that power. He had to resign himself. But you had your father, observed François, who really was intelligent, and not only because Livia said so. True, I had my father. And so, the boy asked, am I really going to end up in one of those places where they put children who have no father or mother?

'That will never happen, I promise you,' said the inspector. And he held out his hand. François shook it, looking him in the eye.

*

When he emerged from the bathroom, all ready to go to work, he saw that François had taken the puzzle apart and was cutting the pieces into different shapes with a pair of scissors. He was trying, in his naive way, to avoid following the set pattern. All of a sudden Montalbano staggered, as if struck by an electrical charge.

'Jesus!' he whispered.

Livia looked over at him and saw him trembling, eyes popping out of his head. She became alarmed.

'My God, Salvo, what is it?'

His only answer was to pick up the boy, lift him over his head, look at him from below, put him back down, and kiss him.

'François, you're a genius!' he said.

*

Entering the office, he nearly slammed into Mimì Augello, who was on his way out.

'Ah, Mimì. Thanks for the puzzle.'

Mimì only gaped at him, dumbfounded.

'Fazio, on the double!'

'At your service, Chief!'

Montalbano explained to him in great detail what he was supposed to do.

'Galluzzo, in my office!'

'Yes, sir.'

He explained to him in great detail what he was supposed to do.

'Can I come in?'

It was Tortorella, pushing the door open with his foot since his hands were busy carrying a stack of papers three feet high.

'What is it?'

'Didìo's complaining.'

Didìo was the administrative manager of the Police

Commissioner's Office of Montelusa. He was nicknamed 'The Scourge of God' and 'The Wrath of God' for his punctiliousness.

'What's he complaining about?'

'Says you're behind. Says you gotta sign some papers.' And he dropped the stack of papers on the desk. 'Better take a deep breath and get started.'

*

After an hour of signing, with his hand already beginning to ache, Fazio came in.

'You're right, Chief. The Vigàta–Fiacca bus makes a stop just outside town, in the Cannatello district. And five minutes later, the bus coming from the other direction, the Fiacca–Vigàta, also stops at Cannatello.'

'So somebody could, in theory, get on the bus for Fiacca in Vigàta, get off at Cannatello, and, five minutes later, get on the Fiacca–Vigàta bus and return to town.'

'Of course.'

'Thanks, Fazio. Well done.'

'Wait a minute, Chief. I brought back the ticket man from the morning line, the Fiacca–Vigàta. His name is Lopipàro. Should I get him to come in?'

'By all means.'

Lopipàro, a reed-thin, surly man of about fifty, was keen to point out at once that he was not a ticket man, but a driver whose duties included collecting tickets. As the tickets were bought in tobacco shops, he did nothing more than collect them once the passengers had boarded the bus.

'Mr Lopìparo, everything that's said in this room must remain confidential.'

The driver/ticket man brought his right hand to his heart, as if taking a solemn oath.

'Silent as the grave,' he said.

'Mr Lopìparo—'

'Lopipàro,' he corrected, stressing the penultimate syllable.

'Mr Lopipàro, do you know Mrs Lapècora, the lady whose husband was murdered?'

'I sure do. She's got a season ticket for that line. She goes back and forth to Fiacca at least three times a week. She goes to visit her sister who's sick; she's always talking about her on the bus.'

'I'm going to ask you to make an effort to remember something.'

'I'll give it my best, since you ask.'

'Last Thursday, did you see Mrs Lapècora?'

'No need to make any effort. I certainly did see her. We even had a little run-in.'

'You quarrelled with Mrs Lapècora?'

'Yessir, I sure did! Mrs Lapècora, as everybody knows, is a little tight. She's cheap. Well, on Thursday morning she caught the six-thirty bus for Fiacca. But when we stopped at Cannatello, she got off and told Cannizzaro, the driver, that she had to go back because she'd forgotten something she was supposed to take to her sister. Cannizzaro, who told me all this that same evening, let her out.

Five minutes later, on my way to Vigàta, I stopped at Cannatello, and the lady got on my bus.'

'What did you argue about?'

'She didn't want to give me a ticket for going from Cannatello to Vigàta. She claimed she shouldn't have to use up two tickets for a little mistake. But I gotta have a ticket for every person on the bus. I couldn't just look the other way, like Mrs Lapècora wanted me to.'

'It's only right,' said Montalbano. 'But tell me something. Let's say the lady manages in half an hour to get what she forgot at home. How's she going to get to Fiacca that same morning?'

'She catches the Montelusa–Trapani bus, which stops in Vigàta at exactly seven-thirty. Which means she would arrive in Fiacca only an hour late.'

*

'Ingenious,' Fazio commented after Lopipàro had left. 'How did you figure it out?'

'The little kid, François, tipped me off when he was working on a jigsaw puzzle.'

'But why did she do it? Was she jealous of the Tunisian maid?'

'No. Mrs Lapècora's a cheapskate, as the man said. She was afraid her husband would spend everything he had on that woman. But there was something else that triggered the whole thing.'

'What was that?'

'I'll tell you later. As Catarella says, "Aravice is a nasty vice". It was greed, you see, that brought her to Lopipàro's attention, when she should have been making every effort to remain unnoticed.'

*

'First it took me half an hour to find out where she lived, then I wasted another half hour trying to persuade the old lady, who didn't trust me. She was afraid of me, but she calmed down when I asked her to come out of the house and she saw the police car. She made a small bundle of her things and then got in the car. You should have heard how the child cried with delight when, to his surprise, she appeared out of nowhere! They gave each other a big hug. And your lady friend was also very moved.'

'Thanks, Gallù.'

'When do you want me to come by to drive her back to Montelusa?'

'Don't worry about it, I'll take care of it.'

Their little family was growing without mercy. Now Grandma Aisha was also at Marinella.

*

He let the phone ring a long time, but nobody answered. The widow Lapècora wasn't home. She must certainly be out shopping. There might, however, be another explanation. He dialled the number to the Cosentino household. The security guard's likeable, moustachioed wife answered, speaking in a soft voice.

'Is your husband asleep?'

'Yes, Inspector. Do you want me to call him?'

'There's no need. You can give him my regards. Listen, signora: I tried calling Mrs Lapècora, but there was no answer. Do you know by any chance if she—'

'You won't find her in this morning, Inspector. She went to Fiacca to see her sister. She went today because tomorrow morning, at ten o'clock, she's got the funeral of the dear—'

'Thanks, signora.'

He hung up. Maybe this would simplify what needed to be done.

'Fazio!'

'At your orders, Chief.'

'Here are the keys to Lapècora's office, Salita Granet 28. Go inside and take the set of keys that are in the middle drawer of the desk. There's a little tag attached to them that says "home". It must be an extra set that he used to keep at the office. Then go to Mrs Lapècora's house and let yourself in with those keys.'

'Wait a second. What if she's there?'

'She's not. She's out of town.'

'What do you want me to do?'

'In the dining room there's a glass cupboard with dishes, cups, trays and whatnot. Take something from it, anything you like, but make sure it's something she can't deny is hers. The ideal thing would be a cup from a complete set. Then bring it here. And don't forget to put the keys back in their drawer at the office.'

'And what if the widow notices a cup is missing when she comes back?'

'We don't give a fuck. Then you must do one more thing. Phone Jacomuzzi and tell him that by the end of the day, I want the knife that was used to kill Lapècora. If he doesn't have anyone who can bring it to me, go and get it yourself.'

*

'Montalbano? This is Valente. Could you be here in Mazàra by four o'clock this afternoon?'

'If I leave immediately. Why?'

'The captain of the fishing boat is coming, and I'd like you to be there.'

'Thanks, I appreciate it. Has your man managed to find anything out?'

'Yes, and it didn't take much. He said the fishermen are quite willing to talk.'

'What did they say?'

'I'll tell you when you get here.'

'No, tell me now, so I can give it some thought on the way.'

'Okay. We're convinced the crew knew little or nothing about the whole business. They all claim the vessel was just outside our territorial waters, that it was a very dark night, and that they clearly saw a vessel approaching them on the radar screen.'

'So why did they keep going?'

'Because it didn't occur to any of the crew that it might

be a Tunisian patrol boat or whatever it was. I repeat, they were in international waters.'

'And then?'

'Then, without warning, came the signal to halt. Our fishing boat – or its crew at least, I can't speak for the captain – thought it was our Customs Police making a routine check. So they stopped, and they heard people speaking Arabic. At this point the Tunisian on the Italian boat went astern and lit a cigarette. And got shot. Only then did the fishing boat turn and flee.'

'And then?'

'And then what, Montalbà? How long is this phone call going to last?'

FOURTEEN

Unlike most men of the sea, Angelo Prestìa, crew chief and owner of the *Santopadre* motor trawler, was a fat, sweaty man. But he was sweating because it was natural for him, not because of the questions Valente was asking him. Actually, in this regard, he seemed not only calm, but even slightly put out.

'I don't understand why you suddenly wanna drag this story out again. It's water under the bridge.'

'We'd merely like to clear up a few small details, then you'll be free to go,' Valente said to reassure him.

'Well, out with it then, for God's sake!'

'You've always maintained that the Tunisian patrol boat was acting illegally, since your vessel was in international waters. Is that correct?'

'Of course it's correct. But I don't see why you're interested in questions that are the concern of the Harbour Office.'

'You'll see later.'

'But I don't need to see anything, if you don't mind!

Did the Tunisian government issue a statement or didn't they? And in this statement, did they say they killed the Tunisian themselves or didn't they? So why do you want to hash it all out again?'

'There's already a discrepancy,' Valente observed.

'Where?'

'You, for example, say the attack occurred in international waters, whereas they say you'd already crossed their border. Is that a discrepancy or isn't it, as you might say?'

'No, sir, it is not a discrepancy. It's a mistake.'

'On whose part?'

'Theirs. They obviously took their bearings wrong.'

Montalbano and Valente exchanged a lightning-quick glance, which was the signal to begin the second phase of their pre-arranged interrogation.

'Mr Prestìa, do you have a criminal record?'

'No, sir.'

'But you have been arrested.'

'You guys really have a thing for old stories, don't you! Yes, sir, I was arrested, because some poof, some sonofabitch had a grudge against me and reported me. But then the judge realized the bastard was a liar, and so he let me go.'

'What were you accused of?'

'Smuggling.'

'Cigarettes or drugs?'

'The second.'

'And your whole crew also ended up in the slammer, didn't they?'

'Yessir, but they all got out 'cause they were innocent like me.'

'Who was the judge that threw the case out of court?'

'I don't remember.'

'Was it Antonio Bellofiore?'

'Yeah, I think it was him.'

'Did you know he was thrown in jail himself a year later for rigging trials?'

'No, I didn't know. I spend more time at sea than on land.'

Another lightning-quick glance, and the ball was passed to Montalbano.

'Let's forget these old stories,' the inspector began. 'Do you belong to a co-operative?'

'Yes, the Mafico.'

'What does it stand for?'

'Mazarese Fishermen's Co-operative.'

'When you sign up a Tunisian fisherman, do you choose him yourself or is he referred to you by the co-operative?'

'The co-op tells us which ones to take,' Prestìa replied, starting to sweat more than usual.

'We happen to know that the co-operative furnished you with a certain name, but you chose Ben Dhahab instead.'

'Listen, I didn't know this Ben Dhahab, never seen 'im before in my life. When he showed up on board five minutes before we put out, I thought he was the one sent by the co-op.'

'You mean Hassan Tarif?'

'I think that was 'is name.'

'Okay. Why didn't the co-operative ask you for an explanation?'

Captain Prestìa smiled, but his face was drawn and by now he was bathed in sweat.

'But this kind of stuff happens every day! They trade places all the time! The important thing is to avoid complaints.'

'So why didn't Hassan Tarif complain? After all, he lost a day's wages.'

'You're asking me? Go ask him.'

'I did,' Montalbano said calmly.

Valente looked at him in astonishment. This part had not been pre-arranged.

'And what did he tell you?' Prestìa asked almost defiantly.

'He said Ben Dhahab came to him the day before and asked if he was signed on with the *Santopadre*, and when he said yes, Dhahab told him not to show up for three days and gave him a whole week's pay.'

'I don't know anything about that.'

'Let me finish. Given this fact, Dhahab certainly didn't sign on because he needed work. He already had money. Therefore he must have come on your boat for another reason.'

Valente paid very close attention to the trap Montalbano was setting. The bit about this mysterious Tarif taking money from Dhahab had clearly been invented by the inspector, and Valente needed to know what he was driving at.

'Do you know who Ben Dhahab was?'

'A Tunisian looking for work.'

'No, my friend, he was one of the biggest names in narcotics traffic.'

While Prestìa was turning pale, Valente understood that it was now his turn. He secretly smiled to himself. He and Montalbano made a formidable duo, like Totò and Peppino.

'Looks like you're in a fix Mr Prestìa,' Valente began in a compassionate, almost fatherly tone.

'But why?'

'Come on, can't you see? A drug trafficker the calibre of Ben Dhahab signs on with your fishing boat, sparing no expense. And you have the past record you do. I, therefore, have two questions. First: what is one plus one? And second: what went wrong that night?'

'You're trying to mess me up! You want to ruin me!'

'You're doing it yourself, with your own two hands.'

'No! No! This has gone too far!' said Prestìa, very upset. 'They guaranteed me that . . .'

He stopped short, wiped off his sweat.

'Guaranteed you what?' Montalbano and Valente asked at the same time.

'That I wouldn't have any trouble.'

'Who did?'

Captain Prestìa stuck his hand in his pocket, dug out his wallet, extracted a calling card, and threw it onto Valente's desk.

*

Having disposed of Prestìa, Valente dialled the number on the calling card. It belonged to the prefecture of Trapani.

'Hello? This is Vice-Commissioner Valente from Mazàra. I'd like to speak with Commendatore Mario Spadaccia, chief of the cabinet.'

'Please hold.'

'Hello, Commissioner Valente. This is Spadaccia.'

'Sorry to disturb you, Commendatore, but I have a question concerning the killing of that Tunisian on the fishing boat—'

'Hasn't that all been cleared up? The government in Tunis—'

'Yes, I know, Commendatore, but—'

'Why are you calling me?'

'Because the crew chief of the fishing boat—'

'He gave you my name?'

'He gave us your card. He was keeping it as some sort of . . . guarantee.'

'Which indeed it was.'

'Excuse me?'

'Let me explain. You see, some time ago, His Excellency . . .' (*Wasn't that title abolished half a century ago?* Montalbano wondered while listening in on an extension.) '. . . His Excellency the prefect received an urgent request. He was asked to give his full support to a Tunisian journalist who wanted to conduct a sensitive investigation among his compatriots here, and who, for this reason, among others, also wished to sign on with one of our fishing boats. His Excellency authorized me to oversee the matter. Captain Prestìa's name was brought to my attention; I was told he was very reliable. Prestìa, however, had some worries about getting in trouble with the employment office. That's why I gave him my card. Nothing more.'

'Commendatore, I thank you very much for your thorough explanation,' said Valente. And he hung up.

They sat there in silence, eyeing each other.

'The guy's either a fuck-up or he's putting one over on us,' said Montalbano.

'This whole thing's beginning to stink,' Valente said pensively.

'Yeah,' said Montalbano.

*

They were discussing what their next move should be when the phone rang.

'I told them I wasn't here for anyone!' Valente shouted angrily. He picked up, listened a moment, then passed the receiver to Montalbano.

Before leaving for Mazàra, the inspector had left word at the office as to where he could be found if needed.

'Hello? Montalbano here. Who's this? Ah, is that you, Mr Commissioner?'

'Yes, it's me. Where have you run off to?'

He was irritated.

'I'm here with my colleague, Vice-Commissioner Valente.'

'He's not your colleague. He's a vice-commissioner and you're not.'

Montalbano started to feel worried.

'What's going on, Commissioner?'

'No, *I'm* asking *you* what the hell is going on?'

Hell? The commissioner said 'hell'?

'I don't understand.'

'What kind of crap have you been digging up?'

Crap? Did the commissioner say 'crap'? Was this the start of the Apocalypse? Would the trumpets of Judgment soon begin to sound?

'But what have I done wrong?'

'Yesterday you gave me a number plate, remember?'

'Yes. AM 237 GW.'

'That's the one. Well, I immediately asked a friend of mine in Rome to look into it, to save time, at your request, and he just called me back, very annoyed. They told him that if he wants to know the name of the car's owner, he must submit a written request specifying in detail the reasons for said request.'

'That's not a problem, Commissioner. I'll explain the whole story to you tomorrow, and you, in the request, can—'

'Montalbano, you don't understand, or perhaps you won't understand. That's a cloaked number.'

'What does that mean?'

'It means the car belongs to the secret services. Is that so hard to understand?'

That was no mere stink, what they had smelled. The air itself was turning foul.

*

As he was telling Valente about Lapècora's murder, Karima's abduction, Fahrid and Fahrid's car, which actually belonged to the secret services, a troubling thought occurred to him. He phoned the commissioner in Montelusa.

'Excuse me, Commissioner, but when you spoke with your friend in Rome about the number plate, did you tell him what it was about?'

'How could I? I don't know the first thing about what you're doing.'

The inspector heaved a sigh of relief.

'I merely said,' the commissioner continued, 'that it involved an investigation that you, Inspector Montalbano, were conducting.'

The inspector retracted his sigh of relief.

*

'Hello, Galluzzo? Montalbano here. I'm calling from Mazàra. I think I'm going to be here late, so, contrary to what I said, I want you to go immediately to Marinella, to my house, pick up the old Tunisian lady, and take her to Montelusa. All right? You haven't got a minute to lose.'

*

'Hello, Livia? Listen very carefully to what I say, and do exactly what I tell you to do, without arguing. I'm in Mazàra at the moment, and I don't think they've bugged our phone yet.'

'Oh my God, what are you saying?'

'I asked you, please don't argue, don't ask questions, don't say anything. You must only listen to what I say. Very soon Galluzzo will be there. He's going to pick up the old woman and take her back with him to Montelusa. No long goodbyes, please; you can tell François he'll see her again soon. As soon as Galluzzo leaves, call my office and ask for Mimì Augello. You absolutely must find him, no matter where he is. And tell him you need to see him at once.'

'What if he's busy?'

'For you, he'll drop everything and come running. You, in the meantime, will pack François's few possessions into a small suitcase, then—'

'But what do you want—'

'Quiet, understand? Quiet. Tell Mimì that, on my orders, the kid must disappear from the face of the earth. Vanish. He should hide him somewhere safe, where he'll be all right. And don't ask where he intends to take him. Is that clear? You mustn't know where François has gone. And don't start crying, it bothers me. Listen closely. Wait for about an hour after Mimì has left with the kid, then call Fazio. Tell him, in tears – you won't have to fake it since you're crying already – tell him the kid has disappeared, maybe he ran off in search of the old lady, you don't know, but in short you want him to help you find him. In the meantime, I'll have returned. And one last thing: call Palermo airport and reserve a seat on the flight to Genoa, the one that leaves around midday tomorrow. That'll give me enough time to find someone to take you there. See you soon.'

He hung up, and his eyes met Valente's troubled gaze.

'You think they'd go that far?'

'Further.'

*

'Is the story clear to you now?' asked Montalbano.

'I think I'm beginning to understand,' replied Valente.

'Let me explain better,' said the inspector. 'All in all, things may have gone as follows: Ahmed Moussa, for his own reasons, has one of his men, Fahrid, set up a base of operations. Fahrid enlists the help – whether freely offered or not, I don't know – of Ahmed's sister, Karima, who's been living in Sicily for a few years. Then they blackmail a man from Vigàta named Lapècora into letting them use his old import-export business as a front. Are you following?'

'Perfectly.'

'Ahmed, who needs to attend an important meeting involving weapons or political support for his movement, comes to Italy under the protection of our secret services. The meeting takes place at sea, but in all likelihood it's a trap. Ahmed didn't have the slightest suspicion that our services were double-crossing him, and that they were in cahoots with the people in Tunis who wanted to liquidate him. Among other things, I'm convinced that Fahrid himself was part of the plan to do away with Ahmed. The sister, I don't think so.'

'Why are you so afraid for the boy?'

'Because he's a witness. He could recognize Fahrid the

way he recognized his uncle on TV. And Fahrid has already killed Karima, I'm sure of it. He killed her after taking her away in a car that turns out to belong to our secret services.'

'What are we going to do?'

'You, for now, are going to sit tight. I'm going to get busy creating a diversion.'

'Good luck.'

'Good luck to you, my friend.'

*

By the time he got back to headquarters it was already evening. Fazio was there waiting for him.

'Have you found François?'

'Did you go home before coming here?' Fazio asked instead of answering.

'No. I came directly from Mazàra.'

'Chief, could we go into your office for a minute?'

Once they were inside, Fazio closed the door.

'Chief, I'm a policeman. Maybe not as good a policeman as you, but still a policeman. How did you know the kid ran away?'

'What's with you, Fazio? Livia phoned me in Mazàra and I told her to call you.'

'See, Chief, the fact is, the young lady told me she was asking me for help because she didn't know where you were.'

'Touché,' said Montalbano.

'And then, she was really and truly crying, no doubt about that. Not because the boy had run away, but for some other reason, which I don't know. So I figured out what it was you wanted me to do, and I did it.'

'And what did I want you to do?'

'To raise a ruckus, make a lot of noise. I went to all the houses in the neighbourhood and asked every person I ran into. Have you seen a little boy like so? Nobody'd seen him, but now they all know he ran away. Isn't that what you wanted?'

Montalbano felt moved. This was real friendship, Sicilian friendship, the kind based on intuition, on what was left unsaid. With a true friend, one never needs to ask, because the other understands on his own and acts accordingly.

'What should I do now?'

'Keep raising a ruckus. Call the carabinieri, call every one of their headquarters in the province, call every police station, hospital, anybody you can think of. But do it unofficially, only by phone, nothing in writing. Describe the boy, show them you're worried.'

'But are we sure they won't end up finding him, Chief?'

'Not to worry, Fazio. He's in good hands.'

*

He took a sheet of paper with the station's letterhead and typed:

TO THE MINISTRY OF TRANSPORTATION AND AUTOMOBILE REGISTRATION:

FOR DELICATE INVESTIGATION INTO ABDUCTION AND PROBABLE

HOMICIDE OF WOMAN ANSWERING TO NAME KARIMA MOUSSA NEED NAME OWNER AUTOMOBILE LICENCE-PLATE NUMBER AM 237 GW. KINDLY REPLY PROMPTLY. INSPECTOR SALVO MONTALBANO.

God only knew why, whenever he had to write a fax, he composed it as if it were a telegram. He re-read it. He'd even written out the woman's name to make the bait more appetizing. They would surely have to come out in the open now.

'Gallo!'

'Yes, sir.'

'Find the fax number for Auto Registration in Rome and send this right away. Galluzzo!'

'At your service.'

'Well?'

'I took the old lady to Montelusa. Everything's taken care of.'

'Listen, Gallù. Tell your brother-in-law to be in the general vicinity of headquarters after Lapècora's funeral tomorrow. And tell him to bring a cameraman.'

'Thanks, Chief, with all my heart.'

'Fazio!'

'I'm listening.'

'It completely slipped my mind. Did you go to Mrs Lapècora's apartment?'

'Sure did. And I took a small cup from a set of twelve. I've got it over there. You wanna see it?'

'What the hell for? Tomorrow I'll tell you what to do

with it. For now, put it in a cellophane bag. Oh, and, did Jacomuzzi send you the knife?'

'Yessirree.'

*

He didn't have the courage to leave the office. At home the hard part awaited him. Livia's sorrow. Speaking of which, if Livia was leaving, then . . . He dialled Adelina's number.

'Adelì? Montalbano here. Listen, the young lady's leaving tomorrow morning; I need to recuperate. And you know what? I haven't eaten a thing all day.'

One had to live, no?

FIFTEEN

Livia was on the veranda, sitting on the bench, utterly still, and seemed to be looking out at the sea. She wasn't crying, but her red, puffy eyes said that she'd used up her supply of tears. The inspector sat down beside her, took one of her hands and squeezed it. To Montalbano it felt as if he'd picked up something dead; he found it almost repulsive. He let it go and lit a cigarette. Livia, he'd decided, should know as little as possible about the whole affair. But it was clear she'd given the matter some thought, and her question went right to the point.

'Do they want to harm him?'

'Actually harm him, probably not. Make him disappear for a while, yes.'

'How?'

'I don't know. Maybe by putting him in an orphanage under a false name.'

'Why?'

'Because he met some people he wasn't supposed to meet.'

Still staring at the sea, Livia thought about Montalbano's last words.

'I don't understand.'

'What don't you understand?'

'If these people François met are Tunisians, perhaps illegal immigrants, couldn't you, as policemen—'

'They're not only Tunisian.'

Slowly, as if making a great effort, Livia turned and faced him.

'They're not?'

'No. And I'm not saying another word.'

'I want him.'

'Who?'

'François. I want him.'

'But, Livia—'

'Shut up. I want him. No one can take him away from me like that, you least of all. I've thought long and hard about this, you know, these last few hours. How old are you, Salvo?'

'Forty-four, I think.'

'Forty-four and ten months. In two months you'll be forty-five. I've already turned thirty-three. Do you know what that means?'

'No. What what means?'

'We've been together for six years. Every now and then we talk about getting married, and then we drop the subject. We both do, by mutual, tacit consent. And we don't resume the discussion. We get along so well just the way things are, and our laziness, our egotism, gets the better of us, always.'

'Laziness? Egotism? What are you talking about? There are objective difficulties which—'

'Which you can stick up your arse,' Livia brutally concluded.

Montalbano, disconcerted, fell silent. Only once or twice in six years had Livia ever used obscenities, and it was always in troubling, extremely tense circumstances.

'I'm sorry,' Livia said softly. 'But sometimes I just can't stand your camouflage and hypocrisy. Your cynicism is more authentic.'

Montalbano, still silent, took it all in.

'Don't try to distract me from what I want to say to you. You're very good at it; it's your job. What I want to know is: when do you think we can get married? Give me a straight answer.'

'If it was only up to me . . .'

Livia leapt to her feet.

'That's enough! I'm going to bed. I took two sleeping pills and my plane leaves Palermo at midday tomorrow. But first I want to finish what I have to say. If we ever get married, it'll be when you're fifty and I'm thirty-eight. In other words, too late to have children. And we still haven't realized that somebody, God or whoever is acting in His place, has already sent us a child, at just the right moment.'

She turned her back and went inside. Montalbano

stayed outside on the veranda, gazing at the sea, but unable to bring it into focus.

*

An hour before midnight, he made sure Livia was sleeping profoundly, then he unplugged the phone, gathered together all the loose change he could find, turned off the lights, and went out. He drove to the telephone booth in the car park of the Marinella Bar.

'Nicolò? Montalbano here. A couple of things. Tomorrow morning, around midday, send somebody along with a cameraman to the neighbourhood of police headquarters. There are some new developments.'

'Thanks. What else?'

'I was wondering, do you have a very small video camera, one that doesn't make any noise? The smaller the better.'

'You want to leave posterity a document of your prowess in bed?'

'Do you know how to use this camera?'

'Of course.'

'Then bring it to me.'

'When?'

'As soon as you've finished your midnight news report. But don't ring the doorbell when you get here, Livia's asleep.'

*

'Hello, is this the prefect of Trapani? Please excuse me for calling so late. This is Corrado Menichelli of the *Corriere della Sera*. I'm calling from Milan. We recently got wind of an extremely serious development, but before publishing our report on it, we wanted to confirm a few things with you personally, since they concern you directly.'

'Extremely serious? What is this about?'

'Is it true that pressure was put on you to accommodate a certain Tunisian journalist during his recent visit to Mazàra? I advise that you think a moment before answering, in your own interest.'

'I don't need to think for even a second!' the prefect exploded. 'What are you talking about?'

'Don't you remember? That's very odd, you know, since this all happened barely three weeks ago.'

'None of this ever happened! No pressure was ever put on me! I don't know anything about any Tunisian journalists!'

'Mr Prefect, we have proof that—'

'You can't have proof of something that never happened! Let me speak immediately to the editor-in-chief!'

Montalbano hung up. The prefect of Trapani was sincere; the head of his cabinet, on the other hand, was not.

*

'Valente? Montalbano here. I just spoke to the prefect of Trapani; I was pretending to be a reporter for the *Corriere della Sera*. He doesn't know anything. The whole thing was set up by our friend, Commendatore Spadaccia.'

'Where are you calling from?'

'Not to worry. I'm calling from a phone booth. Now here's what we should do next, providing that you agree.'

To tell him, he spent every last piece of change but one.

*

'Mimì? Montalbano here. Were you sleeping?'

'No, I was dancing. What the fuck did you expect?'

'Are you mad at me?'

'Hell, yes! After the position you put me in!'

'Me? What position?'

'Sending me to take away the boy. Livia looked at me with hatred. I had to tear him out of her arms. It made me feel sick to my stomach.'

'Where'd you take François?'

'To Calapiàno, to my sister's.'

'Is it safe there?'

'Very safe. She and her husband have a great big house with a farm, three miles from the village, very isolated. My sister has two boys, one of them the same age as François. He'll be fine there. It took me two and a half hours to get there, and two and a half to drive back.'

'Tired, eh?'

'Very tired. I won't be in tomorrow morning.'

'All right, you won't be in, but I want you at my house, in Marinella, by nine at the latest.'

'What for?'

'To pick Livia up and drive her to Palermo airport.'

'Okay.'

'How come you're suddenly not so tired any more, eh, Mimì?'

*

Livia was now having a troubled sleep, groaning from time to time. Montalbano closed the bedroom door, sat down in the armchair, and turned on the television at very low volume. On TeleVigàta, Galluzzo's brother-in-law was saying that the Foreign Ministry in Tunis had issued a statement regarding some erroneous information about the unfortunate killing of a Tunisian fisherman aboard an Italian motor trawler that had entered Tunisian waters. The statement denied the wild rumours according to which the fisherman was not, in fact, a fisherman, but the rather well-known journalist Ben Dhahab. It was an obvious case of two men with the same name, since Ben Dhahab the journalist was alive and well and still working. In the city of Tunis alone, the statement went on to say, there are more than twenty men named Ben Dhahab. Montalbano turned off the television. So the tide had started to turn, and people were running for cover, raising fences, putting up smokescreens.

*

He heard a car pull up and stop in the clearing in front of the house. The inspector rushed to the door to open up. It was Nicolò.

'I got here as fast as I could,' he said, entering.

'Thanks.'

'Livia's asleep?' the newsman asked, looking around.

'Yes. She's leaving for Genoa tomorrow morning.'

'I'm so sorry I won't have a chance to say goodbye to her.'

'Nicolò, did you bring the video camera?'

The newsman reached into his jacket pocket and pulled out a gadget no larger than four packets of cigarettes stacked two by two.

'Here you are. I'm going home to bed.'

'No you're not. First you have to hide this somewhere it won't be visible.'

'How am I going to do that, if Livia's sleeping in the next room?'

'Nicolò, I don't know why you've got it into your head that I want to film myself fucking. I want you to set up the camera in this room.'

'Tell me what it is you want to film.'

'A conversation between me and a man sitting exactly where you are now.'

Nicolò looked straight ahead and smiled.

'Those shelves full of books seem like they were put there for that very purpose.'

Taking a chair from the table, he set it next to the bookcase and climbed up on it. He shuffled a few books, set up the camera, sat back down where he was before, and looked up.

'From here you can't see it,' he said, satisfied. 'Come and check for yourself.'

The inspector checked.

'That seems fine.'

'Stay there,' said Nicolò.

He climbed back up on the chair, fussed about, and got back down.

'What's it doing?' asked Montalbano.

'Filming you.'

'Really? It makes no noise at all.'

'I told you the thing's amazing.'

Nicolò repeated his rigmarole of climbing onto the chair and stepping back down. But this time he had the camera in his hand and showed it to Montalbano.

'Here's how you do it, Salvo. To rewind the tape, you press this button. Now bring the camera up to your eye and press this other button. Go ahead, try.'

Montalbano did as he was told and saw a very tiny image of himself ask in a microscopic voice: 'What's it doing?' Then he heard Nicolò's voice say, 'Filming you.'

'Fantastic,' the inspector said. 'There's one thing, though. Is that the only way to see what you've filmed?'

'Of course not,' Nicolò replied, taking out a normal-looking video cassette that was made differently inside. 'Watch what I do. I remove the tape from the video camera, which as you can see is as small as the one in your answering machine, and I slip it inside this one, which is made for this purpose and can be used in your VCR.'

'Listen, to make it record, what do I do?'

'Push this other button.'

Seeing the inspector's expression, which looked more confused than convinced, Nicolò grew doubtful.

'Will you be able to use it?'

'Come on!' replied Montalbano, offended.

'Then why are you making that face?'

'Because I can't very well climb onto a chair in front of the man I want to film. It would make him suspicious.'

'See if you can reach it by standing on tiptoe.'

He could.

'Then it's simple. Just leave a book out on the table, then casually put it back on the shelf, meanwhile pressing the button.'

*

Dear Livia,

Unfortunately I can't wait for you to wake up. I have to go to Montelusa to see the commissioner. I've already arranged to have Mimì come to take you to the airport. Please try to be as calm and untroubled as possible. I'll phone you this evening. Kisses,

Salvo

A travelling salesman of the lowest rank would have expressed himself with more affection and imagination. He rewrote the note and, strangely, it came out exactly the same as the previous one. Nothing doing. It wasn't true that he had to see the commissioner; he merely wanted to skip the goodbyes. It was therefore a big fat lie, and he had never been able to tell one directly to someone he respected. Little fibs, on the other hand, he was very good at. And how.

*

At headquarters he found Fazio waiting for him, upset.

'I've been trying to call you at home for the last half hour. You must've unplugged the telephone.'

'What's the problem?'

'Some bloke phoned saying he accidentally found the dead body of an old woman in Villaseta, on Via Garibaldi, in the same house where we caught the little boy. That's why I was looking for you.'

Montalbano felt something like an electric shock.

'Tortorella and Galluzzo have already gone there. Galluzzo just phoned and said it was the same old lady he took to your house.'

Aisha.

The punch Montalbano gave himself in the face wasn't hard enough to knock out his teeth, but it made his lip bleed.

'What the hell are you doing, Chief?' said Fazio, flabbergasted.

Aisha was a witness, of course, just like François. But the inspector's eyes and attention had all been on the boy. A fucking idiot, that's what he was. Fazio handed him a handkerchief.

'Here, clean yourself up.'

*

Aisha was a twisted little bundle at the foot of the stairs that led up to Karima's room.

'She apparently fell and broke her neck,' said Dr Pasquano, who'd been summoned by Tortorella. 'But I'll be able to tell you more after the autopsy. Although to send an old lady like this flying, you'd only need to blow on her.'

'And where's Galluzzo?' Montalbano asked Tortorella.

'He went to Montelusa to talk to a Tunisian woman the deceased was staying with. He wanted to ask her why the old lady came back here, to find out if anybody had telephoned her.'

As the ambulance was leaving, the inspector went inside Aisha's house, lifted a stone next to the fireplace, took out the bank book, blew the dust off, and put it in his pocket.

'Chief!'

It was Galluzzo. No, nobody had phoned Aisha. She'd simply decided to go home. She woke up one morning, took the bus, and did not miss her appointment with death.

*

Back in Vigàta, before going to headquarters, he stopped in at the office of a notary named Cosentino, whom he liked.

'What can I do for you, Inspector?'

Montalbano pulled out the bank book and handed it to the notary, who opened it, glanced at it, and asked, 'So?'

The inspector launched into an extremely complicated explanation; he wanted him to know only half the story.

'What I think you're saying,' the notary summarized, 'is that this money belongs to a woman you presume to be dead, and that her son, a minor, is her only heir.'

'Right.'

'And you'd like for this money to be tied up in some

way, so that the child could only enter into possession when he comes of age.'

'Right.'

'But why don't you simply hold on to the booklet yourself, and when the time comes, turn it over to him?'

'What makes you think I'll still be alive in fifteen years?'

'I see,' said the notary. He continued, 'Let's do this: you take the book back with you, I'll give the matter some thought, and let's talk again in a week. It might be a good idea to invest that money.'

'It's up to you,' said Montalbano, standing up.

'Take the book back.'

'You keep it. I might lose it.'

'Then wait and I'll give you a receipt.'

'If you'd be so kind.'

'One more thing.'

'Tell me.'

'You must be absolutely certain, you know, that the mother is dead.'

*

From headquarters, he phoned home. Livia was about to leave. She gave him a rather chilly goodbye, or so it seemed to him. He didn't know what to do about it.

'Is Mimì there yet?'

'Of course. He's waiting in the car.'

'Have a good trip. I'll call you tonight.'

He had to move on, not let Livia tie him up.

'Fazio!'

'At your command.'

'Go to the church where Lapècora's funeral is being held. It must've already started by now. Bring Gallo along. When people are expressing their condolences to the widow, I want you to approach her and, with the darkest look you can muster up, say: 'Signora, please come with us to police headquarters.' If she starts to make a scene, starts screaming and shouting, don't hesitate to use force to put her in the squad car. And one more thing: Lapècora's son is sure to be there in the cemetery. If he tries to defend his mother, handcuff him.'

*

MINISTRY OF TRANSPORTATION AND AUTOMOBILE REGISTRATION: CONCERNING THE EXTREMELY SENSITIVE INVESTIGATION OF HOMICIDE OF TWO WOMEN NAMES KARIMA AND AISHA ABSOLUTELY MUST KNOW PERSONAL PARTICULARS AND ADDRESS OF OWNER OF AUTOMOBILE NUMBER PLATE AM 237 GW STOP PLEASE REPLY PROMPTLY STOP SIGNED SALVO MONTALBANO VIGATA POLICE MONTELUSA PROVINCE.

At the Automobile Registration office, before passing the fax on to the person in charge, they were sure to have a laugh at his expense and think him some kind of idiot for the way he formulated his request. But the person in charge, for his part, would understand the gambit, the challenge hidden in the message, and be forced to make a counter-move. Which was exactly what Montalbano wanted.

SIXTEEN

Montalbano's office was located at the opposite end of the building from the entrance to police headquarters, and yet he still heard all the shouting that broke out when Fazio's car arrived with the widow Lapècora inside. Though there were hardly any journalists or photographers around, dozens of idlers and rubberneckers must have joined their modest number.

'Signora, why were you arrested?'

'Look over here, signora!'

'Out of the way! Out of the way!'

Then there was relative calm and someone knocked at his door. It was Fazio.

'How'd it go?'

'She didn't put up much resistance. But she got upset when she saw the journalists.'

'What about the son?'

'There was a man standing next to her in the cemetery, and everyone was expressing their condolences to him too, so I thought he must be the son. But when I told the widow she had to come with us, he turned his back and walked away. So I guess he wasn't her son.'

'Ah, but he was, Fazio. Too sensitive to witness his mother's arrest. And terrified that he might have to pay her legal fees. Bring the lady in here.'

'Like a thief, that's how you're treating me! Just like a thief!' the widow burst out as soon as she saw the inspector.

Montalbano made a dark face.

'Did you mistreat the lady?'

As if reading from a script, Fazio pretended to be embarrassed.

'Well, since we were arresting her—'

'Who ever said you were arresting her? Please sit down, signora, I apologize for the unpleasant misunderstanding. I won't keep you but a few minutes, only as long as it takes to draw up a report of your answers to a few questions. Then you can go home and that'll be the end of it.'

Fazio went and sat down at the typewriter, while Montalbano sat behind his desk. The widow seemed to have calmed down a little, although the inspector could see her nerves jumping under her skin like fleas on a stray dog.

'Signora, please correct me if I'm wrong. You told me, as you'll remember, that on the morning of your husband's murder, you got out of bed, went into the bathroom, got dressed, took your bag from the dining room, and went out. Is that right?'

'Absolutely.'

'You didn't notice anything abnormal in your apartment?'

'What was I supposed to notice?'

'For example, that the door to the study, contrary to custom, was closed?'

He'd taken a wild guess, but was right on the mark. Initially red, the woman's face blanched. But her voice remained steady.

'I think it was open, since my husband never closed it.'

'No, it was not, signora. When I entered your home with you, upon your return from Fiacca, the door was closed. I reopened it myself.'

'What does it matter if it was open or closed?'

'You're right, it's a meaningless detail.'

The widow couldn't help heaving a long sigh.

'Signora, the morning your husband was murdered, you left for Fiacca to visit your ailing sister. Right?'

'That's what I did.'

'But you forgot something, and for that reason, at the Cannatello junction, you got off the bus, waited for the next bus coming from the opposite direction, and returned to Vigàta. What did you forget?'

The widow smiled; apparently she'd prepared herself for such a question.

'I did not get off at Cannatello that morning.'

'Signora, I have statements from the two bus drivers.'

'They're right, except for one thing. It wasn't that morning, but two mornings before. The bus drivers got their days wrong.'

She was shrewd and quick. He would have to resort to trickery.

He opened a drawer to his desk and took out the kitchen knife in its cellophane bag.

'This, signora, is the knife that was used to murder your husband. With only one stab wound, in the back.'

The widow's expression didn't change. She didn't say a word.

'Have you ever seen it before?'

'You see so many knives like that.'

Very slowly, the inspector again slipped his hand into the drawer, and this time he withdrew another cellophane bag, this one with a small cup inside.

'Do you recognize this?'

'Did you take that yourselves? You made me turn the house upside down looking for it!'

'So it's yours. You officially recognize it.'

'Of course I do. What use could you have for that cup?'

'It's going to help me send you to jail.'

Of all the possible reactions, the widow chose one that, in a way, won the inspector's admiration. In fact, she turned her head towards Fazio and politely, as if paying a courtesy call, asked him, 'Has he gone crazy?'

Fazio, in all sincerity, would have liked to answer that in his opinion the inspector had been crazy since birth, but he said nothing and merely stared out of the window.

'Now I'll tell you how things went,' said Montalbano. 'That morning, hearing the alarm clock, you got up and went into the bathroom. You necessarily passed by the door to the study, which you noticed was closed. At first you thought nothing of it, then you reconsidered. And when you came out of the bathroom, you opened it. But you didn't go in, at least I don't think you did. You waited a moment in the doorway, reclosed the door, went into the kitchen, grabbed the knife, and put it in your bag. Then you went out, you caught the bus, you got off at Cannatello, you got on the bus to Vigàta, you went back home, you opened the door, you saw your husband ready to go out, you argued with him, he opened the door to the lift, which was on your floor because you'd just used it. You followed behind him, you stabbed him in the back, he turned halfway around, fell to the ground, you started the lift, you reached the ground floor, and you got out. And nobody saw you. That was your great stroke of luck.'

'But why would I have done it?' the woman asked calmly. And then, with an irony that seemed incredible at that moment and in that place, 'Just because my husband had closed the door to his study?'

Montalbano, from a seated position, bowed admiringly to her.

'No, signora; because of what was behind that closed door.'

'And what was that?'

'Karima, your husband's mistress.'

'But you said yourself that I didn't go into the room.'

'You didn't need to, because you were assailed by a cloud of perfume, the very stuff that Karima wore in abundance. It's called Volupté. It has a strong, persistent scent. You'd probably smelled it before from time to time on your husband's clothes. It was still there in the study, less strong of course, when I went in that evening, after you came home.'

The widow Lapècora remained silent; she was thinking over what the inspector had just said.

'Would you answer me one question?' she then asked.

'As many as you like.'

'Why, in your opinion, didn't I go into the study and kill that woman first?'

'Because your brain is as precise as a Swiss watch and as fast as a computer. Karima, seeing you open the door, would have put herself on the defensive, ready for anything. Your husband, hearing her scream, would have come running and disarmed you with Karima's help. Whereas by pretending not to notice anything, you could wait and catch him in the act a little later.'

'And how do you explain, just to follow your argument, that my husband was the only one killed?'

'When you returned, Karima was already gone.'

'Excuse me, but since you weren't there, who told you this story?'

'Your fingerprints on the cup and on the knife told me.'

'Not on the knife!' the woman snapped.

'Why not on the knife?'

The woman started biting her lip.

'The cup is mine, the knife isn't.'

'The knife is also yours; it's got one of your fingerprints on it. Clear as day.'

'But that can't be!'

Fazio did not take his eyes off his superior. He knew there were no fingerprints on the knife. This was the most delicate moment of the trick.

'And you're so sure there are no fingerprints on the knife because when you stabbed your husband you were still wearing the gloves you'd put on when you got all dressed up to go out. You see, the fingerprint we took from it was not from that morning, but from the day before, when, after using the knife to clean the fish you had for dinner, you washed it and put it back in the kitchen drawer. In fact, the fingerprint is not on the handle, but on the blade, right where the blade and the handle meet. And now you're going to go into the next room with Fazio, and we're going to take your fingerprints and compare them.'

'He was a son of a bitch,' said Signora Lapècora, 'and he deserved to die the way he did. He brought that whore into my home to get his jollies in my bed all day while I was out.'

'Are you saying you acted out of jealousy?'

'Why else?'

'But hadn't you already received three anonymous letters? You could have caught them in the act at the office on Salita Granet.'

'I don't do that kind of thing. But when I realized he'd brought that whore into my home, my blood started to boil.'

'I think, signora, your blood started to boil a few days before that.'

'When?'

'When you discovered your husband had withdrawn a large sum from his bank account.'

This time, too, the inspector was bluffing. It worked.

'Two hundred million lire!' the widow said in rage and despair. 'Two hundred million for that disgusting whore!'

That explained part of the money in Karima's bank book.

'If I didn't stop him, he was liable to eat up the office, our home and our savings!'

'Shall we put this all in a statement, signora? But first tell me one thing. What did your husband say when you appeared before him?'

'He said: "Get the hell out of my way. I have to go to the office." He'd probably had a spat with the slut, she'd left, and he was running after her.'

*

'Mr Commissioner? Montalbano here. I'm calling to let you know that I've just now managed to get Mrs Lapècora to confess to her husband's murder.'

'Congratulations. Why did she do it?'

'Self-interest, which she's trying to disguise as jealousy. I need to ask a favour of you. Could I hold a press conference?'

There was no answer.

'Commissioner? I asked if I could—'

'I heard you perfectly well, Montalbano. It's just that I was speechless with amazement. *You* want to hold a press conference? I don't believe it!'

'And yet it's true.'

'All right, go ahead. But later you must explain to me what's behind it.'

*

'Are you saying that Mrs Lapècora had long known about her husband's relations with Karima?' asked Galluzzo's brother-in-law in his capacity as a reporter for TeleVigàta.

'Yes. Thanks to no less than three anonymous letters that her husband had sent to her.'

At first they didn't understand.

'Do you mean to say that Mr Lapècora actually denounced himself to his wife?' asked a bewildered journalist.

'Yes. Because Karima had started blackmailing him. He was hoping his wife's reaction would free him from his predicament. But Mrs Lapècora did not intervene. Nor did their son.'

'Excuse me, but why didn't he turn to the police?'

'Because he thought it would create a big scandal. Whereas, with his wife's help, he was hoping matters would stay within the, uh, family circle.'

'But where is this Karima now?'

'We don't know. She escaped with her son, a little boy. Actually one of her friends, who was worried about their disappearance, asked the Free Channel to air a photo of the mother and her son. But so far nobody has come forward.'

They thanked him and left. Montalbano smiled in

satisfaction. The first puzzle had been solved, perfectly, within its specific outline. Fahrid, Ahmed and even Aisha had been left out of it. With them in it, had they been properly used, the puzzle's design would have been entirely different.

✲

He was early for his appointment with Valente. He stopped in front of the restaurant where he'd gone the last time he was in Mazàra. He gobbled up a sauté of clams in breadcrumbs, a heaped dish of spaghetti with white clam sauce, a roast turbot with oregano and caramelized lemon, and he topped it all off with a bitter chocolate timbale in orange sauce. When it was all over he stood up, went into the kitchen, and shook the chef's hand without saying a word, deeply moved. In the car, on his way to Valente's office, he sang at the top of his lungs: '*Guarda come dondolo, guarda come dondolo, col twist . . .*'

✲

Valente showed Montalbano into a room next to his own.

'It's something we've done before,' he said. 'We leave the door ajar, and you, by manipulating this little mirror, can see what's happening in my office, if hearing's not enough.'

'Be careful, Valente. It's a matter of seconds.'

'Leave it to us.'

✲

Commendatore Spadaccia walked into Valente's office. It was immediately clear he was nervous.

'I'm sorry, Commissioner Valente, I don't understand. You could have easily come to the prefecture yourself and saved me some time. I'm a very busy man, you know.'

'Please forgive me, Commendatore,' Valente said with abject humility. 'You're absolutely right. But we'll make up for that at once; I won't keep you more than five minutes. I just need a simple clarification.'

'All right.'

'The last time we met, you told me the prefect had been asked in some way—'

The commendatore raised an imperious hand, and Valente immediately fell silent.

'If that's what I said, I was wrong. His Excellency knows nothing about all this. Anyway, it's the sort of bullshit we see every day. The ministry, in Rome, phoned me; they don't bother His Excellency with this kind of crap.'

Obviously the prefect, after getting the phone call from the bogus *Corriere* reporter, had asked the chief of his cabinet for an explanation. And it must have been a rather lively discussion, the echoes of which could still be heard in the strong words the commendatore was using.

'Go on,' Spadaccia urged.

Valente threw up his hands, a halo hovering over his head.

'That's all,' he said.

Spadaccia, dumbstruck, looked all around as if to verify the reality of what was happening.

'Are you telling me you have nothing more to ask me?'

'That's right.'

Spadaccia slammed his hand down on the desk with such force that even Montalbano jumped in the next room.

'You think you've made an idiot of me, but you'll pay for this, just wait and see!'

He stormed out, fuming. Montalbano ran to the window, nerves taut. He saw the commendatore shoot out of the front door like a bullet towards his car, whose driver was getting out to open the door for him. At that exact moment, the door of a squad car that had just pulled up opened, and out came Angelo Prestìa, who was immediately taken by the arm by a policeman. Spadaccia and the captain of the fishing boat stood almost face to face. They said nothing to each other, and each continued on his way.

The whinny of joy that Montalbano let out now and then when things went right for him terrified Valente, who came running from the next room.

'What's the matter with you?'

'It worked!'

'Sit down here,' they heard a policeman say. Prestìa had been brought into the office.

Valente and Montalbano stayed where they were; each lit a cigarette and smoked it without saying a word to the other. Meanwhile the captain of the *Santopadre* simmered on a low flame.

*

They entered with faces like the bearers of black clouds and bitter cargoes. Valente went and sat behind his desk; Montalbano pulled up a chair and sat down beside him.

'When's this aggravation gonna end?' the captain began.

He didn't realize that with his aggressive attitude, he had just revealed what he was thinking to Valente and Montalbano: that is, he believed that Commendator Spadaccia had come to vouch for the truth of his testimony. He felt at peace, and could therefore be indignant.

On the desk was a voluminous folder on which Angelo Prestìa's name was written in large block letters – voluminous because it was filled with old memos, but the captain didn't know this. Valente opened it and took out Spadaccia's calling card.

'You gave this to us, correct?'

Valente's switch from the politeness of last time to a more police-like bluntness worried Prestìa.

'Of course it's correct. The commendatore gave it to me and said if I had any trouble after taking the Tunisian aboard I could turn to him. Which I did.'

'Wrong,' said Montalbano, fresh as a spring chicken.

'But that's what he told me to do!'

'Of course that's what he told you to do, but as soon as you smelled a rat, you gave that calling card to us instead. And in doing so, you put that good man in a pickle.'

'A pickle? What kind of pickle?'

'Don't you think being implicated in premeditated murder is a pretty nasty pickle?'

Prestìa shut up.

'My colleague Montalbano,' Valente cut in, 'is trying to explain to you why things went as they did.'

'And how did they go?'

'They went as follows: if you had gone directly to Spadaccia and hadn't given us his card, he would have taken care of everything, under the table, of course. Whereas you, by giving us the card, got the law involved. So that left Spadaccia with only one option: deny everything.'

'What?!'

'Yessirree. Spadaccia's never seen you before, never heard your name. He made a sworn statement, which we've added to our file.'

'The son of a bitch!' said Prestìa. Then he asked, 'And how did he explain how I got his card?'

Montalbano laughed heartily to himself.

'He fooled you there, too, pal,' he said. 'He brought us a photocopy of a declaration he made about ten days ago to the Trapani police. Says his wallet was stolen with everything inside, including four or five calling cards, he couldn't remember exactly how many.'

'He tossed you overboard,' said Valente.

'Where the water's way over your head,' Montalbano added.

'How long are you going to manage to stay afloat?' Valente piled it on.

The sweat under Prestìa's armpits formed great big blotches. The office was filled with an unpleasant odour of musk and garlic, which Montalbano saw as rot-green in colour. Prestìa put his head in his hands and muttered:

'They didn't give me any choice.'

He remained awhile in that position, then apparently made up his mind, 'Can I speak with a solicitor?'

'A solicitor?' said Valente, as if greatly surprised.

'Why do you want a solicitor?' Montalbano asked in turn. 'I thought—'

'You thought what?'

'That we were going to arrest you?'

The duo worked perfectly together.

'You're not going to arrest me?'

'Of course not.'

'You can go now, if you like.'

It took Prestìa five minutes before he could get his arse unstuck from the chair and run out the door, literally.

*

'So, what happens next?' asked Valente, who knew they had unleashed a pack of demons.

'What happens next is that Prestìa will go and pester Spadaccia. And the next move will be theirs.'

Valente looked worried.

'What's wrong?' asked Montalbano.

'I don't know . . . I'm not convinced . . . I'm afraid they'll silence Prestìa. And we would be responsible.'

'Prestìa's too visible at this point. Bumping him off would be like putting their signature on the entire operation. No, I'm convinced they *will* silence him, but by paying him off handsomely.'

'Will you explain something for me?'

'Sure.'

'Why are you stepping into this quicksand?'

'And why are you following behind me?'

'First of all, because I'm a policeman, like you, and secondly, because I'm having fun.'

'And my answer is: my first reason is the same as yours. And my second is that I'm doing it for money.'

'And what'll you gain from it?'

'I know exactly what my gain will be. But you want to bet that you'll gain something from it too?'

*

Deciding not to give in to the temptation, he sped past the restaurant where he'd stuffed himself at lunch, doing 120 kilometres an hour. A half kilometre later, however, his resolution suddenly foundered, and he slammed on the brakes, provoking a furious blast of the horn from the car behind him. The man at the wheel, while passing him, glared at him angrily and gave him the finger. Montalbano then made a U-turn, strictly prohibited on that stretch of road, went straight into the kitchen, and, without even saying hello, asked the cook, 'So, exactly how do you prepare your striped mullet?'

SEVENTEEN

The following morning, at eight o'clock sharp, he appeared at the commissioner's office. His boss, as usual, had been there since seven, amid the muttered curses of the cleaning women who felt he prevented them from doing their jobs.

Montalbano told him about Mrs Lapècora's confession, explaining how the poor murder victim, as if trying to sidestep his tragic end, had written anonymously to his wife and openly to his son, but both had let him stew in his own juices. He made no mention of either Fahrid or Moussa – of the larger puzzle, in other words. He didn't want the commissioner, now at the end of his career, to find himself implicated in an affair that stank worse than a pile of shit.

And up to this point it had gone well for him; he hadn't had to pull any wool over the commissioner's eyes. He'd only left a few things out, told a few half-truths.

'But why did you want to hold a press conference, you who usually avoid them like the plague?'

He had anticipated this question, and the answer he

had ready on his lips allowed him another at least partial omission, if not an outright lie.

'This Karima, you see, was a rather unusual sort of prostitute. She went not only with Lapècora, but with other people as well. All well on in years: retirees, businessmen, professors. By limiting the case to Lapècora, I've tried to prevent the poison, the insinuations, from spreading to a bunch of poor wretches who, in the end, didn't really do anything wrong.'

He was convinced it was a plausible explanation. And in fact, the commissioner's only comment was, 'You have strange morals, Montalbano.' And then he asked, 'But has this Karima really disappeared?'

'Apparently, yes. When she learned her lover had been killed, she ran away with her little boy, fearing she might be implicated in the homicide.'

'Listen,' said the commissioner. 'What was that business with the car all about?'

'What car?'

'Come on, Montalbano. The car that turned out to belong to the secret services. They're nasty people, you know.'

Montalbano laughed. He'd practised the laugh the night before, in front of a mirror, persisting until he got it right. Now, however, contrary to his hopes, it rang false, too high-pitched. But if he wanted to keep his excellent superior out of this mess, he no longer had any choice. He had to tell a lie.

'Why do you laugh?' asked the commissioner, surprised.

'Out of embarrassment, believe me. The person who gave me that licence number phoned me the next day and said he'd made a mistake. The letters were right, but he'd got the number wrong. It was 837, not 237. I apologize. I feel mortified.'

The commissioner looked him in the eye for what seemed like an eternity. Then he spoke in a soft voice.

'If you want me to swallow that, I'll swallow it. But be very careful, Montalbano. Those people don't mess about. They're capable of anything, and whenever they slip up, they blame it on certain colleagues who went astray. Who don't exist. They're the ones who go astray. It's in their nature.'

Montalbano didn't know what to say. The commissioner changed subject.

'Tonight you'll have dinner at my house. I don't want to hear any arguments. You'll eat whatever there is. I've got two things I absolutely have to tell you. But I won't say them here, in my office, because that would give them a bureaucratic flavour, which I find unpleasant.'

It was a beautiful day, not a cloud in the sky, and yet Montalbano had the impression that a shadow had fallen across the sun, making the room turn suddenly cold.

*

There was a letter addressed to him on the desk in his office. He checked the postmark, as he always did, to try and discover its provenance, but it was illegible. He opened the envelope and read:

Inspector Montalbano,

You dont know me and I dont know what your like. My name is Arcangelo Prestifilippo and I am your fathers business partner in the vineyard which is producing very well, thank the Lord. Your father never talks about you but I found out he collects all the newspapers that talk about you and when he sees you on tv sometimes he starts crying but tries to not let other people see.

Dear Inspector, I feel my heart give out because the news I got to tell you isnt good. Ever since Signora Giulia, your father's second wife went up to Heaven four years ago, my partner and friend hasnt been the same. Then last year he started feeling bad, he would run out of breath even just from climbing some stairs and he would get dizzy. He didnt want to go to the doctor, nothing doing. And so I took advantage because my son who works in Milan and is a good doctor, came to town, and I took him to your father's house. My son looked at him and got upset because he wanted your father to go to the hospital. He made such a big fuss and talked so much that he convinced your father to go to the hospital with him before he went back to Milan. I went to see him every night and ten days later the doctor told me they did all the tests and your father had that terrible lung disease. And so your father started going in and out of the hospital for treatment which made all his hair fall out but didnt make him one bit better. And he told me specially to not tell you about it, he said he didnt want you getting all worried. But last night I talked to the doctor and he said your father is near the end now, he got only one month maybe, give or take a few days. And so in spiter your dad's strict orders I wanted you to know whats happening. Your fathers in the Clinica Porticelli, the telefone number is 341234. Theres a phone in his room. But its better if you come and see him in person and pretend you dont know nuthin bout him being sick. You already got my phone number, its the same as the vineyard office where I work all day long.

I am very sorry.

Best regards,

Arcangelo Prestifilippo

A slight tremor in his hands made him struggle to put the letter back in the envelope, and so he slipped it into his pocket. A profound weariness came over him, forcing him to lean heavily, eyes closed, against the back of his chair. He had trouble breathing; there seemed suddenly to be no air in the room. He stood up with difficulty, then went into Augello's office.

'What's wrong?' asked Mimì as soon as he saw his face.

'Nothing. Listen, I've got some work to do. I mean, I need a little time alone, some peace and quiet.'

'Anything I can do to help?'

'Yes. Take care of everything yourself. I'll see you tomorrow. Don't let anybody phone me at home.'

*

He passed by the *càlia e simenza* shop, bought a sizable cornet, and began his stroll along the jetty. A thousand thoughts raced through his head, but he was unable to seize a single one. When he arrived at the lighthouse he kept on walking. Directly below the lighthouse was a large rock, slippery with green moss. In danger of falling into the sea with each step, he managed to reach the rock and sat down, cornet in hand. But he didn't open it. He felt a kind of wave surge up from some part of his lower body, ascend towards his chest, and from there continue rising towards his throat, forming a knot that took his breath away. He felt the need to cry, but the tears wouldn't come. Then, amid the jumble of thoughts crowding his brain, a few words forced their way into clarity until they came together in a line of verse:

Father, you die a little more each day . . .

What was it? A poem? By whom? And when had he read it? He repeated the line under his breath, 'Father, you die a little more each day . . .'

And at last, out of his previously blocked, closed throat came the cry, but more than a cry it was the shrill wail of a wounded animal, followed, at once, by a rush of unstoppable, liberating tears.

*

A year before, when he'd been wounded in a shoot-out and ended up in the hospital, Livia had told him his father was phoning every day. He'd come only once to see him in person, when he was convalescing. He must have already been sick at the time. To Montalbano he'd merely looked a little thinner, nothing more. He was, in fact, even better dressed than usual, having always made a point of looking smart. On that occasion he'd asked his son if he needed anything. 'I can help,' he'd said.

*

When had they started to grow silently apart? His father had always been a caring, affectionate parent. That, Montalbano could not deny. He'd done everything in his power to lessen the pain of the loss of his mother. Whenever Montalbano fell ill as an adolescent – which luckily was not very often – his father used to stay at home from work so he wouldn't be alone. What was it, then, that hadn't worked? Perhaps there had always been a nearly total lack of communication between the two; they never could find the words to express their feelings for each other. So often, when very young, Montalbano had thought: *My father is a closed man.* And probably – though he realized it only now – his father had sat on a rock by the sea and thought the same of him. Still, he'd shown great sensitivity; before remarrying, for example, he'd waited for his son to finish university and win the placement competition. And yet when his father finally brought his new wife home, Montalbano had felt offended for no reason. A wall had risen between them; a glass wall, it's true, but a wall nonetheless. And so their meetings had gradually decreased in number to one or two a year. His father would usually arrive with a case of the wines produced by his vineyard, stay half a day, and then leave. Montalbano would always find the wine excellent and proudly offer it to his friends, telling them his father had made it. But had he ever told his father the wine was excellent? He dug deep in his memory. Never. Just as his father collected the newspapers that talked about him and felt like crying whenever he saw him on television, and yet had never, in person, congratulated him on the success of an investigation.

*

He sat on that rock for over two hours, and when he got up to go back into town, his mind was made up. He would not go to visit his father. The sight of him would surely have made his father realize how gravely ill he was. It would have made things worse. Anyway, he didn't really know if his father would be happy to see him. Montalbano, moreover, had a fear, a horror, of the dying. He wasn't sure he could stand the fear and horror of seeing his father die. On the brink of collapse, he might run away.

*

When he got back to Marinella he still had that harsh, heavy feeling of weariness inside. He undressed, put on his bathing suit, and dived into the sea. He swam until his legs began to cramp. Returning home, he realized he was in no condition to go to the commissioner's for dinner.

'Hello? Montalbano here. I'm very sorry, but—'

'You can't come?'

'No, I'm really very sorry.'

'Work?'

Why not tell him the truth?

'No, Mr Commissioner. It's my father. Somebody sent me a letter. It looks like he's dying.'

At first the commissioner said nothing; the inspector only heard him heave a long sigh.

'Listen, Montalbano. If you want to go and see him, even for an extended stay, go ahead, don't worry about anything. I'll find a temporary replacement for you.'

'No, I'm not going. Thanks anyway.'

Again the commissioner didn't speak. He must have been shocked by the inspector's words; but he was a polite, old-fashioned man, and did not bring the subject up again.

'Montalbano, I feel awkward.'

'Please don't, not with me.'

'Do you remember I said I had two things to say to you at dinner?'

'Of course.'

'Well, I'll say them to you over the phone, even though, as I said, I feel awkward doing so. And this probably isn't the most appropriate moment, but I'm afraid you might find out from another source, like the newspapers . . . You don't know this, of course, but almost a year ago I put in a request for early retirement.'

'Oh God, don't tell me they—'

'Yes, they granted it.'

'But why do you want to retire?'

'Because I no longer feel in step with the world, and because I feel tired. To me, the betting service for soccer matches is still called Sisal.'

The inspector didn't understand.

'I'm sorry, I don't get it.'

'What do you call it?'

'Totocalcio.'

'You see? Therein lies the difference. A while ago, some journalist accused Montanelli of being too old, and as proof, he cited the fact that Montanelli still called Totocalcio Sisal, as he used to call it thirty years ago.'

'But that doesn't mean anything! It was only a joke!'

'It means a lot, Montalbano, a lot. It means unconsciously holding on to the past, not wanting to see certain changes, even rejecting them. And I am barely a year away from retirement, anyway. I've still got my parents' house in La Spezia, which I've been having refurbished. If you like, when you come to Genoa to see Miss Livia, you can drop in on us.'

'And when are—'

'When am I leaving? What's today's date?'

'The twelfth of May.'

'I officially leave my job on the tenth of August.'

The commissioner cleared his throat, and the inspector understood that they had now come to the second thing, which was perhaps harder to say.

'About the other matter . . .'

He was hesitant, clearly. Montalbano bailed him out.

'It couldn't possibly be worse than what you just told me.'

'It's about your promotion.'

'No!'

'Listen to me, Montalbano. Your position can no longer be justified. In addition, now that I've been granted early retirement, I'm not, well, in a strong bargaining position. I have to recommend your promotion, and there won't be any obstacles.'

'Will I be transferred?'

'There's a ninety-nine percent chance of it. Bear in mind that if I didn't recommend you for the appointment, with all your successes, the ministry might see that in a negative light and could end up transferring you anyway, but without a promotion. Couldn't you use a raise?'

The inspector's brain was running at full speed, smoking, in fact, trying to find a possible solution. He glimpsed one and pounced on it.

'And what if, from this moment on, I no longer arrested anyone?'

'I don't understand.'

'I mean, what if I pretend not to solve any more cases, if I mishandle investigations, if I let slip—'

'Rubbish, Montalbano, the only thing you're letting slip is idiocies. I just don't understand. Every time I talk to you about promotion, you suddenly regress and start reasoning like a child.'

*

He killed an hour lolling about the house, putting some books back on the shelf and dusting the glass over the five engravings he owned, which Adelina never did. He did not turn on the television. He looked at his watch: almost ten p.m. He got in his car and drove to Montelusa. The three cinemas were showing the Taviani brothers' *Elective Affinities,* Bertolucci's *Stealing Beauty,* and *Travels with Goofy.* Without the slightest hesitation, he chose the cartoon. The cinema was empty. He went back to the man who had torn his ticket.

'There's nobody there!'

'You're there. What do you want, company? It's late. At this hour, all the little kids are asleep. You're the only one still awake.'

He had so much fun that, at one moment, he caught himself laughing out loud in the empty cinema.

*

There comes a moment, he thought, *when you realize your life has changed. But when did it happen? you ask yourself. And you have no answer. Unnoticed events kept accumulating until, one day, a transformation occurred – or perhaps they were perfectly visible events, whose importance and consequences, however, you never took into account. You ask yourself over and over, but the answer to that 'when' never comes. As if it mattered!*

Montalbano, for his part, had a precise answer to that question. My life changed, he would have said, on the twelfth of May.

*

Beside the front door to his house, Montalbano had recently had a small lamp installed that went on automatically when night fell. It was by the light of this lamp that he saw, from the main road, a car stopped in the clearing in front of the house. He turned into the small lane leading to the house, and pulled up a few inches from the other car. As he expected, it was a metallic grey BMW. Its number plate was AM 237 GW. But there wasn't a soul to be seen. The man who'd driven it there was surely hiding somewhere nearby. Montalbano decided it was best to feign indifference. He stepped out of the car, whistling, closed the door, and saw somebody waiting for him. He hadn't noticed him earlier because the man was standing on the far side of the car and was so small in stature that his head did not exceed the height of the car's roof. Practically a midget, or not much more than one. Well dressed, and wearing small, gold-rimmed glasses.

'You've made me wait a long time,' the little man said, coming forward.

Montalbano, keys in hand, moved towards the front door. The quasi-midget stepped in front of him, shaking a kind of identity card.

'My papers,' he said.

The inspector pushed aside the little hand holding the documents, opened the door, and went inside. The man followed behind him.

'I am Colonel Lohengrin Pera,' said the elf.

The inspector stopped dead in his tracks, as if someone had pressed the barrel of a gun between his shoulder blades. He turned slowly around and looked the colonel up and down. His parents must have given him that name to compensate somehow for his stature and surname. Montalbano felt fascinated by the colonel's little shoes, which he must surely have had made to measure; they wouldn't even have fitted in the '*sottouomo*' category, as the shoemakers called it – that is, for 'sub-men'. And yet the services had enlisted him, so he must have been tall enough to make the grade. His eyes, however, behind the lenses, were lively, attentive, dangerous. Montalbano felt certain he was looking at the brains behind the Moussa affair. He went into the kitchen, still followed by the colonel, put the mullets in tomato sauce that Adelina had made for him into the oven, and started setting the table, without once opening his mouth. On the table was a seven-hundred-page book he'd bought from a bookshop and had never opened. He'd been drawn by the title: *The Metaphysics of Partial Being*. He picked it up, stood on tiptoe, and put it on the shelf, pressing the button on the videocamera. As if somebody had said 'roll 'em'. Colonel Lohengrin Pera sat down in the right chair.

EIGHTEEN

Montalbano took a good half hour to eat his mullets, either because he wanted to savour them as they deserved, or to give the colonel the impression that he didn't give a flying fuck about what the man might have to say to him. He didn't even offer him a glass of wine. He acted as if he were alone, to the point where he even once burped out loud. For his part, Lohengrin Pera, once he'd sat down, had stopped moving, limiting himself to staring at the inspector with beady, snake-like eyes. Only when Montalbano had downed a demi-tasse of espresso did the colonel begin to speak.

'You understand, of course, why I've come to see you.'

The inspector stood up, went into the kitchen, placed the little cup in the sink, and returned.

'I'm playing above board,' the colonel continued, after waiting for him to return. 'It's probably the best way, with you. That's why I chose to come in that car, for which you twice requested information on the owner.'

From his jacket pocket he withdrew two sheets of paper,

which Montalbano recognized as the faxes he'd sent to Vehicle Registration.

'Only you already knew who the car belonged to; your commissioner must certainly have told you its number plate was cloaked. So, since you sent me these faxes anyway, it must mean their intention was more than simply to request information, however imprudently. I therefore became convinced – correct me if I'm wrong – that for your own reasons, you wanted us to come out into the open. So here I am: your wish has been granted.'

'Would you excuse me a minute?' Montalbano asked.

Without waiting for an answer, he got up, went into the kitchen and returned with a plate on which was a huge, hard piece of Sicilian *cassata* ice cream. The colonel settled in patiently and waited for him to eat it.

'Please continue,' said the inspector. 'I can't eat it when it's like this. It has to melt a little first.'

'Before we go any further,' resumed the colonel, who apparently had very strong nerves, 'let me clarify something. In your second fax, you mention the murder of a woman named Aisha. We had absolutely nothing to do with that death. It must surely have been an unfortunate accident. If she'd needed to be eliminated, we would have done so immediately.'

'I don't doubt it. I was well aware of that too.'

'So why did you state otherwise in your fax?'

'Just to turn up the heat.'

'Right. Have you read the writings and speeches of Mussolini?'

'He's not one of my favourite authors.'

'In one of his last writings, Mussolini says that the people should be treated like a donkey, with a carrot and a stick.'

'Always so original, that Mussolini! You know something?'

'What?'

'My grandfather used to say the same thing. He was a peasant and, since he wasn't Mussolini, he was referring only to the ass, the donkey, that is.'

'May I continue the metaphor?'

'By all means!'

'Your faxes, as well as your having persuaded Vice-Commissioner Valente of Mazàra to interrogate the captain of the fishing boat and the head of the prefect's cabinet, these and other things were the stick you used to flush us out.'

'So where does the carrot come in?'

'The carrot is in the declarations you made at the press conference you held after arresting Mrs Lapècora for the murder of her husband. You could have dragged us into that one by the hair, but you didn't. You were careful to keep that crime within the confines of jealousy and greed. Still, that was a menacing carrot; it said—'

'Colonel, I suggest you drop the metaphor; at this point we've got a talking carrot.'

'Fine. You, with that press conference, wanted us to know that you had other information in your possession which, at that moment, you were unwilling to show. Am I right?'

The inspector extended a spoon towards the ice cream, filled it, and brought it to his mouth.

'It's still hard,' he said to Lohengrin Pera.

'You discourage me,' the colonel commented, but he went on. 'Anyway, since we're laying our cards on the table, will you tell me everything you know about the case?'

'What case?'

'The killing of Ahmed Moussa.'

He'd succeeded in making him say that name openly, as duly recorded by the tape in the video camera.

'No.'

'Why not?'

'Because I love the sound of your voice, the way you speak.'

'May I have a glass of water?'

To all appearances, Lohengrin Pera was perfectly calm and controlled, but inside he was surely close to the boiling point. The request for water was a clear sign.

'Go and get it yourself from the kitchen.'

While the colonel fussed about in the kitchen with the glass and tap, Montalbano, who was looking at him from behind, noticed a bulge under his jacket, beside the right buttock. Want to bet the midget is armed with a gun twice his size? He decided not to take any chances and brought a very sharp knife, which he had used to cut the bread, closer to him.

'I'll be explicit and brief,' Lohengrin Pera began, sitting

down and wiping his lips with a tiny handkerchief, an embroidered postage stamp. 'A little more than two years ago, our counterparts in Tunis asked us to collaborate with them on a delicate operation aimed at neutralizing a dangerous terrorist, whose name you got me to say just a moment ago.'

'I'm sorry,' said Montalbano, 'but I have a very limited vocabulary. By "neutralizing" do you mean "physically eliminating"?'

'Call it whatever you like. We discussed the matter with our superiors, naturally, and were ordered not to collaborate. But then, less than a month later, we found ourselves in a very unpleasant position, where it was we who had to ask our friends in Tunis for help.'

'What a coincidence!' Montalbano exclaimed.

'Yes. Without any questions, they gave us the help we wanted, and so we found ourselves morally indebted—'

'No!' Montalbano yelled.

Lohengrin Pera gave a start.

'What's wrong?' he asked.

'You said: *morally* indebted.'

'As you wish. Let's say merely "indebted", without the adverb, all right? But excuse me; before going on, I have to make a telephone call. I keep forgetting.'

'Be my guest,' the inspector said, gesturing towards the phone.

'Thanks; I've got a mobile phone.'

Lohengrin Pera was not armed. The bulge on his

buttock was his mobile phone. He punched in a number that Montalbano was unable to read.

'Hello? This is Pera. All's well, we're talking.'

He turned off the phone and left it on the table.

'Our colleagues in Tunis discovered that Ahmed's favourite sister, Karima, had been living in Sicily for years, and that, through her work, she had a vast circle of acquaintances.'

'Vast, no,' Montalbano corrected him. 'Select, yes. She was a respectable prostitute; she inspired confidence.'

'Ahmed's right-hand man, Fahrid, suggested to his chief that they establish a base of operations in Sicily and avail themselves of Karima's services. Ahmed rather trusted Fahrid; he didn't know he'd been bought by the Tunisian secret services. With our discreet assistance, Fahrid came here and made contact with Karima, who, after a careful review of her clients, chose Lapècora. Perhaps by threatening to inform his wife of their relationship, Karima forced Lapècora to reopen his old import-export business, which turned out to be an excellent cover. Fahrid was able to communicate with Ahmed by writing coded business letters to an imaginary company in Tunis. By the way, in your press conference you said that at a certain point Lapècora wrote anonymously to his wife, informing her of his liaison. Why did he do that?'

'Because he smelled something fishy in the whole arrangement.'

'Do you think he suspected the truth?'

'Of course not! At the most, he probably thought they

were trafficking drugs. If he'd discovered he was at the centre of an international intrigue, he'd have been killed on the spot.'

'I agree. At first, our primary concern was to keep the impatience of the Tunisians in check. But we also wanted to be certain that, once we put the bait in the water, the fish would bite.'

'Excuse me, but who was the blond young man who showed up now and then with Fahrid?'

The colonel looked at him with admiration.

'You know that too? He's one of our men who would periodically go and check up on things.'

'And while he was at it, he would fuck Karima.'

'These things happen. Finally, Fahrid persuaded Ahmed to come to Italy by tempting him with the prospect of a big weapons shipment. As always with our invisible protection, Ahmed Moussa arrived at Mazàra, according to Fahrid's instructions. Under pressure from the chief of the prefect's cabinet, the captain of the fishing boat agreed to take Ahmed aboard, since the meeting between Ahmed and the imaginary arms dealer was supposed to take place on the open sea. Without the slightest suspicion, Ahmed Moussa walked into the trap. He even lit a cigarette, as he'd been told to do, so that they might better recognize each other. But Commendatore Spadaccia, the cabinet chief, made a big mistake.'

'He hadn't warned the captain that it would not be a clandestine meeting, but an ambush,' said Montalbano.

'You could say that. The captain, as he'd been told to

do, threw Ahmed's papers into the sea and divided the seventy million lire the Arab had in his pocket with the rest of the crew. Then, instead of returning to Mazàra, he changed course. He had his doubts about us.'

'Oh?'

'You see, we had steered our motor patrols away from the scene of the action, and the captain knew this. If that's the situation, he must have thought, who's to say I won't run into something on the way back in – a missile, a mine, even another motor patrol that would sink my boat to destroy all trace of the operation? That's why he came to Vigàta. He was shuffling the cards.'

'Had he guessed right?'

'In what sense?'

'Was there someone or something waiting for the fishing boat?'

'Come now, Montalbano! That would have been a useless massacre!'

'And you engage only in useful massacres, is that it? And how do you plan to keep the crew quiet?'

'With the carrot and the stick, to quote again that writer you don't appreciate. In any case, I've said everything I had to say.'

'No.'

'What do you mean, no?'

'I mean: that's not everything. You have very cleverly taken me out to sea, but I haven't forgotten those left behind on land. Fahrid, for example. He must have learned, from one of your informers, that Ahmed had been killed;

but the fishing boat had docked at Vigàta, inexplicably – for him. This troubled him. At any rate, he must now proceed to the second part of his assignment. That is, neutralizing, as you put it, Lapècora. So he shows up at the man's front door and, to his amazement and alarm, finds out that somebody got there first. And so he shits in his pants.'

'I beg your pardon?'

'He gets scared, he no longer knows what is happening. Like the captain of the fishing boat, he thinks your people are behind it. It looks to him like you've begun removing from circulation everyone who was in some way involved in the operation. For a moment, perhaps, he suspects it might have been Karima who did away with Lapècora. You may not know this, but Karima, under orders from Fahrid, forced Lapècora to hide her in his apartment; Fahrid didn't want Lapècora to get any brilliant ideas during those critical hours. Fahrid, however, didn't know that once she'd carried out her mission, Karima had gone back home. In any event, at some point that morning, Fahrid met up with Karima, and the two must have had a violent argument in the course of which he told her that her brother had been killed. Karima then tried to escape. She failed, and she was murdered. She would have had to be eliminated anyway, at some later point, on the quiet.'

'As I'd suspected,' said Lohengrin Pera, 'you've worked it all out. Now I ask you to pause and think. You, like me, are a loyal, devoted servant of our state. And so—'

'Stick it up your arse,' Montalbano said softly.

'I don't understand.'

'Let me repeat: you can take our state and stick it up your arse. You and I have diametrically opposed concepts of what it means to be a servant of the state. For all intents and purposes, we serve two different states. So I beg you please not to liken your work to mine.'

'So now you want to play Don Quixote, Montalbano? Every community needs someone to clean the toilets. But this does not mean that those who clean the toilets are not part of the community.'

Montalbano felt his rage growing; one more word would surely have been a mistake. He reached out with one hand, brought the dish of ice cream nearer, and began to eat. By now Lohengrin Pera had got used to the ritual, and once Montalbano started nibbling the ice cream, he stopped talking.

'Karima was killed, correct?' asked Montalbano after a few spoonfuls.

'Unfortunately, yes. Fahrid was afraid that—'

'I'm not interested in why. I'm interested in the fact that she was killed by the authority of a loyal servant of the state such as yourself. What would you call this specific case: neutralization or murder?'

'Montalbano, you can't use the standard of common morality—'

'Colonel, I already warned you once: do not speak of morality in my presence.'

'I merely meant that sometimes, the reason of state—'

'That's enough,' said Montalbano, who had wolfed

down the ice cream in four angry bites. Then, suddenly, he slapped his forehead.

'What time is it, anyway?'

The colonel looked at his wristwatch, a dainty, precious item that looked like a child's toy.

'It's already two o'clock.'

'Why on earth hasn't Fazio arrived?' Montalbano asked himself, pretending to be worried. Then he added, 'I have to make a phone call.'

He got up, went over to the phone on his desk two yards away, and started speaking in a loud voice so that Lohengrin Pera would hear everything.

'Hello, Fazio? Montalbano here.'

Fazio, drowsy with sleep, spoke with difficulty.

'Chief. What is it?'

'Come on, did you forget about the arrest?'

'What arrest?' said Fazio, at sea.

'The arrest of Simone Fileccia.'

Simone Fileccia had been arrested the day before, by Fazio himself. And, in fact, Fazio understood at once.

'What should I do?'

'Come and pick me up at my place, and we'll go and get him.'

'Should I bring my own car?'

'No, better make it a squad car.'

'I'll be right there.'

'Wait.'

The inspector put his hand over the receiver and turned to the colonel.

'How much more time will this take?'

'That's up to you,' said Lohengrin Pera.

'Be here in, say, twenty minutes or so,' the inspector said to Fazio, 'not before. I have to finish talking to a friend.'

He hung up, sat back down. The colonel smiled.

'Since we've got so little time, tell me your price immediately, if you'll forgive the expression.'

'I come cheap, very cheap,' said Montalbano.

'I'm listening.'

'Two things, that's all. Within a week, I want Karima's body to turn up, and in such a way that there can be no mistake as to its identification.'

A billy club to the head would have had less effect on Lohengrin Pera. Opening and closing his mouth, he gripped the edge of the table with his tiny hands, as if afraid he might fall out of his chair.

'Why?' he managed to utter with the voice of a silkworm.

'None of your fucking business,' was the firm, blunt reply.

The colonel shook his little head from left to right and right to left, looking like a spring puppet.

'It's not possible.'

'Why?'

'We don't know where she was . . . buried.'

'And who does know?'

'Fahrid.'

'Has Fahrid been neutralized? You know, I'm starting to like that word.'

'No. He's gone back to Tunisia.'

'Then there's no problem. Just get in touch with his playmates in Tunis.'

'No,' the midget said firmly. 'The matter has been put to rest at this point. We have nothing to gain by stirring things up again with the discovery of a corpse. No, it's not possible. Ask me anything you like, but that is one thing we cannot grant you. Aside from the fact that I can't see the purpose of it.'

'Too bad,' said Montalbano, getting up. Automatically, Lohengrin Pera also stood up, in spite of himself. But he wasn't the type to give in easily.

'Well, just for curiosity's sake, would you tell me what your second demand is?'

'Certainly. The commissioner of Vigàta has put in a request for my promotion to vice-commissioner—'

'We shall have no problem whatsoever having it accepted,' said the colonel, relieved.

'What about having it rejected?'

Montalbano could distinctly hear Lohengrin Pera's world crumble and fall to pieces on top of him, and he saw the colonel hunch over as if trying to shield himself from a sudden explosion.

'You are totally insane,' said the colonel, sincerely terrified.

'You've just noticed?'

'Listen, you can do whatever you like, but I cannot give in to your demand to turn up the body. Absolutely not.'

'Shall we see how the tape came out?' Montalbano asked politely.

'What tape?' said Lohengrin Pera, confused.

Montalbano went over to the bookcase, stood up on tiptoe, took out the video camera, and showed it to the colonel.

'Jesus!' said the colonel, collapsing in a chair. He was sweating. 'Montalbano, for your own good, I implore you . . .'

But the man was a snake, and he behaved like a snake. As he appeared to be begging the inspector not to do anything stupid, his hand had moved ever so slightly and was now within reach of the mobile phone. Fully aware that he would never make it out of there alone, he wanted to call for reinforcements. Montalbano let him get another centimetre closer to the phone, then sprang. With one hand he sent the phone flying from the table, with the other he struck the colonel hard in the face. Lohengrin Pera flew all the way across the room, glasses falling, then slammed against the far wall back first, and slid to the ground. Montalbano slowly drew near and, as he'd seen done in a movie about Nazis, crushed the colonel's little glasses with his heel.

NINETEEN

And while he was at it, he went for broke, pounding the mobile phone violently into the ground with his heel until he'd half-pulverized it.

He finished the job with a hammer he kept in his tool drawer. Then he approached the colonel, who was still on the floor, groaning feebly. As soon as he saw the inspector in front of him, Lohengrin Pera shielded his face with his forearms, as children do.

'Enough, for pity's sake,' he implored.

What kind of man was he? A punch in the face and a trickle of blood from his split lip, and he's reduced to this? Montalbano grabbed him by the lapels of his jacket, lifted him up, and sat him down. With a trembling hand, Lohengrin Pera wiped away the blood with his embroidered postage stamp, closed his eyes, and appeared to faint.

'It's just that . . . blood . . . I can't stand the sight of it,' he muttered.

'Yours or other people's?' Montalbano enquired.

He went into the kitchen, grabbed a half-full bottle of whisky and a glass, and set these in front of the colonel.

'I'm a teetotaller.'

Montalbano felt a little calmer now, having let off some steam.

If the colonel, he thought, wanted to phone for help, then the people who were supposed to come to his rescue must certainly be in the neighbourhood, just a few minutes' drive from the house. That was the real danger. He heard the doorbell ring.

'Chief? It's me, Fazio.'

He opened the door halfway.

'Listen, Fazio, I have to finish talking to that person I mentioned. Wait in the car. I'll call you when I need you. But be careful: there may be some people in the area who are up to no good. Stop anyone you see approaching the house.'

He shut the door and sat back down in front of Lohengrin Pera, who seemed lost in dejection.

'Now try to understand me, because soon you won't be able to understand anything anymore.'

'What do you intend to do to me?' asked the colonel, turning pale.

'No blood, don't worry. I've got you in the palm of my hand, I hope you realize that. You were foolish enough to blab the whole story in front of a video camera. If I have the tape aired on TV, it's going to kick up such a fucking row on the international scene that you'll be selling chickpea sandwiches on a street corner before it's all over. If, on the other hand, you let Karima's body be found and block my promotion – and make no mistake, the two things go hand in hand – I give you my word of honour that I'll destroy the tape. You have no choice but to trust me. Have I made myself clear?'

Lohengrin Pera nodded his little head 'yes', and at that moment the inspector realized that the knife had disappeared from the table. The colonel must have seized it when he was talking to Fazio.

'Tell me something,' said Montalbano. 'Are there such things, that you know of, as poisonous worms?'

Pera gave him a questioning look.

'For your own good, put down the knife you're holding inside your jacket.'

Without a word, the colonel obeyed and set the knife down on the table. Montalbano opened the whisky bottle, filled the glass to the brim, and held it out to Lohengrin Pera, who recoiled with a grimace of disgust.

'I've already told you I'm a teetotaller.'

'Drink.'

'I can't, believe me.'

Squeezing the colonel's cheeks with the thumb and forefinger of his left hand, Montalbano forced him to open his mouth.

*

Fazio heard the inspector call for him after waiting some forty-five minutes in the car, as he was starting to drift off into a leaden sleep. Upon entering the house, he immediately saw a drunken midget, who had vomited all over himself to boot. Unable to stand on his feet, the midget, leaning first against a chair and then against the wall, was trying to sing 'Celeste Aida'. On the floor, Fazio noticed a pair of glasses and a mobile phone, both smashed to pieces. On the table were an empty bottle of whisky, a glass, also empty, and three or four sheets of paper and some identity cards.

'Listen closely, Fazio,' said the inspector. 'I'm going to tell you exactly what happened here, in case anybody questions you. I was returning home this evening, around midnight, when I saw, at the top of the lane that leads to my house, this man's car, a BMW, blocking my path. He was completely drunk. I brought him home with me because he was in no condition to drive. He had no identification in his pockets, nothing. After several attempts to sober him up, I called you for help.'

'Got it,' said Fazio.

'Now, here's the plan. You're going to pick him up – he doesn't weigh much, in any case – put him in his BMW, get behind the wheel, and put him in a holding cell. I'll follow behind you in the squad car.'

'And how are you going to get back home afterwards?'

'You'll have to drive me back. Sorry. Tomorrow morning, as soon as you see he's recovered his senses, you're to set him free.'

*

Back at home, he removed the pistol from the glove compartment of his car where he always kept it, and stuck it in his belt. Then he took a broom and swept up all the fragments of Lohengrin Pera's mobile phone and glasses, and wrapped them in a sheet of newspaper. He took the little shovel that Mimì had given François and dug two deep holes almost directly below the veranda. In one he put the bundle and covered it up, in the other he dumped the papers and documents, now shredded into little pieces. These he sprinkled with petrol and set on fire. When they had turned to ash, he covered up this hole as well. The sky was beginning to lighten. He went into the kitchen, brewed a pot of strong coffee and drank it. Then he shaved and took a shower. He wanted to be completely relaxed when he sat down to enjoy the video tape.

He put the little cassette inside the bigger one, as Nicolò had instructed him to do, then turned on the TV and the VCR. After a few seconds with the screen still blank, he got up and checked the appliances, certain he'd made some wrong connection. He was utterly hopeless with this sort of thing, to say nothing of computers, which terrified him. Nothing doing this time, either. He popped out the larger cassette, opened it, looked at it. The little cassette seemed poorly inserted, so he pushed it all the way in. He put the whole package back into the VCR. Still nothing on the damn screen. What the hell wasn't working? As he was asking himself this, he froze, seized by doubt. He dashed to the phone.

'Hello?' answered the voice at the other end, pronouncing each letter with tremendous effort.

'Nicolò? This is Montalbano.'

'Who the hell else could it be, Jesus fucking Christ?'

'I have to ask you something.'

'Do you know what time it is?'

'I'm sorry, really sorry. Remember the video camera you lent me?'

'Yeah?'

'Which button was I supposed to push to record? The top one or the bottom one?'

'The top one, arsehole.'

He'd pushed the wrong button.

*

He got undressed again, put on his bathing suit, bravely entered the freezing water, and began to swim. After tiring and turning over to float on his back, he started thinking that it was not, in the end, so terrible that he hadn't recorded anything. The important thing was that the colonel believed he had and would continue to do so. He returned to shore, went back in the house, threw himself down on the bed, still wet, and fell asleep.

*

When he woke up it was past nine, and he had the distinct impression he couldn't go back to work and resume his everyday chores. He decided to inform Mimì.

'Hallo! Hallo! Whoozat talkin' onna line?'

'It's Montalbano, Cat.'

'Izzat really 'n' truly you in person, sir?'

'It's really and truly me in person. Let me speak with Inspector Augello.'

'Hello, Salvo. Where are you?'

'At home. Listen, Mimì, I don't think I can come in to work.'

'Are you sick?'

'No. I just don't feel up to it, not today nor tomorrow. I need to rest for four or five days. Can you cover for me?'

'Of course.'

'Thanks.'

'Wait. Don't hang up.'

'What is it?'

'I'm a little concerned, Salvo. You've been acting weird for the last couple of days. What's the matter with you? Don't make me start worrying about you.'

'Mimì, I just need a little rest, that's all.'

'Where will you go?'

'I don't know yet. I'll phone you later.'

*

Actually, he knew exactly where he would go. He packed his bag in five minutes, then took a little longer to select which books to take along. He left a note in block letters for Adelina, the housekeeper, informing her he'd be back within a week. When he arrived at the trattoria in Mazàra, they greeted him like the prodigal son.

'The other day, I believe I understood that you rent rooms.'

'Yes, we've got five upstairs. But it's the off-season now, so only one of 'em's rented.'

They showed him a room, spacious and bright and looking straight onto the sea.

He lay down on the bed, brain emptied of thoughts, chest swelling with a kind of happy melancholy. He was loosing the moorings, ready to sail out to the country of sleep, when he heard a knock on the door.

'Come in, it's unlocked.'

The cook appeared in the doorway. He was a big man of considerable heft, about forty, with dark eyes and skin.

'What are you doing? Aren't you coming down? I heard you were here and so I made something for you that . . .'

What the cook had made, Montalbano couldn't hear, because a sweet, soft melody, a heavenly tune, had started playing in his ears.

*

For the last hour he'd been watching a rowing boat slowly approaching the shore. On it was a man rowing in sharply rhythmic, vigorous strokes. The boat had also been sighted by the owner of the trattoria; Montalbano heard him cry out, 'Luicì! The cavaliere's coming back!'

The inspector then saw Luicino, the restaurateur's sixteen-year-old son, enter the water to push the boat up onto the sand so the passenger wouldn't get his feet wet. The cavaliere, whose name Montalbano did not know, was smartly dressed, tie and all. On his head he wore a white Panama hat, with the requisite black band.

'Cavaliere, did you catch anything?' the restaurateur asked him.

'A pain in the arse, that's what I caught.'

He was a thin, nervy man, about seventy years old. Later, Montalbano heard him bustling about in the room next to his.

*

'I set a table over here,' said the cook as soon as Montalbano appeared for dinner, and he led him into a tiny room with space for only two tables. The inspector felt grateful for this, since the big dining room was booming with the voices and laughter of a large gathering.

'I've set it for two,' the cook continued. 'Do you have any objection if Cavaliere Pintacuda eats with you?'

He certainly did have an objection: he feared he would have to talk while eating.

A few minutes later, the gaunt septuagenarian introduced himself with a bow.

'Liborio Pintacuda, and I'm not a cavaliere,' he said, sitting down. 'There's something I must tell you, even at the risk of appearing rude,' the non-cavaliere continued. 'I, when I'm talking, do not eat. Conversely, when I'm eating, I don't talk.'

'Welcome to the club,' said Montalbano, sighing with relief.

The pasta with crab was as graceful as a first-rate

ballerina, but the stuffed bass in saffron sauce left him breathless, almost frightened.

'Do you think this kind of miracle could ever happen again?' he asked Pintacuda, gesturing towards his now empty plate. They had both finished and therefore recovered the power of speech.

'It'll happen again, don't worry, just like the miracle of the blood of San Gennaro,' said Pintacuda. 'I've been coming here for years, and never, I repeat, never, has Tanino's cooking let me down.'

'At a top-notch restaurant, a chef like Tanino would be worth his weight in gold,' the inspector commented.

'Yes he would. Last year, a Frenchman passed this way, the owner of a famous Parisian restaurant. He practically got down on his knees and begged Tanino to come to Paris with him. But there was no persuading him. Tanino says this is where he's from, and this is where he'll die.'

'Someone must surely have taught him to cook like that. He can't have been born with that gift.'

'You know, up until ten years ago, Tanino was a small-time crook. Petty theft, drug dealing. Always in and out of jail. Then, one night, the Blessed Virgin appeared to him.'

'Are you joking?'

'I try hard not to. As he tells it, the Virgin took his hands in hers, looked him in the eye, and declared that from the next day forward, he would become a great chef.'

'Come on!'

'You, for example, knew nothing of this story of the Virgin, and yet after eating the bass, you specifically used the word "miracle". But I can see you don't believe in the supernatural, so I'll change subject. What brings you to these parts, Inspector?'

Montalbano gave a start. He hadn't told anyone there what he did for a living.

'I saw your press conference on television, after you arrested that woman for killing her husband,' Pintacuda explained.

'Please don't tell anybody who I am.'

'But they all know who you are, Inspector. Since they've gathered that you don't like to be recognized, however, they play dumb.'

'And what do you do of interest?'

'I used to be a professor of philosophy. If you can call teaching philosophy interesting.'

'Isn't it?'

'Not at all. The students get bored. They no longer care enough to learn how Hegel or Kant thought about things. Philosophy should probably be replaced with some subject like, I don't know, "Basic Management". Then it still might mean something.'

'Basic management of what?'

'Life, my friend. Do you know what Benedetto Croce writes in his *Memoirs*? He says that he learned from experience to consider life a serious matter, as a problem to be solved. Seems obvious, doesn't it? But it's not. One would have to explain to young people, philosophically, what it means, for example, to smash their car into another car one Saturday night. And to tell them how, philosophically, this could be avoided. But we'll have time to discuss all this. I'm told you'll be staying here a few days.'

'Yes. Do you live alone?'

'For the fifteen days I spend here, very much alone. The rest of the time I live in a big old house in Trapani with my wife and four daughters, all married, and eight grandchildren, who, when they're not at school, are with me all day. At least once every three months I escape and come here, leaving no phone number or forwarding address. I cleanse myself, take the waters of solitude. For me this place is like a clinic where I detoxify myself of an excess of sentiment. Do you play chess?'

*

On the afternoon of the following day, as he was lying in bed reading Sciascia's *Council of Egypt* for the twentieth time, it occurred to him that he'd forgotten to tell Valente about the odd agreement he'd made with the colonel. The matter might prove dangerous for his colleague in Mazàra if he were to continue investigating. He went downstairs where there was a telephone.

'Valente? Montalbano here.'

'Salvo, where the hell are you? I asked for you at the office and they said they had no news of you.'

'Why were you looking for me? Has something come up?'

'Yes. The commissioner called me out of the blue this morning to tell me my request for a transfer had been accepted. They're sending me to Sestri.'

Valente's wife, Giulia, was from Sestri, and her parents also lived there. Until now, every time the vice-commissioner had asked to be transferred to Liguria, his request had been denied.

'Didn't I say that something good would come out of this affair?' Montalbano reminded him.

'Do you think—?'

'Of course. They're getting you out of their hair, in such a way that you won't object. And they're right. When does the transfer take effect?'

'Immediately.'

'See? I'll come and say goodbye before you leave.'

Lohengrin Pera and his little gang of playmates had moved very fast. It remained to be seen whether this was a good or a bad sign. He needed to do a foolproof test. If they were in such a hurry to put the matter to rest, then surely they had wasted no time in sending him a message as well. The Italian bureaucracy, usually slow as a snail, becomes lightning-quick when it comes to screwing the citizen. With this well-known truth in mind, he called his commissioner.

'Montalbano! For God's sake, where have you run off to?'

'Sorry for not letting you know. I've taken a few days off to rest.'

'I understand. You went to see—'

'No. Were you looking for me? Do you need me?'

'Yes, I was looking for you, but I don't need you for

anything. Just rest. Do you remember I was supposed to recommend you for a promotion?'

'How could I forget?'

'Well, this morning Commendator Ragusa called me from the Ministry of Justice. He's a good friend of mine. He told me that, apparently . . . some obstacles have come up – of what kind, I have no idea. In short, your promotion has been blocked. Ragusa wouldn't, or couldn't, tell me any more than that. He also made it clear that it was useless, and perhaps even unwise, to insist. Believe me, I'm shocked and offended.'

'Not me.'

'Don't I know it! In fact, you're happy, aren't you?'

'Doubly happy, Commissioner.'

'Doubly?'

'I'll explain when I see you in person.'

He set his mind at rest. They were moving in the right direction.

*

The following morning, Liborio Pintacuda, a steaming cup of coffee in hand, woke the inspector up when it was still dark outside.

'I'll wait for you in the boat.'

He'd invited him to a useless half day of fishing, and the inspector had accepted. Montalbano put on a pair of jeans and a long-sleeved shirt. Sitting in a boat with a gentleman dressed to the nines, he would have felt silly in a bathing suit.

Fishing, for the professor, proved to be exactly like eating. He never opened his mouth, except, every now and then, to curse the fish for not biting.

Around nine in the morning, with the sun already high in the sky, Montalbano couldn't hold back any longer.

'I'm losing my father,' he said.

'My condolences,' the professor said without looking up from his fishing line.

The words seemed flat and inappropriate to the inspector.

'He hasn't died yet. He's dying,' he clarified.

'It makes no difference. For you, your father died the very moment you learned he was going to die. Everything else is, so to speak, a bodily formality. Nothing more. Does he live with you?'

'No, he's in another town.'

'By himself?'

'Yes. And I can't summon the courage to go and see him in this state, before he goes. I just can't. The very idea scares me. I'll never have the strength to set foot in the hospital where he's staying.'

The old man said nothing, limiting himself to replacing the bait the fish had eaten with many thanks. Then he decided to talk.

'You know, I happen to have followed an investigation of yours, the one about the "terracotta dog". In that instance, you abandoned an investigation into some weapons trafficking to throw yourself heart and soul into tracking a crime from fifty years ago, even though solving it wasn't going to yield any practical results. Do you know why you did it?'

'Out of curiosity?' Montalbano guessed.

'No, my friend. It was a very shrewd, intelligent way for you to keep practising your unpleasant profession, but by escaping from everyday reality. Apparently this everyday reality sometimes becomes too much for you to bear. And so you escape. As I do when I take refuge here. But the moment I go back home, I immediately lose half of the benefit. The fact of your father's dying is real, but you refuse to confirm it by seeing it in person. You're like the child who thinks he can blot out the world by closing his eyes.'

Professor Liborio Pintacuda, at this point, looked the inspector straight in the eye.

'When will you decide to grow up?'

TWENTY

As he was going downstairs for supper, he decided he would head back to Vigàta the following morning. He'd been away for five days. Luicino had set the table in the usual little room, and Pintacuda was already sitting at his place and waiting for him.

'I'm leaving tomorrow,' Montalbano announced.

'Not me. I need another week of detox.'

Luicino brought the first course at once, and thereafter their mouths were used only for eating. When the second course arrived, they had a surprise.

'Meatballs!' the professor exclaimed, indignant. 'Meatballs are for dogs!'

The inspector kept his cool. The aroma floating up from the dish and into his nose was rich and dense.

'What's with Tanino? Is he sick?' Pintacuda enquired with a tone of concern.

'No sir, he's in the kitchen,' replied Luicino.

Only then did the professor break a meatball in half with his fork and bring it to his mouth. Montalbano hadn't yet made a move. Pintacuda chewed slowly, eyes half closed, and emitted a sort of moan.

'If one ate something like this at death's door, he'd be happy even to go to hell,' he said softly.

The inspector put half a meatball in his mouth, and with his tongue and palate began a scientific analysis that would have put Jacomuzzi to shame. So: fish and, no question, onion, hot pepper, whisked eggs, salt, pepper, breadcrumbs. But two other flavours, hiding under the taste of the butter used in the frying, hadn't yet answered the call. At the second mouthful, he recognized what had escaped him in the first: cumin and coriander.

'*Koftas!*' he shouted in amazement.

'What did you say?' asked Pintacuda.

'We're eating an Indian dish, executed to perfection.'

'I don't give a damn where it's from,' said the professor. 'I only know it's a dream. And please don't speak to me again until I've finished eating.'

*

Pintacuda waited for the table to be cleared and then suggested they play their now customary game of chess that, equally customarily, Montalbano always lost.

'Excuse me a minute; first I'd like to say goodbye to Tanino.'

'I'll come with you.'

The cook was in the process of giving his assistant a serious tongue-lashing for having cleaned the pans poorly.

'When you do that, they end up tasting like yesterday's food and nobody can tell what they're eating anymore.'

'Listen,' said Montalbano, 'is it true you've never been outside Sicily?'

He must have inadvertently assumed a policeman-like tone, because Tanino seemed suddenly to have returned to his days as a delinquent.

'Never, Inspector, I swear! I got witnesses!'

Therefore he could never have learned that dish from some foreign restaurant.

'Have you ever had any dealings with Indians?'

'Like in the movies? Redskins?'

'Never mind,' said Montalbano. And he said goodbye to the miraculous cook, giving him a hug.

*

In the five days he'd been away – as Fazio reported to him – nothing of any importance had happened. Carmelo Arnone, the man with the tobacco shop near the train station, had fired four shots at Angelo Cannizzaro, haberdasher, over a woman. Mimì Augello, who happened to be in the area, had courageously confronted the gunman and disarmed him.

'So,' Montalbano commented, 'Cannizzaro came away with little more than a good scare.'

It was well known to everyone in town that Carmelo Arnone didn't know how to handle a gun and couldn't even hit a cow at point-blank range.

'Well, no.'

'He hit him?' asked Montalbano, stunned.

Actually, Fazio went on to explain, he hadn't hit his target this time either. One of the bullets, though, after striking a lamp post, had ricocheted back and ended up between Cannizzaro's shoulder blades. The wound was nothing, the bullet had lost all its force by then. But in no time the rumour had spread all over town that the cowardly Carmelo Arnone had shot Angelo Cannizzaro in the back. So Cannizzaro's brother, Pasqualino, who dealt in broad beans and wore glasses with lenses an inch thick, armed himself, tracked down Carmelo Arnone, and shot at him, missing twice. That is, he missed both the target and the identity of the target. Deceived by a strong family resemblance, he had mistaken Carmelo's brother Filippo, who owned a fruit and vegetable store, for Carmelo himself. As for missing the target, the first shot had ended up God knows where, while the second had injured the little finger on the left hand of a shopkeeper from Canicattì who'd come to Vigàta on business. At this point the pistol had jammed, otherwise Pasqualino Cannizzarì, firing blindly, would surely have wrought another slaughter of the innocents.

Ah and also, there were two robberies, four bag snatchings and three cars torched. Routine stuff.

There was a knock at the door and Tortorella came in after pushing the door open with his foot, arms laden with a good six or seven pounds of papers.

'Shall we make good use of your time while you're here?'

'Tortorè, you make it sound like I've been away for a hundred years!'

Since he never signed anything without first carefully reading what it was about, Montalbano had barely dispatched a couple of pounds of documents when it was already lunchtime. Though he felt some stirring in the pit of his stomach, he decided not to go to the Trattoria San Calogero. He wasn't ready yet to desecrate the memory of Tanino, the cook directly inspired by the Madonna. The betrayal, when it came, would have to be justified, at least in part, by abstinence.

He finished signing papers at eight that evening, with aches not only in his fingers, but in his whole arm.

*

By the time he got home, he was ravenous; in the pit of his stomach there now was a hole. How should he proceed? Should he open the oven and fridge and see what Adelina had made for him? He reasoned that, if going from one restaurant to another could technically be called a betrayal, to go from Tanino to Adelina certainly could not. Rather, it might be better defined as a return to the family fold after an adulterous interlude. The oven was empty. In the fridge he found ten or so olives, three sardines and a bit of Lampedusan tuna in a small glass jar. On the kitchen table there was some bread wrapped in paper, next to a note from the housekeeper.

> *Since you didna tell me when you was commin back, I cook and cook and then I gotta thro alla this good food away. I'm not gonna cook no more.*

She didn't want to go on wasting things, clearly, but more importantly, she must have felt offended because he hadn't told her where he was going ('All right, so Ima just a maid, sir, but sommatime you treeta me jes like a maid!').

He listlessly ate a couple of olives with bread, which he decided to accompany with some of his father's wine. He turned the television on to the Free Channel. It was time for the news.

Nicolò Zito was finishing up a commentary on the arrest of a town council man in Fela for embezzlement and graft. Then he moved on to the latest stories. On the outskirts of Sommatina, between Caltanissetta and Enna, a woman's body had been recovered in an advanced state of decomposition.

Montalbano sat bolt upright in his armchair.

The woman had been strangled, stuffed into a bag and thrown into a rather deep, dry well. Beside her they found a small suitcase that led to the victim's identification. Karima Moussa, aged thirty-four, a native of Tunis who had moved to Vigàta a few years earlier.

The photo of Karima and François that the inspector had given Nicolò appeared on the screen.

Did the viewing audience remember the Free Channel's report on the woman's disappearance? No trace, meanwhile, had turned up of the little boy, her son. According to Inspector Diliberto, who was conducting the investigation, the killer might have been the Tunisian woman's unknown procurer. There nevertheless remained, in the inspector's opinion, numerous details to be cleared up.

Montalbano whinnied, turned off the TV, and smiled. Lohengrin Pera had kept his word. He stood up, stretched, sat back down and immediately fell asleep in the armchair. An animal slumber, probably dreamless, like a sack of potatoes.

*

The next morning, from his office, he called the commissioner and invited himself to dinner. Then he called police headquarters in Sommatino.

'Diliberto? Montalbano here. I'm calling from Vigàta.'

'Hello, colleague. What can I do for you?'

'I wanted to know about that woman you found in the well.'

'Karima Moussa.'

'Yes. Are you absolutely certain about the identification?'

'Without a shadow of a doubt. In her bag, among other things, we found an ATM card from the Banca Agricola di Montelusa.'

'Excuse me for interrupting, but anyone, you see, could have put—'

'Let me finish. Three years ago, this woman had an accident for which she was given twelve stitches in her right arm at Montelusa Hospital. It checks out. The scar was still visible despite the body's advanced state of decomposition.'

'Listen, Diliberto, I just got back to Vigàta this morning after a few days off. I'm short on news and found out about the body on a local TV station. They reported you still had some questions.'

'Not about the identification. But I'm certain the woman was killed and buried somewhere else, not where we found her after receiving an anonymous tip. So my question is: why did they dig her up and move the body? What need was there to do that?'

'What makes you so sure they did?'

'You see, Karima's suitcase was soiled with bodily waste from its first period alongside the corpse. And in order to carry the suitcase to the well where it was found, they wrapped it in newspaper.'

'So?'

'The newspaper was only three days old. Whereas the woman had been killed at least ten days earlier. The coroner would bet his life on it. So I need to work out why she was moved. And I have no idea; I just can't understand it.'

Montalbano had an idea, but he couldn't tell his colleague what it was. If only those fuckheads in the secret services could do something right for once! Like the time when, wanting to make people believe that a certain Libyan aeroplane had crashed in Sila on a specific day, they staged a show of explosions and flames, and then, in the autopsy, it was determined that the pilot had actually died fifteen days earlier from the impact. The flying cadaver.

*

After a simple but elegant dinner, Montalbano and his superior retired to the study. The commissioner's wife withdrew in turn to watch television.

Montalbano's story was long and so detailed that he

didn't even leave out his voluntary crushing of Lohengrin Pera's little gold eyeglasses. At a certain point, the report turned into a confession. But the commissioner's absolution was slow in coming. He was truly annoyed at having been left out of the game.

'I'm angry with you, Montalbano. You denied me a chance to amuse myself a little before calling it quits.'

*

My dear Livia,

This letter will surprise you for at least two reasons. The first is the letter itself, my having written it and sent it. Unwritten letters I've sent you by the bushel, at least one a day. I realized that in all these years, I've only sent you an occasional miserly postcard with a few 'bureaucratic, inspectorly' greetings, as you called them.

The second reason, which will delight you as much as surprise you, is its content.

Since you left exactly fifty-five days ago (as you can see, I keep track), many things have happened, some of which concern us directly. To say they 'happened', however, is incorrect; it would be more accurate to write that I made them happen.

You reproached me once for a certain tendency I have to play God by altering the course of events (for others) through omissions great and small, and even through more or less damnable falsifications. Maybe it's true. Actually, it most certainly is. But don't you think this, too, is part of my job?

Whatever the case, you should know at once that I'm about to tell you of another supposed transgression of mine, one that was aimed, however, at turning a chain of events in our favour, and was therefore not for or against anyone else. But first I want to tell you about François.

Neither you nor I have even mentioned his name since the last night you spent in Marinella, when you reproached me for not having realized that the boy could become the son we would never have. What's more, you were hurt by the way I had the child taken from you. But, you see, I was terrified, and with good reason. He had become a dangerous witness, and I was afraid they would make him disappear (or 'neutralize' him, as they say euphemistically).

The omission of that name has weighed heavily on our phone conversations, making them evasive and a little loveless. Today I want to make it clear to you that if I never once mentioned François before now, it was to keep you from nurturing dangerous illusions. And if I'm writing to you about him now, it is because this fear has subsided.

Do you remember that morning in Marinella when François ran away to look for his mother? Well, as I was walking him home, he told me he didn't want to end up in an orphanage. And I replied that this would never happen. I gave him my word of honour, and we shook on it. I made a promise, and I will keep it at all costs.

In these fifty-five days Mimì Augello, at my request, has been phoning his sister three times a week to see how the boy is doing. The answers have always been reassuring.

The day before yesterday, in Mimì's company, I went to see him (by the way, you ought to write Mimì a letter thanking him for his generosity and friendship). I had a chance to observe François for a few minutes while he was playing with Mimì's nephew, who's the same age. He was cheerful and carefree. As soon as he saw me (he recognized me at once), his expression changed. He sort of turned sad. Children's memories, like those of the elderly, are intermittent. I'm sure the thought of his mother had come back to him. He gave me a big hug and then, looking at me with bright, tearless eyes – he doesn't seem to me a boy who cries easily – he didn't ask me what I was afraid he'd ask, that is, if I had any news of Karima. In a soft voice, he said only, 'Take me to Livia.'

Not to his mother. To you. He must be convinced he'll never see his mother again. And unfortunately, he's right.

You know that from the very first, based on unhappy experience, I was convinced that Karima had been murdered. To do what I had in mind, I had to make a dangerous move that would bring the accomplices to her murder out in the open. The next step was to force them to produce the woman's body in such a way that, when it was found, it would be certain to be identified. It all went well. And so I was able to act 'officially' on behalf of François, who has now been declared motherless. The commissioner was a tremendous help to me, putting all his many acquaintances to work. If Karima's body had not been found, my steps would have surely been hindered by endless bureaucratic red tape, which would have delayed the resolution of our problem for years and years.

I realize this letter is getting too long, so I'll change register.

1) In the eyes of the law, Italian as well as Tunisian, François is in a paradoxical situation. In fact, he's an orphan who doesn't exist, inasmuch as his birth was never registered either in Sicily or Tunisia.

2) The judge in Montelusa who deals with these questions has sort of straightened out his status, but only for as long as it takes to go through the necessary procedures. He has assigned him temporarily to the care of Mimì's sister.

3) The same judge has informed me that while it is theoretically possible in Italy for an unmarried woman to adopt a child, in reality it's all talk. And he cited the case of an actress who was subjected to years of judicial pronouncements, opinions and decisions, each one contradicting the last.

4) The best way to expedite matters, in the judge's opinion, is for us to get married.

5) So get your papers ready.

A hug and a kiss. Salvo

P.S. A friend of mine in Vigàta who's a notary will administer a fund of one-half billion lire in François's name, which he'll be free to use when he comes legally of age. I find it fitting that our son should be officially born the exact moment he sets foot in our house, and more than fitting that he should be helped through life by his real mother, whose money that was.

*

YOUR FATHER IS NEARING THE END DO NOT DELAY IF YOU EVER WANT TO SEE HIM AGAIN. ARCANGELO PRESTIFILIPPO.

He'd been expecting these words, but when he read them the dull ache returned, as when he'd first found out. Except that now it was compounded by the anguish of knowing what duty required him to do: to bend down over the bed, kiss his father's forehead, feel his dry, dying breath, look him in the eye, say a few comforting words. Would he have the strength? Drenched in sweat, he thought this must be the inevitable test, if indeed it was true that he must grow up, as Professor Pintacuda had said.

I will teach François not to fear my death, he thought. And from this thought, which surprised him by the very fact that he'd had it, he derived a temporary peace of mind.

*

Right outside the gates of Valmontana, after four straight hours of driving, was a road sign indicating the route to follow for the Clinica Porticelli.

He left the car in the well-ordered car park and went in. He felt his heart beating right under his Adam's apple.

'My name is Montalbano. I'd like to see my father who's staying here.'

The person behind the desk eyed him for a moment, then pointed to a small waiting room.

'Please make yourself comfortable. I'll call Dr Brancato for you.'

He sat down in an armchair and picked up one of the magazines that lay on a small table. He put it back down at once. His hands were so sweaty they had wet the cover.

The doctor, a very serious-looking man of about fifty in a white smock, came in and held out his hand to him.

'Mr Montalbano? I am very, very sorry to have to tell you that your father died peacefully two hours ago.'

'Thank you,' said Montalbano.

The doctor looked at him, slightly bewildered. But it wasn't him the inspector was thanking.

Author's Note

One critic, when reviewing my book *The Terracotta Dog,* wrote that Vigàta, the non-existent town in which all my novels are set, is 'the most invented city of the most typical Sicily.'

I cite these words in support of the requisite declaration that all names, places and situations in this book have been *invented* out of whole cloth. Even the number plate.

If fantasy has somehow coincided with reality, the blame, in my opinion, lies with reality.

The novel is dedicated to Flem. He liked stories like this.

Notes

page 3 – ***sardines a beccafico*** – *Sarde a beccafico* are a famous Sicilian speciality named after a small bird, the *beccafico* (*Sylvia borin*, garden warbler in English), which is particularly fond of figs; indeed the name *beccafico* means 'fig-pecker'. The headless, cleaned sardines are stuffed with sautéed breadcrumbs, pine nuts, raisins and anchovies, then rolled up in such a way that, when removed from the oven, they resemble the bird.

page 8 – **'the prefect'** – The *prefetto* is the local representative of the central Italian government; one is assigned to each province. They are part of the national, not local bureaucracy.

page 31 – ***alalonga all'agrodolce*** – *Alalonga* (literally 'longwing') is a particularly delicious species of small tuna. *All'agrodolce* means 'sweet and sour', and in this case involves sautéing a small steak of the fish in a sauce of vinegar, oil, sugar and parsley.

page 31 – **The Northern League . . . towards secession** – The Lega Nord is a right-wing political party based in the northern regions of Italy (Lombardy, Veneto, Piedmont) and known for its prejudices against foreign immigrants and southern Italians. Until recently they had been threatening to constitute a separate national entity under the historically dubious name of Padania (after the Po River, which runs from the Piedmont through Lombardy and the Veneto), and to secede from the Italian republic.

page 40 – **They spread their hands apart, looking sorrowful** – Spreading the hands apart, palms open, is a gesture typical of southern Italians and seen often among Italian Americans, most notably Al Pacino in many of his movie roles. It usually expresses helplessness and resignation to fate.

page 42 – **A smell of stale perfume, burnt straw in colour** – As seen in the first two novels, Montalbano synaesthetically associates colours with smells.

page 54 – ***E te lo vojo dì / che sò stato io*** – 'And I want to say / that it was me.' The lines are a refrain from a popular Italian song of the early 1970s by the Fratelli DeAngelis. In it a man confesses to a friend that it was he who committed an unsolved crime of passion some thirty years before, and that he has kept the truth inside him all these years.

page 54 – **'goat-tied'** – The Sicilian word is *incaprettato* (containing the word for goat, *capra*), and it refers to a particularly cruel method of execution used by the Mafia, where the victim, face down, has a rope looped around his neck and then tied to his feet, which are raised behind his back, as in hog-tying. Fatigue eventually forces him to lower his feet, strangling himself in the process.

page 73 – **'Italy is a Republic founded on construction work'** – A send-up of the first sentence of the Italian constitution: 'Italy is a Republic founded on work.'

page 77 – **a gesture that meant 'gone away'** – Normally this consists of tapping the edge of the right hand against the open left palm, a sign used equally in Italy, France, Spain and North Africa to mean 'let's go' or 'gone'.

page 83 – **Montalbano brought his fingertips together, pointing upwards, artichoke-like** – This is a familiar gesture of questioning used by all Italians.

page 109 – **he was going out to the nearest tobacco shop** – Tobacco products in Italy are distributed by the state monopoly and sold only in licensed shops, bars and cafes.

page 111 – **when Montelusa was called Kerkent** – The fictional Montelusa is modelled on the city of Agrigento (the ancient Agrigentum), called Girgenti by the Sicilians and Kerkent by the Arabs.

page 113 – **children's late-morning snacks** – Lunch in Italy isn't usually eaten until one or one-thirty in the afternoon, and mothers often pack a snack for their children to quell their late-morning hunger.

page 125 – ***torroncini*** – Marzipan pastries filled with pumpkin jam and covered with roasted almonds.

page 127 – **'the Lacapra case'** – Lapécora means 'the sheep', while Lacapra means 'the goat'.

page 128 – ***pasta 'ncasciata*** – A casserole of *pasta corta* (that is, elbow macaroni, penne, ziti, mezzi ziti, or something similar), tomato sauce, ground beef, Parmesan and béchamel.

page 135 – **'By repenting . . . turning state's witness against the Mafia'** – In Italy, Mafia turncoats are called *pentiti*, 'repenters', and many people, like Montalbano, believe they are treated too leniently by the government.

page 135 – ***càlia e simenza*** – A snack food of chickpeas and pumpkin seeds, sometimes with peanuts as well.

page 160 – **'Pippo Baudo'** – A famous Italian television personality and master of ceremonies for a number of different variety shows.

page 163 – **No one must ever know that Inspector Montalbano was rescued by the carabinieri** – The carabinieri, considered not very intelligent in the popular imagination, are a national paramilitary police force. They and the local police forces are often in competition with each other.

page 166 – **'On Saturday'** – Italian children attend school from Monday to Saturday.

pages 183–4 – **Didìo . . . 'The Wrath of God'** – *Di Dio* means 'of God' in Italian.

page 195 – **Totò and Peppino** – Totò, born Antonio de Curtis to a princely family, was one of the greatest comic actors of twentieth-century Italy. He made many famous films with Peppino, born Peppino De Filippo, another great comic and, like Totò, from Naples.

page 196 – **Wasn't that title abolished half a century ago?** – Much used and abused during the Fascist era, the title 'Your Excellency' was finally banned after the Second World War, though many government dignitaries still defy the ban.

page 229 – ***'Guarda come dondolo . . . col twist'*** – 'See how I sway, see how I sway, doing the twist.' Lines from a popular song written and performed by Edoardo Vianello.

page 244 – **'Montanelli'** – Indro Montanelli (1909–2001) was a famous journalist who began his long career during the time of the Fascists, whom he initially supported. He continued to work as a columnist and social critic until his death.

page 248 – **to compensate . . . for his . . . surname** – *Pera* means 'pear' in Italian.

page 267 – **'Celeste Aida'** – A famous aria from Giuseppe Verdi's opera *Aida.*

page 273 – **'the miracle of the blood of San Gennaro'** – San Gennaro (St Januarius) is the patron saint of Naples. Though little is known about him, his celebrity lies in the alleged miracle of the 'liquefaction' of his blood, which is kept in a small glass vial in the eponymous cathedral of that city. The miracle is believed to occur some eighteen times a year, but the main event is on 19 September, the saint's feast day, when large crowds always gather to witness it. Failure to liquefy is believed to be a dire portent.

page 287 – **a certain Libyan aeroplane . . . from the impact** – On 27 June 1980, an Italian airliner crashed into the sea near the Sicilian island of Ustica. All eighty-one people on board died, and the incident has remained shrouded in mystery. The most prevalent theory is that the plane was shot down by a missile during a NATO exercise, but NATO has always denied this. The radar data, meanwhile, has disappeared. Many rumours (never confirmed) have since surfaced saying that an aerial battle had taken place during an attempt by NATO to shoot down the plane in which Colonel Ghaddafi was travelling. Whatever the case, shortly after the incident a fallen Libyan war plane was recovered in the Calabrian mountains, which the Italian secret service said had crashed the same day as the airliner. The only problem was that the pilot would have to have been dead while flying the aeroplane, since a verifiable autopsy (after an earlier one had been proven false) showed that he'd died twelve days before the crash.

Notes compiled by Stephen Sartarelli